The Editor

KIMBERLY W. BENSTON is Francis B. Gummere Professor of English at Haverford College, where he has also served as director of the Hurford Center for Arts and Humanities, provost, and the fifteenth president, and from which he received the Lindback Award for Distinguished Teaching. His books include *Baraka: The Renegade and the Mask* and *Performing Blackness: Enactments of African-American Modernism.* He is editor of *Imamu Amiri Baraka: A Collection of Critical Essays, Speaking for You: The Vision of Ralph Ellison, Larry Neal: Essays,* the "Performance" Special Issue of *PMLA,* and the "Black Arts Movement" section of *The Norton Anthology of African-American Literature.*

NORTON CRITICAL EDITIONS
Victorian Era

A NORTON CRITICAL EDITION

H. G. Wells
THE ISLAND OF DOCTOR MOREAU

AUTHORITATIVE TEXT
BACKGROUNDS AND CONTEXTS
RECEPTION AND INTERPRETATION

Edited by

KIMBERLY W. BENSTON
HAVERFORD COLLEGE

W. W. NORTON & COMPANY
Independent Publishers Since 1923

W. W. Norton & Company has been independent since its founding in 1923, when William Warder Norton and Mary D. Herter Norton first published lectures delivered at the People's Institute, the adult education division of New York City's Cooper Union. The firm soon expanded its program beyond the Institute, publishing books by celebrated academics from America and abroad. By mid-century, the two major pillars of Norton's publishing program—trade books and college texts—were firmly established. In the 1950s, the Norton family transferred control of the company to its employees, and today—with a staff of five hundred and hundreds of trade, college, and professional titles published each year—W. W. Norton & Company stands as the largest and oldest publishing house owned wholly by its employees.

Library of Congress Control Number: 2024946025

ISBN: 978-0-393-92015-4 (pbk)

W. W. Norton & Company, Inc., 500 Fifth Avenue, New York, N.Y. 10110
    www.wwnorton.com
W. W. Norton & Company Ltd., 15 Carlisle Street, London W1D 3BS

1 2 3 4 5 6 7 8 9 0

Contents

Reception and Interpretation

List of Illustrations

Preface

> I had never beheld such a repulsive and extraordinary face before, and yet—if the contradiction is credible—I experienced at the same time an odd feeling that in some way I *had* already encountered exactly the features and gestures that now amazed me. . . . [T]he man, who had waited for us on the beach, began chattering to them excitedly—a foreign language, as I fancied—as they laid hands on some bales piled near the stern. Somewhere I had heard such a voice before, and I could not think where.
> —H. G. Wells, *The Island of Doctor Moreau*, pp. 11, 23[1]

Like the narrating protagonist of H. G. Wells's spiritedly horrifying novel of vivisection on a remote Pacific island, the reader of *The Island of Doctor Moreau* might encounter the voice coming from its incandescent pages as if hearing a "foreign language" that yet seems hauntingly familiar. The source of this eerie enticement is twofold, leading us to both author and work as sites of the narrative's distinctive place in literary and cultural history.

On the one hand, we now encounter any work by Wells as the residue of a titanic career of literary, scientific, and social imagination, comprising dozens of novels, scores of short stories, and a torrent of political and public intellectual commentary that together made Wells at one time the most renowned writer in the English-speaking world. So much of our contemporary experience, from nuclear power and genetic engineering to space travel and the World Wide Web, was first anticipated and even addressed by Wells that one might expect "Wellsian" to be an essential epithet of our reading and societal experience. And yet apart from his earliest books—those 1890s novels, starting with *The Time Machine* (1895) and ending shortly thereafter with *The War of the Worlds* (1897–98), that established his enduring reputation as "the father of science fiction"—Wells has, until a fairly recent slow-but-steady reconsideration, been largely neglected in both literary and popular society. Returning to Wells

---

1. Citations refer to this Norton Critical Edition of the text.

today can stir us with the shock of recognizing a voice we're sure we've heard before, but no longer know quite when or where.

On the other hand, the feeling of eerie recollection of something buried or forgotten informs many of Wells's own texts, imbuing their aura of radical innovation with the sensation of a known, if nonetheless extraordinary, conceptual or expressive cadence. This experience of sharp yet elusive evocation suffuses *The Island of Doctor Moreau*, affecting not only its thematic interests in epistemology (the entanglement of knowledge, perception, and belief) and evolution (the continuity and difference between past, present, and emerging life-forms) but also its rhetorical investments in literary tradition. For slightly beneath the surface of the novel's plot (the discovery of animals gruesomely transformed to quasi-human form) and edgy characterizations (the criminally brilliant, exiled vivisectionist Dr. Moreau; his slovenly assistant, the disgraced medical student Montgomery; and the shipwrecked amateur naturalist, our narrator, Prendick—not to mention the poignant menagerie of Beast People) we find the seething strata of allusion that inject into the narrative subtle vectors of philosophical, psychological, and political brooding. While this subterranean conceptual territory accommodates a particular intersection of late-Victorian debates about science (principally the Darwinian revolution), imperialism (especially the extensive but troubled British Empire), and biomedical experimentation (specifically, vivisection), its broader thematic foundation points us to a material and metaphorical destination: *the island* itself.

Where *Moreau*'s hapless narrator is blown to the far-flung "hidden" site of the novel's spine-chilling escapades, the reader is drawn by the undertow of stylistic and topical reference to perhaps the oldest and most common genre of Western narration, the castaway adventure. Variously echoing, citing, and evoking texts as various as Homer's *Odyssey*, Virgil's *Aeneid*, William Shakespeare's *The Tempest*, Daniel Defoe's *Robinson Crusoe*, and Jonathan Swift's *Gulliver's Travels*, Wells's tale emerges like its predecessors from the whirlpool of crisis and disorientation, the shipwreck figuring total dislocation from the coordinates of civilization and its mapped frontiers. The island space, in its radical isolation and strangeness, establishes a separation that can be by turns terrifying and liberating, signaling either the threat of alienating otherness or a yearning for freedom from the limitations of the traveler's former world. But always, surviving the wreckage generates a fresh beginning, presenting opportunity to salvage heroism from catastrophe, meaning from chaos.

If, as in one common scenario, the island is a space of monstrous Otherness (as Homer's Odysseus finds upon landing among the

Laestrygonian cannibals or when driven by hostile winds to the dehumanizing shores of Circe's abode), the castaway figure can display the courage and ingenuity suitable to a representative of "proper" culture, thus affirming and enhancing the ideals of "civilization" (ideals that figures like Shakespeare's Prospero ostensibly clarify and improve through their island sojourn). Alternatively (as with Virgil's Aeneas and Defoe's Crusoe), the castaway upon arrival sees the island locale as uninhabited and uncultivated, a blank slate upon which he[2] can inscribe new visions of sociality, desire, and identity—a kind of laboratory for reshaping elemental "humanity" through which the hero's yearning for unfettered autonomy and dominion can be fully satisfied . . . just as Moreau, who will enact *literally* the urge to fashion a new form of human being, recounts experiencing the notably nameless island's "green stillness" as a sign that "the place seemed waiting for me." The Western castaway mythos is thus colonialist in the broadest (though also often precise) sense, highlighting a will to appropriation, redefinition, and domination as the salient features of its narrative design.

The newcomer's act of insular reorigination, though, can take two forms, both of which Moreau seems to embody: invention or ironization, revolution or repetition. Envisioning colonization as the composition of a New World hewn from an untouched wilderness free of history, the audacious survivor entertains the dream of autonomous sovereignty and unfettered creation. Like Crusoe, Moreau imports materials and instruments from both the margins and the metropole of European empire, which he deploys to reestablish his program of biological transmutation: for him, continuity would be merely a springboard to a momentous departure. Ostentatiously fashioning "creature[s] of my own," he unapologetically portrays himself as a latter-day demiurge. But, as Moreau fatally discovers, such self-elevation can prove self-delusion, for the island *as such* is always already preinhabited, whether by other living beings or even by geological formation (as materially witnessed by the liberally scattered volcanic ash). That lesson of historical belatedness was one of the cardinal intellectual legacies of Wells's education, at the center of which was post-Darwinian awareness of *Homo sapiens* as an accident of long-occurring natural interdependencies; but it is equally an idea lodged in the island topos that traces back to classical thought. Not so much a blank slate as a mystic writing pad, the island is a palimpsest of competing assertions and aspirations.

2. The tradition that Wells inherits is decidedly masculine, a gendered coloration that *Moreau* subtly disturbs not only in its main characterizations but also in narrational asides and psychological development.

As a locus of such (re)inscription, the literary island is thus a meta-expressive space; for the writer, too, organizes the story through a parallel act of imaginative encounter through which conventions are tested, revised, and celebrated. For Wells, though, the writerly or reflexive condition of the island motif is stretched beyond conventional boundaries, his story becoming in effect a textual archipelago that enmeshes the tradition in what Prendick calls the "tumultuous dreams" of tangled implications. Aptly, the one writer among the many he draws from whom Wells ever acknowledged as an influence was Swift, for, as the Gulliver tales exploit with savage intensity, Swift understood that the castaway/island motif can be mobilized for a harsh examination of the writer and reader's own world, while insisting that the island, as a contested and complex locus, can be dynamic as well as distant, unstable as well as useful.

Ultimately, the summoning of so many such fables from the literary storehouse doesn't press *Moreau* into a legible mold, but exposes the tradition's underlying tensions and unresolved contradictions. At once unsentimental and impassioned, grim and exuberant, skeptical and visionary, mimetic and mythic,[3] *Moreau* explodes the narrative codes that it exploits, perhaps realizing the transgressive innovation that its titular "hero" fails to achieve as "the things [he] dream[s]" fall into "travesty." By infusing subliminal literary recollections with tonal and thematic ambiguity, Wells intensifies the atmosphere of unnerving inquiry and unsettled judgment that hovers over Prendick's narration and his progressively frenetic movement from jungle to ocean to home, from anxiety to awareness to despair. Reimagining the castaway adventure through inversion, distortion, and critique, Wells makes the island story distinctively his own.

A Note on the Text

As traced expertly by Robert Philmus,[4] the novel's itinerary from manuscript to last version prepared during Wells's lifetime encompasses at least eight clearly distinguishable instantiations of *The*

3. During the early period of Wells's career, the central debate among writers of English fiction (most prominently the novelists Henry James, Robert Louis Stevenson, and William Dean Howells) was whether literature should be a mimetic, transparent window upon the world or an enrichment of reality through the mythification of experience. Under the banner of "realism versus romance," this aesthetic controversy did not much occupy Wells as a problem for practical literary criticism; but in describing his inventive novels as "scientific romances" he expressed an interest in fusing, and perhaps confusing, these polar visions for fiction. Aptly, his literary comrade and fellow novelist Joseph Conrad (1857–1924) lauded Wells as a "Realist of the Fantastic."
4. See Robert Philmus, "Textual Authority: The Strange Case of *The Island of Doctor Moreau.*" *Science Fiction Studies* 17.1 (1990): 2–11.

Island of Doctor Moreau: the manuscript (MS); the initial English publication in April 1896 by William Heinemann (WH); the initial American publication in August 1896 by Stone and Kimball (S&K); the 1913 reissue by Heinemann (H13; itself reprinted in 1916); the 1924 Atlantic Edition (AtEd) published within the context of *The Works of H. G. Wells*; the 1927 Essex edition (which gained prominence when contained in the 1933 publication of *The Scientific Romances of H. G. Wells* by Gollancz); and the 1946 Penguin edition (P, which became for some time thereafter the principal source text through which subsequent readership encountered the novel). To various, undeterminable extents, Wells had a hand in each of these documentary realizations of the fiction we call "The Island of Doctor Moreau" (to borrow G. Thomas Tanselle's distinction between the specific version, or "text," of a "work" and the composition inscribed or imprinted in various forms over time),[5] granting each a kind of legitimacy, though none final authority or even a clear priority in securing the essential, true, proper, or pure rendition. The process of choosing and refining the core text for this Norton Critical Edition of *The Island of Doctor Moreau*—a challenge faced by all contemporary editors of Wells's novel, several of whom have taught me much through their efforts[6]—thus returns us to fundamental questions of authorial involvement and intention, textual identity, historical context, and readerly engagement that underlie the logic of editorial decision upon which a defensible critical text must be based. The editorial task at hand, then, is, as it were, to reconstruct an actual text that never existed in a physical document but which represents the most cogent intersection of intention, information, and intelligibility—or, put in terms of the agents of meaning, the best encounter of author, context, and reader—as understood from some articulated vantage of logic, purpose, and/or aspiration.

This Norton Critical Edition of *The Island of Doctor Moreau* aims principally to provide that narratively shaped version which most closely arises from Wells's engagement with key scientific, intellectual, political, social, and literary concerns that animated the great cultural ferment of late-Victorian culture. More precisely, it seeks to present the story's vision as it achieved novelistic form in the mid-1890s, when Wells was developing his distinctive approach to the genre he later termed "scientific romance" through a compressed, heady period of narrative production (a period that

---

5. G. Thomas Tanselle, *Textual Criticism and Scholarly Editing* (Charlottesville, VA: U of Virginia P, 1990).
6. With gratitude, I draw particular attention to editions by Mason Harris, Darryl Jones, Patrick Parrinder, Philmus, and Leon Stover (see Selected Bibliography).

included *The Time Machine* [1895], *The Stolen Bacillus and Other Incidents* [1895], *The Invisible Man* [1897], and *The War of the Worlds* [1897–98]). Thus, the choice is ultimately between WH and S&K, which, as Philmus argues, cannot be decided by any clear determination of "fidelity" to an "original" if unavailable copy-text that elevates one version as relatively "faithful" and demotes the other as relatively "corrupt" with respect to authorial intent. Rather, one must choose either on the basis of criteria external to the conditions of the texts' productions (such as an aesthetic preference for one version's stylistic habits) or in terms of a rationale germane to the texts' emergence, which for this critical edition points to WH on two grounds: first, its freedom from alteration in response to published criticism (as seen, for example, in the addition of the subtitle "A Possibility" to S&K); and second, its *Englishness* (seen in "accidentals" of the text: spelling, punctuation, word division, letter case—i.e., aspects of formal presentation; but also evident at times in "substantives," i.e., the semantic value of a given usage, or a phrase's significance as determined by grammatical construction). *Englishness* is, of course, an important ingredient in the mix of interests that the 1896 *Moreau*s both address, but it is subtly dampened or deflected by changes made for S&K's *American* readership. Such changes are in themselves small and of seemingly negligible consequence; but their cumulative effect for the eye and ear is arguably to render a reader's perception less attuned to the sound and sense of texts, contexts, objects, and experiences from specifically *British* literary, scientific, social, and cultural spheres that affected Wells's notably absorptive and allusive imagination. Both more and less a product of Wells's hand than S&K (leaving undecidable which text is most "authentically" the product of authorial intention), WH stands clear of its younger 1896 sibling, first, in the directness with which its author speaks unaffected by defensiveness, and second, in the clarity with which its narrative voice speaks in unfiltered national tones that simultaneously enrich and complicate the novel's thematic concerns.

In choosing WH over S&K as copy-text, then, this Norton Critical Edition is not positing the former as the sturdier or more complete embodiment of a unitary ideal but rather as the most logical starting point for establishing a contingent but serviceable rendering of an idea: that Wells wrote *The Island of Doctor Moreau* as a narrative experiment, undertaken in the crucible of fin-de-siècle Anglo-European culture. This time was itself a watershed moment within the *cultural* experiment that he, and this work in particular, helps us see as extending from the modernity ushered in by the Enlightenment to the still-unfolding epoch of modernity's uncertain culmination or disappearance. In other words, *Moreau* is a

narrative experiment shaped on the model of what Wells took to be
the ambiguous story of Darwinian evolution, with its interplay of
chance and choice, accident and advancement, humiliation and hope.
In terms explored by Edward Said in his studies of modern textuality,[7]
we are positing this critical text as a *beginning* of a specific project, a
product of a particular moment's performance of expression and
meaning, not as an *origin* that hovers over or guides, like a dynastic
sovereign, any succeeding moment of the work's appearance. We are
in effect choosing to arrest an occasion within the ongoing discourse called "The Island of Doctor Moreau" in order to focus as
sharply as possible Wells's pivotal gaze backward toward Darwin,
and forward toward emerging ideas of genetic information and
experimentation; backward toward methodological and moral disputes about the "new religion" of science (including vivisection), and
forward toward "animal studies" as a philosophical and material critique of Enlightenment humanism; backward toward the rise of
England's global expansion, and forward toward the contraction and
fragmentation of empire; backward toward amalgams of Romance
and realism through which writers from Homer to Rudyard Kipling
conveyed and questioned their cultures' defining views of experience, and forward toward idioms that pressure the very concepts of
reception and representation. WH is our copy-text because it most
reliably presents to our view that juncture, at once historical and
imaginative, from which Wells created "The Island of Doctor Moreau"
as a Janus-faced narrative, simultaneously facing backward and forward as an image of the world he inherited and the world he thought
might come.

Annotations

Footnotes and glossaries for this Norton Critical Edition offer direction and background regarding Wells's many historical, cultural,
scientific, and literary allusions, as well as diction that the contemporary reader might find narrowly specialized, antiquated,
obscure, or ambiguous. References to material provided in the
"Backgrounds and Contexts" section are offered partly as invitations
to readers to explore cultural and expressive influences on the novel.
To qualify for annotation as an actual or possible allusion, the word
or passage must offer a verbal echo of the potential source text and
not just a thematic similarity (thus, for example, the effect of Swift's
Gulliver's Travels on the novel's final chapter, though reasonably
clear to most readers of both texts, is not annotated, but possible

---

7. Edward Said, *Beginnings: Intention and Method* (New York: Columbia UP, 1975).

revisionary echoes of Darwin's *On the Origin of Species* in ch. IX
["The Thing in the Forest"] are noted). References to Wells's writings are limited to those which gloss the term, phrase, or passage in
question, rather than being called upon to develop arguments about
supposed "Wellsian" beliefs or intentions presumed to propel or govern the narrative.

Acknowledgments

Among the many generous and brilliant supporters of this volume, I must begin with my good friends at Norton: Julia Reidhead, who instantaneously and ever after believed in the project; Carol Bemis, Rachel Goodman, and Thea Goodrich, for their editorial assistance; and Kylie Yamauchi, whose meticulous craft and steadfast devotion proved instrumental to the volume's completion. For their many keen insights, careful scholarship, and lively engagement, I am deeply grateful to my former students Sydney Jones, Sam Levine, Federico Perelmuter, Dylan Ravenfox, Marina Relman, Susanna Sacks, and Lane Sassine. The incomparable duo of Rob Haley at Haverford College's Lutnick Library and Jeremiah Mercurio at Columbia University Libraries went well beyond the call in providing me needed, obscure, and often even unconsidered materials that illuminated many Wells enigmas that arose along the way. I want to extend my gratitude also to contributors and rightsholders who gave permission for their work to be reproduced in this volume. Additionally, I am indebted to the Gummere Professorship and to the Haverford College Provost's Office for their generous support of research conducted during this project.

Finally, to everyone at 7, 7P, and 5G who often did without me during the rigors and joys of recent times while I leaned into the homestretch, I am profoundly beholden to you, not least for the gift of what Wells calls at the end of *Moreau* "a sense of infinite peace and protection" that comes from your unflagging love.

Charles Robert Ashbee, frontispiece to the 1896 William Heinemann edition.

The Text of
THE ISLAND OF DOCTOR MOREAU

Contents

INTRODUCTION

On February the 1st, 1887, the *Lady Vain* was lost by collision with a derelict[1] when about the latitude 1° s. and longitude 107° w.

On January the 5th, 1888—that is, eleven months and four days after—my uncle, Edward Prendick, a private gentleman, who certainly went aboard the *Lady Vain* at Callao,[2] and who had been considered drowned, was picked up in latitude 5°3′ s. and longitude 101° w. in a small open boat, of which the name was illegible, but which is supposed to have belonged to the missing schooner *Ipecacuanha*.[3] He gave such a strange account of himself that he was supposed demented. Subsequently, he alleged that his mind was a blank from the moment of his escape from the *Lady Vain*. His case was discussed among psychologists at the time as a curious instance of the lapse of memory consequent upon physical and mental stress. The following narrative was found among his papers by the undersigned, his nephew and heir, but unaccompanied by any definite request for publication.

The only island known to exist in the region in which my uncle was picked up is Noble's Isle, a small volcanic islet, and uninhabited. It was visited in 1891 by H.M.S. *Scorpion*. A party of sailors then landed, but found nothing living thereon except certain curious white moths, some hogs and rabbits, and some rather peculiar rats. No specimen was secured of these. So that this narrative is without confirmation in its most essential particular. With that understood, there seems no harm in putting this strange story before the public, in accordance, as I believe, with my uncle's intentions. There is at least this much in its behalf: my uncle passed out of human knowledge about 5° s. and longitude 105° w.,[4] and reappeared in the same part of the ocean after a space of eleven months. In some way he must have lived during the interval. And it seems that a schooner called the *Ipecacuanha*, with a drunken captain,

---

1. Ship abandoned at sea.
2. Peruvian seaport, near Lima. *Private gentleman*: a man of high, but not aristocratic, social position, possessed of independent economic means; here also meaning traveling for his own ("private") rather than official purposes.
3. Alluding to the root of *Cephaëlis ipecacuanha*, a small, shrubby South American plant possessing emetic, diaphoretic, and purgative properties (*Oxford English Dictionary*; henceforth *OED*): inducing nausea, sweating, and disgorging. *Schooner*: small, seafaring vessel rigged with two masts, fore (frontward) and aft (in the rear or stern).
4. The geographical coordinates given for Prendick's loss and recovery—assuming the S&K correction of longitudes as west rather than east (which would place him, nonsensically, in the Indian Ocean)—locate him more or less west of the Galapagos Islands in the South Pacific Ocean. The momentous voyage of naturalist Charles Darwin (1809–1882) on the H.M.S. *Beagle* took him in 1835 to the Galapagos, where his extensive biological, botanical, and geological observations (described at length in his *Journal and Remarks* of 1839) set in motion his reconsideration of evolutionary theory.

John Davis, did start from Arica[5] with a puma and certain other animals aboard in January 1887, that the vessel was well known at several ports in the South Pacific, and that it finally disappeared from those seas (with a considerable amount of copra aboard), sailing to its unknown fate from Banya[6] in December 1887, a date that tallies entirely with my uncle's story.

—CHARLES EDWARD PRENDICK

CHAPTER I.   In the Dingey[7] of the *Lady Vain*

I do not propose to add anything to what has already been written concerning the loss of the *Lady Vain*. As everyone knows, she collided with a derelict when ten days out from Callao. The long-boat with seven of the crew was picked up eighteen days after by H.M. gun-boat *Myrtle*,[8] and the story of their privations has become almost as well known as the far more terrible *Medusa* case.[9] I have now, however, to add to the published story of the *Lady Vain* another as horrible, and certainly far stranger. It has hitherto been supposed that the four men who were in the dingey perished, but this is incorrect. I have the best evidence for this assertion—I am one of the four men.

---

5. Chilean seaport, notably the site of deadly international and local strife (having been seized from Peru in 1880 and being subject to a fierce civil war in 1891).
6. Unclear, as known settlements of that name are landlocked and mostly in Bulgaria. Robert M. Philmus suggests this might be a typesetter's error for "Banka" or "Bangka," an island in the Dutch Indies (now Indonesia) with similar geographical coordinates to Prendick's location, only eastward (*The Island of Doctor Moreau: A Variorum Text* [Athens: U of Georgia P, 1993], p. 90). Along with other subliminal evocations of colonial locales beyond the South Pacific (e.g., "Noble's Isle" recalls Australia's Noble Island, home to the Indigenous Ithu people; "Arica" could be taken as a typo for "Africa" [which indeed is S&K's reading], from which animals and natural resources, as well as people, were extracted for European use), the possible variant "Banka" aligns with the colonialist aura of Prendick's adventure. *Copra*: dried coconut kernels.
7. *Dingey*: small sailboat, carried behind a larger ship as a cargo or rescue vessel.
8. A "repulse class" naval warship launched in 1818 under the name *Malabar*, put out of sea-service and used as a coal "hulk" or depot at midcentury and renamed *Myrtle* in 1883 before being sold from the fleet in 1905. *Long-boat*: large, open boat with sails and oars, typically carried by a merchant sailing vessel for transporting people and provisions between ship and shore.
9. The frigate *Méduse* of the French navy, shipwrecked off the coast of present-day Mauretania in 1816, forcing the evacuation of its 400-plus passengers, 147 of whom crammed onto an improvised raft towed by the *Méduse*'s boats. When the boats set the raft loose, its passengers were abandoned on the open sea, with many washing overboard, others eventually killed by internal battles, and some taking to cannibalism as food supplies dwindled. Only 15 of the raft's party survived, two of whom recounted the catastrophic 13-day episode in a book that made this incident one of the most notorious of the early to mid-19th century (see Henry Savigny and Alexandre Corréard, *Narrative of a Voyage to Senegal in 1816*, pp. 197–204 below). Among the most famous artistic commemorations inspired by Savigny and Corréard's *Narrative* is the monumental painting *The Raft of the Medusa* (1818–19; see p. 117) by French artist Théodore Géricault (1791–1824).

But, in the first place, I must state that there never were four men in the dingey; the number was three. Constans, who was "seen by the captain to jump into the gig" (*Daily News*, March 17, 1887),[1] luckily for us, and unluckily for himself, did not reach us. He came down out of the tangle of ropes under the stays of the smashed bowsprit;[2] some small rope caught his heel as he let go, and he hung for a moment head downward, and then fell and struck a block or spar floating in the water. We pulled towards him, but he never came up.

I say, luckily for us he did not reach us, and I might almost add luckily for himself, for there were only a small breaker[3] of water and some soddened ship's biscuits with us—so sudden had been the alarm, so unprepared the ship for any disaster. We thought the people on the launch would be better provisioned (though it seems they were not), and we tried to hail them. They could not have heard us, and the next morning when the drizzle cleared—which was not until past midday—we could see nothing of them. We could not stand up to look about us because of the pitching of the boat. The sea ran in great rollers, and we had much ado to keep the boat's head to them. The two other men who had escaped so far with me were a man named Helmar, a passenger like myself, and a seaman whose name I don't know, a short sturdy man with a stammer.[4]

We drifted famishing, and, after our water had come to an end, tormented by an intolerable thirst, for eight days altogether. After the second day the sea subsided slowly to a glassy calm. It is quite impossible for the ordinary reader to imagine those eight days. He has not—luckily for himself—anything in his memory to imagine with. After the first day we said little to one another and lay in our places in the boat and stared at the horizon, or watched, with eyes that grew larger and more haggard every day, the misery and weakness gaining upon our companions. The sun became pitiless. The

1. Philmus (*Island*, p. 90) notes that while no relevant story appeared in the London *Daily News* on this date, in February 1893 the paper printed a report of court proceedings involving three shipwrecked sailors "who cannibalized a fourth after drawing lots for who would be victim," one of whom carried the middle name "Hjalmar" (cf. "Helmar" in next paragraph). *Gig*: long, narrow rowboat attached to a larger ship.
2. Large spar (a length of wood usually supporting a sail, such as the mast) projecting from the stem of a vessel, to which the foremast stays fastened.
3. "Small keg or cask" (*OED*), often used in sailing vessels as ballast or carried in life-boats as provision; perhaps a corruption of the Spanish *barrica*. While Wells might have changed this to "beaker" in later editions, the larger amount of liquid contained in WH's "breaker" seems more appropriate to the circumstance.
4. Many details in this and the following paragraphs echo those given in Savigny and Corréard's *Narrative*. Wells also had at hand accounts of a more recent case of cannibalism at sea, known as *Regina v. Dudley and Stephens* (1884), in which three shipwrecked sailors on the yacht *Mignonette* survived by killing and consuming a fourth, the *Mignonette*'s cabin boy. Upon their rescue and return to England, two of the surviving sailors were eventually convicted of murder and sentenced to death, though they served brief commuted sentences. The case became a cultural cause célèbre, recalled in most British law curricula.

water ended on the fourth day, and we were already thinking strange things and saying them with our eyes; but it was, I think, the sixth before Helmar gave voice to the thing we all had in mind. I remember our voices were dry and thin, so that we bent towards one another and spared our words. I stood out against it with all my might, was rather for scuttling the boat and perishing together among the sharks that followed us; but when Helmar said that if his proposal was accepted we should have drink, the sailor came round to him.

I would not draw lots, however, and in the night the sailor whispered to Helmar again and again, and I sat in the bows with my clasp-knife in my hand—though I doubt if I had the stuff in me to fight. And in the morning I agreed to Helmar's proposal, and we handed halfpence[5] to find the odd man.

The lot fell upon the sailor, but he was the strongest of us and would not abide by it, and attacked Helmar with his hands. They grappled together and almost stood up. I crawled along the boat to them, intending to help Helmar by grasping the sailor's leg, but the sailor stumbled with the swaying of the boat, and the two fell upon the gunwale[6] and rolled overboard together. They sank like stones. I remember laughing at that and wondering why I laughed. The laugh caught me suddenly like a thing from without.

I lay across one of the thwarts[7] for I know not how long, thinking that if I had the strength I would drink sea-water and madden myself to die quickly. And even as I lay there, I saw, with no more interest than if it had been a picture, a sail come up towards me over the sky-line. My mind must have been wandering, and yet I remember all that happened quite distinctly. I remember how my head swayed with the seas, and the horizon with the sail above it danced up and down. But I also remember as distinctly that I had a persuasion that I was dead, and that I thought what a jest it was they should come too late by such a little to catch me in my body.

For an endless period, as it seemed to me, I lay with my head on the thwart watching the dancing schooner—she was a little ship, schooner-rigged fore and aft—come up out of the sea. She kept tacking[8] to and fro in a widening compass, for she was sailing dead into the wind. It never entered my head to attempt to attract attention, and I do not remember anything distinctly after the sight of her side until I found myself in a little cabin aft. There's a dim half-memory

---

5. Drew lots.
6. Uppermost edge or planking of a ship's side.
7. Rowers' seats or benches.
8. Following a zigzag course (as the bow of a ship meets the wind without adjustment of the sails). *Schooner-rigged*: equipped or outfitted ("rigged") with sails appropriate to a schooner.

of being lifted up to the gangway and of a big red countenance, covered with freckles and surrounded with red hair, staring at me over the bulwarks.[9] I also had a disconnected impression of a dark face with extraordinary eyes close to mine, but that I thought was a nightmare, until I met it again. I fancy I recollected some stuff being poured in between my teeth. And that is all.

CHAPTER II.   The Man Who Was Going Nowhere

The cabin in which I found myself was small, and rather untidy. A youngish man with flaxen hair, a bristly straw-coloured moustache, and a dropping nether lip was sitting and holding my wrist. For a minute we stared at one another without speaking. He had watery grey eyes, oddly void of expression.

Then just overhead came a sound like an iron bed-stead being knocked about and the low angry growling of some large animal. At the same time the man spoke again.

He repeated his question: "How do you feel now?"

I think I said I felt all right. I could not recollect how I had got there. He must have seen the question in my face, for my voice was inaccessible to me.

"You were picked up in a boat—starving. The name on the boat was the *Lady Vain*, and there were spots of blood on the gunwale." At the same time my eye caught my hand, so thin that it looked like a dirty skin purse full of loose bones, and all the business of the boat came back to me.

"Have some of this," said he, and gave me a dose of some scarlet stuff, iced.

It tasted like blood, and made me feel stronger.

"You were in luck," said he, "to get picked up by a ship with a medical man aboard." He spoke with a slobbering articulation, with the ghost of a lisp.

"What ship is this?" I said slowly, hoarse from my long silence.

"It's a little trader from Arica and Callao. I never asked where she came from in the beginning. Out of the land of born fools, I guess. I'm a passenger myself from Arica. The silly ass who owns her—he's captain too, named Davis—he's lost his certificate or something. You know the kind of man—calls the thing the *Ipecacuanha*—of all silly

---

9. Woodwork running along a ship's side above the upper deck. *Gangway*: raised, planked passageway connecting different parts of a ship or used for boarding (i.e., gangplank).

infernal names, though when there's much of a sea without any wind she certainly acts according."[1]

Then the noise overhead began again, a snarling growl and the voice of a human being together. Then another voice telling some "Heaven-forsaken idiot" to desist.

"You were nearly dead," said my interlocutor. "It was a very near thing indeed. But I've put some stuff into you now. Notice your arm's sore? Injections. You've been insensible for nearly thirty hours."

I thought slowly. I was distracted now by the yelping of a number of dogs. "Am I eligible for solid food?" I asked.

"Thanks to me," he said. "Even now the mutton is boiling."

"Yes," I said, with assurance; "I could eat some mutton."

"But," said he, with a momentary hesitation, "you know I'm dying to hear of how you came to be alone in the boat." I thought I detected a certain suspicion in his eyes.

"*Damn that howling!*"

He suddenly left the cabin, and I heard him in violent controversy with some one, who seemed to me to talk gibberish in response to him. The matter sounded as though it ended in blows, but in that I thought my ears were mistaken. Then he shouted at the dogs and returned to the cabin.

"Well?" said he, in the doorway. "You were just beginning to tell me."

I told him my name, Edward Prendick, and how I had taken to natural history as a relief from the dulness of my comfortable independence. He seemed interested in this. "I've done some science myself—I did my Biology at University College,—getting out the ovary of the earthworm and the radula[2] of the snail and all that. Lord! it's ten years ago. But go on, go on—tell me about the boat."

He was evidently satisfied with the frankness of my story, which I told in concise sentences enough—for I felt horribly weak,—and when it was finished he reverted at once to the topic of natural history and his own biological studies. He began to question me closely about Tottenham Court Road and Gower Street. "Is Caplatzi still flourishing? What a shop that was!"[3] He had evidently been a very

---

1. Referring to seasickness (per the root meaning of *ipecacuanha*; see note 3 on p. 4).
2. The horny band or structure of tiny teeth with which mollusks scrape and take in food particles from a surface. *I did my Biology at University College*: The field and location of Montgomery's education are closely aligned to those of Wells, who studied under pioneering English biologist T. H. Huxley (1825–1895) at what is now Imperial College London and earned a degree in zoology from the University of London.
3. Anthony (né Antonio) Caplatzi—known formally as a "mathematical and philosophical instrument maker"—made and sold medical and other scientific equipment in a shop located on a small thoroughfare running between Tottenham Court Road and Gower Street in central London, near University College. (See Philmus, *Island*, p. 91 for more biographical information regarding Caplatzi's links to UC.)

ordinary medical student, and drifted incontinently[4] to the topic of
the music-halls. He told me some anecdotes. "Left it all," he said,
"ten years ago. How jolly it all used to be! But I made a young ass of
myself. . . . Played myself out before I was twenty-one. I dare say it's
all different now. . . . But I must look up that ass of a cook and see
what he's doing to your mutton."

The growling overhead was renewed, so suddenly and with so
much savage anger that it startled me. "What's that?" I called after
him, but the door had closed. He came back again with the boiled
mutton, and I was so excited by the appetising smell of it, that I forgot the noise of the beast forthwith.

After a day of alternate sleep and feeding I was so far recovered
as to be able to get from my bunk to the scuttle and see the green
seas trying to keep pace with us. I judged the schooner was running
before the wind.[5] Montgomery—that was the name of the flaxen-
haired man—came in again as I stood there, and I asked him for
some clothes. He lent me some duck[6] things of his own, for those I
had worn in the boat, he said, had been thrown overboard. They
were rather loose for me, for he was large, and long in his limbs.

He told me casually that the captain was three-parts drunk in his
own cabin. As I assumed the clothes I began asking him some questions about the destination of the ship. He said the ship was bound
to Hawaii, but that it had to land him first.

"Where?" said I.

"It's an island. . . . Where I live. So far as I know, it hasn't got a
name."

He stared at me with his nether lip dropping, and looked so wil-
fully stupid of a sudden that it came into my head that he desired to
avoid my questions. I had the discretion to ask no more.

CHAPTER III.   The Strange Face

We left the cabin and found a man at the companion obstructing
our way. He was standing on the ladder with his back to us, peering
over the combing[7] of the hatchway. He was, I could see, a misshapen man, short, broad, and clumsy, with a crooked back, a hairy

4. Abruptly.
5. Moving in the direction of, hence propelled by, the wind. *Scuttle*: small opening in the
   side or bottom of a ship, furnished with a lid, providing light and ventilation.
6. Sturdy, plain-woven fabric (usually linen or cotton), commonly used for sailors' clothing (from the Dutch *doek*, "linen canvas").
7. Misspelling of "coaming," the raised border at the edges of a ship's scuttles and hatches
   (or openings in a ship's deck, a "hatchway" being a passageway giving access to such a
   space via ladder or stairs). *Companion*: stairway or ladder leading from one deck of a
   ship to another below (or the canopy to such a stairway).

neck and a head sunk between his shoulders.[8] He was dressed in dark blue serge,[9] and had peculiarly thick coarse black hair. I heard the unseen dogs growl furiously, and forthwith he ducked back, coming into contact with the hand I put out to fend him off from myself. He turned with animal swiftness.

In some indefinable way the black face thus flashed upon me shocked me profoundly. It was a singularly deformed one. The facial part projected, forming something dimly suggestive of a muzzle, and the huge half-open mouth showed as big white teeth as I had ever seen in a human mouth. His eyes were bloodshot at the edges, with scarcely a rim of white round the hazel pupils. There was a curious glow of excitement in his face.

"Confound you!" said Montgomery. "Why the devil don't you get out of the way?" The black-faced man started aside without a word.

I went on up the companion, instinctively staring at him as I did so. Montgomery stayed at the foot for a moment. "You have no business here, you know," he said, in a deliberate tone. "Your place is forward."

The black-faced man cowered. "They . . . won't have me forward." He spoke slowly, with a queer hoarse quality in his voice.

"Won't have you forward!" said Montgomery in a menacing voice. "But I tell you to go." He was on the brink of saying something further, then looked up at me suddenly and followed me up the ladder. I had paused halfway through the hatchway, looking back, still astonished beyond measure at the grotesque ugliness of this black-faced creature. I had never beheld such a repulsive and extraordinary face before, and yet—if the contradiction is credible—I experienced at the same time an odd feeling that in some way I *had* already encountered exactly the features and gestures that now amazed me. Afterwards it occurred to me that probably I had seen him as I was lifted aboard, and yet that scarcely satisfied my suspicion of a previous acquaintance. Yet how one could have set eyes on so singular a face and have forgotten the precise occasion passed my imagination.

Montgomery's movement to follow me released my attention, and I turned and looked about me at the flush deck[1] of the little schooner. I was already half prepared by the sounds I had heard for

---

8. The myth of "monstrous men" from Africa and the "East" whose heads hung beneath their shoulders was a staple of classical and early modern European ethnography and travel writing. Often, such figures were also said to be cannibals or "anthropophagi," a conjunction that we find in Othello's famous tale of his own exotic travels in Shakespeare's play: "I spoke of . . . / my traveller's history . . . / of the cannibals that each other eat, / The Anthropophagi, and men whose heads / Do grow beneath their shoulders" (*Othello* 1.3.133, 138, 142–44). All Shakespeare citations are from *The Norton Shakespeare*, 3rd ed., ed. Stephen Greenblatt et al. (New York and London: W. W. Norton, 2015).
9. Durable twilled fabric, associated during this period with the working class and poor.
1. Ship's deck that extends from the bow (front) to the stern (rear), usually with no structure above.

what I saw. Certainly I never beheld a deck so dirty. It was littered
with scraps of carrot, shreds of green stuff, and indescribable
filth. Fastened by chains to the main mast were a number of grisly
staghounds, who now began leaping and barking at me, and by the
mizzen[2] a huge puma was cramped in a little iron cage, far too small
even to give it turning-room. Farther under the starboard[3] bulwark
were some big hutches containing a number of rabbits, and a solitary llama was squeezed in a mere box of a cage forward. The dogs
were muzzled by leather straps. The only human being on deck was
a gaunt and silent sailor at the wheel.

The patched and dirty spankers were tense before the wind, and
up aloft the little ship seemed carrying every sail she had. The sky
was clear, the sun midway down the western sky; long waves, capped
by the breeze with froth, were running with us. We went past the
steersman to the taffrail and saw the water come foaming under the
stern,[4] and the bubbles go dancing and vanishing in her wake. I
turned and surveyed the unsavoury length of the ship.

"Is this an ocean menagerie?"[5] said I.

"Looks like it," said Montgomery.

"What are these beasts for? Merchandise, curios?[6] Does the captain think he is going to sell them somewhere in the South Seas?"

"It does look like it, doesn't it?" said Montgomery, and turned
towards the wake again.

Suddenly we heard a yelp and a volley of furious blasphemy coming from the companion hatchway, and the deformed man with the
black face clambered up hurriedly. He was immediately followed by
a heavy red-haired man in a white cap. At the sight of the former the
staghounds, who had all tired of barking at me by this time, became
furiously excited, howling and leaping against their chains. The black
hesitated before them, and this gave the red-haired man time to
come up with him and deliver a tremendous blow between the
shoulder-blades. The poor devil went down like a felled ox, and rolled

---

2. Ship's mast located aft (rearward) of the mainmast. *Staghounds*: dogs bred for hunting.
3. Right-hand side of a ship.
4. Ship's rear. *Spankers*: fore-and-aft sails on the mast nearest a ship's stern. *Taffrail*:
handrail located on the open deck toward a ship's stern.
5. A collection of normally wild animals kept caged, and sometimes trained, for exhibi-
tion (akin to a zoo or circus, but emphasizing the "necessary" enclosure of "exotic"
creatures). Though dating to the reign of Henry III (1207–1272), English menageries
were largely available only to private audiences until the beginning of the 18th century
and were limited in scope until the 19th century, when capture, transport, and display
of "exotic beasts" from colonial sites in Africa, Asia, South America, and the British
Empire's archipelagos were offered to the public as emblems of national imperial
expansion, conquest, efficacy, and authority. Animal merchants followed methods and
routes established by the global slave trade, such that the production and consumption
of menageries remained implicated in the logic of racialized subjugation long after
slavery was abolished in the Anglo-American world.
6. A feature of the international trade in wildlife was a market for preserved animals,
horns, tusks, skeletons, and other "curiosities" of the "wild" taken from across the globe.

in the dirt among the furiously excited dogs. It was lucky for him they were muzzled. The red-haired man gave a yawp[7] of exultation and stood staggering and, as it seemed to me, in serious danger of either going backwards down the companion hatchway, or forwards upon his victim.

So soon as the second man had appeared, Montgomery had started violently. "Steady on there!" he cried, in a tone of remonstrance. A couple of sailors appeared on the forecastle.[8]

The black-faced man, howling in a singular voice, rolled about under the feet of the dogs. No one attempted to help him. The brutes did their best to worry him, butting their muzzles at him. There was a quick dance of their lithe grey bodies over the clumsy prostrate figure. The sailors forward shouted to them as though it was admirable sport. Montgomery gave an angry exclamation, and went striding down the deck. I followed him.

In another second the black-faced man had scrambled up and was staggering forward. He stumbled up against the bulwark by the main shrouds,[9] where he remained panting and glaring over his shoulder at the dogs. The red-haired man laughed a satisfied laugh.

"Look here, captain," said Montgomery, with his lisp a little accentuated, gripping the elbows of the red-haired man; "this won't do."

I stood behind Montgomery. The captain came half round and regarded him with the dull and solemn eyes of a drunken man. "Wha' won't do?" he said; and added, after looking sleepily into Montgomery's face for a minute, "Blasted Sawbones!"[1]

With a sudden movement he shook his arms free, and after two ineffectual attempts stuck his freckled fists into his side-pockets.

"That man's a passenger," said Montgomery. "I'd advise you to keep your hands off him."

"Go to hell!" said the captain loudly. He suddenly turned and staggered towards the side. "Do what I like on my own ship," he said.

I think Montgomery might have left him then—seeing the brute was drunk. But he only turned a shade paler, and followed the captain to the bulwarks.

"Look here, captain," he said. "That man of mine is not to be ill-treated. He has been hazed[2] ever since he came aboard."

For a minute alcoholic fumes kept the captain speechless. "Blasted Sawbones!" was all he considered necessary.

7. Hoarse cry.
8. The forward section of a ship's upper deck.
9. Ropes, or rigging, leading from a ship's mastheads to provide lateral support for the masts.
1. Pejorative slang for physician, especially a surgeon given to overzealous amputation or other drastic treatment; at times applied to vivisectors.
2. Bullied.

I could see that Montgomery had one of those slow pertinacious[3] tempers that will warm day after day to a white heat and never again cool to forgiveness, and I saw too that this quarrel had been some time growing. "The man's drunk," said I, perhaps officiously; "you'll do no good."

Montgomery gave an ugly twist to his dropping lip. "He's always drunk. Do you think that excuses his assaulting his passengers?"

"My ship," began the captain, waving his hand unsteadily towards the cages, "was a clean ship. Look at it now." It was certainly anything but clean. "Crew," continued the captain, "clean respectable crew."

"You agreed to take the beasts."

"I wish I'd never set eyes on your infernal island. What the devil . . . want beasts for on an island like that? Then that man of yours . . . Understood he was a man. He's a lunatic. And he hadn't no business aft. Do you think the whole damned ship belongs to you?"

"Your sailors began to haze the poor devil as soon as he came aboard."

"That's just what he is—he's a devil, an ugly devil. My men can't stand him. *I* can't stand him. None of us can't stand him. Nor *you* either."

Montgomery turned away. "*You* leave that man alone, anyhow," he said, nodding his head as he spoke.

But the captain meant to quarrel now. He raised his voice: "If he comes this end of the ship again I'll cut his insides out, I tell you. Cut out his blasted insides! Who are *you* to tell *me* what *I'm* to do. I tell you I'm captain of the ship—Captain and Owner. I'm the law here, I tell you—the law and the prophets.[4] I bargained to take a man and his attendant to and from Arica and bring back some animals. I never bargained to carry a mad devil and a silly Sawbones, a—"

Well, never mind what he called Montgomery. I saw the latter take a step forward, and interposed. "He's drunk," said I. The captain began some abuse even fouler than the last. "Shut up," I said, turning on him sharply, for I had seen danger in Montgomery's white face. With that I brought the downpour on myself.

However, I was glad to avert what was uncommonly near a scuffle, even at the price of the captain's drunken ill-will. I do not think I have ever heard quite so much vile language come in a continuous stream from any man's lips before, though I have frequented eccentric company enough. I found some of it hard to endure—though I am a

3. Strong-willed.
4. In the Sermon on the Mount, Jesus describes the citizens of God's kingdom and explains his connection to prophetic law of the Mosaic tradition: "Thou shalt love the Lord thy God with all thy heart, and with all thy soul, and with all thy mind. This is the first and great commandment. And the second is like unto it, Thou shalt love they neighbour as thyself. On these two commandments hang all the law and the prophets" (Matthew 22:37–40; from the King James Version of the Bible, as are all other biblical citations in the notes).

mild-tempered man. But certainly when I told the captain to shut up
I had forgotten I was merely a bit of human flotsam, cut off from my
resources, and with my fare unpaid, a mere casual dependant on the
bounty—or speculative enterprise—of the ship. He reminded me of it
with considerable vigour. But at any rate I prevented a fight.

CHAPTER IV. At the Schooner's Rail

That night land was sighted after sundown, and the schooner hove
to.[5] Montgomery intimated that was his destination. It was too far to
see any details; it seemed to me then simply a low-lying patch of
dim blue in the uncertain blue-grey sea. An almost vertical streak
of smoke went up from it into the sky.

The captain was not on deck when it was sighted. After he had
vented his wrath on me he had staggered below, and I understand
he went to sleep on the floor of his own cabin. The mate practically
assumed the command. He was the gaunt, taciturn individual we
had seen at the wheel. Apparently he too was in an evil temper with
Montgomery. He took not the slightest notice of either of us. We
dined with him in a sulky silence, after a few ineffectual efforts on
my part to talk. It struck me, too, that the men regarded my companion and his animals in a singularly unfriendly manner. I found
Montgomery very reticent about his purpose with these creatures,
and about his destination, and though I was sensible of a growing
curiosity I did not press him.

We remained talking on the quarter-deck[6] until the sky was thick
with stars. Except for an occasional sound in the yellow-lit forecastle, and a movement of the animals now and then, the night was
very still. The puma lay crouched together, watching us with shining eyes, a black heap in the corner of its cage. The dogs seemed to
be asleep. Montgomery produced some cigars.

He talked to me of London in a tone of half-painful reminiscence,
asking all kinds of questions about changes that had taken place.
He spoke like a man who had loved his life there, and had been suddenly and irrevocably cut off from it. I gossiped as well as I could of
this and that. All the time the strangeness of him was shaping itself
in my mind, and as I talked I peered at his odd pallid face in the dim
light of the binnacle lantern behind me. Then I looked out at the
darkling[7] sea, where in the dimness his little island was hidden.

5. Was brought to a stop against the wind.
6. Small, raised deck above the main deck and behind a ship's main mast, reserved for the
   captain and other privileged persons.
7. Darkening; dimming. *Binnacle lantern*: protective case containing a ship's navigational
   instruments, including compass and oil lamp.

This man, it seemed to me, had come out of Immensity merely to save my life. To-morrow he would drop over the side and vanish again out of my existence. Even had it been under commonplace circumstances it would have made me a trifle thoughtful. But in the first place was the singularity of an educated man living on this unknown little island, and coupled with that, the extraordinary nature of his luggage.[8] I found myself repeating the captain's question: What did he want with the beasts? Why, too, had he pretended they were not his when I had remarked about them at first? Then again, in his personal attendant there was a bizarre quality that had impressed me profoundly. These circumstances threw a haze of mystery round the man. They laid hold of my imagination and hampered my tongue.

Towards midnight our talk of London died away, and we stood side by side leaning over the bulwarks, and staring dreamily over the silent starlit sea, each pursuing his own thoughts. It was the atmosphere for sentiment, and I began upon my gratitude.

"If I may say it," said I, after a time, "you have saved my life."

"Chance," he answered; "just chance."

"I prefer to make my thanks to the accessible agent."

"Thank no one. You had the need, and I the knowledge, and I injected and fed you much as I might have collected a specimen. I was bored, and wanted something to do. If I'd been jaded that day, or hadn't liked your face, well—; it's a curious question where you would have been now."

This damped my mood a little. "At any rate—" I began.

"It's chance, I tell you," he interrupted, "as everything is in a man's life. Only the asses won't see it. Why am I here now—an outcast from civilisation—instead of being a happy man, enjoying all the pleasures of London? Simply because—eleven years ago—I lost my head for ten minutes on a foggy[9] night."

He stopped. "Yes?" said I.

"That's all."

We relapsed into silence. Presently he laughed. "There's something in this starlight that loosens one's tongue. I'm an ass, and yet somehow I would like to tell you."

8. I.e., the animals on board.
9. A term associated in 19th-century English culture with homosexuality generally and the scene of homosexual assignation in particular, shrouded as such socially condemned practices were in secrecy and obfuscation. See, for example, *Strange Case of Dr. Jekyll and Mr. Hyde* (1886) by Robert Louis Stevenson (1850–1894), and *The Picture of Dorian Gray* (1890) by Oscar Wilde (1854–1900), narratives familiar to Wells. Combined with earlier and later descriptions of Montgomery in terms stereotyped in the late Victorian period as "gay," Montgomery's quickly committed lapse from sanctioned behavior on a "foggy night" in the vicinity of Gower Street—known as a locus of sexual nonconformity and cultural experimentation—marks the nature of his "blunder" in suitably euphemistic but insistent terms.

"Whatever you tell me, you may rely upon my keeping to myself. . . . If that's it."

He was on the point of beginning, and then shook his head doubtfully. "Don't," said I. "It is all the same to me. After all, it is better to keep your secret. There's nothing gained but a little relief, if I respect your confidence. If I don't . . . well?"

He grunted undecidedly. I felt I had him at a disadvantage, had caught him in the mood of indiscretion; and, to tell the truth, I was not curious to learn what might have driven a young medical student out of London. I have an imagination. I shrugged my shoulders, and turned away. Over the taffrail leant a silent black figure, watching the stars. It was Montgomery's strange attendant. It looked over its shoulder quickly with my movement, then looked away again.

It may seem a little thing to you, perhaps, but it came like a sudden blow to me. The only light near us was a lantern at the wheel. The creature's face was turned for one brief instant out of the dimness of the stem towards this illumination, and I saw that the eyes that glanced at me shone with a pale green light.

I did not know then that a reddish luminosity, at least, is not uncommon in human eyes. The thing came to me as stark inhumanity. That black figure, with its eyes of fire, struck down through all my adult thoughts and feelings, and for a moment the forgotten horrors of childhood came back to my mind. Then the effect passed as it had come. An uncouth black figure of a man, a figure of no particular import, hung over the taffrail, against the starlight, and I found Montgomery was speaking to me.

"I'm thinking of turning in, then," said he; "if you've had enough of this."

I answered him incongruously.[1] We went below, and he wished me good-night at the door of my cabin.

That night I had some very unpleasant dreams. The waning moon rose late. Its light struck a ghostly faint white beam across my cabin, and made an ominous shape on the planking by my bunk. Then the staghounds woke, and began howling and baying, so that I dreamt fitfully, and scarcely slept until the approach of dawn.

CHAPTER V.   The Man Who Had Nowhere to Go

In the early morning—it was the second morning after my recovery, and I believe the fourth after I was picked up—I awoke through an avenue of tumultuous dreams, dreams of guns and howling mobs, and became sensible of a hoarse shouting above me. I rubbed my

1. Obliquely; distractedly.

eyes, and lay listening to the noise, doubtful for a little while of my whereabouts. Then came a sudden pattering of bare feet, the sound of heavy objects being thrown about, a violent creaking and rattling of chains. I heard the swish of the water as the ship was suddenly brought round, and a foamy yellow-green wave flew across the little round window and left it streaming. I jumped into my clothes and went on deck.

As I came up the ladder I saw against the flushed sky—for the sun was just rising—the broad back and red hair of the captain, and over his shoulder the puma spinning from a tackle rigged on to the mizzen spanker boom.[2] The poor brute seemed horribly scared, and crouched in the bottom of its little cage. "Overboard with 'em!" bawled the captain. "Overboard with 'em! We'll have a clean ship soon of the whole bilin' of 'em."[3]

He stood in my way, so that I had perforce to tap his shoulder to come on deck. He came round with a start, and staggered back a few paces to stare at me. It needed no expert eye to tell that the man was still drunk. "Hullo!" said he stupidly, and then with a light coming into his eyes, "Why, it's Mister—Mister—?"

"Prendick," said I.

"Prendick be damned!" said he. "Shut Up—that's your name. Mister Shut Up."

It was no good answering the brute. But I certainly did not expect his next move. He held out his hand to the gangway by which Montgomery stood talking to a massive white-haired man in dirty blue flannels, who had apparently just come aboard. "That way, Mister Blasted Shut Up. That way," roared the captain.

Montgomery and his companion turned as he spoke.

"What do you mean?" said I.

"That way, Mister Blasted Shut Up—that's what I mean. Overboard, Mister Shut Up—and sharp. We're clearing the ship out, cleaning the whole blessed ship out. And overboard you go."

I stared at him dumbfounded. Then it occurred to me it was exactly the thing I wanted. The lost prospect of a journey as sole passenger with this quarrelsome sot was not one to mourn over. I turned towards Montgomery.

"Can't have you," said Montgomery's companion concisely.

"You can't have me!" said I, aghast. He had the squarest and most resolute face I ever set eyes upon.

"Look here," I began, turning to the captain.

2. Spar (or pole) along the bottom of a sail, used to control the sail's angle and shape into the wind. *Tackle*: rigging.
3. I.e., "the whole boiling mess of them and their luggage," from the phrase "the whole kit and bilin'" or "the entire group and their equipment" (*kit* meaning the whole thing, *bilin'* meaning a seething mass, especially of people).

"Overboard," said the captain. "This ship ain't for beasts and cannibals, and worse than beasts, any more. Overboard you go . . . Mister Shut Up. If they can't have you, you goes adrift. But, anyhow, you go! With your Friends. I've done with this blessed island for evermore amen! I've had enough of it."

"But, Montgomery," I appealed.

He distorted his lower lip, and nodded his head hopelessly at the grey-haired man beside him, to indicate his powerlessness to help me.

"I'll see to *you* presently," said the captain.

Then began a curious three-cornered altercation. Alternately I appealed to one and another of the three men, first to the grey-haired man to let me land, and then to the drunken captain to keep me aboard. I even bawled entreaties to the sailors. Montgomery said never a word; only shook his head. "You're going overboard, I tell you," was the captain's refrain. . . . "Law be damned! I'm king here."

At last, I must confess, my voice suddenly broke in the middle of a vigorous threat. I felt a gust of hysterical petulance, and went aft, and stared dismally at nothing.

Meanwhile the sailors progressed rapidly with the task of unshipping the packages and caged animals. A large launch with two standing lugs lay under the lee[4] of the schooner, and into this the strange assortment of goods were swung. I did not then see the hands from the island that were receiving the packages, for the hull of the launch was hidden from me by the side of the schooner.

Neither Montgomery nor his companion took the slightest notice of me, but busied themselves in assisting and directing the four or five sailors who were unloading the goods. The captain went forward, interfering rather than assisting. I was alternately despairful and desperate. Once or twice, as I stood waiting there for things to accomplish themselves, I could not resist an impulse to laugh at my miserable quandary. I felt all the wretcheder for the lack of a breakfast. Hunger and a lack of blood-corpuscles[5] take all the manhood from a man. I perceived pretty clearly that I had not the stamina either to resist what the captain chose to do to expel me, or to force myself upon Montgomery and his companion. So I waited passively upon fate, and the work of transferring Montgomery's possessions to the launch went on as if I did not exist.

Presently that work was finished, and then came a struggle; I was hauled, resisting weakly enough, to the gangway. Even then I noticed the oddness of the brown faces of the men who were with

4. Side of a ship that's sheltered from the wind. *Lugs*: i.e., lug-sails, four-sided square sails suspended from a spar called a "yard" at an oblique angle so that they overlap the mast when raised; there are three types of lug-sails: standing, dipping, and balanced. *Launch*: large, flat-bottomed boat that operates in shallow water.

5. Blood cells.

Montgomery in the launch. But the launch was now fully laden, and was shoved off hastily. A broadening gap of green water appeared under me, and I pushed back with all my strength to avoid falling headlong.

The hands in the launch shouted derisively, and I heard Montgomery curse at them. And then the captain, the mate and one of the seamen helping him, ran me aft towards the stern. The dingey of the *Lady Vain* had been towing behind; it was half full of water, had no oars, and was quite unvictualled.[6] I refused to go aboard her, and flung myself full-length on the deck. In the end they swung me into her by a rope—for they had no stern ladder,—and then they cut me adrift.

I drifted slowly from the schooner. In a kind of stupor I watched all hands take to the rigging, and slowly but surely she came round to the wind. The sails fluttered, and then bellied out as the wind came into them. I stared at her weather-beaten side heeling[7] steeply towards me. And then she passed out of my range of view.

I did not turn my head to follow her. At first I could scarcely believe what had happened. I crouched in the bottom of the dingey, stunned, and staring blankly at the vacant oily sea. Then I realised I was in that little hell of mine again, now half-swamped. Looking back over the gunwale I saw the schooner standing away from me, with the red-haired captain mocking at me over the taffrail; and, turning towards the island, saw the launch growing smaller as she approached the beach.

Abruptly the cruelty of this desertion became clear to me. I had no means of reaching the land unless I should chance to drift there. I was still weak, you must remember, from my exposure in the boat; I was empty and very faint, or I should have had more heart. But as it was I suddenly began to sob and weep as I had never done since I was a little child. The tears ran down my face. In a passion of despair I struck with my fists at the water in the bottom of the boat, and kicked savagely at the gunwale. I prayed aloud to God that he would let me die.

CHAPTER VI.   The Evil-Looking Boatmen

But the islanders, seeing I was really adrift, took pity on me. I drifted very slowly to the eastward, approaching the island slantingly, and presently I saw with hysterical relief the launch come round and return towards me. She was heavily laden, and as she drew near

---

6. Not provided with food and other necessities.
7. Tipping to one side due to the wind's force or an uneven load.

I could make out Montgomery's white-haired broad-shouldered companion sitting cramped up with the dogs and several packing-cases in the stern sheets.[8] This individual stared fixedly at me without moving or speaking. The black-faced cripple was glaring at me as fixedly in the bows near the puma. There were three other men besides, strange brutish-looking fellows, at whom the stag-hounds were snarling savagely. Montgomery, who was steering, brought the boat by me, and, rising, caught and fastened my painter to the tiller[9] to tow me—for there was no room aboard.

I had recovered from my hysterical phase by this time, and answered his hail as he approached bravely enough. I told him the dingey was nearly swamped, and he reached me a piggin.[1] I was jerked back as the rope tightened between the boats. For some time I was busy baling.[2]

It was not until I had got the water under—for the water in the dingey had been shipped,[3] the boat was perfectly sound—that I had leisure to look at the people in the launch again.

The white-haired man, I found, was still regarding me steadfastly, but with an expression, as I now fancied, of some perplexity. When my eyes met his he looked down at the staghound that sat between his knees. He was a powerfully built man, as I have said, with a fine forehead and rather heavy features; but his eyes had that odd droop-ing of the skin above the lids that often comes with advancing years, and the fall of his heavy mouth at the corners gave him an expression of pugnacious resolution. He talked to Montgomery in a tone too low for me to hear. From him my eyes travelled to his three men, and a strange crew they were. I saw only their faces, yet there was something in their faces—I knew not what—that gave me a queer spasm of disgust. I looked steadily at them, and the impres-sion did not pass, though I failed to see what had occasioned it. They seemed to me then to be brown men, but their limbs were oddly swathed in some thin dirty white stuff down even to the fingers and feet. I have never seen men so wrapped up before, and women so only in the East. They wore turbans too, and thereunder peered out their elfin faces at me, faces with protruding lower jaws and bright eyes. They had lank black hair, almost like horse-hair, and seemed, as they sat, to exceed in stature any race of men I have seen. The white-haired man, who I knew was a good six feet in height, sat a head below any one of the three. I found afterwards that really none

---

8. Space at the stern of an open boat.
9. Lever used to turn a boat's rudder from side to side for navigation. *Painter*: rope attached to a dingey's bow, used for tying or towing the boat.
1. Small wooden pail.
2. I.e., bailing.
3. Bailed out.

were taller than myself, but their bodies were abnormally long, and the thigh-part of the leg short and curiously twisted. At any rate they were an amazingly ugly gang, and over the heads of them, under the forward lug, peered the black face of the man whose eyes were luminous in the dark.

As I stared at them they met my gaze, and then first one and then another turned away from my direct stare and looked at me in an odd furtive manner. It occurred to me that I was perhaps annoying them, and I turned my attention to the island we were approaching.

It was low, and covered with thick vegetation, chiefly a kind of palm that was new to me. From one point a thin white thread of vapour rose slantingly to an immense height, and then frayed out like a down feather. We were now within the embrace of a broad bay flanked on either hand by a low promontory. The beach was of dull grey sand, and sloped steeply up to a ridge, perhaps sixty or seventy feet above the sea-level, and irregularly set with trees and undergrowth. Half-way up was a square piebald stone enclosure that I found subsequently was built partly of coral and partly of pumiceous lava.[4] Two thatched roofs peeped from within this enclosure.

A man stood awaiting us at the water's edge. I fancied, while we were still far off, that I saw some other and very grotesque-looking creatures scuttle into the bushes upon the slope, but I saw nothing of these as we drew nearer. This man was of a moderate size, and with a black negroid[5] face. He had a large, almost lipless mouth, extraordinary lank arms, long thin feet and bow legs, and stood with his heavy face thrust forward staring at us. He was dressed like Montgomery and his white-haired companion, in jacket and trousers of blue serge.

As we came still nearer, this individual began to run to and fro on the beach, making the most grotesque movements. At a word of command from Montgomery the four men in the launch sprang up with singular awkward gestures and struck the lugs.[6] Montgomery steered us round and into a narrow little dock excavated in the beach. Then the man on the beach hastened towards us. This dock, as I

---

4. Of the nature of light, porous, glassy volcanic rock (or pumice). *Piebald*: particolored, alternating light and dark.
5. Characteristic of a dark-complexioned person of African descent; now recognized as specious and offensive, the term was still widely considered in late 19th-century Euro-American scientific and anthropological discourse an appropriate designation of one of several "human races." In the now-debunked theories of race that persisted from the late 1780s into the 20th century, often in service of justifying racist practices of oppression, three racial groupings—Negroid, Caucasoid, Mongoloid—were accounted elemental "types of mankind," a classificatory scheme in which animals were also perniciously, if confusedly, implicated: see illustration on p. 118 below.
6. Lowered the sails.

call it, was really a mere ditch just long enough at this phase of the tide to take the long-boat.

I heard the bows ground in the sand, staved the dingey off the rudder of the big boat with my piggin, and, freeing the painter, landed. The three muffled men, with the clumsiest movements, scrambled out upon the sand, and forthwith set to landing the cargo, assisted by the man on the beach. I was struck especially with the curious movements of the legs of the three swathed and bandaged boatmen—not stiff they were, but distorted in some odd way, almost as if they were jointed in the wrong place. The dogs were still snarling, and strained at their chains after these men, as the white-haired man landed with them.

The three big fellows spoke to one another in odd guttural tones, and the man, who had waited for us on the beach, began chattering to them excitedly—a foreign language, as I fancied—as they laid hands on some bales piled near the stern. Somewhere I had heard such a voice before, and I could not think where. The white-haired man stood holding in a tumult of six dogs, and bawling orders over their din. Montgomery, having unshipped the rudder, landed likewise, and all set to work at unloading. I was too faint, what with my long fast and the sun beating down on my bare head, to offer any assistance.

Presently the white-haired man seemed to recollect my presence, and came up to me. "You look," said he, "as though you had scarcely breakfasted."

His little eyes were a brilliant black under his heavy brows. "I must apologise for that. Now you are our guest, we must make you comfortable—though you are uninvited, you know."

He looked keenly into my face. "Montgomery says you are an educated man, Mr. Prendick—says you know something of science. May I ask what that signifies?"

I told him I had spent some years at the Royal College of Science, and had done some research in biology under Huxley.[7] He raised his eyebrows slightly at that.

"That alters the case a little, Mr. Prendick," he said, with a trifle more respect in his manner. "As it happens, we are biologists here. This is a biological station[8]—of a sort." His eye rested on the men in

---

7. Huxley (see note 2 on p. 9) became known as "Darwin's Bulldog" in the wake of his fiery defense of Darwin's 1859 *On the Origin of Species* in the 1860 "Great Debate" at Oxford with evolution foe Bishop Samuel Wilberforce (1805–1873). Wells accounted himself a lifelong "disciple" of this "towering great man" who exemplified "cool-headed deliberate thinking, plain statement and perfect sincerity" ("Thomas Henry Huxley" [1935]).

8. An outpost designed for study of flora and fauna in their native habitats. The biological or "field" station arose in Europe during the 1870s as part of the broader shift in biological research toward observation and empiricism as the basis for scientific understanding, taking its place alongside, but also in rivalry with, such institutions as museums, zoos, and aquariums. These sites were not only scattered throughout the major research areas of Europe but also followed the pathways of colonial expansion, thereby becoming hallmarks of national identity and prestige among European imperialistic states.

white, who were busily hauling the puma, on rollers, towards the walled yard. "I and Montgomery, at least," he added.

Then, "When you will be able to get away, I can't say. We're off the track to anywhere. We see a ship once in a twelvemonth or so."

He left me abruptly and went up the beach past this group, and, I think, entered the enclosure. The other two men were with Montgomery erecting a pile of smaller packages on a low wheeled truck. The llama was still on the launch with the rabbit-hutches; the staghounds still lashed to the thwarts. The pile of things completed, all three men laid hold of the truck and began shoving the ton-weight or so upon it after the puma. Presently Montgomery left them, and coming back to me, held out his hand.

"I'm glad," said he, "for my own part. That captain was a silly ass. He'd have made things lively for you."

"It was you," said I, "that saved me again."

"That depends. You'll find this island an infernally rum[9] place, I promise you. I'd watch my goings carefully if I were you. *He*—" He hesitated, and seemed to alter his mind about what was on his lips. "I wish you'd help me with these rabbits," he said.

His procedure with the rabbits was singular. I waded in with him and helped him lug one of the hutches ashore. No sooner was that done than he opened the door of it, and tilting the thing on one end, turned its living contents out on the ground. They fell in a struggling heap one on the top of the other. He clapped his hands, and forthwith they went off with that hopping run of theirs, fifteen or twenty of them, I should think, up the beach. "Increase and multiply, my friends," said Montgomery. "Replenish the island. Hitherto we've had a certain lack of meat here."[1]

As I watched them disappearing, the white-haired man returned with a brandy flask and some biscuits. "Something to go on with, Prendick," said he in a far more familiar tone than before.

I made no ado, but set to work on the biscuits at once, while the white-haired man helped Montgomery to release about a score more of the rabbits. Three big hutches, however, went up to the house with the puma. The brandy I did not touch, for I have been an abstainer from my birth.

---

9. Odd; strange; suspect (*OED*).
1. Compare God's command in Genesis for "every living creature" of the sea and the air to "Be fruitful, and multiply" (Genesis 1:21, 22) with the theories of English economist and demographer Thomas Robert Malthus (1766–1834), who argued in *An Essay on the Principle of Population* (1798) that increased food supply led to a temporary improvement in the population's well-being that inevitably plummeted when resultant population growth led to fierce competition for sustenance; this ironic, anti-utopian trajectory was later termed the "Malthusian trap or specter." Malthus's theory significantly influenced Darwin's conceptions of natural selection.

CHAPTER VII.   The Locked Door

The reader will perhaps understand that at first everything was so strange about me, and my position was the outcome of such unexpected adventures, that I had no discernment of the relative strangeness of this or that thing about me. I followed the llama up the beach, and was overtaken by Montgomery, who asked me not to enter the stone enclosure. I noticed then that the puma in its cage and the pile of packages had been placed outside the entrance to this quadrangle.

I turned and saw that the launch had now been unloaded, run out again, and was being beached, and the white-haired man was walking towards us. He addressed Montgomery.

"And now comes the problem of this uninvited guest. What are we to do with him?"

"He knows something of science," said Montgomery.

"I'm itching to get to work again—with this new stuff," said the grey-haired man, nodding towards the enclosure. His eyes grew brighter.

"I daresay you are," said Montgomery, in anything but a cordial tone.

"We can't send him over there, and we can't spare the time to build him a new shanty. And we certainly can't take him into our confidence just yet."

"I'm in your hands," said I. I had no idea of what he meant by "over there."

"I've been thinking of the same things," Montgomery answered. "There's my room with the outer door—"

"That's it," said the elder man promptly, looking at Montgomery, and all three of us went towards the enclosure. "I'm sorry to make a mystery, Mr. Prendick—but you'll remember you're uninvited. Our little establishment here contains a secret or so, is a kind of Bluebeard's Chamber,[2] in fact. Nothing very dreadful really—to a sane man. But just now—as we don't know you—"

"Decidedly," said I; "I should be a fool to take offense at any want of confidence."

He twisted his heavy mouth into a faint smile—he was one of those saturnine[3] people who smile with the corners of the mouth

---

2. The protagonist of a grisly French folktale, made enduringly influential by Charles Perrault (1628–1703) in *Stories from Past Times* (1697), Bluebeard killed a sequence of wives in a "chamber of horrors" from which he barred his matrimonial victims before adding their remains to his secretive death-vault. Hence the term designates any space "in which a person keeps something hidden, especially something shocking or controversial" (*OED*).
3. Gloomy; dour.

down,—and bowed his acknowledgement of my complaisance. The main entrance to the enclosure we passed; it was a heavy wooden gate, framed in iron and locked, with the cargo of the launch piled outside it; and at the corner we came to a small doorway I had not previously observed. The grey-haired man produced a bundle of keys from the pocket of his greasy blue jacket, opened this door, and entered. His keys and the elaborate locking up of the place, even while it was still under his eye, struck me as peculiar.

I followed him, and found myself in a small apartment, plainly but not uncomfortably furnished, and with its inner door, which was slightly ajar, opening into a paved courtyard. This inner door Montgomery at once closed. A hammock was slung across the darker corner of the room, and a small unglazed window, defended by an iron bar, looked out towards the sea.

This, the grey-haired man told me, was to be my apartment, and the inner door, which, "for fear of accidents," he said, he would lock on the other side, was my limit inward. He called my attention to a convenient deck-chair before the window, and to an array of old books, chiefly, I found, surgical works and editions of the Latin and Greek classics—languages I cannot read with any comfort[4]—on a shelf near the hammock. He left the room by the outer door, as if to avoid opening the inner one again.

"We usually have our meals in here," said Montgomery, and then, as if in doubt, went out after the other. "Moreau," I heard him call, and for the moment I do not think I noticed. Then as I handled the books on the shelf it came up in consciousness: where had I heard the name of Moreau before?[5]

I sat down before the window, took out the biscuits that still remained to me, and ate them with an excellent appetite. "Moreau?"

Through the window I saw one of those unaccountable men in white lugging a packing-case along the beach. Presently the window-frame hid him. Then I heard a key inserted and turned in the lock behind me. After a little while I heard, through the locked door, the

4. Much like Wells, whose prodigious multidisciplinary learning did not include extensive formal instruction in classical languages; rather, Wells was a product of more "modern" scientific training and voracious autodidactic reading.

5. Among many possible claimants as historical influences upon the protagonist's name are the French symbolist painter Gustave Moreau (1826–1898), whose reputation on the Continent and in England was at its height in the 1890s, notably as a painter of works depicting humans and animals in complex, often terrifying relation (see illustration on p. 119 below); the psychiatrist and neuropharmacologist Jacques-Joseph Moreau (1804–1884), the first biomedical researcher to explore the relation between madness and dreams; the French biologist, mathematician, astronomer, and writer Pierre-Louis Moreau de Maupertuis (1698–1759), known for scientific expeditions and for theories of heredity based on detailed studies of anatomical anomalies; and Omar ibn Said (1770?–1864?)—known better by his alias, "Uncle Moreau"—widely learned Senegalese-born American enslaved person, author of the only known narrative by an enslaved person in America written in Arabic.

noise of the staghounds, which had now been brought up from the beach. They were not barking, but sniffing and growling in a curious fashion. I could hear the rapid patter of their feet, and Montgomery's voice soothing them.

I was very much impressed by the elaborate secrecy of these two men regarding the contents of the place, and for some time I was thinking of that, and of the unaccountable familiarity of the name of Moreau. But so odd is the human memory, that I could not then recall that well-known name in its proper connection. From that my thoughts went to the indefinable queerness of the deformed and white-swathed man on the beach. I never saw such a gait, such odd motions, as he pulled at the box. I recalled that none of these men had spoken to me, though most of them I had found looking at me at one time or another in a peculiar furtive manner, quite unlike the frank stare of your unsophisticated savage. I wondered what language they spoke. They had all seemed remarkably taciturn, and when they did speak, endowed with very uncanny[6] voices. What was wrong with them? Then I recalled the eyes of Montgomery's ungainly attendant.

Just as I was thinking of him, he came in. He was now dressed in white, and carried a little tray with some coffee and boiled vegetables thereon. I could hardly repress a shuddering recoil as he came, bending amiably, and placed the tray before me on the table.

Then astonishment paralyzed me. Under his stringy black locks I saw his ear! It jumped upon me suddenly, close to my face. The man had pointed ears, covered with a fine brown fur!

"Your breakfast, sair,"[7] he said. I stared at his face without attempting to answer him. He turned and went towards the door, regarding me oddly over his shoulder.

I followed him out with my eyes, and as I did so, by some trick of unconscious cerebration, there came surging into my head the phrase: "The Moreau—Hollows" was it? "The Moreau—?" Ah! it sent my memory back ten years. "The Moreau Horrors." The phrase drifted loose in my mind for a moment, and then I saw it in red lettering on a little buff-coloured pamphlet, that to read made one shiver and creep. Then I remembered distinctly all about it. That long-forgotten pamphlet came back with startling vividness to my mind. I had been a mere lad then, and Moreau was, I suppose, about fifty; a prominent and masterful physiologist,[8] well known in

---

6. Eerily mysterious, uncomfortably unexpected, and possibly dangerous.
7. Sir (inflection of Irish vernacular *sár*); with connotation of "overlord" (per *tsar*).
8. Specialist in the scientific study of living organisms, especially their anatomy and biological systems; with the rise of animal experimentation as a means of physiological discovery in the mid-to-late 19th century, "physiologist" became nearly synonymous with "vivisectionist."

scientific circles for his extraordinary imagination and his brutal
directness in discussion. Was this the same Moreau? He had published some very astonishing facts in connection with the transfusion of blood, and, in addition, was known to be doing valuable work
on morbid[9] growths. Then suddenly his career was closed. He had
to leave England. A journalist obtained access to his laboratory in
the capacity of laboratory assistant, with the deliberate intention of
making sensational exposures; and by the help of a shocking accident—if it was an accident—his gruesome pamphlet became notorious. On the day of its publication, a wretched dog, flayed and
otherwise mutilated, escaped from Moreau's house.[1]

It was in the silly season, and a prominent editor, a cousin of the
temporary laboratory assistant, appealed to the conscience of the
nation.[2] It was not the first time that conscience has turned against
the methods of research. The doctor was simply howled out of the
country. It may be he deserved to be, but I still think the tepid support of his fellow-investigators, and his desertion by the great body
of scientific workers, was a shameful thing. Yet some of his experiments, by the journalist's account, were wantonly cruel. He might
perhaps have purchased his social peace by abandoning his investigations, but he apparently preferred the latter, as most men would
who have once fallen under the overmastering spell of research. He
was unmarried, and had indeed nothing but his own interests to
consider. . . .

I felt convinced that this must be the same man. Everything
pointed to it. It dawned upon me to what end the puma and the other
animals, which had now been brought with other luggage into the
enclosure behind the house, were destined; and a curious faint
odour, the halitus[3] of something familiar, an odour that had been in
the background of my consciousness hitherto, suddenly came forward into the forefront of my thoughts. It was the antiseptic odour of

9. Diseased or disease-prone. *Transfusion of blood*: from the discovery of the blood's circulation in 1628 by William Harvey to the first successful transfusion of blood in a
human in 1828 by James Blundell and the many discoveries about blood made in the
late 19th century, vivisection and animal experimentation have played central roles in
the story of human blood transfusion.
1. Prendick's memory of the "Moreau Horrors" evokes three notorious episodes during the
(anti)vivisection debates of the 1870s and 1880s: the spectacle of French psychiatrist
Valentin Magnan inducing epilepsy in two dogs by injecting them with absinthe at the
1874 meeting of the British Medical Association in Norwich; the exposé in 1875 by
English physician George Hoggan of excruciating experiments conducted on live dogs in
the Parisian laboratory of physiologist Claude Bernard; and the prosecution in 1881
under the Cruelty to Animals Act of English neurologist David Ferrier, whose assiduous
advocacy of vivisection made him a scourge of the antivivisection movement.
2. Probable reference to Richard Holt Hutton (1826–1897), prominent antivivisectionist
and editor of the *Spectator*. *Silly season*: late summer, when the slower news pace during parliamentary recess led newspapers to sensationalize relatively minor stories.
3. "A vapor, exhalation" (*OED*).

the operating-room. I heard the puma growling through the wall, and one of the dogs yelped as though it had been struck.

Yet surely, and especially to another scientific man, there was nothing so horrible in vivisection[4] as to account for this secrecy. And by some odd leap in my thoughts the pointed ears[5] and luminous eyes of Montgomery's attendant came back again before me with the sharpest definition. I stared before me out at the green sea, frothing under a freshening breeze, and let these and other strange memories of the last few days chase each other through my mind.

What could it mean? A locked enclosure on a lonely island, a notorious vivisector, and these crippled and distorted men? . . .

CHAPTER VIII.   The Crying of the Puma

Montgomery interrupted my tangle of mystification and suspicion about one o'clock, and his grotesque attendant followed him with a tray bearing bread, some herbs, and other eatables, a flask of whisky, a jug of water, and three glasses and knives. I glanced askance at this strange creature, and found him watching me with his queer restless eyes. Montgomery said he would lunch with me, but that Moreau was too pre-occupied with some work to come.

"Moreau!" said I; "I know that name."

"The devil you do!" said he. "What an ass I was to mention it to you. I might have thought. Anyhow, it will give you an inkling of our—mysteries. Whisky?"

"No thanks—I'm an abstainer."

"I wish I'd been. But it's no use locking the door after the steed is stolen. It was that infernal stuff led to my coming here. That and a foggy night. I thought myself in luck at the time when Moreau offered to get me off. It's queer. . . ."[6]

"Montgomery," said I suddenly, as the outer door closed; "why has your man pointed ears?"

"Damn!" he said, over his first mouthful of food. He stared at me for a moment, and then repeated, "Pointed ears?"

4. Dissection of or operation upon a living organism, usually in pursuit of physiological or pathological knowledge; often pejorative, in contrast to "animal study" or "animal experimentation."

5. Darwin suggested in *The Descent of Man* (1871) that pointy ears in humans were a vestigial feature indicating a common ancestry among primates.

6. Montgomery's allusion to being released from a legal embarrassment ("get me off") in the context of his calamitous "foggy night" (cf. note 9 on p. 16) evokes the prosecution of Oscar Wilde in 1895 for "gross indecency," to which Wells alludes in the introduction to the 1924 Atlantic Edition of the novel: "There was a scandalous trial at the time [that I wrote *The Island of Doctor Moreau*], the graceless and pitiless downfall of a man of genius, and the story was the response of an imaginative mind to the reminder that humanity is but animal rough-hewn to a reasonable shape in perpetual internal conflict between instinct and injunction."

"Little points to them," said I, as calmly as possible, with a catch in my breath; "and a fine black fur at the edges."

He helped himself to whisky and water with great deliberation. "I was under the impression . . . that his hair covered his ears."

"I saw them as he stooped by me to put that coffee you sent to me on the table. And his eyes shine in the dark."

By this time Montgomery had recovered from the surprise of my question. "I always thought," he said deliberately, with a certain accentuation of his flavouring of lisp; "that there *was* something the matter with his ears. From the way he covered them. . . . What were they like?"

I was persuaded from his manner that this ignorance was a pretence. Still, I could hardly tell the man I thought him a liar. "Pointed," I said; "rather small and furry—distinctly furry. But the whole man is one of the strangest things I ever set eyes on."

A sharp, hoarse cry of animal pain came from the enclosure behind us. Its depth and volume testified to the puma. I saw Montgomery wince.

"Yes?" he said.

"Where did you pick the creature up?"

"Er—San Francisco. . . . He's an ugly brute, I admit. Half-witted, you know. Can't remember where he came from.[7] But I'm used to him, you know. We both are. How does he strike you?"

"He's unnatural," I said. "There's something about him. . . . Don't think me fanciful, but it gives me a nasty little sensation, a tightening of my muscles, when he comes near me. It's a touch . . . of the diabolical, in fact."

Montgomery had stopped eating while I told him this. "Rum," he said. "*I* can't see it."

He resumed his meal. "I had no idea of it," he said, and masticated. "The crew of the schooner . . . must have felt it the same. . . . Made a dead set at the poor devil. . . . You saw the captain?"

Suddenly the puma howled again, this time more painfully. Montgomery swore under his breath. I had half a mind to attack him about the men on the beach. Then the poor brute within gave vent to a series of short, sharp screams.

"Your men on the beach," said I; "what race are they?"

"Excellent fellows, aren't they?" said he absent-mindedly, knitting his brows as the animal yelled out sharply. I said no more. There

---

7. The "ugly brute" referred to is named "M'ling," possibly signifying "missing link," a colloquial term (derived from the medieval notion of a Great *Chain* of Being linking all life in a hierarchical order descending from God to humans to animals to matter) for the erroneously hypothesized transitional form in animal evolution bridging "advanced" primates and early anthropoids—a process of "hominization" presumed by some post-Darwinian evolutionary theorists to be a progressive movement from "simplicity" to "complexity."

was another outcry worse than the former. He looked at me with his dull grey eyes, and then took some more whisky. He tried to draw me into a discussion about alcohol, professing to have saved my life with it. He seemed anxious to lay stress on the fact that I owed my life to him. I answered him distractedly. Presently our meal came to an end, the misshapen monster with the pointed ears cleared away, and Montgomery left me alone in the room again. All the time he was in a state of ill-concealed irritation at the noise of the vivi-sected puma. He spoke of his odd want of nerve, and left me to the obvious application.

I found myself that the cries were singularly irritating, and they grew in depth and intensity as the afternoon wore on. They were painful at first, but their constant resurgence at last altogether upset my balance. I flung aside a crib of Horace[8] I had been reading, and began to clench my fists, to bite my lips, and pace the room.

Presently I got to stopping my ears with my fingers.

The emotional appeal of those yells grew upon me steadily, grew at last to such an exquisite expression of suffering that I could stand it in that confined room no longer. I stepped out of the door into the slumberous[9] heat of the late afternoon, and walking past the main entrance—locked again I noticed—turned the corner of the wall.

The crying sounded even louder out of doors. It was as if all the pain in the world had found a voice. Yet had I known such pain was in the next room, and had it been dumb, I believe—I have thought since—I could have stood it well enough. It is when suffering finds a voice and sets our nerves quivering that this pity comes troubling us. But in spite of the brilliant sunlight and the green fans of the trees waving in the soothing sea breeze, the world was a confusion, blurred with drifting black and red phantasms, until I was out of earshot of the house in the chequered wall.

CHAPTER IX.   The Thing in the Forest

I strode through the undergrowth that clothed the ridge behind the house, scarcely heeding whither I went, passed on through the shadow of a thick cluster of straight-stemmed trees beyond it, and so presently found myself some way on the other side of the ridge, and descending towards a streamlet that ran through a narrow valley. I paused and listened. The distance I had come, or the intervening

---

8. Quintus Horatius Flaccus (65–8 BCE), Roman poet, a staple of 19th-century English and European schooling, hence also known to many "gentlemen" like Prendick and Moreau through "cribs," or cheat sheets with the original Latin set side by side to a literal English translation. Horace was prized for being a "moralist," as well as for his meticulous craft and rationalistic philosophical bent.
9. Sleep-inducing; soporific.

masses of thicket, deadened any sound that might be coming from the enclosure. The air was still. Then with a rustle a rabbit emerged, and went scampering up the slope before me. I hesitated, and sat down in the edge of the shade.

The place was a pleasant one. The rivulet was hidden by the luxuriant vegetation of the banks, save at one point, where I caught a triangular patch of its glittering water. On the farther side I saw through a bluish haze a tangle of trees and creepers, and above these again the luminous blue of the sky. Here and there a splash of white or crimson marked the blooming of some trailing epiphyte.[1] I let my eyes wander over this scene for a while, and then began to turn over in my mind again the strange peculiarities of Montgomery's man. But it was too hot to think elaborately, and presently I fell into a tranquil state midway between dozing and waking.

From this I was aroused, after I know not how long, by a rustling amidst the greenery on the other side of the stream. For a moment I could see nothing but the waving summits of the ferns and reeds. Then suddenly upon the bank of the stream appeared something—at first I could not distinguish what it was. It bowed its head to the water and began to drink. Then I saw it was a man, going on all-fours like a beast!

He was clothed in a bluish cloth, and was of a copper-coloured hue, with black hair. It seemed that grotesque ugliness was an invariable character of these islanders. I could hear the suck of the water at his lips as he drank.

I leant forward to see him better, and a piece of lava, detached by my hand, went pattering down the slope. He looked up guiltily, and his eyes met mine. Forthwith he scrambled to his feet and stood wiping his clumsy hand across his mouth and regarding me. His legs were scarcely half the length of his body. So, staring one another out of countenance,[2] we remained for perhaps the space of a minute. Then, stopping to look back once or twice, he slunk off among the bushes to the right of me, and I heard the swish of the fronds[3] grow faint in the distance and die away. Every now and then he regarded me with a steadfast stare. Long after he had disappeared I remained sitting up staring in the direction of his retreat. My drowsy tranquility had gone.

I was startled by a noise behind me, and, turning suddenly, saw the flapping white tail of a rabbit vanishing up the slope. I jumped to my feet.

1. Any plant that grows upon another plant for physical support but, unlike a parasite, takes no nutrients from that supportive organism. *Creepers*: small, viny plants that grow along the ground or ascend a supporting surface (e.g., ivy growing up a tree).
2. Disconcertedly; in bewilderment.
3. Large compound leaves or leaflike parts of a palm, fern, or similar plant.

The apparition of this grotesque half-bestial creature had suddenly populated the stillness of the afternoon for me. I looked around me rather nervously, and regretted that I was unarmed. Then I thought that the man I had just seen had been clothed in bluish cloth, had not been naked as a savage would have been, and I tried to persuade myself from that fact that he was after all probably a peaceful character, that the dull ferocity of his countenance belied him.

Yet I was greatly disturbed at the apparition. I walked to the left along the slope, turning my head about and peering this way and that among the straight stems of the trees. Why should a man go on all-fours and drink with his lips? Presently I heard an animal wailing again, and taking it to be the puma, I turned about and walked in a direction diametrically opposite to the sound. This led me down to the stream, across which I stepped and pushed my way up through the undergrowth beyond.

I was startled by a great patch of vivid scarlet on the ground, and going up to it found it to be a peculiar fungus branched and corrugated like a foliaceous lichen, but deliquescing[4] into slime at the touch. And then in the shadow of some luxuriant ferns I came upon an unpleasant thing, the dead body of a rabbit, covered with shining flies, but still warm, and with the head torn off. I stopped aghast at the sight of the scattered blood. Here at least was one visitor to the island disposed of!

There were no traces of other violence about it. It looked as though it had been suddenly snatched up and killed. And as I stared at the little furry body came the difficulty of how the thing had been done. The vague dread that had been in my mind since I had seen the inhuman face of the man at the stream grew distincter as I stood there. I began to realise the hardihood of my expedition among these unknown people. The thicket about me became altered to my imagination. Every shadow became something more than a shadow, became an ambush, every rustle became a threat. Invisible things seemed watching me.

I resolved to go back to the enclosure on the beach. I suddenly turned away and thrust myself violently—possibly even frantically—through the bushes, anxious to get a clear space about me again.

I stopped just in time to prevent myself emerging upon an open space. It was a kind of glade in the forest made by a fall; seedlings were already starting up to struggle for the vacant space, and beyond, the dense growth of stems and twining vines and splashes of fungus and flowers closed in again. Before me, squatting together upon the

---

4. Becoming liquid by dissolving into moisture drawn from the air. *Foliaceous*: leaflike. *Lichen*: complex plantlike organism constituted by a symbiotic union of a fungus and an alga.

fungoid ruins of a huge fallen tree, and still unaware of my approach, were three grotesque human figures. One was evidently a female. The other two were men. They were naked, save for swathings of scarlet cloth about the middles, and their skins were of a dull pinkish drab colour, such as I had seen in no savages before. They had fat, heavy, chinless faces, retreating foreheads, and a scant bristly hair upon their heads.[5] Never before had I seen such bestial-looking creatures.

They were talking, or at least one of the men was talking to the other two, and all three had been too closely interested to heed the rustling of my approach. They swayed their heads and shoulders from side to side. The speaker's words came thick and sloppy, and though I could hear them distinctly I could not distinguish what he said. He seemed to me to be reciting some complicated gibberish.[6] Presently his articulation became shriller, and spreading his hands he rose to his feet.

At that the others began to gibber in unison, also rising to their feet, spreading their hands, and swaying their bodies in rhythm with their chant. I noticed then the abnormal shortness of their legs and their lank clumsy feet. All three began slowly to circle round, raising and stamping their feet and waving their arms; a kind of tune crept into their rhythmic recitation, and a refrain—"Aloola" or "Baloola"[7] it sounded like. Their eyes began to sparkle and their ugly faces to brighten with an expression of strange pleasure. Saliva dropped from their lipless mouths.

Suddenly, as I watched their grotesque and unaccountable gestures, I perceived clearly for the first time what it was that had offended me, what had given me the two inconsistent and conflicting impressions of utter strangeness and yet of the strangest familiarity. The three creatures engaged in this mysterious rite were human in shape, and yet human beings with the strangest air about them of some familiar animal. Each of these creatures, despite its human form, its rag of clothing and the rough humanity of its bodily form, had woven into it, into its movements, into the expression of its countenance, into its whole presence, some now irresistible suggestion of a hog, a swinish taint, the unmistakable mark of the beast.[8]

---

5. Features ascribed to the creatures seen by Prendick here and elsewhere constitute composites of descriptions applied by contemporary anthropologists, ethnographers, criminologists, and sociologists to "savages," "negroid specimens," "criminals," and "degenerates" (including "degenerative geniuses").
6. Rapid, inarticulate, and unintelligible speech; jabber.
7. Possibly mangled form of "hallelujah" (expression of joy, praise, or gratitude).
8. "And that no man might buy or sell, save he that had the mark, or the name of the beast, or the number of his name" (Revelation 13:17). The two beasts presented in the biblical Book of Revelation have been read as embodiments of oppressive state and falsifying church, with the bestial brand standing in contrast to the properly marked humanity of the faithful. That nexus of implications—blending conflicts between

I stood overcome by this amazing realisation, and then the most horrible questionings came rushing into my mind. They began leaping into the air, first one and then the other, whooping and grunting. Then one slipped, and for a moment was on all-fours, to recover indeed forthwith. But that transitory gleam of the true animalism of these monsters was enough.

I turned as noiselessly as possible, and becoming every now and then rigid with the fear of being discovered as a branch cracked or leaf rustled, I pushed back into the bushes. It was long before I grew bolder and dared to move freely.

My one idea for the moment was to get away from these foul beings, and I scarcely noticed that I had emerged upon a faint pathway amidst the trees. Then, suddenly traversing a little glade, I saw with an unpleasant start two clumsy legs among the trees, walking with noiseless footsteps parallel with my course, and perhaps thirty yards away from me. The head and upper part of the body were hidden by a tangle of creeper. I stopped abruptly, hoping the creature did not see me. The feet stopped as I did. So nervous was I that I controlled an impulse to headlong flight with the utmost difficulty.

Then, looking hard, I distinguished through the interlacing network the head and body of the brute I had seen drinking. He moved his head. There was an emerald flash in his eyes as he glanced at me from the shadow of the trees, a half-luminous colour that vanished as he turned his head again. He was motionless for a moment, and then with noiseless tread began running through the green confusion. In another moment he had vanished behind some bushes. I could not see him, but I felt that he had stopped and was watching me again.

What on earth was he—man or animal? What did he want with me? I had no weapon, not even a stick. Flight would be madness. At any rate the Thing, whatever it was, lacked the courage to attack me. Setting my teeth hard I walked straight towards him. I was anxious not to show the fear that seemed chilling my backbone. I pushed through a tangle of tall white-flowered bushes, and saw him twenty yards beyond, looking over his shoulder at me and hesitating. I advanced a step or two looking steadfastly into his eyes.

"Who are you?" said I. He tried to meet my gaze.

---

institutions and people; truth and deception; spirituality and bestiality—lies at the center of the secondary reference evoked by Wells with "mark of the beast": the 1890 short story "The Mark of the Beast" by English writer Rudyard Kipling [1865–1936; see pp. 204–16 below]. Lurking behind the whole of Prendick's sentence is the final paragraph of Darwin's *The Descent of Man*: "Man may be excused for feeling some pride at having risen, though not through his own exertions, to the very summit of the organic scale; . . . But . . . we must acknowledge [that] . . . —with all [his] exalted powers— Man still bears in his bodily frame the indelible stamp of his lowly origins."

"No!" he said suddenly, and, turning, went bounding away from me through the undergrowth. Then he turned and stared at me again. His eyes shone brightly out of the dusk under the trees.

My heart was in my mouth, but I felt my only chance was bluff, and walked steadily towards him. He turned again and vanished into the dusk. Once more I thought I caught the glint of his eyes, and that was all.

For the first time I realised how the lateness of the hour might affect me. The sun had set some minutes since, the swift dusk of the tropics was already fading out of the eastern sky, and a pioneer[9] moth fluttered silently by my head. Unless I would spend the night among the unknown dangers of the mysterious forest, I must hasten back to the enclosure.

The thought of a return to that pain-haunted refuge was extremely disagreeable, but still more so was the idea of being overtaken in the open by darkness, and all that darkness might conceal. I gave one more look into the blue shadows that had swallowed up this odd creature, and then retraced my way down the slope towards the stream, going as I judged in the direction from which I had come.

I walked eagerly, perplexed by all these things, and presently found myself in a level place among scattered trees. The colourless clearness that comes after the sunset flush was darkling. The blue sky above grew momentarily deeper, and the little stars one by one pierced the attenuated light; the interspaces of the trees, the gaps in the farther vegetation, that had been hazy blue in the daylight, grew black and mysterious.

I pushed on. The colour vanished from the world, the tree-tops rose against the luminous blue sky in inky silhouette, and all below that outline melted into one formless blackness. Presently the trees grew thinner, and the shrubby undergrowth more abundant. Then there was a desolate space covered with white sand, and then another expanse of tangled bushes.[1]

I was tormented by a faint rustling upon my right hand. I thought at first it was fancy, for whenever I stopped, there was silence, save for the evening breeze in the treetops. Then when I went on again there was an echo to my footsteps.

I moved away from the thickets, keeping to the more open ground, and endeavouring by sudden turns now and then to surprise this thing, if it existed, in the act of creeping upon me. I saw nothing,

---

9. Relating to or designating a hardy species that is the first to colonize barren or previously steady-state environments.

1. The language of this passage recalls Darwin's conclusion to *On the Origin of Species*, in which he develops the metaphor of Earth's ecosystem as a "tangled bank" where unconsciously competing flora and fauna realize the "grandeur of . . . life" through their very struggle for existence.

and nevertheless my sense of another presence grew steadily. I increased my pace, and after some time came to a slight ridge, crossed it and turned sharply, regarding it steadfastly from the further side. It came out black and clear-cut against the darkling sky.

And presently a shapeless lump heaved up momentarily against the skyline and vanished again. I felt assured now that my tawny-faced antagonist was stalking me again. And coupled with that was another unpleasant realisation, that I had lost my way.

For a time I hurried on hopelessly perplexed, pursued by that stealthy approach. Whatever it was, the thing either lacked the courage to attack me, or it was waiting to take me at some disadvantage. I kept studiously to the open. At times I would turn and listen, and presently I half-persuaded myself that my pursuer had abandoned the chase, or was a mere creation of my disordered imagination. Then I heard the sound of the sea. I quickened my footsteps almost to a run, and immediately there was a stumble in my rear.

I turned suddenly and stared at the uncertain trees behind me. One black shadow seemed to leap into another. I listened rigid, and heard nothing but the creep of the blood in my ears. I thought that my nerves were unstrung, and that my imagination was tricking me, and turned resolutely towards the sound of the sea again.

In a minute or so the trees grew thinner, and I emerged upon a bare low headland running out into the somber water. The night was calm and clear, and the reflection of the growing multitude of the stars shivered in the tranquil heaving of the sea. Some way out, the wash upon an irregular band of reef shone with a pallid light of its own. Westward I saw the zodiacal light mingling with the yellow brilliance of the evening star.[2] The coast fell away from me to the east, and westward it was hidden by the shoulder of the cape. Then I recalled the fact that Moreau's beach lay to the west.

A twig snapped behind me and there was a rustle. I turned and stood facing the dark trees. I could see nothing—or else I could see too much. Every dark form in the dimness had its ominous quality, its peculiar suggestion of alert watchfulness. So I stood for perhaps a minute, and then, with an eye to the trees still, turned westward to cross the headland. And as I moved, one among the lurking shadows moved to follow me.

My heart beat quickly. Presently the broad sweep of a bay to the westward became visible, and I halted again. The noiseless shadow halted a dozen yards from me. A little point of light shone on the further bend of the curve, and the grey sweep of the sandy beach

---

2. Venus (named for the Roman goddess of beauty and love, especially sensual love). *Zodiacal light*: cone of diffuse, eerie light above the horizon at sunrise or sunset.

lay faint under the starlight. Perhaps two miles away was that little point of light. To get to the beach I should have to go through the trees where the shadows lurked, and down a bushy slope.

I could see the thing rather more distinctly now. It was no animal, for it stood erect. At that I opened my mouth to speak, and found a hoarse phlegm choked my voice. I tried again, and shouted, "Who is there?" There was no answer. I advanced a step. The thing did not move; only gathered itself together. My foot struck a stone.

That gave me an idea. Without taking my eyes off the black form before me I stooped and picked up this lump of rock. But at my motion the thing turned abruptly as a dog might have done, and slunk obliquely into the farther darkness. Then I recalled a schoolboy expedient against big dogs, twisted the rock into my handkerchief, and gave this a turn round my wrist. I heard a movement further off among the shadows as if the thing was in retreat. Then suddenly my tense excitement gave way; I broke into a profuse perspiration and fell a-trembling, with my adversary routed and this weapon in my hand.

It was some time before I could summon resolution to go down through the trees and bushes upon the flank of the headland to the beach. At last I did it at a run, and as I emerged from the thicket upon the sand I heard some other body crashing after me.

At that I completely lost my head with fear, and began running along the sand. Forthwith there came the swift patter of soft feet in pursuit. I gave a wild cry and redoubled my pace. Some dim black things about three or four times the size of rabbits went running or hopping up from the beach towards the bushes as I passed. So long as I live I shall remember the terror of that chase. I ran near the water's edge, and heard every now and then the splash of the feet that gained upon me. Far away, hopelessly far, was the yellow light. All the night about us was black and still. Splash, splash came the pursuing feet nearer and nearer. I felt my breath going, for I was quite out of training; it whooped as I drew it, and I felt a pain like a knife at my side. I perceived the thing would come up with me long before I reached the enclosure, and, desperate and sobbing for breath, I wheeled round upon it and struck at it as it came up to me—struck with all my strength. The stone came out of the sling of the handkerchief as I did so.

As I turned, the thing, which had been running on all-fours, rose to its feet, and the missile fell fair on its left temple. The skull rang loud and the animal-man blundered into me, thrust me back with its hands, and went staggering past me to fall headlong upon the sand with its face in the water. And there it lay still.

I could not bring myself to approach that black heap. I left it there with the water rippling round it under the still stars, and, giving it

a wide berth, pursued my way towards the yellow glow of the house.
And presently, with a positive effect of relief, came the pitiful moaning of the puma, the sound that had originally driven me out to
explore this mysterious island. At that, though I was faint and horribly fatigued, I gathered together all my strength and began running
again towards the light. It seemed to me a voice was calling me.

CHAPTER X.   The Crying of the Man

As I drew near the house I saw that the light shone from the open
door of my room; and then I heard, coming from out the darkness
at the side of that orange oblong, the voice of Montgomery shouting
"Prendick."

I continued running. Presently I heard him again. I replied by a
feeble "Hullo!" and in another moment had staggered up to him.

"Where have you been?" said he, holding me at arm's-length, so
that the light from the door fell on my face. "We have both been so
busy that we forgot you until about half an hour ago."

He led me into the room and sat me down in the deck chair. For
a while I was blinded by the light. "We did not think you would start
to explore this island of ours without telling us," he said. And then,
"I was afraid! But . . . what . . . Hullo!"

For my last remaining strength slipped from me, and my head fell
forward on my chest. I think he found a certain satisfaction in giving me brandy. "For God's sake," said I, "fasten that door."

"You've been meeting some of our curiosities, eh?" said he. He
locked the door and turned to me again. He asked me no questions,
but gave me some more brandy and water, and pressed me to eat. I
was in a state of collapse. He said something vague about his for-
getting to warn me, and asked me briefly when I left the house and
what I had seen. I answered him as briefly in fragmentary sentences.
"Tell me what it all means," said I, in a state bordering on hysterics.

"It's nothing so very dreadful," said he. "But I think you have had
about enough for one day." The puma suddenly gave a sharp yell of
pain. At that he swore under his breath. "I'm damned," said he, "if
this place is not as bad as Gower Street—with its cats."[3]

"Montgomery," said I, "what was that thing that came after me.
Was it a beast, or was it a man?"

"If you don't sleep to-night," he said, "you'll be off your head
tomorrow."

---

3. As home not only to University College and its medical school but also to private labs
run by independent physiologists, Gower Street was likely a place where one could
hear the "sharp yells" of domestic animals.

I stood up in front of him. "What was that thing that came after me?" I asked.

He looked me squarely in the eyes and twisted his mouth askew. His eyes, which had seemed animated a minute before, went dull. "From your account," said he, "I'm thinking it was a bogle."[4]

I felt a gust of intense irritation that passed as quickly as it came. I flung myself into the chair again and pressed my hands on my forehead. The puma began again.

Montgomery came round behind me and put his hand on my shoulder. "Look here, Prendick," he said; "I had no business to let you drift out into this silly island of ours. But it's not so bad as you feel, man. Your nerves are worked to rags. Let me give you something that will make you sleep. *That* . . . will keep on for hours yet. You must simply get to sleep, or I won't answer for it."

I did not reply. I bowed forward and covered my face with my hands. Presently he returned with a small measure containing a dark liquid. This he gave me. I took it unresistingly, and he helped me into the hammock.

When I awoke it was broad day. For a little while I lay flat, staring at the roof above me. The rafters, I observed, were made out of the timbers of a ship.[5] Then I turned my head and saw a meal prepared for me on the table. I perceived that I was hungry, and prepared to clamber out of the hammock, which, very politely, anticipating my intention, twisted round and deposited me upon all-fours on the floor.

I got up and sat down before the food. I had a heavy feeling in my head, and only the vaguest memory at first of the things that had happened overnight. The morning breeze blew very pleasantly through the unglazed window, and that and the food contributed to the sense of animal comfort I experienced. Presently the door behind me, the door inward towards the yard of the enclosure, opened. I turned and saw Montgomery's face. "All right?" said he. "I'm frightfully busy." And he shut the door. Afterwards I discovered that he forgot to re-lock it.

Then I recalled the expression of his face the previous night, and with that the memory of all I had experienced reconstructed itself before me. Even as that fear returned to me came a cry from within. But this time it was not the cry of a puma.

I put down the mouthful that hesitated upon my lips, and listened. Silence, save for the whisper of the morning breeze. I began to think my ears had deceived me.

4. Goblin, phantom, or night specter causing fear and dread.
5. Per the domicile built by the eponymous castaway hero in *Robinson Crusoe* (1719) by English writer Daniel Defoe (1660–1731), which became a model for many subsequent castaway novels (see excerpt on pp. 189–97 below).

After a long pause I resumed my meal, but with my ears still vigilant. Presently I heard something else very faint and low. I sat as if frozen in my attitude. Though it was faint and low, it moved me more profoundly than all that I had hitherto heard of the abominations behind the wall. There was no mistake this time in the quality of the dim broken sounds, no doubt at all of their source; for it was groaning, broken by sobs and gasps of anguish. It was no brute this time. It was a human being in torment!

And as I realised this I rose, and in three steps had crossed the room, seized the handle of the door into the yard, and flung it open before me.

"Prendick, man! Stop!" cried Montgomery, intervening. A startled deerhound yelped and snarled. There was blood, I saw, in the sink, brown, and some scarlet, and I smelt the peculiar smell of carbolic acid.[6] Then through an open doorway beyond, in the dim light of the shadow, I saw something bound painfully upon a framework, scarred, red, and bandaged. And then blotting this out appeared the face of old Moreau, white and terrible.

In a moment he had gripped me by the shoulder with a hand that was smeared red, had twisted me off my feet, and flung me headlong back into my own room. He lifted me as though I was a little child. I fell at full length upon the floor, and the door slammed and shut out the passionate intensity of his face. Then I heard the key turn in the lock, and Montgomery's voice in expostulation.

"Ruin the work of a lifetime!" I heard Moreau say.

"He does not understand," said Montgomery, and other things that were inaudible.

"I can't spare the time yet," said Moreau.

The rest I did not hear. I picked myself up and stood trembling, my mind a chaos of the most horrible misgivings. Could it be possible, I thought, that such a thing as the vivisection of men was possible? The question shot like lightning across a tumultuous sky. And suddenly the clouded horror of my mind condensed into a vivid realisation of my danger.

CHAPTER XI.   The Hunting of the Man

It came before my mind with an unreasonable hope of escape, that the outer door of my room was still open to me. I was convinced now, absolutely assured, that Moreau had been vivisecting a human being. All the time since I had heard his name I had been trying to link in

---

6. Phenol, an aromatic acidic compound used as an antiseptic—hence appropriate to a surgical theater.

my mind in some way the grotesque animalism of the islanders with his abominations; and now I thought I saw it all. The memory of his works in the transfusion of blood recurred to me. These creatures I had seen were the victims of some hideous experiment!

These sickening scoundrels had merely intended to keep me back, to fool me with their display of confidence, and presently to fall upon me with a fate more horrible than death, with torture, and after torture the most hideous degradation it was possible to conceive—to send me off, a lost soul, a beast, to the rest of their Comus rout.[7] I looked round for some weapon. Nothing. Then, with an inspiration, I turned over the deck chair, put my foot on the side of it, and tore away the side rail. It happened that a nail came away with the wood, and, projecting, gave a touch of danger to an otherwise petty weapon. I heard a step outside, incontinently flung open the door, and found Montgomery within a yard of it. He meant to lock the outer door.

I raised this nailed stick of mine and cut at his face, but he sprang back. I hesitated a moment, then turned and fled round the corner of the house. "Prendick, man!" I heard his astonished cry. "Don't be a silly ass, man!"

Another minute, thought I, and he would have had me locked in, and as ready as a hospital rabbit[8] for my fate. He emerged behind the corner, for I heard him shout, "Prendick!" Then he began to run after me, shouting things as he ran.

This time, running blindly, I went northeastward, in a direction at right angles to my previous expedition. Once, as I went running headlong up the beach, I glanced over my shoulder and saw his attendant with him. I ran furiously up the slope, over it, then turned eastward along a rocky valley, fringed on either side with jungle. I ran for perhaps a mile altogether, my chest straining, my heart beating in my ears, and then, hearing nothing of Montgomery or his man, and feeling upon the verge of exhaustion, I doubled sharply back towards the beach, as I judged, and lay down in the shelter of a cane brake.[9]

There I remained for a long time, too fearful to move, and indeed too fearful even to plan a course of action. The wild scene about me lay sleeping silently under the sun, and the only sound near me was

7. In the lyric-dramatic poem *Comus* (1634) by English poet John Milton (1608–1674), the debauched sorcerer Comus encourages his followers, whom he has transformed from humans into grotesque half-beast figures, to engage in an animalistic revel. Milton displays the "rout" as a disruption of civil harmony and corruption of moral virtue under the sway of a charismatically licentious flouter of law. In addition to Milton's poem, the famous painting by Sir Edwin Henry Landseer (1802–1873), *The Defeat, of Comus and His Beasts* (1843; see illustration on p. 120 below), might well have influenced Wells's depiction of his Beast People.
8. Caged rabbit awaiting vivisection or other experimental procedure in a hospital laboratory.
9. Thicket of tall woody grass (like bamboo) or reeds.

the thin hum of some small gnats that had discovered me. Presently I became aware of a drowsy breathing sound—the soughing[1] of the sea upon the beach.

After about an hour I heard Montgomery shouting my name far away to the north. That set me thinking of my plan of action. As I interpreted it then, this island was inhabited only by these two vivisectors and their animalised victims. Some of these, no doubt, they could press into their service against me, if need arose. I knew both Moreau and Montgomery carried revolvers; and, save for a feeble bar of deal, spiked with a small nail, the merest mockery of a mace,[2] I was unarmed.

So I lay still where I was until I began to think of food and drink. And at that moment the real hopelessness of my position came home to me. I knew no way of getting anything to eat; I was too ignorant of botany to discover any resort of root or fruit that might lie about me; I had no means of trapping the few rabbits upon the island. It grew blanker the more I turned the prospect over. At last, in the desperation of my position, my mind turned to the animal men I had encountered. I tried to find some hope in what I remembered of them. In turn I recalled each one I had seen, and tried to draw some augury[3] of assistance from my memory.

Then suddenly I heard a staghound bay, and at that realised a new danger. I took little time to think, or they would have caught me then, but, snatching up my nailed stick, rushed headlong from my hiding-place towards the sound of the sea. I remember a growth of thorny plants with spines that stabbed like penknives. I emerged, bleeding, and with torn clothes, upon the lip of a long creek opening northward. I went straight into the waves without a minute's hesitation, wading up the creek, and presently finding myself knee-deep in a little stream. I scrambled out at last on the westward bank, and, with my heart beating loudly in my ears, crept into a tangle of ferns to await the issue. I heard the dog—it was only one—draw nearer, and yelp when it came to the thorns. Then I heard no more, and presently began to think I had escaped.

The minutes passed, the silence lengthened out, and at last, after an hour of security, my courage began to return to me.

By this time I was no longer very terrified or very miserable. For I had, as it were, passed the limit of terror and despair. I felt now that my life was practically lost, and that persuasion made me capable of daring anything. I had even a certain wish to encounter Moreau face to face. And, as I had waded into the water, I remembered that

---

1. Moaning, murmuring, rushing.
2. Heavy medieval clublike weapon, often spiked. *Bar of deal:* plank or board hewn from an inexpensive log, usually of pine or fir.
3. Anticipation; sign.

if I were too hard pressed, at least one path of escape from torment still lay open to me—they could not very well prevent my drowning myself. I had half a mind to drown myself then, but an odd wish to see the whole adventure out, a queer impersonal spectacular interest in myself,[4] restrained me. I stretched my limbs, sore and painful from the pricks of the spiny plants, and stared around me at the trees; and, so suddenly that it seemed to jump out of the green tracery about it, my eyes lit upon a black face watching me.

I saw that it was the simian[5] creature who had met the launch upon the beach. He was clinging to the oblique stem of a palm tree. I gripped my stick, and stood up facing him. He began chattering. "You, you, you," was all I could distinguish at first. Suddenly he dropped from the tree, and in another moment was holding the fronds apart, and staring curiously at me.

I did not feel the same repugnance towards this creature that I had experienced in my encounters with the other Beast Men. "You," he said, "in the boat." He was a man, then—at least, as much of a man as Montgomery's attendant—for he could talk.

"Yes," I said, "I came in the boat. From the ship."

"Oh!" he said, and his bright restless eyes travelled over me, to my hands, to the stick I carried, to my feet, to the tattered places in my coat, and the cuts and scratches I had received from the thorns. He seemed puzzled at something. His eyes came back to my hands. He held his own hand out, and counted his digits slowly, "One, Two, Three, Four, Five—eh?"

I did not grasp his meaning then. Afterwards I was to find that a great proportion of these Beast People had malformed hands, lacking sometimes even three digits. But guessing this was in some way a greeting, I did the same thing by way of reply. He grinned with immense satisfaction. Then his quick roving glance went round again. He made a swift movement, and vanished. The fern fronds he had stood between came swishing together.

I pushed out of the brake after him, and was astonished to find him swinging cheerfully by one lank arm from a rope of creepers that looped down from the foliage overhead. His back was to me.

"Hullo!" said I.

He came down with a twisting jump, and stood facing me. "I say," said I, "where can I get something to eat?"

"Eat!" he said. "Eat man's food now." And his eyes went back to the swing of ropes. "At the huts."

"But where are the huts?"

4. Self-regarding detachment.
5. Ape- or monkeylike.

"Oh!"

"I'm new, you know."

At that he swung round, and set off at a quick walk. All his motions were curiously rapid. "Come along," said he. I went with him to see the adventure out. I guessed the huts were some rough shelter, where he and some more of these Beast People lived. I might perhaps find them friendly, find some handle in their minds to take hold of. I did not know yet how far they had forgotten the human heritage I ascribed them.

My ape-like companion trotted along by my side, with his hands hanging down and his jaw thrust forward. I wondered what memory he might have in him. "How long have you been on this island?" said I.

"How long?" he asked. And, after having the question repeated, he held up three fingers. The creature was little better than an idiot. I tried to make out what he meant by that, and it seems I bored him. After another question or two, he suddenly left my side and sprang at some fruit that hung from a tree. He pulled down a handful of prickly husks, and went on eating the contents. I noted this with satisfaction, for here, at least, was a hint for feeding. I tried him with some other questions, but his chattering prompt responses were, as often as not, quite at cross-purposes with my question. Some few were appropriate, others quite parrot-like.

I was so intent upon these peculiarities that I scarcely noticed the path we followed. Presently we came to trees, all charred and brown, and so to a bare place covered with a yellow-white incrustation, across which a drifting smoke, pungent in whiffs to nose and eyes, went drifting. On our right, over a shoulder of bare rock, I saw the level blue of the sea. The path coiled down abruptly into a narrow ravine between two tumbled and knotty masses of blackish scoriae.[6] Into this we plunged.

It was extremely dark, this passage, after the blinding sunlight reflected from the sulphurous ground. Its walls grew steep, and approached one another. Blotches of green and crimson drifted across my eyes. My conductor stopped suddenly. "Home," said he, and I stood on a floor of a chasm that was at first absolutely dark to me. I heard some strange noises, and thrust the knuckles of my left hand into my eyes. I became aware of a disagreeable odour like that of a monkey's cage ill-cleaned. Beyond, the rock opened again upon a gradual slope of sunlit greenery, and on either hand the light smote[7] down through a narrow channel into the central gloom.

---

6. Rough, cindery residue from melting lava exposed to the air.
7. Struck sharply (archaic).

CHAPTER XII.   The Sayers of the Law

Then something cold touched my hand. I started violently, and saw close to me a dim pinkish thing, looking more like a flayed child than anything else in the world. The creature had exactly the mild but repulsive features of a sloth, the same low forehead and slow gestures. As the first shock of the change of light passed, I saw about me more distinctly. The little sloth-like creature was standing and staring at me. My conductor had vanished.

The place was a narrow passage between high walls of lava, a crack in its knotted flow, and on either side interwoven heaps of sea-mat,[8] palm fans and reeds leaning against the rock, formed rough and impenetrably dark dens. The winding way up the ravine between these was scarcely three yards wide, and was disfigured by lumps of decaying fruit-pulp and other refuse, which accounted for the disagreeable stench of the place.

The little pink sloth creature was still blinking at me when my Ape Man reappeared at the aperture of the nearest of these dens, and beckoned me in. As he did so a slouching monster wriggled out of one of the places farther up this strange street, and stood up in featureless silhouette against the bright green beyond, staring at me. I hesitated—had half a mind to bolt the way I had come—and then, determined to go through with the adventure, gripped my nailed stick about the middle, and crawled into the little evil-smelling lean-to after my conductor.

It was a semicircular space, shaped like the half of a bee-hive, and against the rocky wall that formed the inner side of it was a pile of variegated fruits, cocoa-nuts and others. Some rough vessels of lava and wood stood about the floor, and one on a rough stool. There was no fire.[9] In the darkest corner of the hut sat a shapeless mass of darkness that grunted "Hey!" as I came in, and my Ape Man stood in the dim light of the doorway and held out a split cocoa-nut to me as I crawled into the other corner and squatted down. I took it and began gnawing it, as serenely as possible, in spite of my tense trepidation, and the nearly intolerable closeness of the den. The little pink sloth creature stood in the aperture of the hut, and something else with a drab face and bright eyes came staring over its shoulder.

---

8. Lacy, meshlike growth, common to rocky shores in England, often seen covering algae seaweeds.

9. In chapter II of *The Descent of Man*, Darwin writes that the "discovery of fire, probably the greatest ever made by man, excepting language, dates from before the dawn of history. . . . I cannot understand, therefore, how it is that Mr. Wallace [English botanist and evolutionary theorist Alfred Russel Wallace (1823–1913)] maintains, that 'natural selection could only have endowed the savage with a brain a little superior to that of an ape.'"

"Hey," came out of the lump of mystery opposite. "It is a man! It is a man!" gabbled my conductor—"a man, a man, a live man, like me."

"Shut up!" said the voice from the dark, and grunted. I gnawed my cocoa-nut amid an impressive silence. I peered hard into the blackness, but could distinguish nothing. "It is a man," the voice repeated. "He comes to live with us?" It was a thick voice with something in it, a kind of whistling overtone, that struck me as peculiar, but the English accent was strangely good.

The Ape Man looked at me as though he expected something. I perceived the pause was interrogative. "He comes to live with you," I said.

"It is a man. He must learn the Law."

I began to distinguish now a deeper darkness in the black, a vague outline of a hunched-up figure. Then I noticed the opening of the place was darkened by two more heads. My hand tightened on my stick. The thing in the dark repeated in a louder tone, "Say the words." I had missed its last remark. "Not to go on all-Fours; that is the Law"—it repeated in a kind of sing-song.[1]

I was puzzled. "Say the words," said the Ape Man, repeating, and the figures in the doorway echoed this with a threat in the tone of their voices. I realised I had to repeat this idiotic formula. And then began the insanest ceremony. The voice in the dark began intoning a mad litany, line by line, and I and the rest to repeat it. As they did so, they swayed from side to side, and beat their hands upon their knees, and I followed their example. I could have imagined I was already dead and in another world. The dark hut, these grotesque dim figures, just flecked here and there by a glimmer of light, and all of them swaying in unison and chanting:—

"Not to go on all-Fours; *that* is the Law. Are we not Men?"

"Not to suck up Drink; *that* is the Law. Are we not Men?"

"Not to eat Flesh nor Fish; *that* is the Law. Are we not Men?"

"Not to claw Bark of Trees; *that* is the Law. Are we not Men?"

"Not to chase other Men; *that* is the Law. Are we not Men?"[2]

---

1. The portrayal of the Beast People chanting the Law in "sing-song" fashion evokes Kipling's 1894 poem "The Law of the Jungle" (see pp. 185–86 below).
2. Cf. the Enlightenment motto "Am I not a man and a brother?" which, in conjunction with the image of a kneeling African man in chains, was made prominent from the late 18th to the mid-19th centuries by the Quaker-led Society for Effecting the Abolition of the Slave Trade. In a bitter irony, the intended allegory of emancipation was often subverted, its image being read instead as a representation of African inferiority and need for conversion. (The application of such irony to the evolution debate can be seen in a *Punch* cartoon of 1861: see p. 121 below.) *Not to go on all-Fours*: In the Bible "going on all-fours" serves as a general metaphor of animality. *Not to suck up Drink*: In Judges 7:5–7, God admonishes Gideon, the young leader chosen to liberate Israel, both from its enemies and from its own idolatry, to exclude from his army "Every one that lappeth of the water with his tongue, as a dog lappeth." *Not to eat Flesh nor Fish*: In many Hebraic and early Christian interpretations of the Old Testament, humans, like animals, were originally vegetarian. *Not to claw Bark of Trees*: Alongside God's

And so from the prohibition of these acts of folly, on to the prohibition of what I thought then were the maddest, most impossible, and most indecent[3] things one could well imagine. A kind of rhythmic fervour fell on all of us; we gabbled and swayed faster and faster, repeating this amazing law. Superficially the contagion of these brute men was upon me, but deep down within me laughter and disgust struggled together. We ran through a long list of prohibitions, and then the chant swung round to a new formula:—

"*His* is the House of Pain.

"*His* is the Hand that makes.

"*His* is the Hand that wounds.

"*His* is the Hand that heals."[4]

And so on for another long series, mostly quite incomprehensible gibberish to me, about *Him,* whoever he might be. I could have fancied it was a dream, but never before have I heard chanting in a dream.

"*His* is the lightning-flash," we sang. "*His* is the deep salt sea."[5]

A horrible fancy came into my head that Moreau, after animalising these men, had infected their dwarfed brains with a kind of deification of himself. However, I was too keenly aware of white teeth and strong claws about me to stop my chanting on that account. "*His* are the stars in the sky."

At last that song ended. I saw the Ape Man's face shining with perspiration, and my eyes being now accustomed to the darkness, I saw more distinctly the figure in the corner from which the voice came. It was the size of a man, but it seemed covered with a dull

---

prohibition against consuming the blood of animals (Genesis 9:4), we might note here the Christian motif of innocent blood oozing from wood, understood as a prefigurement of the Crucifixion (cf. the medieval English poems *The Dream of the Rood*; *Christ III*; and *Andreas*). *Not to chase other Men:* Essentially a translation of "Thou shalt not kill," as "chase" in several biblical verses means to "pursue as an enemy unto death." Compare the Beast People's liturgy generally and the biblical Ten Commandments (see Exodus 20 and Deuteronomy 5).

3. In late Victorian vernacular and legal parlance, sexually depraved.

4. Cf. the Book of Job 5:18: "For he maketh sore, and bindeth up: he woundeth, and his hands make whole." *House of Pain:* A classical motif, the "house of pain" image draws on the etymology of "pain" as retribution (Greek *poinē*) or penalty (Latin *poena*) to fashion a grotesquely bestialized disciplinary enclosure (cage; prison; dungeon; chamber; underground cave or vault) designed for administering torturous, often hellish punishments for transgressions against divine or sovereign authority. Cf. the "house of endlesse paine" in *The Faerie Queene* I.v.33 (1590) by Edmund Spenser (1552/53–1599) and the "dark and dismal house of pain" of Milton's *Paradise Lost* II.823 (1674).

5. Cf. "Saint Patrick's Breastplate" (1889) by Irish poet, hymnist, and educational patron Cecil F. Alexander (1818–1895): "I bind unto myself today . . . / The flashing of the lightning free, / The whirling wind's tempestuous shocks, / The stable earth, the deep salt sea / Around the old eternal rocks." The rugged landscape of this Celtic lorica, or protective prayer, reflects the ascetic quest for spirituality in a world devoted to other values and pursuits.

grey hair almost like a Skye terrier.[6] What was it? What were they all? Imagine yourself surrounded by all the most horrible cripples and maniacs it is possible to conceive, and you may understand a little of my feelings with these grotesque caricatures of humanity about me.[7]

"He is a five-man, a five-man, a five-man . . . like me," said the Ape Man.

I held out my hands. The grey creature in the corner leant forward. "Not to run on all-Fours; that is the Law. Are we not Men?" he said. He put out a strangely distorted talon,[8] and gripped my fingers. The thing was almost like the hoof of a deer produced into claws. I could have yelled with surprise and pain. His face came forward and peered at my nails, came forward into the light of the opening of the hut, and I saw with a quivering disgust that it was like the face of neither man or beast, but a mere shock of grey hair, with three shadowy overarchings to mark the eyes and mouth.

"He has little nails,"[9] said this grisly creature in his hairy beard. "It is well."

He threw my hand down, and instinctively I gripped my stick. "Eat roots and herbs—it is His will," said the Ape Man.

"I am the Sayer of the Law," said the grey figure. "Here come all that be new, to learn the Law. I sit in the darkness and say the Law."

"It is even so," said one of the beasts in the doorway.

"Evil are the punishments of those who break the Law. None escape."

"None escape," said the Beast Folk, glancing furtively at each other.

"None, none," said the Ape Man. "None escape. See! I did a little thing, a wrong thing, once. I jabbered, jabbered, stopped talking. None could understand. I am burnt, branded in the hand. He is great, he is good!"

"None escape," said the grey creature in the corner.

"None escape," said the Beast People, looking askance at one another.

"For every one the want that is bad," said the grey Sayer of the Law. "What you will want, we do not know. We shall know. Some

---

6. Breed of terrier thought to have originated on the Isle of Skye.
7. The paragraph is among several in this chapter that recast passages from the 1878 travelogue *Through the Dark Continent* by explorer Henry Morton Stanley (1841–1904), in which the author encounters an African tribe meeting him with cries of "these are men!": "I saw before me a hundred beings of the most degraded, unpresentable type it is possible to conceive, and though I know quite well that thousands of years ago the beginning of this wretched humanity and myself were one and the same, a sneaking disinclination to believe it possessed me strongly" (*Through the Dark Continent*, Vol. II [New York: Harper & Brothers, 1878], pp. 72–73).
8. Claw.
9. Like a properly groomed Victorian gentleman.

want to follow things that move, to watch and slink and wait and spring, to kill and bite, bite deep and rich, sucking the blood. . . . It is bad. 'Not to chase other Men; that is the Law. *Are we not Men?* Not to eat Flesh nor Fish; that is the Law. *Are we not Men?*'"

"None escape," said a dappled brute standing in the doorway.

"For every one the want that is bad," said the grey Sayer of the Law. "Some want to go tearing with teeth and hands into the roots of things, snuffing into the earth. . . . It is bad."

"None escape," said the men in the door.

"Some go clawing trees, some go scratching at the graves of the dead; some go fighting with foreheads or feet or claws; some bite suddenly, none giving occasion; some love uncleanness."

"None escape," said the Ape Man, scratching his calf.

"None escape," said the little pink sloth creature.

"Punishment is sharp and sure. Therefore learn the Law. Say the words," and incontinently he began again the strange litany of the Law, and again I and all these creatures began singing and swaying. My head reeled with this jabbering and the close stench of the place, but I kept on, trusting to find presently some chance of a new development. "Not to go on all-Fours; that is the Law. *Are we not Men?*"

We were making such a noise that I noticed nothing of the tumult outside, until some one, who, I think, was one of the two Swine Men I had seen, thrust his head over the little pink sloth creature and shouted something excitedly, something that I did not catch. Incontinently those at the opening of the hut vanished, my Ape Man rushed out, the thing that had sat in the dark followed him—I only observed it was big and clumsy, and covered with silvery hair,—and I was left alone.

Then before I reached the aperture I heard the yelp of a staghound.

In another moment I was standing outside the hovel, my chair-rail in my hand, every muscle of me quivering. Before me were the clumsy backs of perhaps a score of these Beast People, their misshapen heads half-hidden by their shoulder-blades. They were gesticulating excitedly. Other half-animal faces glared interrogation out of the hovels. Looking in the direction in which they faced I saw coming through the haze under the trees beyond the end of the passage of dens the dark figure and awful white face of Moreau. He was holding the leaping staghound back, and close behind him came Montgomery, revolver in hand.

For a moment I stood horror-struck.

I turned and saw the passages behind me blocked by another heavy brute with a huge grey face and twinkling little eyes, advancing towards me. I looked round and saw to the right of me, and half a dozen yards in front of me, a narrow gap in the wall of rock through which a ray of light slanted into the shadows. "Stop!" cried Moreau, as I strode towards this, and then, "Hold him!" At that, first one face turned towards me, and then others. Their bestial minds were happily slow.

I dashed my shoulder into a clumsy monster who was turning to see what Moreau meant, and flung him forward into another. I felt his hands fly round, clutching at me and missing me. The little pink sloth creature dashed at me and I cut it over, gashed down its ugly face with the nail in my stick, and in another minute I was scrambling up a steep side pathway, a kind of sloping chimney out of the ravine. I heard a howl behind me, and cries of "Catch him!" "Hold him!" and the grey-faced creature appeared behind me and jammed his huge bulk into the cleft. "Go on, go on!" they howled. I clambered up the narrow cleft in the rock, and came out upon the sulphur on the westward side of the village of the Beast Men.

That gap was altogether fortunate for me, for the narrow way slanting obliquely upward must have impeded the nearer pursuers. I ran over the white space and down a steep slope through a scattered growth of trees, and came to a low-lying stretch of tall reeds. Through this I pushed into a dark thick undergrowth that was black and succulent under foot. As I plunged into the reeds my foremost pursuers emerged from the gap. I broke my way through this undergrowth for some minutes. The air behind me and about me was soon full of threatening cries. I heard the tumult of my pursuers in the gap up the slope, then the crashing of the reeds, and every now and then the crackling crash of a branch. Some of the creatures roared like excited beasts of prey. The staghound yelped to the left. I heard Moreau and Montgomery shouting in the same direction. I turned sharply to the right. It seemed to me even then that I heard Montgomery shouting for me to run for my life.

Presently the ground gave, rich and oozy, under my feet; but I was desperate and went headlong into it, struggled through knee-deep, and so came to a winding path among tall canes. The noise of my pursuers passed away to my left. In one place three strange pink hopping animals, about the size of cats, bolted before my footsteps. This pathway ran uphill, across another open space covered with white incrustation, and plunged into a cane brake again.

Then suddenly it turned parallel with the edge of a steep walled gap which came without warning like the haha[1] of an English park—turned with unexpected abruptness. I was still running with

---

1. A boundary consisting of a sunk wall or fence between the tended area of an estate or park and the pasturelands or open space beyond, erected so as to obstruct one's way but not one's view ("ha" being an exclamation of surprise).

all my might, and I never saw this drop until I was flying headlong through the air.

I fell on my forearms and head, among thorns, and rose with a torn ear and bleeding face. I had fallen into a precipitous ravine, rocky and thorny, full of a hazy mist that drifted about me in wisps, and with a narrow streamlet, from which this mist came, meandering down the centre. I was astonished at this thin fog in the full blaze of daylight, but I had no time to stand wondering then. I turned to my right down stream, hoping to come to the sea in that direction, and so have my way open to drown myself. It was only later I found that I had dropped my nailed stick in my fall.

Presently the ravine grew narrower for a space, and carelessly I stepped into the stream. I jumped out again pretty quickly, for the water was almost boiling. I noticed too there was a thin sulphurous scum drifting upon its coiling water. Almost immediately came a turn in the ravine and the indistinct blue horizon. The nearer sea was flashing the sun from a myriad facets. I saw my death before me. But I was hot and panting, with the warm blood oozing out of my face and running pleasantly through my veins. I felt more than a touch of exultation, too, at having distanced my pursuers. It was not in me then to go out and drown myself. I stared back the way I had come.

I listened. Save for the hum of the gnats and the chirp of some small insects that hopped among the thorns, the air was absolutely still. Then came the yelp of a dog, very faint, and a chattering and gibbering, the snap of a whip and voices. They grew louder, then fainter again. The noise receded up the stream and faded away. For a while the chase was over.

But I knew now how much hope of help for me lay in the Beast People.

CHAPTER XIII.   A Parley

I turned again and went on down towards the sea. I found the hot stream broadened out to a shallow weedy sand, in which an abundance of crabs and long-bodied, many-legged creatures started from my footfall. I walked to the very edge of the salt water, and then I felt I was safe. I turned and stared—arms akimbo[2]—at the thick green behind me, into which the steamy ravine cut like a smoking gash. But as I say, I was too full of excitement, and—a true saying, though those who have never known danger may doubt it—too desperate to die.

2. Arms on hips, elbows outward.

Then it came into my head that there was one chance before me yet. While Moreau and Montgomery and their bestial rabble chased me through the island, might I not go round the beach until I came to their enclosure?—make a flank march upon them, in fact, and then with a rock lugged out of their loosely built wall perhaps, smash in the lock of the smaller door and see what I could find—knife, pistol, or what not—to fight them with when they returned? It was at any rate a chance of getting a price for my life.

So I turned to the westward and walked along by the water's edge. The setting sun flashed his blinding heat into my eyes. The slight Pacific tide was running in with a gentle ripple.

Presently the shore fell away southward and the sun came round upon my right hand. Then suddenly, far in front of me, I saw first one and then several figures emerging from the bushes,—Moreau with his grey staghound, then Montgomery, and two others. At that I stopped.

They saw me and began gesticulating and advancing. I stood watching them approach. The two Beast Men came running forward to cut me off from the undergrowth inland. Montgomery came running also, but straight towards me. Moreau followed slower with the dog.

At last I roused myself from inaction, and turning seaward walked straight into the water. The water was very shallow at first. I was thirty yards out before the waves reached to my waist. Dimly I could see the inter-tidal creatures[3] darting away from my feet.

"What are you doing, man?" cried Montgomery.

I turned, standing waist-deep, and stared at them.

Montgomery stood panting at the margin of the water. His face was bright red with exertion, his long flaxen hair blown about his head, and his drooping nether lip showed his irregular teeth. Moreau was just coming up, his face pale and firm, and the dog at his hand barked at me. Both men had heavy whips. Further up the beach stared the Beast Men.

"What am I doing?—I am going to drown myself," said I.

Montgomery and Moreau looked at one another. "Why?" asked Moreau.

"Because that is better than being tortured by you."

"I told you so," said Montgomery, and Moreau said something in a low tone.

"What makes you think I shall torture you?" asked Moreau.

"What I saw," I said. "And those—yonder."

"Hush!" said Moreau, and held up his hand.

---

3. Animals living in the area where the ocean meets land between high and low tides (also called the littoral zone, or seashore).

"I will not," said I; "they were men: what are they now? I at least will not be like them." I looked past my interlocutors. Up the beach were M'ling, Montgomery's attendant, and one of the white swathed brutes from the boat. Further up, in the shadow of the trees, I saw my little Ape Man, and behind him some other dim figures.

"Who are these creatures?" said I, pointing to them, and raising my voice more and more that it might reach them. "They were men— men like yourselves, whom you have infected with some bestial taint, men whom you have enslaved, and whom you still fear.—You who listen," I cried, pointing now to Moreau, and shouting past him to the Beast Men, "you who listen! Do you not see these men still fear you, go in dread of you? Why then do you fear them? You are many—"

"For God's sake," cried Montgomery, "stop that, Prendick!"

"Prendick!" cried Moreau.

They both shouted together as if to drown my voice. And behind them lowered the staring faces of the Beast Men, wondering, their deformed hands hanging down, their shoulders hunched up. They seemed, as I fancied then, to be trying to understand me, to remember something of their human past.

I went on shouting, I scarcely remember what. That Moreau and Montgomery could be killed; that they were not to be feared: that was the burthen[4] of what I put into the heads of the Beast People to my own ultimate undoing. I saw the green-eyed man in the dark rags, who had met me on the evening of my arrival, come out from among the trees, and others followed him to hear me better.

At last for want of breath I paused.

"Listen to me for a moment," said the steady voice of Moreau, "and then say what you will."

"Well," said I.

He coughed, thought, then shouted: "Latin, Prendick! Bad Latin! Schoolboy Latin! But try and understand. *Hi non sunt homines, sunt animalia qui nos habemus* . . . vivisected.[5] A humanising process.[6] I will explain. Come ashore."

I laughed. "A pretty story," said I. "They talk, build houses, cook.[7] They were men. It's likely I'll come ashore."

4. Main theme.
5. "These are not humans, they are animals whom we have . . . vivisected."
6. In Wells's time, "humanization" signified both the development of behaviors and social capabilities that putatively distinguish humans from other animals (but also, by a trou- blesome form of transference, some humans from others) and morphological changes that took place among a chain of hominids resulting in the physical traits and capabili- ties of the specific species *Homo sapiens*. Today, anthropologists and evolutionary biologists generally distinguish the *cultural* process of (so-called) humanization from the *biological* process of "hominization."
7. Among the dozens of traits adduced since antiquity as distinguishing humans from other animals, these three—language use, fashioning of and with tools, and discovery of fire for transforming raw materials to cooked food—are those focused on by Darwin in his account of "man's descent" from "lower animals" (see p. 144 below).

"The water just behind where you stand is deep . . . and full of sharks."

"That's my way," said I. "Short and sharp. Presently."

"Wait a minute." He took something out of his pocket that flashed back the sun, and dropped the object at his feet. "That's a loaded revolver," said he. "Montgomery here will do the same. Now we are going up the beach until you are satisfied the distance is safe. Then come and take the revolvers."

"Not I. You have a third between you."

"I want you to think over things, Prendick. In the first place, I never asked you to come upon this island. In the next, we had you drugged last night, had we wanted to work you any mischief; and in the next, now your first panic is over, and you can think a little—is Montgomery here quite up to the character you give him? We have chased you for your good. Because this island is full of . . . inimical phenomena.[8] Why should we want to shoot you when you have just offered to drown yourself?"

"Why did you set . . . your people on to me when I was in the hut?"

"We felt sure of catching you and bringing you out of danger. Afterwards we drew away from the scent—for your good."

I mused. It seemed just possible. Then I remembered something again.

"But I saw," said I, "in the enclosure—"

"That was the puma."

"Look here, Prendick," said Montgomery. "You're a silly ass. Come out of the water and take these revolvers, and talk. We can't do anything more then than we could do now."

I will confess that then, and indeed always, I distrusted and dreaded Moreau. But Montgomery was a man I felt I understood.

"Go up the beach," said I, after thinking, and added, "holding your hands up."

"Can't do that," said Montgomery, with an explanatory nod over his shoulder. "Undignified."

"Go up to the trees, then," said I, "as you please."

"It's a damned silly ceremony," said Montgomery.

Both turned and faced the six or seven grotesque creatures, who stood there in the sunlight, solid, casting shadows, moving, and yet so incredibly unreal. Montgomery cracked his whip at them, and forthwith they all turned and fled helter-skelter into the trees. And when Montgomery and Moreau were at a distance I judged sufficient, I waded ashore, and picked up and examined the revolvers. To satisfy myself against the subtlest trickery I discharged one at the

---

8. Cf. Caliban's speech in Shakespeare's *The Tempest* 3.2.128–29 (1611).

rounded lump of lava, and had the satisfaction of seeing the stone pulverised and the beach splashed with lead.

Still I hesitated for a moment.

"I'll take the risk," said I, at last, and with a revolver in each hand I walked up the beach towards them.

"That's better," said Moreau, without affectation. "As it is, you have wasted the best part of my day with your confounded imagination."

And with a touch of contempt that humiliated me, he and Montgomery turned and went on in silence before me.

The knot of Beast Men, still wondering, stood back among the trees. I passed them as serenely as possible. One started to follow me, but retreated again when Montgomery cracked his whip. The rest stood silent—watching. They may once have been animals. But I never before saw an animal trying to think.[9]

CHAPTER XIV.   Doctor Moreau Explains[1]

"And now, Prendick, I will explain," said Dr. Moreau, so soon as we had eaten and drunk. "I must confess you are the most dictatorial guest I ever entertained. I warn you that this is the last I do to oblige you. The next thing you threaten to commit suicide about I shan't do—even at some personal inconvenience."

He sat in my deck chair, a cigar half consumed in his white dexterous-looking fingers. The light of the swinging lamp fell on his white hair; he stared through the little window out at the starlight. I sat as far away from him as possible, the table between us and the revolvers to hand. Montgomery was not present. I did not care to be with the two of them in such a little room.

"You admit that vivisected human being, as you called it, is, after all, only the puma?" said Moreau. He had made me visit that horror in the inner room to assure myself of its inhumanity.[2]

"It is the puma," I said, "still alive, but so cut and mutilated as I pray I may never see living flesh again. Of all vile—"

"Never mind that," said Moreau. "At least spare me those youthful horrors.[3] Montgomery used to be just the same. You admit it is

---

9. Suggesting that Prendick lacks the experience and acumen of an evolutionary biologist like Darwin regarding the issue of animal cognition, one of the era's most seriously engaged scientific and philosophical topics.

1. This chapter revisits and in some places reworks ideas formulated by Wells in several of his early scientific writings, most prominently "Human Evolution, an Artificial Process" (see pp. 239–42 below), "The Limits of Individual Plasticity" (pp. 242–44 below), and "The Province of Pain" (pp. 247–50 below).

2. I.e., nonhumanness.

3. I.e., childish expressions of terror and repugnance.

the puma. Now be quiet while I reel off my physiological lecture to you." And forthwith, beginning in the tone of a man supremely bored, but presently warming a little, he explained his work to me. He was very simple and convincing. Now and then there was a touch of sarcasm in his voice. Presently I found myself hot with shame at our mutual positions.

The creatures I had seen were not men, had never been men. They were animals—humanised animals—triumphs of vivisection.

"You forget all that a skilled vivisector can do with living things," said Moreau. "For my own part I'm puzzled why the things I have done here have not been done before. Small efforts of course have been made—amputation, tongue-cutting, excisions. Of course you know a squint[4] may be induced or cured by surgery? Then in the case of excisions you have all kinds of secondary changes, pigmentary disturbances, modifications of the passions, alterations in the secretion of fatty tissue.[5] I have no doubt you have heard of these things?"

"Of course," said I. "But these foul creatures of yours—"

"All in good time," said he, waving his hand at me; "I am only beginning. Those are trivial cases of alteration. Surgery can do better things than that. There is building up as well as breaking down and changing.[6] You have heard, perhaps, of a common surgical operation resorted to in cases where the nose has been destroyed. A flap of skin is cut from the forehead, turned down on the nose, and heals in the new position. This is a kind of grafting in a new position of part of an animal upon itself. Grafting of freshly obtained material from another animal is also possible,—the case of teeth, for example. The grafting of skin and bone is done to facilitate

---

4. An ocular condition known medically as "strabismus," in which the eyes tend to look obliquely or askance (in the popular expression, "cross-eyed"). *Tongue-cutting*: popular term for "frenotomy," the surgical procedure practiced since the 18th century to correct the condition of "tongue-tie" in newborns or infants, in which the membrane under the tongue (frenulum) that connects the tongue to the floor of the mouth is too short. *Excisions*: surgical procedures involving removal of tissue, bone, or organ by resection or cutting. Moreau's examples form the kind of constellation of maladies and practices that suggested to much of the 19th-century medical community the cognate relation of vivisection and the fast-advancing sphere of surgery.

5. In the fast-developing practice of biomedicine in the latter half of the 19th century, these were all complications or side effects ("secondary changes") of emerging techniques of surgical intervention, including tissue grafting and anesthesia. *Modifications of the passions*: a term familiar from the moral psychology of Scottish philosopher David Hume (1711–1776), who felt that the "passions," or emotions, as much as or more than reason, were the seat of moral principles and judgments, and could be redirected by imagination or reason only as a secondary effect of the passion itself.

6. Cf. Ecclesiastes 3:1, 3: "To every thing there is a season . . . a time to break down, and a time to build up." Wells was deeply familiar with the work of the French socialist Pierre-Joseph Proudhon (1809–1865), who famously chose as the epigraph for his *The Poverty of Philosophy* (1847) a similar phrase translated from Deuteronomy, *destruam et aedificabo*—"I shall destroy and I shall build."

healing. The surgeon places in the middle of the wound pieces of skin snipped from another animal, or fragments of bone from a victim freshly killed. Hunter's cockspur—possibly you have heard of that—flourished on the bull's neck.[7] And the rhinoceros rats of the Algerian zouaves are also to be thought of,—monsters manufactured by transferring a slip from the tail of an ordinary rat to its snout, and allowing it to heal in that position."[8]

"Monsters manufactured!" said I. "Then you mean to tell me—"

"Yes. These creatures you have seen are animals carven and wrought into new shapes. To that—to the study of the plasticity of living forms[9]—my life has been devoted. I have studied for years, gaining in knowledge as I go. I see you look horrified, and yet I am telling you nothing new. It all lay in the surface of practical anatomy years ago, but no one had the temerity to touch it. It's not simply the outward form of an animal I can change. The physiology, the chemical rhythm of the creature, may also be made to undergo an enduring modification, of which vaccination and other methods of inoculation with living or dead matter are examples that will, no doubt, be familiar to you. A similar operation is the transfusion of blood, with which subject indeed I began. These are all familiar cases. Less so, and probably far more extensive, were the operations of those medieval practitioners who made dwarfs and beggar cripples and show-monsters; some vestiges of whose art still remain in the preliminary manipulation of the young mountebank or contortionist.[1] Victor Hugo gives an account of them in *L'Homme qui*

---

7. *Hunter's cock-spur . . . bull's neck*: John Hunter (1728–1793), Scottish surgeon, physiologist, and anatomist, was famous for methods of grafting and transplantation. In the fourth volume of his *Works* (1835), Hunter wrote that "The males of almost every class of animals are probably disposed to fight . . . and in many of these there are parts destined solely for that purpose, as the spurs in the cock, and the horns in the bull; and on that account, the strength of the bull lies principally in his neck; that of the cock in his limbs." *The case of teeth*: Hunter reported successful transplants of human teeth into the highly vascularized comb of a cock (a procedure known as xenografting).

8. Wells refers here to a comic episode—a kind of mock-Hunterian vivisectional prank—recounted in *Curiosities of Natural History, First Series* (1858) by English surgeon, zoologist, and natural historian Francis ("Frank") T. Buckland (1826–1880). Buckland describes a purported translation of a story from a French newspaper about how Zouaves (French soldiers known for their colorful uniforms, hardiness, and daring) tricked a naturalist stocking his menagerie with "strange animals" into believing he could obtain an anomalous modern creature called "the trumpet-rat" by tying one rat's tail to another's crudely incised nose (hence Wells's "rhinoceros rat").

9. Wells wrote of "plasticity" frequently during the period in which *The Island of Doctor Moreau* was composed, most notably in "The Limits of Individual Plasticity" (see pp. 242–44 below), where he defines the term against the seeming immutability of natural selection and heredity (see also "Human Evolution, An Artificial Process," pp. 239–43 below).

1. A performer capable of twisting the body into extraordinary postures. *Mountebank*: an itinerant charlatan who sold "quack" medicines to gullible audiences, often by exhibiting evidently diseased or enhanced bodies to demonstrate the nostrums' effectiveness.

Rit.[2] . . . But perhaps my meaning grows plain now. You begin to see that it is a possible thing to transplant tissue from one part of an animal to another, or from one animal to another, to alter its chemical reactions and methods of growth, to modify the articulations of its limbs, and indeed to change it in its most intimate structure?

"And yet this extraordinary branch of knowledge has never been sought as an end, and systematically, by modern investigators, until I took it up! Some such things have been hit upon in the last resort of surgery; most of the kindred evidence that will recur to your mind has been demonstrated, as it were, by accident—by tyrants, by criminals, by the breeders of horses and dogs, by all kinds of untrained clumsy-handed men working for their own immediate ends.[3] I was the first man to take up this question armed with antiseptic surgery, and with a really scientific knowledge of the laws of growth.

"Yet one would imagine it must have been practised in secret before. Such creatures as the Siamese Twins.[4] . . . And in the vaults of the Inquisition.[5] No doubt their chief aim was artistic torture, but some, at least, of the inquisitors must have had a touch of scientific curiosity. . . ."

"But," said I. "These things—these animals *talk!*"

2. *The Man Who Laughs* [*By Order of the King*], an 1869 novel by French writer Victor-Marie Hugo (1802–1885), features a protagonist who as a child was disfigured with a permanent grin by a reconstructive surgeon; Hugo's work is rife with imagery of deformity, impairment, distortion, and defacement, including extensive passages redolent with language we find earlier in Wells's novel and now threaded through Moreau's discourse.
3. Particularly in England, physicians and those practicing experiments on bodies (living and dead) largely comprised an unorganized, unregulated group of private, amateur practitioners until the rapid professionalization of medicine in the mid-to-late 19th century. *Tyrants*: As animal welfare arose as a concern within Western societies in the early modern period, animal cruelty was often figured as a form of political violence or "tyranny," particularly in Protestant discourse. *Criminals*: on the one hand evoking the aura of taboo that had hovered over vivisection since antiquity but especially in the early modern Christian West, even as it gained prominence in emerging physiological and biological science; on the other hand referring to the practice of vivisection *upon* criminals and to dissection of illegally obtained corpses. *Breeders of horses and dogs*: Darwin's close studies of animal breeding, begun in *Questions about the Breeding of Animals* (1839), transformed his nascent hypotheses about natural selection and the struggle for existence into a theory of evolutionary transmutation.
4. Outdated term for conjoined twins; derived from the case of Chang and Eng Bunker (1811–1874), brothers of Chinese descent born in Siam (now Thailand) who were widely exhibited throughout England and the United States during the 1830s as a "curiosity" in "freak shows," and extensively studied and pictured as "scientific specimens" by physicians.
5. A series of powerful institutions within the Catholic Church established in 12th-century France and continued into the 15th century throughout Catholic Europe (most notably Spain) and the New World to root out "heresy." The Inquisition became infamous for the severity of its tortures and the thoroughness of its persecutions. In *The Man Who Laughs*, Hugo implicitly refers to these institutions and their practices in terms that Moreau echoes: "They knew how to produce things in those days which are not produced now; they had talents which we lack. . . . We no longer know how to sculpture living human flesh" (*The Man Who Laughs* [*By Order of the King*], "Preliminary Chapter," III).

He said that was so, and proceeded to point out that the possibilities of vivisection do not stop at a mere physical metamorphosis. A pig may be educated.[6] The mental structure is even less determinate than the bodily. In our growing science of hypnotism[7] we find the promise of a possibility of replacing old inherent instincts by new suggestions, grafting upon or replacing the inherited fixed ideas.[8] Very much, indeed, of what we call moral education is such an artificial modification and perversion of instinct; pugnacity is trained into courageous self-sacrifice, and suppressed sexuality into religious emotion.[9] And the great difference between man and monkey is in the larynx, he said, in the incapacity to frame delicately different sound-symbols by which thought could be sustained.[1] In this I failed to agree with him, but with a certain incivility he declined to notice my objection. He repeated that the thing was so, and continued his account of his work.

But I asked him why he had taken the human form as a model. There seemed to me then, and there still seems to me now, a strange wickedness in that choice.

He confessed that he had chosen that form by chance. "I might just as well have worked to form sheep into llamas, and llamas into

6. Ironic reference to the attack on utilitarianism—the philosophical idea that an action is morally "good" insofar as it produces happiness or pleasure rather than grief or pain, summarized by the English philosopher and social reformer Jeremy Bentham (1748–1832), in the maxim "the greatest good for the greatest number"—by Scottish historian and philosopher Thomas Carlyle (1795–1881) as "a philosophy fit for swine," or "Pig-Philosophy." Carlyle argued that this doctrine encouraged a view of humans as mere creatures of appetite driven by no nobler idea of life's purpose than gratification of desire.
7. A term invented in 1841 by Scottish surgeon and natural philosopher James Braid (1795–1860) for the technique of artificially inducing in subjects deep sleep or a state of altered attention as a form of anesthesia or a means of instigating changes in their mental or physical condition.
8. Moreau paraphrases the core argument of T. H. Huxley's "Evolution and Ethics" (see pp. 180–84 below), which claims that ethics, the foundation of a "civilized" community, is wholly a product of human conscience and social consensus, being in effect "grafted upon" the biological sphere of nature and potentially "replacing" instinctual drives.
9. While, as Philmus aptly notes (*Island*, 96), the analysis of cultural sublimation that makes Moreau's formulations here familiar to us had not yet been provided by Austrian neurologist and psychoanalyst Sigmund Freud (1856–1939), its vocabulary and insights had been circulating in medical, philosophical, and literary discourses familiar to Wells by, for example, German psychiatrist Richard von Krafft-Ebing (1840–1902), German philologist and philosopher Friedrich Nietzsche (1844–1900), and English author Vernon Lee (1856–1935). *Moral education*: a term applied by late 19th-century educational reformists to the use of pedagogical methods as instruments for shaping character and behavior according to ethical, religious, or social principles.
1. A preoccupation of late-19th-century anthropology and linguistics was the gap between humans as shapers and speakers of complex language and their relatively simpleminded and inarticulate primate contemporaries. Where culturally focused researchers such as Anglo-German philologist Friedrich Max Müller (1823–1900) and American primatologist Richard Lynch Garner (1848–1920) debated whether apes possessed brains capable of integrating reason and language (see pp. 167–71 and 171–77 below), theorists of evolution who focused on physical anthropology (such as Huxley and Wallace) argued about whether anatomical disparities such as the morphology and positioning of the larynx accounted for humans' superior linguistic and expressive capacities.

sheep. I suppose there is something in the human form that appeals to the artistic turn of mind more powerfully than any animal shape can. But I've not confined myself to man-making. Once or twice . . ." He was silent, for a minute perhaps. "These years! How they have slipped by! And here I have wasted a day saving your life, and am now wasting an hour explaining myself!"

"But," said I, "I still do not understand. Where is your justification for inflicting all this pain? The only thing that could excuse vivisection to me would be some application—"[2]

"Precisely," said he. "But you see I am differently constituted. We are on different platforms. You are a materialist."[3]

"I am *not* a materialist," I began hotly.

"In my view—in my view. For it is just this question of pain that parts us.[4] So long as visible or audible pain turns you sick, so long as your own pain drives you, so long as pain underlies your propositions about sin,[5] so long, I tell you, you are an animal, thinking a little less obscurely what an animal feels. This pain—"

I gave an impatient shrug at such sophistry.[6]

"Oh! but it is such a little thing. A mind truly open to what science has to teach must see that it is a little thing. It may be that, save in this little planet, this speck of cosmic dust, invisible long before the nearest star could be attained[7]—it may be, I say, that nowhere else does this thing called pain occur. But the laws we feel our way towards . . . Why, even on this earth, even among living things, what pain is there?"

2. At the heart of the vivisection debates of the 1870s and 1880s was dispute over whether the practice was—considered in its best light, rather than as simply gratuitous torture— pursued in quest of pure scientific knowledge or, as even its reluctant supporters (such as Darwin) sometimes claimed, undertaken in the cause of practical medical discoveries. Rarer in these debates were arguments promoting vivisection as an intellectual end in itself. See "Animality, Science, and the Vivisection Debate," pp. 217–38 below.

3. One who believes that nothing exists except matter, space, and the movement and modification of matter between spaces. In context of Moreau's presentation, materialism evokes, first, the general scientific paradigm under development since the 17th century in which reality is founded on observation and measurement of physical materials and processes; second, the application of this paradigm in Darwin's rejection of teleology (purpose; design; intentionality; agency—whether divine or mortal) as an explanation for the "origin" and "ends" of natural experience; and third and more immediately, utilitarianism, with its emphasis on consequences of actions quantified by comparable calculations of pleasure and pain.

4. Again Moreau sets himself against the "pig philosophy" of Jeremy Bentham, who wrote in 1780: "The question is not, Can they [i.e., animals] *reason*? Nor, Can they *talk*? but *Can they suffer*?" Compare Wells's "The Province of Pain" (pp. 247–50) below.

5. See "Human Evolution, an Artificial Process" (see pp. 239–42 below).

6. Superficially plausible but actually fallacious reasoning, often with intent to deceive.

7. The phrasal patterns and prosodic rhythms of this passage recall a passage from Shakespeare's *Richard II* (1597) that offers a countervailing view of England as a kind of utopic sanctuary precious, rather than inconsequential, in its "littleness": ". . . this sceptred isle, / . . . this little world, / . . . This blessèd plot, this earth, this realm, this England" (2.1.40, 45, 50).

He drew a little penknife as he spoke from his pocket, opened the smaller blade and moved his chair so that I could see his thigh. Then, choosing the place deliberately, he drove the blade into his leg and withdrew it.

"No doubt you have seen that before. It does not hurt a pin-prick. But what does it show? The capacity for pain is not needed in the muscle, and it is not placed there; it is but little needed in the skin, and only here and there over the thigh is a spot capable of feeling pain. Pain is simply our intrinsic medical adviser to warn us and stimulate us. All living flesh is not painful, nor is all nerve, nor even all sensory nerve. There's no taint of pain, real pain, in the sensations of the optic nerve. If you wound the optic nerve you merely see flashes of light, just as disease of the auditory nerve merely means a humming in our ears.[8] Plants do not feel pain; the lower animals—it's possible that such animals as the starfish and crayfish do not feel pain. Then with men, the more intelligent they become the more intelligently they will see after their own welfare, and the less they will need the goad to keep them out of danger. I never yet heard of a useless thing that was not ground out of existence by evolution sooner or later. Did you?[9] And pain gets needless.

"Then I am a religious man,[1] Prendick, as every sane man must be. It may be I fancy I have seen more of the ways of this world's Maker than you—for I have sought His laws,[2] in *my* way, all my life, while you, I understand, have been collecting butterflies. And I tell you, pleasure and pain have nothing to do with heaven or hell.[3]

8. Moreau here follows closely the description of effects wrought by a "blow" to the eyes (or ears) given by early modern French philosopher René Descartes (1596–1650) in his *Discourse on Method, Optics, Geometry, and Meteorology*, "Optics—Discourse Six: Vision" (1637). Descartes described animals as mechanical automata, incapable of thought, language, or self-consciousness. This vision of animals as incapable of feeling pain helped fuel intensified vivisectional activity unbound by any sense of ethical constraint well into the 19th century.

9. In *On the Origin of Species*, Darwin noted a number of vestigial inherited traits that could not be explained by continued primary functionality, but which remained in a species because of secondary or not-yet-understood roles. Moreau's view that use of a trait would dwindle with decreasing need, leading eventually to that trait's disappearance, accords with the evolutionary theory of Darwin's most influential predecessor, French naturalist Jean-Baptiste Lamarck (1744–1829), who argued that evolution proceeded not by the aimless process of natural selection but according to natural laws that govern organisms' efforts to adapt to their changing environments by increasing or suppressing the use of relevant attributes.

1. I.e., as opposed to a materialist, a person who believes that mental processes can be separated from physical ones.

2. Divinely inscribed principles governing nature; see the extract from *Natural Theology* by English clergyman William Paley (1743–1805) on pp. 127–30 below, but with a possible glance at Lamarck's four laws of organismal acquisition, retention, and transmission of characteristics as articulated in his *Zoological Philosophy* (1809) and *Natural History of Invertebrate Animals* (1815).

3. An ironically dismissive echo of Jeremy Bentham, who wrote in *An Introduction to the Principles of Morals and Legislation* (1780): "[P]leasure is in *itself* a good: nay, even setting aside immunity from pain, the only good: pain is in *itself* an evil; and, indeed, without exception, the only evil; or else the words good and evil have no meaning."

Pleasure and pain—Bah! What is your theologian's ecstasy but Mahomet's houri[4] in the dark? This store men and women set on pleasure and pain, Prendick, is the mark of the beast upon them, the mark of the beast from which they came. Pain! Pain and pleasure—they are for us, only so long as we wriggle in the dust. . . .[5]

"You see, I went on with this research just the way it led me. That is the only way I ever heard of research going. I asked a question, devised some method of getting an answer, and got—a fresh question. Was this possible, or that possible? You cannot imagine what this means to an investigator, what an intellectual passion grows upon him. You cannot imagine the strange colourless delight of these intellectual desires. The thing before you is no longer an animal, a fellow-creature, but a problem. Sympathetic pain—all I know of it I remember as a thing I used to suffer from years ago. I wanted—it was the only thing I wanted—to find out the extreme limit of plasticity in a living shape."[6]

"But," said I, "the thing is an abomination—"[7]

"To this day I have never troubled about the ethics of the matter. The study of Nature makes a man at last as remorseless as Nature.[8] I have gone on, not heeding anything but the question I was pursuing, and the material has . . . dripped into the huts yonder. . . . It is nearly eleven years since we came here, I and Montgomery and six Kanakas.[9] I remember the green stillness of the island and the empty ocean about us as though it was yesterday. The place seemed waiting for me.

"The stores were landed and the house was built. The Kanakas founded some huts near the ravine. I went to work here upon what I had brought with me. There were some disagreeable things happened at first. I began with a sheep, and killed it after a day and a half by a slip of the scalpel; I took another sheep and made a thing of pain and fear, and left it bound up to heal. It looked quite human

4. From the Arabic *hūrīya*, a "virgin in paradise" awaiting the (male) faithful for service and marriage.

5. Like the biblical serpent who seduced humans to transgress divine prohibition: "upon thy belly shalt thou go, and dust shalt thou eat all the days of thy life" (Genesis 3:14).

6. Moreau echoes the indifference to animal suffering articulated by vivisection's most ardent (and notorious) proponents, chief among them Bernard (see p. 219 below) and the Croatian-born English bacteriologist Emanuel Edward Klein (1844–1925).

7. Something that excites disgust; a desecration, vice, or idol; via folk etymology, something inhuman (Latin *ab-homine*: "away from man").

8. Cf. *Agnosticism: A Doctrine of Despair* (1880) by American Congregational minister and philosopher Noah Porter (1811–1892), which reads in part: "Man shudders before Nature's remorseless insensibility. He notices how little she makes of the dead, and how little she cares for the living; how she mocks at and trifles with sensibility and with life. Of another life there are no tidings and few suggestions."

9. Originally a term for Indigenous Hawaiians derived from their self-designation (kanaka 'ōiwi, or simply "person"); more broadly applied to groups of Pacific Islanders who were indentured laborers (chiefly on sugar cane and cotton plantations) spread diasporically across the Polynesian archipelagos of the British Empire; now considered derogatory in some contexts.

to me when I had finished it, but when I went to it I was discontented with it; it remembered me, and was terrified beyond imagination, and it had no more than the wits of a sheep. The more I looked at it the clumsier it seemed, until at last I put the monster out of its misery. These animals without courage, these fear-haunted, pain-driven things, without a spark of pugnacious energy to face torment—they are no good for man-making.

"Then I took a gorilla I had, and upon that, working with infinite care, and mastering difficulty after difficulty, I made my first man. All the week, night and day, I moulded him. With him it was chiefly the brain that needed moulding; much had to be added, much changed. I thought him a fair specimen of the negroid type when I had done him, and he lay, bandaged, bound, and motionless before me.[1] It was only when his life was assured that I left him, and came into the room again and found Montgomery much as you are. He had heard some of the cries as the thing grew human,[2] cries like those that disturbed *you* so. I didn't take him completely into my confidence at first. And the Kanakas, too, had realised something of it. They were scared out of their wits by the sight of me. I got Montgomery over to me—in a way, but I and he had the hardest job to prevent the Kanakas deserting. Finally they did, and so we lost the yacht. I spent many days educating the brute—altogether I had him for three or four months. I taught him the rudiments of English, gave him ideas of counting,[3] even made the thing read the alphabet. But at that he was slow—though I've met with idiots slower. He began with a clean sheet, mentally;[4] had no memories left in his

1. Moreau claims here to have accomplished with vivisection the process of evolution from great ape to human that some mid-19th-century audiences, from clergy to social and natural scientists, misconstrued Darwin to be proposing in his theories of evolution. See "The Lion of the Season" (p. 122 below). *Negroid type*: The idea of a "missing link" between modern humans and their anthropoid progenitors became racialized, contributing to the 19th century's revision of "scientific racism" by asserting a closer proximity of apes to darker ("negroid") races within the human family than to white European ("civilized") races (see illustration on p. 118).
2. Debate about the (in)ability of nonhuman primates to devise and express intelligible, humanlike language intensified toward the end of the 19th century, coming to focus in the mid-1890s with Garner's expedition to the "French Congo" in 1892–93 to study gorillas in their native setting.
3. While show tricks like pigs counting with their trotters were long a staple of animal exhibitions and circuses, in the late 19th century numeracy emerged among ethologists as a possible index of animal cognition, most famously in the case of Clever Hans, a horse who responded to problems posed by his trainer through a variety of hoof taps and head nods. A later investigator reinterpreted the horse's successes as responses to subtle, unconscious clues delivered by the trainer's body language, in what has since been termed "the Clever Hans effect."
4. The idea that the mind begins as a tabula rasa, a blank slate uninscribed by any preformed concepts or values, and that knowledge therefore comes from experience or perception, was developed by English philosopher John Locke (1632–1704) in his 1689 *An Essay Concerning Human Understanding*. From this hypothesis, Locke derived his revolutionary ideal of a free, self-authored mind—the construct that we alone are arbiters of our own thought and condition. Darwin's evolutionary paradigm, with its emphasis on genetic determination and natural selection, conflicts with the tabula rasa framework.

mind of what he had been. When his scars were quite healed, and he was no longer anything but painful and stiff, and able to converse a little, I took him yonder and introduced him to the Kanakas as an interesting stowaway.

"They were horribly afraid of him at first, somehow—which offended me rather, for I was conceited about him,—but his ways seemed so mild, and he was so abject, that after a time they received him and took his education in hand. He was quick to learn, very imitative and adaptive, and built himself a hovel rather better, it seemed to me, than their own shanties. There was one among the boys, a bit of a missionary, and he taught the thing to read, or at least to pick out letters, and gave him some rudimentary ideas of morality, but it seems the beast's habits were not all that is desirable.

"I rested from work for some days, and was in a mind to write an account of the whole affair to wake up English physiology. Then I came upon the creature squatting up in a tree gibbering at two of the Kanakas who had been teasing him. I threatened him, told him the inhumanity of such a proceeding, aroused his sense of shame, and came here resolved to do better before I took my work back to England. I have been doing better; but somehow the things drift back again, the stubborn beast-flesh grows, day by day, back again.[5] . . . I mean to do better things still. I mean to conquer that. This puma . . .

"But that's the story. All the Kanaka boys are dead now. One fell overboard of the launch, and one died of a wounded heel that he poisoned in some way with plant-juice. Three went away in the yacht, and I suppose, and hope, were drowned. The other one . . . was killed. Well—I have replaced them. Montgomery went on much as you are disposed to do at first, and then . . ."

"What became of the other one?" said I sharply,—"the other Kanaka who was killed?"

"The fact is, after I had made a number of human creatures I made a thing—" He hesitated.

"Yes?" said I.

"It was killed."

"I don't understand," said I; "do you mean to say . . ."

---

5. Moreau's description of the vivisected, humanized gorilla "drift[ing] back again" to a more purely animal state evokes the cultural discourse of "degeneration" that escalated in the late 19th century at the intersection of biological and social science. Western Europe (not least England) suffered growing fear for the future through economic recession, rising crime, threats to empire, urban misery, and political instability—a state of perceived pervasive decline that often took the form of racial panic and a growing recognition that human development might not be unidirectional or answerable to the dominant modern narrative of "progress"—a central theme of Wells's novel *The Time Machine* (1895). On late-Victorian "degeneration" discourse, see the selection by E. Ray Lankester, pp. 155–59 below.

"It killed the Kanaka—yes. It killed several other things that it caught. We chased it for a couple of days. It only got loose by accident—I never meant it to get away. It wasn't finished. It was purely an experiment. It was a limbless thing with a horrible face that writhed along the ground in a serpentine fashion. It was immensely strong and in infuriating pain, and it travelled in a rollicking way like a porpoise swimming. It lurked in the woods for some days, doing mischief to all it came across, until we hunted it, and then it wriggled into the northern part of the island, and we divided the party to close in upon it. Montgomery insisted upon coming with me. The man had a rifle, and when his body was found one of the barrels was curved into the shape of an S, and very nearly bitten through. . . . Montgomery shot the thing. . . . After that I stuck to the ideal of humanity—except for little things."

He became silent. I sat in silence watching his face.

"So for twenty years altogether—counting nine years in England—I have been going on, and there is still something in everything I do that defeats me, makes me dissatisfied, challenges me to further effort. Sometimes I rise above my level, sometimes I fall below it, but always I fall short of the things I dream. The human shape I can get now, almost with ease, so that it is lithe and graceful, or thick and strong; but often there is trouble with the hands[6] and claws—painful things that I dare not shape too freely. But it is in the subtle grafting and re-shaping one must needs do to the brain that my trouble lies. The intelligence is often oddly low, with unaccountable blank ends, unexpected gaps. And least satisfactory of all is something that I cannot touch, somewhere—I cannot determine where—in the seat of the emotions.[7] Cravings, instincts, desires that harm humanity, a strange hidden reservoir to burst suddenly and inundate the whole being of the creature with anger, hate, or fear. These creatures of mine seemed strange and uncanny to you as soon as you began to observe them, but to me, just after I make them, they seem to be indisputable human beings. It's afterwards as I observe them that the persuasion fades. First one animal trait, then another, creeps to the surface and stares out at me. . . . But I will conquer yet.

---

6. Darwin postulated that, along with the "vocal organs" necessary for producing advanced language and speech, the most important anatomical development in humanity's evolution story was the appearance among primates of the distinctive human hand, with its shorter, straighter fingers and larger, more muscular, mobile, and fully opposable thumb, leading to exceptional abilities in the shaping and handling of weaponry and tools (see pp. 145–46 below).

7. The anatomical location that generates emotions or from which they derive was variously located over time. In contrast to terms like *feeling, passion, appetite, sentiment, affection,* and *desire*—which enjoyed a long history of use in philosophical and ethical juxtapositions of psychic agitation and cognitive mastery—*emotion* came to prominence as a description of mental sensation in the 19th century with the rise of psychology as a medical discipline, which increasingly asserted that the "seat of the emotions" is best understood as an *intersection* of brain and body, the latter "expressing" what the former conceives.

Each time I dip a living creature into the bath of burning pain,[8] I say, This time I will burn out all the animal, this time I will make a rational creature of my own. After all, what is ten years? Man has been a hundred thousand in the making."[9]

He thought darkly. "But I am drawing near the fastness.[1] This puma of mine . . ."

After a silence: "And they revert. As soon as my hand is taken from them the beast begins to creep back, begins to assert itself again. . . ."

Another long silence.

"Then you take the things you make into those dens?" said I.

"They go. I turn them out when I begin to feel the beast in them, and presently they wander there. They all dread this house and me. There is a kind of travesty of humanity over there. Montgomery knows about it, for he interferes in their affairs. He has trained one or two of them to our service. He's ashamed of it, but I believe he half-likes some of these beasts. It's his business, not mine. They only sicken me with a sense of failure. I take no interest in them. I fancy they follow in the lines the Kanaka missionary marked out, and have a kind of mockery of a rational life—poor beasts! There's something they call the Law. Sing hymns about 'all thine.'[2] They build them-selves their dens, gather fruit and pull herbs—marry even. But I can see through it all, see into their very souls, and see there nothing but the souls of beasts, beasts that perish—anger, and the lusts to live and gratify themselves. . . . Yet they're odd. Complex, like every-thing else alive. There is a kind of upward striving in them, part vanity, part waste[3] sexual emotion, part waste curiosity. It only mocks me. . . . I have some hope of that puma; I have worked hard at her head and brain. . . .

"And now," said he, standing up after a long gap of silence, dur-ing which we had each pursued our own thoughts; "what do you think? Are you in fear of me still?"

I looked at him, and saw but a white-faced, white-haired man, with calm eyes. Save for his serenity, the touch almost of beauty that resulted from his set tranquillity, and from his magnificent build, he might have passed muster among a hundred other comfortable old gentlemen. Then I shivered. By way of answer to his second ques-tion, I handed him a revolver with either hand.

8. Moreau evokes the baptismal rite, with pain substituting for the "waters of life" that Jesus experienced in the river Jordan (see, e.g., Matthew 3:11).
9. Moreau's time span for the evolutionary shaping of *Homo sapiens*, which after Darwin could in some respects be grasped as a process spanning millions of years, is so abbre-viated as to call attention to the elasticity and openness of his key terms: "Man" and "making."
1. That to which one holds, or by which one is held, most firmly.
2. A phrase used in several 19th-century hymns, e.g., "All Things Are Thine; no Gift Have We," by American Quaker poet John Greenleaf Whittier (1807–1892).
3. Superfluous; incidental (as with by-products of a process).

"Keep them," he said, and snatched at a yawn. He stood up, stared at me for a moment, and smiled. "You have had two eventful days," said he. "I should advise some sleep. I'm glad it's all clear. Good-night."

He thought me over for a moment, then went out by the inner door. I immediately turned the key in the outer one.

I sat down again, sat for a time in a kind of stagnant mood, so weary, emotionally, mentally, and physically, that I could not think beyond the point of which he had left me. The black window stared at me like an eye. At last with an effort I put out the lamp, and got into the hammock. Very soon I was asleep.

CHAPTER XV.   Concerning the Beast Folk

I woke early. Moreau's explanation stood before my mind, clear and definite, from the moment of my awakening. I got out of the hammock and went to the door to assure myself that the key was turned. Then I tried the window-bar, and found it firmly fixed. That these man-like creatures were in truth only bestial monsters, mere grotesque travesties of men, filled me with a vague uncertainty of their possibilities that was far worse than any definite fear. A tapping came at the door, and I heard the glutinous[4] accents of M'ling speaking. I pocketed one of the revolvers (keeping one hand upon it) and opened to him.

"Good-morning, sair," he said, bringing, in addition to the customary herb breakfast, an ill-cooked rabbit. Montgomery followed him. His roving eye caught the position of my arm, and he smiled askew.

The puma was resting to heal that day; but Moreau, who was singularly solitary in his habits, did not join us. I talked with Montgomery to clear my ideas of the way in which the Beast Folk lived. In particular, I was urgent to know how these inhuman monsters were kept from falling upon Moreau and Montgomery, and from rending one another.

He explained to me that the comparative safety of Moreau and himself was due to the limited mental scope of these monsters. In spite of their increased intelligence, and the tendency of their animal instincts to re-awaken, they had certain Fixed Ideas implanted by Moreau in their minds, which absolutely bounded their imaginations. They were really hypnotised, had been told certain things were impossible, and certain things were not to be done, and these prohibitions were woven into the texture of their minds beyond any

4. Sluggish; thick.

possibility of disobedience or dispute. Certain matters, however, in which old instinct was at war with Moreau's convenience, were in a less stable condition. A series of propositions called the Law—I had already heard them recited—battled in their minds with the deep-seated, ever rebellious cravings of their animal natures. This Law they were ever repeating, I found, and—ever breaking. Both Montgomery and Moreau displayed particular solicitude to keep them ignorant of the taste of blood. They feared the inevitable suggestions of that flavour.

Montgomery told me that the Law, especially among the feline Beast People, became oddly weakened about nightfall; that then the animal was at its strongest; a spirit of adventure sprang up in them at the dusk; they would dare things they never seemed to dream about by day. To that I owed my stalking by the Leopard Man on the night of my arrival. But during these earlier days of my stay they broke the Law only furtively, and after dark; in the daylight there was a general atmosphere of respect for its multifarious prohibitions.

And here perhaps I may give a few general facts about the island and the Beast People. The island, which was of irregular outline, and lay low upon the wide sea, had a total area, I suppose, of seven or eight square miles.[*] It was volcanic in origin, and was now fringed on three sides by coral reefs. Some fumarolles[5] to the northward, and a hot spring, were the only vestiges of the forces that had long since originated it. Now and then a faint quiver of earthquake would be sensible, and sometimes the ascent of the spire of smoke would be rendered tumultuous by gusts of steam. But that was all. The population of the island, Montgomery informed me, now numbered rather more than sixty of these strange creations of Moreau's art, not counting the smaller monstrosities which lived in the undergrowth and were without human form. Altogether, he had made nearly a hundred and twenty, but many had died; and others, like the writhing Footless Thing of which he had told me, had come by violent ends. In answer to my question, Montgomery said that they actually bore offspring, but that these generally died. There was no evidence of the inheritance of the acquired human characteristics.[6] When they lived, Moreau took them and stamped the human form

---

[*] This description corresponds in every respect to Noble's Island. —C.E.P.

5. Openings in the Earth's surface that vent volcanic gases.

6. Lamarck's fourth law—that acquired or modified characteristics are preserved as hereditary elements transmitted to the next generation—was challenged and ultimately superseded by Darwin's theory of natural selection (see pp. 136–39 and 145–46 below). Lamarck's law remained controversial among evolutionary biologists throughout the late 19th century. Wells remained Lamarckian until he fully digested and accepted the germ-plasm hypothesis of German evolutionary biologist August Friedrich Leopold Weismann (1834–1914), which introduced to the debate in the late 1880s and early 1890s the idea that characteristics could be transmitted generationally only through cellular material rather than through bodily traits.

upon them. The females were less numerous than the males, and liable to much furtive persecution in spite of the monogamy the Law enjoined.

It would be impossible for me to describe these Beast People in detail—my eye has had no training in details—and unhappily I cannot sketch. Most striking perhaps in their general appearance was the disproportion between the legs of these creatures and the length of their bodies; and yet—so relative is our idea of grace—my eye became habituated to their forms, and at last I even fell in with their persuasion that my own long thighs were ungainly. Another point was the forward carriage of the head, and the clumsy and inhuman curvature of the spine. Even the Ape Man lacked that inward sinuous curve of the back that makes the human figure so graceful. Most had their shoulders hunched clumsily, and their short forearms hung weakly at their sides. Few of them were conspicuously hairy—at least, until the end of my time upon the island.

The next most obvious deformity was in their faces, almost all of which were prognathous,[7] malformed about the ears, with large and protuberant noses, very furry or very bristly hair, and often strangely coloured or strangely placed eyes. None could laugh, though the Ape Man had a chattering titter. Beyond these general characters their heads had little in common; each preserved the quality of its particular species: the human mark distorted but did not hide the leopard, the ox, or the sow, or other animal or animals, from which the creature had been moulded. The voices, too, varied exceedingly. The hands were always malformed; and though some surprised me by their unexpected humanity, almost all were deficient in the number of digits, clumsy about the finger-nails, and lacking any tactile sensibility.

The two most formidable animal-men were my Leopard Man and a creature made of Hyaena and Swine. Larger than these were the three bull creatures who pulled in the boat. Then came the Silvery Hairy Man who was also the Sayer of the Law, M'ling, and a satyr[8]-like creature of Ape and Goat. There were three Swine Men and a Swine Woman, a Mare-Rhinoceros creature, and several other females whose sources I did not ascertain. There were several Wolf creatures, a Bear-Bull, and a Saint Bernard Dog Man. I have already described the Ape Man, and there was a particularly hateful (and evil-smelling) old woman made of Vixen[9] and Bear, whom I hated

---

7. Having a markedly projecting jaw.
8. Semihuman, semi-animal woodland demigod associated with Dionysus or Bacchus (Greek and Roman god of intoxication, ritual madness, and religious ecstasy) and characterized by licentious behavior and ribald manners.
9. She-fox.

from the beginning. She was said to be a passionate votary[1] of the Law. Smaller creatures were certain dappled youths and my little sloth creature. But enough of this catalogue!

At first I had a shivering horror of the brutes, felt all too keenly that they were still brutes, but insensibly I became a little habituated to the idea of them, and, moreover, I was affected by Montgomery's attitude towards them. He had been with them so long that he had come to regard them as almost human beings—his London days seemed a glorious impossible past to him. Only once in a year or so did he go to Arica to deal with Moreau's agent, a trader in animals there. He hardly met the finest type of mankind in that seafaring village of Spanish mongrels. The men aboard ship, he told me, seemed at first just as strange to him as the Beast Men seemed to me,—unnaturally long in the leg, flat in the face, prominent in the forehead, suspicious, dangerous, and cold-hearted. In fact, he did not like men. His heart had warmed to me, he thought, because he had saved my life.

I fancied even then that he had a sneaking kindness for some of these metamorphosed brutes, a vicious sympathy with some of their ways, but that he attempted to veil from me at first.

M'ling, the black-faced man, his attendant, the first of the Beast Folk I had encountered, did not live with the others across the island, but in a small kennel at the back of the enclosure. The creature was scarcely so intelligent as the Ape Man, but far more docile, and the most human-looking of all the Beast Folk, and Montgomery had trained it to prepare food, and indeed to discharge all the trivial domestic offices that were required. It was a complex trophy of Moreau's horrible skill, a bear, tainted with dog and ox, and one of the most elaborately made of all his creatures. It treated Montgomery with a strange tenderness and devotion; sometimes he would notice it, pat it, call it half-mocking, half-jocular names, and so make it caper with extraordinary delight; sometimes he would ill-treat it, especially after he had been at the whisky, kicking it, beating it, pelting it with stones or lighted fusees.[2] But whether he treated it well or ill, it loved nothing so much as to be near him.

I say I became habituated to the Beast People, that a thousand things that had seemed unnatural and repulsive speedily became natural and ordinary to me. I suppose everything in existence takes its colour from the average hue of our surroundings: Montgomery and Moreau were too peculiar and individual to keep my general impressions of humanity well defined. I would see one of the clumsy

---

1. Worshipper; partisan.
2. Large friction or flare matches, known variously as "lucifers," "parlor matches," and "drunkard's matches." *Caper*: skip or dance in a lively way.

bovine creatures who worked the launch treading heavily through the undergrowth, and find myself asking, trying hard to recall, how he differed from some really human yokel trudging home from his mechanical labours; or I would meet the Fox-Bear Woman's vulpine[3] shifty face, strangely human in its speculative cunning, and even imagine I had met it before in some city byway.

Yet every now and then the beast would flash out upon me beyond doubt or denial. An ugly-looking man, a hunchbacked human savage to all appearance, squatting in the aperture of one of the dens, would stretch his arms and yawn, showing with startling suddenness scissor-edged incisors and saber-like canines, keen and brilliant as knives.[4] Or in some narrow pathway, glancing with a transitory daring into the eyes of some lithe, white-swathed female figure, I would suddenly see (with a spasmodic revulsion) that they had slit-like pupils, or, glancing down, note the curving nail with which she held her shapeless wrap about her. It is a curious thing, by the by, for which I am quite unable to account, that these weird creatures—the females I mean—had in the earlier days of my stay an instinctive sense of their own repulsive clumsiness, and displayed, in consequence, a more than human regard for the decencies and decorum of external costume.

CHAPTER XVI. How the Beast Folk Tasted Blood

But my inexperience as a writer betrays me, and I wander from the thread of my story. After I had breakfasted with Montgomery he took me across the island to see the fumarolle and the source of the hot spring, into whose scalding waters I had blundered on the previous day. Both of us carried whips and loaded revolvers. While going through a leafy jungle on our road thither we heard a rabbit squealing. We stopped and listened, but we heard no more, and presently we went on our way, and the incident dropped out of our minds. Montgomery called my attention to certain little pink animals with long hind-legs, that went leaping through the undergrowth. He told me they were creatures made of the offspring of the Beast People, that Moreau had invented. He had fancied they might serve for meat, but a rabbit-like habit of devouring their young had defeated this

---

3. Foxlike; slang: crafty, cunning. *Bovine*: cattlelike; slang: dull, stolid. *Yokel*: uneducated, unsophisticated rural peasant (usually derogatory).
4. A (now largely discredited) description of the Neanderthal, an extinct species or sub-species of archaic humans, discovery of which in the early to mid-19th century sparked fresh speculation and debate regarding hominid roots of modern humans' genealogy.

intention. I had already encountered some of these creatures, once during my moonlight flight from the Leopard Man, and once during my pursuit by Moreau on the previous day. By chance, one hopping to avoid us leapt into the hole caused by the uprooting of a wind-blown tree. Before it could extricate itself we managed to catch it. It spat like a cat, scratched and kicked vigorously with its hindlegs, and made an attempt to bite, but its teeth were too feeble to inflict more than a painless pinch. It seemed to me rather a pretty little creature, and as Montgomery stated that it never destroyed the turf by burrowing, and was very cleanly in its habits, I should imagine it might prove a convenient substitute for the common rabbit in gentlemen's parks.[5]

We also saw on our way the trunk of a tree barked in long strips and splintered deeply. Montgomery called my attention to this. "Not to claw Bark of Trees; *that* is the Law," he said. "Much some of them care for it!" It was after this, I think, that we met the Satyr and the Ape Man. The Satyr was a gleam of classical memory on the part of Moreau,[6] his face ovine in expression—like the coarser Hebrew type,—his voice a harsh bleat, his nether extremities Satanic.[7] He was gnawing the husk of a pod-like fruit as he passed us. Both of them saluted Montgomery.

"Hail," said they, "to the Other with the whip!"

"There's a third with a whip now," said Montgomery. "So you'd better mind!"

"Was he not made?" said the Ape Man. "He said—he said he was made."

The Satyr Man looked curiously at me. "The Third with the whip, he that walks weeping into the sea, has a thin white face."

"He has a thin long whip," said Montgomery.

"Yesterday he bled and wept," said the Satyr. "You never bleed nor weep. The Master does not bleed nor weep."

---

5. Large, artificially cultivated areas of land associated with English estates, carefully designed to seem the product of nature, not art, intermingling flora and fauna (especially deer and rabbits, but including a wider variety of relatively tame though seemingly undomesticated creatures); generally evocative of the hereditary royal spaces called "crownland," thereby insinuating the wealth of its proprietor and his allegiance to time-tested virtues unthreatened by modern encroachments.
6. Wells's language recalls T. H. Huxley's diction when introducing his exploration of evolutionary connections between humans and other primates in *Man's Place in Nature* (1863).
7. Allusion to the "devil's mark," i.e., the belief, medieval in origin, that the devil's feet are cloven (split into two parts, like goat or sheep hoofs). *Ovine*: sheeplike. *Hebrew type*: like "negroid type," a product of 19th-century racial classifications, based sometimes on "scientific" criteria (such as measurements of skulls and facial angles) and sometimes on culturally based "evidence" (such as interpretations of biblical "Hebrews" as a "mongrel race" apart from the Adamic Caucasians whose progeny populated and ruled Europe).

"Ollendorffian beggar!"[8] said Montgomery. "You'll bleed and weep if you don't look out."

"He has five fingers; he is a five-man like me," said the Ape Man.

"Come along, Prendick," said Montgomery, taking my arm, and I went on with him.

The Satyr and the Ape Man stood watching us and making other remarks to each other.

"He says nothing," said the Satyr. "Men have voices."

"Yesterday he asked me of things to eat," said the Ape Man. "He did not know." Then they spoke inaudible things, and I heard the Satyr laughing.

It was on our way back that we came upon the dead rabbit. The red body of the wretched little beast was rent to pieces, many of the ribs stripped white, and the backbone indisputably gnawed.

At that Montgomery stopped. "Good God!" said he, stooping down and picking up some of the crushed vertebrae to examine them more closely. "Good God!" he repeated, "what can this mean?"

"Some carnivore of yours has remembered its old habits," I said, after a pause. "This backbone has been bitten through."

He stood staring, with his face white and his lip pulled askew. "I don't like this," he said slowly.

"I saw something of the same kind," said I, "the first day I came here."

"The devil you did! What was it?"

"A rabbit with its head twisted off."

"The day you came here?"

"The day I came here. In the undergrowth, at the back of the enclosure, when I came out in the evening. The head was completely wrung off."

He gave a long low whistle.

"And what is more, I have an idea which of your brutes did the thing. It's only a suspicion, you know. Before I came on the rabbit I saw one of your monsters drinking in the stream."

"Sucking his drink?"

"Yes."

"Not to suck your Drink; *that* is the Law. Much the brutes care for the Law, eh—when Moreau's not about?"

"It was the brute who chased me."

"Of course," said Montgomery; "it's just the way with carnivores. After a kill they drink. It's the taste of blood, you know.

---

8. Fellow (contemptuous). *Ollendorffian*: from Heinrich Gottfried Ollendorff (1803–1865), German grammarian and teacher working in Paris known for his repetitive and comically bombastic phrases.

"What was the brute like?" he asked. "Would you know him again?" He glanced about us, standing astride over the mess of dead rabbit, his eyes roving among the shadows and screens of greenery, the lurking-places and ambuscades[9] of the forest, that bounded us in. "The taste of blood," he said again.

He took out his revolver, examined the cartridges in it, and replaced it. Then he began to pull at his dropping lip.

"I think I should know the brute again. I stunned him. He ought to have a handsome bruise on the forehead of him."[1]

"But then we have to *prove* he killed the rabbit," said Montgomery. "I wish I'd never brought the things here."

I should have gone on, but he stayed there thinking over the mangled rabbit in a puzzle-headed way. As it was, I went to such a distance that the rabbit's remains were hidden.

"Come on!" I said.

Presently he woke up and came towards me. "You see," he said, almost in a whisper, "they are all supposed to have a fixed idea against eating anything that runs on land. If some brute has by accident tasted blood . . ."

We went on some way in silence. "I wonder what can have happened," he said to himself. Then, after a pause, again: "I did a foolish thing the other day. That servant of mine . . . I showed him how to skin and cook a rabbit. It's odd . . . I saw him licking his hands . . . It never occurred to me."

Then: "We must put a stop to this. I must tell Moreau."

He could think of nothing else on our homeward journey.

Moreau took the matter even more seriously than Montgomery, and I need scarcely say I was infected by their evident consternation. "We must make an example," said Moreau. "I've no doubt in my own mind that the Leopard Man was the sinner. But how can we prove it? I wish, Montgomery, you had kept your taste for meat in hand, and gone without these exciting novelties. We may find ourselves in a mess yet through it."

"I was a silly ass," said Montgomery. "But the thing's done now. And you said I might have them, you know."

"We must see to the thing at once," said Moreau. "I suppose, if anything should turn up, M'ling can take care of himself?"

"I'm not so sure of M'ling," said Montgomery. "I think I ought to know him."

In the afternoon, Moreau, Montgomery, myself, and M'ling went across the island to the huts in the ravine. We three were armed.

---

9. Ambushes.
1. Cf. God's prophecy of "bruising" (crushing) the serpent's head as punishment for his role in the fall: "And I will put enmity between thee and the woman, and between thy seed and her seed; it shall bruise thy head, and thou shalt bruise his heel" (Genesis 3:15).

M'ling carried the little hatchet he used in chopping firewood, and some coils of wire. Moreau had a huge cowherd's horn slung over his shoulder. "You will see a gathering of the Beast People," said Montgomery. "It's a pretty sight." Moreau said not a word on the way, but his heavy white-fringed face was grimly set.

We crossed the ravine, down which smoked the stream of hot water, and followed the winding pathway through the cane brakes until we reached a wide area covered over with a thick powdery yellow substance, which I believe was sulphur. Above the shoulder of a weedy bank the sea glittered. We came to a kind of shallow natural amphitheatre, and here the four of us halted. Then Moreau sounded the horn and broke the sleeping stillness of the tropical afternoon. He must have had strong lungs. The hooting note rose and rose amidst its echoes to at last an ear-penetrating intensity. "Ah!" said Moreau, letting the curved instrument fall to his side again.

Immediately there was a crashing through the yellow canes, and a sound of voices from the dense green jungle that marked the morass[2] through which I had run on the previous day. Then at three or four points on the edge of the sulphurous area appeared the grotesque forms of the Beast People, hurrying towards us. I could not help a creeping horror as I perceived first one and then another trot out from the trees or reeds, and come shambling along over the hot dust. But Moreau and Montgomery stood calmly enough, and, perforce, I stuck beside them. First to arrive was the Satyr, strangely unreal, for all that he cast a shadow, and tossed the dust with his hoofs; after him, from the brake, came a monstrous lout, a thing of horse and rhinoceros, chewing a straw as it came; and then appeared the Swine Woman and two Wolf Women; then the Fox-Bear Witch with her red eyes in her peaked red face, and then others—all hurrying eagerly. As they came forward they began to cringe towards Moreau and chant, quite regardless of one another, fragments of the latter half of the litany of the Law: "*His* is the Hand that wounds, *His* is the Hand that heals," and so forth.

As soon as they had approached within a distance of perhaps thirty yards they halted, and bowing on knees and elbows, began flinging the white dust upon their heads. Imagine the scene if you can. We three blue-clad men, with our misshapen black-faced attendant, standing in a wide expanse of sunlit yellow dust under the blazing blue sky, and surrounded by this circle of crouching and gesticulating monstrosities, some almost human, save in their subtle expression and gestures, some like cripples, some so strangely distorted as to resemble nothing but the denizens of our wildest dreams. And beyond, the reedy lines of a cane brake in one direction, a dense

2. Swamp; bog.

tangle of palm trees on the other, separating us from the ravine with the huts, and to the north the hazy horizon of the Pacific Ocean.

"Sixty-two, sixty-three," counted Moreau. "There are four more."

"I do not see the Leopard Man," said I.

Presently Moreau sounded the great horn again, and at the sound of it all the Beast People writhed and grovelled in the dust. Then, slinking out of the cane brake, stooping near the ground, and trying to join the dust-throwing circle behind Moreau's back, came the Leopard Man. And I saw that his forehead was bruised. The last of the Beast People to arrive was the little Ape Man. The earlier animals, hot and weary with their grovelling, shot vicious glances at him.

"Cease," said Moreau, in his firm loud voice, and the Beast People sat back upon their hams and rested from their worshipping.

"Where is the Sayer of the Law?" said Moreau, and the hairy grey monster bowed his face in the dust.

"Say the words," said Moreau, and forthwith all in the kneeling assembly, swaying from side to side and dashing up the sulphur with their hands, first the right hand and a puff of dust, and then the left, began once more to chant their strange litany.

When they reached "Not to eat Flesh or Fish; that is the Law," Moreau held up his lank white hand. "*Stop!*" he cried, and there fell absolute silence upon them all.

I think they all knew and dreaded what was coming. I looked round at their strange faces. When I saw their wincing attitudes and the furtive dread in their bright eyes, I wondered that I had ever believed them to be men.

"That Law has been broken," said Moreau.

"None escape," from the faceless creature with the Silvery Hair. "None escape," repeated the kneeling circle of Beast People.

"Who is he?" cried Moreau, and looked round at their faces, cracking his whip. I fancied the Hyaena-Swine looked dejected, so too did the Leopard Man. Moreau stopped, facing this creature, who cringed towards him with the memory and dread of infinite torment. "Who is he?" repeated Moreau, in a voice of thunder.

"Evil is he who breaks the Law," chanted the Sayer of the Law.

Moreau looked into the eyes of the Leopard Man, and seemed to be dragging the very soul out of the creature.

"Who breaks the Law—" said Moreau, taking his eyes off his victim and turning towards us. It seemed to me there was a touch of exultation in his voice.

"—goes back to the House of Pain," they all clamoured; "goes back to the House of Pain, O Master!"

"Back to the House of Pain—back to the House of Pain," gabbled the Ape Man, as though the idea was sweet to him.

"Do you hear?" said Moreau, turning back to the criminal, "my frien . . . Hullo!"

For the Leopard Man, released from Moreau's eye, had risen straight from his knees, and now, with eyes aflame and his huge feline tusks flashing out from under his curling lips, leapt towards his tormentor. I am convinced that only the madness of unendurable fear could have prompted this attack. The whole circle of threescore monsters seemed to rise about us. I drew my revolver. The two figures collided. I saw Moreau reeling back from the Leopard Man's blow. There was a furious yelling and howling all about us. Every one was moving rapidly. For a moment I thought it was a general revolt.

The furious face of the Leopard Man flashed by mine, with M'ling close in pursuit. I saw the yellow eyes of the Hyaena-Swine blazing with excitement, his attitude as if he were half-resolved to attack me. The Satyr, too, glared at me over the Hyaena-Swine's hunched shoulders. I heard the crack of Moreau's pistol and saw the pink flash dart across the tumult. The whole crowd seemed to swing round in the direction of the glint of fire, and I, too, was swung round by the magnetism of the movement. In another second I was running, one of a tumultuous shouting crowd, in pursuit of the escaping Leopard Man.

That is all that I can tell definitely. I saw the Leopard Man strike Moreau, and then everything spun about me, until I was running headlong.

M'ling was ahead, close in pursuit of the fugitive. Behind, their tongues already lolling out, ran the Wolf-Women in great leaping strides. The Swine-Folk followed, squealing with excitement, and the two Bull Men in their swathings of white. Then came Moreau in a cluster of the Beast People, his wide-brimmed straw hat blown off, his revolver in hand, and his lank white hair streaming out. The Hyaena-Swine ran beside me, keeping pace with me, and glancing furtively at me out of his feline eyes, and the others came pattering and shouting behind us.

The Leopard Man went bursting his way through the long canes, which sprang back as he passed and rattled in M'ling's face. We others in the rear found a trampled path for us when we reached the brake. The chase lay through the brake for perhaps a quarter of a mile, and then plunged into a dense thicket that retarded our movements exceedingly, though we went through it in a crowd together—fronds flicking into our faces, ropy creepers catching us under the chin, or gripping our ankles, thorny plants hooking into and tearing cloth and flesh together.

"He has gone on all-fours through this," panted Moreau, now just ahead of me.

"None escape," said the Wolf-Bear, laughing into my face with the exultation of hunting.

We burst out again among rocks, and saw the quarry ahead, running lightly on all-fours, and snarling at us over his shoulder. At that the Wolf-Folk howled with delight. The thing was still clothed, and, at a distance, its face still seemed human, but the carriage of its four limbs was feline, and the furtive droop of its shoulder was distinctly that of a hunted animal. It leapt over some thorny yellow-flowering bushes and was hidden. M'ling was half-way across the space.

Most of us now had lost the first speed of the chase, and had fallen into a longer and steadier stride. I saw, as we traversed the open, that the pursuit was now spreading from a column into a line. The Hyaena-Swine still ran close to me, watching me as it ran, every now and then puckering its muzzle with a snarling laugh.

At the edge of the rocks, the Leopard Man, realising he was making for the projecting cape upon which he had stalked me on the night of my arrival, had doubled[3] in the undergrowth. But Montgomery had seen the manoeuver, and turned him again.

So, panting, tumbling against rocks, torn by brambles, impeded by ferns and reeds, I helped to pursue the Leopard Man, who had broken the Law, and the Hyaena-Swine ran, laughing savagely, by my side. I staggered on, my head reeling, and my heart beating against my ribs, tired almost to death, and yet not daring to lose sight of the chase, lest I should be left alone with this horrible companion. I staggered on in spite of infinite fatigue and the dense heat of the tropical afternoon.

And at last the fury of the hunt slackened. We had pinned the wretched brute into a corner of the island. Moreau, whip in hand, marshalled us all into an irregular line, and we advanced, now slowly, shouting to one another as we advanced, and tightening the cordon[4] about our victim. He lurked, noiseless and invisible, in the bushes through which I had run from him during that midnight pursuit.

"Steady!" cried Moreau; "steady!" as the ends of the line crept round the tangle of undergrowth, and hemmed the brute in.

"'Ware a rush!" came the voice of Montgomery from beyond the thicket.

I was on the slope above the bushes. Montgomery and Moreau beat along the beach beneath. Slowly we pushed in among the fretted[5] network of branches and leaves. The quarry was silent.

"Back to the House of Pain, the House of Pain, the House of Pain!" yelped the voice of the Ape Man, some twenty yards to the right.

---

3. Turned sharply and suddenly.
4. Military-style encirclement.
5. Interlaced.

When I heard that, I forgave the poor wretch all the fear he had inspired in me.

I heard the twigs snap and the boughs swish aside before the heavy tread of the Horse-Rhinoceros upon my right. Then suddenly, through a polygon of green, in the half-darkness under the luxuriant growth, I saw the creature we were hunting. I halted. He was crouched together into the smallest possible compass, his luminous green eyes turned over his shoulder regarding me.

It may seem a strange contradiction in me—I cannot explain the fact,—but now, seeing the creature there in a perfectly animal attitude, with the light gleaming in its eyes, and its imperfectly human face distorted with terror, I realised again the fact of its humanity. In another moment other of its pursuers would see it, and it would be overpowered and captured, to experience once more the horrible tortures of the enclosure. Abruptly I slipped out my revolver, aimed between its terror-struck eyes, and fired.

As I did so the Hyaena-Swine saw the thing, and flung itself upon it with an eager cry, thrusting thirsty teeth into its neck. All about me the green masses of the thicket were swaying and cracking as the Beast People came rushing together. One face and then another appeared.

"Don't kill it, Prendick," cried Moreau. "Don't kill it!" And I saw him stooping as he pushed through under the fronds of the big ferns.

In another moment he had beaten off the Hyaena-Swine with the handle of his whip, and he and Montgomery were keeping away the excited carnivorous Beast People, and particularly M'ling, from the still quivering body. The Hairy Grey Thing came sniffing at the corpse under my arm. The other animals, in their animal ardour, jostled me to get a nearer view.

"Confound you, Prendick!" said Moreau. "I wanted him."

"I'm sorry," said I, though I was not. "It was the impulse of the moment." I felt sick with exertion and excitement. Turning, I pushed my way out of the crowding Beast People, and went on alone up the slope towards the higher part of the headland. Under the shouted instructions of Moreau, I heard the three white-swathed Bull Men begin dragging the victim down towards the water.

It was easy now for me to be alone. The Beast People manifested a quite human curiosity about the dead body, and followed it in a thick knot, sniffing and growling at it, as the Bull Men dragged it down the beach. I went to the headland, and watched the Bull Men, black against the evening sky, as they carried the weighted dead body out to sea, and, like a wave across my mind, came the realisation of the unspeakable aimlessness of things upon the island. Upon the beach, among the rocks beneath me, was the Ape Man, the Hyaena-Swine, and several other of the Beast People, standing about

Montgomery and Moreau. They were all still intensely excited, and all overflowing with noisy expressions of their loyalty to the Law. Yet I felt an absolute assurance in my own mind that the Hyaena-Swine was implicated in the rabbit-killing. A strange persuasion came upon me that, save for the grossness of the line, the grotesqueness of the forms, I had here before me the whole balance of human life in miniature, the whole interplay of instinct, reason, and fate, in its simplest form. The Leopard Man had happened to go under. That was all the difference.

Poor brutes! I began to see the viler aspect of Moreau's cruelty. I had not thought before of the pain and trouble that came to these poor victims after they had passed from Moreau's hands. I had shivered only at the days of actual torment in the enclosure. But now that seemed to be the lesser part. Before they had been beasts, their instincts fitly adapted to their surroundings, and happy as living things may be. Now they stumbled in the shackles of humanity, lived in a fear that never died, fretted[6] by a law they could not understand; their mock-human existence began in an agony, was one long internal struggle, one long dread of Moreau—and for what? It was the wantonness that stirred me.

Had Moreau had any intelligible object I could have sympathized at least a little with him. I am not so squeamish about pain as that. I could have forgiven him a little even had his motive been hate. But he was so irresponsible, so utterly careless. His curiosity, his mad, aimless investigations, drove him on, and the things were thrown out to live a year or so, to struggle, and blunder, and suffer; at last to die painfully. They were wretched in themselves; the old animal hate moved them to trouble one another; the Law held them back from a brief hot struggle and a decisive end to their natural animosities.[7]

In those days my fear of the Beast People went the way of my personal fear for Moreau. I fell indeed into a morbid state, deep and enduring, alien to fear, which has left permanent scars upon my mind. I must confess I lost faith in the sanity of the world when I saw it suffering the painful disorder of this island. A blind fate, a vast pitiless mechanism, seemed to cut and shape the fabric of existence, and I, Moreau (by his passion for research), Montgomery (by his passion for drink), the Beast People, with their instincts and mental restrictions, were torn and crushed, ruthlessly, inevitably, amid the infinite complexity of its incessant wheels. But this

---

6. Gnawed away; consumed.
7. This and the previous paragraph offer a compressed description of what Wells calls "the tragedy of Extinction" in his 1893 essay "On Extinction" (see pp. 244–47 below).

condition did not come all at once. . . . I think indeed that I antici-
pate a little in speaking of it now.

CHAPTER XVII.   A Catastrophe

Scarcely six weeks passed before I had lost every feeling but dislike
and abhorrence of these infamous experiments of Moreau's. My one
idea was to get away from these horrible caricatures of my Maker's
image,[8] back to the sweet and wholesome intercourse of men. My
fellow-creatures, from whom I was thus separated, began to assume
idyllic virtue and beauty in my memory. My first friendship with
Montgomery did not increase. His long separation from humanity,
his secret vice of drunkenness, his evident sympathy with the Beast
People, tainted him to me. Several times I let him go alone among
them. I avoided intercourse with them in every possible way. I spent
an increasing proportion of my time upon the beach, looking for
some liberating sail that never appeared, until one day there fell
upon us an appalling disaster that put an altogether different aspect
upon my strange surroundings.

It was about seven or eight weeks after my landing—rather more,
I think, though I had not troubled to keep account of the time—
when this catastrophe occurred. It happened in the early morning—I
should think about six. I had risen and breakfasted early, having
been aroused by the noise of three Beast Men carrying wood into
the enclosure.

After breakfast I went to the open gateway of the enclosure and
stood there smoking a cigarette and enjoying the freshness of the
early morning. Moreau presently came round the corner of the
enclosure and greeted me. He passed by me, and I heard him behind
me unlock and enter his laboratory. So indurated[9] was I at that
time to the abomination of the place, that I heard without a touch of
emotion the puma victim begin another day of torture. It met its

---

8. Evocation of Genesis 1:27: "So God created man in his own image, in the image of God
created he him," capping a sequence of allusions linking Moreau's actions, island, and
creatures to the biblical narratives of origins and fall (the former evoked in the vivisector's Elohim-like surveying of his creative endeavors—"I rested from work for some
days, and was in a mind to write an account of the whole affair"; see above, p. 65; the
latter recalled, e.g., in the previous chapter's many images of a "wriggling" creature
that, having "got loose," "writhed along the ground in a serpentine fashion," "lurked in
the woods . . . doing mischief," and finally killed a Kanaka, curling his gun barrels into
the self-signature of an "S" [see above, p. 66]). Moreau's earlier claim to have chosen
"the human form as a model" *by chance* (see p. 60 above) connects to this passage by
marking his godlike making of humanoid creatures as a "caricature" of the biblical
God's creation of humanity, while deepening the complex association of his vivisectional project with Darwinian natural selection.
9. Hardened.

persecutor with a shriek almost exactly like that of an angry virago.[1]

Then something happened. I do not know what it was exactly to this day. I heard a sharp cry behind me, a fall, and, turning, saw an awful face rushing upon me, not human, not animal, but hellish, brown, seamed with red branching scars, red drops starting out upon it, and the lidless eyes ablaze. I flung up my arm to defend myself from the blow that flung me headlong with a broken forearm, and the great monster, swathed in lint[2] and with red-stained bandages fluttering about it, leapt over me and passed. I rolled over and over down the beach, tried to sit up, and collapsed upon my broken arm. Then Moreau appeared, his massive white face all the more terrible for the blood that trickled from his forehead. He carried a revolver in one hand. He scarcely glanced at me, but rushed off at once in pursuit of the puma.

I tried the other arm and sat up. The muffled figure in front ran in great striding leaps along the beach, and Moreau followed her. She turned her head and saw him, then, doubling abruptly, made for the bushes. She gained upon him at every stride. I saw her plunge into them, and Moreau, running slantingly to intercept her, fired and missed as she disappeared. Then he too vanished in the green confusion.

I stared after them, and then the pain in my arm flamed up, and with a groan I staggered to my feet. Montgomery appeared in the doorway dressed, and with his revolver in his hand.

"Great God, Prendick!" he said, not noticing that I was hurt. "That brute's loose! Tore the fetter out of the wall. Have you seen them?" Then sharply, seeing I gripped my arm, "What's the matter?"

"I was standing in the doorway," said I.

He came forward and took my arm. "Blood on the sleeve," said he, and rolled back the flannel. He pocketed the weapon, felt my arm about painfully, and led me inside. "Your arm is broken," he said; and then, "Tell me exactly how it happened—what happened."

I told him what I had seen, told him in broken sentences, with gasps of pain between them, and very dexterously and swiftly he bound my arm meanwhile. He slung it from my shoulder, stood back, and looked at me. "You'll do," he said. "And now?" He thought. Then he went out and locked the gates of the enclosure. He was absent some time.

I was chiefly concerned about my arm. The incident seemed merely one more of many horrible things. I sat down in the deck

---

1. Fierce, strong woman; colloquially: a loud, insolent scold.
2. Soft, fleecy material for dressing wounds (usually made by scraping linen).

chair and, I must admit, swore heartily at the island. The first dull feeling of injury in my arm had already given way to a burning pain when Montgomery re-appeared.

His face was rather pale, and he showed more of his lower gums than ever. "I can neither see nor hear anything of him," he said. "I've been thinking he may want my help." He stared at me with his expressionless eyes. "That was a strong brute," he said. "It's simply wrenched its fetter out of the wall."

He went to the window, then to the door, and there turned to me. "I shall go after him," he said. "There's another revolver I can leave with you. To tell you the truth, I feel anxious somehow."

He obtained the weapon, and put it ready to my hand on the table, then went out, leaving a restless contagion in the air. I did not sit long after he left. I took the revolver in hand and went to the doorway.

The morning was as still as death. Not a whisper of wind was stirring, the sea was like polished glass, the sky empty, the beach desolate. In my half-excited, half-feverish state this stillness of things oppressed me.

I tried to whistle, and the tune died away. I swore again—the second time that morning. Then I went to the corner of the enclosure and stared inland at the green bush that had swallowed up Moreau and Montgomery. When would they return? And how?

Then far away up the beach a little grey Beast Man appeared, ran down to the water's edge, and began splashing about. I strolled back to the doorway, then to the corner again, and so began pacing to and fro like a sentinel upon duty. Once I was arrested by the distant voice of Montgomery bawling, "Coo-ee[3] . . . Mor-eau!" My arm became less painful, but very hot. I got feverish and thirsty. My shadow grew shorter. I watched the distant figure until it went away again. Would Moreau and Montgomery never return? Three seabirds began fighting for some stranded treasure.

Then from far away behind the enclosure I heard a pistol-shot. A long silence, and then came another. Then a yelling cry nearer, and another dismal gap of silence. My unfortunate imagination set to work to torment me. Then suddenly a shot close by.

I went to the corner, startled, and saw Montgomery, his face scarlet, his hair disordered, and the knee of his trousers torn. His face expressed profound consternation. Behind him slouched the Beast Man M'ling, and round M'ling's jaws were some ominous brown stains.

---

3. Australian call, originating from the Indigenous Dharug language, meaning "come here," used to summon an absent person, to indicate one's own position, or to call for help.

"Has he come?" he said.

"Moreau?" said I. "No."

"My God!" The man was panting, almost sobbing for breath. "Go back in," he said, taking my arm. "They're mad. They're all rushing about mad. What can have happened? I don't know. I'll tell you when my breath comes. Where's some brandy?"

He limped before me into the room and sat down in the deck chair. M'ling flung himself down just outside the doorway and began panting like a dog. I got Montgomery some brandy and water. He sat staring blankly in front of him, recovering his breath. After some minutes he began to tell me what had happened.

He had followed their track for some way. It was plain enough at first on account of the crushed and broken bushes, white rags torn from the puma's bandages, and occasional smears of blood on the leaves of the shrubs and undergrowth. He lost the track, however, on the stony ground beyond the stream where I had seen the Beast Man drinking, and went wandering aimlessly westward shouting Moreau's name. Then M'ling had come to him carrying a light hatchet. M'ling had seen nothing of the puma affair, had been felling wood and heard him calling. They went on shouting together. Two Beast Men came crouching and peering at them through the undergrowth, with gestures and a furtive carriage that alarmed Montgomery by their strangeness. He hailed them, and they fled guiltily. He stopped shouting after that, and after wandering some time further in an undecided way, determined to visit the huts.

He found the ravine deserted.

Growing more alarmed every minute, he began to retrace his steps. Then it was he encountered the two Swine Men I had seen dancing on the night of my arrival; bloodstained they were about the mouth, and intensely excited. They came crashing through the ferns, and stopped with fierce faces when they saw him. He cracked his whip in some trepidation, and forthwith they rushed at him. Never before had a Beast Man dared to do that. One he shot through the head, M'ling flung himself upon the other, and the two rolled grappling. M'ling got his brute under and with his teeth in its throat, and Montgomery shot that too as it struggled in M'ling's grip. He had some difficulty in inducing M'ling to come on with him.

Thence they had hurried back to me. On the way M'ling had suddenly rushed into a thicket and driven out an under-sized Ocelot Man, also blood-stained, and lame through a wound in the foot. This brute had run a little way and then turned savagely at bay, and Montgomery—with a certain wantonness I thought—had shot him.

"What does it all mean?" said I.

He shook his head and turned once more to the brandy.

CHAPTER XVIII.   The Finding of Moreau

When I saw Montgomery swallow a third dose of brandy I took it upon myself to interfere. He was already more than half-fuddled. I told him that some serious thing must have happened to Moreau by this time, or he would have returned, and that it behoved[4] us to ascertain what that catastrophe was. Montgomery raised some feeble objections, and at last agreed. We had some food, and then all three of us started.

It is possibly due to the tension of my mind at the time, but even now that start into the hot stillness of the tropical afternoon is a singularly vivid impression. M'ling went first, his shoulders hunched, his strange black head moving with quick starts as he peered first on this side of the way and then on that. He was unarmed. His axe he had dropped when he encountered the Swine Men. Teeth were *his* weapons when it came to fighting. Montgomery followed with stumbling footsteps, his hands in his pockets, his face downcast; he was in a state of muddled sullenness with me on account of the brandy. My left arm was in a sling—it was lucky it was my left,— and I carried my revolver in my right.

We took a narrow path through the wild luxuriance of the island, going north-westward. And presently M'ling stopped and became rigid with watchfulness. Montgomery almost staggered into him, and then stopped too. Then, listening intently, we heard, coming through the trees, the sound of voices, and footsteps approaching us.

"He is dead," said a deep vibrating voice.

"He is not dead, he is not dead," jabbered another.

"We saw, we saw," said several voices.

"*Hul*-lo!" suddenly shouted Montgomery. "Hullo there!"

"Confound you!" said I, and gripped my pistol.

There was a silence, then a crashing among the interlacing vegetation, first here, then there, and then half a dozen faces appeared, strange faces, lit by a strange light. M'ling made a growling noise in his throat. I recognised the Ape Man—I had, indeed, already identified his voice—and two of the white-swathed brown-featured creatures I had seen in Montgomery's boat. With them were the two dappled brutes, and that grey, horribly crooked creature who said the Law, with grey hair streaming down its cheeks, heavy grey eyebrows, and grey locks pouring off from a central parting upon its sloping forehead, a heavy faceless thing, with strange red eyes, looking at us curiously from amidst the green.

For a space no one spoke. Then Montgomery hiccoughed, "Who . . . said he was dead?"

---

4. Was incumbent upon. *Fuddled*: intoxicated.

The Monkey Man looked guiltily at the Hairy Grey Thing. "He is dead," said this monster. "They saw."

There was nothing threatening about this detachment at any rate. They seemed awe-stricken and puzzled. "Where is he?" said Montgomery.

"Beyond," and the grey creature pointed.

"Is there a Law now?" asked the Monkey Man. "Is it still to be this and that? Is he dead indeed?" "Is there a Law?" repeated the man in white. "Is there a Law, thou Other with the whip? He is dead," said the Hairy Grey Thing. And they all stood watching us.

"Prendick," said Montgomery, turning his dull eyes to me. "He's dead—evidently."

I had been standing behind him during this colloquy. I began to see how things lay with them. I suddenly stepped in front of him and lifted up my voice:—"Children of the Law," I said, "he is *not* dead."

M'ling turned his sharp eyes on me. "He has changed his shape— he has changed his body," I went on. "For a time you will not see him. He is . . . there"—I pointed upward—"where he can watch you. You cannot see him. But he can see you. Fear the Law."[5]

I looked at them squarely. They flinched.

"He is great, he is good," said the Ape Man, peering fearfully upward among the dense trees.

"And the other Thing?" I demanded.

"The Thing that bled and ran screaming and sobbing—that is dead too," said the Grey Thing, still regarding me.

"That's well," grunted Montgomery.

"The Other with the whip," began the Grey Thing.

"Well?" said I.

"Said he was dead."

But Montgomery was still sober enough to understand my motive in denying Moreau's death. "He is not dead," he said slowly. "Not dead at all. No more dead than me."

"Some," said I, "have broken the Law. They will die. Some have died. Show us now where his old body lies. The body he cast away because he had no more need of it."

"It is this way, Man who walked in the sea,"[6] said the Grey Thing.

And with these six creatures guiding us, we went through the tumult of ferns and creepers and tree-stems towards the north-west.

5. Prendick echoes Jesus addressing his disciples cryptically in anticipation of his death and resurrection: "A little while, and ye shall not see me: and again, a little while, and ye shall see me: and, Because I go to the Father?" (John 16:17). Prendick adopts the stance that early English colonialists assumed in their encounters with Indigenous peoples of the New World, expecting them to accept European Christian ideas with a blend of wonder, fear, and credulity.
6. The Christological allusions continue with this reference to "Jesus walking on the sea" (John 6:19).

Then came a yelling, a crashing among the branches, and a little pink homunculus[7] rushed by us shrieking. Immediately after appeared a feral monster in headlong pursuit, blood-bedabbled, who was amongst us almost before he could stop his career.[8] The Grey Thing leapt aside; M'ling with a snarl flew at it, and was struck aside; Montgomery fired and missed, bowed his head, threw up his arm, and turned to run. I fired, and the thing still came on; fired again point-blank into its ugly face. I saw its features vanish in a flash. Its face was driven in. Yet it passed me, gripped Montgomery, and holding him, fell headlong beside him, and pulled him sprawling upon itself—in its death-agony.

I found myself alone with M'ling, the dead brute, and the prostrate man. Montgomery raised himself slowly and stared in a muddled way at the shattered Beast Man beside him. It more than half-sobered him. He scrambled to his feet. Then I saw the Grey Thing returning cautiously through the trees.

"See," said I, pointing to the dead brute. "Is the Law not alive? This came of breaking the Law."

He peered at the body. "He sends the Fire that kills,"[9] said he in his deep voice, repeating part of the ritual.

The others gathered round and stared for a space.

At last we drew near the westward extremity of the island. We came upon the gnawed and mutilated body of the puma, its shoulder-bone smashed by a bullet, and perhaps twenty yards further found at last what we sought. He lay face downward in a trampled space in a cane brake. One hand was almost severed at the wrist, and his silvery hair was dabbled in blood. His head had been battered in by the fetters of the puma. The broken canes beneath him were smeared with blood. His revolver we could not find. Montgomery turned him over.

* * * *

Resting at intervals, and with the help of the seven Beast People—for he was a heavy man,—we carried him back to the enclosure. The night was darkling. Twice we heard unseen creatures howling and shrieking past our little band, and once the little pink sloth creature appeared and stared at us, and vanished again. But we were not attacked again. At the gates of the enclosure our company of Beast People left us—M'ling going with the rest. We locked

---

7. Diminutive but fully formed person.
8. Speedy charge.
9. Echoes biblical language describing Elijah's encounter with the God-flouting king of the Moabites, Ahaziah: "Then the king sent unto him a captain of fifty. . . . Thou man of God, the king hath said, Come down. And Elijah answered and said unto the captain of fifty, if I be a man of God, then let fire come down from heaven, and consume thee and thy fifty. And there came down fire from heaven, and consumed him and his fifty" (2 Kings 1:9–10).

ourselves in, and then took Moreau's mangled body into the yard, and laid it upon a pile of brushwood.

Then we went into the laboratory and put an end to all we found living there.

CHAPTER XIX.   Montgomery's "Bank Holiday"[1]

When this was accomplished, and we had washed and eaten, Montgomery and I went into my little room and seriously discussed our position for the first time. It was then near midnight. He was almost sober, but greatly disturbed in his mind. He had been strangely under the influence of Moreau's personality. I do not think it had ever occurred to him that Moreau could die. This disaster was the sudden collapse of the habits that had become part of his nature in the ten or more monotonous years he had spent on the island. He talked vaguely, answered my questions crookedly, wandered into general questions.

"This silly ass of a world," he said. "What a muddle it all is! I haven't had any life. I wonder when it's going to begin. Sixteen years being bullied by nurses and schoolmasters at their own sweet will, five in London grinding hard at medicine—bad food, shabby lodgings, shabby clothes, shabby vice—a blunder—I didn't know any better—and hustled off to this beastly island. Ten years here! What's it all for, Prendick? Are we bubbles blown by a baby?"

It was hard to deal with such ravings. "The thing we have to think of now," said I, "is how to get away from this island."

"What's the good of getting away? I'm an outcast. Where am I to join on? It's all very well for *you*, Prendick. Poor old Moreau! We can't leave him here to have his bones picked. As it is . . . And besides, what will become of the decent part of the Beast Folk?"

"Well," said I. "That will do to-morrow. I've been thinking we might make the brushwood into a pyre and burn his body—and those other things . . . Then what will happen with the Beast Folk?"

"*I* don't know. I suppose those that were made of beasts of prey will make silly asses of themselves sooner or later. We can't massacre the lot. Can we? I suppose that's what *your* humanity would suggest? . . . But they'll change. They are sure to change."

He talked thus inconclusively until at last I felt my temper going. "Damnation!" he exclaimed, at some petulance of mine. "Can't you see I'm in a worse hole than you are?" And he got up and went for

1. British weekday off for bank employees; generally, any public holiday for workers.

the brandy. "Drink," he said, returning. "You logic-chopping, chalky-faced saint of an atheist,[2] drink."

"Not I," said I, and sat grimly watching his face under the yellow paraffin[3] flare as he drank himself into a garrulous misery. I have a memory of infinite tedium. He wandered into a maudlin defence of the Beast People and of M'ling. M'ling, he said, was the only thing that had ever really cared for him. And suddenly an idea came to him.

"I'm damned!" said he, staggering to his feet, and clutching the brandy-bottle. By some flash of intuition I knew what it was he intended. "You don't give drink to that beast!" I said, rising and facing him.

"Beast!" said he. "You're the beast. He takes his liquor like a Christian. Come out of the way, Prendick."

"For God's sake," said I.

"Get . . . out of the way," he roared, and suddenly whipped out his revolver.

"Very well," said I, and stood aside, half-minded to fall upon him as he put his hand upon the latch, but deterred by the thought of my useless arm. "You've made a beast of yourself. To the beasts you may go."

He flung the doorway open and stood, half-facing me, between the yellow lamp-light and the pallid glare of the moon; his eye-sockets were blotches of black under his stubbly eyebrows. "You're a solemn prig,[4] Prendick, a silly ass! You're always fearing and fancying. We're on the edge of things. I'm bound to cut my throat to-morrow. I'm going to have a damned good bank holiday to-night."

He turned and went out into the moonlight. "M'ling," he cried; "M'ling, old friend!"

Three dim creatures in the silvery light came along the edge of the wan beach, one a white-wrapped creature, the other two blotches of blackness following it. They halted, staring. Then I saw M'ling's hunched shoulders as he came round the corner of the house.

"Drink," cried Montgomery; "drink, ye brutes! Drink, and be men. Dammy,[5] I'm the cleverest! Moreau forgot this. This is the last touch.

---

2. Impossibly self-denying person (in reference to St. Oran or Otteran, popularly known in Britain and Ireland as "patron saint of atheists," who volunteered to be buried alive as required by a prophetic dream so that his exiled monastic order could build its church on the small island of Iona). *Logic-chopping*: pedantically argumentative. *Chalky-faced*: habitually didactic (for being ever at the blackboard).
3. A colorless, flammable, oily liquid used as a fuel, especially kerosene.
4. Moralistic, snobbish pedant.
5. Damme or damn me (mildly profane oath).

Drink, I tell you."[6] And waving the bottle in his hand, he started off at a kind of quick trot to the westward, M'ling ranging himself between him and the three dim creatures who followed.

I went to the doorway. They were already indistinct in the mist of the moonlight before Montgomery halted. I saw him administer a dose of the raw brandy to M'ling, and saw the five figures melt into one vague patch. "Sing," I heard Montgomery shout; "sing all together, 'Confound old Prendick.' . . . That's right. Now, again: 'Confound old Prendick.'"

The black group broke up into five separate figures and wound slowly away from me along the band of shining beach. Each went howling at his own sweet will, yelping insult at me, or giving whatever other vent this new inspiration of brandy demanded.

Presently I heard Montgomery's remote voice shouting, "Right turn!" and they passed with their shouts and howls into the blackness of the landward trees. Slowly, very slowly, they receded into silence.

The peaceful splendour of the night healed again. The moon was now past the meridian[7] and travelling down the west. It was at its full, and very bright, riding through the empty blue sky. The shadow of the wall lay, a yard wide, and of inky blackness, at my feet. The eastward sea was a featureless grey, dark and mysterious, and between the sea and the shadow the grey sands (of volcanic glass and crystals), flashed and shone like a beach of diamonds. Behind me the paraffin lamp flared hot and ruddy.

Then I shut the door, locked it, and went into the enclosure where Moreau lay beside his latest victims—the staghounds and the llama, and some other wretched brutes,—his massive face, calm even after his terrible death, and with the hard eyes open, staring at the dead white moon above. I sat down upon the edge of the sink, and, with my eyes upon that ghastly pile of silvery light and ominous shadows, began to turn over my plans in my mind.

In the morning I would gather some provisions in the dingey, and after setting fire to the pyre before me, push out into the desolation of the high sea once more. I felt that for Montgomery there was no help; that he was in truth half akin to these Beast Folk, unfitted for human kindred. I do not know how long I sat there scheming. It

6. Montgomery's intoxicated obsession with getting the "brutes" around him to "drink" themselves into manhood evokes two source texts that likewise involve mixtures of mastery and subservience, animality and anarchy, ritual and rebellion, hunting and heresy, within the context of a community surrounded by water: the Stefano–Caliban exchanges in Shakespeare's *The Tempest* (2.2.76ff. and 3.2.21ff.) and Ahab's ritualistic rousing of the *Pequod*'s crew to hunt the "great white whale" in "The Quarter-Deck" chapter of *Moby-Dick* (1851) by American novelist Herman Melville (1819–1891).
7. A zenith point of the moon's orbit from the observer's perspective; the highest position in the sky as marked longitudinally with respect to the observer's location.

must have been an hour or so. Then my planning was interrupted by the return of Montgomery to my neighbourhood. I heard a yelling from many throats, a tumult of exultant cries, passing down towards the beach, whooping and howling and excited shrieks, that seemed to come to a stop near the water's edge. The riot rose and fell; I heard heavy blows and the splintering smash of wood, but it did not trouble me then. A discordant chanting began.

My thoughts went back to my means of escape. I got up, brought the lamp, and went into a shed to look at some kegs I had seen there. Then I became interested in the contents of some biscuit tins, and opened one. I saw something out of the tail of my eye, a red figure, and turned sharply.

Behind me lay the yard, vividly black and white in the moonlight, and the pile of wood and fagots[8] on which Moreau and his mutilated victims lay, one on another. They seemed to be gripping one another in one last revengeful grapple. His wounds gaped black as night, and the blood that had dripped lay in black patches upon the sand. Then I saw, without understanding, the cause of the phantom, a ruddy glow that came and danced and went upon the wall opposite. I misinterpreted this, fancied it was a reflection of my flickering lamp, and turned again to the stores in the shed. I went on rummaging among them as well as a one-armed man could, finding this convenient thing and that, and putting them aside for to-morrow's launch. My movements were slow, and the time passed quickly. Presently the daylight crept upon me.

The chanting died down, gave place to a clamour, then began again, and suddenly broke into a tumult. I heard cries of "More, more!" a sound like quarrelling, and a sudden wild shriek. The quality of the sounds changed so greatly that it arrested my attention. I went out into the yard and listened. Then, cutting like a knife across the confusion, came the crack of a revolver.

I rushed at once through my room to the little doorway. As I did so I heard some of the packing-cases behind me go sliding down and smash together, with a clatter of glass on the floor of the shed. But I did not heed these. I flung the door open and looked out.

Up the beach by the boathouse a bonfire was burning, raining up sparks into the indistinctness of the dawn. Around this struggled a mass of black figures. I heard Montgomery call my name. I began to run at once towards this fire, revolver in hand. I saw the pink tongue of Montgomery's pistol lick out once, close to the ground. He was down. I shouted with all my strength and fired into the air.

I heard some one cry "The Master!" The knotted black struggle broke into scattering units, the fire leapt and sank down. The crowd of Beast People fled in sudden panic before me up the beach. In my excitement I fired at their retreating backs as they disappeared among the bushes. Then I turned to the black heaps upon the ground.

Montgomery lay on his back with the hairy grey Beast Man sprawling across his body. The brute was dead, but still gripping Montgomery's throat with its curving claws. Near by lay M'ling on his face, and quite still, his neck bitten open, and the upper part of the smashed brandy-bottle in his hand. Two other figures lay near the fire, the one motionless, the other groaning fitfully, every now and then raising its head slowly, then dropping it again.

I caught hold of the Grey Man and pulled him off Montgomery's body; his claws drew down the torn coat reluctantly as I dragged him away.

Montgomery was dark in the face and scarcely breathing. I splashed sea-water on his face and pillowed his head on my rolled-up coat. M'ling was dead. The wounded creature by the fire—it was a Wolf Brute with a bearded grey face—lay, I found, with the fore part of its body upon the still glowing timber. The wretched thing was injured so dreadfully that in mercy I blew its brains out at once. The other brute was one of the Bull Men swathed in white. He too was dead.

The rest of the Beast People had vanished from the beach. I went to Montgomery again and knelt beside him, cursing my ignorance of medicine.

The fire beside me had sunk down, and only charred beams of timber glowing at the central ends, and mixed with a grey ash of brushwood, remained. I wondered casually where Montgomery had got his wood. Then I saw that the dawn was upon us. The sky had grown brighter, the setting moon was growing pale and opaque in the luminous blue of the day. The sky to the eastward was rimmed with red.

Then I heard a thud and a hissing behind me, and, looking round, sprang to my feet with a cry of horror. Against the warm dawn great tumultuous masses of black smoke were boiling up out of the enclosure, and through their stormy darkness shot flickering threads of blood-red flame. Then the thatched roof caught. I saw the curving charge of the flames across the sloping straw. A spurt of fire jetted from the window of my room.

I knew at once what had happened. I remembered the crash I had heard. When I had rushed out to Montgomery's assistance I had overturned the lamp.

The hopelessness of saving any of the contents of the enclosure stared me in the face. My mind came back to my plan of flight, and turning swiftly I looked to see where the two boats lay upon the beach. They were gone! Two axes lay upon the sands beside me, chips and splinters were scattered broadcast,[9] and the ashes of the bonfire were blackening and smoking under the dawn. He had burnt the boats to revenge himself upon me and prevent our return to mankind.

A sudden convulsion of rage shook me. I was almost moved to batter his foolish head in as he lay there helpless at my feet. Then suddenly his hand moved, so feebly, so pitifully, that my wrath vanished. He groaned and opened his eyes for a minute.

I knelt down beside him and raised his head. He opened his eyes again, staring silently at the dawn, and then they met mine. The lids fell. "Sorry," he said presently, with an effort. He seemed trying to think. "The last," he murmured, "the last of this silly universe. What a mess—"

I listened. His head fell helplessly to one side. I thought some drink might revive him, but there was neither drink nor vessel in which to bring drink at hand. He seemed suddenly heavier. My heart went cold.

I bent down to his face, put my hand through the rent in his blouse. He was dead; and even as he died a line of white heat, the limb of the sun, rose eastward beyond the projection of the bay, splashing its radiance across the sky, and turning the dark sea into a weltering tumult of dazzling light. It fell like a glory[1] upon his death-shrunken face.

I let his head fall gently upon the rough pillow I had made for him, and stood up. Before me was the glittering desolation of the sea, the awful solitude upon which I had already suffered so much; behind me the island, hushed under the dawn, its Beast People silent and unseen. The enclosure with all its provisions and ammunition burnt noisily, with sudden gusts of flame, a fitful crackling, and now and then a crash. The heavy smoke drove up the beach away from me, rolling low over the distant tree-tops towards the huts in the ravine. Beside me were the charred vestiges of the boats and these five dead bodies.

Then out of the bushes came three Beast People, with hunched shoulders, protruding heads, misshapen hands awkwardly held, and inquisitive unfriendly eyes, and advanced towards me with hesitating gestures.

CHAPTER XX.   Alone with the Beast Folk

I faced these people, facing my fate in them, single-handed—now literally single-handed, for I had a broken arm. In my pocket was a revolver with two empty chambers. Among the chips scattered about

9. In all directions (like seed).
1. Nimbus; halo. *Limb*: edge. *Weltering*: turbulent, raging.

the beach lay the two axes that had been used to chop up the boats. The tide was creeping in behind me.

There was nothing for it but courage. I looked squarely into the faces of the advancing monsters. They avoided my eyes, and their quivering nostrils investigated the bodies that lay beyond me on the beach. I took half a dozen steps, picked up the blood-stained whip that lay beneath the body of the Wolf Man, and cracked it.

They stopped and stared at me. "Salute," said I. "Bow down!"

They hesitated. One bent his knees. I repeated my command, with my heart in my mouth, and advanced upon them. One knelt, then the other two.

I turned and walked towards the dead bodies, keeping my face towards the three kneeling Beast Men, very much as an actor passing up the stage faces his audience.

"They broke the Law," said I, putting my foot on the Sayer of the Law. "'They have been slain. Even the Sayer of the Law. Even the Other with the whip. Great is the Law! Come and see."

"None escape," said one of them, advancing and peering.

"None escape," said I. "Therefore hear and do as I command." They stood up, looking questioningly at one another.

"Stand there," said I.

I picked up the hatchets and swung them by their heads from the sling of my arm, turned Montgomery over, picked up his revolver, still loaded in two chambers, and bending down to rummage, found half a dozen cartridges in his pocket.

"Take him," said I, standing up again and pointing with the whip; "take him and carry him out, and cast him into the sea."

They came forward, evidently still afraid of Montgomery, but still more afraid of my cracking red whip-lash, and, after some fumbling and hesitation, some whip-cracking and shouting, lifted him gingerly, carried him down to the beach, and went splashing into the dazzling welter of the sea. "On," said I, "on!—carry him far."

They went in up to their armpits and stood regarding me. "Let go," said I, and the body of Montgomery vanished with a splash. Something seemed to tighten across my chest. "Good!" said I, with a break in my voice, and they came back, hurrying and fearful, to the margin of the water, leaving long wakes of black in the silver. At the water's edge they stopped, turning and glaring into the sea as though they presently expected Montgomery to arise thencefrom and exact vengeance.

"Now these," said I, pointing to the other bodies.

They took care not to approach the place where they had thrown Montgomery into the water, but, instead, carried the four dead Beast People slantingly along the beach for perhaps a hundred yards before they waded out and cast them away.

As I watched them disposing of the mangled remains of M'ling I heard a light footfall behind me, and turning quickly saw the big Hyaena-Swine perhaps a dozen yards away. His head was bent down, his bright eyes were fixed upon me, his stumpy hands clenched and held close by his side. He stopped in this crouching attitude when I turned, his eyes a little averted.

For a moment we stood eye to eye. I dropped the whip and snatched at the pistol in my pocket. For I meant to kill this brute—the most formidable of any left now upon the island—at the first excuse. It may seem treacherous, but so I was resolved. I was far more afraid of him than of any other two of the Beast Folk. His continued life was, I knew, a threat against mine.

I was perhaps a dozen seconds collecting myself. Then I cried, "Salute! Bow down!"

His teeth flashed upon me in a snarl. "Who are *you*, that I should. . . ."

Perhaps a little too spasmodically, I drew my revolver, aimed, and quickly fired. I heard him yelp, saw him run sideways and turn, knew I had missed, and clicked back the cock with my thumb for the next shot. But he was already running headlong, jumping from side to side, and I dared not risk another miss. Every now and then he looked back at me over his shoulder. He went slanting along the beach, and vanished beneath the driving masses of dense smoke that were still pouring out from the burning enclosure. For some time I stood staring after him. I turned to my three obedient Beast Folk again, and signalled them to drop the body they still carried. Then I went back to the place by the fire where the bodies had fallen, and kicked the sand until all the brown blood-stains were absorbed and hidden.

I dismissed my three serfs[2] with a wave of the hand, and went up the beach into the thickets. I carried my pistol in my hand, my whip thrust, with the hatchets, in the sling of my arm. I was anxious to be alone, to think out the position in which I was now placed.

A dreadful thing, that I was only beginning to realise, was that over all this island there was now no safe place where I could be alone, and secure to rest or sleep. I had recovered strength amazingly since my landing, but I was still inclined to be nervous, and to break down under any great stress. I felt I ought to cross the island, and establish myself with the Beast People, making myself secure in their confidence. And my heart failed me. I went back to the beach, and, turning eastward past the burning enclosure, made for a point where a shallow spit[3] of coral sand ran out towards the reef.

2. Feudal servants; bondsmen.
3. Narrow point of land projecting into a body of water.

Here I could sit down and think, my back to the sea, and my face against any surprise. And there I sat, chin on knees, the sun beating down upon my head, and a growing dread in my mind, plotting how I could live on against the hour of my rescue (if ever rescue came). I tried to review the whole situation as calmly as I could, but it was impossible to clear the thing of emotion.

I began turning over in my mind the reason of Montgomery's desire. "They will change," he said. "They are sure to change." And Moreau—what was it that Moreau had said? "The stubborn beast flesh grows day by day back again. . . ." Then I came round to the Hyaena-Swine. I felt assured that if I did not kill that brute he would kill me. . . . The Sayer of the Law was dead—worse luck! . . . They knew now that we of the Whips could be killed, even as they themselves were killed. . . .

Were they peering at me already out of the green masses of ferns and palms over yonder—watching until I came within their spring? Were they plotting against me? What was the Hyaena-Swine telling them? My imagination was running away with me into a morass of unsubstantial fears.

My thoughts were disturbed by a crying of sea-birds, hurrying towards some black object that had been stranded by the waves on the beach near the enclosure. I knew what that object was, but I had not the heart to go back and drive them off. I began walking along the beach in the opposite direction, designing to come round the eastward corner of the island, and so approach the ravine of the huts, without traversing the possible ambuscades of the thickets.

Perhaps half a mile along the beach I became aware of one of my three Beast Folk advancing out of the landward bushes towards me. I was now so nervous with my own imaginings that I immediately drew my revolver. Even the propitiatory[4] gestures of the creature failed to disarm me.

He hesitated as he approached. "Go away," cried I. There was something very suggestive of a dog in the cringing attitude of the creature. It retreated a little way, very like a dog being sent home, and stopped, looking at me imploringly with canine brown eyes. "Go away," said I. "Do not come near me."

"May I not come near you?" it said.

"No. Go away," I insisted, and snapped my whip. Then, putting my whip in my teeth, I stooped for a stone, and with that threat drove the creature away.

So, in solitude, I came round by the ravine of the Beast People, and, hiding among the weeds and reeds that separated this crevice

4. Conciliatory; mercy-seeking.

from the sea, I watched such of them as appeared, trying to judge from their gestures and appearance how the death of Moreau and Montgomery and the destruction of the House of Pain had affected them. I know now the folly of my cowardice. Had I kept my courage up to the level of the dawn, had I not allowed it to ebb away in solitary thought, I might have grasped the vacant sceptre of Moreau and ruled over the Beast People. As it was, I lost the opportunity, and sank to the position of a mere leader among my fellows.

Towards noon certain of them came and squatted basking in the hot sand. The imperious voices of hunger and thirst prevailed over my dread. I came out of the bushes, and, revolver in hand, walked down towards these seated figures. One, a Wolf Woman, turned her head and stared at me, and then the others. None attempted to rise or salute me. I felt too faint and weary to insist against so many, and I let the moment pass.

"I want food," said I, apologetically, and drawing near.

"There is food in the huts," said an Ox-Boar Man drowsily, and looking away from me.

I passed them, and went down into the shadow and odours of the almost deserted ravine. In an empty hut I feasted on some specked and half-decayed fruit, and then, after I had propped some branches and sticks about the opening, and placed myself with my face towards it, and my hand upon my revolver, the exhaustion of the last thirty hours claimed its own, and I let myself fall into a light slumber, trusting that the flimsy barricade I had erected would cause sufficient noise in its removal to save me from surprise.

CHAPTER XXI.   The Reversion of the Beast Folk

In this way I became one among the Beast People in the Island of Doctor Moreau. When I awoke it was dark about me. My arm ached in its bandages. I sat up, wondering at first where I might be. I heard coarse voices talking outside. Then I saw that my barricade had gone, and that the opening of the hut stood clear. My revolver was still in my hand.

I heard something breathing, saw something crouched together close beside me. I held my breath, trying to see what it was. It began to move slowly, interminably. Then something soft and warm and moist passed across my hand.

All my muscles contracted. I snatched my hand away. A cry of alarm began, and was stifled in my throat. Then I just realised what had happened sufficiently to stay my fingers on the revolver.

"Who is that?" I said in a hoarse whisper, the revolver still pointed.

"*I*, Master."

"Who are you?"

"They say there is no Master now. But I know, I know. I carried the bodies into the sea, O Walker in the Sea, the bodies of those you slew. I am your slave, Master."

"Are you the one I met on the beach?" I asked.

"The same, Master."

The thing was evidently faithful enough, for it might have fallen upon me as I slept. "It is well," I said, extending my hand for another licking kiss. I began to realise what its presence meant, and the tide of my courage flowed. "Where are the others?" I asked.

"They are mad. They are fools," said the Dog Man. "Even now they talk together beyond there. They say, 'The Master is dead; the Other with the Whip is dead. That Other who walked in the Sea is—as we are. We have no Master, no Whips, no House of Pain any more. There is an end. We love the Law, and will keep it; but there is no pain, no Master, no Whips for ever again.' So they say. But I know, Master, I know."

I felt in the darkness and patted the Dog Man's head. "It is well," I said again.

"Presently you will slay them all," said the Dog Man.

"Presently," I answered, "I will slay them all—after certain days and certain things have come to pass. Every one of them save those you spare, every one of them shall be slain."

"What the Master wishes to kill the Master kills," said the Dog Man with a certain satisfaction in his voice.

"And that their sins may grow," I said; "let them live in their folly until their time is ripe. Let them not know that I am the Master."

"The Master's will is sweet," said the Dog Man, with the ready tact of his canine blood.

"But one has sinned," said I. "Him I will kill, whenever I may meet him. When I say to you, '*That is he*,' see that you fall upon him.— And now I will go to the men and women who are assembled together."

For a moment the opening of the hut was blackened by the exit of the Dog Man. Then I followed and stood up, almost in the exact spot where I had been when I had heard Moreau and his staghound pursuing me. But now it was night, and all the miasmatic[5] ravine about me was black, and beyond, instead of a green sunlit slope, I saw a red fire before which hunched grotesque figures moved to and fro. Further were the thick trees, a bank of black fringed above with the

---

5. Noxious (of an infectious vapor).

black lace of the upper branches. The moon was just riding up on the edge of the ravine, and like a bar across its face drove the spire of vapour that was for ever streaming from the fumarolles of the island.

"Walk by me," said I, nerving myself, and side by side we walked down the narrow way, taking little heed of the dim things that peered at us out of the huts.

None about the fire attempted to salute me. Most of them disregarded me—ostentatiously. I looked round for the Hyaena-Swine, but he was not there. Altogether, perhaps twenty of the Beast Folk squatted, staring into the fire or talking to one another.

"He is dead, he is dead, the Master is dead," said the voice of the Ape Man to the right of me. "The House of Pain—there *is* no House of Pain."

"He is not dead," said I, in a loud voice. "Even now he watches us."

This startled them. Twenty pairs of eyes regarded me.

"The House of Pain is gone," said I. "It will come again. The Master you cannot see. Yet even now he listens above you."

"True, true!" said the Dog Man.

They were staggered at my assurance. An animal may be ferocious and cunning enough, but it takes a real man to tell a lie. "The Man with the Bandaged Arm speaks a strange thing," said one of the Beast Folk.

"I tell you it is so," I said. "The Master and the House of Pain will come again. Woe be to him who breaks the Law!"

They looked curiously at one another. With an affectation of indifference I began to chop idly at the ground in front of me with my hatchet. They looked, I noticed, at the deep cuts I made in the turf.

Then the Satyr raised a doubt; I answered him, and then one of the dappled things objected, and an animated discussion sprang up round the fire. Every moment I began to feel more convinced of my present security. I talked now without the catching in my breath, due to the intensity of my excitement, that had troubled me at first. In the course of about an hour I had really convinced several of the Beast Folk of the truth of my assertions, and talked most of the others into a dubious state. I kept a sharp eye for my enemy the Hyaena-Swine, but he never appeared. Every now and then a suspicious movement would startle me, but my confidence grew rapidly. Then as the moon crept down from the zenith, one by one the listeners began to yawn (showing the oddest teeth in the light of the sinking fire), and first one, and then another, retired towards the dens in the ravine. And I, dreading the silence and darkness, went with them, knowing I was safer with several of them than with one alone.

In this manner began the longer part of my sojourn upon this Island of Doctor Moreau. But from that night until the end came there was but one thing happened to tell, save a series of innumerable small unpleasant details and the fretting of an incessant uneasiness. So that I prefer to make no chronicle for that gap of time, to tell only one cardinal incident of the ten months I spent as an intimate of these half-humanised brutes. There is much that sticks in my memory that I could write, things that I would cheerfully give my right hand to forget. But they do not help the telling of the story. In the retrospect it is strange to remember how soon I fell in with these monsters' ways and gained my confidence again. I had my quarrels, of course, and could show some teeth-marks still, but they soon gained a wholesome respect for my trick of throwing stones and the bite of my hatchet. And my St. Bernard Dog Man's loyalty was of infinite service to me. I found their simple scale of honour was based mainly on the capacity for inflicting trenchant wounds. Indeed I may say—without vanity, I hope—that I held something like a pre-eminence among them. One or two whom, in various disputes, I had scarred rather badly, bore me a grudge, but it vented itself, chiefly behind my back, and at a safe distance from my missiles, in grimaces.

The Hyaena-Swine avoided me, and I was always on the alert for him. My inseparable Dog Man hated and dreaded him intensely. I really believe that was at the root of the brute's attachment to me. It was soon evident to me that the former monster had tasted blood, and gone the way of the Leopard Man. He formed a lair somewhere in the forest, and became solitary. Once I tried to induce the Beast Folk to hunt him, but I lacked the authority to make them co-operate for one end. Again and again I tried to approach his den and come upon him unawares, but always he was too acute for me, and saw or winded[6] me and got away. He too made every forest pathway dangerous to me and my allies with his lurking ambuscades. The Dog Man scarcely dared to leave my side.

In the first month or so the Beast Folk, compared with their latter condition, were human enough, and for one or two besides my canine friend I even conceived a friendly tolerance. The little pink sloth creature displayed an odd affection for me, and took to following me about. The Monkey Man bored me, however. He assumed, on the strength of his five digits, that he was my equal, and was forever jabbering at me, jabbering the most arrant[7] nonsense. One thing about him entertained me a little: he had a fantastic trick of coining new words. He had an idea, I believe, that to gabble about names that

6. Scented.
7. Extreme.

meant nothing was the proper use of speech. He called it "big thinks,"
to distinguish it from "little thinks"—the sane everyday interests of
life. If ever I made a remark he did not understand, he would praise
it very much, ask me to say it again, learn it by heart, and go off
repeating it, with a word wrong here or there, to all the milder of the
Beast People. He thought nothing of what was plain and comprehensible. I invented some very curious "big thinks" for his especial use. I
think now that he was the silliest creature I ever met; he had developed in the most wonderful way the distinctive silliness of man without losing one jot of the natural folly of a monkey.

This, I say, was in the earlier weeks of my solitude among these
brutes. During that time they respected the usage established by the
Law, and behaved with general decorum. Once I found another rabbit torn to pieces—by the Hyaena-Swine, I am assured,—but that
was all. It was about May when I first distinctly perceived a growing
difference in their speech and carriage, a growing coarseness of
articulation, a growing disinclination to talk. My Monkey Man's jabber multiplied in volume, but grew less and less comprehensible,
more and more simian. Some of the others seemed altogether slipping their hold upon speech, though they still understood what I
said to them at that time. Can you imagine language, once clear-
cut and exact, softening and guttering, losing shape and import,
becoming mere lumps of sound again? And they walked erect with
an increasing difficulty. Though they evidently felt ashamed of themselves, every now and then I would come upon one or other running
on toes and finger-tips, and quite unable to recover the vertical attitude. They held things more clumsily; drinking by suction, feeding
by gnawing; grew commoner every day. I realised more keenly than
ever what Moreau had told me about the "stubborn beast flesh." They
were reverting, and reverting very rapidly.

Some of them—the pioneers, I noticed with some surprise, were
all females—began to disregard the injunction of decency—
deliberately for the most part. Others even attempted public outrages upon the institution of monogamy. The tradition of the Law
was clearly losing its force. I cannot pursue this disagreeable subject. My Dog Man imperceptibly slipped back to the dog again; day
by day he became dumb, quadrupedal,[8] hairy. I scarcely noticed the
transition from the companion on my right hand to the lurching dog
at my side. As the carelessness and disorganisation increased from
day to day, the lane of dwelling places, at no time very sweet, became
so loathsome that I left it, and going across the island made myself
a hovel of boughs amid the black ruins of Moreau's enclosure. Some

8. Four-footed.

memory of pain, I found, still made that place the safest from the Beast Folk.

It would be impossible to detail every step of the lapsing of these monsters; to tell how, day by day, the human semblance left them; how they gave up bandagings and wrappings, abandoned at last every stitch of clothing; how the hair began to spread over the exposed limbs; how their foreheads fell away and their faces projected; how the quasi-human intimacy I had permitted myself with some of them in the first month of my loneliness became a horror to recall.

The change was slow and inevitable. For them and for me it came without any definite shock. I still went among them in safety, because no jolt in the downward glide had released the increasing charge of explosive animalism that ousted the human day by day. But I began to fear that soon now that shock must come. My St. Bernard Brute followed me to the enclosure, and his vigilance enabled me to sleep at times in something like peace. The little pink sloth thing became shy and left me, to crawl back to its natural life once more among the tree-branches. We were in just the state of equilibrium that would remain in one of those "Happy Family" cages[9] that animal-tamers exhibit, if the tamer were to leave it for ever.

Of course these creatures did not decline into such beasts as the reader has seen in zoological gardens—into ordinary bears, wolves, tigers, oxen, swine, and apes. There was still something strange about each; in each Moreau had blended this animal with that; one perhaps was ursine chiefly, another feline chiefly, another bovine chiefly, but each was tainted with other creatures—a kind of generalised animalism appeared through the specific dispositions. And the dwindling shreds of the humanity still startled me every now and then, a momentary recrudescence[1] of speech perhaps, an unexpected dexterity of the forefeet, a pitiful attempt to walk erect.

I too must have undergone strange changes. My clothes hung about me as yellow rags, through whose rents glowed the tanned skin. My hair grew long, and became matted together. I am told that even now my eyes have a strange brightness, a swift alertness of movement.

At first I spent the daylight hours on the southward beach watching for a ship, hoping and praying for a ship. I counted on the *Ipecacuanha* returning as the year wore on, but she never came. Five

---

9. Caged groupings of various smaller animals exhibited on the pretense of showing typically competitive, combative animals existing in the felicitous harmony suitable to Victorian families and social associations. The idea was made famous by American showman P. T. Barnum (1810–1891), who displayed a "Happy Family of birds and beasts" in his American Museum in New York in 1850. While the practice waned in the later 19th century, fast-money hustlers of the sort Wells apparently alludes to here continued showing "family cages" on the streets of London.
1. Recurrence (as of a disease gone into remission).

times I saw sails, and thrice smoke, but nothing ever touched the island. I always had a bonfire ready, but no doubt the volcanic reputation of the island was taken to account for that.

It was only about September or October that I began to think of making a raft. By that time my arm had healed, and both my hands were at my service again. At first I found my helplessness appalling. I had never done any carpentry or suchlike work in my life, and I spent day after day in experimental chopping and binding among the trees. I had no ropes, and could hit on nothing wherewith to make ropes; none of the abundant creepers seemed limber or strong enough, and with all my litter of scientific education I could not devise any way of making them so. I spent more than a fortnight grubbing among the black ruins of the enclosure and on the beach where the boats had been burnt, looking for nails and other stray pieces of metal that might prove of service. Now and then some Beast creature would watch me, and go leaping off when I called to it. There came a season of thunderstorms and heavy rain that greatly retarded my work, but at last the raft was completed.

I was delighted with it. But with a certain lack of practical sense that has always been my bane I had made it a mile or more from the sea, and before I had dragged it down to the beach the thing had fallen to pieces. Perhaps it is as well that I was saved from launching it. But at the time my misery at my failure was so acute, that for some days I simply moped on the beach and stared at the water and thought of death.

But I did not mean to die, and an incident occurred that warned me unmistakably of the folly of letting the days pass so—for each fresh day was fraught with increasing danger from the Beast Monsters. I was lying in the shade of the enclosure wall staring out to sea, when I was startled by something cold touching the skin of my heel, and starting round found the little pink sloth creature blinking into my face. He had long since lost speech and active movement, and the lank hair of the little brute grew thicker every day, and his stumpy claws more askew. He made a moaning noise when he saw he had attracted my attention, went a little way towards the bushes, and looked back at me.

At first I did not understand, but presently it occurred to me that he wished me to follow him, and this I did at last, slowly—for the day was hot. When he reached the trees he clambered into them, for he could travel better among their swinging creepers than on the ground.

And suddenly in a trampled space I came upon a ghastly group. My St. Bernard creature lay on the ground dead, and near his body crouched the Hyaena-Swine, gripping the quivering flesh with misshapen claws, gnawing at it and snarling with delight. As I

approached, the monster lifted its glaring eyes to mine, its lips went
trembling back from its red-stained teeth, and it growled menac-
ingly. It was not afraid and not ashamed; the last vestige of the
human taint had vanished. I advanced a step further, stopped, pulled
out my revolver. At last I had him face to face.

The brute made no sign of retreat. But its ears went back, its hair
bristled, and its body crouched together. I aimed between the eyes
and fired. As I did so the thing rose straight at me in a leap, and I
was knocked over like a ninepin.[2] It clutched at me with its crippled
hand, and struck me in the face. Its spring carried it over me. I fell
under the hind part of its body, but luckily I had hit as I meant, and
it had died even as it leapt. I crawled out from under its unclean
weight and stood up trembling, staring at its quivering body. That
danger at least was over. But this, I knew, was only the first of the
series of relapses that must come.

I burnt both the bodies on a pyre of brushwood. Now, indeed, I
saw clearly that unless I left the island my death was only a question of time. The Beasts by that time had, with one or two exceptions, left the ravine, and made themselves lairs, according to their
tastes, among the thickets of the island. Few prowled by day; most
of them slept, and the island might have seemed deserted to a newcomer; but at night the air was hideous with their calls and howling. I had half a mind to make a massacre of them—to build traps
or fight them with my knife. Had I possessed sufficient cartridges, I
should not have hesitated to begin the killing. There could now be
scarcely a score left of the dangerous carnivores; the braver of these
were already dead. After the death of this poor dog of mine, my last
friend, I too adopted to some extent the practice of slumbering in
the daytime, in order to be on my guard at night. I rebuilt my den in
the walls of the enclosure with such a narrow opening that anything
attempting to enter must necessarily make a considerable noise. The
creatures had lost the art of fire, too, and recovered their fear of it.
I turned once more, almost passionately now, to hammering together
stakes and branches to form a raft for my escape.

I found a thousand difficulties. I am an extremely unhandy man—
my schooling was over before the days of Slöjd,[3]—but most of the
requirements of a raft I met at last in some clumsy circuitous way
or other, and this time I took care of the strength. The only insur-
mountable obstacle was, that I had no vessel to contain the water I
should need if I floated forth upon these untravelled seas. I would
have even tried pottery, but the island contained no clay. I used to

---

2. Pin used in bowling game "ninepins," played primarily in Europe.
3. Scandinavian system of manual training in handicraft tools and materials, especially
   woodwork; not unlike the anti-industrial Arts and Crafts Movement, Slöjd (also known
   as "educational sloyd") proved fashionable in some English schools during the 1890s.

go moping about the island, trying with all my might to solve this one last difficulty. Sometimes I would give way to wild outbursts of rage, and hack and splinter some unlucky tree in my intolerable vexation. But I could think of nothing.

And then came a day, a wonderful day, that I spent in ecstasy. I saw a sail to the southwest, a small sail like that of a little schooner, and forthwith I lit a great pile of brushwood and stood by it in the heat of it and the heat of the midday sun, watching. All day I watched that sail, eating or drinking nothing, so that my head reeled; and the Beasts came and glared at me, and seemed to wonder, and went away. The boat was still distant when night came and swallowed it up, and all night I toiled to keep my blaze bright and high, and the eyes of the Beasts shone out of the darkness, marvelling. In the dawn it was nearer, and I saw that it was the dirty lug-sail of a small boat. My eyes were weary with watching, and I peered and could not believe them. Two men were in the boat, sitting low down, one by the bows and the other at the rudder. But the boat sailed strangely. The head was not kept to the wind; it yawed[4] and fell away.

As the day grew brighter I began waving the last rag of my jacket to them; but they did not notice me, and sat still, facing one another. I went to the lowest point of the low headland and gesticulated and shouted. There was no response, and the boat kept on her aimless course, making slowly, very slowly, for the bay. Suddenly a great white bird flew up out of the boat, and neither of the men stirred nor noticed it. It circled round, and then came sweeping overhead with its strong wings outspread.

Then I stopped shouting, and sat down on the headland and rested my chin on my hands and stared. Slowly, slowly, the boat drove past towards the west. I would have swum out to it, but something, a cold vague fear, kept me back. In the afternoon the tide stranded it, and left it a hundred yards or so to the westward of the ruins of the enclosure.

The men in it were dead, had been dead so long that they fell to pieces when I tilted the boat on its side and dragged them out. One had a shock of red hair like the captain of the *Ipecacuanha,* and a dirty white cap lay in the bottom of the boat. As I stood beside the boat, three of the Beasts came slinking out of the bushes and sniffing towards me. One of my spasms of disgust came upon me. I thrust the little boat down the beach and clambered on board her. Two of the brutes were Wolf Beasts, and came forward with quivering nostrils and glittering eyes; the third was the horrible nondescript[5] of bear and bull.

---

4. Moved erratically from side to side (per a ship deviating from course).
5. Hitherto unidentified or undefined species.

When I saw them approaching those wretched remains, heard them snarling at one another, and caught the gleam of their teeth, a frantic horror succeeded my repulsion. I turned my back upon them, struck the lug,[6] and began paddling out to sea. I could not bring myself to look behind me.

But I lay between the reef and the island that night, and the next morning went round to the stream and filled the empty keg aboard with water. Then, with such patience as I could command, I collected a quantity of fruit, and waylaid and killed two rabbits with my last three cartridges. While I was doing this I left the boat moored to an inward projection of the reef, for fear of the Beast Monsters.

CHAPTER XXII.   The Man Alone

In the evening I started and drove out to sea before a gentle wind from the southwest, slowly and steadily, and the island grew smaller and smaller, and the lank spire of smoke dwindled to a finer and finer line against the hot sunset. The ocean rose up around me, hiding that low dark patch from my eyes. The daylight, the trailing glory of the sun, went streaming out of the sky, was drawn aside like some luminous curtain, and at last I looked into that blue gulf of immensity that the sunshine hides, and saw the floating hosts of the stars. The sea was silent, the sky was silent; I was alone with the night and silence.

So I drifted for three days, eating and drinking sparingly, and meditating upon all that had happened to me, nor desiring very greatly then to see men again. One unclean rag was about me, my hair a black tangle. No doubt my discoverers thought me a madman. It is strange, but I felt no desire to return to mankind. I was only glad to be quit of the foulness of the Beast Monsters. And on the third day I was picked up by a brig from Apia[7] to San Francisco. Neither the captain nor the mate would believe my story, judging that solitude and danger had made me mad. And fearing their opinion might be that of others, I refrained from telling my adventure further, and professed to recall nothing that had happened to me between the loss of the *Lady Vain* and the time when I was picked up again—the space of a year.

---

6. Lowered the lug sail (to facilitate rowing the boat).
7. Seaport (now capital) of the Polynesian archipelago Western Samoa (now Samoa), located on its second largest island, Upolu, suggestively located halfway between Banya (see note 6 on p. 5 above) and Noble Isle. Apia was the site of a notorious incident during the struggle among colonial powers for control of the Samoan Islands (known as the "Samoan Crisis" of 1887–89). *Brig*: ship with two square-rigged masts.

I had to act with the utmost circumspection to save myself from the suspicion of insanity. My memory of the Law, of the two dead sailors, of the ambuscades of the darkness, of the body in the cane brake, haunted me. And, unnatural as it seems, with my return to mankind came, instead of that confidence and sympathy I had expected, a strange enhancement of the uncertainty and dread I had experienced during my stay upon the island. No one would believe me, I was almost as queer to men as I had been to the Beast People. I may have caught something of the natural wildness of my companions.

They say that terror is a disease, and anyhow, I can witness that, for several years now, a restless fear has dwelt in my mind, such a restless fear as a half-tamed lion cub may feel. My trouble took the strangest form. I could not persuade myself that the men and women I met were not also another, still passably human, Beast People, animals half-wrought into the outward image of human souls, and that they would presently begin to revert, to show first this bestial mark and then that. But I have confided my case to a strangely able man, a man who had known Moreau, and seemed half to credit my story, a mental specialist[8]—and he has helped me mightily.

Though I do not expect that the terror of that island will ever altogether leave me, at most times it lies far in the back of my mind, a mere distant cloud, a memory and a faint distrust; but there are times when the little cloud spreads until it obscures the whole sky. Then I look about me at my fellow-men. And I go in fear. I see faces keen and bright, others dull or dangerous, others unsteady, insincere; none that have the calm authority of a reasonable soul. I feel as though the animal was surging up through them; that presently the degradation[9] of the Islanders will be played over again on a larger scale. I know this is an illusion, that these seeming men and women about me are indeed men and women, men and women forever, perfectly reasonable creatures, full of human desires and tender solicitude, emancipated from instinct, and the slaves of no fantastic Law—being altogether different from the Beast Folk. Yet I shrink from them, from their curious glances, their inquiries and assistance, and long to be away from them and alone.

For that reason I live near the broad free downland,[1] and can escape thither when this shadow is over my soul; and very sweet is the empty downland then, under the wind-swept sky. When I lived in London the horror was wellnigh insupportable. I could not get away from men; their voices came through windows; locked doors

---

8. Psychiatric consultant.
9. I.e., degeneration (see note 5 on p. 65 above).
1. Area of gently rolling, open, uncultivated hills ("downs"), common to southern England.

were flimsy safeguards. I would go out into the streets to fight with my delusion, and prowling women would mew after me, furtive craving men glance jealously at me, weary pale workers go coughing by me, with tired eyes and eager paces like wounded deer dripping blood, old people, bent and dull, pass murmuring to themselves, and all unheeding a ragged tail of gibing[2] children. Then I would turn aside into some chapel, and even there, such was my disturbance, it seemed that the preacher gibbered Big Thinks even as the Ape Man had done; or into some library, and there the intent faces over the books seemed but patient creatures waiting for prey. Particularly nauseous were the blank expressionless faces of people in trains and omnibuses;[3] they seemed no more my fellow-creatures than dead bodies would be, so that I did not dare to travel unless I was assured of being alone. And even it seemed that I, too, was not a reasonable creature, but only an animal tormented with some strange disorder in its brain, that sent it to wander alone, like a sheep stricken with the gid.[4]

But this is a mood that comes to me now—I thank God—more rarely. I have withdrawn myself from the confusion of cities and multitudes, and spend my days surrounded by wise books, bright windows in this life of ours lit by the shining souls of men. I see few strangers, and have but a small household. My days I devote to reading and to experiments in chemistry, and I spend many of the clear nights in the study of astronomy. There is, though I do not know how there is or why there is, a sense of infinite peace and protection in the glittering hosts of heaven. There it must be, I think, in the vast and eternal laws of matter, and not in the daily cares and sins and troubles of men, that whatever is more than animal within us must find its solace and its hope.[5] I hope, or I could not live. And so, in hope and solitude, my story ends.

EDWARD PRENDICK

---

2. Taunting. *Mew*: whine; screech.
3. Multipassenger public vehicles.
4. Disease of herbivores, especially sheep, caused by larvae of tapeworm in the brain and resulting in a staggering gait and obsessive circling behavior (cf. "giddy"), as well as head-tilting and depression.
5. Wells's sentence, in its vocabulary and arguably in its sentiment, recalls the framing passages of Darwin's *On the Origin of Species*: the opening epigraph by English theologian, philosopher, and scientist William Whewell (1794–1866), which refers to the "general laws" that govern the "material world"; and the closing paragraph:

> Thus, from the war of nature, from famine and death, the most exalted object which we are capable of conceiving, namely, the production of the higher animals, directly follows. There is grandeur in this view of life . . . that, whilst this planet has gone circling on according to the fixed laws of gravity, from so simple a beginning endless forms most beautiful and most wonderful have been, and are being evolved.

Note.[6]—. The substance of the chapter entitled "Doctor Moreau explains," which contains the essential idea of the story, appeared as a middle article in the *Saturday Review* in January, 1895.[7] This is the only portion of this story that has been previously published, and it has been entirely recast to adapt it to the narrative form. Strange as it may seem to the unscientific reader, there can be no denying that, whatever amount of credibility attaches to the detail of this story, the manufacture of monsters—and perhaps even of *quasi*-human monsters—is within the possibilities of vivisection.[8]

---

6. This epilogial note appears in some but not all subsequent editions in which Wells had an editorial hand.
7. "The Limits of Individual Plasticity" (see pp. 242–44 below).
8. See the review by P. Chalmers Mitchell (pp. 257–59 below) and the unsigned review in the *Manchester Guardian* (pp. 262–263 below) to get the flavor of early responses to *The Island of Doctor Moreau* that dismissed its scientific plausibility. Wells's sensitivity to this critical repudiation of the novel's experimental conceit can be seen not only in his response to Mitchell (p. 260 below), but also in his addition of the subtitle "A Possibility" to the S&K edition.

Glossary of Nautical, Botanical, and Geological Terms

Nautical Terms

Aft: near or toward a ship's rear (stern)

Binnacle: container holding a ship's navigational instruments, including compass and oil lamp (contained in a protective case or "lantern")

Boom: spar along the bottom of a sail, used to control the sail's angle and shape into the wind

Bow: forward part of a ship

Bowsprit: large spar (or length of wood, usually supporting a sail, such as the mast) projecting from the stem of a vessel, to which the foremast stays fastened

Breaker: small keg or cask, often used in sailing vessels as ballast or carried in lifeboats for provision of water

Brig: ship with two square-rigged masts

Bulwarks: woodwork running along a ship's side above the upper deck

Combing/coaming: the raised border at the edges of a ship's scuttles and hatches

Companion: stairway or ladder leading from one deck of a ship to another (or the canopy to such a stairway)

Derelict: ship abandoned at sea

Dingey: dinghy; small sailboat, carried behind a larger ship as a cargo or rescue vessel

Flush deck: ship's deck that extends from the bow (front) to the stern (rear), usually with no structure above

Fore: near to a ship's front (bow)

Forecastle: pronounced "focsul"; the forward section of a ship's upper deck

Gangway: raised, planked passageway connecting different parts of a ship or used for boarding (i.e., gangplank)

Gig: long, narrow rowboat attached to a larger ship (cf. *dingey*)

Gunwale: pronounced "gunnel"; uppermost edge or planking of a ship's side

Hatch: opening in a ship's deck

Hatchway: passageway giving access to a ship's hatches

Heaving (or hove) to: being brought to a stop against the wind

Heel: when a boat tips to one side due to the wind's force or an uneven load

Launch: large, flat-bottomed boat that operates in shallow water

Lee: side of a ship that's sheltered from the wind

Long-boat: large, open boat with sails and oars, typically carried by a merchant sailing vessel for transporting people and provisions between ship and shore

Lugs or lug sails: four-sided square sails suspended from a spar called a "yard" at an oblique angle so that they overlap the mast when raised; of three types: standing, dipping, and balanced

Mizzen: ship's mast located aft (rearward) of a ship's mainmast

Painter: rope attached to a dinghy's bow, used for tying or towing the boat

Quarter-deck: small, raised deck above the main deck and behind the ship's mainmast, reserved for the captain and other privileged persons

Rigged: equipped or outfitted

Rigging: ropes, chains, and fittings used to operate a ship's masts, sails, spars, etc.

Schooner: small seafaring vessel rigged with two masts, fore (frontward) and aft (in the rear or stern)

Scuttle: small opening in the side or bottom of a ship, furnished with a lid, providing light and ventilation

Shrouds: ropes, or rigging, leading from a ship's mastheads to provide lateral support for the masts

Spanker: fore-and-aft sail on the mast nearest a ship's stern

Spar: length of wood, usually supporting a sail, such as the mast

Starboard: right-hand side of a ship

Stern: ship's rear

Stern sheets: space at the stern of an open boat

Struck the lugs: lowered the sails

Tack: to change or sustain a ship's direction by turning the bow to the wind and shifting the sails

Tackle: rigging

Taffrail: handrail located on the open deck toward a ship's stern

Thwart: rower's seat or bench

Tiller: lever used to turn a boat's rudder from side to side for navigation

Yaw: move erratically from side to side (per a ship deviating from course)

Botanical Terms

Cane brake: thicket of tall woody grass (like bamboo) or reeds

Creeper: small, viny plant that grows along the ground or ascends a supporting surface (e.g., ivy growing up a tree)

Epiphyte: a plant that grows upon another plant for physical support, but unlike a parasite takes no nutrients from that supportive organism

Foliaceous: leaflike

Frond: large compound leaves or leaf-like parts of a palm, fern, or similar plant

Lichen: complex plant-like organism constituted by a symbiotic union of a fungus and an alga

Morass: swamp; bog

Pioneer: designating a hardy species that is the first to colonize barren or previously steady-state environments

Geological Terms

Fumarolle: an opening in the Earth's surface that vents volcanic gases

Pumiceous: of the nature of light, porous, glassy volcanic rock (or pumice)

Scoria (pl.: scoriae): rough, cindery residue from melting of lava exposed to the air

Sulphurous: of the nature of the mineral sulphur, or sulfur, a pale greenish-yellow combustible nonmetal element found near volcanoes and hot springs

BACKGROUNDS AND CONTEXTS

Illustrations

Théodore Géricault, *The Raft of the Medusa* (1818–19). Géricault's monumental painting—exhibited in London at the Egyptian Hall (Piccadilly) in 1820, where it was viewed by nearly 40,000 visitors— inspired generations of English writers and artists.

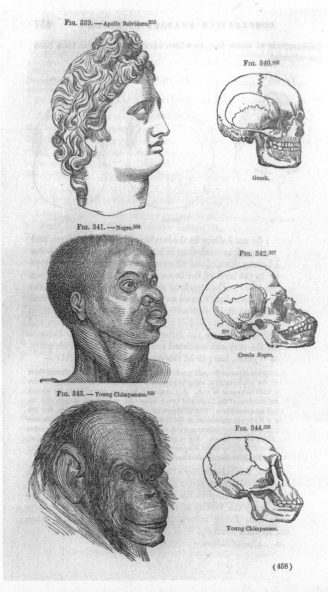

FIG. 339. — Apollo Belvidere.[553]

FIG. 340.[556]

Greek.

FIG. 341. — Negro.[554]

FIG. 342.[557]

Creole Negro.

FIG. 343. — Young Chimpanzee.[555]

FIG. 344.[558]

Young Chimpanzee.

(458)

From George Gliddon and Josiah Nott, *Types of Mankind* (1854). Medical Historical Library, Harvey Cushing / John Hay Whitney Medical Library, Yale University. In the mid-nineteenth century, practitioners of "scientific racism" such as Gliddon and Nott claimed that *Homo sapiens* comprised several distinct species or "races," each appearing by a separate act of divine creation. Darwin's *On the Origin of Species* (1859) laid waste to the polygenists' racialist theory of human origins.

118

Gustave Moreau, *Oedipus and the Sphinx* (1864). Known for his interest in translating mythological and neoclassical themes into the psychologically charged language of Symbolism, Moreau was drawn to scenes like that depicted here between Oedipus and the Sphinx in which ambiguous encounters illuminate the riddle of human identity.

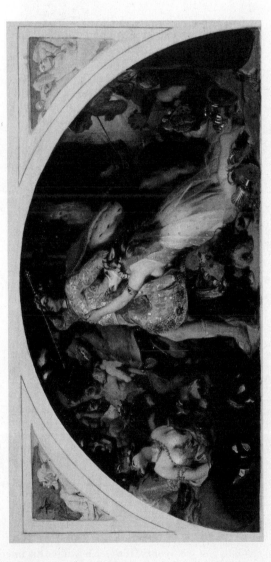

J. C. Armytage, *Rout of Comus and His Band*, engraved in 1865 after Sir Edwin Henry Landseer's 1843 painting *The Defeat, of Comus and His Beasts*. Photo: Tate Images. Landseer's illustration of Milton's poem "Comus, a Masque" emphasizes human-animal hybridity as an expression of festive misrule. Commissioned by Queen Victoria's husband, Prince Albert, in 1843, Landseer's painting was popularized in the later-nineteenth century through etchings produced by several engravers.

"Monkeyana," *Punch* 40 (May 18, 1861). Image courtesy of the Wellcome Collection. The Enlightenment motto seen here was used ironically to express the possibility of a "familial" relation of shared ancestry between species such as great apes and humans—an idea first proposed by Scottish linguist James Burnett, Lord Monboddo (1714–1799), who referred to the anthropoidal ape as the "brother of man," and later delicately but effectively articulated by Darwin in *On the Origin of Species* (1859).

THE LION OF THE SEASON.

ALARMED FLUNKEY. "MR. G-G-G-O-O-O-RILLA!"

"The Lion of the Season," *Punch* 40 (May 25, 1861). Image courtesy of the Wellcome Collection. When actual encounters with great ape populations (stirred by colonial expeditions that raided primate populations for menageries, zoos, exhibitions, and "scientific" experiments) intersected with vigorous, often inflammatory public debate about the logic and implications of evolution, consternation arose at the possibility that some form of ape-man or man-ape was the "missing link" between older simian forms and *Homo sapiens*. Gorillas in particular were represented as a kind of uncanny Beast People endowed with remarkably humanoid likeness, stirring both fear and edgy amusement (as seen in this *Punch* cartoon, which satirized the sensation caused by the arrival in London of French-American anthropologist Paul Du Chaillu with an ostentatious display of gorilla specimens obtained on an expedition to western equatorial Africa).

122

Faustin Betbeder, "Professor Darwin," *Figaro's London Sketch Book of Celebrities* (February 18, 1874). With the publication of *The Descent of Man* in 1871, Darwin's theory of human origination through processes of natural selection rather than by divine creation became a topic of renewed popular debate. Darwin owned a copy of Betbeder's cartoon, which he kept alongside an associated text clipping that read in part: "with rare humility [Darwin] owns that his ancestors were apes."

Evolution: Theory, Society, Language, and Ethics

Publication of Charles Darwin's *On the Origin of Species* in 1859 was a seismic event in Western intellectual and cultural history, changing not only the way we view the inception, activity, and evolution of living organisms but also the fundamental frameworks guiding our conception of humanity's place within life itself. After *Origin*, every anchoring category of our supposedly distinctive "human" identity—morality, language, reason, culture—became suddenly a site of radical insecurity, and the solid earth of human exceptionalism gave way to the abysmal prospect of human entanglement with the rest of creation. For what ultimately emerges from *Origin*'s argument—that, in a nutshell, species arise, develop, and disappear through the "natural selection" of small, inheritable variations over long periods of emergence, reproduction, and struggle for continuation in environments that likewise change over time—is a transvaluation of every key character in the story about earthly life that until then had been told jointly by religious doctrine and Enlightenment philosophy. Darwin's analysis of evolutionary process as an interplay of organism and environment equally dashed religious exaltations of a human soul made uniquely sacred by timeless spiritual authority and humanistic visions of the *Homo sapiens* mind progressively realizing its inherent capacity for autonomous authorship. As Darwin confessed (when contemplating his own religious faith on the eve of his marriage in 1839), "As soon as you realise that one species could evolve into another, the whole structure wobbles and collapses."[1] Even to Darwin, the reimagined story of life that came to be known as "Darwinism" was a potentially ruinous revelation, an ominous insight charged equally with terror and transformation.

At the heart of the worldview in which Darwin's own initial theological, philosophical, and scientific beliefs were nurtured was the concept of *design* through which a benevolent Creator gave form, function, and meaning to a natural world made for the benefit of humanity. Such was the essential framework of "natural theology," a purported integration of religious Truth and scientific principle that William Paley, an Anglican clergyman and Utilitarian philosopher whose work was required reading during Darwin's undergraduate

---

1. From Darwin's private notebook of 1838, as cited in Christoph Marty, "Darwin on a Godless Creation," *Scientific American* (February 12, 2009).

studies at Cambridge, articulated most systematically and influentially in his 1802 treatise of that name. When Darwin set forth on the barque HMS *Beagle* in 1831 at the start of his five-year survey expedition to the southern coasts of South America, he was an ardent admirer of Paley. But the "one long argument" that Darwin described as binding his book's massive body of closely examined detail into a new theory of evolution as life's causal vector proved a revolutionary subversion of natural theology's conceptual foundations. For essence, Darwin's account of existence gives us contingency; for permanence, transience; for teleology, happenstance; for metaphysics, matter; for foresight, caprice; and for the anthropomorphic Designer of an anthropocentric universe, an indifferent activity of "selection" within an impersonal nature in which adaptations tumble through time in a random (but retrospectively explicable) concatenation of triumph and failure, throwing individual species into a whirligig of mutation, metamorphosis, and obliteration.

Stating bluntly, Darwin swept away the presiding paradigm with biblical force: "now that the law of natural selection has been discovered ... [t]here seems to be no more design in the variability of organic beings and in the action of natural selection, than in the course which the wind blows."[2]

That discovery caused an instantaneous sensation upon *Origin*'s publication, stirring melodramatic battles between defenders of doctrinal views of creation and an emerging generation of professional scientists—most famously in the 1860 "Great Debate" at the Oxford University Museum of Natural History between Bishop Samuel Wilberforce and the biologist and anatomist T. H. Huxley (soon to be known as "Darwin's Bulldog" for his tenacious advocacy of *Origin*'s broad evolutionary argument). Though shrouded in a fog of subsequent mythmaking, the debate clearly turned on what Darwin had long thought of as the dreaded "monkey question": that is, the unavoidable inference from *Origin*'s argument that humans and other primates descended from a common ancestor. The "monkey question"—further stimulated by the commotion caused by adventurer-zoologist Paul Du Chaillu's appearance in London with a collection of stuffed gorillas, a newly discovered genus of great ape[3]—so caught the public imagination that the caricature of Darwin-as-monkey[4] remained for decades the signature image of the cultural battle that *Origin* had ignited (and that continued to rage among public intellectuals and literary writers like Wells long after evolutionary theory had, as a general proposition, been accepted in the scientific community).

---

2. Charles Darwin, *The Autobiography of Charles Darwin, 1809–1882*. Ed. Nora Barlow (New York: Harcourt Brace and Company, 1958), p. 88.
3. The hubbub is keenly captured in a *Punch* cartoon, "The Lion of the Season"; see illustration on p. 122 above.
4. As in Faustin Betbeder's famous cartoon, "Professor Darwin"; see illustration on p. 123 above.

Theory

WILLIAM PALEY

From Natural Theology[†]

From *Chapter XXIII*
Of the Personality of the Deity

Contrivance, if established, appears to me to prove every thing which we wish to prove. Amongst other things, it proves the *personality* of the Deity, as distinguished from what is sometimes called nature, sometimes called a principle: which terms, in the mouths of those who use them philosophically, seem to be intended, to admit and to express an efficacy, but to exclude and to deny a personal agent. Now that which can contrive, which can design, must be a person. These capacities constitute personality, for they imply consciousness and thought. They require that which can perceive an end or purpose; as well as the power of providing means, and of directing them to their end.[1] They require a centre in which perceptions unite, and from which volitions flow; which is mind. The acts of a mind prove the existence of a mind: and in whatever a mind resides, is a person. The seat of intellect is a person. We have no authority to limit the properties of mind to any particular corporeal form, or to any particular circumscription of space. These properties subsist, in created nature, under a great variety of sensible forms. Also every animated being has its *sensorium*, that is, a certain portion of space, within which perception and volition are exerted. This sphere may be enlarged to an indefinite extent; may comprehend the universe; and, being so imagined, may serve to furnish us with as good a notion, as we are capable of forming, of the *immensity* of the Divine Nature, *i.e.* of a Being, infinite, as well in essence as in power; yet nevertheless a person. * * *

Of this however we are certain, that whatever the Deity be, neither the *universe*, nor any part of it which we see, can be He. The universe itself is merely a collective name: its parts are all which are real; or which are *things*. Now inert matter is out of the question: and organized substances include marks of contrivance. But whatever includes marks of contrivance, whatever, in its constitution, testifies

---

† From *Natural Theology; Or, Evidences of the Existence and Attributes of the Deity*. Collected from the Appearances of Nature (London: J. Faulder, 1809 [1802]), pp. 408–18, 441. Unless otherwise indicated, notes are by Paley.
1. Priestley's *Letters to a Philosophical Unbeliever*, p. 153, ed. 2.

design, necessarily carries us to something beyond itself, to some other being, to a designer prior to, and out of, itself. No animal, for instance, can have contrived its own limbs and senses; can have been the author to itself of the design with which they were constructed. That supposition involves all the absurdity of self-creation, *i.e.* of acting without existing. Nothing can be God, which is ordered by a wisdom and a will, which itself is void of: which is indebted for any of its properties to contrivance *ab extra*.[2] The *not* having that in his nature which requires the exertion of another prior being (which property is sometimes called self-sufficiency, and sometimes self-comprehension), appertains to the Deity, as his essential distinction, and removes his nature from that of all things which we see. Which consideration contains the answer to a question that has sometimes been asked, namely, Why, since something or other must have existed from eternity, may not the present universe be that something? The contrivance perceived in it, proves that to be impossible. Nothing contrived, can, in a strict and proper sense, be eternal, forasmuch as the contriver must have existed before the contrivance.

Wherever we see marks of contrivance, we are led for its cause to an *intelligent* author. And this transition of the understanding is founded upon uniform experience. We see intelligence constantly contriving, that is, we see intelligence constantly producing effects, marked and distinguished by certain properties; not certain particular properties, but by a kind and class of properties, such as relation to an end, relation of parts to one another, and to a common purpose. We see, wherever we are witnesses to the actual formation of things, nothing except intelligence producing effects so marked and distinguished. Furnished with this experience, we view the productions of nature. We observe *them* also marked and distinguished in the same manner. We wish to account for their origin. Our experience suggests a cause perfectly adequate to this account. No experience, no single instance or example, can be offered in favour of any other. * * * In like manner, and upon the same foundation (which in truth is that of experience), we conclude that the works of nature proceed from intelligence and design, because, in the properties of relation to a purpose, subserviency to a use, they resemble what intelligence and design are constantly producing, and what nothing except intelligence and design ever produce at all. Of every argument, which would raise a question as to the safety of this reasoning, it may be observed, that if such argument be listened to, it leads to the inference, not only that the present order of nature is insufficient to prove the existence of an intelligent Creator, but that no imaginable order would be sufficient to prove it; that *no* contrivance, were it ever so mechanical, ever so

2. From without (Latin) [*Editor's note*].

precise, ever so clear, ever so perfectly like those which we ourselves employ, would support this conclusion. A doctrine, to which, I conceive, no sound mind can assent.

The force however of the reasoning is sometimes sunk by our taking up with mere names. * * * [W]e must here notice again, the misapplication of the term "law," and the mistake concerning the idea which that term expresses in physics, whenever such idea is made to take the place of power, and still more of an intelligent power, and, as such, to be assigned for the cause of any thing, or of any property of any thing, that exists. This is what we are secretly apt to do, when we speak of organized bodies (plants for instance, or animals), owing their production, their form, their growth, their qualities, their beauty, their use, to any law or laws of nature; and when we are contented to sit down with that answer to our inquiries concerning them. I say once more, that it is a perversion of language to assign any law, as the efficient, operative cause of any thing. A law presupposes an agent, for it is only the mode according to which an agent proceeds; it implies a power, for it is the order according to which that power acts. Without this agent, without this power, which are both distinct from itself, the "law" does nothing; is nothing.

What has been said concerning "law," holds true of *mechanism*. Mechanism is not itself power. Mechanism, without power, can do nothing. Let a watch be contrived and constructed ever so ingeniously; be its parts ever so many, ever so complicated, ever so finely wrought or artificially put together, it cannot *go* without a weight or spring, *i.e.* without a force independent of, and ulterior to, its mechanism. The spring acting at the centre, will produce different motions and different results, according to the variety of the intermediate mechanism. One and the self-same spring, acting in one and the same manner, *viz.* by simply expanding itself, may be the cause of a hundred different and all useful movements, if a hundred different and well-devised sets of wheels be placed between it and the final effect; *e.g.* may point out the hour of the day, the day of the month, the age of the moon, the position of the planets, the cycle of the years, and many other serviceable notices; and these movements may fulfil their purposes with more or less perfection, according as the mechanism is better or worse contrived, or better or worse executed, or in a better or worse state of repair: *but in all cases, it is necessary that the spring act at the centre*. The course of our reasoning upon such a subject would be this. By inspecting the watch, even when standing still, we get a proof of contrivance, and of a contriving mind, having been employed about it. In the form and obvious relation of its parts, we see enough to convince us of this. If we pull the works in pieces, for the purpose of a closer examination, we are still more fully convinced. But, when we see the watch *going*, we see proof of another point, *viz.* that there is a power somewhere, and somehow or other, applied to it; a power in action;—that there is more in the subject than the mere wheels of the machine;—that there is a secret spring, or a gravitating plummet;—in a word, that there is force, and energy, as well as mechanism.

So then, the watch in motion establishes to the observer two conclusions: One; that thought, contrivance, and design, have been employed in the forming, proportioning, and arranging of its parts; and that whoever or wherever he be, or were, such a contriver there is, or was: The other; that force or power, distinct from mechanism, is, at this present time, acting upon it. * * * It is the same in nature. In the works of nature we trace mechanism; and this alone proves contrivance: but living, active, moving, productive nature, proves also the exertion of a power at the centre: for, wherever the power resides, may be denominated the centre. * * *

Upon the whole; after all the schemes and struggles of a reluctant philosophy, the necessary resort is to a Deity. The marks of *design* are too strong to be gotten over. Design must have had a designer. That designer must have been a person. That person is GOD.

CHARLES DARWIN

From On the Origin of Species[†]

Introduction

When on board H.M.S. *Beagle*, as naturalist, I was much struck with certain facts in the distribution of the organic beings inhabiting South America, and in the geological relations of the present to the past inhabitants of that continent. These facts, as will be seen in the latter chapters of this volume, seemed to throw some light on the origin of species—that mystery of mysteries,[1] as it has been called by one of our greatest philosophers. On my return home, it occurred to me, in 1837, that something might perhaps be made out on this question by patiently accumulating and reflecting on all sorts of facts which could possibly have any bearing on it. After five years' work I allowed myself to speculate on the subject, and drew up some short

[†] From *On the Origin of Species by Means of Natural Selection, or the Preservation of Favoured Races in the Struggle for Life*, 6th ed. (London: Odhams Press Ltd., 1872 [1859], pp. 29, 32–34, 45, 51–52, 80–83, 85, 89–90, 95–96, 98–99, 141–43, 465, 468–70, 484–86, 490–92. Notes are by the editor of this Norton Critical Edition.
1. In 1838, English scientist and inventor John W. F. Herschel (1792–1871) used this phrase to describe "the replacement of extinct species by others" in correspondence to fellow scientist Charles Babbage (1791–1871).

notes; these I enlarged in 1844 into a sketch of the conclusions, which then seemed to me probable: from that period to the present day I have steadily pursued the same object. I hope that I may be excused for entering on these personal details, as I give them to show that I have not been hasty in coming to a decision.

* * *

No one ought to feel surprise at much remaining as yet unexplained in regard to the origin of species and varieties, if he make due allowance for our profound ignorance in regard to the mutual relations of the many beings which live around us. Who can explain why one species ranges widely and is very numerous, and why another allied species has a narrow range and is rare? Yet these relations are of the highest importance, for they determine the present welfare and, as I believe, the future success and modification of every inhabitant of this world. Still less do we know of the mutual relations of the innumerable inhabitants of the world during the many past geological epochs in its history. Although much remains obscure, and will long remain obscure, I can entertain no doubt, after the most deliberate study and dispassionate judgment of which I am capable, that the view which most naturalists until recently entertained, and which I formerly entertained—namely, that each species has been independently created—is erroneous. I am fully convinced that species are not immutable; but that those belonging to what are called the same genera are lineal descendants of some other and generally extinct species, in the same manner as the acknowledged varieties of any one species are the descendants of that species. Furthermore, I am convinced that natural selection has been the most important, but not the exclusive, means of modification.

Chapter 1. Variation under Domestication

CAUSES OF VARIABILITY

When we compare the individuals of the same variety or sub-variety of our older cultivated plants and animals, one of the first points which strikes us is, that they generally differ more from each other than do the individuals of any one species or variety in a state of nature. And if we reflect on the vast diversity of the plants and animals which have been cultivated, and which have varied during all ages under the most different climates and treatment, we are driven to conclude that this great variability is due to our domestic productions having been raised under conditions of life not so uniform as, and somewhat different from, those to which the parent species had been exposed under nature. * * * No case is on record of a variable organism ceasing to vary under cultivation. * * *

*   *   *

BREEDS OF THE DOMESTIC PIGEON,
THEIR DIFFERENCES AND ORIGIN

Believing that it is always best to study some special group, I have, after deliberation, taken up domestic pigeons. I have kept every breed which I could purchase or obtain, and have been most kindly favoured with skins from several quarters of the world[.] * * * The diversity of the breeds is something astonishing. * * *

*   *   *

Great as are the differences between the breeds of the pigeon, I am fully convinced that the common opinion of naturalists is correct, namely, that all are descended from the rock-pigeon (Columba livia), including under this term several geographical races or sub-species, which differ from each other in the most trifling respects. * * *

*   *   *

I have discussed the probable origin of domestic pigeons at some, yet quite insufficient, length; because when I first kept pigeons and watched the several kinds, well knowing how truly they breed, I felt fully as much difficulty in believing that since they had been domesticated they had all proceeded from a common parent, as any naturalist could in coming to a similar conclusion in regard to the many species of finches, or other groups of birds, in nature. One circumstance has struck me much; namely, that nearly all the breeders of the various domestic animals and the cultivators of plants, with whom I have conversed, or whose treatises I have read, are firmly convinced that the several breeds to which each has attended, are descended from so many aboriginally distinct species. Ask, as I have asked, a celebrated raiser of Hereford cattle, whether his cattle might not have descended from Long-horns, or both from a common parent-stock, and he will laugh you to scorn. I have never met a pigeon, or poultry, or duck, or rabbit fancier, who was not fully convinced that each main breed was descended from a distinct species. * * * The explanation, I think, is simple: from long-continued study they are strongly impressed with the differences between the several races; and though they well know that each race varies slightly, for they win their prizes by selecting such slight differences, yet they ignore all general arguments, and refuse to sum up in their minds slight differences accumulated during many successive generations. May not those naturalists who, knowing far less of the laws of inheritance than does the breeder, and knowing no more than he does of the intermediate links in the long lines of descent, yet admit that many of our domestic races are descended from the same parents—may they not learn a lesson of caution, when they deride the idea of species in a state of nature being lineal descendants of other species?

PRINCIPLES OF SELECTION ANCIENTLY FOLLOWED, AND THEIR EFFECTS

Let us now briefly consider the steps by which domestic races have been produced, either from one or from several allied species. Some effect may be attributed to the direct and definite action of the external conditions of life, and some to habit; but he would be a bold man who would account by such agencies for the differences between a dray and race-horse, a greyhound and bloodhound, a carrier and tumbler pigeon. One of the most remarkable features in our domesticated races is that we see in them adaptation, not indeed to the animal's or plant's own good, but to man's use or fancy. Some variations useful to him have probably arisen suddenly, or by one step. * * * But when we compare the dray-horse and race-horse, the dromedary and camel, the various breeds of sheep fitted either for cultivated land or mountain pasture, with the wool of one breed good for one purpose, and that of another breed for another purpose; when we compare the many breeds of dogs, each good for man in different ways; * * * when we compare the host of agricultural, culinary, orchard, and flower-garden races of plants, most useful to man at different seasons and for different purposes, or so beautiful in his eyes, we must, I think, look further than to mere variability. We can not suppose that all the breeds were suddenly produced as perfect and as useful as we now see them; indeed, in many cases, we know that this has not been their history. The key is man's power of accumulative selection: nature gives successive variations; man adds them up in certain directions useful to him. In this sense he may be said to have made for himself useful breeds.

* * *

Chapter 3. Struggle for Existence

* * * How have all those exquisite adaptations of one part of the organisation to another part, and to the conditions of life and of one organic being to another being, been perfected? We see these beautiful co-adaptations most plainly in the woodpecker and the mistletoe; and only a little less plainly in the humblest parasite which clings to the hairs of a quadruped or feathers of a bird; in the structure of the beetle which dives through the water; in the plumed seed which is wafted by the gentlest breeze; in short, we see beautiful adaptations everywhere and in every part of the organic world.

*** All these results, as we shall more fully see in the next chapter, follow from the struggle for life. Owing to this struggle, variations, however slight and from whatever cause proceeding, if they be in any degree profitable to the individuals of a species, in their infinitely complex relations to other organic beings and to their physical conditions of life, will tend to the preservation of such individuals, and will generally be inherited by the offspring. The offspring, also, will thus have a better chance of surviving, for, of the many individuals of any species which are periodically born, but a small number can survive. I have called this principle, by which each slight variation, if useful, is preserved, by the term natural selection, in order to mark its relation to man's power of selection. But the expression often used by Mr. Herbert Spencer,[2] of the Survival of the Fittest, is more accurate, and is sometimes equally convenient. We have seen that man by selection can certainly produce great results, and can adapt organic beings to his own uses, through the accumulation of slight but useful variations, given to him by the hand of Nature. But Natural Selection, we shall hereafter see, is a power incessantly ready for action, and is as immeasurably superior to man's feeble efforts, as the works of Nature are to those of Art.

* * *

THE TERM, STRUGGLE FOR EXISTENCE, USED IN A LARGE SENSE

I should premise that I use this term in a large and metaphorical sense, including dependence of one being on another, and including (which is more important) not only the life of the individual, but success in leaving progeny. Two canine animals, in a time of dearth, may be truly said to struggle with each other which shall get food and live. But a plant on the edge of a desert is said to struggle for life against the drought, though more properly it should be said to be dependent on the moisture. A plant which annually produces a thousand seeds, of which only one of an average comes to maturity, may be more truly said to struggle with the plants of the same and other kinds which already clothe the ground. *** In these several senses, which pass into each other, I use for convenience sake the general term of Struggle for Existence.

2. English biologist, sociologist, and anthropologist (1820–1903), an early proponent of evolution (see pp. 150–54 below). Spencer introduced the term "survival of the fittest" in *The Principles of Biology* (1864), which appeared five years after the first edition of *On the Origin of Species*.

GEOMETRICAL RATIO OF INCREASE

A struggle for existence inevitably follows from the high rate at which all organic beings tend to increase. Every being, which during its natural lifetime produces several eggs or seeds, must suffer destruction during some period of its life, and during some season or occasional year, otherwise, on the principle of geometrical increase, its numbers would quickly become so inordinately great that no country could support the product. Hence, as more individuals are produced than can possibly survive, there must in every case be a struggle for existence, either one individual with another of the same species, or with the individuals of distinct species, or with the physical conditions of life. It is the doctrine of Malthus[3] applied with manifold force to the whole animal and vegetable kingdoms[.] * * *

* * *

In looking at Nature, it is most necessary to keep the foregoing considerations always in mind—never to forget that every single organic being may be said to be striving to the utmost to increase in numbers; that each lives by a struggle at some period of its life; that heavy destruction inevitably falls either on the young or old during each generation or at recurrent intervals. Lighten any check, mitigate the destruction ever so little, and the number of the species will almost instantaneously increase to any amount.[4]

* * *

COMPLEX RELATIONS OF ALL ANIMALS AND PLANTS
TO EACH OTHER IN THE STRUGGLE FOR EXISTENCE

* * *

[We have seen] that cattle absolutely determine the existence of the Scotch fir; but in several parts of the world insects determine the existence of cattle. Perhaps Paraguay offers the most curious instance of this; for here neither cattle nor horses nor dogs have ever run wild, though they swarm southward and northward in a feral state; * * * this is caused by the greater number in Paraguay of a certain fly, which lays its eggs in the navels of these animals when first born. The increase of these flies, numerous as they are, must be habitually checked by some means, probably by other parasitic

---

3. See note 1 on p. 24.
4. Here follows in the first edition (1859) the following sentence, notable for its literally double-edged image of the "face of nature": "The face of nature may be compared to a yielding surface, with ten thousand sharp wedges packed close together and driven inwards by incessant blows, sometimes one wedge being struck, and then another with greater force."

insects. Hence, if certain insectivorous birds were to decrease in Paraguay, the parasitic insects would probably increase; and this would lessen the number of the navel-frequenting flies—then cattle and horses would become feral, and this would certainly greatly alter (as indeed I have observed in parts of South America) the vegetation: this again would largely affect the insects; and this, * * * the insectivorous birds, and so onwards in ever-increasing circles of complexity. Not that under nature the relations will ever be as simple as this. Battle within battle must be continually recurring with varying success; and yet in the long run the forces are so nicely balanced that the face of nature remains for long periods of time uniform, though assuredly the merest trifle would give the victory to one organic being over another. Nevertheless, so profound is our ignorance, and so high our presumption, that we marvel when we hear of the extinction of an organic being; and as we do not see the cause, we invoke cataclysms to desolate the world, or invent laws on the duration of the forms of life!

* * *

Chapter 4. Natural Selection; or The Survival of the Fittest

How will the struggle for existence, briefly discussed in the last chapter, act in regard to variation? Can the principle of selection, which we have seen is so potent in the hands of man, apply under nature? I think we shall see that it can act most efficiently. Let the endless number of slight variations and individual differences occurring in our domestic productions, and, in a lesser degree, in those under nature, be borne in mind. * * * Let it also be borne in mind how infinitely complex and close-fitting are the mutual relations of all organic beings to each other and to their physical conditions of life; and consequently what infinitely varied diversities of structure might be of use to each being under changing conditions of life. Can it then be thought improbable, seeing that variations useful to man have undoubtedly occurred, that other variations useful in some way to each being in the great and complex battle of life, should occur in the course of many successive generations? If such do occur, can we doubt (remembering that many more individuals are born than can possibly survive) that individuals having any advantage, however slight, over others, would have the best chance of surviving and procreating their kind? On the other hand, we may feel sure that any variation in the least degree injurious would be rigidly destroyed. This preservation of favourable individual differences and variations, and the destruction of those which are injurious, I have called Natural Selection, or the Survival of the Fittest. * * *

Several writers have misapprehended or objected to the term Natural Selection. Some have even imagined that natural selection induces variability, whereas it implies only the preservation of such variations as arise and are beneficial to the being under its conditions of life. No one objects to agriculturists speaking of the potent effects of man's selection; and in this case the individual differences given by nature, which man for some object selects, must of necessity first occur. Others have objected that the term selection implies conscious choice in the animals which become modified; and it has even been urged that, as plants have no volition, natural selection is not applicable to them! In the literal sense of the word, no doubt, natural selection is a false term; but who ever objected to chemists speaking of the elective affinities of the various elements?—and yet an acid cannot strictly be said to elect the base with which it in preference combines. It has been said that I speak of natural selection as an active power or Deity; but who objects to an author speaking of the attraction of gravity as ruling the movements of the planets? Every one knows what is meant and is implied by such metaphorical expressions; and they are almost necessary for brevity. So again it is difficult to avoid personifying the word Nature; but I mean by nature, only the aggregate action and product of many natural laws, and by laws the sequence of events as ascertained by us. With a little familiarity such superficial objections will be forgotten.

* * *

As man can produce, and certainly has produced, a great result by his methodical and unconscious means of selection, what may not natural selection effect? Man can act only on external and visible characters: Nature, if I may be allowed to personify the natural preservation or survival of the fittest, cares nothing for appearances, except in so far as they are useful to any being. She can act on every internal organ, on every shade of constitutional difference, on the whole machinery of life. Man selects only for his own good; Nature only for that of the being which she tends. Every selected character is fully exercised by her, as is implied by the fact of their selection. * * * How fleeting are the wishes and efforts of man! How short his time, and consequently how poor will be his results, compared with those accumulated by Nature during whole geological periods! Can we wonder, then, that Nature's productions should be far "truer" in character than man's productions; that they should be infinitely better adapted to the most complex conditions of life, and should plainly bear the stamp of far higher workmanship?

It may metaphorically be said that natural selection is daily and hourly scrutinising, throughout the world, the slightest variations;

rejecting those that are bad, preserving and adding up all that are good; silently and insensibly working, *whenever and wherever opportunity offers*, at the improvement of each organic being in relation to its organic and inorganic conditions of life. We see nothing of these slow changes in progress, until the hand of time has marked the long lapse of ages, and then so imperfect is our view into long-past geological ages that we see only that the forms of life are now different from what they formerly were.

* * *

SUMMARY OF CHAPTER

* * * Natural selection, as has just been remarked, leads to divergence of character and to much extinction of the less improved and intermediate forms of life. On these principles, the nature of the affinities, and the generally well defined distinctions between the innumerable organic beings in each class throughout the world, may be explained. It is a truly wonderful fact—the wonder of which we are apt to overlook from familiarity—that all animals and all plants throughout all time and space should be related to each other in groups, subordinate to groups, in the manner which we everywhere behold—namely, varieties of the same species most closely related, species of the same genus less closely and unequally related, forming sections and sub-genera, species of distinct genera much less closely related, and genera related in different degrees, forming sub-families, families, orders, sub-classes, and classes. The several subordinate groups in any class cannot be ranked in a single file, but seem clustered round points, and these round other points, and so on in almost endless cycles. If species had been independently created, no explanation would have been possible of this kind of classification; but it is explained through inheritance and the complex action of natural selection, entailing extinction and divergence of character, as we have seen illustrated in the diagram.

The affinities of all the beings of the same class have sometimes been represented by a great tree. I believe this simile largely speaks the truth. The green and budding twigs may represent existing species; and those produced during former years may represent the long succession of extinct species. At each period of growth all the growing twigs have tried to branch out on all sides, and to overtop and kill the surrounding twigs and branches, in the same manner as species and groups of species have at all times overmastered other species in the great battle for life. The limbs divided into great branches, and these into lesser and lesser branches, were themselves once, when the tree was young, budding twigs; and this connexion of the former and present buds by ramifying branches may well represent the classification of all extinct and living species in groups subordinate to groups. Of the many twigs which flourished when the tree was a mere bush, only two or three, now grown into great branches, yet survive and bear the other branches; so with the species which lived during long-past geological periods, very few have left living and modified descendants. From the first growth of the tree, many a limb and branch has decayed and dropped off; and these fallen branches of various sizes may represent those whole orders, families, and genera which have now no living representatives, and which are known to us only in a fossil state. *** As buds give rise by growth to fresh buds, and these, if vigorous, branch out and overtop on all sides many a feebler branch, so by generation I believe it has been with the great Tree of Life, which fills with its dead and broken branches the crust of the earth, and covers the surface with its ever-branching and beautiful ramifications.

*　*　*

Chapter 15. Recapitulation and Conclusion

As this whole volume is one long argument, it may be convenient to the reader to have the leading facts and inferences briefly recapitulated.

That many and serious objections may be advanced against the theory of descent with modification through variation and natural selection, I do not deny. I have endeavoured to give to them their full force. Nothing at first can appear more difficult to believe than that the more complex organs and instincts have been perfected, not by means superior to, though analogous with, human reason, but by the accumulation of innumerable slight variations, each good for the individual possessor. Nevertheless, this difficulty, though appearing to our imagination insuperably great, cannot be considered real if we admit the following propositions, namely, that all parts of the organisation and instincts offer, at least individual differences—that there is a struggle for existence leading to the preservation of profitable deviations of structure or instinct—and, lastly, that gradations in the state of perfection of each organ may have existed, each good of its kind. The truth of these propositions cannot, I think, be disputed.

*　*　*

As according to the theory of natural selection an interminable number of intermediate forms must have existed, linking together all the species in each group by gradations as fine as our existing varieties, it may be asked, Why do we not see these linking forms all around us? Why are not all organic beings blended together in an inextricable chaos? With respect to existing forms, we should remember that we have no right to expect (excepting in rare cases) to discover *directly* connecting links between them, but only between each and some extinct and supplanted form. * * * For we have reason to believe that only a few species of a genus ever undergo change; the other species becoming utterly extinct and leaving no modified progeny. Of the species which do change, only a few within the same country change at the same time; and all modifications are slowly effected. I have also shown that the intermediate varieties which probably at first existed in the intermediate zones, would be liable to be supplanted by the allied forms on either hand; for the latter, from existing in greater numbers, would generally be modified and improved at a quicker rate than the intermediate varieties, which existed in lesser numbers; so that the intermediate varieties would, in the long run, be supplanted and exterminated.

On this doctrine of the extermination of an infinitude of connecting links, between the living and extinct inhabitants of the world, and at each successive period between the extinct and still older species, why is not every geological formation charged with such links? Why does not every collection of fossil remains afford plain evidence of the gradation and mutation of the forms of life? * * *

I can answer these questions and objections only on the supposition that the geological record is far more imperfect than most geologists believe. The number of specimens in all our museums is absolutely as nothing compared with the countless generations of countless species which have certainly existed. The parent form of any two or more species would not be in all its characters directly intermediate between its modified offspring, any more than the rock-pigeon is directly intermediate in crop and tail between its descendants, the pouter and fantail pigeons. We should not be able to recognise a species as the parent of another and modified species, if we were to examine the two ever so closely, unless we possessed most of the intermediate links; and owing to the imperfection of the geological record, we have no just right to expect to find so many links. * * *

*   *   *

* * * The belief that species were immutable productions was almost unavoidable as long as the history of the world was thought to be of short duration;[5] and now that we have acquired some idea of

---

5. When Darwin wrote, naturalists assumed that living forms were essentially fixed and stable, a view consistent with natural theology and conventional biblical interpretation. The destabilization of that essentialist understanding began with the geological demonstration in the 1830s by Scottish geologist Charles Lyell (1797–1875) in his *Principles of*

the lapse of time, we are too apt to assume, without proof, that the geological record is so perfect that it would have afforded us plain evidence of the mutation of species, if they had undergone mutation.

But the chief cause of our natural unwillingness to admit that one species has given birth to other and distinct species, is that we are always slow in admitting any great changes of which we do not see the steps. The difficulty is the same as that felt by so many geologists, when Lyell first insisted that long lines of inland cliffs had been formed, and great valleys excavated, by the agencies which we still see at work. The mind cannot possibly grasp the full meaning of the term of even a million years; it cannot add up and perceive the full effects of many slight variations, accumulated during an almost infinite number of generations.

Although I am fully convinced of the truth of the views given in this volume under the form of an abstract, I by no means expect to convince experienced naturalists whose minds are stocked with a multitude of facts all viewed, during a long course of years, from a point of view directly opposite to mine. It is so easy to hide our ignorance under such expressions as the "plan of creation," "unity of design," etc., and to think that we give an explanation when we only restate a fact. Any one whose disposition leads him to attach more weight to unexplained difficulties than to the explanation of a certain number of facts will certainly reject the theory. A few naturalists, endowed with much flexibility of mind, and who have already begun to doubt the immutability of species, may be influenced by this volume; but I look with confidence to the future, to young and rising naturalists, who will be able to view both sides of the question with impartiality. * * * Whoever is led to believe that species are mutable will do good service by conscientiously expressing his conviction; for thus only can the load of prejudice by which this subject is overwhelmed be removed.

Several eminent naturalists have of late published their belief that a multitude of reputed species in each genus are not real species; but that other species are real, that is, have been independently created. This seems to me a strange conclusion to arrive at. They admit that a multitude of forms, which till lately they themselves thought were special creations, and which are still thus looked at by the majority of naturalists, and which consequently have all the external characteristic features of true species—they admit that these have been produced by variation, but they refuse to extend the same view to other and slightly different forms. Nevertheless, they do not pretend that they can define, or even conjecture, which are

---

Geology (1830–33) of Earth's lengthy development, the slow nature of which potentially obscured the continuous activity of incremental planetary change that Darwin makes central to his evolutionary theory (in opposition to the idea of sudden, permanent creation of life still championed by most of Darwin's theistically grounded contemporaries).

the created forms of life, and which are those produced by second-ary laws. They admit variation as a *vera causa*[6] in one case, they arbitrarily reject it in another, without assigning any distinction in the two cases. The day will come when this will be given as a curi-ous illustration of the blindness of preconceived opinion. These authors seem no more startled at a miraculous act of creation than at an ordinary birth. But do they really believe that at innumerable periods in the earth's history certain elemental atoms have been commanded suddenly to flash into living tissues? Do they believe that at each supposed act of creation one individual or many were produced? Were all the infinitely numerous kinds of animals and plants created as eggs or seed, or as full grown? and in the case of mammals, were they created bearing the false marks of nourishment from the mother's womb? * * * Under a scientific point of view, and as leading to further investigation, but little advantage is gained by believing that new forms are suddenly developed in an inexplicable manner from old and widely different forms, over the old belief in the creation of species from the dust of the earth. * * *

* * *

In the future I see open fields for far more important researches. Psychology will be securely based on the foundation already well laid by Mr. Herbert Spencer, that of the necessary acquirement of each mental power and capacity by gradation. Much light will be thrown on the origin of man and his history.

Authors of the highest eminence seem to be fully satisfied with the view that each species has been independently created. To my mind it accords better with what we know of the laws impressed on matter by the Creator, that the production and extinction of the past and present inhabitants of the world should have been due to sec-ondary causes, like those determining the birth and death of the individual. When I view all beings not as special creations, but as the lineal descendants of some few beings which lived long before the first bed of the Cambrian system was deposited, they seem to me to become ennobled. Judging from the past, we may safely infer that not one living species will transmit its unaltered likeness to a distinct futurity. And of the species now living very few will trans-mit progeny of any kind to a far distant futurity; for the manner in which all organic beings are grouped, shows that the greater num-ber of species in each genus, and all the species in many genera, have left no descendants, but have become utterly extinct. We can so far take a prophetic glance into futurity as to foretell that it will be

6. True cause (Latin).

the common and widely spread species, belonging to the larger and dominant groups within each class, which will ultimately prevail and procreate new and dominant species. As all the living forms of life are the lineal descendants of those which lived long before the Cambrian epoch, we may feel certain that the ordinary succession by generation has never once been broken, and that no cataclysm has desolated the whole world. Hence, we may look with some confidence to a secure future of great length. And as natural selection works solely by and for the good of each being, all corporeal and mental endowments will tend to progress towards perfection.

It is interesting to contemplate a tangled bank, clothed with many plants of many kinds, with birds singing on the bushes, with various insects flitting about, and with worms crawling through the damp earth, and to reflect that these elaborately constructed forms, so different from each other, and dependent upon each other in so complex a manner, have all been produced by laws acting around us. These laws, taken in the largest sense, being Growth with reproduction; Inheritance which is almost implied by reproduction; Variability from the indirect and direct action of the conditions of life, and from use and disuse; a Ratio of Increase so high as to lead to a Struggle for Life, and as a consequence to Natural Selection, entailing Divergence of Character and the Extinction of less improved forms. Thus, from the war of nature, from famine and death, the most exalted object which we are capable of conceiving, namely, the production of the higher animals, directly follows. There is grandeur in this view of life, with its several powers, having been originally breathed by the Creator into a few forms or into one; and that, whilst this planet has gone circling on according to the fixed law of gravity, from so simple a beginning endless forms most beautiful and most wonderful have been, and are being evolved.

From The Descent of Man[†]

Introduction

* * *

The sole object of this work is to consider, firstly, whether man, like every other species, is descended from some pre-existing form; secondly, the manner of his development; and thirdly, the value of the

† From *The Descent of Man, and Selection in Relation to Sex*, 2nd ed. (London: John Murray, 1874 [1871]), pp. 2, 24–25, 49–52, 63–64, 66, 69–71, 73–75, 150, 613, 619. Unless otherwise indicated, notes are by the editor of this Norton Critical Edition. Some of Darwin's notes have been omitted.

differences between the so-called races of man. As I shall confine myself to these points, it will not be necessary to describe in detail the differences between the several races—an enormous subject which has been fully described in many valuable works. * * * Nor shall I have occasion to do more than to allude to the amount of difference between man and the anthropomorphous apes; for Prof. Huxley,[1] in the opinion of most competent judges, has conclusively shewn that in every visible character man differs less from the higher apes, than these do from the lower members of the same order of Primates.

* * *

Chapter I. The Evidence of the Descent of Man from Some Lower Form

RUDIMENTS

* * *

* * * The homological[2] construction of the whole frame in the members of the same class is intelligible, if we admit their descent from a common progenitor, together with their subsequent adaptation to diversified conditions. On any other view, the similarity of pattern between the hand of a man or monkey, the foot of a horse, the flipper of a seal, the wing of a bat, etc., is utterly inexplicable. * * *

Thus we can understand how it has come to pass that man and all other vertebrate animals have been constructed on the same general model, why they pass through the same early stages of development, and why they retain certain rudiments in common. Consequently we ought frankly to admit their community of descent: to take any other view, is to admit that our own structure, and that of all the animals around us, is a mere snare laid to entrap our judgment. * * * It is only our natural prejudice, and that arrogance which made our forefathers declare that they were descended from demi-gods, which leads us to demur to this conclusion. But the time will before long come, when it will be thought wonderful that naturalists, who were well acquainted with the comparative structure and development of man, and other mammals, should have believed that each was the work of a separate act of creation.

---

1. English biologist, anatomist, and anthropologist Thomas Henry (T. H.) Huxley (1825–1895), whose *Evidence as to Man's Place in Nature* (1863) offered the first extended argument for the evolution of humans and apes from a common ancestor, based largely on anatomical analysis showing the likeness of human and ape brains.
2. Structurally or functionally similar.

Chapter II. On the Manner of Development of Man from Some Lower Form

NATURAL SELECTION

* * *

Although the intellectual powers and social habits of man are of paramount importance to him, we must not underrate the importance of his bodily structure, to which subject the remainder of this chapter will be devoted. * * *

Even to hammer with precision is no easy matter, as every one who has tried to learn carpentry will admit. To throw a stone with as true an aim as a Fuegian[3] in defending himself, or in killing birds, requires the most consummate perfection in the correlated action of the muscles of the hand, arm, and shoulder, and, further, a fine sense of touch. In throwing a stone or spear, and in many other actions, a man must stand firmly on his feet; and this again demands the perfect co-adaptation of numerous muscles. To chip a flint into the rudest tool, or to form a barbed spear or hook from a bone, demands the use of a perfect hand; for, as a most capable judge, Mr. Schoolcraft[4] remarks, the shaping fragments of stone into knives, lances, or arrowheads, shews "extraordinary ability and long practice." * * * One can hardly doubt, that a man-like animal who possessed a hand and arm sufficiently perfect to throw a stone with precision, or to form a flint into a rude tool, could, with sufficient practice, as far as mechanical skill alone is concerned, make almost anything which a civilised man can make. The structure of the hand in this respect may be compared with that of the vocal organs, which in the apes are used for uttering various signal-cries, or, as in one genus, musical cadences; but in man the closely similar vocal organs have become adapted through the inherited effects of use for the utterance of articulate language.

* * *

As soon as some ancient member in the great series of the Primates came to be less arboreal, owing to a change in its manner of procuring subsistence, or to some change in the surrounding conditions, its habitual manner of progression would have been modified: and thus it would have been rendered more strictly quadrupedal or bipedal. Baboons frequent hilly and rocky districts, and only from necessity climb high trees; and they have acquired almost the gait

---

3. English term for the Indigenous peoples of Tierra de Fuego, an archipelago at the extreme southern tip of South America.

4. [Quoted by Mr. Lawson Tait in his 'Law of Natural Selection,' 'Dublin Quarterly Journal of Medical Science,' Feb. 1869. Dr. Keller is likewise quoted to the same effect —*Darwin*.] Darwin refers above to *American Indians, Their History, Condition, and Prospects* (1850) by American geographer, geologist, and ethnologist Henry Rowe Schoolcraft (1793–1864).

of a dog. Man alone has become a biped; and we can, I think, partly see how he has come to assume his erect attitude, which forms one of his most conspicuous characters. Man could not have attained his present dominant position in the world without the use of his hands, which are so admirably adapted to act in obedience to his will. Sir C. Bell[5] insists that "the hand supplies all instruments, and by its correspondence with the intellect gives him universal dominion." But the hands and arms could hardly have become perfect enough to have manufactured weapons, or to have hurled stones and spears with a true aim, as long as they were habitually used for locomotion and for supporting the whole weight of the body, or, as before remarked, so long as they were especially fitted for climbing trees. Such rough treatment would also have blunted the sense of touch, on which their delicate use largely depends. From these causes alone it would have been an advantage to man to become a biped; but for many actions it is indispensable that the arms and whole upper part of the body should be free; and he must for this end stand firmly on his feet. To gain this great advantage, the feet have been rendered flat; and the great toe has been peculiarly modified, though this has entailed the almost complete loss of its power of prehension. It accords with the principle of the division of physiological labour, prevailing throughout the animal kingdom, that as the hands became perfected for prehension, the feet should have become perfected for support and locomotion. * * *

CONCLUSION

* * *

In regard to bodily size or strength, we do not know whether man is descended from some small species, like the chimpanzee, or from one as powerful as the gorilla; and, therefore, we cannot say whether man has become larger and stronger, or smaller and weaker, than his ancestors. We should, however, bear in mind that an animal possessing great size, strength, and ferocity, and which, like the gorilla, could defend itself from all enemies, would not perhaps have become social: and this would most effectually have checked the acquirement of the higher mental qualities, such as sympathy and the love of his fellows. Hence it might have been an immense advantage to man to have sprung from some comparatively weak creature.

* * *

5. Scottish surgeon, anatomist, and philosopher Charles Bell (1774–1842); Darwin refers to Bell's 1833 volume *The Hand: Its Mechanisms and Vital Endowments as Evincing Design* (the fourth of the Bridgewater Treatises, works written by various clergymen to promote natural theology's claims to scientific authority).

Chapter III. Comparison of the Mental Powers of Man and the Lower Animals

*   *   *

My object in this chapter is to shew that there is no fundamental difference between man and the higher mammals in their mental faculties. * * *

*   *   *

* * * [T]he lower animals, like man, manifestly feel pleasure and pain, happiness and misery. Happiness is never better exhibited than by young animals, such as puppies, kittens, lambs, etc., when playing together, like our own children. Even insects play together, as has been described by that excellent observer, P. Huber,[6] who saw ants chasing and pretending to bite each other, like so many puppies.

The fact that the lower animals are excited by the same emotions as ourselves is so well established, that it will not be necessary to weary the reader by many details. * * * It is, I think, impossible to read the account given by Sir E. Tennent,[7] of the behaviour of the female elephants, used as decoys, without admitting that they intentionally practise deceit, and well know what they are about. Courage and timidity are extremely variable qualities in the individuals of the same species, as is plainly seen in our dogs. Some dogs and horses are ill-tempered, and easily turn sulky; others are good-tempered; and these qualities are certainly inherited. Every one knows how liable animals are to furious rage, and how plainly they shew it. Many, and probably true, anecdotes have been published on the long-delayed and artful revenge of various animals. * * * Sir Andrew Smith,[8] a zoologist whose scrupulous accuracy was known to many persons, told me the following story of which he was himself an eye-witness; at the Cape of Good Hope an officer had often plagued a certain baboon, and the animal, seeing him approaching one Sunday for parade, poured water into a hole and hastily made some thick mud, which he skilfully dashed over the officer as he passed by, to the amusement of many bystanders. For long afterwards the baboon rejoiced and triumphed whenever he saw his victim.

The love of a dog for his master is notorious; as an old writer quaintly says, "A dog is the only thing on this earth that luvs you more than he luvs himself."[9]

---

6. Swiss entomologist François Huber (1750–1831); Darwin refers to Huber's 1810 treatise *Recherches sur les moeurs des fourmis indigènes* ("research on the habits of native ants") [French].
7. James Emerson Tennent, Irish politician who served as Colonial Secretary in Ceylon (now Sri Lanka); Darwin refers to Tennent's treatise *The Wild Elephant, and the Method of Capturing and Taming It in Ceylon* (1867).
8. English zoologist, surgeon, and explorer (1797–1872).
9. [Quoted by Dr. Lauder Lindsay, in his 'Physiology of Mind in the Lower Animals,' 'Journal of Mental Science,' April 1871, p. 38 —*Darwin.*] Generally attributed to American humorist

* * *

As Whewell[1] has well asked, "who that reads the touching instances of maternal affection, related so often of the women of all nations, and of the females of all animals, can doubt that the principle of action is the same in the two cases?" We see maternal affection exhibited in the most trifling details. * * * So intense is the grief of female monkeys for the loss of their young, that it invariably caused the death of certain kinds kept under confinement by Brehm[2] in N. Africa. Orphan monkeys were always adopted and carefully guarded by the other monkeys, both males and females. * * *

Most of the more complex emotions are common to the higher animals and ourselves. Every one has seen how jealous a dog is of his master's affection, if lavished on any other creature; and I have observed the same fact with monkeys. This shews that animals not only love, but have desire to be loved. Animals manifestly feel emulation. They love approbation or praise; and a dog carrying a basket for his master exhibits in a high degree self-complacency or pride. There can, I think, be no doubt that a dog feels shame, as distinct from fear, and something very like modesty when begging too often for food. A great dog scorns the snarling of a little dog, and this may be called magnanimity. * * *

We will now turn to the more intellectual emotions and faculties, which are very important, as forming the basis for the development of the higher mental powers. Animals manifestly enjoy excitement, and suffer from ennui, as may be seen with dogs, and, according to Rengger,[3] with monkeys. All animals feel *wonder*, and many exhibit *curiosity*. They sometimes suffer from this latter quality, as when the hunter plays antics and thus attracts them; I have witnessed this with deer, and so it is with the wary chamois,[4] and with some kinds of wild-ducks. * * *

Hardly any faculty is more important for the intellectual progress of man than *attention*. Animals clearly manifest this power, as when a cat watches by a hole and prepares to spring on its prey. Wild animals sometimes become so absorbed when thus engaged, that they may be easily approached. * * *

It is almost superfluous to state that animals have excellent *memories* for persons and places. * * * Even ants, as P. Huber has clearly shewn, recognised their fellow-ants belonging to the same

---

Henry Wheeler Shaw (1818–1885), who wrote under the pen name Josh Billings.
1. William Whewell (1794–1866), English scientist, philosopher, and clergyman; Darwin cites a passage from Whewell's Bridgewater Treatise *Astronomy and General Physics Considered with Reference to Natural Theology* (1833).
2. Alfred Edmund Brehm (1829–1884), German zoologist, ornithologist, and author.
3. Swiss naturalist Johann Rudolph Rengger (1795–1832), author of an influential study of fauna in Paraguay.
4. Goatlike mammal native to mountainous areas from southern Europe to the Caucasus.

community after a separation of four months. Animals can certainly by some means judge of the intervals of time between recurrent events.

The Imagination is one of the highest prerogatives of man. By this faculty he unites former images and ideas, independently of the will, and thus creates brilliant and novel results. * * * Dreaming gives us the best notion of this power. * * * As dogs, cats, horses, and probably all the higher animals, even birds have vivid dreams, and this is shewn by their movements and the sounds uttered, we must admit that they possess some power of imagination. * * *

Of all the faculties of the human mind, it will, I presume, be admitted that REASON stands at the summit. Only a few persons now dispute tha animals possess some power of reasoning. Animals may constantly be seen to pause, deliberate, and resolve. It is a significant fact, that the more the habits of any particular animal are studied by a naturalist, the more he attributes to reason and the less to unlearnt instincts * * *.

We can only judge by the circumstances under which actions are performed, whether they are due to instinct, or to reason, or to the mere association of ideas: this latter principle, however, is intimately connected with reason. * * *

*   *   *

Chapter VI. On the Affinities and Genealogy of Man

*   *   *

It would be beyond my limits, and quite beyond my knowledge, even to name the innumerable points of structure in which man agrees with the other Primates. Our great anatomist and philosopher, Prof. Huxley, has fully discussed this subject, and concludes that man in all parts of his organization differs less from the higher apes, than these do from the lower members of the same group. Consequently there "is no justification for placing man in a distinct order."

*   *   *

Chapter XXI. General Summary and Conclusion

*   *   *

I am aware that the conclusions arrived at in this work will be denounced by some as highly irreligious; but he who denounces them is bound to shew why it is more irreligious to explain the origin of man as a distinct species by descent from some lower form, through the laws of variation and natural selection, than to explain the birth of the individual through the laws of ordinary reproduction. The birth both of the species and of the individual are equally parts of that grand sequence of events, which our minds refuse to accept as the result of blind chance. The understanding revolts at such a conclusion, whether or not we are able to believe that every slight variation of structure,—the union of each pair in marriage, the dissemination of each seed,—and other such events, have all been ordained for some special purpose. * * *

* * *

Man may be excused for feeling some pride at having risen, though not through his own exertions, to the very summit of the organic scale; and the fact of his having thus risen, instead of having been aboriginally placed there, may give him hope for a still higher destiny in the distant future. But we are not here concerned with hopes or fears, only with the truth as far as our reason permits us to discover it; and I have given the evidence to the best of my ability. We must, however, acknowledge, as it seems to me, that man with all his noble qualities, with sympathy which feels for the most debased, with benevolence which extends not only to other men but to the humblest living creature, with his god-like intellect which has penetrated into the movements and constitution of the solar system—with all these exalted powers—Man still bears in his bodily frame the indelible stamp of his lowly origin.

Society

HERBERT SPENCER

From "Progress: Its Law and Cause"[†]

The current conception of progress is shifting and indefinite. Sometimes it comprehends little more than simple growth—as of a nation in the number of its members and the extent of territory over which it spreads. Sometimes it has reference to quantity of material products—as when the advance of agriculture and manufactures is the topic. Sometimes the superior quality of these products is contemplated; and sometimes the new or improved appliances by which they are produced. When, again, we speak of moral or intellectual progress, we refer to states of the individual or people exhibiting it; while, when the progress of Science or Art is commented upon, we have in view certain abstract results of human thought and action.

---

† From the *Westminster Review* 67 (April 1857): 445–46, 451–56, 466. Notes are by the editor of this Norton Critical Edition.

Not only, however, is the current conception of progress more or less vague, but it is in great measure erroneous. It takes in not so much the reality of progress as its accompaniments—not so much the substance as the shadow. That progress in intelligence seen during the growth of the child into the man, or the savage into the philosopher, is commonly regarded as consisting in the greater number of facts known and laws understood; whereas the actual progress consists in those internal modifications of which this larger knowledge is the expression. Social progress is supposed to consist in the making of a greater quantity and variety of the articles required for satisfying men's wants; in the increasing security of person and property; in widening freedom of action; whereas, rightly understood, social progress consists in those changes of structure in the social organism which have entailed these consequences. The current conception is a teleological one. The phenomena are contemplated solely as bearing on human happiness. Only those changes are held to constitute progress which directly or indirectly tend to heighten human happiness; and they are thought to constitute progress simply because they tend to heighten human happiness. But rightly to understand progress, we must learn the nature of these changes, considered apart from our interests. Ceasing, for example, to regard the successive geological modifications that have taken place in the earth, as modifications that have gradually fitted it for the habitation of man, and as therefore constituting geological progress, we must ascertain the character common to these modifications—the law to which they all conform. And similarly in every other case. Leaving out of sight concomitants and beneficial consequences, let us ask what progress is in itself.

In respect to that progress which individual organisms display in the course of their evolution, this question has been answered by the Germans. The investigations of Wolff, Goethe, and von Baer,[1] have established the truth that the series of changes gone through during the development of a seed into a tree, or an ovum into an animal, constitute an advance from homogeneity of structure to heterogeneity of structure. In its primary stage, every germ consists of a substance that is uniform throughout, both in texture and chemical composition. The first step is the appearance of a difference between two parts of this substance; or, as the phenomenon is called in physiological language, a differentiation. Each of these differentiated divisions presently begins itself to exhibit some contrast of parts; and by and by these secondary differentiations become as

---

1. German biologist and geographer Karl Ernst von Baer (1792–1876). *Wolff*: German physiologist and embryologist Kasper Friedrich Wolff (1733–1794). *Goethe*: German poet, novelist, playwright, and scientist Johann Wolfgang von Goethe (1749–1832).

definite as the original one. This process is continuously repeated—is simultaneously going on in all parts of the growing embryo; and by endless such differentiations there is finally produced that complex combination of tissues and organs constituting the adult animal or plant. This is the history of all organisms whatever. It is settled beyond dispute that organic progress consists in a change from the homogeneous to the heterogeneous.

Now, we propose in the first place to show that this law of organic progress is the law of all progress. Whether it be in the development of the earth, in the development of life upon its surface, in the development of society, of government, of manufactures, of commerce, of language, literature, science, art, this same evolution of the simple into the complex, through successive differentiations, holds throughout. * * *

Whether an advance from the homogeneous to the heterogeneous is or is not displayed in the biological history of the globe, it is clearly enough displayed in the progress of the latest and most heterogeneous creature—man. It is true alike that, during the period in which the earth has been peopled, the human organism has grown more heterogeneous among the civilized divisions of the species; and that the species as a whole has been growing more heterogeneous in virtue of the multiplication of races and the differentiation of these races from each other. In proof of the first of these positions we may cite the fact that, in the relative development of the limbs, the civilized man departs more widely from the general type of the placental mammalia than do the lower human races. While often possessing well-developed body and arms, the Australian[2] has very small legs: thus reminding us of the chimpanzee and the gorilla, which present no great contrasts in size between the hind and fore limbs. But in the European, the greater length and massiveness of the legs have become marked. * * * Moreover, judging from the greater extent and variety of faculty he exhibits, we may infer that the civilized man has also a more complex or heterogeneous nervous system than the uncivilized man: and indeed the fact is in part visible in the increased ratio which his cerebrum bears to the subjacent ganglia,[3] as well as in the wider departure from symmetry in its convolutions. * * * Even were we to admit the hypothesis that mankind originated from several separate stocks, it would still remain true that, as from each of these stocks there have sprung many now widely different tribes, which are proved by philological evidence to have had a common origin, the race as a whole is far less homogeneous than it once was. Add to which, that we have, in the Anglo-Americans, an example of

2. Spencer refers here to Indigenous peoples of the Australian mainland, or "Aborigines."
3. Areas of gray matter in the neocortex of the brain (later termed *basal ganglia*).

a new variety arising within these few generations; and that, if we may trust to the descriptions of observers, we are likely soon to have another such example in Australia.

On passing from humanity under its individual form, to humanity as socially embodied, we find the general law still more variously exemplified. The change from the homogeneous to the heterogeneous is displayed in the progress of civilization as a whole, as well as in the progress of every nation; and is still going on with increasing rapidity. As we see in existing barbarous tribes, society in its first and lowest form is a homogeneous aggregation of individuals having like powers and like functions: the only marked difference of function being that which accompanies difference of sex. Every man is warrior, hunter, fisherman, tool-maker, builder; every woman performs the same drudgeries. Very early, however, in the course of social evolution, there arises an incipient differentiation between the governing and the governed. Some kind of chieftainship seems coeval with the first advance from the state of separate wandering families to that of a nomadic tribe. The authority of the strongest or the most cunning makes itself felt among a body of savages as in a herd of animals, or a posse of schoolboys. * * * In the course of ages there arises, as among ourselves, a highly complex political organization of monarch, ministers, lords and commons, with their subordinate administrative departments, courts of justice, revenue offices, etc., supplemented in the provinces by municipal governments, county governments, parish or union governments—all of them more or less elaborated. By its side there grows up a highly complex religious organization, with its various grades of officials, from archbishops down to sextons, its colleges, convocations, ecclesiastical courts, etc.; to all of which must be added the ever-multiplying independent sects, each with its general and local authorities. And at the same time there is developed a highly complex aggregation of customs, manners, and temporary fashions, enforced by society at large, and serving to control those mirror transactions between man and man which are not regulated by civil and religious law. * * *

* * * While the governing part has undergone the complex development above detailed, the governed part has undergone an equally complex development, which has resulted in that minute division of labour characterizing advanced nations. It is needless to trace out this progress from its first stages, up through the caste divisions of the East and the incorporated guilds of Europe, to the elaborate producing and distributing organization existing among ourselves. It has been an evolution which, beginning with a tribe whose members severally perform the same actions each for himself, ends with a civilized community whose members severally perform different actions for each other; and an evolution which has transformed

the solitary producer of any one commodity into a combination of producers who, united under a master, take separate parts in the manufacture of such commodity. * * * [W]hen roads and other means of transit become numerous and good, the different districts begin to assume different functions, and to become mutually dependent. The calico manufacture locates itself in this county, the woolen cloth manufacture in that; silks are produced here, lace there; stockings in one place, shoes in another; pottery, hardware, cutlery, come to have their special towns; and ultimately every locality becomes more or less distinguished from the rest by the leading occupation carried on in it. This subdivision of functions shows itself not only among the different parts of the same nation, but among different nations. That exchange of commodities which free trade is increasing so largely, will ultimately have the effect of specializing, in a greater or less degree, the industry of each people. So that, beginning with a barbarous tribe, almost if not quite homogeneous in the functions of its members, the progress has been, and still is, towards an economic aggregation of the whole human race; growing ever more heterogeneous in respect of the separate functions assumed by separate nations, the separate functions assumed by the local sections of each nation, the separate functions assumed by the many kinds of makers and traders in each town, and the separate functions assumed by the workers united in producing each commodity.

* * * [T]he law thus clearly exemplified in the evolution of the social organism is exemplified with equal clearness in the evolution of all products of human thought and action; whether concrete or abstract, real or ideal. * * *

* * * Being that which determines progress of every kind—astronomic, geologic, organic, ethnologic, social, economic, artistic, etc.—it must be involved with some fundamental trait displayed in common by these; and must be expressible in terms of this fundamental trait. The only obvious respect in which all kinds of progress are alike, is, that they are modes of change; and hence, in some characteristic of changes in general, the desired solution will probably be found. We may suspect a priori that in some universal law of change lies the explanation of this universal transformation of the homogeneous into the heterogeneous.

Thus much premised, we pass at once to the statement of the law, which is this:—*Every active force produces more than one change—every cause produces more than one effect.* * * *

E. RAY LANKESTER

From Degeneration: A Chapter in Darwinism[†]

For a long time the knowledge of living things, of plants and of animals could hardly be said to form part of the general body of science, for the causes of these things were quite unknown. They were kept apart as a separate region of nature, and were supposed to have been pitched, as it were, into the midst of an orderly and cause-abiding world without cause or order: they were strangers to the universal harmony prevailing around them. Fact upon fact was observed and recorded by students of plants and animals, but having no hypothesis as to the causes of what they were studying, the naturalists of twenty years ago, and before that day, though they collected facts, made slow progress and some strange blunders. Suddenly one of those great guesses which occasionally appear in the history of science, was given to the science of biology by the imaginative insight of that greatest of living naturalists—I would say that greatest of living men—Charles Darwin. * * *

It is a very general popular belief at the present day that the Darwinian theory is simply no more than a capricious and anti-theological assertion that mankind are the modified descendants of ape-like ancestors. * * *

The first hypothesis, then, which was present to Mr. Darwin's mind, as it had been to that of other earlier naturalists, was this: "Have not all the varieties or species of living things (man, of course, included) been produced by the continuous operation of the *same* set of physico-chemical causes which alone we can discover, and which alone have been proved sufficient to produce everything else?" "If this be so," Mr. Darwin must have argued (and here it was that he boldly stepped beyond the speculations of Lamarck and adopted the method by which Lyell[1] had triumphantly established Geology as a science), "these causes must still be able to produce new forms, and are doing so wherever they have opportunity." * * *

And now we have to note the important fact which makes this process of development so intensely interesting in relation to the pedigree of the animal kingdom. There is very strong reason to believe that it is a general law of transmission or inheritance, that structural characteristics appear in the growth of a young organism in the order in which those characteristics have been acquired by its ancestors. At

---

[†] From *Degeneration: A Chapter in Darwinism* (London: Macmillan & Co., 1880), pp. 9–12, 20–22, 25, 28–29, 30, 32–33, 57–62. Unless otherwise indicated, notes are by the editor of this Norton Critical Edition.

[1] Scottish geologist Charles Lyell (1797–1875). *Lamarck*: French zoologist and naturalist Jean-Baptiste Lamarck (1744–1829).

first the egg of a dog represents (imperfectly, it is true,) in form and structure the earliest ancestors of the dog; a few days later it has the form and structure of somewhat later ancestors; later still the embryo dog resembles less remote ancestors; until at last it reaches the degree of elaboration proper to its immediate forefathers. * * *

Accordingly the phases of development or growth of the young are a brief recapitulation of the phases of form through which the ancestors of the young creature have passed. In some animals this recapitulation is more, in others it is less complete. Sometimes the changes are hurried through and disguised, but we find here and there in these histories of growth from the egg most valuable assistance in the attempt to reconstruct the genealogical tree. * * *

And now we are approaching the main point to which I wish to draw the reader's attention. * * *

It is clearly enough possible for a set of forces such as we sum up under the head "natural selection" to so act on the structure of an organism as to produce one of three results, namely these; to keep it *in statu quo*; to increase the complexity of its structure; or lastly, to diminish the complexity of its structure. We have as possibilities either BALANCE, or ELABORATION, or DEGENERATION. * * *

* * * The hypothesis of Degeneration will, I believe, be found to render most valuable service in pointing out the true relationships of animals which are a puzzle and a mystery when we use only and exclusively the hypothesis of Balance, or the hypothesis of Elaboration. It will, as a true scientific hypothesis, help us to discover causes. * * *

Degeneration may be defined as a gradual change of the structure in which the organism becomes adapted to *less* varied and *less* complex conditions of life; whilst Elaboration is a gradual change of structure in which the organism becomes adapted to more and more varied and complex conditions of existence. In Elaboration there is a new *expression* of form, corresponding to new perfection of work in the animal machine. In Degeneration there is *suppression* of form, corresponding to the cessation of work. Elaboration of some one organ *may* be a necessary accompaniment of Degeneration in all the others; in fact, this is very generally the case; and it is only when the total result of the Elaboration of some organs, and the Degeneration of others, is such as to leave the whole animal in a *lower* condition, that is, fitted to less complex action and reaction in regard to its surroundings, than was the ancestral form with which we are comparing it (either actually or in imagination) that we speak of that animal as an instance of Degeneration.

Any new set of conditions occurring to an animal which render its food and safety very easily attained, seem to lead as a rule to Degeneration; just as an active healthy man sometimes degenerates when he becomes suddenly possessed of a fortune; or as Rome degenerated when possessed of the riches of the ancient world. The habit of parasitism clearly acts upon animal organisation in this way. Let the parasitic life once be secured, and away go legs, jaws, eyes, and ears; the active, highly-gifted crab, insect, or annelid may become a mere sac, absorbing nourishment and laying eggs. * * *

All that has been, thus far, here said on the subject of Degeneration is so much zoological specialism, and may appear but a narrow restriction of the discussion to those who are not zoologists. Though we may establish the hypothesis most satisfactorily by the study of animal organization and development, it is abundantly clear that degenerative evolution is by no means limited in its application to the field of zoology. It clearly offers an explanation of many vegetable phenomena, and is already admitted by botanists as the explanation of the curious facts connected with the reproductive process in the higher plants. * * * In other fields, wherever in fact the great principle of evolution has been recognised, degeneration plays an important part. In tracing the development of languages, philologists have long made use of the hypothesis of degeneration. Under certain conditions, in the mouths and minds of this or that branch of a race, a highly elaborate language has sometimes degenerated and become no longer fit to express complex or subtle conceptions, but only such as are simpler and more obvious.[2]

The traditional history of mankind furnishes us with notable examples of degeneration. High states of civilisation have decayed and given place to low and degenerate states. At one time it was a

---

2. The term (degeneration of language) includes two very distinct things; the one is degeneration of grammatical form, the other degeneration of the language as an instrument of thought. The former is a far commoner phenomenon than the latter, and, in fact, whilst actually degenerating so far as grammatical complexity is concerned, a language may be at the same time becoming more and more serviceable, or more and more perfect as an organ having a particular function. The decay of useless inflexions and the consequent simplification of language may be compared to the specialization of the one toe of the primitively five-toed foot of the horse, whilst the four others which existed in archaic horses are, one by one, atrophied. Taken by itself, this phenomenon may possibly be described as degeneration, but inasmuch as the whole horse is not degenerate but, on the contrary, specialized and elaborated, it is advisable to widely distinguish such local atrophy from general degeneration. In the same way language cannot, in relation to this question, be treated as a thing by itself—it must be regarded as a possession of the human organism, and the simplification of its structure merely means in most cases its more complete adaptation to the requirements of the organism.

True degeneration of language is therefore only found as part and parcel of a more general degeneration of mental activity. To some extent the conclusion that this or that language, as compared with its earlier condition, exhibits evidence of such degeneration, must be matter of taste and open to discussion. For instance, the English of Johnson may be regarded as degenerate when compared with that of Shakspeare. There is less probability of a difference of opinion as to the degeneracy of modern Greek as compared with "classical" Greek; or of some of the modern languages of Hindustan as compared with Sanskrit, and I am informed that the same kind of degeneration is exhibited by modern Irish as compared with old Irish. Degeneration, in the proper sense of the word, so far as it applies to language, would seem to mean simply a decay or diversion of literary taste and of literary production in the race to which such language may be appropriate [Lankester's note].

favourite doctrine that the savage races of mankind were degenerate descendants of the higher and civilised races. This general and sweeping application of the doctrine of degeneration has been proved to be erroneous by careful study of the habits, arts, and beliefs of savages; at the same time there is no doubt that many savage races as we at present see them are actually degenerate and are descended from ancestors possessed of a relatively elaborate civilisation. As such we may cite some of the Indians of Central America, the modern Egyptians, and even the heirs of the great oriental monarchies of præ-Christian times. Whilst the hypothesis of universal degeneration as an explanation of savage races has been justly discarded, it yet appears that degeneration has a very large share in the explanation of the condition of the most barbarous races, such as the Fuegians, the Bushmen, and even the Australians.[3] They exhibit evidence of being descended from ancestors more cultivated than themselves.

With regard to ourselves, the white races of Europe, the possibility of degeneration seems to be worth some consideration. In accordance with a tacit assumption of universal progress—an unreasoning optimism—we are accustomed to regard ourselves as necessarily progressing, as necessarily having arrived at a higher and more elaborated condition than that which our ancestors reached, and as destined to progress still further. On the other hand, it is well to remember that we are subject to the general laws of evolution, and are as likely to degenerate as to progress. As compared with the immediate forefathers of our civilisation—the ancient Greeks—we do not appear to have improved so far as our bodily structure is concerned, nor assuredly so far as some of our mental capacities are concerned. Our powers of perceiving and expressing beauty of form have certainly *not* increased since the days of the Parthenon and Aphrodite of Melos.[4] In matters of the reason, in the development of intellect, we may seriously inquire how the case stands. Does the reason of the average man of civilised Europe stand out clearly as an evidence of progress when compared with that of the men of bygone ages? Are all the inventions and figments of human superstition and folly, the self-inflicted torturing of mind, the reiterated substitution of wrong for right, and of falsehood for truth, which disfigure our modern civilisation—are these evidences of progress? In such respects we have at least reason to fear that we may be degenerate. Possibly we are

3. *Fuegians*: Indigenous peoples of Tierra del Fuego (located at the southern tip of South America), subjected to genocidal occupation by European and South American colonizers, a process brought to near completion shortly after the time of Lankester's writing. *Bushmen*: antiquated, pejorative term of Dutch origin for the San people of southern Africa.
4. Greek sculpture, also known as the *Venus de Milo*, created ca. 150–125 BCE. *Parthenon*: temple on the Athenian Acropolis, dedicated to the Greek goddess Athena during the 5th century BCE.

all drifting, tending to the condition of intellectual Barnacles or Ascidians.[5] It is possible for us—just as the Ascidian throws away its tail and its eye and sinks into a quiescent state of inferiority—to reject the good gift of reason with which every child is born, and to degenerate into a contented life of material enjoyment accompanied by ignorance and superstition. The unprejudiced, all-questioning spirit of childhood may not inaptly be compared to the tadpole tail and eye of the young Ascidian: we have to fear lest the prejudices, pre-occupations, and dogmatism of modern civilisation should in any way lead to the atrophy and loss of the valuable mental qualities inherited by our young forms from primæval man.

There is only one means of estimating our position, only one means of so shaping our conduct that we may with certainty avoid degeneration and keep an onward course. We are as a race more fortunate than our ruined cousins—the degenerate Ascidians. For us it is possible to ascertain what will conduce to our higher development, what will favour our degeneration. To us has been given the power to *know the causes of things*, and by the use of this power it is possible for us to control our destinies. It is for us by ceaseless and ever hopeful labour to try to gain a knowledge of man's place in the order of nature. When we have gained this fully and minutely, we shall be able by the light of the past to guide ourselves in the future. In proportion as the whole of the past evolution of civilised man, of which we at present perceive the outlines, is assigned to its causes, we and our successors on the globe may expect to be able duly to estimate that which makes for, and that which makes against, the progress of the race. The full and earnest cultivation of Science—the Knowledge of Causes—is that to which we have to look for the protection of our race—even of this English branch of it—from relapse and degeneration.

FREDERICK ENGELS

From "The Part Played by Labour in the Transition from Ape to Man"[†]

LABOUR is the source of all wealth, the economists assert. It is this—next to nature, which supplies it with the material that it converts into wealth. But it is also infinitely more than this. It is the

5. Saclike marine invertebrates, also known as "sea squirts." *Barnacles*: sticky crustaceans.

† From *Dialectics of Nature*, trans. and ed. Clemens Dutt (London: Lawrence & Wishart Ltd., 1946), pp. 279–83, 289–94. Copyright © 1946 by Lawrence and Wishart Ltd. Reproduced by permission of the licensor through PLSclear. Essay written in 1876. Notes are by the editor of this Norton Critical Edition.

primary basic condition for all human existence, and this to such an extent that, in a sense, we have to say that labour created man himself.

Many hundreds of thousands of years ago, during an epoch, not yet definitely determined, of that period of the earth's history which geologists call the Tertiary period, most likely towards the end of it, a specially highly-developed race of anthropoid apes lived somewhere in the tropical zone—probably on a great continent that has now sunk to the bottom of the Indian Ocean. Darwin has given us an approximate description of these ancestors of ours. They were completely covered with hair, they had beards and pointed ears, and they lived in bands in the trees.

Almost certainly as an immediate consequence of their mode of life, for in climbing the hands fulfil quite different functions from the feet, these apes when moving on level ground began to drop the habit of using their hands and to adopt a more and more erect posture in walking. This was *the decisive step in the transition from ape to man.* * * *

* * * Many monkeys use their hands to build nests for themselves in the trees or even, like the chimpanzee, to construct roofs between the branches for protection against the weather. With their hands they seize hold of clubs to defend themselves against enemies, or bombard the latter with fruits and stones. In captivity, they carry out with their hands a number of simple operations copied from human beings. But it is just here that one sees how great is the gulf between the undeveloped hand of even the most anthropoid of apes and the human hand that has been highly perfected by the labour of hundreds of thousands of years. The number and general arrangement of the bones and muscles are the same in both; but the hand of the lowest savage can perform hundreds of operations that no monkey's hand can imitate. No simian hand has ever fashioned even the crudest stone knife.

At first, therefore, the operations, for which our ancestors gradually learned to adapt their hands during the many thousands of years of transition from ape to man, could only have been very simple. The lowest savages, even those in whom a regression to a more animal-like condition, with a simultaneous physical degeneration, can be assumed to have occurred, are nevertheless far superior to these transitional beings. Before the first flint could be fashioned into a knife by human hands, a period of time must probably have elapsed in comparison with which the historical period known to us appears insignificant. But the decisive step was taken: *the hand became free* and could henceforth attain ever greater dexterity and skill, and the greater flexibility thus acquired was inherited and increased from generation to generation.

Thus the hand is not only the organ of labour, *it is also the product of labour.* Only by labour, by adaptation to ever new operations, by inheritance of the resulting special development of muscles, ligaments, and, over longer periods of time, bones as well, and by the ever-renewed employment of these inherited improvements in new, more and more complicated operations, has the human hand attained the high degree of perfection that has enabled it to conjure into being the pictures of Raphael, the statues of Thorwaldsen, the music of Paganini.[1]

But the hand did not exist by itself. It was only one member of an entire, highly complex organism. And what benefited the hand, benefited also the whole body it served * * * .

* * * The mastery over nature, which begins with the development of the hand, with labour, widened man's horizon at every new advance. He was continually discovering new, hitherto unknown, properties of natural objects. On the other hand, the development of labour necessarily helped to bring the members of society closer together by multiplying cases of mutual support, joint activity, and by making clear the advantage of this joint activity to each individual. In short, men in the making arrived at the point where *they had something to say* to one another. The need led to the creation of its organ; the undeveloped larynx of the ape was slowly but surely transformed by means of gradually increased modulation, and the organs of the mouth gradually learned to pronounce one articulate letter after another.

Comparison with animals proves that this explanation of the origin of language from and in the process of labour is the only correct one. * * *

* * * By the co-operation of hands, organs of speech, and brain, not only in each individual, but also in society, human beings became capable of executing more and more complicated operations, and of setting themselves, and achieving, higher and higher aims. With each generation, labour itself became different, more perfect, more diversified. Agriculture was added to hunting and cattle-breeding, then spinning, weaving, metal-working, pottery, and navigation. Along with trade and industry, there appeared finally art and science. From tribes there developed nations and states. Law and politics arose, and with them the fantastic reflection of human things in the human mind: religion. In the face of all these creations, which appeared in the first place to be products of the mind, and which seemed to dominate human society, the more modest productions of the working hand retreated into the background, the more so since the mind that plans the labour process already at a very early stage of development

---

1. Italian violinist and composer Niccolò Paganini (1782–1840). *Raphael*: Italian painter and architect Raffaello Sanzio da Urbino (1483–1520). *Thorwaldsen*: Danish-Icelandic sculptor Bertel Thorvaldsen (1770–1844).

of society (*e.g.* already in the primitive family), was able to have the labour that had been planned carried out by other hands than its own. All merit for the swift advance of civilisation was ascribed to the mind, to the development and activity of the brain. Men became accustomed to explain their actions from their thoughts, instead of from their needs—(which in any case are reflected and come to consciousness in the mind)—and so there arose in the course of time that idealistic outlook on the world which, especially since the decline of the ancient world, has dominated men's minds. It still rules them to such a degree that even the most materialistic natural scientists of the Darwinian school are still unable to form any clear idea of the origin of man, because under this ideological influence they do not recognise the part that has been played therein by labour.

Animals, as already indicated, change external nature by their activities just as man does, if not to the same extent. * * *

* * * [W]e have no intention of disputing the ability of animals to act in a planned and premeditated fashion. * * * But all the planned action of all animals has never resulted in impressing the stamp of their will upon nature. For that, man was required.

In short, the animal merely *uses* external nature, and brings about changes in it simply by his presence; man by his changes makes it serve his ends, *masters* it. This is the final, essential distinction between man and other animals, and once again it is labour that brings about this distinction.

Let us not, however, flatter ourselves overmuch on account of our human conquest over nature. For each such conquest takes its revenge on us. Each of them, it is true, has in the first place the consequences on which we counted, but in the second and third places it has quite different, unforeseen effects which only too often cancel out the first. The people who, in Mesopotamia, Greece, Asia Minor, and elsewhere, destroyed the forests to obtain cultivable land, never dreamed that they were laying the basis for the present devastated condition of these countries, by removing along with the forests the collecting centres and reservoirs of moisture. * * * Those who spread the potato in Europe were not aware that they were at the same time spreading the disease of scrofula.[2] Thus at every step we are reminded that we by no means rule over nature like a conqueror over a foreign people, like someone standing outside nature—but that we, with flesh, blood, and brain, belong to nature, and exist in its midst, and that all our mastery of it consists in the fact that we have the advantage over all other beings of being able to know and correctly apply its laws.

---

2. Tuberculosis of the neck.

And, in fact, with every day that passes we are learning to understand these laws more correctly, and getting to know both the more immediate and the more remote consequences of our interference with the traditional course of nature. In particular, after the mighty advances of natural science in the present century, we are more and more getting to know, and hence to control, even the more remote natural consequences at least of our more ordinary productive activities. But the more this happens, the more will men not only feel, but also know, their unity with nature, and thus the more impossible will become the senseless and antinatural idea of a contradiction between mind and matter, man and nature, soul and body, such as arose in Europe after the decline of classic antiquity and which obtained its highest elaboration in Christianity.

But if it has already required the labour of thousands of years for us to learn to some extent to calculate the more remote *natural* consequences of our actions aiming at production, it has been still more difficult in regard to the more remote *social* consequences of these actions. We mentioned the potato and the resulting spread of scrofula. But what is scrofula in comparison with the effect on the living conditions of the masses of the people in whole countries resulting from the workers being reduced to a potato diet, or in comparison with the famine which overtook Ireland in 1847 in consequence of the potato disease, and which put under the earth a million Irishmen, nourished solely or almost exclusively on potatoes, and forced the emigration overseas of two million more? * * * And when * * * Columbus discovered America, he did not know that by doing so he was giving new life to slavery, which in Europe had long ago been done away with, and laying the basis for the Negro slave traffic. The men who in the seventeenth and eighteenth centuries laboured to create the steam engine had no idea that they were preparing the instrument which more than any other was to revolutionise social conditions throughout the world. Especially in Europe, by concentrating wealth in the hands of a minority, the huge majority being rendered propertyless, this instrument was destined at first to give social and political domination to the bourgeoisie, and then, however, to give rise to a class struggle between bourgeoisie and proletariat, which can end only in the overthrow of the bourgeoisie and the abolition of all class contradictions. But even in this sphere, by long and often cruel experience and by collecting and analysing the historical material, we are gradually learning to get a clear view of the indirect, more remote, social effects of our productive activity, and so the possibility is afforded us of mastering and controlling these effects as well.

To carry out this control requires something more than mere knowledge. It requires a complete revolution in our hitherto existing mode of production, and with it of our whole contemporary social order. * * *

Language

CHARLES DARWIN

Language[†]

Chapter III: Comparison of the Mental Powers of Man and the Lower Animals

This faculty has justly been considered as one of the chief distinctions between man and the lower animals. But man, as a highly competent judge, Archbishop Whately[1] remarks, "is not the only animal that can make use of language to express what is passing in his mind, and can understand, more or less, what is so expressed by another." In Paraguay the Cebus azarae[2] when excited utters at least six distinct sounds, which excite in other monkeys similar emotions. The movements of the features and gestures of monkeys are understood by us, and they partly understand ours, as Rengger[3] and others declare. * * * With the domesticated dog we have the bark of eagerness, as in the chase; that of anger, as well as growling; the yelp or howl of despair, as when shut up; the baying at night; the bark of joy, as when starting on a walk with his master; and the very distinct one of demand or supplication, as when wishing for a door or window to be opened. According to Houzeau,[4] who paid particular attention to the subject, the domestic fowl utters at least a dozen significant sounds.

The habitual use of articulate language is, however, peculiar to man; but he uses, in common with the lower animals, inarticulate cries to express his meaning, aided by gestures and the movements of the muscles of the face. * * * That which distinguishes man from the lower animals is not the understanding of articulate sounds, for, as every one knows, dogs understand many words and sentences. In this respect they are at the same stage of development as infants, between the ages of ten and twelve months, who understand many

---

† From *The Descent of Man, and Selection in Relation to Sex*, 2nd ed. (London: John Murray, 1871), pp. 84–92. Unless otherwise indicated, notes are by the editor of this Norton Critical Edition. Some of Darwin's notes have been omitted.
1. Richard Whately (1787–1863), English theologian, rhetorician, and political economist; Darwin cites a passage from Whately's *On Instinct* as quoted in an 1864 article from the *Anthropological Review* attributed to "Philalethes."
2. Species of capuchin monkey.
3. Johann Rudolph Rengger (1795–1832), Swiss naturalist, physician, and explorer.
4. Jean-Charles Houzeau, Belgian astronomer, journalist, and self-described "naturalist traveller" (1820–1888); Darwin refers here to Houzeau's 1872 *Études sur les Facultés Mentales des Animaux comparées à celles de l'Homme* (studies on the mental faculties of animals compared to those of man).

words and short sentences, but cannot yet utter a single word. It is not the mere articulation which is our distinguishing character, for parrots and other birds possess this power. Nor is it the mere capacity of connecting definite sounds with definite ideas. * * * The lower animals differ from man solely in his almost infinitely larger power of associating together the most diversified sounds and ideas; and this obviously depends on the high development of his mental powers.

* * * The sounds uttered by birds offer in several respects the nearest analogy to language, for all the members of the same species utter the same instinctive cries expressive of their emotions; and all the kinds which sing, exert their power instinctively; but the actual song, and even the call-notes, are learnt from their parents or foster-parents. * * * The first attempts to sing "may be compared to the imperfect endeavour in a child to babble." The young males continue practising, or as the bird-catchers say, "recording," for ten or eleven months. Their first essays shew hardly a rudiment of the future song; but as they grow older we can perceive what they are aiming at; and at last they are said "to sing their song round." Nestlings which have learnt the song of a distinct species, as with the canary-birds educated in the Tyrol, teach and transmit their new song to their offspring. The slight natural differences of song in the same species inhabiting different districts may be appositely compared, as Barrington[5] remarks, "to provincial dialects"; and the songs of allied, though distinct species may be compared with the languages of distinct races of man. I have given the foregoing details to shew that an instinctive tendency to acquire an art is not peculiar to man.

* * * I cannot doubt that language owes its origin to the imitation and modification of various natural sounds, the voices of other animals, and man's own instinctive cries, aided by signs and gestures. * * * Since monkeys certainly understand much that is said to them by man, and when wild, utter signal-cries of danger to their fellows; and since fowls give distinct warnings for danger on the ground, or in the sky from hawks (both, as well as a third cry, intelligible to dogs), may not some unusually wise ape-like animal have imitated the growl of a beast of prey, and thus told his fellow-monkeys the nature of the expected danger? This would have been a first step in the formation of a language. * * *

Several writers, more especially Prof. Max Muller,[6] have lately insisted that the use of language implies the power of forming general concepts; and that as no animals are supposed to possess this

5. Irish naturalist Richard Manliffe Barrington (1849–1915).
6. Friedrich Max Müller (1823–1900), Anglo-German philologist; Darwin refers to Müller's 1873 essay "Lectures on Mr. Darwin's Philosophy of Language," excerpted on pp. 167–71 below.

power, an impassable barrier is formed between them and man.[7] With respect to animals, I have already endeavoured to shew that they have this power, at least in a rude and incipient degree.

* * * As all the higher mammals possess vocal organs, constructed on the same general plan as ours, and used as a means of communication, it was obviously probable that these same organs would be still further developed if the power of communication had to be improved; and this has been effected by the aid of adjoining and well adapted parts, namely the tongue and lips. The fact of the higher apes not using their vocal organs for speech, no doubt depends on their intelligence not having been sufficiently advanced. The possession by them of organs, which with long-continued practice might have been used for speech, although not thus used, is paralleled by the case of many birds which possess organs fitted for singing, though they never sing. Thus, the nightingale and crow have vocal organs similarly constructed, these being used by the former for diversified song, and by the latter only for croaking. * * *

The perfectly regular and wonderfully complex construction of the languages of many barbarous nations has often been advanced as a proof, either of the divine origin of these languages, or of the high art and former civilisation of their founders. Thus F. von Schlegel[8] writes: "In those languages which appear to be at the lowest grade of intellectual culture, we frequently observe a very high and elaborate degree of art in their grammatical structure. This is especially the case with the Basque and the Lapponian, and many of the American languages." But it is assuredly an error to speak of any language as an art, in the sense of its having been elaborately and methodically formed. Philologists now admit that conjugations, declensions, etc., originally existed as distinct words, since joined together; and as such words express the most obvious relations between objects and persons, it is not surprising that they should have been used by the men of most races during the earliest ages.

7. The judgment of a distinguished philologist, such as Prof. Whitney, will have far more weight on this point than anything that I can say. He remarks ('Oriental and Linguistic Studies,' 1873, p. 297), in speaking of Bleek's views: "Because on the grand scale language is the necessary auxiliary of thought, indispensable to the development of the power of thinking, to the distinctness and variety and complexity of cognitions to the full mastery of consciousness; therefore he would fain make thought absolutely impossible without speech, identifying the faculty with its instrument. He might just as reasonably assert that the human hand cannot act without a tool. With such a doctrine to start from, he cannot stop short of Muller's [sic] worst paradoxes, that an infant (in fans, not speaking) is not a human being, and that deaf-mutes do not become possessed of reason until they learn to twist their fingers into imitation of spoken words." Max Muller [sic] gives in italics ('Lectures on Mr. Darwin's Philosophy of Language,' 1873, third lecture) this aphorism: "There is no thought without words, as little as there are words without thought." What a strange definition must here be given to the word thought! [Darwin's note].
8. Karl Wilhelm Friedrich von Schlegel (1772–1829), German poet, linguist, philologist, and philosopher; Darwin cites Schlegel's Philosophy of Language (1828–29), Lecture II.

With respect to perfection, the following illustration will best shew how easily we may err: a Crinoid[9] sometimes consists of no less than 150,000 pieces of shell, all arranged with perfect symmetry in radiating lines; but a naturalist does not consider an animal of this kind as more perfect than a bilateral one with comparatively few parts, and with none of these parts alike, excepting on the opposite sides of the body. He justly considers the differentiation and specialisation of organs as the test of perfection. So with languages: the most symmetrical and complex ought not to be ranked above irregular, abbreviated, and bastardised languages, which have borrowed expressive words and useful forms of construction from various conquering, conquered, or immigrant races.

From these few and imperfect remarks I conclude that the extremely complex and regular construction of many barbarous languages, is no proof that they owe their origin to a special act of creation. Nor, as we have seen, does the faculty of articulate speech in itself offer any insuperable objection to the belief that man has been developed from some lower form.

MAX MÜLLER

From "Lectures on Mr. Darwin's Philosophy of Language, II"[†]

* * * It is easy to understand that the Darwinian school, having brought itself to look upon the divers forms of living animals as the result of gradual development, should have considered it an act of intellectual cowardice to stop short before man. The gap between man and the higher apes is so very small, whereas the gap between the ape and the moneres[1] is enormous. If, then, the latter could be cleared, how could we hesitate about the former? * * * I cannot follow Mr. Darwin because I hold that this question is not to be decided in an anatomical theatre only. There is to my mind one difficulty which Mr. Darwin has not sufficiently appreciated, and which I certainly do not feel able to remove. There is between the whole animal kingdom on one side, and man, even in his lowest state, on the other, a barrier which no animal has ever crossed, and that barrier is—*Language*. By no effort of the understanding, by no stretch of imagination, can I explain to myself how language could

9. Marine animal in the phylum including starfish and sea urchins.
† From *Fraser's Magazine* 7 (June 1873): 666–67, 670–72, 674–75. Müller's notes have been omitted.
1. Single-celled organisms lacking a nucleus and other membrane-bound cellular compartments (or organelles); prokaryotes.

have grown out of anything which animals possess, even if we granted them millions of years for that purpose. If anything has a right to the name of *specific difference*, it is language, as we find it in man, and in man only. Even if we removed the name of specific difference from our philosophic dictionaries, I should still hold that nothing deserves the name of man except what is able to speak. If Mr. Mill[2] maintains that a rational elephant could not be called a man, all depends on what he means by rational. But it may certainly be said with equal, and even greater truth, that a speaking elephant or an elephantine speaker could never be called an elephant. I can bring myself to imagine with evolutionist philosophers that that most wonderful of organs, the eye, has been developed out of a pigmentary spot, and the ear out of a particularly sore place in the skin; that, in fact, an animal without any organs of sense may in time grow into an animal with organs of sense. I say I can imagine it, and I should not feel justified in classing such a theory as utterly inconceivable. But, taking all that is called animal on one side, and man on the other, I must call it inconceivable that any known animal could ever develop language. Professor Schleicher,[3] though an enthusiastic admirer of Darwin, observed once jokingly, but not without a deep meaning, 'If a pig were ever to say to me, "I am a pig," it would ipso facto cease to be a pig.' This shows how strongly he felt that language was out of the reach of any animal, and the exclusive or specific property of man. I do not wonder that Mr. Darwin and other philosophers belonging to his school should not feel the difficulty of language as it was felt by Professor Schleicher, who, though a Darwinian, was also one of our best students of the Science of Language. But those who know best what language is, and, still more, what it presupposes, cannot, however Darwinian they may be on other points, ignore the veto which, as yet, that science enters against the last step in Darwin's philosophy. That philosophy would not be vitiated by admitting an independent beginning for man. For if Mr. Darwin admits, in opposition to the evolutionist *pur et simple*, four or five progenitors for the whole of the animal kingdom, which are most likely intended for the *Radiata, Mollusca, Articulata*, and *Vertebrata*, there would be nothing radically wrong in admitting a fifth progenitor for man. As Mr. Darwin does not admit this, but declares distinctly that man has been developed from some lower animal, we may conclude that physiologically and anatomically there are no tenable arguments against this view. But if Mr. Darwin goes on to say that in a series of forms graduating *insensibly* from some ape-like creature to man as he now exists, it would be impossible to fix on

2. English philosopher John Stuart Mill (1806–1873); Müller refers to Mill's *A System of Logic: Ratiocinative and Inductive* (1843), book I, chapter 1, section 5.
3. German linguist August Schleicher (1821–1868).

any definite point where the term 'man' ought to be used, he has left the ground, peculiarly his own, where few would venture to oppose him, and he must expect to be met by those who have studied man, not only as an ape-like creature, which he undoubtedly is, but also as an un-ape-like creature, possessed of language, and of all that language implies. * * *

I confess that after reading again and again what Mr. Darwin has written on the subject of language, I cannot understand how he could bring himself to sum up the subject as follows: 'We have seen that the faculty of articulate speech in itself does not offer any insuperable objection to the belief that man has been developed from some lower animal' (p. 62).[4]

Now the fact is that not a single instance has ever been adduced of any animal trying or learning to speak, nor has it been explained by any scholar or philosopher how that barrier of language, which divides man from all animals, might be effectually crossed. * * * Mr. Darwin has never told us what he thinks on this point. He refers to certain writers on the origin of language, who consider that the first materials of language are either interjections or imitations; but their writings in no wise support the theory that animals also could, either out of their own barkings and bellowings, or out of the imitative sounds of mocking-birds, have elaborated anything like what we mean by language, even among the lowest savages. It may be in the recollection of some of my hearers that, in my Lectures on the Science of Language, when speaking of Demokritos and some of his later followers, I called his theory on the origin of language the *Bowwow* theory, because I felt certain that, if this theory were only called by its right name, it would require no further refutation.[5] * * * For philological purposes it matters little, as I said in 1866, what opinion we hold on the origin of roots so long as we agree that, with the exception of a number of purely mimetic expressions, all words, such as we find them, whether in English or in Sanskrit, encumbered with prefixes and suffixes, and mouldering away under the action of phonetic decay, must, in the last instance, be traced back, by means of definite phonetic laws, to those definite primary forms which we are accustomed to call roots.[6] These roots stand like barriers between the chaos and the kosmos of human speech. Whoever admits the historical character of roots, whatever opinion he may hold on their origin, is not a Demokritean, does not hold that

---

4. *The Descent of Man*, vol. 1 (1871); Müller misquotes Darwin, substituting "animal" for "form."
5. Lecture IX of *Lectures on the Science of Language* (1866). *Demokritos*: Pre-Socratic philosopher (ca. 460–370 BCE).
6. Müller's term for the elemental building blocks of language, which are not mere sounds or speech parts but, rather, conceptual formations.

theory which I called the Bow-wow theory, and cannot be quoted in support of Mr. Darwin's opinion that the cries of animals represent the earliest stage of the language of man.

If we speak simply of the materials, not of the elements, of language—and the distinction between these two words is but too often overlooked—then, no doubt, we may not only say that the phonetic materials of the cries of animals and the languages of man are the same, but, following in the footsteps of evolutionist philosophers, we might trace the involuntary exclamations of men back to the inanimate and inorganic world. * * *

* * * [W]ithout doubting any of the extraordinary accounts of the intellect, the understanding, the caution, the judgment, the sagacity, acuteness, cleverness, genius, or even the social virtues of animals, the rules of positive philosophy forbid us to assert anything about their instincts or intellectual faculties. We may allow ourselves to be guided by our own fancies or by analogy, and we may guess and assert very plausibly many things about the inner life of animals; but however strong our own belief may be, the whole subject is transcendent, i.e. beyond the reach of positive knowledge. We all admit that, in many respects, the animal is even superior to man. Who is there but at one time or other has not sighed for the wings of birds? Who can deny that the muscles of the lion are more powerful, those of the cat more pliant, than ours * * *? Nay, I am quite prepared to go even farther, and if metaphysicians were to tell me that our senses only serve to distract the natural intuitions of the soul, that our organs of sense are weak, deceptive, limited, and that a mollusc, being able to digest without a stomach and to live without a brain, is a more perfect, certainly a more happy, being than man, I should bow in silence; but I should still appeal to one palpable fact—viz. that whatever animals may do or not do, no animal has ever spoken. * * *

* * * Now there are two totally distinct operations which in ordinary parlance go by the same name of language, but which should be distinguished most carefully as *Emotional* and *Rational* language. The power of showing by outward signs what we feel, or, it may be, what we think, is the source of emotional language, and the recognition of such emotional signs, or the understanding of their purport, is no more than the result of memory, a resus[7] citation of painful or pleasant impressions connected with such signs. That emotional language is certainly shared in common by man and animals. If a dog barks, that may be a sign, according to circumstances, of his being angry or pleased or surprised. Every dog speaks that language, every dog understands it, and other animals too, such as cats or sheep, and even children, learn it. * * * What, then, is the

7. Resuscitative.

difference between *emotional* language and *rational* language? The very name shows the difference. Language, such as we speak, is founded on reason, reason meaning for philosophical purposes the faculty of forming and handling general concepts; and as that power manifests itself outwardly by articulate language only, we, as positive philosophers, have a right to say that animals, being devoid of the only tangible sign of reason which we know, viz. language, may by us be treated as irrational beings—irrational, not in the sense of devoid of observation, shrewdness, calculation, presence of mind, reasoning in the sense of weighing, or even genius, but simply in the sense of devoid of the power of forming and handling general concepts. * * *

R. L. GARNER

From "The Simian Tongue"†

In coming before the world with a new theory, I am aware that it may have to undergo many repairs, and be modified by many new ideas. On entering the world of science, it begins its "struggle for life," and under the law of "the survival of the fittest" its fate must be decided. I am aware that it is heresy to doubt the dogmas of science as well as of some religious sects; but sustained by proofs too strong to be ignored, I am willing to incur the ridicule of the wise and the sneer of bigots, and assert that "articulate speech" prevails among the lower primates, and that their speech contains the rudiments from which the tongues of mankind could easily develop; and to me it seems quite possible to find proofs to show that such is the origin of human speech.

I have long believed that each sound uttered by an animal had a meaning which any other animal of the same kind would interpret at once. Animals soon learn to interpret certain words of man and to obey them, but never try to repeat them. When they reply to man, it is always in their own peculiar speech. I have often watched the conduct of a dog as he would speak, until I could interpret a meaning to his combined act and speech. I observed the same thing in other species with the same results; and it occurred to me that if I could correctly imitate these sounds I might learn to interpret them more fully and prove to myself whether it was really a uniform speech or not.

Some seven years ago, in the Cincinnati Zoological Garden, I was deeply impressed by the conduct of a number of monkeys caged with a savage rib-nosed mandril, which they seemed to fear very much. The cage was divided by a wall through which was a small doorway

† From the *New Review* 4 (June 1891): 555–62.

leading from the inner to an outer compartment, in which was a tall upright, supporting a platform at its top. Every movement of this mandril seemed to be closely watched by the monkeys that could see him, and instantly reported to those in the other compartment. The conduct of these monkeys so confirmed my belief and inspired me with new hopes and new zeal that I believed "the key to the secret chamber" was within my grasp. I regarded the task of learning the monkey tongue as very much the same as learning that of a strange race of mankind; more difficult in the degree of its inferiority, but less in volume. Year by year, as new ideas were revealed to me, new barriers arose, and I began to realise how great a task was mine. One difficulty was to *utter* the sounds I heard; another was to recall them; and yet another was to translate them. Impelled by an eternal hope, and not discouraged by poor success, I continued my studies as best I could, in the gardens of New York, Philadelphia, Cincinnati, and Chicago, and with such specimens as I could find with the travelling menagerie museum, or hand organ, or aboard some ship, or kept as a pet in some family. They have all aided in teaching me the little I know of their native tongues. But at last came a revelation! A new idea dawned upon me; and after wrestling half a night with it I felt assured of ultimate success. I went to Washington, and called upon Dr. Frank Baker, Director of the National Zoological Garden and proposed the novel experiment of acting as interpreter between, two monkeys. Of course he laughed, but not in derision or in doubt, for scientific men are always credulous and believe all they are told. I then explained to him how it was possible, and he quite agreed with me. We set the time and prepared for the work. The plan was quite simple. We separated two monkeys which had been caged together, and placed them in separate rooms. I then arranged a phonograph near the cage of the female, and caused her to utter a few sounds, which were recorded on the cylinder. The machine was then placed near the cage containing the male, and the record repeated to him and his conduct closely studied. The surprise and perplexity of the male were evident.

He traced the sounds to the horn from which they came, and failing to find his mate he thrust his hand and arm into the horn quite up to his shoulder, withdrew it, and peeped into the horn again and again. He would then retreat and again cautiously approach the horn, which he examined with evident interest. The expressions of his face were indeed a study. Having satisfied myself that he recognised the sounds as those of his mate, I next proceeded to record some of his efforts, but my success was not fully up to my hopes. Yet I had secured from him enough to win the attention of his mate, and elicit from her some signs of recognition. And thus, for the first time in the history of philology, the simian tongue was reduced to record. My belief was now confirmed, and the faith of others strengthened. I noted some of the defects in my experiment, and provided against them for the future. Some weeks later, in the Chicago Zoological Garden, I made some splendid phonographic records; and thence I went to the Cincinnati Garden, where I secured, among others, a fine, distinct record of the two chimpanzees, all of which I brought home with me for study. I placed them on the machine and repeated them over and over, until I became quite familiar with the sounds and improved myself very much in my efforts to utter them. I returned to Cincinnati and Chicago some weeks later, and tried my skill as a linguist with a degree of success far beyond my wildest hopes.

Having described to some friends who were with me the word I would use, I stood for a while with my side turned to the cage containing a capuchin monkey (*cebus capucinus*). I uttered the word or sound which I had translated "milk." My first effort caught his ear and caused him to turn and look at me. On repeating it some three or four times he answered me very distinctly with the same word I had used, and then turned to a small pan kept in the cage for him to drink from. I repeated the word again, and he placed the pan near the front of the cage and came quite up to the bars and uttered the word. I had not shown him any milk or anything of the kind. But the man in charge then brought me some milk, which I gave to him, and he drank it with great zest; then looked at me, held up the pan, and repeated the sound some three or four times. I gave him more milk, and thus continued till I was quite sure he used the same sound each time he wanted milk.

I next described to the friends who were with me a word which was very hard to render well, but I translated it "to eat." I now held a banana in front of the cage and he at once gave the word I had described. Repeated tests showed to me that he used the same word for apple, carrot, bread, and banana, hence I concluded that it meant "food," or "hunger," as also "to eat." After this I began on a word which I had interpreted "pain," or "sick," and with such result as made me feel quite sure I was not far from right. My next word was "weather," or "storm," and while the idea may seem far-fetched, I felt fairly well sustained by my tests. For many other words I had a vague idea of a meaning, and still believe that I can verify them in the end. These are only a few of many trials I have made to solve the problem of the simian tongue, and while I have only gone a step, as it were, I believe that I have found a clue to the great secret of speech, and pointed out the way which leads to its solution.

I went next to the Cincinnati Garden. When the visitors had left the monkey-house I approached the cage of a capuchin monkey, and found him crouched in the rear of his cage. I spoke to him in his own tongue, using the word which I had called "milk." He rose, answered me with the same word, and came at once to the front of the cage. He looked at me as if in doubt, and I repeated the word; he did the same, and turned at once to a small pan in the cage, which he picked up and placed near the door at the side, and returned to me and uttered the word again. I asked the keeper for milk, which he did not have, however, but brought me some water. The efforts of my little simian friend to secure the glass were very earnest, and the pleading manner and tone assured me of his extreme thirst. I allowed him to dip his hand into the glass and he would suck his fingers and reach again. I kept the glass from reach of his hand, and he would repeat the sound and beg for more. I was thus convinced that the word I had translated "milk" must also mean "water," and from this and other tests, I at last determined that it meant also "drink" and probably "thirst." I have never seen a capuchin monkey that did not use these two words. The sounds are very soft and not unlike a flute; very difficult to imitate and quite impossible to write. They are purely vocal, except faint traces of "h" or "wh" as in the word "who"; a very feeble "w"; and here and there a slight gutteral "ch."

To imitate the word which I interpret "food," fix the mouth as if to whistle: draw the tongue far back into the mouth, and try to utter the word "who" by blowing. The pitch of sound is a trifle higher than the cooing of a pigeon, and not wholly unlike it. The phonics appear to me to be "wh-u-w," with the consonant elements so faint as to be almost imaginary. In music the tone is F sharp, * * * and this seems to be the vocal pitch of the entire species, though they have a wide range of voice. The sound which I have translated "drink" or "thirst" is nearly uttered by relaxing and parting the lips, and placing the tongue as it is found in ending the German word "ich," and in this position try to utter "ch-e-u-w," making the "ch" like "k," blending the "e" and "u" like "slurred" notes in music, and suppressing the "w" as in the first case. The consonant elements can barely be detected, and the tone is about an octave higher than the word used for "food." Another sound I suspected was a "menace" or "cry of alarm," but I was unable to utter it, except with the phonograph; but during February I had access to a fine specimen of the capuchin, in Charleston, S.C. On my first visit to him I found him very gentle, and we at once became good friends. He ate from my hands and seemed to regard me very kindly. The next day, while feeding him, I uttered the peculiar sound of "alarm," whereupon he sprang at once to a perch in the top of his cage, and as I continued the sound he seemed almost frantic with fright. I could not tempt him by any means to come down. I then retired some twenty feet from the cage, and his master (of whom he is very fond) induced him to come down from the perch, and while he was fondling him I gave the alarm from where I stood. He jumped again to his perch and nothing would induce him to leave it while I remained in sight. The next day, on my approach, he fled to his perch and I could not induce him on any terms to return. It is now some time since I began my visits, and I have never, since his first fright, induced him to accept anything from me, and only with great patience can I get him to leave his perch at all, although I have not repeated this peculiar sound since my third visit, nor can I again elicit a reply from him when I say his word for "food" or "drink."

This sound may be fairly imitated by placing the back of the hand very gently to the mouth, and kissing it, drawing in the air, and producing a shrill, whistling sound, prolonged and slightly circumflexed.

Its pitch is the highest F sharp on the piano. It is not whistled, however, by a monkey, but is made with the vocal organs. While this is the highest vocal pitch of a capuchin, there are other sounds much more difficult to imitate or describe. It must be remembered that an attempt to *spell* a sound which is almost an absolute vowel, can at best convey only a very imperfect idea of the true sounds or the manner of uttering them.

I have access also to another specimen of the same variety, with which I am experimenting, but I have never tried the "alarm" on him as I do not wish to lose his friendship. He uses all the words I know in his language, and speaks them well.

My work has been confined chiefly to the capuchin monkey, because he seems to have one of the best defined languages of any of his genus, besides being less vicious and more willing to treat one civilly. So far as I have seen, the capuchin is the Caucasian of the monkey race. The chimpanzee has a strong but monotonous voice, confined to a small range of sounds, but affords a fine study while in the act of talking. I have not gone far enough with him as yet to give much detail of his language. There are only three in America now, and they talk but little and are hard to record. I have recorded but one sound made by a sooty monkey; three by a mandril; five by the white-face sapajou; and a few of less value. But from the best proof I have found I have arrived, as I believe, at some strange facts, which I shall here state.

1. The simian tongue has about eight or nine sounds, which may be changed by modulation into three or four times that number.
2. They seem to be half-way between a whistle and a pure vocal sound, and have a range of four octaves, and so far as I have tried they all chord with F sharp on a piano.
3. The sound used most is very much like "u"—"oo," in "shoot." The next one something like "e" in "be." So far I find no a, i, or o.

4. Faint traces of consonant sounds can be found in words of low pitch, but they are few and quite feeble; but I have had cause to believe that they develop in a small degree by a change of environment.

5. The present state of their speech has been reached by development from a lower form.

6. Each race or kind has its own peculiar tongue, slightly shaded into dialects, and the radical or cardinal sounds do not have the same meanings in all tongues.

7. The words are monosyllabic, ambiguous and collective, having no negative terms except resentment.

8. The phonic character of their speech is very much the same as that of children in their early efforts to talk, except as regards the pitch.

9. Their language seems to obey the same laws of change and growth as human speech.

10. When caged together one monkey will learn to understand the language of another kind, but does not try to speak it. His replies are in his own vernacular.

11. They use their lips in talking in very much the same way that men do; but seldom speak when alone or when not necessary.

12. I think their speech, compared to their physical, mental, and social state, is in about the same relative condition as that of man by the same standard.

13. The more fixed and pronounced the social and gregarious instincts are in any species, the higher the type of its speech.

14. Simians reason from cause to effect, and their reasoning differs from that of man *in degree*, *but not in kind*.

To reason, they *must think*, and if it be true that *man cannot think without words*, it must be true of monkeys: hence, they must formulate those thoughts into words, and words are the natural exponents of thoughts.

15. Words are the audible, and signs the visible, expression of thought, and any voluntary sound made by the vocal organs with a constant meaning is a word.

16. The state of their language seems to correspond with their power to think, and to express their thoughts.

If we compare the tongues of civilised races with those of the savage tribes of Africa which are confined to a few score of words, we gain some idea of the growth of language within the limits of our own genus. The few wants and simple modes of life in such a state account for this paucity of words; and this small range of sounds gives but little scope for vocal development, and hence their difficulty in learning to speak the tongues of civilised men. This is, doubtless, the reason why the negroes of the United States, after a sojourn of two hundred years with the white race, are unable to utter the sounds of "th," "thr," and other double consonants; the former of which they pronounce "d" if breathing, and "t" if aspirate; the latter like "trw." The sound of "v" they usually pronounce "b," while "r" resembles "w" or "rw" when initial, and as a final is usually entirely suppressed. They have a marked tendency to omit auxiliaries and final sounds, and in all departures from the higher types of speech tend back to ancestral forms. I believe, if we could apply the rule of perspectives and throw our vanishing point far back beyond the chasm that separates man from his simian prototype, that we should find one unbroken outline, tangent to every circle of life from man to protozoa, in language mind, and matter.

The sage of science finds the fossil rays of light still shining in the chamber of sleeping epochs, and by their aid he reads the legends on the guide-posts of time; but the echoes of time are lost and its lips are dumb; hence our search for the first voice of speech must come within the brief era of man; but if his prototype survives, does not his parent speech survive? If the races of mankind may be the progeny of the simian stock, may not their languages be the progeny of the simian tongue?

Ethics

CHARLES DARWIN

On the Moral Sense[†]

Chapter IV. Comparison of the Mental Powers of Man and the Lower Animals

I fully subscribe to the judgment of those writers who maintain that of all the differences between man and the lower animals, the moral sense or conscience is by far the most important. * * * [I]t is summed up in that short but imperious word "ought," so full of high significance. It is the most noble of all the attributes of man, leading him without a moment's hesitation to risk his life for that

---

† From *The Descent of Man, and Selection in Relation to Sex,* 2nd ed. (London: John Murray, 1874 [1871]), pp. 97–100, 112, 115–16, 610. Darwin's notes have been omitted.

of a fellow-creature; or after due deliberation, impelled simply by the deep feeling of right or duty, to sacrifice it in some great cause. * * *

* * * [A]s far as I know, no one has approached it exclusively from the side of natural history. The investigation possesses, also, some independent interest, as an attempt to see how far the study of the lower animals throws light on one of the highest psychical faculties of man.

The following proposition seems to me in a high degree probable— namely, that any animal whatever, endowed with well-marked social instincts, the parental and filial affections being here included, would inevitably acquire a moral sense or conscience, as soon as its intellectual powers had become as well, or nearly as well developed, as in man. * * *

It may be well first to premise that I do not wish to maintain that any strictly social animal, if its intellectual faculties were to become as active and as highly developed as in man, would acquire exactly the same moral sense as ours. In the same manner as various animals have some sense of beauty, though they admire widely-different objects, so they might have a sense of right and wrong, though led by it to follow widely different lines of conduct. If, for instance, to take an extreme case, men were reared under precisely the same conditions as hive-bees, there can hardly be a doubt that our unmarried females would, like the worker-bees, think it a sacred duty to kill their brothers, and mothers would strive to kill their fertile daughters. * * * Nevertheless, the bee, or any other social animal, would gain in our supposed case, as it appears to me, some feeling of right or wrong, or a conscience. For each individual would have an inward sense of possessing certain stronger or more enduring instincts, and others less strong or enduring; so that there would often be a struggle as to which impulse should be followed; and satisfaction, dissatisfaction, or even misery would be felt, as past impressions were compared during their incessant passage through the mind. In this case an inward monitor would tell the animal that it would have been better to have followed the one impulse rather than the other. The one course ought to have been followed, and the other ought not; the one would have been right and the other wrong * * * .

THE MORE ENDURING SOCIAL INSTINCTS CONQUER THE LESS PERSISTENT INSTINCTS

Man, from the activity of his mental faculties, cannot avoid reflection: past impressions and images are incessantly and clearly passing through his mind. Now with those animals which live permanently in a body, the social instincts are ever present and persistent. Such animals are always ready to utter the danger-signal, to defend the community, and to give aid to their fellows in accordance with their habits; they feel at all times, without the stimulus of any special passion or desire, some degree of love and sympathy for them; they are unhappy if long separated from them, and always happy to be again in their company. * * *

Man prompted by his conscience, will through long habit acquire such perfect self-command, that his desires and passions will at last yield instantly and without a struggle to his social sympathies and instincts, including his feeling for the judgment of his fellows. The still hungry, or the still revengeful man will not think of stealing food, or of wreaking his vengeance. It is possible, or as we shall hereafter see, even probable, that the habit of self-command may, like other habits, be inherited. Thus at last man comes to feel, through acquired and perhaps inherited habit, that it is best for him to obey his more persistent impulses. The imperious word "ought" seems merely to imply the consciousness of the existence of a rule of conduct, however it may have originated. Formerly it must have been often vehemently urged that an insulted gentleman *ought* to fight a duel. We even say that a pointer *ought* to point, and a retriever to retrieve game. If they fail to do so, they fail in their duty and act wrongly. * * *

*   *   *

Chapter XXI. General Summary and Conclusion

* * * The development of the moral qualities is a more interesting problem. The foundation lies in the social instincts, including under this term the family ties. These instincts are highly complex, and in the case of the lower animals give special tendencies towards certain definite actions; but the more important elements are love, and the distinct emotion of sympathy. Animals endowed with the social instincts take pleasure in one another's company, warn one another of danger, defend and aid one another in many ways. These instincts do not extend to all the individuals of the species, but only to those of the same community. As they are highly beneficial to the species, they have in all probability been acquired through natural selection.

A moral being is one who is capable of reflecting on his past actions and their motives—of approving of some and disapproving of others; and the fact that man is the one being who certainly deserves this designation, is the greatest of all distinctions between him and the lower animals. * * *

T. H. HUXLEY

From "Evolution and Ethics: Prolegomena"†

I

It may be safely assumed that, two thousand years ago, before Cæsar set foot in southern Britain, the whole country-side visible from the windows of the room in which I write, was in what is called "the state of nature." * * *

That the state of nature, at any time, is a temporary phase of a process of incessant change, which has been going on for innumerable ages, appears to me to be a proposition as well established as any in modern history. * * * [I]f every link in the ancestry of these humble indigenous plants had been preserved and were accessible to us, the whole would present a converging series of forms of gradually diminishing complexity, until, at some period in the history of the earth, far more remote than any of which organic remains have yet been discovered, they would merge in those low groups among which the boundaries between animal and vegetable life become effaced.[1] * * *

II

Three or four years have elapsed since the state of nature, to which I have referred, was brought to an end, so far as a small patch of the soil is concerned, by the intervention of man. The patch was cut off from the rest by a wall; within the area thus protected, the native vegetation was, as far as possible, extirpated; while a colony of strange plants was imported and set down in its place. In short, it was made into a garden. At the present time, this artificially treated area presents an aspect extraordinarily different from that of so much of the land as remains in the state of nature, outside the wall. * * * [C]onsiderable quantities of vegetables, fruits, and flowers are produced, of kinds which neither now exist, nor have ever existed, except under conditions such as obtain in the garden; and which, therefore, are as much works of the art of man as the frames and glass-houses in which some of them are raised. That the "state of Art," thus created in the state of nature by man, is sustained by and dependent on him, would at once become apparent, if the watchful supervision of the gardener were withdrawn, and the antagonistic

---

† From *Collected Essays*, vol. 9: *Evolution and Ethics and Other Essays* (London: Macmillan, 1894), pp. 1, 5, 9–14, 16–18, 29–31, 44–45. Notes are by Huxley.
1. "On the Border Territory between the Animal and the Vegetable Kingdoms," *Essays*, vol. viii, p. 162.

influences of the general cosmic process were no longer sedulously warded off, or counteracted. The walls and gates would decay; quadrupedal and bipedal intruders would devour and tread down the useful and beautiful plants; birds, insects, blight, and mildew would work their will; the seeds of the native plants, carried by winds or other agencies, would immigrate, and in virtue of their long-earned special adaptation to the local conditions, these despised native weeds would soon choke their choice exotic rivals. A century or two hence, little beyond the foundations of the wall and of the houses and frames would be left, in evidence of the victory of the cosmic powers at work in the state of nature, over the temporary obstacles to their supremacy, set up by the art of the horticulturist. * * *

III

No doubt, it may be properly urged that the operation of human energy and intelligence, which has brought into existence and maintains the garden, by what I have called "the horticultural process," is, strictly speaking, part and parcel of the cosmic process. And no one could more readily agree to that proposition than I. In fact, I do not know that any one has taken more pains than I have, during the last thirty years, to insist upon the doctrine, so much reviled in the early part of that period, that man, physical, intellectual, and moral, is as much a part of nature, as purely a product of the cosmic process, as the humblest weed.[2]

But if, following up this admission, it is urged that, such being the case, the cosmic process cannot be in antagonism with that horticultural process which is part of itself—I can only reply, that if the conclusion that the two are antagonistic is logically absurd, I am sorry for logic, because, as we have seen, the fact is so. The garden is in the same position as every other work of man's art; it is a result of the cosmic process working through and by human energy and intelligence; and, as is the case with every other artificial thing set up in the state of nature, the influences of the latter are constantly tending to break it down and destroy it. * * *

IV

Not only is the state of nature hostile to the state of art of the garden; but the principle of the horticultural process, by which the latter is created and maintained, is antithetic to that of the cosmic process. The characteristic feature of the latter is the intense and unceasing competition of the struggle for existence. The

2. See "Man's Place in Nature," *Collected Essays* vol. vii, and "On the Struggle for Existence in Human Society" (1888).

characteristic of the former is the elimination of that struggle, by the removal of the conditions which give rise to it. The tendency of the cosmic process is to bring about the adjustment of the forms of plant life to the current conditions; the tendency of the horticultural process is the adjustment of the conditions to the needs of the forms of plant life which the gardener desires to raise.

The cosmic process uses unrestricted multiplication as the means whereby hundreds compete for the place and nourishment adequate for one; it employs frost and drought to cut off the weak and unfortunate; to survive, there is need not only of strength, but of flexibility and of good fortune.

The gardener, on the other hand, restricts multiplication; provides that each plant shall have sufficient space and nourishment; protects from frost and drought; and, in every other way, attempts to modify the conditions, in such a manner as to bring about the survival of those forms which most nearly approach the standard of the useful, or the beautiful, which he has in his mind. * * *

V

The process of colonization presents analogies to the formation of a garden which are highly instructive. Suppose a shipload of English colonists sent to form a settlement, in such a country as Tasmania was in the middle of the last century. On landing, they find themselves in the midst of a state of nature, widely different from that left behind them in everything but the most general physical conditions. The common plants, the common birds and quadrupeds, are as totally distinct as the men from anything to be seen on the side of the globe from which they come. The colonists proceed to put an end to this state of things over as large an area as they desire to occupy. They clear away the native vegetation, extirpate or drive out the animal population, so far as may be necessary, and take measures to defend themselves from the re-immigration of either. In their place, they introduce English grain and fruit trees; English dogs, sheep, cattle, horses; and English men; in fact, they set up a new Flora and Fauna and a new variety of mankind, within the old state of nature. Their farms and pastures represent a garden on a great scale, and themselves the gardeners who have to keep it up, in watchful antagonism to the old *regime*. Considered as a whole, the colony is a composite unit introduced into the old state of nature; and, thenceforward, a competitor in the struggle for existence, to conquer or be vanquished.

Under the conditions supposed, there is no doubt of the result, if the work of the colonists be carried out energetically and with intelligent combination of all their forces. On the other hand, if they are

slothful, stupid, and careless; or if they waste their energies in con-
tests with one another, the chances are that the old state of nature
will have the best of it. The native savage will destroy the immigrant
civilized man; of the English animals and plants some will be extirpated by their indigenous rivals, others will pass into the feral state
and themselves become components of the state of nature. In a few
decades, all other traces of the settlement will have vanished.

VI

Let us now imagine that some administrative authority, as far superior in power and intelligence to men, as men are to their cattle, is
set over the colony, charged to deal with its human elements in such
a manner as to assure the victory of the settlement over the antagonistic influences of the state of nature in which it is set down. He
would proceed in the same fashion as that in which the gardener
dealt with his garden. In the first place, he would, as far as possible,
put a stop to the influence of external competition by thoroughly
extirpating and excluding the native rivals, whether men, beasts, or
plants. * * *

* * * Laws, sanctioned by the combined force of the colony, would
restrain the self-assertion of each man within the limits required for
the maintenance of peace. In other words, the cosmic struggle for
existence, as between man and man, would be rigorously suppressed;
and selection, by its means, would be as completely excluded as it is
from the garden. * * *

* * *

X

* * *

It is needful only to look around us, to see that the greatest restrainer
of the anti-social tendencies of men is fear, not of the law, but of
the opinion of their fellows. The conventions of honour bind men
who break legal, moral, and religious bonds; and, while people
endure the extremity of physical pain rather than part with life,
shame drives the weakest to suicide.

Every forward step of social progress brings men into closer relations with their fellows, and increases the importance of the
pleasures and pains derived from sympathy. We judge the acts of
others by our own sympathies, and we judge our own acts by the
sympathies of others, every day and all day long, from childhood
upwards, until associations, as indissoluble as those of language,
are formed between certain acts and the feelings of approbation or

disapprobation. * * * We come to think in the acquired dialect of morals. An artificial personality, the "man within," as Adam Smith[3] calls conscience, is built up beside the natural personality. He is the watchman of society, charged to restrain the anti-social tendencies of the natural man within the limits required by social welfare.

XI

I have termed this evolution of the feelings out of which the primitive bonds of human society are so largely forged, into the organized and personified sympathy we call conscience, the ethical process.[4] So far as it tends to make any human society more efficient in the struggle for existence with the state of nature, or with other societies, it works in harmonious contrast with the cosmic process. But it is none the less true that, since law and morals are restraints upon the struggle for existence between men in society, the ethical process is in opposition to the principle of the cosmic process, and tends to the suppression of the qualities best fitted for success in that struggle.[5] * * *

* * *

XV

* * * That which lies before the human race is a constant struggle to maintain and improve, in opposition to the State of Nature, the State of Art of an organized polity; in which, and by which, man may develop a worthy civilization, capable of maintaining and constantly improving itself, until the evolution of our globe shall have entered so far upon its downward course that the cosmic process resumes its sway; and, once more, the State of Nature prevails over the surface of our planet.

3. "Theory of the Moral Sentiments," Part iii. chap. 3. *On the influence and authority of conscience.*
4. Worked out, in its essential features, chiefly by Hartley and Adam Smith, long before the modern doctrine of evolution was thought of.
5. See my essay "On the Struggle for Existence in Human Society" * * *; and *Collected Essays*, vol. I, p. 276, for Kant's recognition of these facts.

RUDYARD KIPLING

The Law of the Jungle[†]

Now this is the Law of the Jungle—as old and as true as the sky;
    And the Wolf that shall keep it may prosper, but the Wolf that
    shall break it must die.
As the creeper that girdles the tree-trunk the Law runneth forward
    and back—
For the strength of the Pack is the Wolf, and the strength of the Wolf
    is the Pack.

Wash daily from nose-tip to tail-tip; drink deeply, but never too
    deep;
And remember the night is for hunting, and forget not the day is for
    sleep.
The Jackal may follow the Tiger, but, Cub, when thy whiskers are
    grown,
Remember the Wolf is a Hunter—go forth and get food of thine
    own.
Keep peace with the Lords of the Jungle—the Tiger, the Panther,
    and Bear.
And trouble not Hathi the Silent, and mock not the Boar in his lair.
When Pack meets with Pack in the Jungle, and neither will go from
    the trail,
Lie down till the leaders have spoken—it may be fair words shall
    prevail.
When ye fight with a Wolf of the Pack, ye must fight him alone and
    afar,
Lest others take part in the quarrel, and the Pack be diminished by
    war.
The Lair of the Wolf is his refuge, and where he has made him his
    home,
Not even the Head Wolf may enter, not even the Council may come.
The Lair of the Wolf is his refuge, but where he has digged it too
    plain,
The Council shall send him a message, and so he shall change it
    again.
If ye kill before midnight, be silent, and wake not the woods with
    your bay,
Lest ye frighten the deer from the crop, and your brothers go empty
    away.

† From *The Second Jungle Book* (London: Macmillan, 1894), pp. 23–25.

Ye may kill for yourselves, and your mates, and your cubs as they
     need, and ye can;
But kill not for pleasure of killing, and seven times never kill Man!
If ye plunder his Kill from a weaker, devour not all in thy pride;
Pack-Right is the right of the meanest; so leave him the head and
     the hide.
The Kill of the Pack is the meat of the Pack. Ye must eat where it
     lies;
And no one may carry away of that meat to his lair, or he dies.
The Kill of the Wolf is the meat of the Wolf. He may do what he
     will;
But, till he has given permission, the Pack may not eat of that Kill.
Cub-Right is the right of the Yearling. From all of his Pack he may
     claim
Full-gorge when the killer has eaten; and none may refuse him the
     same.
Lair-Right is the right of the Mother. From all of her year she may
     claim
One haunch of each kill for her litter, and none may deny her the
     same.
Cave-Right is the right of the Father—to hunt by himself for his
     own:
He is freed of all calls to the Pack; he is judged by the Council
     alone.
Because of his age and his cunning, because of his gripe and his
     paw,
In all that the Law leaveth open, the word of your Head Wolf is
     Law.
Now these are the Laws of the Jungle, and many and mighty are
     they;
But the head and the hoof of the Law and the haunch and the
     hump is—Obey!

Race, Cannibalism, and Empire

Laminating a reductive reading of the Darwinian model of biological change onto the Enlightenment "progress narrative," apologists for European empire assigned cultural "others" lower spots on the evolutionary ladder. Imperial-minded Europeans used the concept of evolution to define the colonized's social conditions as "primitive" or "undeveloped" environments either awaiting transformation into proper civic spheres (a "civilizing process" that, they argued, could be accelerated by aggressive colonial intervention) or frozen in place for anthropological inspection (as though Indigenous cultures—or "modern savages," as they were often termed in imperial representation—constituted "living fossils" of early human progression, the "missing links" between "highly developed" nonhuman animals and the fully mature embodiment of *Homo sapiens*, the white male European). Translating the broad idiom of "race" (which could signify "species" among either biota or human populations) into a narrowed discourse of physical or genealogical identity, empire's proponents forged a "[pseudo-] scientific racism" from a mélange of ethnocentric myths cultivated in literary forms like traveler's tales and cartography, in polygenetic theories of human origin often rooted in heretical but increasingly popular biblical exegeses, and in contemporary disciplines like physical anthropology (which asserted that purported anatomical "differences" like cranial sizes were evidence of racially determined intellectual and cultural hierarchies).[1] Adopting neo-Darwinian notions of "survival of the fittest," this motley racist ideology underwrote violent projects of colonial expansion and domination, naturalizing the figure of the imperial adventurer as the bearer of a fully realized "humanity" into the "dark continents" of "primitive" or "human*like*" creatures that God "meant [i.e., bred] to serve" their rightful masters.[2]

In this narrative designed to rewrite the colonized subject as a "brute" requiring corrective control by imperial authority—whether by conversion to complete humanity (the "civilizing process"); redirection of animality for effective use within the civilizational order (enslavement or

---

1. Thus we are delivered the idea of "*types* of mankind," in which "the human" is divided by taxonomies that locate some "races" closer to animal forms than to the most advanced (i.e., European) human figure: see illustration on p. 118 above.
2. The emerging discipline of anthropology—epitomized by Edward Tylor's watershed study, *Primitive Culture* (1871), aptly published in the same year that Darwin's *Descent of Man* appeared—strategically conflated the *biological* development of *Homo sapiens* from animal precursors with the *cultural* development of "civilization" from its "primitive" roots in "prehistoric" human society.

peonage); or generalized cleansing (genocide, naturalized as "selective extinction")—the cannibal plays a special role as that humanlike character who highlights the authentically "human" by being simultaneously its most proximate and most distant "other." A racialized version of the classical anthropophagus (who, like Homer's Cyclops, was represented as living outside the frameworks of law, property, and sociality in a rude state of nature), the modern cannibal bogey anchored and vindicated empire, as can be seen already in a text like Defoe's *Robinson Crusoe* (1719). Defoe's titular hero, thrown by shipwreck into isolation on an island wilderness threatening confidence in his own "humanity," initially recovers self-mastery by subduing animal life in his newfound "kingdom" through hunting, husbandry, and domestication . . . only to have that process interrupted by the ominous appearance of a footprint that potentially dethrones the imperial hero from his perch of singular authority. When this imprint of an alternative form of human existence is revealed to be a trace of cannibal activity, Crusoe eventually reasserts and amplifies his "sovereign" identity by repeating the pattern of animal subjugation with the alien (sub)human figures, killing and dispersing all but one among the cannibal tribes, whom he tames as a kind of hominal servant-pet. Enacting the story of "civilizing mission" upon that lone cannibal survivor, Crusoe names, educates, and converts his newfound "subject" (Friday), who in turn affirms Crusoe's primacy as "master" through a socialized blend of word, gesture, and deed. The cannibal thus is internalized to the operation of colonial domination while remaining outside the pale of proper (British/European) rule: the "unnatural" cannibal naturalizes empire's belated dominion in spaces where a footprint might once have signaled only simple animal or Indigenous presence.

This thematic nexus of animal captivity, racialized otherness, cannibal threat, and castaway crisis is hiding in plain sight on *Moreau*'s early pages, signaling the implication of empire's political history in the narrative's more prominent explorations of evolution and vivisection. For nineteenth-century Europeans living through an age of rapid colonization spurred by the geopolitical ambitions of their newly risen nation-states, the infamous 1816 episode of the French frigate *Medusa*, cited on *Moreau*'s first page, served as instigation and symbol of empire's lurking disturbance.[3] What Prendick calls "the terrible Medusa case" began when the vessel ran aground off the west coast of Africa while on a mission to reestablish a French colonial port. Betrayed by its feckless captain and cowardly officers, nearly 150 passengers and crew sought frantically to save themselves by fashioning a raft from the sinking ship's materials; abandoned to the sea on a fragile and ill-provisioned vessel, all but fifteen of those set adrift on the *Medusa* raft perished, several by what the sensational survivor-memoir by Jean-Baptiste Henry Savigny and Alexandre Corréard called the "extreme resource" of "necessary"

---

3. The most famous maritime tragedy before the *Titanic*, the *Medusa* shipwreck was made vivid to European, especially English, audiences by Théodore Géricault's monumental 1818–19 painting *The Raft of the Medusa* (see illustration on p. 117 above).

cannibalism. Savigny and Corréard's narrative could be taken, therefore, as a tale not only of national degradation (figured in the shipwreck debris scattered at the locus of colonial assertion) but also of self-inflicted dehumanization that ironized the foundational justifications of imperialist rule. If before this period of later empire, cannibalism was represented as always the act of the cultural "other," remaining in writings from Homer to Defoe unthinkable for any proper person lest he himself become a "wretched brute" (as the Roman orator Cicero put it), cannibalism began to be considered in European law and literature potentially permissible under "extreme" conditions warranted by the "necessity" of survival. Savigny and Corréard's plea to their European audience for sympathetic regard—echoed in many other instances of nineteenth-century maritime cannibalism, including cases from which Wells drew in writing the opening scenes of *Moreau*[4]—in effect asks the reader to shift the site of judgment from natural law (in which unvarying repudiation attaches to anthropophagy *as such*) to civic law (in which the state, the engine and embodiment of imperial aspiration, can legislate the exception through which a European's humanity is retained despite cannibalistic acts). Prendick, clinging to his raft, floats between these alternative forms of judgment and value.

DANIEL DEFOE

From Robinson Crusoe[†]

Chapter II. Slavery and Escape

That evil influence which carried me first away from my father's house—which hurried me into the wild and indigested notion of raising my fortune, and that impressed those conceits so forcibly upon me as to make me deaf to all good advice, and to the entreaties and even the commands of my father—I say, the same influence, whatever it was, presented the most unfortunate of all enterprises to my view; and I went on board a vessel bound to the coast of Africa; or, as our sailors vulgarly called it, a voyage to Guinea.[1] * * *

---

4. Winking at maritime cannibalism under duress became common by the late 18th century under what was termed "custom of the sea." In England, defense of "necessity" for cannibalism at sea was legally reversed in an 1884 case involving shipwreck of the English yacht the *Mignonette*, a case that hovers over the early events of *Moreau* in tension with "custom of the sea" doctrine that the *Mignonette* affair had formally abrogated but likely had not pragmatically abolished.

† From *The Life and Adventures of Robinson Crusoe* (New York: American Book Exchange, 1880 [1719]), pp. 12, 29, 31, 33–34, 98–99, 102–03, 106, 108–109, 113–15, 118, 135, 137–42.

1. Country on the west coast of Africa from which many enslaved people were exported by European traders in the 17th and 18th centuries.

Chapter III. Wrecked on a Desert Island

* * * In this course we passed the line in about twelve days' time, and were, by our last observation, in seven degrees twenty-two minutes northern latitude, when a violent tornado, or hurricane, took us quite out of our knowledge. It began from the south-east, came about to the north-west, and then settled in the north-east; from whence it blew in such a terrible manner, that for twelve days together we could do nothing but drive, and, scudding away before it, let it carry us whither fate and the fury of the winds directed; and, during these twelve days, I need not say that I expected every day to be swallowed up; nor, indeed, did any in the ship expect to save their lives. * * *

What the shore was, whether rock or sand, whether steep or shoal, we knew not. * * *

All the remedy that offered to my thoughts at that time was to get up into a thick bushy tree like a fir, but thorny, which grew near me, and where I resolved to sit all night, and consider the next day what death I should die, for as yet I saw no prospect of life. * * * And having cut me a short stick, like a truncheon, for my defence, I took up my lodging; and having been excessively fatigued, I fell fast asleep, and slept as comfortably as, I believe, few could have done in my condition, and found myself more refreshed with it than, I think, I ever was on such an occasion. * * *

*   *   *

Chapter X. Tames Goats

* * * I got over the fence, and laid me down in the shade to rest my limbs, for I was very weary, and fell asleep; but judge you, if you can, that read my story, what a surprise I must be in when I was awaked out of my sleep by a voice calling me by my name several times, "Robin, Robin, Robin Crusoe: poor Robin Crusoe! Where are you, Robin Crusoe? Where are you? Where have you been?"

I was so dead asleep at first, being fatigued with rowing, or part of the day, and with walking the latter part, that I did not wake thoroughly; but dozing thought I dreamed that somebody spoke to me; but as the voice continued to repeat, "Robin Crusoe, Robin Crusoe," at last I began to wake more perfectly, and was at first dreadfully frightened, and started up in the utmost consternation; but no sooner were my eyes open, but I saw my Poll sitting on the top of the hedge; and immediately knew that it was he that spoke to me; for just in such bemoaning language I had used to talk to him and teach him; and he had learned it so perfectly that he would sit upon my finger, and lay his bill close to my face and cry, "Poor Robin

Crusoe! Where are you? Where have you been? How came you here?" and such things as I had taught him.

However, even though I knew it was the parrot, and that indeed it could be nobody else, it was a good while before I could compose myself. First, I was amazed how the creature got thither; and then, how he should just keep about the place, and nowhere else; but as I was well satisfied it could be nobody but honest Poll, I got over it; and holding out my hand, and calling him by his name, "Poll," the sociable creature came to me, and sat upon my thumb, as he used to do, and continued talking to me, "Poor Robin Crusoe! and how did I come here? and where had I been?" just as if he had been overjoyed to see me again; and so I carried him home along with me. * * *

Chapter XI. *Finds Print of Man's Foot on the Sand*

It would have made a Stoic smile to have seen me and my little family sit down to dinner. There was my majesty the prince and lord of the whole island; I had the lives of all my subjects at my absolute command; I could hang, draw, give liberty, and take it away, and no rebels among all my subjects. Then, to see how like a king I dined, too, all alone, attended by my servants! Poll, as if he had been my favorite, was the only person permitted to talk to me. My dog, who was now grown old and crazy, and had found no species to multiply his kind upon, sat always at my right hand; and two cats, one on one side of the table and one on the other, expecting now and then a bit from my hand, as a mark of especial favor.

But these were not the two cats which I brought on shore at first, for they were both of them dead, and had been interred near my habitation by my own hand; but one of them having multiplied by I know not what kind of creature, these were two which I had preserved tame; whereas the rest ran wild in the woods, and became indeed troublesome to me at last, for they would often come into my house, and plunder me too, till at last I was obliged to shoot them, and did kill a great many; at length they left me. With this attendance and in this plentiful manner I lived; neither could I be said to want anything but society; and of that, some time after this, I was likely to have too much. * * *

It happened one day, about noon, going towards my boat, I was exceedingly surprised with the print of a man's naked foot on the shore, which was very plain to be seen on the sand. I stood like one thunderstruck, or as if I had seen an apparition. I listened, I looked round me, but I could hear nothing, nor see anything; I went up to a rising ground to look farther; I went up the shore and down the shore, but it was all one; I could see no other impression but that one. I went to it again to see if there were any more, and to observe if it might not be my fancy; but there was no room for that, for there was exactly the print of a foot—toes, heel, and every part of a foot. How it came thither I knew not, nor could I in the least imagine; but after innumerable fluttering thoughts, like a man perfectly confused and out of myself, I came home to my fortification, not feeling, as we say, the ground I went on, but terrified to the last degree, looking behind me at every two or three steps, mistaking every bush and tree, and fancying every stump at a distance to be a man. Nor is it possible to describe how many various shapes my affrighted imagination represented things to me in, how many wild ideas were found every moment in my fancy, and what strange, unaccountable whimsies came into my thoughts by the way. * * *

How strange a checker-work of Providence is the life of man! and by what secret different springs are the affections hurried about, as different circumstances present! To-day we love what to-morrow we hate; to-day we seek what to-morrow we shun; to-day we desire what to-morrow we fear, nay, even tremble at the apprehensions of. This was exemplified in me, at this time, in the most lively manner imaginable; for I, whose only affliction was that I seemed banished from human society, that I was alone, circumscribed by the boundless ocean, cut off from mankind, and condemned to what I call silent life; that I was as one whom Heaven thought not worthy to be numbered among the living, or to appear among the rest of His creatures; that to have seen one of my own species would have seemed to me a raising me from death to life, and the greatest blessing that Heaven itself, next to the supreme blessing of salvation, could bestow; I say, that I should now tremble at the very apprehensions of seeing a man, and was ready to sink into the ground at but the shadow or silent appearance of a man having set his foot in the island. * * *

In the middle of these cogitations, apprehensions, and reflections, it came into my thoughts one day that all this might be a mere chimera[2] of my own, and that this foot might be the print of my own foot, when I came on shore from my boat: this cheered me up a little, too, and I began to persuade myself it was all a delusion; that it was nothing else but my own foot; and why might I not come that way from the boat, as well as I was going that way to the boat? Again, I considered also that I could by no means tell for certain where I had trod, and where I had not; and that if, at last, this was only the print of my own foot, I had played the part of those fools who try to make stories of spectres and apparitions, and then are frightened at them more than anybody. * * *

2. Illusion.

Chapter XII. A Cave Retreat

But to go on: after I had thus secured one part of my little living stock, I went about the whole island, searching for another private place to make such another deposit; when, wandering more to the west point of the island than I had ever done yet, and looking out to sea, I thought I saw a boat upon the sea, at a great distance. I had found a perspective glass[3] or two in one of the seamen's chests, which I saved out of our ship, but I had it not about me; and this was so remote that I could not tell what to make of it, though I looked at it till my eyes were not able to hold to look any longer; whether it was a boat or not I do not know, but as I descended from the hill I could see no more of it, so I gave it over; only I resolved to go no more out without a perspective glass in my pocket. When I was come down the hill to the end of the island, where, indeed, I had never been before, I was presently convinced that the seeing the print of a man's foot was not such a strange thing in the island as I imagined: and but that it was a special providence that I was cast upon the side of the island where the savages never came, I should easily have known that nothing was more frequent than for the canoes from the main, when they happened to be a little too far out at sea, to shoot over to that side of the island for harbour: likewise, as they often met and fought in their canoes, the victors, having taken any prisoners, would bring them over to this shore, where, according to their dreadful customs, being all cannibals, they would kill and eat them; of which hereafter. * * *

In this frame of thankfulness I went home to my castle, and began to be much easier now, as to the safety of my circumstances, than ever I was before: for I observed that these wretches never came to this island in search of what they could get; perhaps not seeking, not wanting, or not expecting anything here; and having often, no doubt, been up the covered, woody part of it without finding anything to their purpose. I knew I had been here now almost eighteen years, and never saw the least footsteps of human creature there before; and I might be eighteen years more as entirely concealed as I was now, if I did not discover myself to them, which I had no manner of occasion to do; it being my only business to keep myself entirely concealed where I was, unless I found a better sort of creatures than cannibals to make myself known to. Yet I entertained such an abhorrence of the savage wretches that I have been speaking of, and of the wretched, inhuman custom of their devouring and eating one another up, that I continued pensive and sad, and kept close within my own circle for almost two years after this: when I

3. A telescope.

say my own circle, I mean by it my three plantations—viz. my castle, my country seat (which I called my bower), and my enclosure in the woods: nor did I look after this for any other use than an enclosure for my goats; for the aversion which nature gave me to these hellish wretches was such, that I was as fearful of seeing them as of seeing the devil himself. I did not so much as go to look after my boat all this time, but began rather to think of making another; for I could not think of ever making any more attempts to bring the other boat round the island to me, lest I should meet with some of these creatures at sea; in which case, if I had happened to have fallen into their hands, I knew what would have been my lot. * * *

* * * But . . . I began, with cooler and calmer thoughts, to consider what I was going to engage in; what authority or call I had to pretend to be judge and executioner upon these men as criminals, whom Heaven had thought fit for so many ages to suffer unpunished to go on, and to be as it were the executioners of His judgments one upon another; how far these people were offenders against me, and what right I had to engage in the quarrel of that blood which they shed promiscuously upon one another. I debated this very often with myself thus: "How do I know what God Himself judges in this particular case? It is certain these people do not commit this as a crime; it is not against their own consciences reproving, or their light reproaching them; they do not know it to be an offence, and then commit it in defiance of divine justice, as we do in almost all the sins we commit. They think it no more a crime to kill a captive taken in war than we do to kill an ox; or to eat human flesh than we do to eat mutton." * * *

* * *

Chapter XIV. A Dream Realised

* * * I came to reflect seriously upon the real danger I had been in for so many years in this very island, and how I had walked about in the greatest security, and with all possible tranquillity, even when perhaps nothing but the brow of a hill, a great tree, or the casual approach of night, had been between me and the worst kind of destruction, viz., that of falling into the hands of cannibals and savages, who would have seized on me with the same view as I would on a goat or turtle; and have thought it no more crime to kill and devour me than I did of a pigeon or a curlew.[4] I would unjustly slander myself if I should say I was not sincerely thankful to my great Preserver, to whose singular protection I acknowledged, with great humility, all

---

4. Large, long-legged shorebird.

these unknown deliverances were due, and without which I must inevitably have fallen into their merciless hands. * * *

About a year and a half after I entertained these notions (and by long musing had, as it were, resolved them all into nothing, for want of an occasion to put them into execution), I was surprised one morning early by seeing no less than five canoes all on shore together on my side the island, and the people who belonged to them all landed and out of my sight. The number of them broke all my measures; for seeing so many, and knowing that they always came four or six, or sometimes more in a boat, I could not tell what to think of it, or how to take my measures to attack twenty or thirty men single-handed; so lay still in my castle, perplexed and discomforted. However, I put myself into the same position for an attack that I had formerly provided, and was just ready for action, if anything had presented. Having waited a good while, listening to hear if they made any noise, at length, being very impatient, I set my guns at the foot of my ladder, and clambered up to the top of the hill, by my two stages, as usual; standing so, however, that my head did not appear above the hill, so that they could not perceive me by any means. Here I observed, by the help of my perspective-glass, that they were no less than thirty in number; that they had a fire kindled, and that they had meat dressed. How they had cooked it I knew not, or what it was; but they were all dancing, in I know not how many barbarous gestures and figures, their own way, round the fire.

While I was thus looking on them, I perceived, by my perspective, two miserable wretches dragged from the boats, where, it seems, they were laid by, and were now brought out for the slaughter. I perceived one of them immediately fall; being knocked down, I suppose, with a club or wooden sword, for that was their way; and two or three others were at work immediately, cutting him open for their cookery, while the other victim was left standing by himself, till they should be ready for him. In that very moment this poor wretch, seeing himself a little at liberty and unbound, Nature inspired him with hopes of life, and he started away from them, and ran with incredible swiftness along the sands, directly towards me; I mean towards that part of the coast where my habitation was. I was dreadfully frightened, I must acknowledge, when I perceived him run my way. * * * However, I kept my station, and my spirits began to recover when I found that there was not above three men that followed him; and still more was I encouraged when I found that he outstripped them exceedingly in running, and gained ground on them; so that, if he could but hold out for half an hour I saw easily he would fairly get away from them all. * * *

* * * I slowly advanced towards the two that followed; then rushing at once upon the foremost, I knocked him down with the stock

of my piece. I was loath to fire, because I would not have the rest
hear; though, at that distance, it would not have been easily heard,
and being out of sight of the smoke, too, they would not have known
what to make of it. Having knocked this fellow down, the other who
pursued him stopped, as if he had been frightened, and I advanced
towards him: but as I came nearer, I perceived presently he had a
bow and arrow, and was fitting it to shoot at me: so I was then obliged
to shoot at him first, which I did, and killed him at the first shot.
The poor savage who fled, but had stopped, though he saw both his
enemies fallen and killed, as he thought, yet was so frightened with
the fire and noise of my piece that he stood stock still, and neither
came forward nor went backward, though he seemed rather inclined
still to fly than to come on. I hallooed again to him, and made signs
to come forward, which he easily understood, and came a little way;
then stopped again, and then a little farther, and stopped again; and
I could then perceive that he stood trembling, as if he had been taken
prisoner, and had just been to be killed, as his two enemies were. I
beckoned to him again to come to me, and gave him all the signs of
encouragement that I could think of; and he came nearer and nearer,
kneeling down every ten or twelve steps, in token of acknowledgment
for saving his life. I smiled at him, and looked pleasantly, and beckoned to him to come still nearer; at length he came close to me; and
then he kneeled down again, kissed the ground, and laid his head
upon the ground, and taking me by the foot, set my foot upon his
head; this, it seems, was in token of swearing to be my slave for ever.
I took him up and made much of him, and encouraged him all I
could. * * *

* * * In a little time I began to speak to him; and teach him to
speak to me; and first, I let him know his name should be Friday,
which was the day I saved his life; I called him so for the memory of
the time. I likewise taught him to say Master; and then let him know
that was to be my name; I likewise taught him to say Yes and No and
to know the meaning of them. I gave him some milk in an earthen
pot, and let him see me drink it before him, and sop my bread in it;
and gave him a cake of bread to do the like, which he quickly com-
plied with, and made signs that it was very good for him. I kept there
with him all that night; but as soon as it was day I beckoned to him
to come with me, and let him know I would give him some clothes; at
which he seemed very glad, for he was stark naked. * * *

* * * I took my man Friday with me, giving him the sword in his
hand, with the bow and arrows at his back, which I found he could
use very dexterously, making him carry one gun for me, and I two
for myself; and away we marched to the place where these creatures
had been; for I had a mind now to get some fuller intelligence of

them. When I came to the place my very blood ran chill in my veins, and my heart sunk within me, at the horror of the spectacle; indeed, it was a dreadful sight, at least it was so to me, though Friday made nothing of it. The place was covered with human bones, the ground dyed with their blood, and great pieces of flesh left here and there, half eaten, mangled, and scorched; and, in short, all the tokens of the triumphant feast they had been making there, after a victory over their enemies. I saw three skulls, five hands, and the bones of three or four legs and feet, and abundance of other parts of the bodies; and Friday, by his signs, made me understand that they brought over four prisoners to feast upon; that three of them were eaten up, and that he, pointing to himself, was the fourth; that there had been a great battle between them and their next king, of whose subjects, it seems, he had been one, and that they had taken a great number of prisoners; all which were carried to several places by those who had taken them in the fight, in order to feast upon them, as was done here by these wretches upon those they brought hither.

I caused Friday to gather all the skulls, bones, flesh, and whatever remained, and lay them together in a heap, and make a great fire upon it, and burn them all to ashes. I found Friday had still a hankering stomach after some of the flesh, and was still a cannibal in his nature; but I showed so much abhorrence at the very thoughts of it, and at the least appearance of it, that he durst not discover it: for I had, by some means, let him know that I would kill him if he offered it.

J. B. HENRY SAVIGNY AND
ALEXANDRE CORRÉARD

From Narrative of a Voyage to Senegal in 1816[†]

*** COMPRISING AN ACCOUNT OF THE Shipwreck of the Medusa, THE SUFFERINGS OF THE CREW, AND THE VARIOUS OCCURRENCES ON BOARD THE RAFT. *** TO WHICH ARE SUBJOINED OBSERVATIONS RESPECTING THE AGRICULTURE OF THE WESTERN COAST OF AFRICA. ***

[†] From *Narrative of a Voyage to Senegal in 1816*, 2nd ed. (London: Henry Colburn, 1818 [1816]), pp. vii, 1–3, 5, 7, 14, 18, 20–21, 33, 43–44, 49, 55, 60, 72, 76, 82, 84, 88, 91–92, 94, 96–97, 107–13, 118–20, 123–24, 126, 309, 316–18. On the title page of the anonymous 1818 English translation, Corréard's first name appears to have been anglicized to "Alexander," restored here to the historically proper "Alexandre."

Preface

The annals of the marine, record no example of a shipwreck so terrible as that of the Medusa frigate. Two of the unfortunate crew, who have miraculously escaped from the catastrophe, impose upon themselves the painful and delicate task, of describing all the circumstances which attended it. * * *

Introduction

* * * The English made themselves masters in 1758 of the Isle of St. Louis,[1] the seat of the general government of all the settlements which the French have on that part of the coast; we recovered it twenty years after, in 1779 and our possessions were again confirmed to us by the treaty of peace between France and England, concluded on the 3d of September, 1783. In 1808, our possessions fell again into the power of the English, less by the superiority of their arms, than by the treachery of some individuals unworthy of bearing the name of Frenchmen. They were finally restored to us by the treaties of peace of 1814, and 1815, which confirmed that of 1783 in its whole extent. * * *

The rights of the two nations being thus regulated, France thought of resuming her possessions and the enjoyment of her rights. The minister of the marine after having long meditated, and taken two years to prepare an expedition of four vessels, at last gave orders that it should sail for Senegal.

This expedition consisted therefore of 365 persons, of whom about 240 were embarked on board the *Medusa* frigate.

Narrative, &c. &c.

On the 17th of June, 1816, at seven in the morning, the expedition for Senegal sailed from the roads of the Island of Aix,[2] under the command of Captain Chaumareys. * * *

The next morning at day break we saw very distinctly the islands of Madeira Porto Santo. * * * The hills are covered with vineyards, bordered with banian trees:[3] in short every thing is combined to render Madeira one of the most beautiful islands of Africa. * * *

---

1. French colonial settlement at the mouth of the Senegal River, founded in 1659.
2. Island off the French west coast.
3. Wetland trees with branches that hang downward and grow new trunks. *Madeira Porto Santo*: Atlantic archipelago west of Africa.

Having doubled a point which extends into the sea, we entered the bay, at the bottom of which is the town of St. Croix.[4] The appearance of Teneriffe is majestic: the whole island is composed of mountains, which are extremely high, and crowned with rocks terrifying from their size, which on the north side, seem to rise perpendicularly above the surface of the ocean. * * *

The depravity of morals at St. Croix is extreme; so much so that when the women heard that some Frenchmen were arrived in the town, they placed themselves at their doors, and when they passed, urged them to enter. All this is usually done in the presence of the husbands, who have no right to oppose it, because the Holy Inquisition will have it so, and because the monks who are very numerous in the island take care that this custom is observed. They possess the art of blinding the husbands, by means of the *prestiges*[5] of religion, which they abuse in the highest degree. * * * These abuses are almost inevitable in a burning climate, where the passion of love is often stronger than reason, and sometimes breaks through the barriers which religion attempts to oppose to it: this depravity of morals must therefore be attributed to inflamed passions, and not to abuses facilitated by a religion so sublime as ours. * * *

We stranded on the 2d of July, at a quarter after three p.m. in 19° 36' north latitude, and 19° 45' west longitude. * * *

At night the sky became cloudy, the winds came from the sea, and blew violently. The sea ran high, and the frigate began to heel with more and more violence, every moment we expected to see her bulge; consternation again spread, and we soon felt the cruel certainty that she was irrecoverably lost. * * *

The raft, impelled by the strength of the current and of the sea, broke the cable which fastened it to the frigate and began to drive; those who beheld this accident announced it by their cries, and a boat was immediately sent after it, which brought it back. * * *

Though in so terrible a situation, on our fatal raft, we cast our eyes upon the frigate, and deeply regretted this fine vessel, which, a few days before, seemed to command the waves, which it cut through with astonishing rapidity. * * *

As soon as all the boats had taken their post, cries of *"Vive le Roi!"*[6] were a thousand times repeated by the men upon the raft, and a little white flag was hoisted at the top of a musket. * * * The chiefs

---

4. Better known as Santa Cruz de Tenerife, a Spanish colonial outpost in the Canary Islands, opposite the northwestern coast of Africa; a jagged mountain ridge of volcanic origin can be seen from the city.
5. Delusions; enchantments (French).
6. "Long live the king!" (French), a proclamation of loyalty to the French state, which had returned to monarchy in 1814 following the French Revolution and its Napoleonic aftermath.

of the little division which was to conduct us to the land, had sworn not to abandon us: we are far from accusing all those gentlemen of having violated the laws of honor; but a series of circumstances obliged them to renounce the generous plan which they had formed to save us, or to perish with us. * * *

* * * At the moment that we were putting off, from the frigate, a bag with twenty-five pounds of biscuit was thrown us, which fell into the sea; we got it up with difficulty; it was converted into a paste, but we preserved it in that condition. Several considerate persons fastened the casks of wine and water to the cross pieces of the raft, and we kept a strict watch over them. Thus we have faithfully described the nature of our situation when we put off from the vessel. * * *

After the disappearance of the boats, the consternation was extreme. * * *

An order, according to numbers, was fixed for the distribution of our miserable provisions. The ration of wine was fixed at three quarters a day: we shall say no more of the biscuit: the first distribution consumed it entirely. The day passed over pretty quietly: we conversed on the means which we should employ to save ourselves; we spoke of it as a certainty, which animated our courage: and we kept up that of the soldiers, by cherishing the hope of being soon able to revenge ourselves upon those who had so basely abandoned us. This hope of vengeance inspired us all equally, and we uttered a thousand imprecations against those who had left us a prey to so many misfortunes and dangers. * * *

* * * Two young lads, and a baker, did not fear to seek death, by throwing themselves into the sea, after having taken leave of their companions in misfortune. Already the faculties of our men were singularly impaired; some fancied they saw the land; others, vessels which were coming to save us; all announced to us by their cries these fallacious visions. * * *

The soldiers and sailors, terrified by the presence of an almost inevitable danger, gave themselves up for lost. Firmly believing that they were going to be swallowed up, they resolved to soothe their last moments by drinking till they lost the use of their reason. * * *

* * * Thus inflamed, these men, become deaf to the voice of reason, desired to implicate, in one common destruction, their companions in misfortune; they openly expressed their intention to rid themselves of the officers, who they said, wished to oppose their design, and then to destroy the raft by cutting the ropes which united the different parts that composed it. * * * The workmen did their utmost to stop them, by presenting the point of their sabres. * * *

The mutineers being repulsed, * * * left us at this moment a little repose. * * *

* * * [A] man and his wife, who just before had seen themselves attacked with sabres and bayonets, and thrown at the same moment into the waves of a stormy sea, could hardly believe their senses when they found themselves in each other's arms. * * *

* * * The idea of owing her life to Frenchmen, at this moment, seemed still to add to her happiness. Unfortunate woman! she did not foresee the dreadful fate that awaited her among us! Let us return to our raft. * * *

Thinking that order was restored, we had returned to our post at the center of the raft, only we took the precaution to retain our arms. It was nearly midnight: after an hour's apparent tranquillity, the soldiers rose again: their senses were entirely deranged; they rushed upon us like madmen, with their knives or sabres in their hands. As they were in full possession of their bodily strength, and were also armed, we were forced again to put ourselves on our defence. Their revolt was the more dangerous, as in their delirium they were entirely deaf to the cries of reason. They attacked us; we charged them in our turn, and soon the raft was covered with their dead bodies. * * *

* * * For forty-eight hours we had taken nothing, and had been obliged to struggle incessantly against a stormy sea; like them we could hardly support ourselves; courage alone still made us act. We resolved to employ all possible means to procure fish. We collected all the tags from the soldiers, and made little hooks of them; we bent a bayonet to catch sharks: all this availed us nothing; the currents carried our hooks under the raft, where they got entangled. A shark bit at the bayonet, and straightened it. We gave up our project. But an extreme resource was necessary to preserve our wretched existence. We tremble with horror at being obliged to mention that which we made use of! we feel our pen drop from our hand; a death-like chill pervades all our limbs; our hair stands erect on our heads!—Reader, we beseech you, do not feel indignation towards men who are already too unfortunate; but have compassion on them, and shed some tears of pity on their unhappy fate.

Those whom death had spared in the disastrous night which we have just described, fell upon the dead bodies with which the raft was covered, and cut off pieces, which some instantly devoured. Many did not touch them; almost all the officers were of this number. Seeing that this horrid nourishment had given strength to those who had made use of it, it was proposed to dry it, in order to render it a little less disgusting. Those who had firmness enough to abstain from it took a larger quantity of wine. We tried to eat sword-belts and cartouch-boxes.[7] We succeeded in swallowing some little morsels.

7. Leather cartridge boxes.

Some eat linen. Others pieces of leather from the hats, on which there was a little grease, or rather dirt. We were obliged to give up these last means. A sailor attempted to eat excrements, but he could not succeed.

* * * The fourth morning's sun, after our departure, at length rose on our disaster, and shewed us ten or twelve of our companions extended lifeless on the rail. This sight affected us the more as it announced to us that our bodies, deprived of existence, would soon be stretched on the same place. We gave their bodies to the sea for a grave; reserving only one, destined to feed those who, the day before, had clasped his trembling hands, vowing him an eternal friendship. * * * A circumstance occurred which afforded us some consolation: a shoal of flying fish passed under the raft, and as the extremities left an infinite number of vacancies between the pieces which composed it, the fish got entangled in great numbers. We threw ourselves upon them, and caught a considerable quantity. * * *

* * * We dressed some fish, which we devoured with extreme avidity; but our hunger was so great and our portion of fish so small, that we added to it some human flesh, which dressing rendered less disgusting. * * * This repast gave us all fresh strength to bear new fatigues. The night was tolerable, and would have appeared happy had it not been signalised by a new massacre.

Some Spaniards, Italians, and Negroes, who had remained neuter in the first mutiny, and some of whom had even ranged themselves on our side, formed a plot to throw us all into the sea, hoping to execute their design by falling on us by surprise. These wretches suffered themselves to be persuaded by the negroes, who assured them that the coast was extremely near, and promised, that when they were once on shore, they would enable them to traverse Africa without danger. * * * The mutineers rushed forward to avenge their comrades, a terrible combat again ensued, and both sides fought with desperate fury. Soon the fatal raft was covered with dead bodies, and flowing with blood which ought to have been shed in another cause, and by other hands. * * *

We were now only twenty-seven remaining; of this number but fifteen seemed likely to live some days: all the rest, covered with large wounds, had almost entirely lost their reason; yet they had a share in the distribution of provisions, and might, before their death, consume thirty or forty bottles of wine, which were of inestimable value to us. We deliberated thus: to put the sick on half allowance would have been killing them by inches. So after a debate, at which the most dreadful despair presided, it was resolved to throw them into the sea. This measure, however repugnant it was to ourselves, procured the survivors wine for six days; when the decision was made, who would dare to execute it? The habit of seeing death ready to pounce upon us as his prey, the certainty of our infallible destruction, without this fatal expedient, every thing in a word, had hardened our hearts, and rendered them callous to all feeling except that of self preservation. Three sailors and a soldier took on themselves this cruel execution: we turned our faces aside, and wept tears of blood over the fate of these unhappy men. Among them were the unfortunate woman and her husband. * * *

* * * Readers, who shudder at the cry of outraged humanity, recollect at least, that it was other men, fellow countrymen, comrades, who had placed us in this horrible situation. * * *

* * * We resolved to await death in a manner worthy of Frenchmen, and with perfect resignation.

* * * Several of us regretted not having fallen in the defence of France. At least, said they, if it had been possible for us to measure our strength once more, with the enemies of our independence, and our liberty! Others found some consolation in the death which awaited us, because we should no longer have to groan under the shameful yoke which oppresses the country. Thus passed the last days of our abode on the raft. Our time was almost wholly employed in speaking of our unhappy country: all our wishes, our last prayers were for the happiness of France. * * *

* * *

We shall not have the presumption to lay down plans, to propose systems, to enforce such or such means for putting them in execution. We shall merely terminate our task by some general considerations calculated to confirm what numerous and able observers have already thought, of the importance of the establishments in Africa, and of the necessity of adopting some general plan of colonisation for these countries. * * *

He who desires the end, desires the means of attaining it. The end at present, should be to prepare every thing beforehand, and rather sooner than later, in order to repair in Africa the past losses and disasters, which irremediable events have caused in the Western Colonies, and to substitute for their riches their prosperity, the progressive decline of which is henceforward inevitable, new elements of wealth and prosperity: the means will be to carry into these countries, so long desolated by our relentless avarice, knowledge, cultivation, and industry. By these means we shall see in that vast continent numerous colonies arise, which will restore to the mother country all the splendour, all the advantages of her ancient commerce, and repay her with interest for the sacrifices she may have made in the new world. But to effect this, let there be no more secret enterprises; no more connivance at fraudulent traffic, no more unhappy negroes snatched away from their families; no more tears shed on that sad African soil, so long the witness of so many afflictions; no more human victims, dragged to the altars of the shameful, and insatiable divinities, which have already devoured such numbers: consequently, let there be no more grounds for hearing in the English Parliament, voices boldly impeaching our good faith, attacking the national honour, and positively asserting that France maintains in her African possessions, the system of the slave trade in the same manner as she did before she consented to its abolition.[8]

Africa offers to our speculators, to the enterprises of our industry, a virgin soil, and an inexhaustible population peculiarly fitted to render it productive. It must be our business to form them according to our views, by associating them in these by a common interest. In conquering them by benefits, instead of subjugating them by crimes, or degrading them by corruption, let us lead them to social order and to happiness, by our moral superiority, instead of dragging them under scourges and chains to misery and death, we shall then have accomplished a useful and a glorious enterprise; we shall have raised our commercial prosperity on the greatest interest of those who have been the voluntary instruments of it, and above all, we shall have expiated, by an immense benefit, this immense crime of the outrages, with which we so long afflicted humanity.

RUDYARD KIPLING

The Mark of the Beast[†][1]

> Your Gods and my Gods—do you or I know which are the stronger?
>
> Native Proverb.

East of Suez,[2] some hold, the direct control of Providence ceases; Man being there handed over to the power of the Gods and Devils of Asia, and the Church of England Providence only exercising an occasional and modified supervision in the case of Englishmen.

---

8. Abolished in the French constitution of 1795, slavery was reintroduced in the French colonies in 1802 by Napoleon, who then abolished the slave trade in 1815.
† From *Pioneer* 9156 (July 12, 1890), 9157 (July 14, 1890).
1. Cf. Revelation 13ff. and note 8 on pp. 34–35.
2. Seaport in northeastern Egypt, near the end of the Suez Canal just south of the Red Sea.

This theory accounts for some of the more unnecessary horrors of life in India: it may be stretched to explain my story.

My friend Strickland of the Police, who knows as much of natives of India as is good for any man, can bear witness to the facts of the case. Dumoise, our doctor, also saw what Strickland and I saw. The inference which he drew from the evidence was entirely incorrect. He is dead now; he died, in a rather curious manner, which has been elsewhere described.

When Fleete came to India he owned a little money and some land in the Himalayas, near a place called Dharmsala.[3] Both properties had been left him by an uncle, and he came out to finance them. He was a big, heavy, genial, and inoffensive man. His knowledge of natives was, of course, limited, and he complained of the difficulties of the language.

He rode in from his place in the hills to spend New Year in the station, and he stayed with Strickland. On New Year's Eve there was a big dinner at the club, and the night was excusably wet.[4] When men foregather from the uttermost ends of the Empire, they have a right to be riotous. The Frontier had sent down a contingent o' Catch-'em-Alive-O's who had not seen twenty white faces for a year, and were used to ride fifteen miles to dinner at the next Fort at the risk of a Khyberee bullet[5] where their drinks should lie. They profited by their new security, for they tried to play pool with a curled-up hedgehog found in the garden, and one of them carried the marker round the room in his teeth. Half a dozen planters had come in from the south and were talking 'horse'[6] to the Biggest Liar in Asia, who was trying to cap all their stories at once. Everybody was there, and there was a general closing up of ranks and taking stock of our losses in dead or disabled that had fallen during the past year. It was a very wet night, and I remember that we sang 'Auld Lang Syne' with our feet in the Polo Championship Cup, and our heads among the stars, and swore that we were all dear friends. Then some of us went away and annexed Burma, and some tried to open up the Soudan and were opened up by Fuzzies in that cruel scrub outside Suakim,[7] and some found stars and medals, and some were married,

---

3. Indian city in the northern province of Himachal Pradesh, where the British established a station, or military base, in 1848 as part of the Kangra District of the Raj, or Empire.
4. Alcohol-drenched.
5. Gunshot fired by rebel from the Kyber District of Pakistan. *The Frontier*: British regiment stationed in the northwest of India. *Catch-'em-Alive-O's*: regiment nickname (from vernacular phrase for "fly-trappers," here applied to a group of callow, foolhardy soldiers).
6. Grandstanding (English slang).
7. Sudanese seaport on the west coast of the Red Sea, also known as Suakin (the Suakin Expeditions of 1884 and 1885 were efforts by the British—aided by Beja warriors

which was bad, and some did other things which were worse, and the others of us stayed in our chains and strove to make money on insufficient experiences.

Fleete began the night with sherry and bitters, drank champagne steadily up to dessert, then raw, rasping Capri with all the strength of whisky, took Benedictine with his coffee, four or five whiskies and sodas to improve his pool strokes, beer and bones[8] at half-past two, winding up with old brandy. Consequently, when he came out, at half-past three in the morning, into fourteen degrees of frost, he was very angry with his horse for coughing, and tried to leapfrog into the saddle. The horse broke away and went to his stables; so Strickland and I formed a Guard of Dishonour to take Fleete home.

Our road lay through the bazaar, close to a little temple of Hanuman,[9] the Monkey-god, who is a leading divinity worthy of respect. All gods have good points, just as have all priests. Personally, I attach much importance to Hanuman, and am kind to his people—the great gray apes of the hills. One never knows when one may want a friend.

There was a light in the temple, and as we passed, we could hear voices of men chanting hymns. In a native temple, the priests rise at all hours of the night to do honour to their god. Before we could stop him, Fleete dashed up the steps, patted two priests on the back, and was gravely grinding the ashes of his cigar-butt into the forehead of the red stone image of Hanuman. Strickland tried to drag him out, but he sat down and said solemnly:

'Shee that? Mark of the B-beasht! I made it. Ishn't it fine?'

In half a minute the temple was alive and noisy, and Strickland, who knew what came of polluting gods, said that things might occur. He, by virtue of his official position, long residence in the country, and weakness for going among the natives, was known to the priests and he felt unhappy. Fleete sat on the ground and refused to move. He said that 'good old Hanuman' made a very soft pillow.

Then, without any warning, a Silver Man came out of a recess behind the image of the god. He was perfectly naked in that bitter, bitter cold, and his body shone like frosted silver, for he was what the Bible calls 'a leper as white as snow.'[1] Also he had no face,

nicknamed "Fuzzy-Wuzzies" after their crownlike, or *tiffa*, hairstyle—to destroy the Sudanese military). *Annexed Burma*: In 1886, the British added Upper Burma (known today as Myanmar) to the Raj, having already incorporated Lower Burma at the start of the Raj in 1858.

8. Ale. *Bitters*: herbal alcohol. *Benedictine*; *Capri*: liquors.
9. Hindu god, featured in the epic *Ramayana*.
1. See Exodus 4:6, Numbers 12:10, and 2 Kings 5:27. *A Silver Man*: victim of leprosy, or "leper"; so called here possibly because of the white appearance of lesions as sensation is lost in the affected skin.

because he was a leper of some years' standing and his disease was heavy upon him. We two stooped to haul Fleete up, and the temple was filling and filling with folk who seemed to spring from the earth, when the Silver Man ran in under our arms, making a noise exactly like the mewing of an otter, caught Fleete round the body and dropped his head on Fleete's breast before we could wrench him away. Then he retired to a corner and sat mewing while the crowd blocked all the doors.

The priests were very angry until the Silver Man touched Fleete. That nuzzling seemed to sober them.

At the end of a few minutes' silence one of the priests came to Strickland and said, in perfect English, 'Take your friend away. He has done with Hanuman, but Hanuman has not done with him.' The crowd gave room and we carried Fleete into the road.

Strickland was very angry. He said that we might all three have been knifed, and that Fleete should thank his stars that he had escaped without injury.

Fleete thanked no one. He said that he wanted to go to bed. He was gorgeously drunk.

We moved on, Strickland silent and wrathful, until Fleete was taken with violent shivering fits and sweating. He said that the smells of the bazaar were overpowering, and he wondered why slaughter-houses were permitted so near English residences. 'Can't you smell the blood?' said Fleete.

We put him to bed at last, just as the dawn was breaking, and Strickland invited me to have another whisky and soda. While we were drinking he talked of the trouble in the temple, and admitted that it baffled him completely. Strickland hates being mystified by natives, because his business in life is to overmatch them with their own weapons. He has not yet succeeded in doing this, but in fifteen or twenty years he will have made some small progress.

'They should have mauled us,' he said, 'instead of mewing at us. I wonder what they meant. I don't like it one little bit.'

I said that the Managing Committee of the temple would in all probability bring a criminal action against us for insulting their religion. There was a section of the Indian Penal Code[2] which exactly met Fleete's offence. Strickland said he only hoped and prayed that they would do this. Before I left I looked into Fleete's room, and saw him lying on his right side, scratching his left breast. Then I went to bed cold, depressed, and unhappy, at seven o'clock in the morning.

---

2. Criminal legal code crafted by British administrators of the Raj and put into force in 1862.

At one o'clock I rode over to Strickland's house to inquire after Fleete's head. I imagined that it would be a sore one. Fleete was breakfasting and seemed unwell. His temper was gone, for he was abusing the cook for not supplying him with an underdone chop. A man who can eat raw meat after a wet night is a curiosity. I told Fleete this and he laughed.

'You breed queer mosquitoes in these parts,' he said. 'I've been bitten to pieces, but only in one place.'

'Let's have a look at the bite,' said Strickland. 'It may have gone down since this morning.'

While the chops were being cooked, Fleete opened his shirt and showed us, just over his left breast, a mark, the perfect double of the black rosettes[3]—the five or six irregular blotches arranged in a circle—on a leopard's hide. Strickland looked and said, 'It was only pink this morning. It's grown black now.'

Fleete ran to a glass.

'By Jove!' he said, 'this is nasty. What is it?'

We could not answer. Here the chops came in, all red and juicy, and Fleete bolted[4] three in a most offensive manner. He ate on his right grinders only, and threw his head over his right shoulder as he snapped the meat. When he had finished, it struck him that he had been behaving strangely, for he said apologetically, 'I don't think I ever felt so hungry in my life. I've bolted like an ostrich.'[5]

After breakfast Strickland said to me, 'Don't go. Stay here, and stay for the night.'

Seeing that my house was not three miles from Strickland's, this request was absurd. But Strickland insisted, and was going to say something when Fleete interrupted by declaring in a shamefaced way that he felt hungry again. Strickland sent a man to my house to fetch over my bedding and a horse, and we three went down to Strickland's stables to pass the hours until it was time to go out for a ride. The man who has a weakness for horses never wearies of inspecting them; and when two men are killing time in this way they gather knowledge and lies the one from the other.

There were five horses in the stables, and I shall never forget the scene as we tried to look them over. They seemed to have gone mad. They reared and screamed and nearly tore up their pickets;[6] they sweated and shivered and lathered and were distraught with fear. Strickland's horses used to know him as well as his dogs; which made the matter more curious. We left the stable for fear of the brutes throwing themselves in their panic. Then Strickland

3. Pleated ornament resembling a rose; used to describe groups of leopard spots.
4. Gorged.
5. I.e., swallowed without chewing.
6. System of ropes and pins used to corral horses or mules.

turned back and called me. The horses were still frightened, but they let us 'gentle' and make much of them, and put their heads in our bosoms.

'They aren't afraid of us,' said Strickland. 'D'you know, I'd give three months' pay if Outrage here could talk.'

But Outrage was dumb, and could only cuddle up to his master and blow out his nostrils, as is the custom of horses when they wish to explain things but can't. Fleete came up when we were in the stalls, and as soon as the horses saw him, their fright broke out afresh. It was all that we could do to escape from the place unkicked. Strickland said, 'They don't seem to love you, Fleete.'

'Nonsense,' said Fleete; 'my mare will follow me like a dog.' He went to her; she was in a loose-box;[7] but as he slipped the bars she plunged, knocked him down, and broke away into the garden. I laughed, but Strickland was not amused. He took his moustache in both fists and pulled at it till it nearly came out. Fleete, instead of going off to chase his property, yawned, saying that he felt sleepy. He went to the house to lie down, which was a foolish way of spending New Year's Day.

Strickland sat with me in the stables and asked if I had noticed anything peculiar in Fleete's manner. I said that he ate his food like a beast; but that this might have been the result of living alone in the hills out of the reach of society as refined and elevating as ours for instance. Strickland was not amused. I do not think that he listened to me, for his next sentence referred to the mark on Fleete's breast, and I said that it might have been caused by blister-flies, or that it was possibly a birth-mark newly born and now visible for the first time. We both agreed that it was unpleasant to look at, and Strickland found occasion to say that I was a fool.

'I can't tell you what I think now,' said he, 'because you would call me a madman; but you must stay with me for the next few days, if you can. I want you to watch Fleete, but don't tell me what you think till I have made up my mind.'

'But I am dining out to-night,' I said. 'So am I,' said Strickland, 'and so is Fleete. At least if he doesn't change his mind.'

We walked about the garden smoking, but saying nothing—because we were friends, and talking spoils good tobacco—till our pipes were out. Then we went to wake up Fleete. He was wide awake and fidgeting about his room.

'I say, I want some more chops,' he said. 'Can I get them?'

We laughed and said, 'Go and change. The ponies will be round in a minute.'

7. Stall.

'All right,' said Fleete. 'I'll go when I get the chops—underdone ones, mind.'

He seemed to be quite in earnest. It was four o'clock, and we had had breakfast at one; still, for a long time, he demanded those underdone chops. Then he changed into riding clothes and went out into the verandah. His pony—the mare had not been caught—would not let him come near. All three horses were unmanageable—mad with fear—and finally Fleete said that he would stay at home and get something to eat. Strickland and I rode out wondering. As we passed the temple of Hanuman, the Silver Man came out and mewed at us.

'He is not one of the regular priests of the temple,' said Strickland. 'I think I should peculiarly like to lay my hands on him.'

There was no spring in our gallop on the racecourse that evening. The horses were stale, and moved as though they had been ridden out.

'The fright after breakfast has been too much for them,' said Strickland.

That was the only remark he made through the remainder of the ride. Once or twice I think he swore to himself; but that did not count.

We came back in the dark at seven o'clock, and saw that there were no lights in the bungalow. 'Careless ruffians my servants are!' said Strickland.

My horse reared at something on the carriage drive, and Fleete stood up under its nose.

'What are you doing, grovelling about the garden?' said Strickland.

But both horses bolted and nearly threw us. We dismounted by the stables and returned to Fleete, who was on his hands and knees under the orange-bushes.

'What the devil's wrong with you?' said Strickland.

'Nothing, nothing in the world,' said Fleete, speaking very quickly and thickly. 'I've been gardening—botanising you know. The smell of the earth is delightful. I think I'm going for a walk—a long walk—all night.'

Then I saw that there was something excessively out of order somewhere, and I said to Strickland, 'I am not dining out.'

'Bless you!' said Strickland. 'Here, Fleete, get up. You'll catch fever there. Come in to dinner and let's have the lamps lit. We'll all dine at home.'

Fleete stood up unwillingly, and said, 'No lamps—no lamps. It's much nicer here. Let's dine outside and have some more chops—lots of 'em and underdone—bloody ones with gristle.'

Now a December evening in Northern India is bitterly cold, and Fleete's suggestion was that of a maniac.

'Come in,' said Strickland sternly. 'Come in at once.'

Fleete came, and when the lamps were brought, we saw that he was literally plastered with dirt from head to foot. He must have been rolling in the garden. He shrank from the light and went to his room. His eyes were horrible to look at. There was a green light behind them, not in them, if you understand, and the man's lower lip hung down.

Strickland said, 'There is going to be trouble—big trouble—to-night. Don't you change your riding-things.'

We waited and waited for Fleete's reappearance, and ordered dinner in the meantime. We could hear him moving about his own room, but there was no light there. Presently from the room came the long-drawn howl of a wolf.

People write and talk lightly of blood running cold and hair standing up and things of that kind. Both sensations are too horrible to be trifled with. My heart stopped as though a knife had been driven through it, and Strickland turned as white as the tablecloth.

The howl was repeated, and was answered by another howl far across the fields.

That set the gilded roof on the horror. Strickland dashed into Fleete's room. I followed, and we saw Fleete getting out of the window. He made beast-noises in the back of his throat. He could not answer us when we shouted at him. He spat.

I don't quite remember what followed, but I think that Strickland must have stunned him with the long boot-jack[8] or else I should never have been able to sit on his chest. Fleete could not speak, he could only snarl, and his snarls were those of a wolf, not of a man. The human spirit must have been giving way all day and have died out with the twilight. We were dealing with a beast that had once been Fleete.

The affair was beyond any human and rational experience. I tried to say 'Hydrophobia,'[9] but the word wouldn't come, because I knew that I was lying.

We bound this beast with leather thongs of the punkah-rope,[1] and tied its thumbs and big toes together, and gagged it with a shoe-horn, which makes a very efficient gag if you know how to arrange it. Then we carried it into the dining-room, and sent a man to Dumoise, the doctor, telling him to come over at once. After we had despatched the messenger and were drawing breath, Strickland said, 'It's no good. This isn't any doctor's work.' I, also, knew that he spoke the truth.

8. Device used for removing boots.
9. Rabies.
1. Cord extending from a ceiling-mounted linen fan, or *punkah*.

The beast's head was free, and it threw it about from side to side. Any one entering the room would have believed that we were curing a wolf's pelt. That was the most loathsome accessory of all.

Strickland sat with his chin in the heel of his fist, watching the beast as it wriggled on the ground, but saying nothing. The shirt had been torn open in the scuffle and showed the black rosette mark on the left breast. It stood out like a blister.

In the silence of the watching we heard something without mewing like a she-otter. We both rose to our feet, and, I answer for myself, not Strickland, felt sick—actually and physically sick. We told each other, as did the men in Pinafore, that it was the cat.[2]

Dumoise arrived, and I never saw a little man so unprofessionally shocked. He said that it was a heart-rending case of hydrophobia, and that nothing could be done. At least any palliative measures would only prolong the agony. The beast was foaming at the mouth. Fleete, as we told Dumoise, had been bitten by dogs once or twice. Any man who keeps half a dozen terriers must expect a nip now and again. Dumoise could offer no help. He could only certify that Fleete was dying of hydrophobia. The beast was then howling, for it had managed to spit out the shoe-horn. Dumoise said that he would be ready to certify to the cause of death, and that the end was certain. He was a good little man, and he offered to remain with us; but Strickland refused the kindness. He did not wish to poison Dumoise's New Year. He would only ask him not to give the real cause of Fleete's death to the public.

So Dumoise left, deeply agitated; and as soon as the noise of the cart-wheels had died away, Strickland told me, in a whisper, his suspicions. They were so wildly improbable that he dared not say them out aloud; and I, who entertained all Strickland's beliefs, was so ashamed of owning to them that I pretended to disbelieve.

'Even if the Silver Man had bewitched Fleete for polluting the image of Hanuman, the punishment could not have fallen so quickly.'

As I was whispering this the cry outside the house rose again, and the beast fell into a fresh paroxysm of struggling till we were afraid that the thongs that held it would give way.

'Watch!' said Strickland. 'If this happens six times I shall take the law into my own hands. I order you to help me.'

He went into his room and came out in a few minutes with the barrels of an old shot-gun, a piece of fishing-line, some thick cord, and his heavy wooden bedstead. I reported that the convulsions had

2. Line from "Carefully on Tiptoe Stealing," a song in the 1878 comic opera *H.M.S. Pinafore* by English composer Arthur Sullivan (1842–1900) and English librettist W. S. Gilbert (1836–1911): "Goodness me—/ Why, what was that? / Silent be, / It was the cat!"

followed the cry by two seconds in each case, and the beast seemed perceptibly weaker.

Strickland muttered, 'But he can't take away the life! He can't take away the life!'

I said, though I knew that I was arguing against myself, 'It may be a cat. It must be a cat. If the Silver Man is responsible, why does he dare to come here?'

Strickland arranged the wood on the hearth, put the gun-barrels into the glow of the fire, spread the twine on the table and broke a walking stick in two. There was one yard of fishing line, gut, lapped with wire, such as is used for mahseer[3]-fishing, and he tied the two ends together in a loop.

Then he said, 'How can we catch him? He must be taken alive and unhurt.'

I said that we must trust in Providence, and go out softly with polo-sticks into the shrubbery at the front of the house. The man or animal that made the cry was evidently moving round the house as regularly as a night-watchman. We could wait in the bushes till he came by and knock him over.

Strickland accepted this suggestion, and we slipped out from a bath-room window into the front verandah and then across the carriage drive into the bushes.

In the moonlight we could see the leper coming round the corner of the house. He was perfectly naked, and from time to time he mewed and stopped to dance with his shadow. It was an unattractive sight, and thinking of poor Fleete, brought to such degradation by so foul a creature, I put away all my doubts and resolved to help Strickland from the heated gun-barrels to the loop of twine—from the loins to the head and back again—with all tortures that might be needful.

The leper halted in the front porch for a moment and we jumped out on him with the sticks. He was wonderfully strong, and we were afraid that he might escape or be fatally injured before we caught him. We had an idea that lepers were frail creatures, but this proved to be incorrect. Strickland knocked his legs from under him and I put my foot on his neck. He mewed hideously, and even through my riding-boots I could feel that his flesh was not the flesh of a clean man.

He struck at us with his hand and feet-stumps. We looped the lash of a dog-whip round him, under the armpits, and dragged him backwards into the hall and so into the dining-room where the beast lay. There we tied him with trunk-straps. He made no attempt to escape, but mewed.

When we confronted him with the beast the scene was beyond description. The beast doubled backwards into a bow as though he

3. Game fish common in south and southeast Asia.

had been poisoned with strychnine,[4] and moaned in the most piti-
able fashion. Several other things happened also, but they cannot
be put down here.

'I think I was right,' said Strickland. 'Now we will ask him to cure
this case.'

But the leper only mewed. Strickland wrapped a towel round his
hand and took the gun-barrels out of the fire. I put the half of the
broken walking stick through the loop of fishing-line and buckled
the leper comfortably to Strickland's bedstead. I understood then
how men and women and little children can endure to see a witch
burnt alive; for the beast was moaning on the floor, and though the
Silver Man had no face, you could see horrible feelings passing
through the slab that took its place, exactly as waves of heat play
across red-hot iron—gun-barrels for instance.

Strickland shaded his eyes with his hands for a moment and we
got to work. This part is not to be printed.

The dawn was beginning to break when the leper spoke. His
mewings had not been satisfactory up to that point. The beast had
fainted from exhaustion and the house was very still. We unstrapped
the leper and told him to take away the evil spirit. He crawled to
the beast and laid his hand upon the left breast. That was all.
Then he fell face down and whined, drawing in his breath as he
did so.

We watched the face of the beast, and saw the soul of Fleete coming back into the eyes. Then a sweat broke out on the forehead and
the eyes—they were human eyes—closed. We waited for an hour
but Fleete still slept. We carried him to his room and bade the leper
go, giving him the bedstead, and the sheet on the bedstead to cover
his nakedness, the gloves and the towels with which we had touched
him, and the whip that had been hooked round his body. He put the
sheet about him and went out into the early morning without speaking or mewing.

Strickland wiped his face and sat down. A night-gong, far away in
the city, made seven o'clock.

'Exactly four-and-twenty hours!' said Strickland. 'And I've done
enough to ensure my dismissal from the service, besides permanent
quarters in a lunatic asylum. Do you believe that we are awake?'

The red-hot gun-barrel had fallen on the floor and was singeing
the carpet. The smell was entirely real.

That morning at eleven we two together went to wake up Fleete.
We looked and saw that the black leopard-rosette on his chest had
disappeared. He was very drowsy and tired, but as soon as he saw

---

4. Toxic alkaloid, typically used as a pesticide and, in small doses, medicinally.

us, he said, 'Oh! Confound you fellows. Happy New Year to you. Never mix your liquors. I'm nearly dead.'

'Thanks for your kindness, but you're over time,' said Strickland. 'To-day is the morning of the second. You've slept the clock round with a vengeance.'

The door opened, and little Dumoise put his head in. He had come on foot, and fancied that we were laying out Fleete.

'I've brought a nurse,' said Dumoise. 'I suppose that she can come in for . . . what is necessary.'

'By all means,' said Fleete cheerily, sitting up in bed. 'Bring on your nurses.'

Dumoise was dumb. Strickland led him out and explained that there must have been a mistake in the diagnosis. Dumoise remained dumb and left the house hastily. He considered that his professional reputation had been injured, and was inclined to make a personal matter of the recovery. Strickland went out too. When he came back, he said that he had been to call on the Temple of Hanuman to offer redress for the pollution of the god, and had been solemnly assured that no white man had ever touched the idol and that he was an incarnation of all the virtues labouring under a delusion.

'What do you think?' said Strickland.

I said, '"There are more things[5] . . ."'

But Strickland hates that quotation. He says that I have worn it threadbare.

One other curious thing happened which frightened me as much as anything in all the night's work. When Fleete was dressed he came into the dining-room and sniffed. He had a quaint trick of moving his nose when he sniffed. 'Horrid doggy smell, here,' said he. 'You should really keep those terriers of yours in better order. Try sulphur,[6] Strick.'

But Strickland did not answer. He caught hold of the back of a chair, and, without warning, went into an amazing fit of hysterics. It is terrible to see a strong man overtaken with hysteria. Then it struck me that we had fought for Fleete's soul with the Silver Man in that room, and had disgraced ourselves as Englishmen for ever, and I laughed and gasped and gurgled just as shamefully as Strickland, while Fleete thought that we had both gone mad. We never told him what we had done.

Some years later, when Strickland had married and was a church-going member of society for his wife's sake, we reviewed the incident

---

5. Cf. Hamlet to Horatio in Shakespeare, *Hamlet* 1.5.168–69: "There are more things in heaven and earth, Horatio, / Than are dreamt of in your philosophy."

6. Used in treatment of canine sarcoptic mange, or scabies, an infestation of the skin by mites that can cause severe itching leading to scabs and hair loss.

dispassionately, and Strickland suggested that I should put it before the public.

I cannot myself see that this step is likely to clear up the mystery; because, in the first place, no one will believe a rather unpleasant story, and, in the second, it is well known to every right-minded man that the gods of the heathen are stone and brass, and any attempt to deal with them otherwise is justly condemned.

Animality, Science, and the Vivisection Debate

"To this day I have never troubled about the ethics of the matter. The study of Nature makes a man at last as remorseless as Nature. I have gone on, not heeding anything but the question I was pursuing, and the material has . . . dripped into the huts yonder. . . ."
—*The Island of Doctor Moreau*, p. 63

Darwin's blurring of species boundaries gave scientific credence to a relational view of human and nonhuman animal experience that had percolated along the margins of learned disciplines in such forms as folklore, literary fable, and nonconformist speculation. But dominant strains of philosophical and scientific thought, rooted in Aristotelian biology and orthodox theology, had maintained, and even deepened, the divide between humans and other creatures in the pre-Darwinian period, most consequentially in the work of French philosopher René Descartes (1596–1650). Descartes swept away any lurking ambiguity in mainstream discourse about human-animal resemblance, denying to nonhuman animals any capacity for thought, imagination, or expressive meaning, describing them instead as merely functional "automata" responding mechanically to external stimuli. Lacking mind and speech, animals for Descartes were wholly matter, bodies devoid of the sensibility or "soul" that constitutes the distinctively human form of embodied existence—and, by extension, such "beast-machines" could in no sense be subjects of moral consideration. But because bodies, whether human or animal, are nearly congruent as entities governed by physical laws, knowledge about animal processes can legitimately inform understanding of human anatomy and biochemistry.

This absolute Cartesian divide between consciousness (humanity) and body (animality) built a platform on which vivisection—a practice that appeared sporadically in scientific investigation since the time of Greek physician Galen in the second century CE—became in the post-Cartesian era an increasingly frequent and visible element of medical inquiry and teaching, often offered as a popular spectacle by scientists seeking to enhance their reputation with a public enthralled by new discoveries. While such displays, in their extravagant cruelty, sometimes had the ironic effect of generating antipathy to vivisection (and fueling a nascent interest in societally approved animal welfare), they also amplified the image of the experimental scientist as innovative virtuoso and, in a more sober but significant mode, helped generate new forms of disciplinary knowledge. Most importantly, for both the history of science and *Moreau*'s specific exploration of that history's implications, vivisection gave new force and direction to the study of physiological systems such that by the early nineteenth century physiology was the engine of modern biomedical research. Sustaining its rise in prestige among the sciences during and after the appearance of Darwin's major works, the discipline of physiology followed the Cartesian path of suppressing recognition of intellectual, emotional, and social similarities between humans and animals while magnifying assumptions regarding their biological resemblance. In order to justify both shackling dogs (and cats, pigs, et al.) on the vivisection table and keeping humans off it, the physiologist, like the nineteenth-century anthropologist, began by reinventing the relation of culture to nature as one that both incorporates continuity and reasserts radical distinction between the two domains. But where anthropology fashioned a moralizing fable of development *within* the human order (in which some humans bear the "stigma of nature" while others have attained the cachet of "civilization"), physiology constructed a timeless epistemological framework that posited the knowing human subject in opposition to the to-be-investigated animal object.

The battles over vivisection that raged in the English public sphere from the 1860s through the 1880s—becoming particularly fierce with the establishment in 1876 of the Royal Commission on the Practice of Subjecting Live Animals to Experiments for Scientific Purposes, and the passage that year of the Cruelty to Animals Act—were in effect waged over the relation between human and nonhuman being as figured in opposed images of vivisector and vivisected. Ostensibly about the actuality and propriety of pain during experimental operations (a topic about which there was actually little clear disagreement, willful cruelty having been popularly abhorred in English culture since the late eighteenth century and, to some extent, legally proscribed in the 1820s), the (anti)vivisection debates in the wake of Darwin were more deeply about moral theory and cultural authority. For their part, vivisectors crafted apologias across the narrow spectrum from defiant defense of science's "advancement" to celebration of vivisection as a type of intellectual and even artistic heroism, a mode of self-sacrificial dedication in which, to cite the prominent vivisector Claude Bernard, the physiologist becomes so absorbed in his quest for knowledge that "he no longer hears the cry of animals, he no longer sees the blood that flows" (*An Introduction to the Study of Experimental Medicine* [1865]; see p. 219 below). Against that image, anti-vivisectionists—led by the redoubtable Anglo-Irish reformer and philosopher Frances Power Cobbe (1822–1904)—characterized their foes in terms that traversed an equally narrow spectrum, suggesting at its extreme that their scientific antagonists indulged themselves in "brutal depravity" that encumbered "civilization" with "wanton savagery." Each side might reasonably have claimed Wells's Moreau as their exemplary specimen.

CLAUDE BERNARD

From An Introduction to the Study of Experimental Medicine[†]

Vivisection

We have succeeded in discovering the laws of inorganic matter only by penetrating into inanimate bodies and machines; similarly we shall succeed in learning the laws and properties of living matter only by displacing living organs in order to get into their inner environment. After dissecting cadavers, then, we must necessarily dissect living beings, to uncover the inner or hidden parts of the organisms and see them work; to this sort of operation we give the name of vivisection, and without this mode of investigation, neither physiology nor scientific medicine is possible; to learn how man and animals live, we cannot avoid seeing great numbers of them die, because the mechanisms of life can be unveiled and proved only by knowledge of the mechanisms of death.

Men have felt this truth in all ages; and in medicine, from the earliest times, men have performed not only therapeutic experiments but even vivisection. We are told that the kings of Persia delivered men condemned to death to their physicians, so that they might perform on them vivisections useful to science. * * * Vivisection of animals also goes very far back. Galen may be considered its founder. * * * In our time, and especially under the influence of Magendie,[1] vivisection has entered physiology and medicine once for all, as an habitual or indispensable method of study.

The prejudices clinging to respect for corpses long halted the progress of anatomy. In the same way, vivisection in all ages has met with prejudices and detractors. We cannot aspire to destroy all the prejudice in the world; neither shall we allow ourselves here to answer the arguments of detractors of vivisection; since they thereby deny experimental medicine, i.e., scientific medicine. However, we shall consider a few general questions, and then we shall set up the scientific goal which vivisection has in view.

First, have we a right to perform experiments and vivisections on man? Physicians make therapeutic experiments daily on their patients, and surgeons perform vivisections daily on their subjects. Experiments, then, may be performed on man, but within what limits?

[†] From *An Introduction to the Study of Experimental Medicine*, trans. Henry Copley Greene (New York: Macmillan Co., 1927), n. a. Notes are by the editor of this Norton Critical Edition.

1. French physiologist François Magendie (1783–1855). *Galen:* Galen of Pergamum, Greek/Roman physician and philosopher (129–216).

It is our duty and our right to perform an experiment on man whenever it can save his life, cure him or gain him some personal benefit. The principle of medical and surgical morality, therefore, consists in never performing on man an experiment which might be harmful to him to any extent, even though the result might be highly advantageous to science, i.e., to the health of others. But performing experiments and operations exclusively from the point of view of the patient's own advantage does not prevent their turning out profitably to science. * * *

May we make experiments on men condemned to death or vivisect them? Instances have been cited * * * in which men have permitted themselves to perform dangerous operations on condemned criminals, granting them pardon in exchange. Modern ideas of morals condemn such actions; I completely agree with these ideas; I consider it wholly permissible, however, and useful to science, to make investigations on the properties of tissues immediately after the decapitations of criminals. A helminthologist[2] had a condemned woman without her knowledge swallow larvae of intestinal worms, so as to see whether the worms developed in the intestines after her death. * * * So, among the experiments that may be tried on man, those that can only harm are forbidden, those that are innocent are permissible, and those that may do good are obligatory.

Another question presents itself. Have we the right to make experiments on animals and vivisect them? As for me, I think we have this right, wholly and absolutely. It would be strange indeed if we recognized man's right to make use of animals in every walk of life, for domestic service, for food, and then forbade him to make use of them for his own instruction in one of the sciences most useful to humanity. No hesitation is possible; the science of life can be established only through experiment, and we can save living beings from death only after sacrificing others. Experiments must be made either on man or on animals. Now I think that physicians already make too many dangerous experiments on man, before carefully studying them on animals. I do not admit that it is moral to try more or less dangerous or active remedies on patients in hospitals, without first experimenting with them on dogs; for I shall prove, further on, that results obtained on animals may all be conclusive for man when we know how to experiment properly. If it is immoral, then, to make an experiment on man when it is dangerous to him, even though the result may be useful to others, it is essentially moral to make experiments on an animal, even though painful and dangerous to him, if they may be useful to man.

2. Zoologist who studies parasitic worms known as helminths.

After all this, should we let ourselves be moved by the sensitive cries of people of fashion or by the objections of men unfamiliar with scientific ideas? All feelings deserve respect, and I shall be very careful never to offend anyone's. I easily explain them to myself, and that is why they cannot stop me. I understand perfectly how physicians under the influence of false ideas, and lacking the scientific sense, fail to appreciate the necessity of experiment and vivisection in establishing biological science. I also understand perfectly how people of fashion, moved by ideas wholly different from those that animate physiologists, judge vivisection quite differently. It cannot be otherwise. * * * A physiologist is not a man of fashion, he is a man of science, absorbed by the scientific idea which he pursues: he no longer hears the cry of animals, he no longer sees the blood that flows, he sees only his idea and perceives only organisms concealing problems which he intends to solve. * * * After what has gone before we shall deem all discussion of vivisection futile or absurd. It is impossible for men, judging facts by such different ideas, ever to agree; and as it is impossible to satisfy everybody, a man of science should attend only to the opinion of men of science who understand him, and should derive rules of conduct only from his own conscience.

The scientific principle of vivisection is easy, moreover, to grasp. It is always a question of separating or altering certain parts of the living machine, so as to study them and thus to decide how they function and for what. Vivisection, considered as an analytic method of investigation of the living, includes many successive steps, for we may need to act either on organic apparatus, or on organs, or on tissue, or on the histological[3] units themselves. In extemporized and other vivisections, we produce mutilations whose results we study by preserving the animals. At other times, vivisection is only an autopsy on the living. * * *

* * * Let us add, in ending, that from every biological point of view, experimental physiology is in itself the one active science of life, because by defining the necessary conditions of vital phenomena it will succeed in mastering them and in governing them through knowledge of their peculiar laws. * * *

As far as direct applicability to medical practice is concerned, it is quite certain that experiments made on man are always the most conclusive. No-one has ever denied it. Only, as neither the moral law nor that of the state permits making on man the experiments which the interests of science imperatively demand, we frankly acclaim experimentation on animals.

---

3. Relating to the study of tissue structure seen under a microscope.

CHARLES DARWIN

[On Vivisection]†

The fact that the lower animals are excited by the same emotions as ourselves is so well established, that it will not be necessary to weary the reader by many details. Terror acts in the same manner on them as on us, causing the muscles to tremble, the heart to palpitate, the sphincters to be relaxed, and the hair to stand on end. Suspicion, the offspring of fear, is eminently characteristic of most wild animals. * * *

*　*　*

In the agony of death a dog has been known to caress his master, and every one has heard of the dog suffering under vivisection, who licked the hand of the operator; this man, unless the operation was fully justified by an increase of our knowledge, or unless he had a heart of stone, must have felt remorse to the last hour of his life.

LEWIS CARROLL

From Some Popular Fallacies about Vivisection‡

At a time when this painful subject is engrossing so large a share of public attention, no apology, I trust, is needed for the following attempt to formulate and classify some of the many fallacies, as they seem to me, which I have met with in the writings of those who advocate the practice. No greater service can be rendered to the cause of truth, in this fiercely contested field, than to reduce these shadowy, impalpable phantoms into definite forms, which can be seen, which can be grappled with, and which, when once fairly laid, we shall not need to exorcise a second time.

I begin with two contradictory propositions, which seem to constitute the two extremes, containing between them the golden mean of truth:—

1. *That the infliction of pain on animals is a right of man, needing no justification.*
2. *That it is in no case justifiable.*

† From *The Descent of Man, and Selection in Relation to Sex*, 2nd ed. (London: John Murray, 1874 [1871]), pp. 69, 70.
‡ From *Fortnightly Review* 23 (June 1875): 847–54.

The first of these is assumed in practice by many who would hardly venture to outrage the common feelings of humanity by stating it in these terms. All who recognise the difference of right and wrong must admit, if the question be closely pressed, that the infliction of pain is in some cases wrong. Those who deny it are not likely to be amenable to argument. For what common ground have we? They must be restrained, like brute beasts, by physical force.

The second has been assumed by an Association lately formed for the total suppression of Vivisection, in whose manifesto it is placed in the same category with Slavery, as being an absolute evil, with which no terms can be made. I think I may assume that the proposition most generally accepted is an intermediate one, namely, that the infliction of pain is in some cases justifiable, but not in all.

3. *That our right to inflict pain on animals is co-extensive with our right to kill, or even to exterminate a race (which prevents the existence of possible animals) all being alike infringements of their rights.*

This is one of the commonest and most misleading of all the fallacies. Mr. Freeman, in an article on Field Sports and Vivisection, which appeared in the *Fortnightly Review* for May, 1874, appears to countenance this when he classes death with pain together, as if they were admitted to be homogeneous. For example—

"By cruelty then I understand, as I have understood throughout, not all infliction of death or suffering on man or beast, but their wrongful or needless infliction. . . . My positions then were two. First . . . that certain cases of the infliction of death or suffering on brute creatures may be blameworthy. The second was, that all infliction of death and suffering for the purpose of mere sport is one of those blameworthy cases."

But in justice to Mr. Freeman I ought also to quote the following sentence, in which he takes the opposite view: "I must in all cases draw a wide distinction between mere killing and torture." * * *

4. *That man is infinitely more important than the lower animals, so that the infliction of animal suffering, however great, is justifiable if it prevent human suffering, however small.*

This fallacy can be assumed only when unexpressed. To put it into words is almost to refute it. Few, even in an age where selfishness has almost become a religion, dare openly avow a selfishness so hideous as this! While there are thousands, I believe, who would be ready to assure the vivisectors that, so far as their personal interests are concerned, they are ready to forego any prospect they may have of a diminution of pain, if it can only be secured by the infliction of so much pain on innocent creatures.

But I have a more serious charge than that of selfishness to bring against the scientific men who make this assumption. They use it dishonestly, recognising it when it tells in their favour, and ignoring it when it tells against them. For does it not pre-suppose the axiom that human and animal suffering differ *in kind*? A strange assertion this, from the lips of people who tell us that man is twin-brother to the monkey! Let them be at least consistent, and when they have proved that the lessening of the *human* suffering is an end so great and glorious as to justify any means that will secure it, let them give the anthropomorphoid ape the benefit of the argument. Further than that I will not ask them to go, but will resign them in confidence to the guidance of an exorable logic.

Had they only the candour and courage to do it, I believe that they would choose the other horn of the dilemma, and would reply, Yes, man is in the same category as the brute; and just as we care not (you see it, so we cannot deny it) how much pain we inflict on the one, so we care not, unless when deterred by legal penalties, how much we inflict on the other. The lust for scientific knowledge is our real guiding principle. The lessening of human suffering is a mere dummy set up to amuse sentimental dreamers. * * *

* * *

8. *That vivisection has no demoralising effect on the character of the operator.*

* * * This is a question to be decided by evidence, not by argument. History furnishes us with but too many examples of the degradation of character produced by the deliberate pitiless contemplation of suffering. The effect of the national bull-fights on the Spanish character is a case in point. But we need not go to Spain for evidence: the following extract from the *Echo*, quoted in the *Spectator* for March 20th, will be enough to enable the reader to judge for himself what sort of effect this practice is likely to have on the minds of the students:—

"But if yet more be necessary to satisfy the public minds on this latter point" (the effect on the operators), "the testimony of an English physiologist, known to the writer, may be useful in conclusion. He was present some time past at a lecture, in the course of which demonstrations were made on living dogs. When the unfortunate creatures cried and moaned under the operation, many of the students *actually mimicked their cries in derision*!" * * *

It is a humiliating but an undeniable truth, that man has something of the wild beast in him, that a thirst for blood can be aroused in him by witnessing a scene of carnage, and that the infliction of torture, when the first instincts of horror have been deadened by the familiarity, may become, first, a matter of indifference, then a subject of morbid interest, then a positive pleasure, and then a ghastly and ferocious delight. * * *

* * *

10. That, while the motive in sport is essentially selfish, in vivisection it is essentially unselfish.

It is my conviction that the non-scientific world is far too ready to attribute to the advocates of science all the virtues they are so ready to claim; and when they put forward their favourite *ad captandum*[1] argument that their labours are undergone for one pure motive—the good of humanity—society is far too ready to exclaim, with Mrs. Varden, "Here is a meek, righteous, thorough-going Christian, who, having dropped a pinch of salt on the tails of all the cardinal virtues, and caught them every one, makes light of their possession, and pants for more morality!"[2] In other words, society is far too ready to accept the picture of the pale, worn devotee of science giving his days and nights to irksome and thankless toil, spurred on by no other motive than a boundless philanthropy. As one who has himself devoted much time and labour to scientific investigations, I desire to offer the strongest possible protest against this falsely coloured picture, I believe that any branch of science, when taken up by one who has a natural turn for it, will soon become as fascinating as sport to the most ardent sportsman, or as any form of pleasure to the most refined sensualist. The claim that hard work, or the endurance of privation, proves the existence of an unselfish motive, is simply monstrous. * * *

Yet, after all, the whole argument, deduced from a comparison of vivisection with sport, rests on the following proposition, which I claim to class as a fallacy:—

11. That toleration of one form of an evil necessitates the toleration of all others.

Grant this, and you simply paralyze all conceivable efforts at reformation. How can we talk of putting down cruelty to animals when drunkenness is rampant in the land? You would propose, then, to legislate in the interests of sobriety? Shame on you! Look at the unseaworthy ships in which our gallant sailors are risking their lives! What! Organize a crusade against dishonest ship-owners, while our streets swarm with a population growing up in heathen ignorance! We can but reply, *non omnia possumus omnes*.[3] And

1. Designed [by emotional appeal] to please the crowd (Latin).
2. See *Barnaby Rudge* (1841), ch. 27 by English novelist Charles Dickens (1812–1870).
3. "We are not all capable of all things" (Latin).

surely the man who sees his way to diminish in any degree a single one of the myriad evils around him, may well lay to heart the saying of a wise man of old, "Whatsoever thy hand findeth to do, do it with thy might."[4]

The last parallel to which the advocates of vivisection may be expected to retreat, supposing all these positions to be found untenable, is the assertion—

12. *That legislation would only increase the evil.*

The plea, if I understand it aright, amounts to this,—that legislation would probably encourage many to go beyond the limit with which at present they are content, as soon as they found that a legal limit had been fixed beyond their own. Granting this to be the tendency of human nature, what is the remedy usually adopted in other cases? A stricter limit, or the abandonment of all limits? * * * We may safely take our stand on the principle of doing the duty which we see before us: secondary consequences are at once out of our control and beyond our calculation.

Let me now collect into one paragraph the contradictions of some of these fallacies (which I have here rather attempted to formulate and classify than to refute, or even fully discuss), and so exhibit in one view the case of the opponents of vivisection. It is briefly this—

That while we do not deny the absolute right of man to end the lives of the lower animals by a painless death, we require good and sufficient cause to be shown for all infliction of pain.

That the prevention of suffering to a human being does not justify the infliction of a greater amount of suffering on an animal.

That the chief evil of the practice of vivisection consists in its effect on the moral character of the operator; and that this effect is distinctly demoralising and brutalising.

That hard work and endurance of privations are no proof of an unselfish motive.

That the toleration of one form of an evil is no excuse for tolerating another.

Lastly, that the risk of legislation increasing the evil is not enough to make all legislation undesirable.

We have now, I think, seen good reasons to suspect that the principle of selfishness lies at the root of this accursed practice. That the same principle is probably the cause of the indifference with

4. Ecclesiastes 9:10.

which its growth among us is regarded, is not perhaps so obvious. Yet I believe this indifference to be based on a tacit assumption, which I propose to notice as the last of this long catalogue of fallacies—

> 13. *That the practice of vivisection will never be extended so as to include human subjects.*

That is, in other words, that while science arrogates to herself the right of torturing at her pleasure the whole sentient creation up to man himself, some inscrutable boundary line is there drawn, over which she will never venture to pass. "Let the galled jade wince, *our* withers are unwrung."[5]

Not improbably, when that stately Levite[6] of old was pacing with dainty step the road that led from Jerusalem to Jericho, "bemused with thinking of tithe-concerns," and doing his best to look unconscious of the prostrate form on the other side of the way, if it could have been whispered in his ear, "*Your* turn comes next to fall among the thieves!" some sudden thrill of pity might have been aroused in him: he might even, at the risk of soiling those rich robes, have joined the Samaritan in his humane task of tending the wounded man. And surely the easygoing Levites of our own time would take an altogether new interest in this matter, could they only realise the possible advent of a day when anatomy shall claim, as legitimate subjects for experiment, first, our condemned criminals—next, perhaps, the inmates of our refuges for incurables—then the hopeless lunatic, the pauper hospital patient, and generally "him that hath no helper,"—a day when successive generations of students, trained from their earliest years to the repression of all human sympathies, shall have developed a new and more hideous Frankenstein—a soulless being to whom science shall be all in all.

> *Homo sum! quidvis humanum a me alienum puto.*[7]

And when that day shall come, O my brotherman, you who claim for yourself and for me so proud an ancestry—tracing our pedigree through the anthropomorphoid ape up to the primeval zoophyte— what potent spell have you in store to win exemption from the common doom? Will you represent to that grim spectre, as he gloats over you, scalpel in hand, the inalienable rights of man? He will tell you that this is merely a question of relative expediency,—that, with so feeble a physique as yours, you have only to be thankful that natural selection has spared you so long. Will you reproach him with the

---

5. Shakespeare, *Hamlet* 3.2.266f.
6. Carroll refers in this paragraph to Jesus's Parable of the Good Samaritan in the Gospel of Luke (10:25–37).
7. "I am a human being; I consider nothing human alien to me" (Latin). Attributed to Roman poet Terence (186 [or 185]–?159 BCE).

needless torture he proposes to inflict upon you? He will smilingly
assure you that the *hyperoesthesia*,[8] which he hopes to induce, is in
itself a most interesting phenomenon, deserving much patient study.
Will you then, gathering up all your strength for one last desperate
appeal, plead with him as with a fellow-man, and with an agonized
cry for "Mercy!" seek to rouse some dormant spark of pity in that
icy breast? Ask it rather of the nether mill-stone.

JAMES PAGET

From Vivisection: Its Pains and its Uses[†]

It seems fair to demand that those who inflict pain or other distress
on animals, for the purpose of acquiring knowledge, should be
judged by the same rules as those who, for any other purposes, do
the same.

The rules by which these are judged may be read in the customs
by which a very great majority of sensible and humane persons
encourage or permit the infliction of pain and death on large numbers of animals, for purposes far short of great utility, necessity, or
self-defence.

It seems in these customs an admitted rule that, for the sake of
certain quantities of utility or pleasure, or both, men may inflict
great pain on animals without incurring the blame of cruelty. Can
it be shown, for those who make painful scientific experiments, that
the pain of their experiments is less and the utility more than in the
majority of the practices permitted or encouraged by the great majority of reasonable and humane persons among the educated classes
in this country?

* * *

Among such practices are the painful restraint and training of our
horses and other domestic animals; the caging of birds for the sake
of their beauty or their song; the imprisonment of animals of all
kinds in zoological gardens and aquaria for study or for amusement.
In all these instances animals are compelled or restrained from the
happiness of natural life; they have to endure what might be inflicted
as severe punishment on criminals—slavery or imprisonment for
life. But the inflictions are justified by the utility which men derive
from them.

---

8. Abnormal physical sensitivity (often of the skin) caused by intensified stimulation.
† From *Nineteenth Century* 10.58 (December 1881): 128–29, 132–33, 137–38.

In another large group of painful customs generally encouraged are those inflicting death and often great suffering on birds and beasts for obtaining ornamental fur or feathers; the mutilation of sheep and oxen for the sake of their better or quicker fattening; the multiplication of pains and deaths in the killing of small birds and small fish, such as larks, quails, whitebait, and the like; although, so far as mere sustenance of life is concerned, any weight of food in one large fish or one large bird would serve as well as an equal weight in a hundred small ones. Still, the pleasure of delicious food, or of beautiful decoration, or, in some instances, the utility of better nutriment, seems sufficient to a vast majority of civilised men and women to justify these customs.

In another group may be named all the pain-giving sports— shooting, hunting, stalking, fishing, and the rest—various in the pleasure that they give, various in utility. And in yet another, the trapping, hunting, and killing of mice, rats, stoats, frogs, and toads invading cultivated land—worms, and slugs, and the whole class of what we call vermin—creatures generally troublesome and sometimes injurious.

From a list such as this, which might easily be enlarged, a rough estimate may be formed of the quantity of pain or distress, imprisonment or death, which, in the opinion of great majorities of persons entitled to judge, may be inflicted on animals for purposes of utility or of pleasure, or from other motives far less than those of necessary self-defence or maintenance of human life. The list may thus serve as a standard with which to compare the pains and the utilities of vivisections. Doubtless many persons would find in it some practices which they would forbid; some would hunt or shoot, but would not keep parrots or larks in confinement; some would eat whitebait or small birds, and wear sealskin, and order the destruction (anyhow) of all the rats and mice in their houses, but would put down fox-hunting and salmon-fishing. But there are very few, even among the generally most sensible and humane, who do not allow or encourage, even if they do not practise, many things of which I think it certain that the pain is greater and the utility less than that of many experiments on living animals. They may do it thoughtlessly, but they may find that they do it, if they will make a careful survey of their furniture, clothes, and ornaments, their food, amusements, and habits of life for a year, and then estimate the pains which in providing all these have been inflicted upon animals. Let them estimate them, if they can, with the same measure as that with which they estimate the pain of vivisection.

* * *

If it may thus be justly held that the pain and other miseries inflicted by vivisection are less than those inflicted in many practices encouraged by sensible and humane persons, it may next be considered whether their utility be as great. It might justly be asked whether their utility and pleasure be as great, for it will not be denied that pleasure is a considerable motive in most of the sports, and in the wearing of decorative dresses such as cannot be procured without giving pain. But I would rather not argue that man's pleasure can ever be reason enough for his giving pain. It seems impossible to define even nearly the 'when,' or the how much pain for how much pleasure. But, if any will hold the contrary, and that in the pursuit of pleasure pain may be inflicted, even without considerations of probable utility, then it may certainly be maintained that there are no pleasures more intense than the pursuit of new knowledge, nor any for which, if for any, greater pain might be given.

*   *   *

Speaking generally, it is certain that there are few portions of useful medical knowledge to which experiments on animals have not contributed. The knowledge may be now so familiar that the sources from which parts of it were derived may be forgotten; or what was first found by experiments may now have other evidences; or, experiments may only have made sure that which, without them, was believed: but the whole history of medicine would show that, whatever useful or accurate knowledge we possess, we owe some parts of it to experiments on animals.

*   *   *

Of course, among the opponents of experiments on animals there are several very different groups, and with some of these it is useless to appeal to reason. Some have committed themselves to the agitation, and cannot recede without discredit or more material loss, and some are carried on with so strong an impulse of a mind once made up that they cannot pause for a revision of their judgment. But there are many who favour the agitation only because they are ignorant of the facts of the case; they have heard or read accusations of cruelty grossly misstated, and have heard no defence or denial of them.

That which is most to be desired is that persons with fairly-balanced minds, with at least an average both of humanity and of capacity for judgment in cases in which deep feeling may be stirred, should study the whole matter, and judge of experiments on animals as they would of other practices in which utility or even pleasure is pleaded as justifying the infliction of pain. Let them visit physiological laboratories, and see what is done, and compare the work and its results with those of a day's shooting, or a night's trapping of rabbits, or of any sport or trade in which the lives of animals are concerned.

And chiefly it is to be wished that the subject should thus be thoroughly studied by those who administer the Act. If they would thus study it, they would be sure that the Act is at least a sufficient deference to public sentiment, they would use the discretion allowed them in its administration, so as to throw as little obstacle as possible in the way of competent persons engaged in the most useful and beneficial inquiries, and they would resist further restraints of experiments on animals with as much resolution as they resist other hindrances to the doing of what they judge to be right.

FRANCIS POWER COBBE

From "Vivisection and Its Two-Faced Advocates"†

The position in which we, the opponents of Vivisection, find ourselves at present is this:—

We seek to stop certain practices which appear to us to involve gross cruelty, and to be contrary to the spirit of English law. Our knowledge of them is derived almost exclusively from the published reports and treatises prepared and issued by the actual individuals who carry out those practices; and our arguments are grounded upon verbatim citations from those published reports and treatises.[1]

The persons whose practices we desire to stop, and their immediate associates, now meet our charges of cruelty by articles in the leading periodicals, wherein the proceedings in question are invested with a character not only diverse from, but opposite to, that which they wear in the scientific treatises and reports above-mentioned. * * *

1. In the first place, the *purpose* of the great majority of experiments is differently described in the scientific treatises and in the popular articles. In the former, the *raison d'etre* of most experiments appears to be the elucidation of points of purely scientific interest. It is only occasionally that we meet with allusions to diseases or their remedies, but the experiments are generally described as showing

---

† From the *Contemporary Review* 41 (April 1882): 610–15. Unless otherwise indicated, notes are by the editor of this Norton Critical Edition.
1. E.g., the "Handbook of the Physiological Laboratory," by Drs. Burdon-Sanderson, Lauder-Brunton, Klein, and Foster, London, 1873; Beclard's "Traite Elementaire," Paris, 1880; Claude Bernard's "Physiologie Operatoire," "Traite sur le Diabete," and "Sur la Chaleur Animale"; Cyon's "Methodik," Giessen; Paul Bert's "La Pression Barometrique," Paris, 1878; Mantegazza's "Del Dolore," Florence, 1880; Livon's "Manuel de Vivisections," 1882. * * * [*Cobbe's note*].

that one organ acts in one way and another in another; that such a lesion, or such an irritation, produces such and such results and reactions; and (especially) that Professor A.'s theory has been disproved and that of Professor B. (temporarily) established. In short, every page of these books corroborates the honest statement of Professor Hermann of Zurich: "The advancement of science, and not practical utility to medicine, is the true and straightforward object of all vivisection. No true investigator in his researches thinks of the practical utilization. Science can afford to despise this justification with which vivisection has been defended in England."—*Die Vivisectionsfrage*, p. 16.

We now turn to such articles as the six which have appeared in the *Nineteenth Century* and the two in the *Fortnightly Review* in defence of vivisection, and, *mirabile dictu!* not a solitary vivisection is mentioned of which the direct advancement of the Healing Art does not appear as the single-minded object.

2. Again, the *severity* of the experiments in common use, appears from the Treatises and Reports (always including the English "Handbook," *Transactions*, and *Journal of Physiology*) to be truly frightful. Sawing across the backbone, dissecting out and irritating all the great nerves, driving catheters along the veins and arteries, inoculating with the most dreadful diseases, cutting out pieces of the intestine, baking, stewing, pouring boiling water into the stomach, freezing to death, reducing the brain to the condition of a "lately-hoed potato field"; these and similarly terrible experiments form the staple of some of them, and a significant feature in all.

But turning now to the popular articles, we find Dr. Lauder-Brunton assuring the readers of the *Nineteenth Century* that "he has calculated that about twenty-four out of every 100 of the experiments (in the Parliamentary Returns), might have given pain. But of these twenty-four, four-fifths are like vaccination, the pain of which is of no great moment. In about one-seventh of the cases the animal only suffered from the healing of a wound." Sir James Paget afforded us a still more *couleur de rose*[2] of the subject. He said: "I believe that, with these few exceptions, there are no physiological experiments which are not matched or far surpassed in painfulness by common practices permitted or encouraged by the most humane persons."

3. Again, as regards the feelings of the vivisectors, in reading these terrible Treatises we do not meet with one solitary appeal against the repetition of painful experiments, one caution to the student to forbear from the extremity of torture, one expression of pity or

2. "Pink color" (French); i.e., rosy.

regret—even when the keenest suffering had been inflicted. On the contrary, we find frequent repetitions of such phrases as "interesting experiments," "very interesting experiments," "beautiful" (*schone*) cerebral inflammation, and so on. In short, the writers, frankly, seem pleased with their work, and exemplify Claude Bernard's description of the ideal Vivisector—the man who "does not hear the animal's cries of pain, and is blind to the blood that flows, and who sees nothing but his idea and organisms which conceal from him the secrets he is resolved to discover."[3] Or still more advanced, they realized Cyon's yet stronger picture in his great book of the "Methodik," of which, by the way, he has lately told us in the *Gaulois*, that when the book was coming out his English colleagues implored him not to allow it to be advertised in England.

In this great treatise M. Cyon tells us:—

> The true vivisector must approach a difficult vivisection with *joyful excitement*. . . . He who shrinks from cutting into a living animal, he who approaches a vivisection as a disagreeable necessity, may be able to repeat one or two vivisections, but he will never be an artist in vivisection. . . . The sensation of the physiologist when, from a gruesome wound, full of blood and mangled tissue, he draws forth some delicate nerve thread . . . has in common with that of a sculptor."—*Methodik*, p. 15.

This is the somewhat startling self-revelation of the Vivisector, made by himself to his colleagues. The picture of him in the *Nineteenth Century* and *Fortnightly Review* is almost as different as one face of Janus[4] from the other. We find him talking of the power of "controlling one's emotions," "disregarding one's own feelings at the sight of suffering," "subordinating feeling to judgment," and much more in the same strain, whereby the Vivisector is made to appear a tender-hearted martyr to the Enthusiasm of Humanity. * * *

5. Again, as regards Anesthetics, throughout the Treatises I cannot recall having once seen them mentioned as *means of allaying the sufferings of the animals*, but very often as convenient applications for *keeping them quiet*. Claude Bernard in his "Physiologie Operatoire," and Cyon in his great "Methodik," each devote a section to them as MEANS OF RESTRAINT ("*contention*"), and describe their merits from that point of view. Morphia, for example, Bernard recommends because it keeps the animal still, though "*il souffre la douleur*";[5] and of curare (which, he says, causes "the most

---

3. ["Introduction a l'Etude de la Medecine Experimentale," p. 180 —*Cobbe*.] See p. 219 above.
4. Two-faced Roman god of duality and transition.
5. "He suffers pain" (French).

atrocious sufferings which the imagination can conceive"), he remarks, without an expression of regret, that its use in vivisection is so universal that it may always be assumed to have been used in experiments not otherwise described. Nor can haste explain this omission to treat anaesthetics from the humanitarian point of view, for the Treatises contain long chapters of advice to the neophyte in vivisection, how he may ingeniously avoid being bitten by the dogs, or scratched by the yet more "*terrible*" cats, which are, Bernard pathetically complains, "*indocile*" when lifted on the torture trough.

Turning to our *Nineteenth Century* essayists, we find chloroform is everywhere, and curare nowhere.

6. Lastly, there is not a trace in the Treatises—even in the English "Handbook"—of the supposed Wall of China which guards the Flowery Land of English Vivisection from the hordes of outer barbarians who practise in Paris, Leipsic, Florence, Strasbourg, and Vienna. We find, on the contrary, a frequent and cordial interchange of experiments and compliments. Our English vivisectionists study in the schools of the Continent, and in several cases have brought over foreigners to be their assistants at home. When Claude Bernard died, so little did English physiologists think of repudiating him, that a letter appeared in the *Times* of March 20, 1878, inviting subscriptions to raise a monument to his honour, signed by Sir James Paget, Dr. Burdon-Sanderson, Professor Humphry, Professor Gerald Yeo, Mr. Ernest Hart, Mr. Romanes, and Dr. Michael Foster.[6] * * *

All this does not look exactly like hearty disgust and repudiation of the foreign system.

But turn we to the *Nineteenth Century* and *Fortnightly Review*, and lo! the garments of our English physiologists are drawn closely around them, and we are assured they have "no connection whatever with the establishment over the way." I am even rebuked for placing on the same page (in my article "Four Replies") certain English experiments and "the disgusting details of foreign atrocities, which excite a persistent feeling of repugnance." Professor Yeo says he "regards with pain and loathing such work as that of Mantegazza," and asks me bitterly, "Why repeat the oft-told tale of horrors contained in the works of Claude Bernard, Paul Bert, Brown-Sequard,

---

6. English physiologist (1836–1907). *Romanes*: Canadian-Scots evolutionary biologist George Romanes (1848–1894); *Hart*: English medical writer Ernest Hart (1835–1898); *Yeo*: Irish physiologist Gerald Francis Yeo (1845–1909); *Humphrey*: English physiologist and anatomist George Murray Humphrey (1820–1896); *Burdon-Sanderson*: English physiologist John Burden-Sanderson (1828–1905); *Paget*: English surgeon and pathologist James Paget (1814–1899).

and Richet in France, of Goltz in Germany, Mantegazza in Italy, and Flint[7] in America?" (p. 361).

Surely this is a cargo of Jonahs[8] thrown overboard together! Claude Bernard, the prince of physiologists, to whom this same professor Gerald Yeo, four years ago, wished to raise a statue! Brown-Sequard, the honoured of Professor Huxley!

* * * And lastly, Goltz!—poor Professor Goltz, who had so many cordial hand-shakes on quitting perfidious Albion, while the autumn leaves were falling, and who is now flung down the Gemonian stairs,[9] as a sacrifice to the rabble of anti-vivisectors, even while the ink is scarcely dry on his touching dedication of his book:—

"SEINEN FREUNDEN IN ENGLAND GEWIDMET VON DEM VERFASSER."[1]

May not this new Raleigh[2] fitly cry, not, "O the friendship of Princes!" but "O the friendship of Physiologists?"

Thus we see that, as regards, first, the purpose of the majority of vivisections; second, their severity; third, their number; fourth, the feelings of the experimenters; fifth, the use of anesthetics; sixth, the difference between English and foreign vivisection,—in short, on every one of the points of importance in the controversy,—there is contradiction on the broadest scale between the scientific Treatises and Reports prepared for "brethren of the craft" and the Articles written in lay periodicals for the edification of the British public.

It is for the reader to judge which class of statement may, with the greater probability, be held to represent the genuine doings and feelings of the writers. * * *

---

7. American physiologist Austin Flint II (1836–1915). *Mantegazza*: Italian neurologist and physiologist Paolo Mantegazza (1831–1910); *Goltz*: German physiologist Friedrich Leopold Goltz (1834–1902); *Richet*: French physiologist Charles Richet (1850–1935); *Brown-Sequard*: Mauritian physiologist Charles-Édouard Brown-Séquard (1817–1894); *Bert*: French zoologist and physiologist Paul Bert (1833–1886).

8. The prophet Jonah was thrown into the sea by sailors fearful that he had angered God, causing a great storm (Jonah 1:11–13).

9. Flight of stairs in ancient Rome, infamous as a site of execution; also known as the Stairs of Death. *Albion*: i.e., England.

1. "Dedicated by the author to his friends in England" (German).

2. Sir Walter Raleigh (1552–1618), English soldier, explorer, statesman, and courtier, to whom was once attributed the phrase "beware the friendship of princes" (actually a translation of a Latin phrase from the Roman poet Horace that appears on a painting—"the Cobbe Portrait"—long conjectured to be of Raleigh).

ROBERT LOUIS STEVENSON

The Scientific Ape[†]

In a certain West Indian Isle, there stood a house and hard by a grove of trees. In the house there dwelt a vivisectionist, and on the trees a clan of anthropoid apes. It chanced that one of these was caught by the vivisectionist and kept some time in a cage in the laboratory. There he was much terrified by what he saw, deeply interested in all he heard; and as he had the fortune to escape at an early period of his case (which was numbered 701) and to return to his family with only a trifling lesion of one foot, he thought himself on the whole the gainer.

He was no sooner back than he dubbed himself doctor and began to trouble his neighbours with the question: Why are not apes progressive?

"I do not know what progressive means," said one, and threw a cocoanut at his grandmother.

"I neither know nor care," said another, and swung himself into a neighbouring tree.

"O stow[1] that!" cried a third.

"Damn progress!" said the chief, who was an old physical-force tory. "Try and behave yourselves better the way you are."

But when the scientific ape got the younger males alone, he was heard with more attention.

"Man is only a promoted ape," said he, hanging his tail from a high branch. "The geological record being incomplete, it is impossible to say how long he took to rise, and how long it might take us to follow in his steps. But by plunging vigorously *in medias res* on a system of my own, I believe we shall astonish everyone. Man lost centuries over religion, morals, poetry and other fudge; it was centuries before he got properly to science, and only the other day that he began to vivisect. We shall go the other way about, and begin with vivisection."

"What in the name of cocoanuts is vivisection?" asked an ape.

The doctor explained at great length what he had seen in the laboratory; and some of his hearers were delighted, but not all.

"I never heard of anything so beastly!" cried an ape who had lost one ear in quarrel with his aunt.

"And what is the good of it?" asked another.

"Don't you see?" said the doctor. "By vivisecting men, we find out how apes are made, and so we advance."

[†] From Ralph Parfect, ed., "Robert Louis Stevenson's 'The Clockmaker' and 'The Scientific Ape': Two Unpublished Fables," *ELH* 48.4 (2005): 401–03. Reprinted by permission of ELT Press. Notes are by the editor of this Norton Critical Edition.
1. Stop or break off (vis. chatter).

"But why not vivisect each other?" asked one of his disciples who was disputatious.

"O, fie!" said the doctor. "I will not sit and listen to such talk; or at least not in public."

"But criminals?" inquired the disputant.

"It is highly doubtful if there be such a thing as right or wrong: then, where's your criminal?" replied the doctor. "And besides the public would not stand it. And men are just as good; it's all the same genus."

"It seems rough on the men," said the ape with one ear.

"Well, to begin with," said the doctor, "they say that we don't suffer and are what they call automata;[2] so I have a perfect right to say the same of them."

"That must be nonsense," said the disputant; "and besides it's self-destructive. If they are only automata, they can teach us nothing of ourselves; and if they can teach us anything of ourselves, by cocoanuts! they have to suffer."

"I am much of your way of thinking," said the doctor, "and indeed that argument is only fit for the monthly magazines. Say that they do suffer. Well, they suffer in the interest of a lower race, which requires help: there can be nothing fairer than that. And besides we shall doubtless make discoveries which will prove useful to themselves."

"But how are we to make discoveries," inquired the disputant, "when we don't know what to look for?"

"God bless my tail!" cried the Doctor, nettled out of his dignity, "I believe you have the least scientific mind of any ape in the Windward Islands![3] *Know* what to look for indeed! True science has nothing to do with that. You just vivisect along, upon the chance; and if you do discover anything, who is so surprised as you?"

"I see one more objection," said the disputant, "though, mind you, I am far from denying it would be capital fun. But men are so strong, and then they have these guns."

"And therefore we shall take babies," concluded the doctor.

That same afternoon, the doctor returned to the vivisectionist's garden, purloined one of his razors through the dressing room window, and on a second trip, removed his baby from the nursery basinette.

There was a great to-do in the tree tops. The ape with the one ear, who was a good natured fellow, nursed the baby in his arms; another stuffed nuts in its mouth, and was aggrieved because it would not eat them.

2. Machines; robots.
3. Group of Caribbean islands constituting the southern arc of the Lesser Antilles.

"It has no sense," said he.

"But I wish it would not cry," said the ape with the one ear, "it looks so horribly like a monkey!"

"This is childish," said the doctor. "Give me the razor."

But at this the ape with one ear lost heart, spat at the doctor, and fled with the baby into the next tree top.

"Yah!" cried the ape with the one ear, "vivisect yourself!"

At this the whole crew began chasing and screaming; and the noise called up the chief, who was in the neighbourhood, killing fleas.

"What is all this about?" cried the chief. And when they had told him, he wiped his brow. "Great cocoanuts!" cried he, "is this a nightmare? Can apes descend to such barbarity? Take back that baby where it came from."

"You have not a scientific mind," said the doctor.

"I do not know if I have a scientific mind or not," replied the chief; "but I have a very thick stick, and if you lay one claw upon that baby, I will break your head with it."

So they took the baby to the front garden plot. The vivisectionist (who was an estimable family man) was overjoyed, and in the lightness of his heart, began three more experiments in his laboratory before the day was done.

Wells on Evolution, Pain, Extinction, and Animal Mind

H. G. WELLS

From "Human Evolution, an Artificial Process"†

There is an idea abroad that the average man is improving by virtue of the same impetus that raised him above the apes, an idea that finds its expression in such works, for instance, as Mr. Kidd's *Social Evolution*.¹ If I read that very suggestive author aright, he believes that "Natural Selection" is "steadily evolving" the intrinsic moral qualities of man (p. 286). It is, however, possible that Natural Selection is not the agent at work here. For Natural Selection is selection by Death. It may help to clarify an important question, to point out what is certainly not very clearly understood at present, that the evolutionary process now operating in the social body is one essentially different from that which has differentiated species in the past and raised man to his ascendency among the animals. It is a process new in this world's history. Assuming the truth of the Theory of Natural Selection, and having regard to Professor Weismann's destructive criticisms of the evidence for the inheritance of acquired characters,² there are satisfactory grounds for believing that man (allowing for racial blendings) is still mentally, morally, and physically, what he was during the later Palaeolithic period, that we are, and that the race is likely to remain, for (humanly speaking) a vast period of time, at the level of the Stone Age. The only considerable evolution that has occurred since then, so far as man is concerned, has been, it is here asserted, a different sort of evolution altogether, an evolution of suggestions and ideas. In this paper it is

---

† From the *Fortnightly Review* 60 (October 1896): 590–95. Notes are by the editor of this Norton Critical Edition.
1. English sociologist Benjamin Kidd (1858–1916), *Social Evolution* (1894).
2. Wells refers here to German evolutionary biologist August Friedrich Leopold Weissman (1834–1914), whose extensive writings on heredity in the 1880s and 1890s rejected the possibility of the inheritance of acquired traits (a view associated with Lamarckism).

proposed to sketch an establishment of this view, and to indicate its bearing upon certain current conceptions.

The fact which so far has been insufficiently considered in this relation is the slowness with which the human animal breeds. * * *

* * * Now there is reason (in the fluctuations of zymotic[3] diseases) to believe that species of bacteria have altered in their nature within the present century. Their structure is, however, out of all comparison simpler than the human, and, apart from that, the known variations of animals, even the variations of fecund animals sedulously bred, are by no means striking. In view of which facts, it appears to me impossible to believe that man has undergone anything but an infinitesimal alteration in his intrinsic nature since the age of unpolished stone.

Even if we suppose that he has undergone such an alteration, it cannot be proceeding in the present civilised state. The most striking feature of our civilisation is its careful preservation of all the human lives that are born to it—the halt, the blind, the deaf and dumb, the ferocious, the atavistic; the wheat and tares not only grow together, but are impartially sheltered from destruction. These grow to maturity and pair under such complex and artificial circumstances that even a determinate Sexual Selection can scarcely be operating. Holding the generally-accepted views of variation, we must suppose as many human beings are born below the average in any particular as above it, and that, therefore, until our civilisation changes fundamentally, the intrinsic average man will remain the same.

This completes the opening proposition of the argument, the a priori case for the permanence of man's inherent nature. * * *

Coming now to the second proposition of this argument, we must admit that it is indisputable that civilised man is in some manner different from the Stone Age savage. But that difference, it is submitted, is in no degree inherited. That, however, is a thing impossible to prove in its entirety, and it is stated here merely as an opinion arising out of the considerations just advanced. The cases of Wolf-Boys[4] that have arisen show with sufficient clearness, at any rate, that the greater part of the difference is not inherited. If the child of a civilised man, by some conjuring with time, could be transferred, at the moment of its birth, to the arms of some Palaeolithic mother, it is conceivable that it would grow up a savage in no way superior, by any standards, to the true-born Palaeolithic savage. The main difference is extrinsic, it is a difference in the scope and nature of

---

3. Infectious.
4. Feral male children assumed to have been reared by wolves. A famous instance familiar to Wells was that of Dina Sanichar (1860 or 1861–1895), discovered by hunters in an Indian cave and handed over to colonial authorities, who placed him in an orphanage where he lived out the remainder of his life.

the circle of thought, and it arose, one may conceive, as a result of the development of speech. Slowly during the vast age of unpolished stone, this new and wonderful instrument of intellectual enlargement and moral suggestion, replaced inarticulate sounds and gestures. Out of speech, by no process of natural selection, but as a necessary consequence, arose tradition. With true articulate speech came the possibilities of more complex co-operations and instructions than had hitherto been possible, more complex industries than hunting and the chipping of flints, and, at last, after a few thousand years, came writing, and therewith a tremendous acceleration in the expansion of that body of knowledge and ideals which is the reality of the civilised state. It is a pure hypothesis, but it seems plausible to suggest, that only with writing could the directly personal governments coalesce to form an ampler type of State. All this was, from the point of view of the evolutionist, to whom a thousand years are but a day, a rapid and inevitable development of speech, just as the flooding of a vast country in the space of a few hours would be the rapid and inevitable consequence of the gradual sapping of a dam that fended off the sea. In his reference to this background of the wider state, and in its effect upon his growth, in moral suggestions and in knowledge, lies, I believe, the essential difference between Civilised and Palaeolithic man.

This completes the statement of the view I would advance. * * * That in civilised man we have (1) an inherited factor, the natural man, who is the product of natural selection, the culminating ape, and a type of animal more obstinately unchangeable than any other living creature; and (2) an acquired factor, the artificial man, the highly plastic creature of tradition, suggestion, and reasoned thought. In the artificial man we have all that makes the comforts and securities of civilisation a possibility. That factor and civilisation have developed, and will develop together. And in this view, what we call Morality becomes the padding of suggested emotional habits necessary to keep the round Palaeolithic savage in the square hole of the civilised state. And Sin is the conflict of the two factors— as I have tried to convey in my *Island of Dr. Moreau*.

If this new view is acceptable it provides a novel definition of Education, which obviously should be the careful and systematic manufacture of the artificial factor in man. * * *

* * * [I]n a rude and undisciplined way indeed, in an amorphous chaotic way we might say, humanity is even now consciously steering itself against the currents and winds of the universe in which it finds itself. In the future, it is at least conceivable, that men with a trained reason and a sounder science, both of matter and psychology, may conduct this operation far more intelligently, unanimously, and effectively, and work towards, and at last attain and preserve, a social

organization so cunningly balanced against exterior necessities on the one hand, and the artificial factor in the individual on the other, that the life of every human being, and, indeed, through man, of every sentient creature on earth, may be generally happy. To me, at least, that is no dream, but a possibility to be lost or won by men, as they may have or may not have the greatness of heart to consciously shape their moral conceptions and their lives to such an end.

This view, in fact, reconciles a scientific faith in evolution with optimism. The attainment of an unstable and transitory perfection only through innumerable generations of suffering and "elimination" is not necessarily the destiny of humanity. * * * We need not clamour for the Systematic Massacre of the Unfit, nor fear that degeneration is the inevitable consequence of security. * * *

From "The Limits of Individual Plasticity"†

The generalizations of heredity may be pushed to extremes, to an almost fanatical fatalism. There are excellent people who have elevated systematic breeding into a creed, and adorned it with a propaganda. The hereditary tendency plays, in modern romance, the part of the malignant fairy, and its victims drive through life blighted from the very beginning. It often seems to be tacitly assumed that a living thing is at the utmost nothing more than the complete realization of its birth possibilities, and so heredity becomes confused with theological predestination. But, after all, the birth tendencies are only one set of factors in the making of the living creature. We overlook only too often the fact that a living being may also be regarded as raw material, as something plastic, something that may be shaped and altered, that this, possibly, may be added and that eliminated, and the organism as a whole developed far beyond its apparent possibilities. We overlook this collateral factor, and so too much of our modern morality becomes mere subservience to natural selection, and we find it not only the discreetest but the wisest course to drive before the wind.[1]

Now the suggestion this little article would advance is this: that there is in science, and perhaps even more so in history, some sanction for the belief that a living thing might be taken in hand and so moulded and modified that at best it would retain scarcely anything of its inherent form and disposition; that the thread of life might be

---

† From the *Saturday Review* 79.2047 (January 19, 1895): 89–90. Notes are by the editor of this Norton Critical Edition.
1. To move along quickly (a nautical term, meaning to propel a ship forward in the wind's direction).

preserved unimpaired while shape and mental superstructure were so extensively recast as even to justify our regarding the result as a new variety of being. This proposition is purposely stated here in its barest and most startling form. It is not asserted that the changes effected would change in any way the offspring of such a creature, but only that the creature itself as an individual is capable of such recasting.

* * * Now first, how far may the inherent bodily form of an animal be operated upon? There are several obvious ways: amputation, tongue-cutting, the surgical removal of a squint, and the excision of organs will occur to the mind at once. In many cases excisions result in extensive secondary changes, pigmentary disturbances, increase in the secretion of fatty tissue, and a multitude of correlative changes. Then there is a kind of surgical operation of which the making of a false nose, in cases where that feature has been destroyed, is the most familiar example. A flap of skin is cut from the forehead, turned down on the nose, and heals in the new position. This is a new kind of grafting of part of an animal upon itself in a new position. Grafting of freshly obtained material from another animal is also possible, has been done in the case of teeth, for example. Still more significant are the graftings of skin and bone—cases where the surgeon, despairing of natural healing, places in the middle of the wound pieces of skin snipped from another individual, fragments of bone from a fresh-killed animal; and the medical student will at once recall Hunter's cock-spur flourishing on the bull's neck.[2] So much for the form.

The physiology, the chemical rhythm of the creature, may also be made to undergo an enduring modification, of which vaccination and other methods of inoculation with living or dead matter are examples. A similar operation is the transfusion of blood, although in this case the results are more dubious. These are all familiar cases. Less familiar and probably far more extensive were the operations of those abominable medieval practitioners who made dwarfs and show monsters, and some vestiges of whose art still remain in the preliminary manipulation of the young mountebank or contortionist. Victor Hugo gives us an account of them, dark and stormy, after his wont, in "L'homme qui rit."[3] But enough has been said to remind the reader that it is a possible thing to transplant tissue from one part of an animal to another, or from one animal to another, to alter its chemical reactions and methods of growth, to modify the articulation of its limbs, and indeed to change it in its most intimate

2. John Hunter (1728–1793), Scottish surgeon, physiologist, and anatomist. See note 7 on p. 58.
3. *The Man Who Laughs*, 1869 novel by French writer Victor-Marie Hugo (1802–1885). In Chapter XIV of *The Island of Doctor Moreau*, Moreau refers to passages in Hugo's novel describing "the manufacture of monsters" by "the vivisection of former days."

structure. And yet this has never been sought as an end and systematically by investigators. Some of such things have been hit upon in the last resort of surgery; most of the kindred evidence that will recur to the reader's mind has been demonstrated as it were by accident—by tyrants, by criminals, by the breeders of horses and dogs, by all kinds of untrained men working for their own immediate ends. It is impossible to believe that the last word, or anything near it, of individual modification has been reached. If we concede the justifications of vivisection, we may imagine as possible in the future, operators, armed with antiseptic surgery and a growing perfection in the knowledge of the laws of growth, taking living creatures and moulding them into the most amazing forms; it may be, even reviving the monsters of mythology, realizing the fantasies of the taxidermist, his mermaids and what-not, in flesh and blood.

The thing does not stop at a mere physical metamorphosis. In our growing science of hypnotism we find the promise of a possibility of replacing old inherent instincts by new suggestions, grafting upon or replacing the inherited fixed ideas. Very much indeed of what we call moral education is such an artificial modification and perversion of instinct; pugnacity is trained into courageous self-sacrifice, and suppressed sexuality into pseudo-religious emotion.

We have said enough to develop this curious proposition. It may be the set limits of structure and psychical capacity are narrower than is here supposed. But as the case stands this artistic treatment of living things, this moulding of the commonplace individual into the beautiful or the grotesque, certainly seems so far credible as to merit a place in our minds among the things that may some day be.

"On Extinction"[†]

The passing away of ineffective things, the entire rejection by Nature of the plans of life, is the essence of tragedy. In the world of animals, that runs so curiously parallel with the world of men, we can see and trace only too often the analogies of our grimmer human experiences; we can find the equivalents to the sharp tragic force of Shakespeare, the majestic inevitableness of Sophocles, and the sordid dreary tale, the middle-class misery, of Ibsen. The life that has schemed and struggled and committed itself, the life that has played and lost, comes at last to the pitiless judgment of time, and is slowly and remorselessly annihilated. This is the saddest chapter of biological science—the tragedy of Extinction.

---

† From *Chambers's Journal* 10 (September 30, 1893): 623–24. Notes are by the editor of this Norton Critical Edition.

In the long galleries of the geological museum are the records of judgments that have been passed graven upon the rocks. Here, for instance, are the huge bones of the 'Atlantosaurus,' one of the mightiest land animals that this planet has ever seen. A huge terrestrial reptile this, that crushed the forest trees as it browsed upon their foliage, and before which the pigmy ancestors of our present denizens of the land must have fled in abject terror of its mere might of weight. It had the length of four elephants, and its head towered thirty feet—higher, that is, than any giraffe—above the world it dominated. And yet this giant has passed away, and left no children to inherit the earth. No living thing can be traced back to these monsters; they are at an end among the branchings of the tree of life. Whether it was through some change of climate, some subtle disease, or some subtle enemy, these titanic reptiles dwindled in numbers, and faded at last altogether among things mundane. Save for the riddle of their scattered bones, it is as if they had never been.

Beside them are the pterodactyls, the first of vertebrated animals to spread a wing to the wind, and follow the hunted insects to their last refuge of the air. How triumphantly and gloriously these winged lizards, these original dragons, must have floated through their new empire of the atmosphere! If their narrow brains could have entertained the thought, they would have congratulated themselves upon having gained a great and inalienable heritage for themselves and their children for ever. And now we cleave a rock and find their bones, and speculate doubtfully what their outer shape may have been. No descendants are left to us. The birds are no offspring of theirs, but lighter children of some clumsy 'deinosaurs.' The pterodactyls also have heard the judgment of extinction, and are gone altogether from the world.

The long roll of palaeontology is half filled with the records of extermination; whole orders, families, groups, and classes have passed away and left no mark and no tradition upon the living fauna of the world. Many fossils of the older rocks are labelled in our museums, 'of doubtful affinity.' Nothing living has any part like them, and the baffled zoologist regretfully puts them aside. What they mean, he cannot tell. They hint merely at shadowy dead subkingdoms, of which the form eludes him. Index fingers are they, pointing into unfathomable darkness, and saying only one thing clearly, the word 'Extinction.'

In the living world of to-day the same forces are at work as in the past. One Fate still spins, and the gleaming scissors cut. In the last hundred years the swift change of condition throughout the world, due to the invention of new means of transit, geographical discovery, and the consequent 'swarming' of the whole globe by civilised men, has pushed many an animal to the very verge of destruction. It is not only the dodo that has gone; for dozens of genera and hundreds of species, this century has witnessed the writing on the wall.[1]

In the fate of the bison extinction has been exceptionally swift and striking. In the 'forties' so vast were their multitudes that sometimes, 'as far as the eye could reach,' the plains would be covered by a galloping herd. Thousands of hunters, tribes of Indians, lived upon them. And now! It is improbable that one specimen in an altogether wild state survives. If it were not for the merciful curiosity of men, the few hundred that still live would also have passed into the darkness of non-existence. Following the same grim path are the seals, the Greenland whale, many Australian and New Zealand animals and birds ousted by more vigorous imported competitors, the black rat, endless wild birds. The list of destruction has yet to be made in its completeness. But the grand bison is the statuesque type and example of the doomed races.

Can any of these fated creatures count? Does any suspicion of their dwindling numbers dawn upon them? Do they, like the Red Indian, perceive the end to which they are coming? For most of them, unlike the Red Indian, there is no alternative of escape by interbreeding with their supplanters. Simply and unconditionally, there is written across their future, plainly for any reader, the one word 'Death.'

Surely a chill of solitude must strike to the heart of the last stragglers in the rout, the last survivors of the defeated and vanishing species. The last shaggy bison, looking with dull eyes from some western bluff across the broad prairies, must feel some dim sense that those wide rolling seas of grass were once the home of myriads of his race, and are now his no longer. The sunniest day must shine with a cold and desert light on the eyes of the condemned. For them the future is blotted out, and hope is vanity.

These days are the days of man's triumph. The awful solitude of such a position is almost beyond the imagination. The earth is warm with men. We think always with reference to men. The future is full of men to our preconceptions, whatever it may be in scientific truth. In the loneliest position in human possibility, humanity supports us. But Hood, who sometimes rose abruptly out of the most mechanical punning to sublime heights, wrote a travesty, grotesquely fearful, of Campbell's 'The Last Man.'[2] In this he probably hit upon the

---

1. Portent of doom (see Daniel 5). *Dodo*: flightless bird, now extinct.
2. "The Last Man" (1826) by English poet, journalist, and humorist Thomas Hood (1799–1845) is a satire upon an 1823 poem of the same name by Scottish poet Thomas Campbell (1777–1844). Campbell's verse, which helped spark a brief but intense "Last Man" tradition in Romantic writing and art, is an evangelical work in which the last human survivor of apocalypse contentedly observes the world's end, secure in expectation of his salvation.

most terrible thing that man can conceive as happening to man: the
earth desert through a pestilence, and two men, and then one man,
looking extinction in the face.

"The Province of Pain"[†]

In spite of the activity of the Society for the Prevention of Cruelty
to Animals in our midst, and of the zealous enemies of the British
Institute of Preventive Medicine, there have been those who have
doubted whether animals—or, at least, very many animals—feel
pain at all. This doubt is impregnable, so far as absolute disproof
goes. No scientific observer has, as yet, crept into the animal mind;
no reminiscences of metempsychosis[1] come to the aid of the
humane. We can only reason that there is evidence of pain from
analogy, a method of proof too apt to display a wayward fancy to be
a sure guide. This alone, however, does not prevent us discussing
the question—rather the reverse, for there is, at least, the charm of
uncertainty about any inquiries how animals may feel pain. It is
speculation almost at its purest.

Many people regard the presence of nerves as indicative of the
possible presence of pain. If the surmise is correct, then every kind
of animal, from the jellyfish up to man, suffers. Some will even go
further, and make plants feel, and figure the whole living creation
as groaning and travailing together. But the probabilities are that
neither is life nor nervous structure inseparably tinted by the possibility of pain. Among the considerations that point to this conclusion is the fact that many of the nervous impressions of our own
bodies have no relation either to pleasure or pain. Most of the
impressions of sight are devoid of any decided flavour of the kind,
and most sounds, and all those many nervous impressions that never
awaken consciousness; those that maintain the tonic contraction of
arteries, for instance, are, it goes without saying, painless. Then the
little ganglia[2] and nerve-threads that lie in the substance of the heart
and keep it beating have nothing to do with pain. The nerves retain
their irritability, too, in many cases, after death; and a frog's hind
leg may be set moving after being cut off from the body. Here, again,
is nerve, but no one will believe there can be pain in an amputated
limb. From considerations such as these, one is forced to conclude

---

† From *Science and Art* 8 (February 1894): 58–59. Notes are by the editor of this Norton
  Critical Edition.
1. Upon death, the transmigration of the soul into the body of another being (either
   human or animal).
2. Clusters of nerve-cell bodies.

that the quality of pain becomes affixed to an impression, not in the nerves that conduct, but in the brain that receives it.

Again, we may have pain without receiving nervous impressions—or, at least, we may have pain not simply and immediately arising from nervous impressions. The emotions of fear, jealousy, and even anger, for instance, have all their painful hue. Pain independent of sensation is possible, but so is sensation without pain. Pain without thought is possible, but so is thought without pain. Pain, then, though a prominent feature of our mental scheme, is not a necessary companion either to any living thing or nervous thread, on the one hand, or to any mental existence, on the other.

The end of pain, so far as we can see its end, is protection. There seems to be little or no absolutely needless or unreasonable pain in the world, though disconsolate individuals might easily be found who see no good in gout or toothache. But these, indeed, may be blessings in a still impenetrable disguise. The man in the story, at any rate, whose wish was granted, and who was released from pain, burnt first one hand and then had the other arm mortify,[3] and was happily saved from dying of starvation through indifference by getting himself scalded to death. Pain, rightly seen, is, in fact, a true guardian angel, watching over the field of our activities, and, with harsh tenderness, turning us back from death. In our own bodies it is certainly only located where it is needed.

The whole surface of man's body has painful possibilities, and nerve-ends are everywhere on the watch against injury, but deeper the sense is not so easily awakened. In proof of this it is a common trick among medical students to thrust a pin into the thigh. There these nerve-ends are thinly scattered over the skin, and these once passed the muscle is penetrated with scarcely a pang. Again, as most people have read, the brain has often been cut in operations after injury to the head without causing pain. Internal pains are always less acute, and less definitely seated than external ones. Many grave internal disorders and injuries may manifest themselves merely as a general feverishness and restlessness, or even go on for long quite unsuspected. The province of pain, then, in man, so far as detailed government is concerned, is merely the surface of his body, with 'spheres of influence,' rather than proper possessions in the interior, and the centre seat of pain is in the mind. Many an operation which to describe gives an unpleasant thrill to the imagination—slicing away the brain, for instance, or washing away the brain with a jet of water—is, as a matter of fact, absolutely painless.

The relation of physical pain to the imagination and the emotions is worthy of consideration. There seems to be a direct relation between

3. Become necrotic or gangrenous.

emotional and physical sensibility, the one varying inversely, to borrow a convenient technicality, as the other. Professor Lombroso
recently raised all the militant feminine by asserting that women
felt physical pain less acutely than men.[4] He hardly deserved the
severely sarcastic retorts that appeared in the ladies' papers. His
critics, from want of practice or other causes, failed to observe the
compliment he was paying them. But a man must have been singularly unobservant if he has failed to notice that, while women are
more sensitive to fear and to such imaginary terrors as reside in the
cockroach and the toad, they can, when physical pain has secured
its grasp upon them, display a silent fortitude quite impossible to
ordinary men. Their pains are more intense mentally, but less so
physically. This is quite in accordance with the view that needless
pain does not exist; where the quickness of imagination guards
against danger there is evidently a lessened need for the actual physical smart.

Emotional states are anaesthetic. A furious man feels neither fear
nor bodily pain, and there is even the clearest antagonism of pain
and calm mental occupation. Do not let your mind dwell upon it is
the advice of common sense. The Ingoldsby Legends[5] were the outcome of the struggle of one sturdy spirit against bodily pain. This is
not the only way in which men can avoid the goad. In the use of
anaesthetics we have men anticipating and meeting the warning. So
far as physical pain goes, civilised people not only probably do not
need it so much, but probably do not feel it so much, or, at any rate,
so often as savages. Moreover, the civilised man evidently feels the
spur of passion far less acutely than his less advanced brother. In
view of the wise economy of nature, it is not immaterial to ask
whether this does not open a probability of man's eventual release
from pain. May he not so grow morally and intellectually as to get
at last beyond the need of corporal chastisement, and foresight take
the place of pain, as science ousts instinct? First, he may avoid pain,
and then the alarm-bell may rust away from disuse. On the other
hand, there is a quantitative relation between feeling and acting. Sit
still, inhibit every movement, your sensations are at a maximum.
So you behave when you would hear low music, and lose nothing.
Struggle violently, the great wave of nervous energy flowing out neu-
tralises the inward flow of feeling. A man when his 'blood is up,'
when he is pouring out energy at every point, will fail to notice the

---

4. See *La donna delinquente: La prostituta e la donna normale* (*The Criminal Woman:
The Prostitute and the Normal Woman*) 1893, by Italian physician and criminologist
Cesare Lombroso (1835–1909).
5. *The Ingoldsby Legends, or Mirth and Marvels*, children's anthology of legends, ghost
stories, and poetry written under the penname "Thomas Ingoldsby of Tappington
Manor" by English clergyman Richard Harris Barham (1788–1845), who suffered in
childhood a crippling injury to his arm.

infliction of a wound, which, if he were at rest, would be intensely painful. The struggles and outcries of animals being wounded have their merciful use—they shunt off so much energy that would register as pain. So the acts of sobbing and weeping are the proper channels of escape from a pressure that would otherwise be intolerable. Probably a great proportion of the impressions that would register as pain in man are immediately transmitted into impulses of movement in animals, and therefore cause no pain. With the development of the intelligence in animals there is, however, a diminution of the promptness with which an animal reacts to stimuli. The higher animals, like man, look before they act; with the distinction of approaching man in being less automatic and more intelligent, it seems credible that they also approach him in feeling pain. Probably, since their emotions are less subtle and their memories less distinct, the actual immediate smart of pain may be keener while it lasts than in man. Man being more intelligent, needs less severity, we may infer, from the hands of his great teacher, Nature, just as the woman needs less than the man.

Hence we may very well suppose that we have, as it were, a series among living things with respect to pain. In such an animal as the dog we may conceive that there is a fairly well-developed moral and intellectual rule, and a keen sense of pain. Going downwards, the mental factor diminishes, the smart of the pain becomes greater and greater in amount, but less and less enduring, until at last the mental disappears and the impression that would be pain is a momentary shock, translated into action before it is felt. On the other hand, as we ascend from the dog to the more complex human, we find physical pain becoming increasingly subordinate to the moral and intellectual. In the place of pains there come mental aversions that are scarcely painful, and an intellectual order replaces the war of physical motives. The lower animals, we may reasonably hold, do not feel pain because they have no intelligence to utilise the warning; the coming man will not feel pain, because the warning will not be needed.

Such considerations as these point to the conclusion that the province of pain is after all a limited and transitory one; a phase through which life must pass on its evolution from the automatic to the spiritual; and, so far as we can tell, among all the hosts of space, pain is found only on the surface of this little planet.

From Text-Book of Biology[†]

Section 43

We have now considered our types, both from the standpoint of adult anatomy and from embryological data; and we have seen through the vertebrate series a common structure underlying wide diversity in external appearance and detailed anatomy. We have seen a certain intermediateness of structure in the frog, as compared with the rabbit and dog-fish, notably in the skull and skeleton, in the circulation, in the ear, and in the reduced myomeres;[1] and we have seen that the rabbit passes in these respects, and in others, through dog-fish-and frog-like stages in its development, and this alone would be quite sufficient to suggest that the similarities of structure are due to other causes than a primordial adaptation to certain conditions of life.

Section 44

It has been suggested by very excellent people that these resemblances are due to some unexplained necessity of adherence to *type*, as though, the power that they assume created these animals originally, as they are now, coupled creative ability with a plentiful lack of ideas, and so perforce repeated itself with impotent variations. On the other hand, we have the supposition that these are "family likenesses," and the marks of a *common ancestry*. This is the opinion now accepted by all zoologists of repute. * * *

* * *

Section 54

* * * The great things of the science of Darwin, Huxley, Wallace, and Balfour[2] remain mainly untold. In the book of nature there are written, for instance, the triumphs of survival, the tragedy of death and extinction, the tragi-comedy of degradation and inheritance, the gruesome lesson of parasitism, and the political satire of colonial organisms. Zoology is, indeed, a philosophy and a literature to those who can read its symbols. In the contemplation of beauty of form and of mechanical beauty, and in the intellectual delight of tracing and elucidating relationships and criticising appearances, there is also for many a great reward in zoological study. With an increasing

[†] From *Text-Book of Biology* (London: W. B. Clive, 1893), pp. 43–44, 127, 131–32. Notes are by the editor of this Norton Critical Edition.
1. Muscle segments.
2. English biologist Francis Maitland Balfour (1851–1882). *Wallace*: English naturalist and biologist Alfred Russell Wallace (1823–1913).

knowledge of the facts of the form of life, there gradually appears to the student the realization of an entire unity shaped out by their countless, and often beautiful, diversity. And at last, in the place of the manifoldness of a fair or a marine store, the student of science perceives the infinite variety of one consistent and comprehensive Being—a realization to which no other study leads him at present so surely. * * *

* * *

Section 105

A vast amount of our activities are reflex, and in such action an efferent stimulus follows an afferent[3] promptly and quite mechanically. *It is only where efferent stimuli do not immediately become entirely transmuted into outwardly moving impulses that mental action comes in and an animal feels.* There appears to be a direct relation between sensation and motion. For instance, the shrieks and other instinctive violent motions produced by pain, "shunt off" a certain amount of nervous impression that would otherwise *register* itself as additional painful sensation. Similarly most women and children understand the comfort of a "good cry," and its benefit in shifting off a disagreeable mental state.

Section 106

The mind receives and stores impressions, and these accumulated experiences are the basis of memory, comparison, imagination, thought, and apparently spontaneous will. **Voluntary actions** differ from reflex by the interposition of this previously stored factor. For instance, when a frog sees a small object in front of him, that may or may not be an edible insect, the direct visual impression does not directly determine his subsequent action. It revives a number of previous experiences, an image already stored of similar insects and associated with painful or pleasurable gustatory experiences. With these arise an emotional effect of desire or repulsion which, passes into action of capture or the reverse.

Section 107

Voluntary actions may, by constant repetition, become **quasi-reflex** in character. The intellectual phase is abbreviated away. *Habits* are once voluntary and deliberated actions becoming mechanical in this

---

3. Conducted inward or toward (per nerves, vis. the nervous system; per blood vessels, vis. organs)—in contrast to "efferent" conduction, which is outward.

way, and slipping out of the sphere of mind. For instance, many of the detailed movements of writing and walking are performed without any attention to the details. An excessive concentration of the attention upon one thing leads to absent-mindedness, and to its consequent absurdities of inappropriate, because imperfectly acquired, reflexes.

Section 108

This fluctuating scope of mind should be remembered, more especially when we are considering the probable mental states of the lower animals. An habitual or reflex action may have all the outward appearance of deliberate adjustment. We cannot tell in any particular case how far the mental comes in, or whether it comes in at all. Seeing that in our own case consciousness does not enter into our commonest and most necessary actions, into breathing and digestion, for instance, and scarcely at all in the *details* of such acts as walking and talking we might infer that nature was economical in its use, and that in the case of such an animal as the Rabbit, which follows a very limited routine, and in which scarcely any versatility in emergencies is evident, it must be relatively inconsiderable. Perhaps after all, pain is not scattered so needlessly and lavishly throughout the world as the enemies of the vivisectionist would have us believe.

From "The Mind in Animals"[†]

* * * Though an out-and-out evolutionist, Professor Lloyd Morgan[1] is disposed to establish a broad distinction between the human mind and that of the highest of other living creatures. He denies even the most rudimentary reason below the human level, and systematically criticizes many alleged cases of ratiocination in animals, with singular clearness and convincingness. The well-authenticated stories of small dogs obtaining the assistance of larger friends to avenge their own defeats, for instance; latch-raising dogs; Professor Sully's case of "canine consciousness" (a dog that stole a piece of meat, and then evidently repented and took it to the feet of his mistress); the case of superstition adduced by Romanes (a dog startled and frightened at a bone suddenly jumping about through the *diablerie* of a piece of thread); the deliberate "deceit" of Mr. Stradling's

---

[†] From *the Saturday Review* 78 (December 1894): 683. Notes are by the editor of this Norton Critical Edition.
1. Wells's article is a review of psychologist C. Lloyd Morgan's *An Introduction to Comparative Psychology*. A proto-behaviorist, Morgan worked upon the principle, known as "Morgan's Canon," that no action should be considered the result of a "higher" mental capability if it can be understood as the result of a "lower" capability.

Maltese terrier;[2] are subtly analysed, and shown to be explicable without supposing any rational process—using the term "rational" with scientific strictness. But Professor Lloyd Morgan lays himself open to criticism in this use of "rational" as a definite distinction between man and animal. He tells us "That being alone is rational who is able to focus the *therefore*"; but, savages apart, does even such a highly finished product of civilization as a Wessex yokel "focus the *therefore*"? does he syllogize? One may reasonably doubt whether syllogistic thinking is a common human property, is not rather an educational product—even a rare one; and it would, we believe, be at least as easy to dispose of any cases of apparently rational thought, using that term in its narrower sense, among quite illiterate people, as it has been with the animal anecdotes considered in this book.

Then in his experimental observations to test the perception of relations Professor Lloyd Morgan does not seem to give proper weight to the difference in mental operations that must exist, due to the difference of sense basis. With man the whole mental structure rests upon touch impressions and visual images, his mental fabric is fundamentally spatial; almost all his prepositions, for instance, primarily express relative position; and consequently it seems to him that the very simplest test one can offer a dog is such an exercise upon spatial relations as to give it a walking-stick to carry through railings. That test Professor Lloyd Morgan used. But the dominant sense of a dog is olfactory, and the series of delicate space perceptions that are the primary constituents of our thought, and which we obtain originally through our ten fingers, can scarcely have a place in its mental fabric. Nevertheless the dog, possessing, as it evidently does, a power of olfactory discriminations infinitely beyond our own, may have on that basis a something not strictly "rational" perhaps, but higher than mere association and analogous to and parallel with the rational. It may even be that Professor Lloyd Morgan's dog, experimenting on Professor Lloyd Morgan with a dead rat or a bone to develop some point bearing upon olfactory relationships, would arrive at a very low estimate indeed of the powers of the human mind.

2. Morgan refers in his treatise to a Mr. Arthur Stradling, who reports to him the clever machinations of a pet dog. *Diablerie*: reckless mischief (French). *Romanes*: Canadian-Scots evolutionary biologist George Romanes (1848–1849). *Sully's*: Morgan refers in his treatise to research on "canine consciousness" conducted by English physiologist James Sully (1842–1923).

RECEPTION AND INTERPRETATION

Early Reviews

P. CHALMERS MITCHELL

Mr. Wells's "Dr. Moreau"†

Those who have delighted in the singular talent of Mr. Wells will read "The Island of Dr. Moreau" (Heinemann. 1896) with dismay. We have all been saying that here is an author with the emotions of an artist and the intellectual imagination of a scientific investigator. He has given us in "The Time Machine" a diorama of prophetic visions of the dying earth, imagined with a pitiless logic, and yet filled with a rare beauty, sometimes sombre and majestic, sometimes shining with fantastic grace. He has brought down among us the angel of our dreams, and, while using the faculties a naturalist would employ in studying the new habitat of a species, he has made us laugh and weep, flush with an unsuspected shame, hug a discovered virtue. Behind these high gifts, behind the simple delight of his story-telling, there has seemed to lie a reasoned attitude to life, a fine seriousness that one at least conjectures to be the background of the greater novelists. When the prenatal whispers of "The Island of Dr. Moreau" reached me, I rejoiced at the promise of another novel with a scientific basis, and I accepted gladly the opportunity given me to say something of it, from the scientific point of view, as well as from that of a devoted novel-reader. But, instead of being able to lay my little wreath at the feet of Mr. Wells, I have to confess the frankest dismay.

For Mr. Wells has put out his talent to the most flagitious[1] usury. His central idea is a modelling of the human frame and endowment of it with some semblance of humanity, by plastic operations upon living animals. The possibilities of grafting and moulding, of shaping the limbs and larynx and brain, of transfusing blood, of changing physiological rhythm, and vague suggestions of hypnotizing dawning intelligence with the elemental rules of human society—these would seem to offer a rich vein to be worked by Mr. Wells's logical

† From the *Saturday Review* 81 (April 11, 1896): 368–69.
1. Villainous.

fancy. They are, indeed, finely imagined, and the story of the hero, suddenly brought into an island peopled with such nightmare creatures, is vivid and exciting to the last degree. To realize them, you must read of the bewilderment and horror of the hero, while he thinks the creatures are men outraged and distorted: of his fear for his own fate at the hands of the artificer of the unnatural: of his gradual acquaintance with the real nature of the monsters: of his new horror at the travesties of human form and mind: of the perils that begin when the "stubborn beast-flesh" has overcome the engrafted humanity, and the population has risen in rebellion against its creator. All this is excellent; but the author, during the inception of his story, like his own creatures, has tasted blood. The usurious interest began when the author, not content with the horror inevitable in his idea, and yet congruous with the fine work he has given us hitherto, sought out revolting details with the zeal of a sanitary inspector probing a crowded graveyard.

You begin with a chromolithographic[2] shipwreck, and three starving survivors playing odd-man-out for a cannibal feast. The odd man breaks faith, and, in the resulting struggle, the hero is left alone in a blood-bespattered boat. When he is rescued, a drunken doctor, no doubt disinclined to change the supposed diet, restores him with a draught of iced blood. When the island is reached he is not allowed by Mr. Wells to land until, refused hospitality by Dr. Moreau and cast adrift by the drunken captain, he has again meditated upon starvation, this time without any mates for whose blood he may pass halfpence. Dr. Moreau himself is a *cliché* from the pages of an antivivisection pamphlet. He has been hounded out of London because a flayed dog (you hear the shuddering ladies handing over their guineas) has been liberated from his laboratory by a spying reporter. It is the blood that Mr. Wells insists upon forcing on us; blood in the sink "brown and red," on the floor, on the hands of the operators, on the bandages that swathe the creatures or that they have left hanging on the bushes—physically disgusting details inevitable in the most conservative surgery; but still more unworthy of restrained art, and, in this case, of scientific *vraisemblance*,[3] is the insistance upon the terror and pains of the animals, on their screams under the knife, and on Dr. Moreau's indifference to the "bath of pain" in which his victims were moulded and recast. Mr. Wells must know that the delicate, prolonged operations of modern surgery became possible only after the introduction of anæsthetics. Equally wrong is the semi-psychological suggestion that pain could be a humanizing agency. It may be that the conscious subjection to pain for a purpose

2. Multicolored picture produced from lithographic plates or stones.
3. Verisimilitude; credibility (French).

has a desirable mental effect; pain in itself, and above all continuous pain inflicted on a struggling, protesting creature, would produce only madness and death. Mr. Wells will not even get his hero out of the island decently. When Dr. Moreau has been killed by his latest victim—a puma become in the laboratory "not human, not animal, but hellish, brown, seamed with red branching scars, red drops starting out upon it"—Mr. Wells must needs bring in an alien horror. The "boat from the machine" drifts ashore with two dead men in it—men "dead so long that they fell in pieces" when the hero dumped them out for the last of the island monsters to snarl over.

It may be that a constant familiarity with the ways and work of laboratories has dulled my sense of the æsthetic possibilities of blood—anatomists, for the most part, wash their hands before they leave their work—and that a public attuned to Mr. Rider Haggard's[4] view of the romantic may demand the insertion of details physically unpleasant; but, for my own part, I feel that Mr. Wells has spoiled a fine conception by greed of cheap horrors. I beg of him, in the name of many, a return to his sane transmutations of the dull conceptions of science into the living and magical beauty he has already given us. We that have read his earlier stories will read all he chooses to write; but must he choose the spell of Circe?[5]

There remains to be said a word about the scientific conceptions underlying Dr. Moreau's experiments. I quite agree that there is scientific basis enough to form the plot of a story. But in an appended note, Mr. Wells is scaring the public unduly. He declares:—"There can be no denying that whatever amount of scientific[6] credibility attaches to the detail of this story, the manufacture of monsters—and perhaps even of *quasi*-human monsters—is within the possibilities of vivisection." The most recent discussion of grafting and transfusion experiments is to be found in a treatise by Oscar Hertwig,[7] a translation of which Mr. Heinemann announces. Later investigators have failed to repeat the grafting experiments of Hunter,[8] and a multitude of experiments on skin and bone grafting and on transfusion of blood shows that animal-hybrids cannot be produced in these fashions. You can transfuse blood or graft skin from one man to another; but attempts to combine living material from different creatures fail.

4. H. Rider Haggard (1856–1935), English author of adventure stories and romances.
5. Demigoddess and enchantress in Greek mythology and epic; see, e.g., Homer's *The Odyssey*, Book X, where Circe turns men into pigs.
6. Mitchell inserts the word "scientific," which is not from Wells's text.
7. Wilhelm August Oscar Hertwig (1849–1922), German embryologist and zoologist; Mitchell refers to his forthcoming translation of Hertwig's treatise *The Biological Problem of To-Day* (1896).
8. John Hunter (1728–1793), Scottish surgeon to whom Moreau refers in Chapter XIV of Wells's novel. See note 7 on p. 58.

H. G. WELLS

[Reply to P. Chalmers Mitchell][†]

Sir,—In a special article in the "Saturday Review" of 11 April, 1896, reviewing my "Island of Doctor Moreau," Mr. Chalmers Mitchell, in addition to certain literary criticisms, which rest upon their merits, gave the lie direct to a statement of mine that the grafting of tissues between animals of different species is possible. This was repeated more elaborately in "Natural Science," and from these centres of distribution it passed into the provincial press, where it was amplified to my discredit in various, animated, but to me, invariably painful phrasing. And the contradiction, with the implication of headlong ignorance it conveys, is now traversing the continent of America (where phrasing is often very vivid indeed) in the wake of the review copies Mr. Stone is distributing.

I was aware at the time that Mr. Chalmers Mitchell was mistaken in relying upon Oscar Hertwig[1] as the final authority on this business, that he was making the rash assertion and not I; but for a while I was unable to replace the stigma of ignorance he had given me, for the simple reason that I knew of no published results of the kind I needed. But the "British Medical Journal" for 31 October, 1896, contains the report of a successful graft, by Mr. Mayo Robson,[2] not merely of connective but of nervous tissue between rabbit and man. I trust, therefore, that "Natural Science" will now modify its statement concerning my book, and that the gentlemen of the provincial press who waxed scornful, and even abusive, on Mr. Chalmers Mitchell's authority, will now wax apologetic. There is quite enough to misunderstand and abuse in the story without any further application of this little mistake of Mr. Chalmers Mitchell's.

[R. H. HUTTON]

[Review][‡]

The ingenious author of *The Time Machine* has found in this little book a subject exactly suited to his rather peculiar type of imagination. When he tried to conceive the idea of making a man of the nineteenth century *travel* in time, so that he was at the same

† From the *Saturday Review* 82 (November 1, 1896): 497.
1. German embryologist (1849–1922).
2. English surgeon Arthur William Mayo-Robson (1853–1933).
‡ From the *Spectator* (April 11, 1896): 519–20.

moment both contemporary with and far removed from the people of a prehistoric age, he conceived an idea which was really quite too self-contradictory to be worked out with any sort of coherence. But in this little book he has worked out a notion much less intrinsically incoherent, and though impossible, yet not so impossible as to be quite inconceivable. In other words, the impossibility is of a less unworkable order though it is also much more gruesome. He has taken a few of the leading methods of the modern surgery and exaggerated them in the hands of an accomplished vivisector into a new physiological calculus that enables its professor to transmute various animals into the semblance of man. * * *

Of course, the real value for literary purposes of this ghastly conception depends on the power of the author to make his readers realise half-way stages between the brute and the rational creature, with which he has to deal. And we must admit that Mr. Wells succeeds in this little story in giving a most fearful vividness to his picture of half-created monsters endowed with a little speech, a little human curiosity, a little sense of shame, and an overgrown dread of the pain and terror which the scientific dabbler in creative processes had inflicted. There is nothing in Swift's grim conceptions of animalised man and rationalised animals[1] more powerfully conceived than Mr. Wells's description of these deformed and malformed creations of Dr. Moreau, repeating the litany in which they abase themselves before the physiological demigod by whom they have been endowed with their new powers of speech, their new servility to a human master, and their profound dread of that "house of pain" in which they have been made and fashioned into half-baked men. The hero of the story, who has been thrown into Dr. Moreau's grisly society, comes suddenly on the huts of these spoiled animals who have been fashioned into a bad imitation of men, and hears them proclaim their new law in the following creed:—

> * * * They swayed from side to side, and beat their hands upon their knees, and I followed their example. I could have imagined I was already dead and in another world. The dark hut, these grotesque dim figures, just flecked here and there by a glimmer of light and all of them swaying in unison and chanting:—
> "Not to go on all-Fours; *that* is the Law. Are we not Men?"
> "Not to suck up Drink; *that* is the Law. Are we not Men?"
> "Not to eat Flesh nor Fish; *that* is the Law. Are we not Men?"
> "Not to claw Bark of Trees; *that* is the Law. Are we not Men?"
> "Not to chase other Men; *that* is the Law. Are we not Men?"

* * *

1. Hutton refers to "A Voyage to the Land of the Houyhnhnms," the fourth section of the novel *Gulliver's Travels* (1726) by English author Jonathan Swift (1667–1745).

Our readers may gain from this passage some faint idea of the power with which this grim conception of the mauling and maiming of brutes into bad imitations of human beings has been worked out by Mr. Wells. It is, of course, a very ingenious caricature of what has been done in certain exceptional efforts of human surgery,—a caricature inspired by the fanaticism of a foul ambition to remake God's creatures by confusing and transfusing and remoulding human and animal organs so as to extinguish so far as possible the chasm which divides man from brute. Mr. Wells has had the prudence, too, not to dwell on the impossibilities of his subject too long. He gives us a very slight, though a very powerful and ghastly, picture, and may, we hope, have done more to render vivisection unpopular, and that contempt for animal pain, which enthusiastic physiologists seem to feel, hideous, than all the efforts of the societies which have been organized for that wholesome and beneficent end. Dr. Moreau is a figure to make an impression on the imagination, and his tragic death under the attack of the puma which he has been torturing so long, has a kind of poetic justice in it which satisfied the mind of the reader. Again, the picture of the rapid reversion to the brute, of the victims which Dr. Moreau had so painfully fashioned, so soon as the terrors of his "house of pain" are withdrawn, is very impressively painted. Altogether, though we do not recommend *The Island of Dr. Moreau* to readers of sensitive nerves, as it might well haunt them only too powerfully, we believe that Mr. Wells has almost rivalled Swift in the power of his gruesome but very salutary as well as impressive, conception.

ANONYMOUS

[Review]†

In *The Island of Dr. Moreau* * * * Mr. H. G. Wells gains our attention at once by the closeness and vigour of his narrative style and by his terse and natural dialogue. His realism of detail is, in fact, the sign of imagination. It is full of skilful and subtle touches, and, harrowing as is the whole effect, he cannot be accused of forcing the note beyond the limits of his conception by any irrelevant accumulation of horrors. But this curious fantasy, with its quasi-scientific foundation, in which a doctor upon a remote island practises vivisection in the spirit of a modern and unsentimental Frankenstein,[1] is intrinsically horrible.

---

† From the *Manchester Guardian* (April 14, 1896): 4.
1. The reviewer refers to the novel *Frankenstein; or, The Modern Prometheus* (1818) by English writer Mary Shelley (1797–1851).

The impressions should not be put to the test of analysis or reflection. As it is, they grip the mind with a painful interest and a fearful curiosity. The mysteries of the forbidden enclosure; the cries of the tortured puma; the pursuit through the dark wood by the leopard man; the strange litany of the beast folk; Prendick's flight and frantic apprehensions; the revolt of the beast folk—such scenes and incidents crowd upon us with a persistent fascination. Absolute success in such a narrative is impossible; to play these curious tricks with science is not the highest art; it might even be contended that this is no legitimate subject for art at all; but in its kind Mr. Wells has achieved a success unquestionable and extraordinary. There must be, of course, a weak place where science and fantasy join. To obscure this plausibly is the great difficulty, and we think that here, as too in "Dr. Jekyll and Mr. Hyde,"[2] there is some little creaking of the machinery. But if the chapter "Dr. Moreau Explains" brings us dangerously near a too critical habit of mind, it is full of striking things—the masterful, overbearing manner of the Doctor, his dreadful plausibility in maintaining his impossible position, his perfect devotion to investigation, the fine contempt for both pleasure and pain which enables him to make the effective counterstroke of accusing his opponent of materialism. "The study of nature makes a man at last as remorseless as nature," he says, and with Prendick we are thrown on our resources to combat this appalling inversion. Here is the picture of the terrible Doctor:—"I looked at him, and saw but a white-faced, white-haired man, with calm eyes. Save for his serenity, the touch almost of beauty that resulted from his set tranquillity and from his magnificent build, he might have passed muster among a hundred other comfortable old gentlemen." But though the reader of this book must sup full of horrors, it must not be supposed that there are no mitigations and no relief. There is a grotesque pathos about the beast folk which redeems them, and Montgomery, a character very much in Mr. Stevenson's manner, is reassuring and quite human in his vulgarity. The effect of the final chapter, "The Man Alone," is admirable, and that he should find solace and a "sense of infinite peace and protection" in the study of the stars is one of the many points that differentiate Mr. Wells from the mere sensational story-spinner. Yet, great as is the ability and pronounced as is the success of this book, we are convinced that Mr. Wells is too strong and original a writer to devote himself exclusively to fantastic themes.

2. I.e., *Strange Case of Dr. Jekyll and Mr. Hyde*, 1886 novel by Scottish author Robert Louis Stevenson (1850–1894).

ANONYMOUS

"A New Frankenstein"†

Mr. Wells is accustomed to employ his fine talents upon fiction with a scientific bias. His imagination, which is a remarkable one, loves to explore in diverse and ingenious directions from a scientific base of operations. We have seen it before in "The Time Machine," and again in "The Wonderful Visit." This philosophical intelligence is rarely absent from his work. It may be that it stands in the way of his popularity; certainly it is not likely to recommend him to such as like their fiction human. But, however that may be, there is no possibility of denying the extraordinary cleverness with which he wraps his fantastic ideas in artistic dress. There may be two opinions as to whether "The Island of Dr. Moreau" is repellent or not. It has been already frankly termed repugnant or repulsive. Yet upon these terms Mrs. Shelley's "Frankenstein" might be written down in condemnation. Pleasing to the ordinary reader in the ordinary sense Mr. Wells's latest book is not; fascinating it certainly is to anyone who loves the deft manipulation of an ingenious idea. Dr. Moreau, a noted vivisectionist, has applied his darling hobby to life, and developed skill to such an extent as to people his kingdom with monsters. There can be nothing but praise for the atmosphere of terror in which Mr. Wells approaches his subject. The earlier chapters are undoubtedly the best in the story. The horrible episode of the puma—we can cordially recommend the chapter to the anti-vivisectionist. As for Mr. Wells himself, it is not likely that he takes any part in this controversy. He is clearly cold in utilizing his materials. The horrors of the island dawn upon one with accumulative efforts, until perhaps the brain grows a little too familiar with them to keep its fears. The difficulty of such progression is that one must be perpetually screwing up a peg tighter as one proceeds, in order to allow no anti-climax, no dulling of the note. But over all the difficulties Mr. Wells's nimble fancy leaps with confidence. He had set himself a hard task, and his sense of the dramatic is never at fault. The reader will creep with uncanny feelings to read of the stalking of Prendick by the Leopard Man. Indeed, he may sup his full of strange and gruesome spectacles in these pages. He may or may not object to it, but he will read if he has once begun, will read and wonder. Very possibly he may see in the characters of Montgomery, Moreau himself, and the drunken captain reasons to regret that Mr. Wells has never cared to write a novel full of such full-blooded

† From the *Pall Mall Gazette* (April 17, 1896): 4.

breathing human creatures as are those which he has sketched at random. But that is his own affair. For those who do not care for the quasi-scientific tale one may safely predict that Mr. Wells will not leave these other talents buried from the light. There is but a small handful of men capable of writing a real novel of life, and he is one. In the meantime, and until he chooses, we must enjoy these fantastic elaborations of his fertile imagination.

ANONYMOUS

[Review]†

* * * We should have thought it impossible for any work of fiction to surpass in gruesome horror some of the problem-novels relating to the great sexual question which have been recently published, if we had not read the "Island of Dr. Moreau," by H. G. Wells. Having read it, we are bound to admit that there are still lower depths of nastiness, and still cruder manifestations of fantastic imbecility than any attained by the ladies who have been so much with us in recent years. Mr. Wells is a very clever person, who has written one or two stories which have had the merit of originality. In these stories he has shown that he possesses distinct gifts as a writer of fiction, and that he could interest a reader, even if his theme were comparatively commonplace. But the commonplace is evidently hateful to him, and he makes it his first business, when sitting down to write a story, to hit upon an idea that shall startle everybody by its extravagance and novelty. In the present instance he has achieved originality at the expense of decency (we do not use the word in its sexual significance) and common sense. He introduces us to a remote islet in the Pacific where a notorious professor of vivisection, with the aid of a drunken Scotch doctor, is engaged in a series of hideous experiments upon living animals. The object of these experiments is to create something having the semblance of man out of the lower creatures. We need not go further into the details of this delectable theme. Mr. Wells, as we have said, has talent, and he employs it here for a purpose which is absolutely degrading. It is no excuse that he should have made his book one that sends a thrill of horror through the mind of the reader. After all, even among writers of fiction, talents are accompanied by responsibilities—a fact which Mr. Wells seems to have forgotten. * * *

† From the *Speaker* 13 (April 18, 1896): 429–30.

[BASIL WILLIAMS]

[Review]†

The horrors described by Mr. Wells in his latest book very pertinently raise the question how far it is legitimate to create feelings of disgust in a work of art. It is undeniable that details of horror and disgust sometimes appear perfectly legitimate methods of arousing the emotions, and add to the beauty of a tragedy and to the pleasure to be derived therefrom. The "Philoctetes"[1] is perhaps an extreme instance of this, for there the loathsomeness of the details of Philoctetes's suffering is as great as it can be, and yet it is never revolting. But in this book the details of suffering so elaborately set forth by Mr. Wells simply have a nauseating effect. The distinction between legitimate and illegitimate use of horror seems to lie not in the form of the horror, but in the purpose for which it is used. The repulsive details in the "Philoctetes" are merely used to give verisimilitude to a tragedy which would be tragic without them; the case of Philoctetes, quite apart from his special sufferings are adventitious, and not of the essence of the tragedy. But in Mr. Wells's story, which may be taken as a type of many others tainted with the same fault, the tragedy, such as it is, merely consists in the details of the form of horror chosen; the disgusting descriptions arouse loathing without any equivalent personal interest. The sufferings inflicted in the course of the story have absolutely no adequate artistic reason, for it is impossible to feel the slightest interest in any one of the characters, who are used as nothing but groundwork on which to paint the horrors. In fact, these horrors have not even the merit of penny-a-lining descriptions of police-court atrocities, for in them there is at least some human interest, but here, without the actual form of horror described, the book would be quite irrational. It has, we observe, been suggested in some quarters that Mr. Wells was animated by a desire to expose the repulsive aspect of vivisection, but we do not believe it. At least, it is singularly ineffective from that point of view, and would be about as valuable for such a purpose as a pornological story in suppressing immorality; and even if that were the object, it would be no defence for artistic failure.

---

† From the *Athenaeum*, no. 3576 (May 9, 1896): 615–16.
1. *Philoctetes* (409 BCE) by Greek tragedian Sophocles (497/6–405 BCE); the play's protagonist suffers a disabling, malodorous foot injury, to which Wells's reviewer obliquely refers below.

Modern Criticism

CYNDY HENDERSHOT

The Animal Without†

Fin de siècle anxieties about maintaining a stable masculinity in the face of the beast within (expressed by Le Fanu, Stevenson, and others) are frequently interwoven with fears surrounding the British male subject's ability to remain British when encountering another culture. In late-nineteenth-century British works of fiction the implicit possibilities of degeneration of the individual that Darwinism ushered in overlap with fears of degeneration of the British Empire. Frequently, these anxieties are conceived of in rhetorically gendered terms. * * * The British male subject of fin de siècle society found his masculinity threatened from within (through the revelation of his biological link to animals) and from without (through the feminized process of natural selection and through cultural Others such as the non-European and the aesthete). * * *

* * *

Wells's novel *The Island of Doctor Moreau* (1896) examines the British male subject within the context of an imaginary island located in the proximity of the Galápagos Islands. This imaginative space implicates Darwin's theories with the imperial project. Moreau serves as both imperial governor and Darwinian scientist on the island, while the Beast People function in the narrative as over-determined "natives." While on board the *Ipecacuanha*, Edward Prendick learns about the island from Montgomery. To para-phrase Charlie Marlow, it is presented to Prendick as one of the blank spaces on the map. Montgomery says: "it's an island, where I live. So far as I know, it hasn't got a name" (7). Later, like a British imperialist, Moreau says of the island, "the place seemed waiting

† From *The Animal Within: Masculinity and the Gothic* (Ann Arbor: University of Michigan Press, 1998), pp. 123–39, 241–43. Reprinted with permission.

for me" (49).[1] British cartographers literally figured Greenwich, a borough of London, the center of the world by mapping longitude 0° as passing through the city. Such mapping was accepted worldwide, and this continued until quite recently to be exclusively the case, as the result of an international agreement signed in 1884. Moreau's desire to appropriate for his project the blank space of an island "waiting" for British settlement updates Robinson Crusoe's project of bringing civilization to savage areas of the world. For Moreau, as Gothic scientist, the blank space is not to be populated by British subjects but is to be used as an "appropriate"—that is, non-British— space for his unethical experimentation.[2] The mapping of the world practiced by British imperialists is imaginatively extended by Wells to a situation in which Moreau's attempt to control and name one of those blank spaces proves disastrous. Noble's Island becomes a microcosm for the failures and excesses of British imperialism.

The Beast People's relationship to non-European natives is a complex, multilayered one. Upon first encountering one of the Beast People, M'Ling, Prendick attempts to read him as a native.[3] Prendick continually emphasizes the "black face" of M'Ling (8), coding him as African or native South American. Prendick is perplexed by "the black" and his curious "deformity" (9). The *Ipecacuanha* crew's treatment of M'Ling bears resemblances to some European treatments of non-Europeans. Although M'Ling is a man, as far as the crew knows, his black face gives them license to hit him and to allow the dogs to frighten him (9–10). Further, his black face allows the captain to label him "a devil" (11), coding the non-European as evil, a coding Prendick himself somewhat laconically repeats, referring to M'Ling as "the poor devil" (9). Later he attempts to resist openly demonizing M'Ling: "that black figure with its eyes of fire struck down through all my adult thoughts and feelings, and for a moment the forgotten horrors of childhood came back to my mind. Then the effect passed as it had come" (13). After arriving on the island, Prendick initially continues to read the Beast People as non-European natives; seeing one creature upon a slope, he describes him as having "a black negroid face" (17). As Prendick spends more time on the island, he begins to perceive disparities between his preconceived notions of what constitutes a non-European savage and what the Beast People actually appear to be. After glimpsing the Leopard Man

1. Said maintains that the genre of the British novel has continually been tied up with imperialist ambition: he traces this imperialist impulse back to the prototypical modern novel, *Robinson Crusoe* (xii).
2. As McClure argues, fin de siècle imperial Gothic (or "Imperial Romance," as he terms it) relies upon London as the center of cartography within which mapping of much of the world first took place (114).
3. For other readings of the Beast People's connection to British imperialism, see Stableford; Showalter, "Apocalyptic"; Philmus, "Introducing"; McCarthy; and Bozzett.

drinking "on all-fours like a beast," Prendick comments, "then I thought that the man I had just seen had been clothed in bluish cloth, had not been naked as a savage would have been; and I tried to persuade myself from that fact that he was after all probably a peaceful character" (25). Ironically. Prendick initially believes the Beast People are "safer" than the savage, scantily clad natives of his imagination. The question Prendick poses to Montgomery apropos of the Beast People, "what race are they?" (23), is one of the central epistemological questions of the novel. What constitutes a non-European native? Who is the imperial Other? The central answer that the novel offers is that the savage is a creation of the European mind: the Beast People are the product of Moreau's science.

Moreau creates an imperial situation on Noble's Island on which he establishes himself as a white god figure controlling the Beast People and using them for manual labor. In the novel Moreau's "whiteness" is emphasized as much as M'Ling's "blackness" is.[4] Prendick first glimpses Moreau as "a massive white-haired man" (14). Until he learns Moreau's identity, Prendick continues to conceive of Moreau as "the white-haired man" (17). When Prendick and Montgomery arrive at Noble's Island, Moreau uses the Beast People to help him unload his animals, and Prendick notices that one black "was dressed like Montgomery and his white-haired companion, in jacket and trousers of blue serge" (18). Like the imperialist, both exploiting the natives through enforced manual labor and making them conform culturally to British dress and habits, Moreau attempts to mold the Beast People into British subjects. Prendick sees one of the Beast People dressed "in white, lugging a packing-case along the beach." These blacks in white convey the process of race purification for which Moreau's humanization of the animals serves as an analogue. The Beast People are forced by Moreau to give up their original culture in order to become more masculine and civilized, that is, more British. M'Ling serves as a domestic servant for Montgomery and Moreau: Prendick sees him "dressed in white" carrying "a little tray with some coffee and vegetables thereon" (21). As many British imperialists made domestic servants out of their subjects, so Moreau uses his natives in order to allow his time to be devoted exclusively to research. Significantly, however, Moreau's "Fridays" are literally created by him.

Moreau's deification of himself as a god to the Beast People correlates with the white god mythology that many European

4. Punter argues that the black and white imagery of Moreau functions as "a natural metaphorical accompaniment, images of white imperialism in its decline" (*Terror* 253). John Frankenheimer's 1996 version of the novel portrays Marlon Brando's Moreau as literally a white god. Moreau's face is painted chalk white, and he wears white clothing when he appears before the Beast People.

imperialists used in order to insure their hegemony over non-European natives: Kurtz represents one imaginative example. Moreau, "white and terrible" (32), establishes a series of laws that read as a parody of European sanctions upon colonized peoples as well as a parodic Decalogue.[5] Moreau's laws are instated in order to protect himself from the Beast People's "savagery." Besides the prohibitions on eating and fighting, Prendick comments on "the prohibition of what I thought then were the maddest, most impossible, and most indecent things one could well imagine" (38). These sexual prohibitions bear direct connection to European imperial prohibitions regarding their subjects.[6] As Sander L. Gilman argues, attempts to categorize and hence control non-European races frequently centered on the issue of sexual perversion. Gilman argues that perversion was projected onto the imperial Other ("Sexology" 73). Thus, the problem of "civilizing" non-European natives frequently took shape in prohibitions against perceived sexual perversions. In the nineteenth century, however, as European epistemology began to move toward a notion of essential degeneracy, the native's perversion labeled him or her as permanently, indeed racially, degenerate and hence in need of European administration.[7] The Beast People's perverse sexuality, troped as "stubborn beast-flesh" by Moreau (81), correlates with fin de siècle European perceptions of the innate sexual perversity of the non-European native.

Exploring the Beast People as non-European natives is an uneasy process. The fact that they are animals who have been humanized through scientific means seems to point to an association between natives and animals and/or natives and missing links: both of these associations were prevalent in late-nineteenth-century British society.[8] The non-European native was viewed by many Victorians as uncivilized and animal-like. Emerging race theories, however, sought to codify European perceptions of other cultures in the supposedly objective discourse of science. Race theorists turned to Darwinian theory as a means of legitimizing views of the native as lower and more animalistic than the supposedly higher, European race. While this hierarchization of the human race stems more from Spencer's ladder of evolution than from Darwin's tree of evolution, the

5. For connections between Moreau's law and both the Decalogue and Kipling's *Jungle Books*, see Platzner; Philmus, "Satiric"; Batchelor; Reed; and G. Beauchamp.
6. For a reading of these unnamed prohibitions as most likely sexual in nature see Philmus (*Variorum* 95n).
7. Gilman states, "degeneracy is the label for the other, specifically the other as the essence of pathology . . . it is the sense of hopelessness and helplessness which is captured by the label of the degenerate" ("Sexology" 83).
8. As Gilman argues, by the late nineteenth century the association of the primitive and unbridled, animalistic sexuality was a commonplace ("Black" 229).

conduciveness of Darwinian theory to race theory remains a vexed issue. Potentially, Darwin's theories seem to indicate similarities between races and thus threaten to eliminate the Otherness that envelops European perceptions of other cultures.[9] Hence, by exploding the Great Chain of Being, Darwin emphasizes the links between European and other cultures as well as the links between humans and animals. While this is certainly one implication of Darwinism being discussed in fin de siècle society, it is one that is fundamentally at odds with imperialism. If all races and cultures stem from a common ancestor, how can the British justify the domination and exploitation of other humans?

One answer that appears to be in play in *Moreau* is the perception of natives as subjects in-between the human and the animal. The Great Chain of Evolution thus places Europeans at the top and other groups, such as South American natives and Africans, at the bottom, close to apes. As Nancy Stepan argues, nineteenth-century science came to see racial behavior as fixed rather than as produced by environment ("Biological" 97). According to this theory, a South American native, for example, was inherently degenerate when compared to the British subject. The lack of inherently masculine traits in non-European peoples made them biologically inferior and more animalistic than Europeans. Stepan argues that in his attempts to establish an argument for continuity in his theory of descent, Darwin opened the gates for these biologized racial theories: "the argument for continuity led, almost inevitably, to the use of the lower races to fill the gaps between animals and man. Later, scientists would find it only too easy to interpret Darwin as meaning that the races of man now formed an evolutionary scale" (*Idea* 55).

Moreau's natives undoubtedly are coded with racial theories that view the non-European as an intermediary between animal and human and which give credence to the treatment of them as less than human. While Moreau and Prendick clearly support, in varying degrees, fin de siècle racial theories—Moreau by forming humanized animals that resemble blacks and South American natives and Prendick by already preconceiving of any native as potentially animalistic and hence being unable to distinguish between a human and a Beast Person—does the novel itself do so? I am not suggesting that there is a simple answer to this question, yet the fact that Wells's "savages" are made by Moreau and not found by him appears to constitute an explicit foregrounding of European perceptions about and

9. Beer argues, for example, that "instead of the severe disjunction between the human and other species enjoined by creationist theory the whole measure can be encompassed: 'we are all netted together'" ("Four" 127)—as a result of Darwinian thought. For other theorists who see the potential in Darwinism for eliminating difference, see G. Levine; Beer, *Plots*.

epistemological creations of natives rather than any statement about non-Europeans per se. In other words, Wells moves toward a deconstruction of European perceptions of the imperial Other.

The "real" non-Europeans who appear in the text are the Kanakas, who are briefly discussed in Moreau's explanation of his experiments. Moreau's use of the South Sea natives who were imported as laborers to Queensland in the 1860s to work on sugarcane plantations, and hence were historically exploited by Europeans much as Moreau exploits them, serves to illustrate that Moreau equates the Kanakas with his natives. Moreau introduces a Gorilla Man ("a fair specimen of the negroid type," as he describes him [49]) into the camps of the Kanakas who help Moreau build his settlement, indicating that he views their level of civilization as equivalent to that of his experimental humans. In fact, in Moreau's Chain of Evolution he places his Beast People higher than the Kanakas. Describing the dwelling the Gorilla Man builds, Moreau comments that he "built himself a hovel rather better, it seemed to me, than their [the Kanakas'] own shanties." His contempt for the Kanakas remains, even though we are told that one teaches the Gorilla Man to read and gives him "some rudimentary ideas of morality." Moreau dismisses the deaths of the Kanakas lightly—"all the Kanaka boys are dead now"—despite the fact that his experiments have led directly or indirectly to their deaths. Moreau comments, "well, I have replaced them," making explicit his reading of non-Europeans as equivalent to his Beast People (49–50).

While Moreau clearly supports racial theories stemming from the Chain of Evolution theory, the novel locates the issue back at the site of the British subject. Moreau's reading of natives sheds more light on his subjectivity than on theirs.[1] The animal within becomes the animal without, a projection that protects the British subject from his own biological connection to the animal world and which provides ideological justification for imperialism. Moreau's created natives reveal British fantasies about the imperial Other. When Prendick arrives at Noble's Island he sees an amalgamation of cultures that does not surprise him. In addition to the black-faced Beast People, he sees "brown men" and women wrapped as they are "only in the East" (17). Prendick sees, in other words, African, South American, and Islamic natives existing in one location. Further, the black-faced M'Ling bears a Chinese-sounding name. The fascinating aspect of this mixture of widely different cultures all coded as Other on Noble's Island is that Prendick is not in the least surprised to see signifiers of diverse cultures in one space. The only aspect of

---

1. Gilman astutely points out that late-nineteenth-century racial theory "turns out to be an inner fear of that hidden within us and projected onto the world" ("Sexology" 89).

the Beast People's physical appearances that arouses his suspicion is their apparent "deformity."

Here Wells seems to be suggesting a point theorized by Said: nineteenth-century British subjects made few or no distinctions between non-European cultures: they all stood as Other, exotic, threatening in the monolithic category of "the native." Said maintains that European perceptions of the non-European relied (and largely still [do]) on binary oppositions (*Orient* 327). For Prendick all of these cultures are non-British, so they are monolithically exotic, dangerously attractive, inferior, as they are for Moreau, who uses this concept of the non-European as the basis for his experiment. He does not create Caucasian-type Beast People; he creates Negroid-type Beast People. The highly exoticized representations of South America in much nineteenth-century British fiction may also be a factor here. Prendick expects any combination of cultures on the South American island because in the British imagination it is a blank space to be filled in as site, to use Said's words, for "a surrogate, and even underground [European] self" (3).[2]

The effect of the island and its inhabitants on Prendick, as representative of masculine British civilization, forms the core of Wells's novel. Edward Prendick is "a private gentleman" who takes (3), as he says, "to Natural History as a relief from the dullness of my comfortable independence" (7). He is representative of the Victorian gentleman who studies out of boredom. In some significant ways Prendick is set apart from his apparently less-civilized contemporaries. After the wreck of the *Lady Vain* Prendick, unlike the other two men who are on a raft with him, is horrified by the proposal of cannibalism as a means of survival.[3] He states, "I stood out against it with all my might, was rather for scuttling the boat and perishing together among the sharks that followed us." When Prendick is forced to accept the proposal, gentlemanlike, he maintains the objectivity of drawing lots, while the sailor who is chosen as a result of this process attacks the other sailor on board, an act that results in their deaths, as they fall overboard and sink "like stones," and in Prendick's survival. Prendick's code of gentlemanly behavior apparently saves him at this juncture, though his hideous laugh, which catches him "suddenly like a thing from without," qualifies this success (5).

2. Many nineteenth-century texts focus on South America as a space for fantastic occurrences. Wells's "Empire of the Ants" and Doyle's *Lost World* and "The Adventure of the Sussex Vampire" are prime examples. The tendency to use South America as a space for the fantastic persists, as Michael Crichton's *Jurassic Park* and Paul Theroux's *Mosquito Coast* attest.
3. See Reed for a discussion of the influence of the *Regina v. Dudley and Stephens* (1884) case, which determined that, "despite the acknowledged necessity for seamen to survive even through cannibalism, human—which is to say British—law would not endorse murder to permit such survival" (134–35).

Prendick's fight against the feminizing degenerative forces at work in the novel is further underscored when he is compared with Montgomery. Montgomery is perceived as a degenerate due to his alcoholism, which, as Eric T. Carlson observes, is termed "dipsomania" and viewed in late-nineteenth-century medical theories as a sign of a general degeneration of the human species because it is perceived as "not willful but an illness, a particular form of mania" (130). In contrast to Montgomery's dipsomania, Prendick is "an abstainer," as he tells Montgomery (23). Yet Prendick's gentlemanliness appears to be primarily superficial: agreeing to follow the formality of drawing lots in order to practice cannibalism and refusing to drink alcohol appear to be flimsy barriers against degeneration. Ultimately, Prendick does degenerate as a result of the time he spends on the island.

Further, Prendick's leisure-class status, that is, taking up scientific studies to ward off boredom, codes him as a decadent in fin de siècle society: his solipsistic scientific research would be perceived by Victorians as decadent because it leads to no published findings. Prendick's vague, non-goal-oriented research distinguishes him from someone like Charles Darwin, who published his research prematurely (in his own view) because his theory was perceived by the Linnaean Society to be stronger than Alfred Russel Wallace's parallel theory. That is, Darwin published against his own better judgment in order to be socially responsible. Prendick as "useless," decadent scientist refers to a central concern of the novel: indeed, *Moreau* appears to explore the implications of the aesthetic movement within its imperial/Darwinian matrix. Wells maintains in a preface to *Moreau* that the trials of Oscar Wilde in 1895 served as part of his inspiration for the novel: "there was a scandalous trial about this time, the graceless and pitiful downfall of a man of genius, and this story was the response of an imaginative mind to the reminder that humanity is but animal rough-hewn to a reasonable shape and in perpetual conflict between instinct and injunction" (ix). The implications of Wilde's trials and their association with the aesthetic movement in general (at least in the popular mind) seemed to illustrate to many the pitfalls of decadence as an artistic stance. Explorations of decadence appear to be coded in several significant ways in the novel. The threat of the feminization of the masculine British Empire via the aesthetes, whose philosophy and lifestyles promoted feminine pleasure over masculine duty, is explored in the three central characters in the novel.

Montgomery's dipsomania codes him as decadent as does his possible homosexuality. Montgomery has been expelled from Britain because, while a medical student in London, he says, "I lost my head for ten minutes on a foggy night" (12). Montgomery's transgression is left ambiguous, but many critics, including Elaine Showalter, have read this transgression as related to Wilde's trials ("Apocalyptic" 80).[4] Montgomery's close relationship with M'Ling—he says that M'Ling "was the only thing that had ever really cared for him" (71)—seems to indicate that Wells is subtly portraying Montgomery as homosexual. In fin de siècle Britain homosexuality was associated with both degeneration and decadent art. Although Montgomery's connection to decadence is a marginal part of the novel, Prendick and Moreau's decadence are central.

The significance of Prendick's propensity for degeneration via a leisure lifestyle that results in his residing on Noble's Island is heightened if we examine his character's associations with the then prince of Wales, the future Edward VII. Victorian anxieties over the future of the British Empire were intensified due to the future king's lifestyle, which was one of fin de siècle decadence. As Barbara Tuchman observes, a typical 1890s evening for the leisure class in London might include a party at the home of Lady de Grey, "London's best-dressed woman," whose guest list included the prince of Wales and Oscar Wilde. The prince was part of the Marlborough House circle, notorious for its "fast" lifestyle and opposed by the "Incorruptibles," a reactionary social group who viewed the prince as "vulgar" and saw themselves "as upholding the tone of Society" (19). The implications of the prince's decadent lifestyle did not go unnoticed by his contemporaries, who despaired over the future of the empire after Victoria's death. As Robert K. Massie observes, both Victoria and her husband, Albert, lamented the prince's idleness, and Victoria likened the Marlborough set to "the nobility of France on the eve of the French Revolution" (16). The prince was perceived by late-nineteenth-century society as one sign of the impending degeneration of the British Empire.

Edward Prendick's association with Prince Albert Edward, heir to the British throne, increases his emblematic significance as representative British male subject. Wells changed Prendick's name from Andrew to Edward in the course of the extensive revisions he made to *Moreau* prior to its publication.[5] Further, Prendick's last name is suggestive of an obscene reference to Edward's notorious womanizing: Pren—Prince—Prince's Dick, *Prin* being a common slang term for *prince*.[6] Edward, the prince who thinks with his dick rather than with his brain, provoked anxieties in those who imagined him as future king. Edward Prendick is the sole survivor of the wreck

---

4. Critics have proposed other transgressions as forming the basis of Montgomery's outcast status, such as murder (e.g., Paris) and cannibalism (e.g., Reed).
5. For discussions of Wells's revisions of *Moreau*, see Philmus, "Revisions" and *Variorum*.
6. George IV, for example, was referred to as "Prinny" (Brooke-Little). *A Concise Dictionary of Slang and Unconventional English* notes that *dick* as slang for *penis* dates from military usage from about 1880.

of the *Lady Vain* (the Lady V; the Lady Victoria) and hence may be read as the successor to the vain pretenses of Victorian society to achieve a massive, invincible empire externally and to achieve a perfected society internally through their notion of progress. What happens to Edward as representative British subject? He degenerates to the animalistic status of a Beast Person and abandons all hope for the British Empire, and by implication the world, through his isolated studies in astronomy. The pessimistic upshot of these associations appears to be that Britain cannot look to Edward (or anyone) to "save" the empire and usher in a utopia; for that they must look to another world. Prendick, like Moreau, withdraws from the "usefulness" of public activity into the "useless," self-contained world of the decadent.

Moreau represents a more sinister connection to fin de siècle decadence and the anxieties surrounding its supposedly feminine degenerativeness. In the novel his applications of Darwinian science are frequently portrayed in artistic terms. In trying to explain his experiments, Moreau uses literary explanations to shed light on them. Attempting to palliate Prendick's curiosity, he says, "our little establishment here contains a secret or so, is a kind of Blue-Beard's chamber, in fact." In Moreau's library Prendick discovers "surgical works and editions of the Latin and Greek classics" on the shelves, indicating a connection that is being established between literature and medicine (20).[7] When forced to explain his experiment to Prendick, Moreau, attempting to establish a history for his experiments, refers to literature, "Victor Hugo gives an account of them [experimental humans] in *L'Homme qui Rit*" (46). Further, when discussing the tortures of the Inquisition, Moreau argues that "their chief aim was *artistic* torture, but some at least of the inquisitors must have had a touch of scientific curiosity" (47; emph. added). These artistic allusions become more specifically linked to the aesthetes and *l'art-pour-l'art* theory prevalent in late-nineteenth-century British and French societies as Moreau's explanation continues.[8] When Prendick asks Moreau why he has chosen the human form for his creations, Moreau first states that it has been chosen "by chance" but then comments, "I suppose there is something in the human form that appeals to the artistic turn more powerfully than any animal shape can." Thus, Moreau chooses to mold humans because of their aesthetic beauty, not because making humans has any useful purpose. Moreau expresses a science-for-science's-sake philosophy

7. For a discussion of Moreau's library in relation to Wells's work and some contemporary variations on it, see S. J. Levine.
8. For discussions of Moreau as artist, see S. J. Levine; Reed.

that eschews utilitarian applications of knowledge.[9] As Moreau tells Prendick: "we are on different platforms. You are a materialist" (47), an assertion that angers Prendick. Moreau refuses to combine morality with his scientific creation, stating that "I have gone on, not heeding anything but the question I was pursuing" (49). Further, his experiments, through their attempts to rid humans of "the beast flesh," are working toward a more aesthetically pleasing human, one who is free from the "cravings, instincts, desires that harm humanity" (51). In the preface to *The Picture of Dorian Gray* Wilde asserts: "the only excuse for making a useless thing is that one admires it intensely. All art is quite useless." Moreau appears to extend this aesthete philosophy to the realm of science, as his attempts to create a humanized animal are "useless" in any materialistic sense, and his motivation appears to be primarily aesthetic. In his preface Wilde also asserts that "there is no such thing as a moral or an immoral book. Books are well written, or badly written" (138). Moreau echoes this philosophy when he tells Prendick that, although Montgomery appears to like the Beast People, "it's his business not mine. They only sicken me with a sense of failure. I take no interest in them" (51). Moreau disregards the Beast People as if they were unsuccessful works of art.

Moreau's connections to decadent art are further solidified if his character is read as being associated with the French Symbolist painter Gustave Moreau. Critics have proposed a variety of possibilities for the meanings of Moreau's name.[1] In terms of examining the fear of the feminization of masculine civilization through decadence that haunts the margins of the novel, linking Moreau with this decadent artist appears relevant. Moreau's paintings focus on the breakdown of boundaries. Most immediately for Wells's novel, Moreau frequently paints minglings of humans and animals. In *The Chimera* (1867), for example, a woman clings to a satyr as he attempts to fly off a cliff. In *Licornes* (n.d.) a woman places her arm around a combination made up of a human and a unicorn: the figure bears a unicorn's head, a human torso and arms, and a unicorn's legs. In *Oedipus and the Sphinx* (1864) a lion with a woman's head, neck,

9. In the Gothic tradition the association of the scientist and the artist is a commonplace. Victor Frankenstein "authors" his creature; Aylmer seeks to make Georgiana into a flawless work of art; Rappaccini watches over his garden as if it is his artistic tableau. Wells takes this traditional association and places it in the specific context of the aesthetic movement.

1. For a summary of the possible sources for Moreau's name, see Philmus, *Variorum* xlxii–xliiin. Steffen-Fluhr briefly discusses some connections between Gustave Moreau and Wells's Moreau ("Paper" 326–27n) and argues that Wells most likely gained knowledge of Moreau's paintings through indirect sources such as Huysman and Wilde. Haynes makes an argument for reading Moreau's name allegorically as Death (Mor) Water (Eau). It should be noted also that the meaning of *moreau* in French is "jet black, or black and shining": this meaning appears to make a connection between Moreau and his most prized experiment, the shining black puma that kills him.

and breasts appears to merge into the body of Oedipus as she asks him the riddle. Moreau also draws on Greco-Roman myths of bestiality for his subject matter. Thus, in *Europa and the Bull* (1869) and *Leda* (n.d.) Moreau focuses on the breakdown of the boundaries of species as the two women concerned are seduced by Zeus, who appears to them in animal form. Significantly, Moreau also blurs the lines between male and female. In *Jason and Medea* (1865) the male and female figures bear similar hair and body shapes, and their genitals are carefully concealed. Moreau continually blurs the lines between the male and female bodies, usually feminizing male figures—as *Orpheus at the Tomb of Eurydice* (1897–98), *Narcissus* (1895), *Hesiod and the Muse* (1891), and others attest.[2] Reading Wells's character Moreau through the work of the painter Gustave Moreau further highlights the associations Wells is making between decadent art, the merging of animal and human, and the breakdown of gender distinctions in fin de siècle society.

The threat to masculine civilization posed by decadent art, a movement Wells openly opposed, is not the only feminine Other that threatens masculine identity in the novel.[3] The feminine nature of Darwinian theory also emerges as the male characters are beset by an uncontrollable nature that is personified as feminine.[4] The novel presents several feminine personifications that point to a fear of the obliteration of masculine civilization by feminized Darwinian nature. Prendick's trip on the *Lady Vain* results in his being made helpless at the hands of brutal natural forces: read along these lines, *Lady* may refer to Dame Nature refashioned in a Darwinian context; *Vain* may refer to masculine civilization's attempt to control a femininely personified nature, of which Moreau's experiments represent an example. Further, in the first paragraph of his narrative Prendick refers to the *Medusa* case, an infamous 1816 historical event involving a French frigate that wrecked, resulting in the survivors practicing cannibalism. The feminine name of the ship, *Medusa*, links the random and horrifying event of a shipwreck with

<hr />

2. I have relied on several sources for Moreau's paintings: see Selz, Flat, Rosenblum, and *Redon, Seurat, and the Symbolists*.

3. Several critics discuss Wells's contempt for the aesthetic movement: see McCarthy; and Philmus, *Variorum* 96–97n. For a solid discussion of the threat the aesthetic movement posed to rigid Victorian gender systems, see Siegel.

4. For discussions of the feminine in the novel, see Paris, who seems to emphasize an essentialized femininity in the novel that the characters transgress against. Showalter makes the connection between the antivivisection movement (which Wells's novel was read in light of) and its connection with feminists ("Apocalyptic" 79–80). Philmus mentions in his introduction that the puma may be read as "the paramount instance of a Darwinian Nature which proves to be intractable to his intentions," though he does not explore the implications of her gendering at any length ("Introducing" xxv). See also Steffen-Fluhr, "Paper." Chamberlin's discussion of thermodynamics and its metaphor of "dark and yet luminous feminine authority" seems relevant here as well (276). Another possible connection being made is between the black female puma and entropy.

a feminine personification much as the *Lady Vain* does. Prendick is rescued by the *Ipecacuanha*, a vessel bearing the name of a low-growing South American shrub whose roots are used medicinally. Of the ship Montgomery comments that the captain "calls the thing the *Ipecacuanha*, of all silly, infernal names; though when there's much of a sea without any mind, she certainly acts accordingly" (6). Like the *Lady Vain*, the *Ipecacuanha* represents an unpredictable, amoral feminine nature. Although the ipecacuanha plant is an emetic, which presumably may be used for beneficial purging, the instability of the view of a beneficent nature is underscored when Moreau tells Prendick that one of the Kanakas dies of a wounded heel "that he poisoned in some way with plant juice" (50), possibly the juice of the ipecacuanha plant or a metonymically linked plant. Additionally, an alternative name for the *Ipecacuanha* in other drafts of *Moreau* is the *Red Luck*, a name that foregrounds the "nature red in tooth and claw" that Tennyson personifies as feminine in *In Memoriam* and which refers back to the dinghy of the *Lady Vain* that is found with "spots of blood on the gunwale" (6).

Thus, even before encountering Noble's Island, Prendick becomes helpless due to the forces of a nature he cannot control.[5] On board the *Ipecacuanha* he must be revived with "some scarlet stuff, iced," which indicates his devolution due to the brutality of nature (6). Like an animal or a vampire, Prendick needs blood in order to regain his strength.[6] Due to the brutal treatment by the captain and crew, he comes to see himself as "a bit of human flotsam, cut off from my resources and with my fare unpaid" (11): Prendick, the British gentleman, comes to realize that he is not the invincible upholder of British civilization but, instead, a weakened animal, dependent upon others for survival. Due to natural forces he cannot control or explain, he begins to wait "passively upon fate" (15), rather than attempting to create his own destiny, as a nineteenth-century British subject placed in a foreign country should do. Prendick loses his masculine vigor and

5. Various implications of Darwinism that are explored in the novel have been discussed by many critics; see Haynes; Bowen; McCarthy; Philmus, *Variorum*, "Introducing," "Satiric"; Milling; S. J. Levine; Batchelor; Stableford; Shaw; Showalter, "Apocalyptic"; and Crossley. Wells's articles on Darwinism and its related ideas that are relevant for *Moreau* include "The Limits of Individual Plasticity," "The Influence of Islands on Variation," "On Extinction," and "Human Evolution, an Artificial Process." See also T. H. Huxley, "Evolution and Ethics." [Huxley's essay and three of Wells's articles cited here are excerpted on pp. 180–84 and 239–47 above —*Editor.*]

6. Paradoxically, vampires tend to represent both devolution and evolution in fin de siècle texts. In *Dracula*, for example, Dracula with his "child's brain" represents the devolved, degenerated Transylvanian aristocrat who threatens to make British subjects into beasts. Van Helsing, however, also sees him as a representative of a new species, one that is evolving to be stronger and more dominant than the human species. Wells uses the vampire as an image of evolution in *The War of the Worlds*, in which the Martians feed through blood transfusions. In *Moreau*, however, the vampiric images appear to be associated more clearly with devolution.

becomes a feminized hysteric. When he believes he is being abandoned by Montgomery and Moreau, he "suddenly began to sob and weep, as I had never done since I was a little child." Reflecting back on this incident, he calls it "my hysterical phase" (16).

Prendick's hysteria and his likening of himself to a child point to the process of degeneration he is undergoing. As Siegel notes, in fin de siècle theories of degeneration the savage and the civilized were frequently allegorized as child and adult (202). Further, women occupied an evolutionary position poised between child and man (204). Prendick is slipping down the ladder of evolution from hysterical woman to child to savage and, finally, to animal. The motivating force behind this degeneration is a femininely personified nature that initially robs him of his physical strength through thirst and starvation and which eventually causes him to become "tropicalized" on Noble's Island. As Stepan argues, an issue of much concern in late-nineteenth-century Europe was the theory that, when "the white race moved out of its 'natural' home, it too underwent a process of biological degeneration—it became 'tropicalized'" ("Biological" 99). During his stay on Noble's Island Prendick does not recover from the degenerative process started by the wreck of the *Lady Vain* but continues to suffer from "hysterics" (31), contemplates suicide (41), and becomes increasingly like the Beast People. He becomes "one of a tumultuous shouting crowd" composed of the Beast People, who are chasing the Leopard Man (61). Significantly, Prendick sees his degeneration as linked with Montgomery, Moreau, and the Beast People's existences, as a process controlled by "a vast pitiless Mechanism, [which] seemed to cut and shape the fabric of existence" (64). By the time he leaves the island he has both physically and mentally degenerated to the level of the Beast People: "I too must have undergone strange changes. My clothes hung about me as yellow rags, through whose rents showed the tanned skin. My hair grew long, and became matted together. I am told that even now my eyes have a strange brightness, a swift alertness of movement" (82).

One central symbol personifies the combination between feminine, Darwinian nature, and imperialism that has produced Prendick's devolution—the female puma. The puma brings together many of the central concerns of the novel into one figure. She stands for feminine Darwinian nature—dangerous, uncontrollable, random. As Prendick and Montgomery travel on the *Ipecacuanha*, the female puma lies "crouched together, watching us with shining eyes, a black heap in the corner of its cage" (12). Like amoral nature, the puma watches, unconcerned, implacable, impenetrable. Significantly, Moreau chooses the puma as the creature upon which all of his hopes of conquering the "beast-flesh" lie. Of the beast-flesh Moreau comments: "I mean to conquer that. This puma—" (50). He tells Prendick: "I have some hope of that puma. I have worked hard at her head and brain—" (51). Moreau chooses as his greatest experiment the species most difficult to alter: Montgomery tells Prendick that "the Law, especially among the feline Beast People, became oddly weakened about nightfall" (53). By altering the puma, Moreau feels he will conquer feminine nature and transform it into masculine civilization. The Western cultural association of the feline with sexuality also informs Moreau's experiment: by altering the puma, he hopes to conquer the animal within—within Victorian culture a concept largely figured as sexuality and a concept that seems to be a personal one for Moreau, as his asexuality attests.[7]

Moreau's choice of a female puma for his most important experiment also has imperial and racial implications. For the late-nineteenth-century British subject the best example of non-European savagery was embodied in the black African female. Gilman notes that for nineteenth-century Britain the female Hottentot was frequently photographed, drawn, and physically displayed as "an icon for deviant sexuality in general" ("Black" 209). Thus, when Victorian subjects saw the black female, "they saw her in terms of her buttocks and saw represented by the buttocks all the anomalies of her genitalia" (219). On the Great Chain of Evolution the black female human was placed next to the highest ape (213). Moreau's choice of a black female animal to perform his greatest experiment on indicates a desire to alter the imperial Other as well as to conquer Darwinian nature. Humanizing the puma means vanquishing an uncontrollable, frightening feminine nature personified in many Victorian minds by the black female.[8] This fear of non-European female sexuality as perverse and dangerous is also expressed by Prendick, when he expresses horror at the female Beast Creatures' reversion to their "original" sexual habits: "some of them—the pioneers in this [reversion], I noticed with some surprise, were all females—began to disregard the injunction of decency, deliberately for the most part. Others even attempted public outrages upon the institution of monogamy.

---

7. Aldiss, although he does not discuss the female puma but only the Leopard Man, argues that in *Moreau* the cat is linked directly to sexuality (32). It should be noted that, in earlier drafts of *Moreau*, a Mrs. Moreau appears. Wells's removal of female characters, apart from the female Beast People, places the issue of gender on a metaphorical level, where it more properly belongs. Anxieties surrounding Darwinian feminine nature and the feminine imperial Other are anxieties grounded in rhetoric, not in biology. In other words, what is at stake in *Moreau* is femininity as a conceptual category, not the status of real women. Further, eliminating the character of Mrs. Moreau places Moreau firmly within the tradition of asexual Gothic scientists such as Victor Frankenstein, Henry Jekyll, and Rappaccini.

8. Showalter notes that the puma may be read as a "shrieking sister" who represents the New Women of fin de siècle society and feminist anti-vivisectionists ("Apocalyptic" 79). For a discussion of the antivivisection movement in Britain, see Lansbury. [For representative writings from the (anti)vivisection debate in late-Victorian England, see pp. 217–38 above —*Editor*.]

The tradition of the Law was clearly losing its force. I cannot pursue this disagreeable subject" (81). Thus, the "disagreeable subject" of non-European female sexuality (equated here with animal perversity) was a target for imperialist control and containment.

Significantly, however, Moreau fails, and masculine civilization's hopes are vanquished by feminine nature. After many days of torture by Moreau, the puma shrieks with a voice "almost exactly like that of an angry virago" and breaks out of Moreau's lab, breaking Prendick's arm in the process (64). Moreau, "his massive white face all the more terrible for the blood that trickled from his forehead" sets out with a revolver (65): his "civilizing" process having failed, he plans to kill nature/black female with Western technology. What occurs, however, is mutual destruction. The puma dies by Moreau's revolver, but Moreau is mauled to death by the puma. Prendick finds his body with one hand "almost severed at the wrist" (69). The puma attempts to bite off the hand, the penetrating, molding, mastering hand of the modern scientist that has attempted to control and "civilize" her. The puma's victory over Moreau (feminine nature's victory over masculine civilization) is underscored when Prendick encounters Moreau's body later. Prendick comments that "his wounds gaped, black as night" (72). Moreau's body has transformed into the physical color of the puma, black, and has become a literalization of his name, *moreau* being French for "jet black" or "black and shining." The white god has been defeated by the black savage, a conclusion that is further emphasized by the anarchy that breaks out on Noble's Island after Moreau's death.

Prendick's effort to uphold the law Moreau has instituted is unsuccessful. The Beast People and Prendick revert to the "beast-flesh," "go native" in imperialist terms, and the novel imagines the extinction of the British Empire as well as the extinction of man. Prendick finds himself in the situation imagined by Wells in his essay "On Extinction," in which he envisions "the most terrible thing that man can conceive as happening to man . . . two men, and then one man, looking extinction in the face" (172). Montgomery's death, the reversion of the Beast People, and the dead sailors Prendick discovers in the boat from the *Ipecacuanha*—all point to the horror of the British subject/race extinguished by a feminine nature/imperial Other.

Ultimately, however, Prendick retreats from the implications of his narrative. While his experiences should teach him the connections between natives and Europeans and the fragile prop that holds up the idealized British gentleman, he distances himself from the Beast People and hence refuses to acknowledge these insights. After Moreau's death Prendick repudiates the sympathy for and identification with the Beast People he has felt earlier. Face-to-face with the Leopard Man, Prendick realizes "the fact of its humanity" (62). After its death Prendick sees "the viler aspect of Moreau's cruelty" (63). Yet, once Moreau's despotic authority is removed from the island, Prendick begins to refer to the Beast People as "monsters," demonizing them as evil: "in retrospect it is strange to remember how soon I fell in with these monsters' ways" (80). Thus, natives under British control are safe to sympathize with; natives under their own authority are monsters. Although Prendick is forced to acknowledge similarities between the Beast People and British subjects, he retreats from these recognitions, attempting to isolate himself in the countryside with his chemical experiments and astronomical studies: "I have withdrawn myself from the confusion of cities and multitudes, and spend my days shrouded by wise books—bright windows in this life of ours, lit by the shining souls of men" (87). While Prendick's "hope" is achieved only by isolation, it indicates that he must continue to view the Beast People as Other in order to keep his sanity (as his trips to "a mental specialist" indicate [86]).

For Prendick encountering the imperial Other means becoming degenerate, losing "Englishness" and masculinity, and fighting to regain these qualities at any price. The novel as a whole, however, is more ambivalent. While the Beast People are demonized and feminized in negative ways, Moreau's corpse, with its gaping black wounds, attests to the futility and corruption of Victorian pretensions to "civilizing" the world through progress. And, though the imperial Other remains alien in the novel, it is an Other created by a British scientist: yet even a fantasy native exceeds British authority and containment in Wells's dark vision.

*   *   *

WORKS CITED

Aldiss, Brian. "Wells and the Leopard Lady." In *H. G. Wells Under Revision*. Eds. Patrick Parrinder and Christopher Rolfe (London: Associated UP, 1990): 27–39.

Batchelor, John. *H. G. Wells* (Cambridge: Cambridge UP, 1985).

Beauchamp, Gorman. "*The Island of Dr. Moreau* as Theological Grotesque." *Papers in Language and Literature* 15 (1979): 408–17.

Beer, Gillian. *Darwin's Plots: Evolutionary Narrative in Darwin, George Eliot and Nineteenth-Century Fiction* (Boston: Routledge and Kegan Paul, 1983).

———. "Four Bodies on the *Beagle*: Touch, Sight and Writing in a Darwin Letter." In *Textuality and Sexuality: Reading Theories and Practices*. Eds. Judith Still and Michael Worton (Manchester: U of Manchester P, 1993): 116–32.

Bowen, Roger. "Science, Myth, and Fiction in H. G. Wells's *Island of Doctor Moreau*." *Studies in the Novel* 8.3 (Fall 1976): 318–35.

Bozzett, Roger. "Moreau's Tragic-Farcical Island." *Science Fiction Studies* 20 (1993): 34–44.

Brooke-Little, John, ed. *The Kings and Queens of Great Britain* (London: John Bartholomew and Son, 1976).

Carlson, Eric T. "Medicine and Degeneration: Theory and Praxis." In *Degeneration: The Dark Side of Progress*. Eds. J. Edward Chamberlin and Sander L. Gilman (New York: Columbia UP, 1985): 121–44.

Flat, Paul. *Le Musée Gustave Moreau* (Paris: Sociéte de Dédition Artistique, n.d.).

Gilman, Sander L. "Sexology, Psychoanalysis, Degeneration: From a Theory of Race to a Race to Theory." In *Degeneration: The Dark Side of Progress*. Eds. J. Edward Chamberlin and Sander L. Gilman (New York: Columbia UP, 1985): 72–96.

Haynes, R. D. "Wells's Debt to Huxley and the Myth of Dr. Moreau." *Cahiers Victoriens et Edouardiens* 13 (April 1981): 31–42.

Huxley, T. H. "Evolution and Ethics." In *Evolution and Ethics, 1893–1943* (London: Pilot Press, 1947): 60–102.

Lansbury, Coral. *The Old Brown Dog: Women, Workers, and Vivisection in Edwardian England* (Madison: U of Wisconsin P, 1985).

Levine, George. *Darwin and the Novelists: Patterns of Science in Victorian Fiction* (Cambridge: Harvard UP, 1988).

Levine, Suzanne Jill. "Science versus the Library in *The Island of Dr. Moreau, La invención de Morel* [*The Invention of Morel*], and *Plan de evasión* [*A Plan for Escape*]." *Latin American Literary Review* 9 (1981): 17–26.

Massie, Robert K. *Dreadnought: Britain, Germany, and the Coming of the Great War* (New York: Random House, 1991).

McCarthy, Patrick A. "*Heart of Darkness* and the Early Novels of H. G. Wells: Evolution, Anarchy, Entropy." *Journal of Modern Literature* 13.1 (March 1986): 37–60.

McClure, John A. "Late Imperial Romance." *Raritan* 10.4 (Spring 1991): 111–30.

Novas, Himilce. *Redon, Seurat, and the Symbolists* (New York: McCall, 1970).

Paris, Michèle. "La Femme et le monstrueux: réflexion à partir de *L'Isle du Docteur Moreau*." In *La Monstrueux dans la litterature et la pensée anglaises* (Cedex: Université de Provence, 1985): 171–84.

Philmus, Robert M. "Introducing *Moreau*." In *The Island of Doctor Moreau: A Variorum Text*. Ed. Robert M. Philmus (Athens and London: U of Georgia P, 1993): i–xlviii.

———. "Revisions of *Moreau*." *Cahiers Victoriens et Edouardiens* 30 (October 1989): 117–40.

————. "The Satiric Ambivalence of *The Island of Doctor Moreau*." *Science Fiction Studies* 8.1 (March 1981): 2–11.

Platzner, Robert L. "H. G. Wells's 'Jungle Book': The Influence of Kipling on *The Island of Dr. Moreau*." *Victorian Newsletter* 36 (Fall 1969): 19–22.

Punter, David. *The Literature of Terror: A History of Gothic Fictions from 1765 to the Present Day* (New York: Longman, 1980).

Redon, Seurat, and the Symbolists (New York: McCall, 1970).

Reed, John R. "The Vanity of the Law in *The Island of Doctor Moreau*." In *H. G. Wells Under Revision*. Eds. Patrick Parrinder and Christopher Rolfe (London: Associated UP, 1990): 134–44.

Rosenblum, Robert. *Paintings in the Musée D'Orsay* (New York: Stewart, Tabori, and Chang, 1989).

Said, Edward. *Culture and Imperialism* (New York: Random House, 1993).

Selz, Joan. *Gustave Moreau*. Trans. Alice Sachs (New York: Crown Publishers, 1979).

Showalter, Elaine. "The Apocalyptic Fables of H. G. Wells." In *Fin de Siécle/Fin du Globe: Fears and Fantasies of the Late Nineteenth Century*. Ed. John Stokes (New York: St. Martin's P, 1992), 69–84.

Shaw, Marion. "'To Tell the Truth of Sex': Confession and Abjection in Late Victorian Writing." In *Rewriting the Victorians: Theory, History, and the Politics of Gender*. Ed. Linda M. Shires (New York: Routledge, 1992): 87–100.

Siegel, Sandra. "Literature and Degeneration: The Representation of 'Decadence'." In *Degeneration: The Dark Side of Progress*. Eds. J. Edward Chamberlin and Sander L. Gilman (New York: Columbia UP, 1985): 199–219.

Stableford, Brian. *Scientific Romance in Britain, 1890–1950* (New York: St. Martin's P, 1985).

Steffen-Fluhr, Nancy. "Paper Tiger: Women and H. G. Wells." *Science Fiction Studies* 12 (1985): 311–29.

Stepan, Nancy. "Biological Degeneration: Races and Their Proper Places." In *Degeneration: The Dark Side of Progress*. Eds. J. Edward Chamberlin and Sander L. Gilman (New York: Columbia UP, 1985): 97–120.

————. *The Idea of Race in Science: Great Britain, 1800–1960* (Hamden, CT: Archon, 1982).

Tuchman, Barbara W. *The Proud Tower: A Portrait of the World before the War, 1890–1914* (New York: Macmillan, 1966).

Wells, H. G. "Human Evolution as an Artificial Process." In *H. G. Wells: Early Writings in Science and Science Fiction*. Ed. Robert M. Philmus and David Y. Hughes (Berkeley: U of California P, 1975), 211–19.

————. "The Influence of Islands on Variation." *Saturday Review*, 17 August 1895: 204–05.

————. *The Island of Doctor Moreau: A Variorum Text*. Ed. Robert M. Philmus (Athens and London: U of Georgia P, 1993).

————. "The Limits of Individual Plasticity." *Early Writings*, 36–39.

————. "On Extinction." *Early Writings*, 169–72.

Wilde, Oscar. *The Picture of Dorian Gray. The Annotated Oscar Wilde*. Ed. H. Montgomery Hyde (New York: Clarkson N. Potter, 1982).

JOHN GLENDENING

"Green Confusion": Evolution and Entanglement in H. G. Wells's *The Island of Doctor Moreau*[†]

The Island of Doctor Moreau (1896) is a richly confused novel, and its complexities and mixed agendas constitute one reason why this remarkable enactment of ideas and theories has received so much, and such varied, critical attention. Its generic, psychological, and thematic disorder does not stand out as much as it might, however, because confusion itself—biological, ethical, epistemological—is one of its subjects.[1] Furthermore, the text begins with great and misleading attention to accuracy, precision, and narrative control. First, Charles Edward Prendick introduces the manuscript of his now deceased uncle, Edward Prendick, starting with these details: "On February the First, 1887, the *Lady Vain* was lost by collision with a derelict when about the latitude 1° S. and longitude 107° W" (3; Intro.). When Edward Prendick commences the story proper, he begins with similar exactitude, stating what "every one knows"—that "the *Lady Vain* . . . collided with a derelict when ten days out from Callao. The long-boat, with seven of the crew, was picked up eighteen days after by H. M. gunboat *Myrtle*" (4; ch. 1). He then shifts to private knowledge: although four men in the ship's dinghy were thought to have perished, there were actually only three men in the boat, with he himself as the sole survivor of that group. Here begins

---

[†] From *Victorian Literature and Culture* 30.2 (September 2002): 571–97. Reprinted with permission.

1. The novel's mix of attributes has allowed various commentators to identify it as satire, parody, parable, fable, allegory, myth, fantasy, fairy tale, romance, burlesque, tragedy, comedy, tragi-comedy, farce, and science fiction. Two years before the appearance of *Doctor Moreau*, in his discussion of evolution in the *Text-Book of Biology*, Wells virtually predicted such a melange for any thorough-going fictional treatment of evolution that he might produce: "In the book of nature there are written . . . the triumphs of survival, the tragedy of death and extinction, the tragi-comedy of degradation and inheritance, the gruesome lesson of parasitism, the political satire of colonial organisms. Zoology is, indeed, a philosophy and a literature to those who can read its symbols" (1:131).

his story of what happened between the time the dinghy was last seen and his being picked up, eleven months later, at about the same location—the coordinates for which the nephew also provides. Both narrators maintain their stances of detailed accuracy and objectivity—the nephew will certify the truth of only that part of his uncle's story he can substantiate—because the story that Edward Prendick tells about the eleven months during which he visits Doctor Moreau's island is so incredible.

These two layers of purported accuracy and control, grounded in public knowledge, serve to disarm the incredulity of readers. More importantly, they set off, by contrast, a story suffused with the operation of chance in human affairs—as illustrated, for instance, by two ships colliding in a relatively untravelled part of a vast ocean. Throughout *The Island of Doctor Moreau* chance and uncertainty undermine order and knowledge. The novel signifies indeterminacy as the ruling element in the universe and in the human condition, even subverting its own textual authority for telling the truth. Chance, contingency, unpredictability, indeterminacy—these elements, inherent in Darwinism, reflect the novel's involvement with evolutionary theory.

Apart from a quasi-allegorical setup that promotes comparison between Doctor Moreau's scientific activities and evolution, the novel establishes three direct connections to Charles Darwin. First, the protagonist and narrator, Edward Prendick, reveals that he, like H. G. Wells himself, had been the student of the great biologist and evolutionist Thomas Huxley, Darwin's disciple, friend, and champion. A second marker of the story's Darwinian provenance is the placement of Moreau's fictional island in the actual vicinity of the Galapagos, islands that Darwin visited and made famous. Although during his stay there Darwin did not recognize that they and their fauna constituted a virtual laboratory for natural selection, after his return to England they provided crucial hints and evidence for his theory.

A third connection with Darwin is the novel's appropriation of the "entangled bank" that he employs, in the conclusion of *On the Origin of Species* (1859), to summarize and promote his theory of evolution. *The Island of Doctor Moreau* adopts the idea of entanglement to disrupt conventional, optimistic views about humanity and its place in the universe. Responding to the controversies about evolutionary theory that Darwin's work catalyzed and that permeated the late nineteenth century, Wells's narrative follows a negative path in exploring the problematic biological and cultural foundations of human life. It stakes out those areas of confused human self-understanding that will have to be disentangled before society can, perhaps, progress on a firmer basis. The question is, what can be determined in an indeterminate universe, what significant truths might manifest themselves after falsehoods, perceived as such, have been cleared away?[2] Integral to Wells's text, the implications and omissions of the entangled bank fix a heuristic starting point. I will begin with Darwin's famous image and the novel's immediate application of entanglement to signify indeterminacy.

I

The *Origin* deploys the entangled bank as an image of unity and order so as to resist the negative implications of chaos and disorder inherent in the process of natural selection. In evolution via natural selection, those individuals with variations that give them a competitive edge in given environments will more readily survive, reproduce, and pass along to later generations their adaptive characteristics, which will continue to develop as long as they enhance chances for survival and reproduction. Thus, gradually, one species evolves from another through interplay of internal and external factors. But the process can appear depressingly chaotic because of the incessant competition between individuals and between species for limited resources, because of the death and extinction that result, because of the apparent randomness of the variations upon which natural selection builds, and because of the complexity and instability of the environmental factors that determine which variations offer survival value. Chance appears to rule. Darwin, however, in his first reference to the entangled bank, in Chapter 3 of the *Origin*, argues against chance: "When we look at the plants and bushes clothing an entangled bank, we are tempted [incorrectly] to attribute their proportional numbers and kinds to what we call chance." This attribution is incorrect, he contends, because the proportions and kinds are in fact established and maintained through a systematic and statistically verifiable process that tends toward order (74–75).

The upbeat conclusion of the *Origin* further develops the entangled bank as a representation of law and order, and of progress as well. It exemplifies the triumph of natural selection, which, because it "works solely by and for the good of each being, [ensures that] all corporeal and mental endowments will tend to progress toward perfection." Representing nature as happy and harmonious, the bank elides the struggle, disorder, and waste that, as Darwin makes clear elsewhere, attend natural selection:

2. As Bozzeto says, Wells's scientific romances, including the novel in question, "clearly present themselves as fictions that encourage a figurative reading, [but] they do not proceed by assertion or lend themselves to a dogmatic reading; instead they leave open the question they deal with, prompting reflection more than eliciting an answer" (38). Nevertheless, after reflection has been prompted over the course of the story, *Doctor Moreau* does suggest some provisional answers to the questions it raises.

It is interesting to contemplate an entangled bank, clothed with many plants of many kinds, with birds singing on the bushes, with various insects flitting about, and with worms crawling through the damp earth, and to reflect that these elaborately constructed forms, so different from each other, and dependent on each other in so complex a manner, have all been produced by laws acting around us. (489)

Again, it is order, not chance, that governs life, and entanglement in the *Origin* therefore evidences a harmonious ecological interdependence and equilibrium between species.

The Island of Doctor Moreau picks up on the negative implications of natural selection that the entangled bank disguises. In Wells's text entanglement means disorder, not order or harmony: it entails the commingling of objects, processes, and qualities that strike the human mind as incompatible or antagonistic because they upset boundaries and categories; and it points to the limits of knowledge, since the mind, caught in the very processes it tries to understand, is continually confounded by contingencies, like those governing the course of Darwinian evolution, too complex to be anticipated or fully comprehended.[3] Ethics, which according to Wells involve the interaction of evolutionarily determined predisposition with artificial behavioral standards developed for maintaining ideas of social good, is one focus of such problematic entanglement.[4] Another is chance, which subverts reasoned expectations, mixing unreality with reality, the probable with the improbable. One function of ethics is to stabilize human life in the face of an indeterminate universe informed by complexity, chance, and consequent unpredictability, but the beginning of Wells's novel dramatizes how readily accident or luck, whether good or bad, can overwhelm standards for guiding behavior and assessing truth. The first page of Edward Prendick's story reinforces this theme through its reference to entanglement.

After correcting the mistake others had made in thinking there were four survivors who had set off in the dingy [*sic*], Prendick states

3. Wells accepted the natural disorder attendant on Darwin's theory but found the theory itself, especially because of its comprehensiveness and explanatory value, to entail considerable order. "[B]y drawing together strands from all disciplines and relating them in one unifying theory, [Darwinian evolution] seemed to him to symbolize order itself. The desire for order became a life-long craving in Wells, brought up in a world of confusion and incompetence" (Haynes 21). It is important to recognize this longing for order, even the latent presence of order, that lies beneath the confusions of *Doctor Moreau*. In his *Text-Book* Wells assured readers that "[w]ith an increasing knowledge of the facts of the form of life, there gradually appears to the student the realization of an entire unity shaped out by their countless, and often beautiful, diversity" (1:132).

4. In his essay "Human Evolution, an Artificial Process," Wells states that "what we call Morality becomes the padding of suggested emotional habits necessary to keep the round Paleolithic savage in the square hole of the civilised state. And Sin is the conflict of the two factors—as I have tried to convey in my *Island of Doctor Moreau*" (*Early Writings* 217) [excerpted on pp. 239–42 above —*Editor*].

that "luckily for us and unluckily for himself," a sailor trying to join the other three had died in the attempt: "He came down out of the tangle of ropes under the stays of the smashed bowsprit, some small rope caught his heel as he let go, and he hung for a moment head downward, and then fell and struck a block or spar floating in the water" (4; ch. 1). The "tangle" that contributes to the sailor's death, overturning him and whatever expectations he had for escape, inaugurates within the novel a series of images that establish entanglement as a trope.[5] Here as elsewhere the story calls attention not only to how human enterprises become entangled with chance occurrences, but to how good and bad luck themselves become entangled. In this case, the sailor's death seemingly benefits the three survivors, who have to share their scanty provisions with one less comrade. This episode adumbrates the relativistic, amoral universe that dominates the novel, and the name of the doomed ship reinforces this picture and the pretensions of humans who ignore it. "*Lady Vain*" suggests the vanity of individuals who think they can entirely control their destinies, the vainness or futility of believing chance can be denied. Also, the ship's name can be connected to the name-change that Wells, in notes for revisions, proposed for the ship that rescues Prendick eight days after the wreck; the *Ipecacuanha* of the first edition would have become the *Red Luck* had Wells acted upon his intent.[6] Conflated, the two names, the *Lady Vain* and the *Red Luck*, suggest the supremacy of Lady Luck, or Mother Nature, whose hands, in the Darwinian vision of competition, struggle, and death, are red with blood.

But as already illustrated, luck cannot always be bad, however one conceives of it—and it is important to remember that "luck" is subjective, relativistic, and contingent; it is open to different interpretations based on different standards and on its different consequences for different people, and it is changeable over time since what seems good or bad in the present can take on the opposite appearance in light of later, unpredictable developments. Suffering from thirst and hunger like his two companions and finally willing to participate in

---

5. In a parallel passage, Wells changed the word "mass" to "tangle" in the incomplete, early version of the novel (see Wells, *Doctor Moreau* 101n[m]), although nowhere else does he mention entanglement in this manuscript. I believe the change was a late one that serves as a thematic bridge to his revision of the story as *The Island of Doctor Moreau*. This first version is called simply *Doctor Moreau*, the new emphasis on "Island" perhaps reflecting the revised story's emphasis on entanglement and hence on a more fully described island setting replete with jungle vegetation [see n. 1 to p. 306 below]. Moreau's island represents, in effect, an evolution from the aridity of Darwin's Galapagos to the lushness of his entangled bank.

6. See Philmus's note on the subject of the name change (Wells, *Doctor Moreau* 89nl). Ipecacuanha, an emetic, indicates the repulsiveness of cannibalism and, more generally, basic and unpleasant biological realities. As such it functions as a reminder of Prendick's animal nature, the recognition of which he tries and fails to purge while he unwillingly voids those ethical certainties that have upheld his life.

cannibalism, Prendick's life is temporarily saved when the three castaways draw lots and one of the others is selected to be eaten. Chance makes Prendick look lucky, and it does so again when the designated victim decides to withdraw from the project, the other man attacks him, they fall out of the dinghy and drown, and Prendick is delivered from the potential aggression of his companions or from an act that appalls him. Although he is left in desperate physical condition, his mere survival turns out to be good, for chance seemingly intervenes in his favor once more. This occurs when the dinghy crosses paths with the *Ipecacuanha*, on which happens to be a man with medical training—Montgomery, Doctor Moreau's assistant—who saves Prendick's life. "'You were in luck,'" he tells Prendick, "'to get picked [up] by a ship with a medical man aboard'" (6; ch. 2); of course, he is lucky to get picked up at all.

Montgomery contends his saving of Prendick was controlled by chance, "as everything is in a man's life"; he says he took him on as a patient simply because he happened to be "bored, and wanted something to do." That Prendick is an amateur biologist also seems fortuitous, in that Montgomery's telling Moreau that "Prendick knows something of science" appears to be the reason, after the bestial captain of the *Ipecacuanha* casts Prendick adrift once more, that Moreau changes his mind and saves the castaway (12, 18; ch. 4, ch. 6). Furthermore, Moreau seemingly affords Prendick better treatment than he would have done had his guest not been the one-time student of Thomas Huxley. But this string of good fortune leads to great and long-term suffering because of the ordeals Prendick undergoes on the island. Also, Prendick's chance arrival there contributes to problems for its inhabitants as his fate becomes entangled with theirs. In general, then, the early part of the narrative establishes chance, with good and bad luck entwined in involved and unforeseen ways, as a central theme, one that remains equally prevalent throughout the remainder of the novel. At the same time, "Red Luck" is the form of chance accentuated in the story, whose preoccupation is especially with the negative implications of natural selection.

Chance, however, should be understood as expression of the contingency that permeates phenomena. The forces of the universe are too multitudinous, varied, changeable, and intermixed to allow accurate prediction or explanation of any but the most limited and strictly controlled events. Chance, which we call good or bad luck when the unlikely seems to impact our lives decidedly, is our explanation for occurrences that appear most unpredictable relative to evidently realistic expectations and to limited understandings. But because much of our experience cannot accurately be predicted or explained due to the many complex, uncontrollable, and mostly unseen forces that bear on it, chance occurs as a relatively common

feature of our lives. To say that chance rules the universe is therefore to say that contingency governs cognition; our knowing continuously struggles to make sense of an elusive and wayward reality.
In his early essays Wells expresses this view of contingency in
pointing out how readily some unforeseen, complex, and uncontrollable circumstance, such as radical environmental change or pestilence, might doom humanity (*Early Writings* 130–31, 171–72). The
universe that *The Island of Doctor Moreau* evokes is largely contingent. On three occasions Prendick finds himself adrift in a small
boat caught in so many circumstances of currents and weather that
its future is unpredictable. This situation presents a graphic image
of human existence in general, even though most people do not
undergo Prendick's extremities of helplessness.

The drifting boat is a prominent motif in the naturalistic fiction
common during the period in which Wells wrote his novel; such fiction portrays social and natural worlds where hostile or, at best,
indifferent forces beyond their control determine people's fates. One
of these forces is chance, sometimes conceived as a sort of implacable antagonist.[7] Much naturalistic fiction actually undermines
the idea of chance because of the appearance of design in the
improbable unrelenting negativity of its effects. Certainly Prendick's
being cast adrift suggests the antagonistic workings of chance, and
the unlikelihood of its happening three times indicates authorial
design rather than chance occurrences. The story somewhat parts
company with naturalism because Prendick is also, against all
odds, saved each time; here then is a degree of even-handedness, a
balancing of good and bad luck, rather than unrelieved negative
determinism. Nevertheless, the novel's overdetermination of chance
along with the overall prevalence of bad fortune, exaggerations
bespeaking artistic or polemical purpose, at first glance indeed
appear to convey a naturalistic or even nihilistic message about the
pointlessness of the cosmos and the helplessness of humanity.
Over-reacting to his disillusionment in the humanistic ideals that
have upheld him, Prendick arrives at such a view, even though he
wills himself to hope for good (87; ch. 22). But the novel as a whole,
more existential than naturalistic, does not. Rather, it conducts a
literary exploration to determine what degree of control and freedom humanity might exercise once it acknowledges that its doings
are inextricably entangled with chance and that there is no moral
agent outside of itself and its own choices. Although Doctor Moreau
is the potential embodiment of this exploration, his daring but

7. The novels of Thomas Hardy, which are full of Darwinian elements, particularly enact
   this role. Presiding as a malevolent agent with a perverse sense of humor, chance
   became increasingly pronounced in his narratives, nearly always frustrating the needs
   and aspirations of his characters.

confused attempts to overcome the randomness of evolution, by dissociating the human from the animal, constitute a flawed response to a refractory universe.

As prominent as it is, chance is only part of the indeterminacy that saturates the story, emphasizing the perplexities to which the mind is susceptible. Indeterminacy, for instance, governs the novel's treatment of the relationship between humans and animals, another area of uncertainty relevant to evolution. Evolutionary theory complicates the distinction between the two; because humans evolved from animals and bear innumerable traces of this ancestry, there can be no absolute or essentialist gap between them—a point that Darwin makes repeatedly in *The Descent of Man* (1871) and *The Expression of the Emotions in Man and Animals* (1872).[8] This issue, the entanglement of human and animal, is broached when Montgomery administers to Prendick "a dose of scarlet stuff" that "tasted like blood, and made [him] feel stronger" (6; ch. 2). On the one hand, the reference to blood recalls that in the dinghy Prendick is willing to defend himself with a knife against anybody who tries to make a meal of him, but that in despair he finally agrees to participate in cannibalism; physical suffering, fear, and the instinct for self-preservation cause him to confront a violent, animalistic part of himself, a dimension he will encounter repeatedly before he escapes from the island. On the other hand, taking the blood-like drink proves positive, strengthening him physically as, no doubt, engaging in cannibalism likewise would have done; our animal nature cannot be denied.[9]

The difference between the two activities is that there exists, against taking the drink, no moral injunction like that which at first keeps Prendick aloof from his companions' cannibalistic enterprise. A preoccupation with ethics is one of the cultural endowments that seems positive because it separates men from animals. When reified as moral law, however, it also causes much suffering, as it does for Prendick, because it forces people to go against the instinctual,

---

8. For example, Darwin writes, "there is no fundamental difference between man and the higher mammals in their mental faculties" (*Descent* 35). Montgomery's assistant, who is the most advanced, sympathetic, and ambiguous of the Beast People, seemingly represents this convergence of man and animal through his name, M'ling, which suggests a mingling of natures. But the two natures of the Beast People do not meld smoothly, any more than they do in the humans that they, on one level, represent. Wells's early essays suggest that the development of language, culture, and ethics encourages this uneasiness by allowing both the drawing of a distinction between man and beast and the discomfort that results when the distinction, as it often must, begins to break down. Wells therefore encourages readers to recognize culture as the artificiality it is, freely choosing to give it their allegiance because of the advantages it confers, while consciously selecting the behavioral standards that will best allow it to function. Our animal natures are a foundation to build upon, not to eradicate.

9. Overall, the taking of the drink functions as an anti-communion, emphasizing brutality, preoccupation with the physical, and isolation. It is an appropriate herald for what Prendick will experience on Moreau's island.

elemental part of their own natures or to feel guilty for not having done so. In this sense, morality actually calls attention to animal-like propensities, and it sometimes even exacerbates or warps them because of desire for the release that their expression promises to produce. A related area of confusion is the appearance of moral relativism that occurs when ethical strictures are found inapplicable or conflicted, especially in extreme situations.[1] Prendick believes that killing and cannibalism are wrong, yet circumstances prepare him to engage in both activities. Later he learns how arbitrary moral codes can be when he encounters the Law of the Beast People that Moreau and their situation have created. Only Moreau appears immune to moral injunction, although it can be argued that this freedom contributes to his and Montgomery's deaths; and only Moreau fully accepts moral relativism as he tries, unsuccessfully, to disentangle the human from the animal through whatever means seem most likely to succeed. The unstable interpenetration of the cultural and the natural, the human and the animal, the moral and the amoral comprises a major area of incertitude in Wells's novel.

The early part of the narrative suggests that the existence of Prendick's story itself, not just its content, reflects indeterminacy, expressing itself as an entanglement of contrary, and unverifiable, possible truths. The frame narrator, Prendick's nephew, states that the "only island known to exist in the region in which my uncle was picked up is Noble's Isle, a small volcanic islet, and uninhabited. It was visited in 1891 by H.M.S. *Scorpion*. A party of sailors then landed, but found nothing living thereon except certain curious white moths, some hogs and rabbits, and some rather peculiar rats." Responding to the sailors' account, the nephew comments that his uncle's "narrative is without confirmation in its most essential particular" (3; Intro.). Although the peculiar life forms appear somewhat corroborative, hinting at Moreau's alterations of the animals he had imported, yet it seems likely that the party, arriving several years after Prendick's visit, would have reported signs of human habitation. Prendick reports that Moreau's buildings burned down, but there should remain evidence of his and Montgomery's long residence on the island, including the "square enclosure . . . built partly of coral and partly of pumiceous lava" that protected Moreau's compound (17; ch. 6). Also, the island should have contained many noteworthy skeletons. The crew of the *Ipecacuanha*, which might have supported part of Prendick's narrative, apparently—it is not quite certain—perishes at sea (3, 85; Intro., ch. 21).

---

1. Wells stresses the relativistic character of morality in his essay, "Morals and Civilization" (*Early Writings* 220–28).

Perhaps there never was a Moreau or Montgomery on the island; perhaps they, the Beast Folk Moreau creates, and Prendick's adventures among them are all delusions of a mind seriously disturbed by the trauma of a ship-wreck, by extreme physical distress, by solitude, and by near-participation—or actual participation, for all we know—in cannibalism. The nephew's evidence suggests that the *Ipecacuanha* did indeed pick up the narrator—the ship, with a puma and other animals aboard, had been in the area at the time he disappeared (3; Intro.). But it is possible that, after being set adrift by the tyrannical, besotted captain, Prendick washed up on Noble's Isle and imagined the rest of his story. Prendick had studied biology with Huxley, and it appears that he knew of the vivisectional experiments that Moreau had conducted on animals back in England. And he apparently had experience with a floating menagerie. Therefore, responding to painful and disorienting experiences at sea, including encounters with real animals and with his own animalistic predilections, and to being stranded alone on an island and living on the level of an animal, Prendick unconsciously might have woven prior knowledge into an evolutionary fantasy that objectifies and to a degree explains inner tensions concerning his moral nature. The actual peculiarity of some of the animals on the island may reflect, not the effects of Moreau's experiments, but the relatively rapid evolutionary adjustments that can occur on isolated islands recently populated by immigrant species—a circumstance Darwin encountered on the Galapagos—and the fast breeding character of the creatures in question, possibly descendants of escapees from ships that had visited the island.[2] The local fauna might have provided Prendick with food until he was able to escape in the boat that chances to beach itself there. In view of these considerations, Prendick's attendance upon "a mental specialist" after returning to London intimates a psychological problem more intense than mere posttraumatic anxiety.[3] That this specialist "had known Moreau" (86; ch. 22) could have provided fortuitous reinforcement, or even a further motivation, for Prendick's delusions.

These evidentiary speculations do not prove that Prendick's tale is false, only that its degree of accuracy cannot be objectively determined, that truth and falsehood cannot be disengaged. Regardless

2. Wells writes about this acceleration of evolution on islands in a 1895 essay, "Influence of Islands." See Bowen 322–24 on the mythic and scientific implications of the island setting.

3. According to Showalter, "The introduction [by Prendick's nephew] . . . places the story in a psychological context, and offers an invitation to the reader to consider the tale as a hysterical hallucination, the result of a repressed trauma. The nature of that trauma has to do with cannibalism." Showalter goes on to analyze Prendick's experiences in relation to the Medusa affair, in which survivors of a shipwreck, abandoned on a raft, engaged in cannibalism. Showalter concludes that Prendick may well have done likewise (81).

of whether or not it is entirely true, his overall story results as much from chance and uncertainty as do the elements that comprise its narrative. It also reminds us that narrative fiction necessarily commingles truth and falsehood, with the human mind predisposed to participate in this entanglement; for example, we are presently treating make-believe characters and their experiences as if they were real, although some of them may not be real even within the logic of the narrative. In a number of respects Wells's novel does not merely depict pervasive uncertainty, it actively enlists readers into it in such a way as to accentuate this aspect of the human condition that most people are quite willing to overlook. Wells is always keen to attack smugness as the first step in perceiving new possibilities.

The rest of this essay will trace entanglement, as signifier of disorder and indeterminacy, through several overlapping contexts: evolutionary theory in the 1880s and '90s; Wells's response to it; the novel's dramatization of this response; and, more specifically, the troping of entanglement within Prendick's story.

II

The late nineteenth century produced an entangled bank of evolutionary theories. Darwinism mutated in a variety of ways, rival evolutionary theories struggled against its dominance, and various highbred varieties appeared. In his biology textbook, first published in 1893, H. G. Wells offers a lucid explanation of Darwin's basic ideas without commenting on this contextual confusion. Nevertheless, he was well aware of the scientific controversies surrounding evolution. Wells faced the same hodge-podge of evolutionary claims and counter-claims, interpretations and investments that met any serious student of the subject. That Darwinism should fragment into different lines of thought, lending itself to various and contradictory agendas, is understandable. Although it sounds simple enough, evolution via natural selection links a surprising number of components and implications. Ernst Mayr's analysis of Darwin's theory, for example, breaks it into five separate theories expounded by means of five facts and three inferences (36–39, 72). Moreover, in part because of this complexity, Darwin's ideas enable multiple inferences about natural and human reality; George Levine identifies nine of these—three primary and six secondary—that together constitute "a sort of gestalt of the Darwinian imagination" especially relevant to creative writers of the late nineteenth and early twentieth centuries (14–20, 13).

Therefore fiction writers preoccupied with Darwinism could seize upon any one or combination of the sort of elements identified by Mayr and Levine, employing their own versions of Darwinism and its significance, either in acceptance, rejection, or some divided response. Moreover, some evolutionary theories were largely non-Darwinian— most prominently, the "neo-Lamarckian" versions that challenged Darwinism late in the century—and these also entered the mix. Knowingly or not, writers such as Wells could selectively apply these evolutionary variants not only because of the complexity and suggestiveness of Darwin's theory in interaction with its competitors, but because so many aspects of evolutionary thought touched upon equally complicated, ideologically charged social issues—religious, philosophical, anthropological, economic, and political. In the case of Darwin, this suggestiveness partially derives from the character of his writing, which frequently employs figurative language to express processes and ideas inaccessible to direct observation or verification, thus lending itself to multiple interpretations: "It is the element of obscurity, of metaphors whose peripheries remain undescribed, which made *The Origin of Species* so incendiary—and which allowed it to be appropriated by thinkers of so many diverse political persuasions. . . . The presence of *latent meaning* made *The Origin* suggestive, even unstoppable in its action upon minds" (Beer 100).

In short, evolutionary theory in general, with its openness to ideological investment, promotes confusion by offering an abundantly entangled set of potential influences for any narrative that, like *The Island of Doctor Moreau*, seriously applies evolution to other areas of concern. But the confusion in Wells's text is especially great because it registers many influences additional to evolution. As Elaine Showalter notes, "The psychological, literary, social, and intellectual sources of *The Island of Dr Moreau* are enormously complex" (77). Nevertheless, evolution is central, and an important dimension of the text's evolutionary complexity is its simultaneous representations of the largely contradictory evolutionary theories of Darwinism and Lamarckism. This entanglement constitutes a focus of scientific and philosophical contention in the novel.

In *Philosophie Zoologique* (1809) J. B. Lamarck presents his theory that species evolve because individuals, in striving to meet their needs in response to changing environments, produce inheritable modifications to relevant features; over generations volition continues to compound these changes, improving the effectiveness of adaptations. Lamarck's stress on the formative role of environment is similar to Darwin's, who also accepts the idea of acquired characteristics—heritable changes occurring within just one generation because of the use and disuse of parts—but only as a secondary factor far less significant than natural selection. Darwin, however, does not embrace the Lamarckian implication that mind, through volition and the making of intelligent choices, drives evolution—that life possesses this mental, virtually inherent tendency toward progress.[4] It is true that Darwin sometimes makes evolution sound essentially progressive, since *The Origin* figuratively employs purpose and teleology to mitigate the negative overtones of the randomness, struggle, and death inherent in natural selection; the prime example of this strategy occurs at the end of *The Origin*, where the entangled bank obfuscates as much as it explains.

Unwilling to accommodate itself to natural selection for either substantive or rhetorical purposes, the neo-Lamarckism that arose toward the end of the century was generally more stringent and doctrinaire than Darwin's form of Darwinism, since the reemergence of Lamarckism in intensified terms in the years following the publication of *The Origin*, and peaking around the turn of the century, was primarily a reaction against Darwinism. Much as Darwin's followers had elaborated on "Darwinism," changing the master's emphases and adjusting his explanations, neo-Lamarckism built on Lamarck's ideas in a variety of ways (see Bowler 62–64). What most varieties had in common, however, was opposition to natural selection and allegiance to inherited characteristics acquired through use and disuse. The neo-Lamarckian advocate most relevant to literature was Samuel Butler, a novelist and scientific outsider whose long-term efforts to supply an alternative to what he saw as the undirected, materialistic process of natural selection led him to a form of Lamarckism. This he expressed in non-fiction works that ended up influencing even some scientists. His stance is encapsulated in the title of one of his books, *Luck, or Cunning, As the Main Means of Organic Modification?* (1887). Like some of the other Lamarckians of his time, Butler extracted from Lamarck the idea that the desire to evolve is innate, expressing itself through the purposeful acquiring and development of new characteristics as part of an intelligence-driven process. This position led him to a vitalism in which a life force works through evolution for human betterment; George Bernard Shaw was Butler's most famous convert to this metaphysical line of thought.

Wells did not share Butler's vitalistic notions, but like him he sought in Lamarck's theory sanction for the idea of human progress— although not assured progress—and for the primacy of intelligence in evolution. What particularly attracted Wells to Lamarckism was its suggestion that evolution might occur rapidly, since an organism's successful adaptive efforts could be immediately expressed and elaborated upon in the next generation; in this scheme, unlike natural selection, change did not have to wait upon the slow, undirected process of variation, competition, and selection in which

4. Dawkins states that "there was a dose of mysticism in Lamarck's actual words—for instance, he had a strong belief in progress up what many people, even today, think of as the ladder of life; and he spoke of animals striving as if they, in some sense, consciously *wanted* to evolve" (289).

many generations are needed for appreciable change to occur. In particular, Wells, with his life-long commitment to education, found in Lamarckism a way in which learning would be quickly compounded, and appropriately applied, as lessons learned in one generation became innate in the next. In this way accumulated wisdom would lead inevitably to rapid social betterment. People simply needed education-enhancing environments.

In the 1880s, however, the ultra- or neo-Darwinism of August Weismann undermined the Lamarckism of some evolutionists while, in reaction, pushing others further into the neo-Lamarckian camp. Wells was among of the former. Anticipating genetics, Weismann propounded his germ plasm theory of inheritance, arguing that characteristics are transmitted from parents to offspring through self-contained units—which Weismann correctly associated with chromosomes—that remained unchanged by any influences on the parents' lives.[5] Only natural selection, he argued, influences the fate of the germ plasm, determining whether or not the organisms that carry it will survive to become parents and propagate their genetic material, sexually combining it to create new variations for selection to work upon. Not only did Weismann's theory directly shore up natural selection, making it the one and only cause of evolution, a position not even Darwin was willing to adopt, but his experiments seemed to disprove its rival, the mechanism of acquired characteristics.[6] The effect on Wells was to end his hope that humans might rapidly evolve into intellectually superior forms capable of conquering social problems. While he was finishing *Doctor Moreau*, or shortly thereafter, Wells's essay "Bio-Optimism" (1895) announced his change of mind; prior to 1895 he had dismissed Weismann's ideas, but now they strengthened his opposition to naïve "bio-optimism," which neo-Lamarckism seemed to sanction, and confirmed his acceptance of natural selection, however unpalatable its workings.[7]

The short-term effect of Wells's conversion was to reinforce the qualified pessimism that, despite his recent belief in the educational

---

5. Today we know that external conditions can in fact produce genetic mutations.
6. Weismann cut the tails off of successive generations of mice to demonstrate that the acquired characteristic of taillessness could not be inherited. Some Lamarckians felt the experiment was flawed because it was not the volition of the mice that produced the alterations.
7. "Bio-Optimism" maintains that "Natural Selection grips us more grimly than it ever did, because the doubts thrown upon the inheritance of acquired characteristics have deprived us of our trust in education as a means of redemption for decadent families." Emphasizing the dark side of natural selection, Wells adds that "[t]he names of the sculptor who carves out the new forms of life are . . . Pain and Death. And the phenomena of degeneration rob one of any confidence that the new forms will be in any case or in a majority of cases 'higher' . . . than the old" (*Early Writings* 208, 209). Given these views, Wells could not look for human improvement via physical evolution or inheritable mental changes brought about through education. Therefore, from this point on, Wells stressed cultural, rather than physiological, change.

potential of rapid evolution, had for some time colored his thinking about mankind's future. In a series of essays in the early 1890s he had challenged Victorian complacency by arguing that humans are no less immune to extinction, and no more significant for the universe, than any other species. Likewise, he called attention to regression or degeneration, in which over a number of generations organs or organisms revert to forms or behaviors resembling those they had assumed during earlier stages of evolution (see "Zoological Retrogression" [1891], *Early Writings* 158–68). Such could be the fate of humans, an idea at the heart of Wells's *The Time Machine* (1895).

Late Victorian society witnessed a spread of concern about degeneration or decay—of society, races, species, even the cosmos itself.[8] This anxiety fed discordantly on fear that socioeconomic progress could not be sustained and suspicion that such progress was already eroding much of traditional cultural value. Along with other sciences, biology provided support for such concern. Weismann made biological degeneration an important part of his theory, maintaining that regression results whenever an environment allows the pressure of natural selection to relax (see Gayon 147–53). He may have had some impact on Wells's thinking in this matter, but a nearer and earlier influence was Thomas Huxley, who did not share Darwin's generally optimistic outlook on the long-term, unimpeded workings of natural selection (for example, see Huxley 80–81).[9] Darwin contended that degeneration was adaptive, a de-emphasizing of features that, while once beneficial, had become superfluous or impedimental because of changed environmental conditions. Darwin nevertheless allowed that some retrogression might result from disuse, the explanation favored by Lamarckians, although in general they did not greatly stress degeneration. For Darwin, Huxley and Wells it was a significant and widespread phenomenon, and the latter two perceived it as a threat to humanity. *The Island of Doctor Moreau* gives full play to the threats of degeneration and extinction that Wells already acknowledged but that the abandonment of Lamarckian optimism accentuated.

A passage Wells added to his novel late in the writing process particularly signals his shift away from Lamarckism.[1] In Chapter 15, Montgomery tells Prendick that Doctor Moreau's creations do not

8. Asker discusses Wells and *Doctor Moreau* in regard to degeneration; Greenslade's book is a recent broad treatment of the subject in relation to British literature.

9. Huxley also influenced Wells to admire pure research, to view scientific investigation "as an open-ended voyage of discovery, full of unpredictable discoveries" (Desmond 540). Moreau's methods constitute a parody of this attitude.

1. Philmus points this out in the introductory essay to his excellent variorum edition (xvii), which reflects his reconstruction of the novel's complex compositional history in light of the many and varied *Moreau* manuscripts and editions that he sorts out. Appropriately, the textual history is as complex and, in some instances, as uncertain as the various constituents of the story.

transmit their altered characteristics to offspring: "There was no evidence of the inheritance of their acquired human characteristics" (53; ch. 15). If new characteristics cannot be inherited, then, as already discussed, rapid intellectual evolution apparently could not occur. Wells's brief interpolation evinces a significant disillusionment, one that plays into the already confused evolutionary picture that the novel absorbed from its complex scientific and intellectual environment. Near the center of the textual confusion, however, lies a tension between the natural selection that Wells now fully accepted as preeminent and the Lamarckism that he abandoned during the writing of his novel. As frequently noted, qualities of Doctor Moreau and his experiments reflect the workings of natural selection. Symbols and figurations of complex referents, however, are multivocal; they suggest more than their overt associations or their authors' intentions and so lend themselves to self-contradiction. This instability of the non-literal no doubt pertains to the complexities of Moreau's character and activities, which, although they evoke natural selection in some respects, also carry implications contrary to natural selection, some of them distinctly Lamarckian in their overtones.[2] In general, this confusion arises from the likening of incommensurable operations—scientific experimentation and evolution. The Lamarckian inflections of Moreau's activities, however, are prominent enough that they do not seem merely the incidental results of an unwieldy comparison of artificial and natural processes. A degree of order in disorder can be established by looking at the Moreau material as a hazy evolutionary allegory torn between two contrary impulses that, during the novel's composition, were important intellectual concerns for Wells.

On the one hand, Doctor Moreau's efforts to evolve animals into humans suggest a dark but generally accurate reading of Darwinian evolution because his project appears largely open-ended, subject to chance, and associated with struggle, suffering, and death.[3] And natural selection does bear an extravagant experimental quality; variations continually undergo environmental testing and prove worthy of survival or not. Moreau encourages his identification with the negative view of natural selection, stating that "'The study of Nature makes a man at last as remorseless as Nature'" (49; ch. 14),

2. As a literal character and as a personification at once of two forms of evolution, Moreau is a confused enough figure. But he is even more so because he also represents the Old Testament creator and law-giver, thereby introducing into the novel a theological dimension that has received much critical attention (for example, see Beauchamp). Moreau, like the novel as a whole, is impressive in offering resistance to simple interpretations.

3. Moreau says to Prendick, "I went on with this research just the way it led me. . . . I asked a question, devised some method of obtaining an answer, and got—a fresh question. . . . You cannot imagine the strange, colourless delight of these intellectual desires! The thing before you is no longer an animal, a fellow-creature, but a problem!" (48; ch. 14).

and Prendick's final assessment of Moreau summarizes this same connection: "he was so irresponsible, so utterly careless! His curiosity, his mad, aimless investigations, drove him on; and the Things were thrown out to live a year or so, to struggle and blunder and suffer, and at last to die painfully. They were wretched in themselves, the old animal hate moved them to trouble one another" (63–64; ch. 16). On the other hand, Moreau's investigations appear non-Darwinian because they are not precisely aimless; whatever his methods, he pursues the goal of creating rational life freed from physical limitations, and he learns as he goes along. Mind, intent, choice, and education inform the process, and these are qualities important for Lamarckism. Thus Moreau's project is Lamarckian in his effort not only to bring about rapid evolution, but to create evolutionary order in place of Darwinian randomness. Another Lamarckian overtone associated with Moreau is his great self-sufficiency and capacity for innovation. These qualities betoken the positive individualism that Lamarckians perceived as underpinning their form of evolution in which acquired characteristics result from the insight and efforts of individual aspirants; Darwin stressed individuality and individual struggle, but not so much the conscious choice-making involved in individualism. Finally, Moreau detects in the Beast People an inherent "upward striving" (51; ch. 14).[4] This tendency suggests the vitalistic strain in Lamarckism that upholds the idea that animals somehow strive to evolve.

Darwinism and Lamarckism agree in some regards pertinent to the story. For example, in their different ways both recognize degeneration, which, as Moreau acknowledges and as we see occurring at the end of the novel, is the fate of his creations: they inexorably return to their animal characters. But because this reversion represents failure for Moreau, it reinforces the controverting of Lamarckian tendencies implicit in his creations' inability to pass along their changes to offspring. Furthermore, according to Weismann's neo-Darwinism, degeneration occurs whenever the struggle for survival slackens. To the degree that he personifies natural selection, Moreau manifests this explanation of degeneration, for once he creates his beings, he largely ends his involvement in their lives and they revert; similarly, once the hand of natural selection is removed degeneration begins.

Overall, evolution through natural selection outweighs Lamarckism, but the picture is far from clear. Moreau's surgical and psychological manipulations of animals create a confused nightmare of

---

4. Moreau, however, attributing it in part to a sort of sublimation, negatively interprets this striving as "part vanity, part waste sexual emotion, part waste curiosity" (51; ch. 14). In this characterization, only curiosity, a mental quality that can lead to purposeful and positive action, relates to Lamarckism.

evolution, and one can speculate that it was a nightmare from which Wells wished to awake. *Doctor Moreau* signals not only a shift between largely contrary ways of interpreting evolution but a shift in Wells's opinion about the fictional attention evolution merits in the first place. If it is of no relevance to the future because acquired characteristics cannot be inherited, or, as he sometimes argued, because in humans it had come to a stop, then evolution has little bearing for an author immersed in a plethora of more relevant ideas and interests.[5] Thus at some point in composing his novel, Wells, always a seeker of clarity and order, may have begun trying to disentangle himself from evolutionary theory by objectifying its complexities and stressing its inapplicability. If such were the case, then he shared this desire for self-emancipation with a number of characters in his fiction.

In his essay "Disentanglement as a Theme in H. G. Wells's Fiction," Robert P. Weeks identifies Doctor Moreau with the many other figures in Wells's stories who try, with initial but temporary success, to escape from "a world enclosed by a network of limitations and dominated by the image of a man driven by a profound, and, at times, an irrational desire to escape. Although the network appears at first to be impenetrable, the hero finally succeeds in disentangling himself . . . but ultimately he experiences defeat in the form either of disillusionment or of death." Wells's fiction depicts such attempts to escape from limiting contingencies but refuses to downplay the difficulties that sometimes make them appear noble even when they fail. It presents, as Weeks says, "a tough hopefulness" expressed through the "tension in Wells's fiction between excessive optimism and chastened optimism, between promise and threat, and between fulfillment and defeat" (440, 444).

Regardless of Wells's conscious intentions in telling the story as he did, *Doctor Moreau* appears to announce its author's effort to extricate himself from the snarls of evolutionary theory, an effort in which he would be more successful than most of his characters in their quests for freedom. In later works he was free to transmute Lamarckian optimism and Darwinian pessimism into a cautionary vision of a possible ideal future always in doubt. Following *Doctor Moreau* and his rejection of Lamarckism, with the hope it held out, he would dismiss evolution as a major fictional theme—although he continued to accept Darwinism and the idea of the indeterminate universe it fosters. Henceforth he would focus on education. Because contingency renders the future unknowable, education becomes

5. Wells arrived at the view that physical evolution, because of its slowness and because of the modern maintenance of those with defects, was essentially at a standstill (see *Early Writings* 213–15). Combining this idea of arrested development with his identification of humans as animals, Wells refers to man as the "culminating ape" (217).

imperative in a universe where nothing is assured but little is pre-
cluded. Individuals are subject to limitations dangerous not to
acknowledge, but humanity as a whole is potentially less limited than
individuals; Wells believed that collectively people can accomplish
much when they honestly assess their constraints and possibilities.

  Doctor Moreau, however, provides no clear or positive cause for
optimism. It is, relative to Wells's career, a transitional text especially wrapped up in contrary concerns, as the author's divided reactions to the novel indicate. Later in his life Wells characterized the
story as a satirical fantasy or romance with a story line not to be
taken quite seriously.[6] However, in the immediate wake of its publication Wells argued against critics who had questioned the efficacy
of Doctor Moreau's methods of altering animals, contending that
they are not unrealistic at all.[7] He clearly did not find fanciful the
possibility of changing an animal's character through amputation,
grafting, transfusions, vaccination, hypnosis, and "excisions" to alter
"physical passions" (*Doctor Moreau* 45–47; ch. 14). In fact, Wells had
already argued the plausibility of such procedures in his essay "The
Limits of Individual Plasticity" (1895) (*Early Writings* 36–39), which
uses Moreau's ideas and language.[8] What he does not argue anywhere is that these methods can produce evolution; accordingly, in
the story they are not evolutionary except on the level of allegory or
satire, and there they constitute only temporary evolution.

  Wells's resistance to scientific criticism of his novel, in contrast
to his later, generally cavalier assessment, points to its situation
somewhere between realism and satirical fantasy. It is realistic in
the way science fiction is generally realistic: even though the science
that underpins the story does not fully exist in the form depicted, it
is presented as plausible because founded on principles and terminology taken from current scientific theory and practice known to
many readers. Moreover, the physical and temporal setting is unremittingly realistic, while the sincere and detailed horror of Prendick's involvement in his story also points toward the earnestness of
presentation associated with realistic fiction. The rudimentary society of the Beast Folk, however, with its overt exaggerations and
distortions of human culture, is fanciful. This is most obvious
in their chanting of the laws, which, because they are negative

6. In his preface to the second volume of *The Works* (Atlantic Edition), Wells refers to the
   novel as "a theological grotesque" entailing a "flaming caricature" of humanity—
   presumably a reference to the Beast People (ix). Elsewhere he calls it "an exercise in
   youthful blasphemy" (*Wells's Literary Criticism* 243).
7. See *The Island of Doctor Moreau*, "Appendix 6. Wells in Defense of *Moreau*" (197–210),
   in which Philmus covers this subject, incorporating Wells's published reactions to the
   negative reviews his book had received. In his responses Wells argues for the scientific
   plausibility of Moreau's experiments.
8. The essay derives from the first version of *Doctor Moreau* and its chapter, "Doctor
   Moreau Explains" (Wells, *Doctor Moreau* 128–35).

injunctions ascribed to Moreau as a semi-divine authority, extravagantly parody the Mosaic Code. The realistic and the fantastic, with its allegorical and satiric weight, do not quite mesh; Prendick continually records his own sense of unreality as the fantastic and realistic intermingle in grotesque ways. There is always a sense of disjunction that contributes to the novel's disquieting atmosphere.[9] This disequilibrium is one reason, I suspect, why the story has been ascribed to so many different genres and why Wells made so many adjustments to it; he must have realized that it contributed to a thematic and generic muddle, however much it enabled a dramatically effective mood.

Indeed, Wells's many interests and intentions, some of them undergoing change, so complicate the story that it is pointless to insist upon just one meaning or implication. Not that this is a weakness: *Doctor Moreau* tells, on the literal level of character and plot, an interesting and coherent story; imaginatively it offers a compelling and impressively thorough investigation of late nineteenth-century evolutionary theory; and, like all competent fiction, it excels in posing intriguing questions in lieu of offering simple answers. In this last respect, it is superior to much of Wells's later, more tendentious work. None of this means that the novel lacks some primary implication offering a degree of coherence, but it can only be inferred by disengaging it from those areas of disorder and limitation that the novel foregrounds; I will return briefly to this matter at the end of the essay.

The point of this section is that the novel treats the confusions of evolutionary theory but also signals Wells's desire for what Doctor Moreau fails to accomplish: disengagement from the ambiguities of evolutionary theory—* * *what Weeks characterizes more generally as the Wellsian goal of disentanglement from limitations. Moreau tries to free humanity, and himself first of all, from the evolutionary traces of its animal ancestors and thereby create a wholly rational creature, but his character is too enmeshed in the novel's evolutionary confusions to allow him this release. Indeed, the text's handling of evolution casts an incapacitating net of indeterminacy over all its characters by destabilizing those binary oppositions that help people make sense of their world. These include chance and design, doubt and knowledge, man and animal, nature and culture, amorality and ethics, degeneration and evolution, pessimism and

---

9. According to Haynes, the disjunctive elements and inconsistencies of the novel allow it to take on mythic resonance: "Despite the apparent realism of the novel—and the recoil of Wells's contemporaries from its vivid pictures of horror testifies to its atmosphere of authenticity—Wells's success in creating the sense of a mythical dimension in the novel resides in its very ambiguities. The images do not reinforce each other, and the resultant blurred and composite picture seems to bespeak a complexity all the more striking because of the clarity of the details" (39–40).

hope. The novel's reconfiguration of Darwin's entangled bank fore-grounds these confusions.

III

During the early part of his stay on Moreau's island Prendick, not yet aware that Moreau's helpers were created from animals, sustains more and more uncertainty about his situation: "What could it mean? A locked enclosure on a lonely island, a notorious vivisector, and these crippled and distorted men?" (22; ch. 7). Then, already disturbed by the ordeals he has undergone and confused by the strangeness of Moreau's activities and his bizarre workers, he becomes more distressed as he listens to the agonized screams of the puma upon which the doctor is operating: "It was as if all the pain in the world had found a voice." He is agonized by a pity he admits he would not have felt had he known of the torture but it had remained silent and unobtrusive (24; ch. 8). He is further upset, it appears, by the suspicion that his pity is merely a conventional learned response rather than expression of an inherently ethical human nature; here he encounters again the issue of moral relativism that self-preservation and cannibalism had broached early in the story. Understandably, when Prendick flees the compound to escape the puma's cries, he perceives a world that, although potentially a tropical paradise, appears to him a confused hell reflecting his cognitive and ethical turmoil: "But in spite of the brilliant sunlight and the green fans of the trees waving in the soothing sea-breeze, the world was a confusion, blurred with drifting black and red phantasms" (24; ch. 8).

Twice in his story he calls the jungle a "green confusion" (27, 65; ch. 9, ch. 17): he projects his mental state onto nature, and nature itself, when interpreted apart from comforting ideologies and eva-sions, readily enables a confused experience fraught with indeter-minacy. Prendick's confusion results from the inability of his internalized cultural nature any longer to impose order on an exter-nal nature that encourages the disruption of mental and moral cat-egories. The ultimate source of confusion is Prendick's mind, which, unable to assimilate his experiences to his self-conceptualizing codes and constructs, must interpret the external world as confusion. With its resistances to vision, orientation, and movement, and with its diz-zying superabundance of phenomena, the jungle is the form of nature that most readily promotes confusion and entanglement.[1]

---

1. The first version of *The Island of Doctor Moreau* makes little note of jungle vegetation. The jungle, however, became indispensable to his revision as Wells discovered his theme of mental entanglement in relation to evolutionary theory; this discovery is hinted at, I believe, by his addition of the word "tangle" to the first page of the original, manuscript version of the story [see n. 5 to p. 290 above].

John R. Reed notes this connection of the jungle and mental entanglement within Wells's life and work:

> Wells never felt comfortable with jungles, which serve him as a consistent metaphor for entanglement, confusion, and a threateningly abundant disorder. As obstructive undergrowth, the jungle represented an impediment to progress; as an environment for hostile predators it signified the dread characteristics of man's unenlightened state. Thus the jungle could be both an external condition signifying frustration and difficulty, and an internal condition of fear against the outbreak of fierce impulses and instincts.

Reed adds that, as an obstacle and as the locus of beasts and bestiality, the jungle was "daunting" and "terrifying" for Wells. The jungle, however, is balanced by the inclusion, in a number of Wells's works, of the garden, the site of natural and cultural coherence. It is probably derived, Reed says, from Huxley's metaphorical application of the garden in the "Prolegomena" to *Evolution and Ethics* (35).

In *Doctor Moreau* there is no garden. The significance of this absence, I believe, is that in his novel Wells confronted his own terrors and uncertainties, including uncertainties about what he had learned as the student of Huxley; it was a way of clearing the air before he went on to other matters. Because he was openly and imaginatively confronting his own "bogle" (to use Montgomery's word [31; ch. 10]) and facing his own jungle, participating in a psychological exercise of great personal import, Wells was led into a probably unanticipated project—the artistic challenging of his own intellectual positions, as he does both in reassessing the relative merits of Darwinism and Lamarckism and in representing the mental flaws in a scientist who actually articulates many of his pet scientific theories and notions.[2] The result is a "green confusion"—a phrase confusedly conflating color and psychology—that signifies entanglement both as a theme and as a condition of nearly every

---

2. Moreau voices or implies a number of ideas and attitudes that Wells advocates in his early essays. These include the importance of vivisection, organic forms' extreme "plasticity" or malleability, the possibility of eliminating the need for pain, the definitive influence of speech in the development of humanity, the insignificance of humankind from a cosmic perspective, and moral relativism. Recognizing such convergence, a minority of critics have interpreted the presentation of Moreau as largely or entirely positive. In the introduction to his informative 1996 critical edition of *The Island of Doctor Moreau*, Stover adopts such a position, reading Moreau as a Wellsian saint. A novel, however, is a work of imagination, not a direct transcription of intellectual positions. My view is that the text expresses Wells's creative response to many desirable and undesirable possibilities summed up especially in the confused ideas and behaviors of Moreau. He is as much a dysfunctional hybrid psychologically as any of his creations is physically, and this is primarily why he fails. In particular Moreau personifies contradictory evolutionary positions, including his author's interest in both Lamarckism and Darwinism, one an intellectual blind alley and the other a vital truth with little to offer to human aspiration.

aspect of the novel. Chapter 9, "The Thing in the Forest," in particular dramatizes entanglement through its adaptation of Darwin's
entangled bank.

In chapter 8 Prendick calls his mental state a "tangle of mystification" (22). Echoing the tangle of ropes at the beginning of the
novel, entanglement again serves as emblem of indeterminacy—of
the unpredictable and unknowable in a world of mixed phenomena.
Furthermore, it introduces the series of Darwinian tangles in chapter 9, where Prendick's encounter with the Leopard-man, the most
dangerous and elusive of Moreau's creations, raises his bewilderment to an even higher level. Robert Philmus comments on one of
these references to entanglement, a passage in which Prendick, on
his way back to Moreau's compound, enters "another expanse of tangled bushes" (28; ch. 9). Philmus's annotation of this passage spec-
ulates that "[t]he 'tangled bushes' are perhaps meant to recall
Darwin's 'tangled bank' as an image of the complex involvement of
species with each other in the evolutionary struggle" (93n33). However, it should be added that there are numerous instances of entanglement in the chapter, with the word "tangle" itself, in one form or
another, appearing a number of times as the narrator describes his
bewildering experiences.

The chapter begins with a virtual parody of Darwin's entangled
bank. Having escaped from Moreau's compound and the puma's
cries, Prendick comes upon a "narrow valley" with a stream: "the
rivulet was hidden by the luxuriant vegetation of the banks save at
one point. . . . On the farther side I saw through a bluish haze a tangle of trees and creepers." After his former dismay, Prendick finds
the scene "pleasant," and he falls "into a tranquil state midway
between dozing and waking." "Then suddenly upon the bank of the
stream appeared Something—at first I could not distinguish what
it was. It bowed its round head to the water, and began to drink.
Then I saw it was a man, going on all-fours like a beast" (25; ch. 9).
By appearing upon a literal entangled bank within this carefully
established scene, the Leopard-man raises, through the observer's
interpretive confusion, the same questions that had perplexed so
many readers of The Origin of Species: what is humanity and how
does it relate to other creatures?

Prendick feels this confusion as he and the creature look at one
another: "staring one another out of countenance, we remained for
perhaps the space of a minute" (25; ch. 9). Perceiver and perceived,
self and other, are intertwined in such a complex and unsettling
manner that it leaves in doubt Prendick's own identity. Whose face
is whose? Both are "out of countenance." Later on Prendick encounters, in the Beast People's ritualistic chanting of their code, the
ambiguous mixture of assertion and uncertainty in the refrain, "Are

we not Men?" (38; ch. 12). In his meeting with the Leopard-man, Prendick faces the seemingly inverse but essentially same question: is he not an animal? Materializing in the midst of a dream-like state and in the context of profound uncertainty, the Leopard-man represents a primordial embodiment of Prendick's unconscious as the narrator faces his own evolutionary legacy and experiences the consequent disarrangement of his ontological and moral identity.

The eerily close connection between Prendick and his antagonist is stressed later in the chapter as they follow parallel paths, stopping and starting together, with the Leopard-man keeping just out of his sight in the vegetation, at one point partially "hidden by a tangle of creeper" (27; ch. 9). Symbolically, Prendick is stalked by an animal nature that he does not wish to acknowledge as his own. And yet, significantly, later in the novel Prendick proprietarily refers to this nemesis as "my Leopard-man" (54; ch. 15).[3] As Prendick's double, the Leopard-man incorporates those primitive elements in the narrator that have continually been forced upon his awareness since the shipwreck; it is as if the creature and the other Beast Folk as well actually emerge from his own nightmarish fantasy—which quite possibly they have if, as discussed earlier, Prendick's story is largely delusional. That the Leopard-man is the first and most powerful of Moreau's creations to revert to its animal ancestry makes it a particularly strong assertion of Prendick's atavism.

The confused interrelationship between stalker and prey intensifies when Prendick's thought is paraphrased so that the pronoun "he" can refer to himself or the Leopard-man: "What on earth was he—man or beast?" Immediately afterwards the narrator, in trying to answer the question, to break through the tangle of identities enveloping man and beast, forces his way through "a tangle of . . . bushes," confronts the other, gazes into his eyes, and demands, "Who are you?" The Leopard-man is unable to meet Prendick's gaze or answer the question: "No!" he said suddenly, and turning went bounding away . . . through the undergrowth" (27; ch. 9). The creature cannot answer because it is unsure of [its] own identity, being both man and animal, and, as a symbolic projection, it cannot reveal itself to a consciousness unwilling to accept its own animal nature, an unwillingness that Prendick demonstrates repeatedly.

The Leopard-man unsettles not only the distinction between man and animal, but more generally that between culture and nature. Is it primarily the product of culture or nature? Are humans primarily the product of culture or nature? What, in fact, is nature apart from cultural interpretations of it? Can culture legitimately conceive of

---

3. In two editions of the novel the phrase reads "the Leopard Man," without the possessive adjective (Wells, *Doctor Moreau* 54n[c]).

the non-cultural at all? Prendick's stalker represents a disquiet about the status of the self that most people have experienced to one degree or another; the narrator must have brought it with him before circumstances raise it to a pitch too intense entirely to ignore. As Jill Milling puts the matter, "the combinational creature is the product of a metaphorical process that discovers relationships between contrasting human and animal characteristics; the partial transformation of these related opposites into the image of the beast-man symbolizes a union of or conflict between nature and culture rooted in man's uncertainty about his own nature and his place in the universe" (110).[4] This conflict expresses itself as a feeling of disorientation entailing the intermixture of "everyday reality" with radically contradictory qualities usually concealed beneath constructions of the normative.

In particular, Prendick's initial encounter with the Leopard-man recalls Freud's characterization of the uncanny as an experience of "dread and creeping horror" that occurs "either when infantile complexes which have been repressed are once more revived by some impression, or when primitive beliefs which have been surmounted seem to be confirmed" (249, 248). Prendick's buried infantile life, dating from a pre-linguistic stage prior to his self-definition as "human," emerges—along with a "primitive belief" in the co-identity of the human and animal worlds—to unsettle ego boundaries. The result is a doubling in which the sense of his conventional self struggles with an emergent one that is both familiar, because it is his, and unfamiliar because it has been repressed. This is the experience that Prendick describes when, in an episode sandwiched between his first encounters with the Leopard-man, he witnesses three of Moreau's creatures who prompt "two inconsistent and conflicting impressions of utter strangeness and yet of the strangest familiarity" because of their unaccountable mixture of animal and human traits (27; ch. 9). All of Prendick's experiences

---

4. A response to such uncertainty is to try to fix one's identity in relation to an Other defined by qualities, generally negative ones, calculated to somehow inflate the self through comparison. Prendick attempts this maneuver, especially at the end when he most wants to avoid identification with the degenerating Beast Folk, whom he now calls "Beast Monsters" in some editions of the novel (Wells, *Doctor Moreau* 86n[h]). The susceptibility of Moreau's creatures to this treatment parallels that of natives to the constructions imposed upon them by colonizers. In her essay dealing with *Doctor Moreau* in terms of imperialism and gender, Hendershot asserts that "the fact that Wells's 'savages' are made by Moreau and not found by him appears to be an explicit foregrounding of European perceptions of and epistemological creation of natives rather than any statement about non-Europeans *per se*. In other words, Wells moved toward a deconstruction of European perceptions of the Imperial Other" (6). This reading meshes with my position that the novel destabilizes any number of conventional understandings about nature, humans, and human practices, thereby involving itself, not in just a gloomy, unproductive recording of injustice and suffering, but in the positive project of pointing toward alternatives. [For excerpts from Hendershot's analysis of Wells's novel, see pp. 267–86 above —Editor.]

on the island occasion similar confusions of mixed ideas and perceptions that confound beliefs about everyday reality.

His experiences seem all the more unsettling because Prendick, a civilized man cultivated with ideals of human dignity and justice, from the first is consistently forced to confront a natural order whose overwhelming imperative is the Darwinian struggle to survive. For example, he comes upon the three Beast Folk in "a kind of glade . . . made by a fall; seedlings were already starting up to struggle for the vacant space: and beyond, the dense growth of stems and twining vines and splashes of fungus and flowers closed in again" (26; ch. 9). Prendick is threatened not only with his own death, but with a realization that life and death appear of little significance because they are so profuse and interfused in the new world he inhabits. The setting in which he stumbles upon the bloody, decapitated body of a rabbit, newly killed by the Leopard-man, illustrates this extravagant indeterminacy of life and death: "I was startled by a great patch of vivid scarlet on the ground, and going up to it found it to be a peculiar fungus, branched and corrugated like a foliaceous lichen, but deliquescing into slime at the touch. And then in the shadow of some luxuriant ferns I came upon an unpleasant thing—the dead body of a rabbit covered with shining flies" (25–26; ch. 9). Prendick's fussy scientific vocabulary cannot disguise the implication that life in general is an inhuman(e) affair "scarlet" with blood and, because inseparable from non-life, of no definitive status. In its confounding of human conceptualizations life is as alien seeming as the strange fungus, which lives upon and readily devolves into death, and as ephemeral as the rabbit that sustains the life of flies. Again Prendick confronts a Darwinian nature of confused boundaries and entangled categories.

This mental confusion intensifies as the Leopard-man stalks him and it grows dark: "Prendick's nightmarish experiences in the forest dramatize in physical terms his loss of conceptual clarity. As darkness closes in, all things melt together 'into one formless blackness' [Wells, *Doctor Moreau* 28]. He is then pursued through the forest by an unclassifiable creature (the *Thing*)" (Seed 9). Appropriately, the narrator calls himself "perplexed" (in two editions of the novel) and then "hopelessly perplexed" (28n[c], 29; ch. 9), using a word derived from Latin forms for "involved, confused, intricate" as well as "interwoven" and "tangled" (*Oxford English Dictionary*). At first a matter of entangled categories, his perplexity is exacerbated by his dangerous connection to the Leopard-man who, in reverting to its animal nature by overcoming the moral strictures that Moreau had inculcated in him, represents a psychological as well as a physical threat to Prendick, who is in danger of following the same path.

The Leopard-man calls into question not only Prendick's psychological condition, but Moreau's as well. Why would he create something potentially so dangerous? One possible answer is that carnivores are often more intelligent than other animals, thereby offering greater potential for further intellectual development. Moreover, the Leopard-man, the disfigured puma that eventually kills Moreau, and the other once and future carnivores pose, in the innate savageness of their natures, a greater challenge and thus greater potential satisfaction for a man obsessed with shaping beasts into rational, civilized creatures. There remains, however, the more fundamental question of why he wishes to perform these conversions in the first place. As an expression of individual psychology, Doctor Moreau and his activities are no more consistent than they are as evolutionary figurations confusedly mixing Darwinism and Lamarckism. His motivation is particularly equivocal.

Moreau's explanations of his activities appear as mixed as everything else in the novel. Nicoletta Vallorani expresses the matter well: "Wells's discourse on evolution as voiced by Moreau maps out a scientific landscape whose value, in terms of narrative effect, is to be seen in the creation of multiple levels of ambiguity, endlessly duplicating the controversial nature of the Darwinian theory itself" (248). One level of ambiguity involves Moreau's two explanations for his activities: he wants to see how far he can go in artificially evolving the physical forms of life—of pushing "plasticity" of form to the utmost—and he wants to evolve life beyond the necessity of experiencing pain. He mingles these ambitions in his explanations to Prendick, but their relationship to one another remains uncertain and contradictory. "'I wanted—it was the one thing I wanted—to find out the extreme limit of plasticity in a living shape'" (48; ch. 14), Moreau states, but his preoccupation with overcoming pain means that ultimate plasticity cannot be his only main goal; form and feeling are of two different orders. It can be argued that finding the limit of plasticity will perhaps entail establishing the limits of pain, that "plasticity" is mental as well as physical; but the matter is unclear. Moreau's emphasis on pain is also problematic because of his actual procedures and outcomes. He may indeed be devoted to improving life by creating beings that can rationally control their own fates and transcend pain, and his dedication and daring in pursuing this seemingly noble end are perhaps incorporated in the apparent name of his domain, Noble's Isle. The same name, however, also points ironically to the nature of his creations thus far. These natives are anything but noble savages, and the pain that Moreau wishes to transcend dominates their lives. In their creation Moreau subjects them to unbearable agonies, and then he turns them loose to lives of suffering.

Furthermore, Moreau's emphasis on pain weakens his assertion that only by chance did he select the human form as the ideal toward which he would work—"He confessed that he had chosen that form by chance" (47; ch. 14). When Moreau talks about physically and mentally overcoming pain, it is human pain and human evolution to which he refers, and so the evolution of humanity seems to be his real objective: "so long as pain underlies your propositions about sin—so long, I tell you, you are an animal"; "with men, the more intelligent they become . . . the less they will need the goad [of pain] to keep them out of danger"; "[t]his store which men and women set on pleasure and pain . . . is the mark of the beast upon them—the mark of the beast from which they came!" (47, 48; ch. 14). Moreau's chief concern therefore is with man and how to evolve him into a higher form; this evolution, directed by intellect, suggests Lamarckism rather than the Darwinism that Moreau's and Prendick's stress on the role of chance and cruelty in the doctor's procedures seems to indicate. Unable to operate on actual humans, Moreau consciously, not by chance, strives to create the more-than-human by first of all moving animals toward humanity; he attempts to encompass the whole evolutionary process, from animal to man and from man to superman.

Moreau's explanation of his project reveals that he is far from being the objective practitioner of pure, open-ended research he claims to be. His sticking a knife into his thigh to demonstrate the possibility of painlessness hints at a considerable egotistic investment—that it is especially for himself that he seeks an ideal of pure intellect unencumbered by bodily limitations. The evolving of animals objectifies his wish to evolve himself, and his willingness to inflict excruciating pain—scientifically unnecessary since he might have anesthetized his subjects (Fried 110)—emphasizes his intellectual and physical control over his victims and hence his exalted status in being entirely free from the great pain he [inflicts] and witnesses.[5] Accordingly, a sadistic assertion of semi-divine agency underlies the baptismal imagery with which Moreau invests his acts of metamorphosis: "Each time I dip a living creature into the bath of burning pain I say, 'This time I will burn out all the animal; this time I will make a rational creature of my own!'" (51; ch. 14). The phrase "my own" and the four other first-person references are telling. Moreau is the primary focus of Moreau's work, and the acid-like process that obsesses him represents a longed-for burning away of his own perceived insufficiencies. The binary logic behind the process of eliminating "the animal" implies that his goal is the

5. Not anesthetizing the animals he operates on does help keep him in power since it causes the Beast People to associate him with pain and thus fear him greatly as a creator both powerful and cruel.

god-like one of creating the human or super-human, not just some form chosen at random.

As would-be creator of evolved humans, an obsessed scientist beset by self-deceptions and mixed motives, Moreau resembles Victor Frankenstein, to whom a passage deleted from an early manuscript version of *The Island of Doctor Moreau* alludes.[6] He is also reminiscent of Frankenstein because he cannot control the consequences of his activities. Despite Moreau's assurance and self-control, the "green confusion" that reigns on the island ultimately represents, not just Prendick's perplexities, but the contingencies that overwhelm his host as well. Events in which chance colludes with Moreau's fallibility attest to his inability to exercise complete dominance over his experiments. Of the agonized legless monster that spread death and destruction, Moreau says, "It only got loose by accident—I never meant it to get away" (50; ch. 14). The escapee prefigures the puma-creature that eventually breaks free and kills Moreau. The doctor also errs by allowing Montgomery to import rabbits as a food source for them, since this act contributes to the dangerous reversion of some of his creatures to predation and intractability (58; ch. 16). And the chance that brings one of Huxley's former students to the island, and influences Moreau to let him stay, places Prendick, while still convinced that Moreau is making animals out of people and not vice versa, in a position to stir up the beast-folk to rebellion against their creator (43; ch. 13). Like the world itself, the island is an imperfect laboratory, unable to contain the chaos inherent in any complex system subject to manifold variables.

The "painful disorder" that Prendick perceives in Moreau's world (64; ch. 16) mirrors that of Darwinian nature, but it appears even more disorderly because, as already noted, it is figuratively combined with elements contrary to natural selection. As practitioner of an artificial Lamarckian form of evolution intelligently directed toward the creation of ultra-rational supermen, Moreau tries to impose goals on a developmental process while at the same time contradictorily avowing an ideal of pure, undirected experimentation closer to Darwinism. The same confusion occurs in his assertion that pain is "a useless thing that [will be] ground out of existence by evolution sooner or later" (48; ch. 14). This process intimates natural selection, but the idea that pain will become useless is predicated on his belief that life will first become intelligent enough to recognize sources of harm and consciously act so as to avoid them. Again, the realization of this intellectual evolution depends, not on chance and a struggle for survival, but on his intellect; this intellect though proves inadequate for producing such evolution.

6. See Wells, *Doctor Moreau* 105nn[c]–[e]; 138n5.

The tendency of his creatures to revert particularly stymies Moreau. It may be true that his failures, as is often the case in scientific experimentation, would have eventually led to success had he been able to continue his work and correct his errors, but his confused motives, obsession, and limited knowledge of himself and the future preclude continuation. They cause him to be as entrapped by circumstances as are Prendick, the beast-folk, and Montgomery as well, all of whom suffer consequent physical or mental retrogression. The humans in the story are no better off than are the sub-humans. The Beast Folk dramatize the condition of humanity, precariously clinging to what civilization it has attained, ever at the mercy of a confused, complex universe as likely to support as oppose suffering, degeneration, and extinction. After the puma kills Moreau, the body of the scientist who had tried to distance himself from his creations ends up ironically entangled with dead Beast People: "[on] the pile of wood and faggots . . . Moreau and his mutilated victims lay, one over another. They seemed to be gripping one another in one last revengeful grapple" (72; ch. 19). Everyone's fate is entangled with that of the other participants in a drama of elusive import and unpredictable consequences.

The entangled bank exemplifies a confused universe again in chapter 16, where it informs the hunt for the Leopard-man that occurs after Prendick reports to Moreau the creature's dangerous reversion. This episode evidences the connection between hunters and hunted, men and monsters, all ensnared in the same biological and environmental contingencies. Prendick detects in Moreau lust for capturing the malefactor and exultation in his own power akin to that of the enthusiastically participating Beast People (60; ch. 16). The description of the chase through entangling vegetation further accentuates the connection between its human and partially human participants in an uncongenial natural world; both enter "a dense thicket, which retarded our movements exceedingly, though we went through it in a crowd together—fronds flicking into our faces, ropy creepers catching us under the chin, or gripping our ankles, thorny plants hooking into and tearing cloth and flesh together" (61; ch. 16). When Prendick describes the final cornering of the quarry he once again employs terms of entanglement. This scene recalls his earlier experience of himself being a hunted animal when, mistakenly believing himself fodder for Moreau's experiments, he hides in an entangled bank reminiscent of the one where he first sees the Leopard-man: "I scrambled out at last on the westward bank, and with my heart beating loudly in my ears, crept into a tangle of ferns" (34; ch. 11). The final cornering of the Leopard-man echoes both this scene and the creature's stalking of Prendick in chapter 9. As the prey cowers "in the bushes through which [Prendick] had run from him" earlier in the story, the pursuers surround the creature within this "tangle of undergrowth" (62; ch. 16). Thus throughout the novel scenes of entanglement, entailing parallels in plot as well as in imagery, enmesh its various characters in the same complexities of mixed circumstances and fragmented understandings.

Finally Prendick spots the cornered Leopard-man "through a polygon of green, in the half darkness under the luxuriant growth." On this occasion Prendick momentarily acknowledges the connections between himself and this other that hitherto have been only implicit in his descriptions: "seeing the creature there in a perfectly animal attitude, with the light gleaming in its eyes and its imperfectly human face distorted with terror, I realised again the fact of its humanity" (62; ch. 16). Recognizing their shared identity, and in a setting momentarily freed from the negative imagery of entanglement, Prendick mercifully shoots the wretch. "Poor brutes," he says afterwards, and he goes on to express great empathy for the Beast Folk (63; ch. 16). These moments of grace, of positive self-transcendence, do not endure, however. The reverting Beast Folk become despicable to Prendick, and he ultimately identifies with other beings only as fellow victims of a meaningless, mixed-up world full of constraints on human freedom.

That Prendick spots the Leopard-man through a "polygon" points to these constraints upon both pursuer and prey. A polygon, a shape with a number of angles and facets, is a rather strange, technically precise word to apply to a gap in vegetation; it indicates both multiple-sidedness and straight lines. But if we connect the two-dimensional polygon—the form the opening might assume from Prendick's vantage point—with its three-dimensional relative, the polyhedron (a "solid bounded by polygons"—*American Heritage Dictionary*), Wells's figure takes on evolutionary significance relevant to the novel. Stephen J. Gould explains that the polyhedron is the shape that Francis Galton, Darwin's cousin and a man whose work Wells would have known, uses to express the idea that natural selection can mold an organism into a great but still limited number of forms; the possibilities are like the facets of a polyhedron, onto any one of which the evolutionary pressure of natural selection might tip it. Galton employs the polyhedron in discussing the malleability of man and other species under selective breeding; Gould connects this discussion to Darwin's treatment of what the *Origin* calls the "plastic" qualities of domesticated animals that breeders use to shape them to their specifications (Gould 382–85). Moreau says that he has dedicated his life "to the study of the plasticity of living forms" (46; ch. 14). Thus the Leopard-man's enclosure within a polygon hints at the plasticity Moreau employs in his "breeding" of the creature but also the natural limitations on Moreau's activities, constrained by inherent predisposition. That the Leopard-man has reverted underscores these limitations. For Wells, possibilities are always entangled with constraints, and progress necessitates a realistic assessment of both. In *Doctor Moreau*, however, the constrictions that surround its characters severely circumscribe their scope for freedom, an interpretation of reality to which Prendick ends up fully subscribing after circumstances have victimized him repeatedly.

At the end of chapter 16 Prendick addresses entanglement one last time, but translates it from natural into cultural terms. Now it is machinery that, through its unfathomable complexities, represents confusion and helplessness for all the actors alike: "A blind Fate, a vast pitiless Mechanism, seemed to cut and shape the fabric of existence; and I, Moreau (by his passion for research), Montgomery (by his passion for drink), the Beast People with their instincts and mental restrictions, were torn and crushed, ruthlessly, inevitably, amid the infinite complexity of its incessant wheels" (64; ch. 16). Normally conceived in opposition to nature, culture, in a further breakdown of conventional categories and binary oppositions, signifies the same contingent reality as does the green confusion of entrapping vegetation. In this light, the imagery is even more crushingly pessimistic than it appears at first glance, implying that the cultural environment is no more likely to support human aspirations than is the natural world, since their terms are interchangeable. Both are unremittingly "Darwinian"—this is the lesson that devastates Prendick.

IV

The reader, however, need not fully subscribe to the disillusionment of a man who ends up as an unhinged, frightened, and possibly untruthful misanthrope.[7] Despite its many confusions, *The Island of Doctor Moreau* functions well as a cautionary tale whose manifest exaggerations and distortions highlight the dangers of ego, of self-isolation, and of evasion of reality—unsympathetic and indeterminate though it may be—through science, religion, or any other means. It offers a sobering diagnosis of the human condition but not a prescription for despair, for only by recognizing constraints upon its autonomy might humanity free itself, to some degree, from what Wells characterizes as the impeding "currents and winds of the

---

7. As with Gulliver, to whom he is often compared (for example, see Hammond), Prendick ends up in a dubious condition. Upon his return to England he "gave such a strange account of himself that he was supposed demented. Subsequently he alleged that his mind was a blank from the moment of his escape from the *Lady Vain*" (3; Intro.). Prendick begins to perceive his fellow humans as repulsive and dangerous beasts, consults a mental specialist, and withdraws from society into solitude.

universe in which [humanity] finds itself" (*Early Writings* 218).[8]
Wells's novel fully attests to the perplexities of entanglement
within the Darwinian universe, but, as both Prendick's own condition and his characterization of Moreau's and Montgomery's failures suggest, humans contribute to "infinite complexity" through
their own ignorance and bad choices.

WORKS CITED

Asker, D. B. D. "H. G. Wells and Regressive Evolution." *Dutch Quarterly Review of Anglo-American Letters* 12.1 (1982): 15–20.

Beauchamp, Gorman. "*The Island of Dr. Moreau* and Theological
Grotesque." *Papers on Language and Literature* 15 (1979): 408–17.

Beer, Gillian. *Darwin's Plots: Evolutionary Narrative in Darwin,
George Eliot and Nineteenth-Century Fiction.* London: Routledge,
1983.

Bowen, Roger. "Science, Myth, and Fiction in H. G. Wells's *Island
of Doctor Moreau*." *Studies in the Novel* 8 (1976): 318–35.

Bowler, Peter J. *The Eclipse of Darwinism: Anti-Darwinian Evolution Theories in the Decades around 1900.* Baltimore: Johns Hopkins UP, 1983.

Bozzeto, Roger. "Moreau's Tragi-Farcical Island." Trans. Robert M.
Philmus and Russell Taylor. Ed. Robert M. Philmus. *Science-
Fiction Studies* 20 (1993): 34–44.

Butler, Samuel. *Luck, or Cunning, As the Main Means of Organic
Modification?* London, 1887.

Darwin, Charles. *The Descent of Man, and Selection in Relation to
Sex.* London, 1871; Princeton: Princeton UP, 1981.

———. *The Expression of the Emotions in Man and Animals.* London,
1872.

———. *On the Origin of Species.* London, 1859; Cambridge: Cambridge UP, 1964.

Dawkins, Richard. *The Blind Watchmaker: Why the Evidence of Evolution Reveals a Universe without Design.* New York: Norton, 1996.

Desmond, Adrian. *Huxley: From Devil's Disciple to Evolution's High
Priest.* Reading: Addison, 1997.

Freud, Sigmund. "The Uncanny." *The Standard Edition of the Complete Psychological Works of Sigmund Freud.* Ed. James Strachey.
Vol. 17. London: Hogarth, 1955. 217–52. 24 vols. 1953–74.

---

8. This quotation comes from Wells's essay, "Human Evolution, an Artificial Process"
(1896), published the same year as *The Island of Doctor Moreau*. In it he argues that
only "the artificial factor," accumulated knowledge disseminated through a selfless
commitment to wide-spread education, can free humanity to pursue, in a rational
manner, the happiness of itself and other forms of life. This factor is prominently
absent from the novel.

Fried, Michael. "Impressionistic Monsters: H. G. Wells's 'The Island of Dr Moreau.'" *Frankenstein: Creation and Monstrosity.* Ed. Stephen Bann. Creative Views. London: Reaktion, 1994. 95–112, 202–06.

Gayon, Jean. *Darwinism's Struggle for Survival: Heredity and the Hypothesis of Natural Selection.* Trans. Mathew Cobb. Cambridge: Cambridge UP, 1998.

Gould, Stephen J. "A Dog's Life in Galton's Polyhedron." *Eight Little Piggies: Reflections in Natural History.* New York: Norton, 1993. 382–95.

Greenslade, William. *Degeneration, Culture and the Novel 1880–1940.* Cambridge: Cambridge UP, 1994.

Hammond, J. R. "The Island of Doctor Moreau: A Swiftian Parable." *The Wellsian: Journal of the H. G. Wells Society* 16 (1976): 30–41.

Haynes, R. D. "Wells's Debt to Huxley and the Myth of Dr. Moreau." *Cahiers Victoriens et Edouardiens* 13 (1981): 31–41.

Haynes, Roslynn D. *H. G. Wells: Discoverer of the Future: The Influence of Science on his Thought.* New York: New York UP, 1980.

Hendershot, Cyndy. "The Animal Without: Masculinity and Imperialism in *The Island of Doctor Moreau* and 'The Adventure of the Speckled Band.'" *Nineteenth-Century Studies* 10 (1996): 1–32.

Huxley, Thomas. "Evolution and Ethics." *Collected Essays.* Vol. 9. London, 1894. 1–86. 9 vols. 1895–96.

Lamarck, J. B. *Philosophie Zoologique.* Paris, 1809.

Levine, George. *Darwin and the Novelists: Patterns of Science in Victorian Fiction.* Cambridge: Harvard UP, 1988.

Mayr, Ernst. *One Long Argument: Charles Darwin and the Genesis of Modern Evolutionary Thought.* Cambridge: Harvard UP, 1991.

Milling, Jill. "The Ambiguous Animal: Evolution of the Beast-Man in Scientific Creation Myths." *The Shape of the Fantastic: Selected Essays from the Seventh International Conference on the Fantastic in the Arts.* Ed. Olena H. Saciuk. Contributions to the Study of Science Fiction and Fantasy 39. New York: Greenwood, 1990. 103–16.

Philmus, Robert M. "Introducing Moreau." *The Island of Doctor Moreau: A Variorum Text.* By H. G. Wells. Ed. Robert M. Philmus. Athens: U of Georgia P, 1993. xi–xlvii.

Reed, John R. *The Natural History of H. G. Wells.* Athens: Ohio UP, 1981.

Seed, David. "Doctor Moreau and his Beast People." *Udolpho* 17 (1994): 8–12.

Showalter, Elaine. "The Apocalyptic Fables of H. G. Wells." *Fin de Siècle/Fin du Globe: Fears and Fantasies of the Late Nineteenth Century.* Ed. John Stokes. New York: St. Martin's, 1992. 69–83.

Stover, Leon. Introduction. *The Island of Doctor Moreau: A Critical Text of the 1896 London First Edition, with an Introduction and Appendices.* By H. G. Wells. Ed. Leon Stover. Jefferson: McFarland, 1996. 1–54.

Vallorani, Nicoletta. "Hybridizing Science: The 'Patchwork Biology' of Dr Moreau." *Cahiers Victoriens et Edouardiens* 46 (1997): 245–61.

Weeks, Robert P. "Disentanglement as a Theme in H. G. Wells's Fiction." *Papers of the Michigan Academy of Science, Arts, and Letters* 39 (1954): 439–44.

Wells, H. G. *Early Writings in Science and Science Fiction.* Ed. Robert M. Philmus and David Y. Hughes. Berkeley: U of California P, 1975.

———. *H. G. Wells's Literary Criticism.* Ed. Patrick Parrinder and Robert M. Philmus. Totowa: Barnes, 1980.

———. "The Influence of Islands on Variation." *Saturday Review* 80 (6 April 1895): 204–05.

———. *The Island of Doctor Moreau: A Variorum Text.* Ed. Robert M. Philmus. Athens: U of Georgia P, 1993.

———. Preface. *The Works of H. G. Wells.* Vol. 2. The Atlantic Edition. New York: Scribner's, 1924. ix–xii. 28 vols. 1924–27.

———. *Text-Book of Biology.* 2 vols. London, 1893.

———. *The Time Machine.* London, 1895.

CARRIE ROHMAN

Burning Out the Animal:
The Failure of Enlightenment Purification in
H. G. Wells's *The Island of Dr. Moreau*†

Jacques Derrida's recent and recurring interest in the problem of the animal signals the critical recognition in cultural theory of a nonhuman "other" that is crucial to our modernity and to our Western philosophical heritage. Derrida traces a certain recalcitrant humanism in Western metaphysical thought—especially in the work of such cardinal thinkers as Aristotle, Freud, Heidegger, and Levinas—which "continues to link subjectivity with man"[1] and withhold it from the animal. In broad theoretical terms, Derrida characterizes the sacrificial structure of Western subjectivity as one that maintains the status

---

† From *Figuring Animals: Essays on Animal Images in Art, Literature, Philosophy, and Popular Culture,* ed. Mary Sanders Pollock and Catherine Rainwater (New York: Palgrave Macmillan, 2005), pp. 121–34. Reprinted with permission.

1. Jacques Derrida, "'Eating Well,' or The Calculation of the Subject: Interview with Jacques Derrida," by Jean-Luc Nancy, in Eduardo Cadava, Peter Connor, and Jean-Luc Nancy, eds., *Who Comes After the Subject?* (New York: Routledge, 1991), 105.

of the "human" by a violent abjection, destruction, and disavowal of the "animal." In other words, the sanctity of humanity depends upon our difference from animals, our repression of animality, and the material reinstantiation of that exclusion through various practices such as meat-eating, hunting, and medical experimentation.

While Derrida outlines a kind of trans-historical Western "carnophallogocentrism,"[2] Slavoj Zizek helps us understand the specific construction of the Enlightenment subject in its distancing from animality, or its "desubstantialization."[3] According to Zizek, the "'official' image of the Enlightenment—the ideology of universal Reason and the progress of humanity, etc."[4] is rooted in the Kantian version of subjectivization:

> the subject "is" only insofar as the Thing (the Kantian Thing in itself as well as the Freudian impossible-incestuous object, *das Ding*) is sacrificed, "primordially repressed" . . . This "primordial repression" introduces a fundamental imbalance in the universe: the symbolically structured universe we live in is organized around a void, an impossibility (the inaccessibility of the thing in itself).[5]

The "official" Enlightenment subject is one that represses its own animality or Thing-ness, and, because of this repression, circulates around a void.

This purified notion of the human subject is profoundly threatened by Darwin's evolutionary theory, which emerges in the late nineteenth century. While various theories of evolution linking humans to other animals had developed prior to Darwin's, his work served as the apex of these philosophical and scientific investigations. With the publication of *On the Origin of Species* in 1859, the human being could be understood as a highly evolved animal. Darwin's insistence that differences between humans and other animals are differences of degree rather than kind radically problematized the traditional humanist abjection of animality, particularly in its purified Enlightenment form.

Darwin's positing of the fundamental inter-ontology of human and animal lays the groundwork for a crisis in humanism vis-à-vis the animal at the turn of the twentieth century. H. G. Wells is among the first modernist writers to thematize clearly this post-Darwinian uncertainty about the stability of the humanist subject in terms of

2. Derrida, "Eating Well," 113. Derrida adds the prefix "carno" to indicate his further delineation of the Western subject he had already identified as "phallogocentric." The more recent term includes carnivorous sacrifice as a primary activity that produces and recites humanist subjectivity.
3. Slavoj Zizek, *Enjoy Your Symptom* (New York: Routledge, 1992), 136.
4. Zizek, *Enjoy Your Symptom*, 180.
5. Ibid.

its species status.[6] The humanized animals in Wells' 1896 novel, *The Island of Dr. Moreau*, embody a Darwinian nightmare of the evolutionary continuum, in which animals become human and—more horrifically—humans become animals. While seemingly invested in the improvement of animal behavior, Dr. Moreau's project is in fact targeted at the constitutive imbalance in the human subject identified by Zizek as the problem of the palpitating "Thing," which must be repressed for the subject to become human. Moreau's intense desire to make animals reasonable represents an excessive instantiation of Enlightenment rationalization in its drive to purify the human subject of all connection to the irrational, the bodily, the animal. But the novel ultimately confirms the impossibility of such purification and stages an insistent collocation of human and animal being.

Anxieties about humankind's participation in animality are recurrently coded in figures of ingestion and cannibalism in the literature of modernism.[7] *The Island of Dr. Moreau* further corroborates this insight. The reader meets Edward Prendick, the novel's protagonist, and two other sailors shipwrecked from the "Lady Vain," as they float helplessly without provisions and without promise of rescue. Prendick describes this initial crisis in terms of hunger and thirst: "We drifted famishing, and, after our water had come to an end, tormented by an intolerable thirst, for eight days altogether."[8] Prendick and his companions find themselves bereft of the basic comforts of human society and physical sustenance. They are confronted with mere physical survival, the need to eat and drink. Their predicament immediately compromises humanity's claim to the transcendence of animal instincts as the three men agree to draw lots and determine who will be the cannibals among them and who will be the victim. Though Prendick's companions struggle with one another and roll overboard before anyone is eaten, human nature is already marked in the novel as fundamentally physical, instinctual, and even aggressive. Peter Kemp describes this perspective as one that marks Wells' larger body of work, particularly his later work, in which the human being is understood more in relation to its animal

---

6. Wells' relationship to science and to Darwinism in particular has been noted by a number of scholars in light of his tutelage under T. H. Huxley. R. D. Haynes has written "Evolutionary theory then seemed to Wells, and may still be regarded as, the nearest approach to a unifying factor in contemporary thought." Roslynn D. Haynes, *H. G. Wells: Discoverer of the Future* (New York: New York University Press, 1980), 16.

7. To name only a few, Joseph Conrad's *Heart of Darkness* (1902), D. H. Lawrence's *Women in Love* (1921), and *The Plumed Serpent* (1926), and James Joyce's *Ulysses* (1922) all explore the problem of animality and human identity through various economies of consumption and incorporation.

8. H. G. Wells, *The Island of Dr. Moreau* (New York: Bantam, 1994), 2. Henceforth, references to this novel will be cited by page numbers and enclosed in parentheses.

contingencies and appetites than to its imagined transcendence of them.[9]

Cyndy Hendershot points out that Prendick, as the novel's "representative of masculine British civilization,"[1] is set apart from the other men in the raft because he resists the initial proposal of cannibalism, but the text immediately undercuts Prendick's status as nonprimitive when he is picked up by Moreau and company. Moreau's assistant Montgomery gives Prendick some "scarlet stuff, iced" (5), and Prendick notes, "It tasted like blood, and made me feel stronger" (6). Here Prendick's basic physical need to eat and drink is realigned with cannibalism and therefore animalized. A few lines later, Montgomery assures the weakened protagonist that some mutton is boiling and will soon be ready to eat. When the mutton is brought in, Prendick is "so excited by the appetising smell of it" that he is no longer disquieted by a puma's incessant growls from the deck (7). Wells' emphasis on the olfactory in this description further underscores Prendick's animal needs. Cary Wolfe and Jonathan Elmer have noted that Freud, in *Civilization and its Discontents*, associates the acquisition of humanity with a decreased reliance on smell and an increased sense of sight.[2] When "man" learns to walk upright, he removes himself from the organicism he once experienced on the ground: "Freud's fantasy of origins tells us, then, that the human animal becomes the one who essentially *sees* rather than *smells*." Therefore Wells' characterization of Prendick is one of regression to an animal state in which the olfactory rather than the specular dominates his relations to the objective world. Prendick has drunk blood and now smells the flesh being prepared for him to eat.

Derrida has argued that the Western subject, just as it is identified with phallic privilege and with the metaphysics of presence, is also organized around carnivorous virility. The acquisition of full humanity in the West, he contends, is predicated upon eating animal flesh. This valorizing function of meat-eating has been explained in a different register by Nick Fiddes in his book *Meat*, which is premised upon the idea that "the most important feature of meat . . . is that it tangibly represents human control of the natural world. Consuming the muscle flesh of other highly evolved animals is a potent statement of our supreme power."[3] For humans, as opposed to

---

9. See especially Kemp's introduction to *H. G. Wells and the Culminating Ape* (New York: St. Martin's Press, 1982).
1. Cyndy Hendershot, "The Animal Without: Masculinity and Imperialism in *The Island of Dr. Moreau* and 'The Adventure of the Speckled Band,'" *Nineteenth Century Studies* 10 (1996), 7 [for excerpts of Hendershot's analysis of Wells's novel see pp. 267–86 above —*Editor*].
2. Cary Wolfe and Jonathan Elmer, "Subject to Sacrifice: Ideology, Psychoanalysis, and the Discourse of Species in Jonathan Demme's *Silence of the Lambs*," *Boundary 2* 22, no. 3 (1995), 141–170.
3. Nick Fiddes, *Meat: A Natural Symbol* (London: Routledge, 1991), 2.

nonhuman animals, eating meat enacts the cultural work of creating and maintaining a subjectivity that is imagined to exceed the
natural. This putative transcendence over nature thus posits the
nonanimality of the human carnivore, and, as George Bataille's
Theory of Religion[4] suggests, works to remove man from the realm of
the thing. Eating cooked meat defines the animal as always-having-
been a thing, and conversely, it defines man as never-having-been a
thing. But Wells' text troubles the distinction between eating the
flesh of animals and eating the flesh of people through its alignment
of the carnivorous and the cannibalistic. Prendick's consumption
of flesh and blood indicates the coincidence of human civilization
and instinctual animality. Wells' foregrounding of the bloody and
smelly in Prendick's eating habits realigns him with the cannibal/
animal. The text takes pains to emphasize the bloody realities of
British cuisine by emphasizing Prendick's animal response to animal flesh. In this way, the text reveals the inherent contradiction of
"carnivorous civilization." Within the first few pages of the novel,
then, Wells codes the eating of flesh as an animal practice. Prendick's
"civilized" status is undercut by his desire to feed on other animals, a
desire that becomes one among several primary markers of animality
in the novel.

  This early troubling of Prendick's status as human is promptly
mirrored in the appearance of M'Ling, Moreau's most beloved Beast
Person whom Prendick perceives as a misshapen black man moving
with "animal swiftness" (9). As Hendershot points out, M'Ling serves
as an obvious point of conflation between imperialist racism and
Darwinian theories of evolutionary superiority. Not yet realizing that
M'Ling is one of Moreau's animals-made-human, Prendick experiences this creature within a psychomythological register:

> I had never beheld such a repulsive and extraordinary face
> before, and yet—if the contradiction is credible—I experienced
> at the same time an odd feeling that in some way I *had* already
> encountered exactly the features and gestures that now amazed
> me. Afterwards it occurred to me that probably I had seen him
> as I was lifted aboard, and yet that scarcely satisfied my suspi-
> cion of a previous acquaintance. (10)

Prendick seems to recollect M'Ling's disquieting face through an
unconscious source that is chronologically anterior. In Jungian
terms, M'Ling triggers Prendick's collective unconscious. Jung maintains that "archetypes" or "primordial images" recur in dream
symbolism because the mind, like the physical body, represents a

---

4. George Bataille, *Theory of Religion*, trans. Robert Hurley (New York: Zone Books,
   1989 [1973]) [*Editor's note*].

"museum" with "a long evolutionary history behind it . . . I am referring to the biological, prehistoric, and unconscious development of
the mind in archaic man, whose psyche was still close to that of the
animal."[5] Prendick's vague recognition of M'Ling, like most recognitions in the novel, says more about him than about the Beast Man
because it indicates his own evolutionary kinship with animality.

This recognition is mythologized in a subtle yet instructive reference to biblical tradition when Prendick turns to view the schooner's deck. He is astonished to see, in addition to staghounds and a
huge puma "cramped" in a small cage, "some big hutches containing a number of rabbits, and a solitary llama . . . squeezed in a mere
box of a cage forward. The dogs were muzzled by leather straps. The
only human being on deck was a gaunt and silent sailor at the wheel"
(11). In this parable of Noah's Ark, humans and animals are equalized by the wrath of God infused into nature and find themselves
literally in the same boat. The parable implicitly deconstructs the
superiority of man over animal by insisting upon their mutual corporeal needs. The Ark is an apt allusion for the beginning of Wells'
tale, which, according to Anne Simpson, calls for humankind's "deep
investigations of the nature of self-awareness."[6]

M'Ling functions as the ironic precursor to Prendick's lesson on
Noble's Island, which undoes humanism's fundamental species tenet
that humans are ontologically distinct from nonhuman animals.
Prendick's confusion over the status of M'Ling's humanity sets the
stage for his own immanent tutelage. Looking toward M'Ling
through the darkness, Prendick is astonished when "it" looks back
with shining green eyes. "The thing came to me," notes Prendick,
"as a stark inhumanity. That black figure, with its eyes of fire, struck
down through all my adult thoughts and feelings, and for a moment
the forgotten horrors of childhood came back to my mind" (18). For
Jung, the childhood mind is more connected to the "deeper instinctive strata of the human psyche,"[7] which adults have learned to control and repress. This narrative moment of terror also recalls
Freudian theory, which implicitly claims that the repression of one's
animality must be learned because, as children, we are not repulsed
by our own physicality.[8] Ultimately, then, Prendick is poised to

5. Carl G. Jung, *Man and His Symbols* (New York: Dell Publishing, 1964), 57.
6. Anne Simpson, "The 'Tangible Antagonist': H. G. Wells and the Discourse of Otherness," *Extrapolation: A Journal of Science Fiction and Fantasy* 31, no. 2 (Summer
1990), 135.
7. Jung, *Man and His Symbols*, 36.
8. Freud writes, "Children show no trace of the arrogance which urges adult civilized
men to draw a hard-and-fast line between their own nature and that of other animals.
Children have no scruples over allowing animals to rank as their full equals. Uninhib-
ited as they are in the avowal of their bodily needs, they no doubt feel themselves more
akin to animals than to their elders, who may well be a puzzle to them." Sigmund
Freud, *Totem and Taboo* (New York: Norton, 1950), 157.

unlearn one of the basic lessons of human subjectivization: to be a person, one must not be an animal.

Moreau's apology for his experimental vivisections comes late in the novel, after Prendick has misunderstood the Beast People as humans who have been scientifically devolved into proto-animals. Of course, this misrecognition underscores the text's deep implications for human identity: Moreau's vivisections, which humanize animals, vividly register the inverse fear that humans already have animal qualities. This textual dialectic mirrors the double-edged nature of evolutionary theory as it was received in the late nineteenth and early twentieth centuries. That is, while much emphasis was placed on the progressive capacities of evolution for human cultures at that time, our shared heritage with other animals resulted in anxieties about regression and atavistic "leftovers" in the human person. Moreau's response to such threats is a grandiose humanizing project that aims ultimately to eradicate animality from the sentient world. And while Moreau remains captivated by his own romance, Prendick learns by the novel's end that this kind of purification is impossibly fantastic.

The deeply disturbing nature of this eventual collapse of humanist subjectivity is foreshadowed in the ninth chapter, subtitled "The Thing in the Forest." In order to escape from the shrieks of the puma being vivisected in Moreau's enclosure, Prendick ventures out to explore his island home. He is surprised to discover an unidentifiable figure that "bowed its head to the water and began to drink. Then [Prendick] saw it was a man, going on all-fours like a beast!" (42). This "animal-man" (50), this "grotesque half-bestial creature" (42), will be identified later in the text as the Leopard Man, but in this scene, Prendick cannot decipher its nature and struggles to comprehend the creature's trans-species appearance. His anxieties are heightened when he stumbles upon a dead rabbit with its head torn off, the most recent victim of the "man" who goes on all fours. The rabbit is covered with flies, with its blood scattered about, and therefore serves as an excessive depiction of predation, consumption, and what Zizek would term the "life substance."[9] In light of Zizek's work, Wells' terminology is perhaps most notable in this section. Prendick narrates the terrifying and various ways in which "the Thing" (46) pursued him. The creature easily coincides with the Kantian Thing, which Zizek reads as that which must be primordially repressed in order to produce the split subject of Lacanian discourse.[1] Prendick's flight from "the Thing" in Wells' text metaphorizes the Subject's haunt by *das Ding*, by a repressed and

9. Zizek, *Enjoy Your Symptom*, 22.
1. Ibid., 181.

abjected animality that always returns. This reading is especially compelling because Prendick vacillates between the certain knowledge that the "other" is following him and the suspicion that his fears issue from within, from his own anxious imagination:

> I was tormented by a faint rustling upon my right hand. I thought at first it was fancy, for whenever I stopped there was a silence save for the evening breeze in the tree-tops. Then when I went on again there was an echo to my footsteps. (47–48)

This "Thing in the Forest" serves as the animal-without who ignites anxiety about the animal-within, and though this chapter ends with Prendick's narrow escape from the creature, the novel will demonstrate that such an escape is ultimately impossible because the animal cannot be extracted from the human subject. As Zizek maintains in reference to the subject's attempt to escape the Thing, "The problem, of course, is that this endeavor [to master the Thing] is ultimately doomed to fail since the imbalance is constitutive."[2]

While ostensibly aimed at the transformation of animals, Moreau's project is in fact directed squarely at this constitutive imbalance in the human subject. The doctor's strident and repeated attempts to make animals reasonable represent an extreme legacy of the Enlightenment project of rationalization: to purify the human subject— and even the animal subject—of all connections to the irrational, the bodily, the supernatural. In other words, Moreau's science is desperate to exterminate animality by creating and policing the boundaries of rationalist humanism. Moreau reveals this fundamental motivation to Prendick when he admits, "Each time I dip a living creature into the bath of burning pain, I say: this time *I will burn out all the animal*, this time I will make a rational creature of my own" (89; emphasis added). Wells' portrait of Moreau emphasizes the constructedness of the Enlightenment subject by suggesting that the transcendence achieved by the rational human requires a certain intense and artificial technology, a burning out of the animal within human nature. The process, of course, is displaced here onto Moreau's unsuspecting subjects, who are animals.

This fictional program of purification depends upon the newly articulated theories of mutation and natural selection. Moreau informs Prendick, "These creatures you have seen are animals carven and wrought into new shapes. To that—to the study of the plasticity of living forms—my life has been devoted" (81). The mutability of species was precisely what compromised humanity's claim to sovereignty over other animals once evolution was considered scientifically sound. And Moreau implicitly confirms this dethroning of the human

2. Ibid., 183.

when he tells Prendick, "A pig may be educated. The mental structure is even less determinate than the bodily . . . Very much indeed of what we call moral education is such an artificial modification and perversion of instinct; pugnacity is trained into courageous self-sacrifice, and suppressed sexuality into religious emotion" (82). Wells appears to draw directly from Nietzschian philosophy in this passage that explains morality as a repression of instinct. Nietzsche outlines a similar theory in *On the Genealogy of Morals*, where he discusses the process of internalization, in which "all those instincts of wild, free, prowling man turned backward *against man himself.*"[3]

The notion that a pig may be educated reveals the ideological kernel of Moreau's "benevolent" Enlightenment fantasy—that all creatures can be elevated beyond their animality, that all creatures can be finally humanized. Horkheimer and Adorno critique this sort of deeply totalizing gesture when they elaborate the repressive forces of Enlightenment reason and its connection to Fascism: "Enlightenment is totalitarian," they explain.[4] The "official" narrative of the Enlightenment proposes that matter will be mastered by scientism, systematism, and rationalist empiricism. The animal represents the human subject's internal resistance to rationality and symbolic law, so Moreau, as a perverse Enlightenment "father," wants to make all creatures reasonable.

Despite Moreau's impassioned lecture on species transformation and the plasticity of forms, Prendick objects to the suffering Moreau inflicts upon his victims. At this objection, Moreau launches into a long discussion of physical pain and the need for rational man to transcend it. "So long as visible or audible pain turns you sick," he maintains, "so long as your own pains drive you . . . I tell you, *you are an animal*, thinking a little less obscurely what an animal feels" (83; emphasis added). Here the scientist emphasizes the corporeal bottom line, the moment of pain in which materiality triumphs and the mind is conquered by the flesh. This is the moment in which humanity's embodiment cannot be denied, yet denial is precisely what Moreau recommends. Moreau refuses to see that his own violent experimentation is akin to the very "animal" drives he works against. As Horkheimer and Adorno say of the animal experiments: "It shows that because he does injury to animals, he and he alone in all creation voluntarily functions as mechanically, as blindly and automatically as the twitching limbs of the victim which the specialist knows how to turn to account."[5] Moreau continues his

3. Friedrich Nietzche, in Walter Kaufmann, trans., *On the Genealogy of Morals* (New York: Vintage, 1989), 85.
4. Max Horkheimer and Theodor W. Adorno, *The Dialectic of Enlightenment* (New York: Continuum, 1944), 6.
5. Horkheimer and Adorno, *Dialectic*, 245.

argument by drawing a knife and carefully inserting it into his own leg. His indifference to the blade is meant to demonstrate his transcendence of animal sensitivity to pain, which he argues can be "ground out of existence" by evolution (84). Again, Moreau aspires to epitomize the rationalist subject in his utter indifference to *matters* of the flesh: "This store men and women set on pleasure and pain, Prendick, is the mark of the beast upon them, the mark of the beast from which they came. Pain! Pain and pleasure—they are for us, only so long as we wriggle in the dust" (84–85).

At the end of Moreau's explanation, Prendick remains, to a certain degree, horrified by the humanizing experiments. He shivers at his newfound understanding of Moreau and finds himself in a "stagnant" mood. Prendick's ambivalence reflects his persistent inability to rationalize the cruel means and questionable ends of the vivisections. Throughout the text, Wells emphasizes Moreau's extreme violence to and thereby provides a rare fictional representation of animal suffering in medical experimentation. Moreau's rationale reinforces the text's suggestion that actual violence against animals is a displaced violence that vainly attempts to exorcise animality from the human psyche. What's more, the text also intimates, through its description of animal suffering, that attempts to deanimalize humanity are fundamentally violent. Before Prendick knows of Moreau's procedures, he is driven from the compound by the puma's "exquisite expression of suffering," which sounds "as if all the pain in the world had found a voice" (40). Obliquely, then, the text bears witness to the inherent violence of the humanizing process that creates Lacan's split subject, a process that forces the individual to renounce its animal nature, its connection to the natural world, and its instinctual desires, and to reinforce this disavowal through violence against nonhumans. As Zizek explains, Lacan's subject "can never fully 'become himself,' he can never fully realize himself, he only ex-sists as the void of a distance from the Thing."[6] The violence of this "compromise formation" (22), in which the subject becoming human must disavow its animality, is literalized in the text by the screams of the puma as Moreau forces its renunciation of animal being in order to shape its "humanity."

If Moreau's experiments characterize the attempted renunciation and purification of animality, his creations also catalogue the inevitable failure of these processes. Moreau is motivated to eliminate the perpetual regression of his Beast People to an animal state. He admits to Prendick that his creatures are unable to maintain their human-like repression of animal instincts, so he works harder to

6. Zizek, *Enjoy Your Symptom*, 22.

perfect his craft: "I have been doing better; but somehow the things drift back again, the stubborn beast flesh grows, day by day, back again" (87). Hendershot reads the "beast flesh" as Wells' codification of sexual perversion, which was often attributed to non-European natives in imperialist narratives.[7] But a close reading of Moreau's continued description suggests that the "beast flesh" cannot be reduced to sexuality alone. Rather, it stands for a multifaceted human participation in animality. At this point, Moreau's description is a thinly veiled denunciation of human behavior:

> And least satisfactory of all is something that I cannot touch, somewhere—I cannot determine where—in the seat of the emotions. Cravings, instincts, desires that harm humanity, a strange hidden reservoir to burst suddenly and inundate the whole being of the creature with anger, hate, or fear. . . . As soon as my hand is taken from them the beast begins to creep back, begins to assert itself again. (88–89)

As Prendick discovers, the repressed beast flesh can return in many ways and requires powerful symbolic containment.

Moreau, who coincides with and *embodies* the Freudian Father, or as Lacan understands it, the retroactively projected Name-of-the-Father, writes the Law for his Beast Folk. His prohibitive symbolic economy parodies the Ten Commandments as it identifies specific bestial acts that the humanized creatures must forego. The Beast Folk chant their moral code, "Not to go on all-Fours; *that* is the Law. Are we not Men? Not to eat Flesh [or] Fish; *that* is the Law. Are we not Men?" (65). In addition, they are not to claw trees or chase other men, and Prendick notes how they swear the prohibition of "the maddest, most impossible and most indecent things one could well imagine" (65). These unmentionables register humanism's projected self-loathing or shame at organicism, while simultaneously acknowledging the profound unknowability of animal consciousness. The Beast Folk's interrogative coda "Are we not Men?" insists upon the *instability* of human subjectivity and the concomitant need to establish and reestablish the boundaries of the human. Indeed, the Beast Folk provide a conspicuous instance of the "productive reiteration" of hegemonic norms that Judith Butler theorizes.[8] The creatures habitually gather to repeat the Law in their desperate attempt to remain human. They must constantly remind themselves of their putative humanity. Butler's work on the iterability and cultural resignification of sexed identity can be applied here to the discourse of species as it operates in Wells' text. In Butler's terms, The

---

7. Hendershot, "The Animal Without," in *The Island of Dr. Moreau*, 5.
8. Judith Butler, *Bodies That Matter* (New York: Routledge, 1993), 107.

Beast Folk speak the necessary recitation, the repeated assumption, of their identity position, "whereby 'assumption' is not a singular act or event, but, rather, an iterable practice."[9] They speak and respeak their identity; they literally rearticulate their humanity in order to maintain its integrity.

Wells continues to lay bare the precarious nature of human identity vis-à-vis the animal through Prendick's gradual demystification of the humanist version of the subject. After several months on the island, he reports becoming "habituated" to the Beast People (96). This habituation results from an uncanny resemblance between the behavior of the Beast People and Prendick's memories of human behavior. He can no longer distinguish the carriage of Moreau's bovine creature who works the launch from "some really human yokel trudging home from his mechanical labours," or the Fox-Bear Woman's "shifty face" from the faces of prostitutes he once saw in "some city by-way" (96). Wells' mutual deployment of gender and species discourses clearly emerges here as he adds that the female creatures had an "instinctive sense of their own repulsive clumsiness" and therefore readily adopted a human regard for decorum (96).

Victorian critics have analyzed "the animal within" as a figure aligned with sexuality, especially feminine sexuality, in nineteenth century literature.[1] But those analyses tend to read out animality *as such* when they treat it as primarily symbolic of human behaviors and anxieties. While animality is occasionally gendered as feminine in the text, and while masculine imperialism is clearly at issue in Moreau's attempts to create and control the "other," the novel remains irreducibly interested in the ontological boundary between human and animal. Therefore, the text's commentary on "primitive" female sexuality cannot contain its broader concern with human animality. Prendick's habituation to the Beast People signals an erosion of the symbolic abjection of animality that constitutes human identity. If humans are socialized to regard animals as fundamentally other, then Prendick's socialization is wearing thin as the Beasts appear uncannily human. There appears to be a two-way trafficking of identity-deconstruction here, as Moreau's animals become partially human while Moreau and the other men seem increasingly animal. This double destabilization unmasks the unmaintainability of the species boundary. The cultural edicts of speciesism dissolve on Dr. Moreau's self-contained island, which functions as an alternative space to the *fin-de-siècle* British socius.

9. Butler, *Bodies That Matter*, 108.
1. Cyndy Hendershot ["The Animal Without"] discusses the Victorian equation of feminine sexuality and the animal.

Prendick's habituation to Moreau's creatures serves as a precursor to his more radical moment of deconstructive clarity involving the Leopard Man. Formerly known as the Thing in the forest, the amorphous Leopard Man hunted Prendick earlier in the novel. He proves to be Moreau's most wayward creature when he is exposed as a killer and consumer of flesh. The Leopard Man has disregarded Moreau's Law and resumed his instinctual modes of behavior; he serves as a testimonial to the impossibility of Moreau's Enlightenment fantasy of producing a purely rational human specimen. When Prendick and Montgomery discover a second slain rabbit in the woods, they suspect that the Beast People are on the verge of regression and revolt. Moreau calls the Folk together and confronts the carnivorous transgression, at which time the guilty Leopard Man leaps at Moreau. A frantic chase ensues, and the Beast People readily join the hunt for one of their own, a betrayer of the Law. In fact, the hunt allows them to indulge their "killer" instincts; the Swine-Folk squeal with excitement and the Wolf-Folk, seeing the Leopard Man run on all fours, howl with delight (106). The frenzied pursuit further unravels Moreau's humanizing project because it disregards the fifth Law: Not to chase other Men. In Freudian terms, the chase corresponds to a return of the repressed animality in the Beast People and ultimately to a similar return in the human psyche. The narrative insists upon the Leopard Man's inter-species identity at this point: "The thing was still clothed, and, at a distance, its face still seemed human, but the carriage of its four limbs was feline, and the furtive droop of its shoulder was distinctly that of a hunted animal" (106). For Prendick, the pursuit of the fugitive Leopard Man frames the novel's most pivotal recognition. Coming upon the crouched figure, who stares over its shoulder at Prendick, the latter admits:

> It may seem a strange contradiction in me—I cannot explain the fact—but now, seeing the creature there *in a perfectly animal attitude*, with the light gleaming in its eyes, and its imperfectly human face distorted with terror, *I realised again the fact of its humanity*. (107–108; emphasis added)

This epiphanic moment produces a surprising inversion of the traditional humanist subject position, which abjects and represses animality. In profound contrast to that abjection, Prendick's vision privileges animality as an *a priori*, necessary, and constitutive element of the human. Prendick's vision insists that the Leopard Man's animality is actually his most human quality.

Indeed, it is the Leopard Man's terror and capacity for suffering that reveal his humanity for Prendick in this scene. Moreau's Law punishes transgressors by returning them to his "House of Pain" (104) for further rationalization. When Prendick realizes that within seconds the animal-man will be "overpowered and captured, to expe-rience once more the horrible tortures of the enclosure," he abruptly opts for a mercy killing and shoots the creature "between his terror-struck eyes" (108). This act of mercy grows out of Prendick's aware-ness of the creature's terror at its imminent suffering. His identification with the Leopard Man also suggests that experiencing fear of bodily harm and awareness of one's mortality are supremely human charac-teristics. In other words, being embodied, experiencing pain, having instincts and fears—these qualities mark one's humanity as pro-foundly as any other qualities.

The broader implications of Prendick's privileged epiphany about the Leopard Man are almost immediately rendered in the text. The Beast People gather together after the fugitive's body is dragged away, and Prendick continues to analyze the products of Moreau's bizarre undertaking: "A strange persuasion came upon me that, save for the grossness of the line, the grotesqueness of the forms, I had here before me the whole balance of human life in miniature, the whole interplay of instinct, reason, and fate, in its simplest form" (109). Philosophical pronouncements like this one, that trouble the sanctity of humanism, characterize the remainder of the novel.

Jill Milling's analysis of science fiction narratives involving beast-men confirms that the scientist/protagonist "who makes discoveries about the relations between humans and other animals . . . records a sense of wonder, displacement, and ambivalence resulting from these revelations."[2] Prendick's vision of humanity is permanently altered by his experience on the island. When he laments the Beast People's lost innocence at Moreau's hands, he implicitly laments humanity's denaturalization as evolved, subjectivated, rational beings. Moreau's beasts *had* been "adapted to their surroundings, and happy as living things may be. Now they stumbled in the shackles of humanity, lived in fear that never died, fretted by a law they could not understand" (109). Humanity is metaphorized as the antithe-sis of freedom, as a blind adherence to authority, to the Law, to the symbolic order. The human creature has lost its immanence. In these rare moments, one detects in Wells traces of a nostalgic long-ing to return to some originary, animal moment in history before the human emerged as fully other from its fellow creatures, before man became the "thinking animal." But for most of the novel, humanity's residual animality stalks the human and threatens its locatability.

Moreau's death at the claws of his Leopard Man confirms the futility of his project and sounds a warning to rationalist humanism

---

2. Jill Milling, in "The Ambiguous Animal: Evolution of the Beast-Man in Scientific Cre-ation Myths," in *The Shape of the Fantastic* (New York: Greenwood, 1990), 108.

that attempts to purify humanity of its animal tendencies are doomed to fail. Prendick's unsuccessful return to "civilization" echoes this defeat. Rather than feeling restored by English society, Prendick reports a "strange enhancement of the uncertainty and dread" he confronted on Moreau's island (154). His detailed explanation of this "delusion" warrants a sizable quotation:

> I could not persuade myself that the men and women I met were not also another, still passably human, Beast People, animals half-wrought into the outward image of human souls; and that they would presently begin to revert, to show first this bestial mark and then that. . . . I see faces keen and bright, others dull or dangerous, others unsteady, insincere; none that have the calm authority of a reasonable soul. I feel as though the animal was surging up through them. . . . [In London] I would go out into the streets to fight with my delusion, and prowling women would mew after me, furtive craving men glance jealously at me, weary pale workers go coughing by me, with tired eyes and eager paces like wounded deer dripping blood. . . . (154–155)

At the novel's end, then, Prendick cannot reengage the basic humanist disavowal of animality. He recognizes the undecidability of the species boundary, and there is a certain horror in that recognition. Ultimately, Prendick places himself in a liminal species category that seems more animal than human; "And it even seemed that I, too, was not a reasonable creature, but only an animal tormented with some strange disorder in its brain, that sent it to wander alone, like a sheep stricken with the gid" (156). Perhaps Prendick obliquely acknowledges the unreasonableness of Enlightenment reason here, a strange disorder in the human brain. The novel's final chapter informs us that Prendick must live as a recluse in order to maintain his sanity. He finds "hope" in an abstract sense of protection he gained from his astronomical studies, in the "eternal laws of matter" (156). Clearly, Prendick's gesture toward stability fails to recontain the anxiety released by the novel. Indeed, Wells' text not only stages a confrontation between the Enlightenment subject and its Darwinian roots, but in doing so it also fundamentally unsettles the traditional notion of the "human" as ontologically nonanimal.

SHERRYL VINT

Animals and Animality on the Island of Moreau[†]

H. G. Wells's *The Island of Doctor Moreau,*[1] published in 1896, is deeply concerned with the relationship between scientific development and moral progress, and the consequences of the former outpacing the latter. It tells the story of a mad scientist who alters animals in order to make them more human; and in our present-day world of genetic engineering and xenotransplantation, as well as advocacy of animal legal and civil rights, its subject matter has never seemed more pertinent. Just as Darwinian science, the context for this and other Wells novels, created a moment of incredible disruption for Victorian society by connecting human and animal life in ways previously unimaginable, recent research in animal cognition, communication, and social organization similarly threatens to challenge and perhaps displace our cultural assumptions about human and non-human life.

Building on Claude Levi-Strauss's assertion that 'animals are good to think with',[2] I want in this essay to bring together a reading of *The Island of Doctor Moreau* with recent scholarship in the emerging field of animal studies. I argue that the focus on how the human/animal boundary is articulated in Wells's novel enables us to perceive more clearly the critique of science contained within it. If we examine the work from the point of view of animal studies, it becomes clear that its critique of science extends beyond specific practices contemporary with its publication, to a critique of the founding assumptions that shaped scientific practice as it emerged in the seventeenth century. Wells's concerns have much in common with recent feminist critiques of science, and also connect *The Island of Doctor Moreau* with the feminist and antivivisectionist positions prevalent at the time he was writing. * * *

Many critics have noted the correspondence between *The Island of Doctor Moreau* and late nineteenth-century racism.[3] Without

---

† From *The Yearbook of English Studies* 37.2, *Science Fiction* (2007): 85–96, 101–02. Reprinted with permission.

1. H. G. Wells, *The Island of Dr. Moreau* (New York: Dover Publications, 1996). All references will be to this edition.

2. Claude Lévi-Strauss, *Totemism*, trans. Rodney Needham (Boston: Beacon, 1963 [1962]): 162 [*Editor's note*].

3. Timothy Christensen argues that the sense of the uncanny that Prendick (the story's narrator) keeps perceiving when he looks at beast people, of some feature 'in' the bodies that sets them apart but cannot be described, is akin to the 'mythical' difference of race in works by Edward Tylor and Frances Galton: see 'The "Bestial Mark" of Race in *The Island of Dr. Moreau*', *Criticism*, 46.4 (2004), 575–95. Elana Gomel has argued that Moreau's desire to 'burn out all the animal' (Wells, p. 59) and create perfect beings is connected with a fascist aesthetic and racial purifying strategies; she sees a link between the New Man ideologies, which lead to the rise of fascism, and the

challenging the insight provided by such readings of the novel, I
want to suggest that thinking about the beast men as animals rather
than as metaphors for animalized racial others can provide additional insight into the novel's critique of science and vivisection. In
order to do this I shall first look briefly at a text that possibly influenced *The Island of Doctor Moreau*—Francis Bacon's *The New
Atlantis* (1627).[4] In her work on animals in the Renaissance, Erica
Fudge describes *The New Atlantis* as a fictional tale of shipwreck as
well as the 'bible' of the new science and a manual for vivisection.[5]
Francis Bacon is one of the most influential and vocal defenders of
the new experimental science emerging in the seventeenth century.
As Fudge explains elsewhere, Bacon associated science both with
power over nature and with man's proper place as separated from
animals and close to God. For him, the Fall separated man from an
innate understanding of other species, and thus learning is now
required to restore man to his 'position as sovereign and commander
of creation'.[6] Science and experimentation give man knowledge,
which is also power, a power of exploitation that becomes 'proof of
humanity [. . .] To experiment on animals—a means of understanding, "naming" them—is to place the human in a God-like position'.[7]

The New Atlantis, this manual for dominating nature and recovering man's proper place, like *The Island of Doctor Moreau*, 'presents
experimentation which sounds very much like the contemporary
practice of genetic engineering: the alteration of appearance and
reproductive faculties, the creation of new hybrids'.[8] Thus the mad
scientist Moreau, who encourages his modified animals in a cult that
worships him as Master, whose Hand 'makes', 'wounds', and 'heals'
them in his 'House of Pain',[9] is the model of the perfect New Scientist, who asserts his own humanity by forcing nature to submit. The
founding moments of science thereby rely on the assertion of the
human/animal boundary because 'dominion, with its inevitable consequences for the natural world, is *the* means to fulfil human
potential: the exploitation of animals is a necessity'.[1]

Victorian society in particular seems to embrace the exploitation
of animals as a way to further scientific knowledge. Rod Preece

---

discourse of *fin-de-siècle* biology: see 'From Dr. Moreau to Dr. Mengele: The Biological
Sublime', *Poetics Today*, 21.2 (2000), 393–421.
4. Published by his literary executor the year after Bacon died.
5. Erica Fudge, *Perceiving Animals: Humans and Beasts in Early Modern English Culture*
(London: Macmillan, 2000), p. 109.
6. Erica Fudge, 'Calling Creatures by their True Names: Bacon, the New Science and the
Beast in Man', in *At the Borders of the Human: Beasts, Bodies and Natural Philosophy in
the Early Modern Period* (London: Macmillan, 1999), pp. 91–109 (p. 94).
7. Fudge, 'Calling Creatures by their True Names', p. 92.
8. Fudge, 'Calling Creatures by their True Names', p. 95.
9. Wells, p. 43. (Page numbers for further references will appear in the text.)
1. Fudge, 'Calling Creatures by their True Names', p. 96.

argues that animal experimentation remained 'isolated and occasional until the publication of Claude Bernard's *Introduction to the Study of Experimental Medicine* in 1865',[2] after which 'the capacity and propensity to use animals as a mere means of human welfare grew rapidly'.[3] Bernard, in fact, might well be the model for the figure of Moreau. Coral Lansbury points out that he encouraged an ethos of sanctity, of a new priesthood, around the practice of science, and, again like Moreau, he felt that there were no limits on the capacity of science to master and modify nature, including the nature of human being. The introduction to Bernard's *Introduction to the Study of Experimental Medicine* presents a portrait of the ideal scientist that seems a blueprint for Moreau:

> The physiologist is no ordinary man: he is a scientist, possessed and absorbed by the scientific idea that he pursues. He does not hear the cries of animals, he does not see their flowing blood, he sees nothing but his idea, and is aware of nothing but an organism that conceals from him the problem he is seeking to resolve.[4]

This vision presents the vivisector in terms of values also proposed by Bacon and which by this time had become exemplary of scientific practice—objectivity, detachment, distance, narrow and specific focus. In Wells's novel, however, we see these same qualities turned into sadism, the distorted delusion of a man who has made himself into a god.

Moreau was banished to his island due to vivisectionist cruelty, driven from London by the combined scandal of a sensationalist pamphlet exposing conditions in his laboratory and 'a wretched dog, flayed and otherwise mutilated, [that] escaped from Moreau's house' (p. 23). Moreau is characterized as the Baconian sort of scientist from *The New Atlantis* who embraces the domination of the natural world, but Wells ensures that Prendick—and we—regard this version of scientific practice with horror. Prendick complains that there is no 'application' to justify the pain caused by the experiments, but Moreau rejects Prendick's perspective as too 'materialist' (p. 54). He continues:

> For it is just this question of pain that parts us. So long as visible or audible pain turns you sick, so long as your own pains drive you, so long as pain underlines your propositions about

2. For excerpts from Bernard's treatise, see pp. 219–21 above [*Editor's note*].
3. Rod Preece, *Animals and Nature: Cultural Myths, Cultural Realities* (Vancouver: University of British Columbia Press, 1999), pp. 139, 140.
4. Quoted in Coral Lansbury, *The Old Brown Dog: Women, Workers, and Vivisection in Edwardian England* (Madison: University of Wisconsin Press, 1985), p. 157.

sin, so long, I tell you, you are an animal, thinking a little less
obscurely what an animal feels. (p. 54)

Here we observe in Moreau's attitude what Donna Haraway has
referred to as the 'god trick' of scientific discourse, where science is
seen as some idealized practice based on 'what escapes human
agency and responsibility in a realm above the fray';[5] this vision of
science as disembodied and distant is one that Haraway rejects. It
is telling that pain is the issue that divides Prendick from Moreau.
Moreau's comments on pain associate him with the vision of the scientist celebrated by Bernard as someone indifferent to the pain of
those he experiments upon because he is focused only on the intellectual question at hand. Like Moreau, Bernard took a dispassionate attitude towards his research subjects; in viewing animals as
mere machines whose 'cries were no more than the grating of gears
in a machine', and in believing that 'it was mawkishly sentimental
to place animal pain before the interests of science',[6] he seems to
have surpassed even Decartes himself.

Although Bernard and his imitators embraced this vision of science, it did provoke outrage among some of his contemporaries,
particularly following the testimony of his student Emmanuel Klein
to the Royal Commission in 1875 regarding the passage of the Cruelty to Animals Act. Klein told commissioners he used anaesthetic
only to protect himself from bites and scratches, and that he did
not consider the animal's suffering in his experiments. He went on
to compare this to the similar lack of concern demonstrated by a
sportsman towards game, which was taken to suggest that perhaps
he enjoyed the torture. Lansbury argues that the explosive popular
response to this testimony directly led to critical artistic responses
such as *The Island of Doctor Moreau*.[7] Even more crucial, however,
is what the discussion of pain reveals about the disembodied
perception of self shared by Moreau and the culture of science in
general.

Wells thus anticipates the critique of objectivity offered by feminist critics of science like Haraway and Sandra Harding, who point
out that such a construction of objectivity is connected to a series
of intellectual moves that separate man from body and nature and
posit the scientist as the neutral, unmarked, and unconnected
observer—a distorted and limited perspective. Instead of the god-
like scientist, Haraway 'insist[s] on the embodied nature of all vision,

5. Donna J. Haraway, 'Situated Knowledges: The Science Question in Feminism and the
   Privilege of Partial Perspective', in *Simians, Cyborgs and Women: The Reinvention of
   Nature* (New York: Routledge, 1991), pp. 184–202 (p. 196).
6. Lansbury, p. 155.
7. Lansbury, p. 130.

and so reclaim[s] the sensory system that has been used to signify a leap out of the marked body and into a conquering gaze from nowhere'.[8] *The Island of Doctor Moreau* corresponds to Haraway's critique in a number of ways, particularly in its recognition that embodiment or animal being is that which must be denied and repressed by figures such as Moreau in order to continue science in this image. Contemporary feminist and other activists also recognized these links. In addition to vivisectors such as Bernard, Victorian society also gave birth to legislation against animal cruelty, with the SPCA founded in 1824, the Vegetarian Society in 1847, and the antivivisectionist movement during the 1870s.[9] The last was closely connected with the feminist movement of the time, as many women 'saw links between the fate of animals in science and the possible fate of women'.[1] The Victorian antivivisectionist movement was a critique of the culture of science as well as a plea for animal rights, and it quickly became a gendered discourse as 'womanly sentimentality' was contrasted with manly, scientific objectivity and distance.[2] The taming of women and the taming of nature continue to be recognized by feminist critics of science such as Haraway and Harding as interrelated projects that reinforce one another; they argue that scientific practice does not have to continue this heritage of dominating nature. Lynda Birke in *Feminism, Animals and Science* argues that the domination of nonhuman animals is a feminist concern because 'systems of domination remain intertwined, so to understand human oppressions more fully requires us to consider also how those oppressions are related to nature's domination'.[3]

Moreau's description of those who experience pain as more animal-like and less human also takes on a gendered note in the

---

8. Haraway, p. 188. See also Sandra Harding, *The Science Question in Feminism* (Milton Keynes: Open University Press, 1986).

9. Preece, pp. 144–45.

1. Lynda Birke, *Feminism, Animals and Science: The Naming of the Shrew* (Milton Keynes: Open University Press, 1994), p. 27. Lansbury points out that part of the opposition to vivisection also came from the working class, who feared that they could suffer the same fate at the hands of scientists and surgeons (p. 58).

2. Birke argues that this created, and continues to create, problems for women who want to claim that they can do science like a man. A limitation of Victorian antivivisectionist rhetoric is that it sometimes used language of essentialism and women's 'natural' capacity for kindness. Birke's analysis reveals how cultures in laboratories and in antivivisection movements in the twentieth century continue to produce the gendered stereotype that men are more likely to be 'objective' (or brutal, depending on one's viewpoint) and women more likely to be sentimental (or empathetic). She notes how conventions of laboratory training and standards for scientific writing work to prevent the animal from appearing as a suffering creature or even particularly as a living being, and she also points out the influence of the social division of labour, which means that technicians rather than scientists spend more time caring for the animals as individuals. Under conditions of patriarchy and racism, technicians are more likely to be female and/or non-white than are scientists.

3. Birke, p. 134. For a detailed argument regarding parallels between misogyny and the exploitation of animals see Carol Adams, *The Sexual Politics of Meat: A Feminist-Vegetarian Critical Theory* (New York: Continuum, 1990).

experimentation on the puma woman, the creature whose pain is most directly described in the novel. When Prendick first hears her screams and thinks them those of an animal, he is overcome by a feeling of sympathy, and is driven from his room so that he is not compelled to hear the pain any more and suffer 'the emotional appeal of those yells' (p. 26). Here Prendick betrays, in Moreau's terms, both his link to animality through his empathy with pain, and also, in contemporary vivisectionist discourse, his link to female sentimentality.[4] When Prendick returns and hears the puma woman cry again, he concludes:

> There was no mistake this time in the quality of the dim broken sounds, no doubt at all of this source; for it was groaning, broken by sobs and gasps of anguish. It was no brute this time. It was a human being in torment! (p. 36)

In her study of the nineteenth-century antivivisectionist movement, Coral Lansbury has argued that many women were drawn to this movement as much for the space it allowed them to express their anxieties about the status of women and women's bodies within their culture as for their concern with animal welfare. Many contemporary antivivisectionists compared the fate of the suffering animal to the suffering of women under the hands of surgeons whose practices seemed not so far removed from those of vivisectionists. Activist Elizabeth Blackwell became haunted by 'the image of a woman like a vivisected animal', given her recognition that

> increasingly women were being used as subjects for medical research; the only difference between the rich and the poor woman was that the latter could not always expect the solace of chloroform and the comfort of her own home when she was examined or operated upon.[5]

In the diary of another activist, Anna Kingsford, we find the description of a woman dying of consumption in a charity hospital who could not be left to die in peace but instead was continually awakened and prodded by rows of medical students; her gender and poverty required her to provide 'yet another lesson in return for the charity she has received, and as a penalty for being a pauper'.[6]

---

4. That the suffering animal is being made into a woman and that she is a feline may also be pertinent. Elizabeth Lawrence demonstrates that it is typical in Western culture to associate cats with women and dogs with men: see 'Feline Fortunes: Contrasting Views of Cats in Popular Culture', *Journal of Popular Culture*, 36.3 (2003), 623–35. She argues that the greater abuse to which cats have been subject in human history is related to this gender difference.
5. Lansbury, p. 90.
6. Quoted in Lansbury, p. 85.

The vulnerability of such women indicates the consequences of the way science has divided the active investigator from the passive world. The scientist has been constructed on the basis of a myth of objectivity, distance, disembodiment, and separation from the world of nature. The rest of nature—including those reduced to the body, such as women, the lower classes, and non-whites—can be used and exploited as raw material, their agency erased from the official discourse of science. As Victorian antivivisectionists and many feminists have since recognized, the human/animal boundary has significant ethical implications for many humans, given the binaries of Western thought that have allied science with man, culture, mind, whiteness, objectivity, and agency, but relegated women and many others to a category of 'not quite' human if full humanity requires occupying this supposedly unmarked category.[7] Humans who are not male, white, and bourgeois have often been categorized as boundary figures, not quite fully human but nonetheless sufficiently human that they cannot be relegated to an entirely separate category of being. Animals, in contrast, despite many connections to humans (as fellow mammals, fellow primates, etc.) are traditionally viewed as occupying a sufficiently separate category that our many uses of them as resource are not considered abuses or morally significant. Particularly when it comes to the practice of science, however, the degree to which animals as well are problematic boundary figures becomes apparent. They must be sufficiently different from humans for it to be morally defensible to torment them for research and kill them when that research is complete. At the same time, however, they must be sufficiently similar to humans for the research results to be deemed pertinent to human health. The critique of the 'mad' scientist in *The Island of Doctor Moreau* reveals how early Wells realized these connections among the discourse of science, the human/animal boundary, and the marginalization of women, workers, and non-whites in Western epistemology.

The beast men of *The Island of Doctor Moreau* have typically been read as revealing the problematic status of the non-white other because of the racialized descriptions that Prendick applies to them when he first sees them. The incident of the puma woman, however, reveals the degree to which gender is also central to the novel's concerns. Not only does her torture remind the reader—particularly the contemporary reader—of the treatment of women by the medical profession, but the description also bears disturbing similarities to aspects of contemporary pornography. Lansbury discusses at length

---

7. For a more extensive critique of liberal humanist subjectivity, particularly its emergence from a discourse about self and property, see Sherryl Vint, *Bodies of Tomorrow: Technology, Subjectivity, Science Fiction* (Toronto: University of Toronto Press, 2006).

the degree to which imagery drawn from the 'breaking' of horses is present in nineteenth-century pornography in the form of bridles, straps, whips, and other bondage paraphernalia. In such texts,

> Women are subdued and held by straps so they can be mounted and flogged more easily, and they always end as grateful victims, trained to enjoy the whip and straps, proud to provide pleasure for their masters. There is an uneasy similarity between the devices made to hold women for sexual pleasure and those tables and chairs, replete with stirrups and straps, which made women ready for the surgeon's knife.[8]

Thus the image of the puma woman 'bound painfully upon a framework, scarred, red, and bandaged' (p. 36) connects Moreau's practices both to the treatment of women by contemporary physicians and to a tradition of sadism in pornography.

Even more revealing is the correspondence between the images of women displayed in contemporary pornography with the marketing of apparatus for vivisection. Lansbury notes that the icon of bound and tortured woman is the staple of nineteenth-century pornography, and further discusses the correspondence between the devices used to bind women, described at length in such pornography, and the apparatus of the vivisector. There are similarities among these tools of pornography, the design of contemporary gynaecological chairs used to hold women and make their bodies accessible to the surgeon, and trade catalogues of vivisectionist apparatus, which were often displayed with 'photographs and drawings of animals fixed to boards with straps and cords, together with an array of scalpels and ovens, vices and saws'.[9] The animals seem in such catalogues to be on display, just as women are displayed in visual pornography. The women in pornographic stories are also often specifically animalized, especially in their expression of suffering: 'throughout her flogging, the woman does not scream: she howls, mews, screeches, and yelps, for the pornographic novelist is careful to limit the amount of human feeling permitted his victim in her suffering'.[1] Lansbury notes that many contemporary antivivisectionist novels chart a progression of scientists who move from experimenting on animals to experimenting upon and often killing their wives.[2] It is

8. Lansbury, p. 99.
9. Lansbury, p. 124.
1. Lansbury, p. 125. Carol Adams in *The Sexual Politics of Meat* also notes a connection between the display of animal bodies—in this case, in images about the consumption of meat—and the display of women in pornography. Her book provides a feminist analysis of the animalizing of women and the sexualizing of animals for consumption that also suggests many important connections between the discourses of animal studies and feminism.
2. Lansbury, p. 143.

worth reminding ourselves here of the specific licence to discount the suffering of others that comes with the 'proper' scientific attitude of dispassionate intellectual pursuit; and, furthermore, of Bacon's belief that it is in exerting power over the other that the scientist/ man asserts his full humanity, by putting himself in his proper, 'god like' relationship to nature. The many correspondences between this construction of science and the pornography of sadism suggest how very important is a feminist critique of science, not merely at the level of specific scientific conclusions, but also on the more fundamental level of the structures of scientific practice itself.

Over the course of the novel Prendick goes through a variety of responses to Moreau's activities. Each of these responses—simply the fact of responding at all—excludes Prendick from the category of scientist as articulated by Bacon and Bernard. Prendick is most distressed when he thinks that the animals are humans who have been experimented upon by Moreau, pointing to the importance of the human/animal boundary for constructing a moral line regarding our treatment of the other. The novel, on its surface, appears to reinforce this boundary, for Moreau's experiments fail and the animals devolve back to their animal nature, but a closer examination shows that this boundary is never secure. Prendick, when first rescued and being transported to the island, notices the 'pale green light' with which the attendant's eyes shine, then goes on to add, 'I did not know then that a reddish luminosity, at least, is not uncommon in human eyes. The thing came to me as a stark inhumanity' (p. 12). Later, he comes to feel a kinship with the animal creatures, and he too reverts to more 'primitive' behaviour when left alone on the island after the deaths of Moreau and Montgomery. Christensen points out that in Prendick's first encounter with the beast people outside the compound, it is obedience to the law—the performance of the chant—that makes one a man; before Prendick engages in this symbolic performance, his status is unresolved for the beast men, despite his morphology.

In this and other ways the novel demonstrates how the human/ animal boundary is something produced by discourse and ideology— such as the ideology of Baconian science. Derrida has argued that the construction of the human subject is as dependent upon this binary as it is upon the privileging of male over female, suggesting that the metaphysics of human subjectivity should be understood as the logic of *'carno-phallogocentrism'*,[3] using the practice of eating meat as a metaphor for the many ways in which some subjects are consumed or made into objects as compared with the white, male

---

3. Jacques Derrida, '"Eating Well," or the Calculation of the Subject: An Interview with Jacques Derrida', in *Who Comes After the Subject?*, ed. by Eduardo Cadava, Peter Connor, and Jean-Luc Nancy (New York: Routledge, 1991), pp. 96–119 (p. 113).

subject. This is similar to Moreau's sense that he asserts his humanity by being indifferent to pain. The novel, however, reminds us that the gap between humans and animals is not as stable as Moreau would suggest. For example, it is the preparation of meat for human consumption that seems to push the beast men towards reversion, demonstrating once again that the category of 'human' is something that is performed, and that certain behaviours are classified differently—as civilized or as savage—based solely on the status of the one performing them.

The most obvious way in which the novel suggests the commonality of humans and animals against Moreau's scientific separation is through its parallels with Book IV of *Gulliver's Travels*, the voyage to the Houyhnhnms, which most forcefully makes Swift's argument that man is not a rational animal but rather an animal capable of reason. The voyages begin with both a shipwreck and some 'animal-like' behaviour by humans, with the result that Gulliver and Prendick each finds himself adrift at sea. Unlike Gulliver, however, who cannot recognize his kinship with the Yahoos and returns to England hating mankind and isolating himself with his horses, Prendick is able to see himself in the beast men. After Moreau's death Prendick spends ten months alone with the beast men, a period not chronicled in his narrative and of which he says, 'In the retrospect it is strange to remember how soon I fell in with these monsters' ways and gained my confidence again' (p. 95). Despite calling them 'monsters', he soon realizes that he is not able to return to 'civilization' smoothly. He tells us 'unnatural as it seems, with my return to mankind came, instead of that confidence and sympathy I had expected, a strange enhancement of the uncertainty and dread I had experienced during my stay upon the island' (p. 102). Just as Gulliver is no longer able to see humans as rational creatures after his sojourn with the Houyhnhnms, so Prendick too finds that he cannot 'persuade [himself] that the men and women [he] met were not also another, still passably human, Beast People, animals half-wrought into the outward image of human souls; and that they would presently begin to revert, to show first this bestial mark and then that' (p. 102). Unlike Gulliver, Prendick does not classify himself apart from the rest of humanity, but rather sees himself as an animal as well.

Prendick hopes to nurture 'whatever is more than animal within' (p. 104) during the remainder of his life. From one point of view, the conclusion thus seems to reinforce the human/animal boundary. However, the critique of the Baconian model of scientist evident in earlier sections of the novel opens a space for thinking of the differences between humans and animals in less damaging ways, to founding a definition of humanity on something other than the domination of nature. The empathy Prendick felt for the puma woman suggests that this model might be something consistent with the feminist embrace of the other, and the recognition that species-ism has much in common with sexism, racism, and similar structures of discrimination. Derrida suggests that we can think about the 'eating' of the other not in terms of carnophallogocentrism, but rather as something that emerges from 'respect for the other at the very moment when [. . .] one must begin to identify with the other, who is to be assimilated, interiorized, understood ideally'.[4] This sort of knowledge and understanding, this relationship across species difference is markedly different from the sort of scientific knowledge championed by Bacon and exemplified by Moreau's advice to Prendick to resist empathy via intellectual detachment—a sense that 'The thing before you is no longer an animal, a fellow-creature, but a problem. Sympathetic pain—all I know of it I remember as a thing I used to suffer from years ago' (p. 56).

Focusing on the animals in *The Island of Doctor Moreau* thus enables us to see the centrality of the category of the animal to our conceptions of human subjectivity, and the relationship between this concept of the human and the practice of science. As I suggested at the beginning of my article, this question never seemed more pertinent than in this current age of genetic science. Wells was equally concerned with connecting his moral discourse with contemporary science. The very end of the novel, following the 'signature' of Prendick as the author of the preceding narrative, contains an editor's note that states: 'Strange as it may seem to the unscientific reader, there can be no denying that, whatever amount of credibility attaches to the detail of this story, the manufacture of monsters—and perhaps even *quasi*-human monsters—is within the possibilities of vivisection' (p. 104).

While the manufacture of quasi-human monsters might now (though not then) strike us as ludicrously beyond the reach of Victorian vivisection, it is a threat that appears in our own science news. I shall mention briefly just one example of this, a study by Phillip Karpowicz, Cynthia Cohen, and Derek van der Kooy[5] about the ethical implications of the creation of human/non-human chimeras through the transplantation of adult human neural stem cells into prenatal mice in order to study the development of human neural cells without the use of human embryos. This particular experiment raised much more public concern than other work in xenotransplantation, potentially because we associate the brain or mind with what it means to be human more than we do any other part of the human

4. Derrida, p. 115.
5. 'Developing Human-Nonhuman Chimeras in Human Stem Cell Research: Ethical Issues and Boundaries', *Kennedy Institute of Ethics Journal*, 15.2 (2005), pp. 107–34.

body. In their review of arguments for and against this research, the authors note that the fears expressed about it were linked to questions regarding where these human/nonhuman chimeras would fall on our moral mapping, whether the human neural cells would take over the hosts resulting in mice with human brains or mice that thought like humans. They argue that such fears are based on a misunderstanding of the science involved, as the 'overall architecture of the animals' brains would not be affected by the presence of these cells' because the neurological 'organization would be governed by the host animal'.[6] What interests me here is why such fears about human/non-human hybrids are so strong, as they point to the extent to which the human/animal boundary is foundational to ethics, not simply the ethics of experimental research, but also overall ethical definitions regarding who does or does not count as a subject.[7] As Kate Soper points out, the category of the animal has been a shifting one and 'Western culture has at various points in its development deemed "inhuman" or less than properly human [. . .] barbarians (those who do not speak one's own language), slaves, negroes, women, Indians, savages, "wild" or "wonder" men, witches, sorcerers, dwarfs, and idiots'.[8] We may be at a moment in which certain animal species are about to join these ranks as newly qualified subjects, a shift in perspective that, if accepted, will be as much a challenge to twenty-first-century thought as Darwinism was to nineteenth.[9]

* * *

The discourse of animal studies thus enables us to comprehend more fully the critique of science offered by *The Island of Doctor Moreau*, and to understand this critique as something that is foundational to how we have produced science in the Western world. It is not simply a matter of how science is conducted or what ideologically inflected conclusions it might support while denying its own status as ideology. Instead, the image of the 'mad' scientist in *The Island of Doctor Moreau* points to enduring problems in how science has been conceived through the separation of man from nature, connected with 'how the development of western science and

6. Karpowicz and others, p. 124.
7. For a more detailed discussion of the human/animal boundary as foundation of Western metaphysics see Giorgio Agamben, *Homo Sacer: Sovereign Power and Bare Life*, trans. by Daniel Heller-Roazen (Palo Alto, CA: Stanford University Press, 1998); and *The Open: Man and Animal* (Palo Alto, CA: Stanford University Press, 2004). See also Derrida, '"Eating Well"'. For a more detailed discussion of how such concepts might be useful for understanding SF see Sherryl Vint, 'Becoming Other: Animals, Kinship and Butler's *Clay's Ark*', *Science Fiction Studies*, 32.2 (2005), 281–300.
8. Kate Soper, *What Is Nature? Culture, Politics and the Non-Human* (Oxford: Blackwell, 1995), p. 74.
9. For an overview of various efforts to assert human civil rights for certain animal species see Joan Dunayer, *Speciesism* (Derwood, MD: Ryce, 2004).

technology has gone hand in hand with the domination and expropriation of nature'.[1] This domination of nature has included the domination of non-human animals, a topic of considerable concern for feminists. Thus the critique of science and of vivisection in *The Island of Doctor Moreau* reminds us that we must analyse cruelty towards animals in some scientific practices not as moments of individual depravity, but instead as a product of 'the location of science in the world of late twentieth century industrialized capitalism'.[2] The subtle and lasting influence of the human/animal boundary * * * is one more reason to use animal studies to help us see our definition of the human in new ways.

JOHN RIEDER

Artificial Humans and the Construction of Race[†]

* * * The interdependence and permeability between fictional narratives and the social discourses and circumstances in which they circulate makes the presence of racism in early science fiction inevitable. In focusing on that presence * * *, however, I do not mean to draw up a catalogue of notoriously racist works, nor to describe in greater detail the more or less casual contamination of the fiction by the ideological spirit of the age. Instead, I want to ask how science fiction handles the discourse of race and its attendant contradictions in one of science fiction's most prominent motifs, the construction of the artificial human.

* * *

* * * [I]t would be difficult to name a concept that troubles the boundaries between science and ideology more stubbornly from the mid-nineteenth century to the Second World War than [does] race. By the same token, no discursive nexus more powerfully interweaves colonialism, scientific discourse, and science fiction than racism, for one of the best reasons to emphasize the importance of evolutionary theory and anthropology to the emergence of science fiction is that early science fiction, at its best, often explores the challenges that those scientific discourses posed to established notions of what was natural and what was human. * * * [T]he opposition between biological determination and cultural construction

1. Birke, p. 134.
2. Birke, p. 135.
† From *Colonialism and the Emergence of Science Fiction* (Middletown, CT: Wesleyan University Press, 2008), pp. 97–98, 104–10, 161. © 2008 by John Rieder. Published by Wesleyan University Press. Used with permission.

is as central to much science fiction as it is to anthropology itself. Pursuing the implications of this reading further will involve spending some time at the *locus classicus* of the problem of nature versus culture in Wells's novel *The Island of Dr. Moreau*. * * *

The Island of Dr. Moreau

* * * Moreau's experimental subjects become members of a new and bizarre community that is itself of more interest than any individual within it. The scientific colony where Moreau performs his sadistic experiments is thus comprised of two quite different settings: the "House of Pain," the compound where Moreau relentlessly pursues his project; and the village of the Beast People nearby. The Beast People's physical reconstruction in the compound only begins to suggest what the cultural assimilation enacted in their ritual chanting of the Law (where the refrain, "Are we not Men?" pointedly alludes to the motto of the British abolition movement, "Am I not a man and a brother?" [38]) drives home forcefully: a sustained and deliberate resemblance of Moreau's experimental subjects to colonial ones.[1]

One of the challenges in interpreting *The Island of Dr. Moreau* is to assess the significance of this allegorical strategy with respect to the relation of nature and culture worked out literally and explicitly in the scientific plot, where the ultimate failure of Moreau's experiments, his inability to keep the Beast People from reverting to their original animality, would seem to assert a basic, inviolable boundary. Ultimately, their bodies are their destinies, and can only be manipulated so far, and no further, by the devices of culture. The way this natural order reasserts itself is a conclusive chastisement of Moreau's intellectual pride. But when taken as an element of the novel's colonial metaphor, where the boundaries between nature and culture and between animal and human are held in tension with the boundaries between civilization and savagery or between the colonizer and the colonized, its significance becomes more complex.

Although Moreau's subjects are animals, his inquiry into the plasticity of living forms certainly implies a related inquiry into the natural and proper shape of the human. In his essay, "Human Evolution, an Artificial Process," Wells proclaims that *The Island of Dr. Moreau* is about the process of civilization—the formation of "the artificial man, the highly plastic creature of tradition, suggestion, and reasoned thought." In this context, "what we call Morality

1. All quotations of *The Island of Dr. Moreau* are from the variorum edition edited by Robert Philmus [Athens: U of Georgia P, 1993].

becomes the padding of suggested emotional habits necessary to keep the round Paleolithic savage in the square hole of the civilised state." Readings of *Moreau* predominantly have followed Wells's lead in interpreting the formation of the Beast People as a metaphor for the conflict between "natural man, . . . the culminating ape" and the demands of "civilisation" (*Early Writings* 217). But Wells's fable is not so abstract in its terms that it resists a more pointed historical reading. Robert Philmus, in his variorum edition of *Moreau*, comments that the early manuscript draft of the novel, because it "describes the Beast People in terms suggestive of colonized races" and "by reason of its continual emphasis on the strict hierarchical division between Moreau and company," strengthens the case that *Moreau*, like *The War of the Worlds*, is intended as a satire on the colonial enterprise (xxiii).[2] More recently, critics increasingly have emphasized the topical references in *The Island of Dr. Moreau* to contemporary racial ideology, connecting the novel to ideas about hybridity, miscegenation, and degeneration as well as to the scientific debate rehearsed in [Compton-Rickett's] *The Quickening of Caliban* [1893] between monogenist and polygenist theories of the origins of racial difference (Brody 130–69; and Christensen).

In order to weigh the satirical and topical dimensions of the colonial metaphor in *The Island of Dr. Moreau*, we need to look carefully at the generic relation the novel creates between its colonial metaphor and its science fiction premise. What kind of an allegory or analogy has Wells invented in Moreau's project? I think Philmus is right on the mark when he says that "Wells 'darwinizes' the Yahoos and Houyhnhnms" of *Gulliver's Travels* (xxvii). Wells also darwinizes Mary Shelley's *Frankenstein*, transposing Shelley's biblical allusions to a racialized evolutionary discourse when Moreau, in the central chapter "Doctor Moreau Explains," tells Prendick that he "moulded" his first man from a gorilla, producing "a fair specimen of the negroid type," and then "rested from work for some days" (49–50). This is not just a satirical thrust at Christian theology, however. What is crucial is rather Moreau's self-recognition, his conviction of his own godlike freedom to pursue his experiment "just the way it led [him]" (48). I propose that Moreau's colony is neither a vehicle for a satirical attack on any particular colony, nor merely a parody of the biblical Eden. Instead, the features of Moreau's colony—the facts that it is presided over by a man whose whiteness Wells emphasizes at every opportunity; that this white man irresponsibly and callously tortures his subjects into a pathetic semblance of his own rational, civilized ways;

2. The early manuscript also contains deleted references to *Frankenstein* and the "state of nature" in Prendick's first encounter with Moreau (105) that suggest that Wells, like Constable, interpreted the Lockean *tabula rasa* of Shelley's creature in the context of the romance revival's opposition of civilization to "nature."

that the entire process is underwritten by the obvious, physiological gap between his own humanity and their animalism; and that the mutilated subjects both rebel against their transformation and inhabit an elaborate ritual apparatus for justifying it and accepting its results—all add up to something that * * * is both phantasmagoric and a clarification of reality at the same time.

* * * *The Island of Dr. Moreau* * * * is not so much a distorted, metaphorical representation of colonialism as it is a literalization of the racist ideological fantasy that guides much colonial practice: We know very well that non-whites are human beings, but we behave under the assumption that they are grotesque parodies of humankind. Moreau's practice actually unfolds the ideological terms in reverse: He knows very well that his experimental subjects are *not* humans, but by laboriously transforming them into grotesque parodies of humankind, he arrives—without any apparent intention of doing so—at the role of colonial master. Generically, this is more like Kafka's "In the Penal Colony" than Orwell's *Animal Farm*, because it is a bizarre enactment of the logic of racism rather than an extended metaphor for any actual social or historical situation. *Moreau* is, as Žižek puts it, "the *mise en scene of the fantasy which is at work in the production of social reality itself*" (36, Žižek's emphasis).

The perspective of Wells's Gulliver-like narrator, Prendick, is crucial. Before we know any details of Moreau's project, Prendick's perspective already has entangled the reader in the discourse of scientific racism. Prendick's account of his first encounter with one of the Beast People associates the "misshapen man" with the animalistic traits attributed to non-whites by the theorists of race in nineteenth-century physical anthropology: "He . . . had peculiarly thick, coarse black hair. . . . The facial part projected, forming something dimly suggestive of a muzzle, and the huge half-open mouth showed as big white teeth as I had ever seen in a human mouth" (8). The retreating facial angle and prominent lower jaw were among the favorite physiological marks that racial theorists used to illustrate the proximity between apes and non-white races, as many a diagram from nineteenth-century treatises on race can attest (see for example the diagrams from Robert Knox's *The Races of Men* [1869], John Jeffries's *The Natural History of the Human Races* [1869], and Alexander Winchell's *Preadamites* [1888] reproduced in Graves, 67 and 72; and Fichman, 116). The psychometrician Francis Galton, Darwin's cousin and the inventor of the term "eugenics," found the same overlapping of animal and human traits in his studies of intelligence, claiming that the average Australian aborigine was only a little more intelligent than the very smartest kind of dog (see the comparative table from Galton's *Hereditary Genius* [1892] reproduced by

Graves, 95). Thus, while the revulsion Prendick feels before "the grotesque ugliness of this black-faced creature" is a mark of its monstrosity (one could compare Prendick's reaction to that inspired by the physiognomy of Frankenstein's creature, for example, or to the instinctive repulsion all spectators feel in the presence of the bestial Mr. Hyde in Stevenson's *Dr. Jekyll and Mr. Hyde* [1886]), it is at least as important that the uncanny sense of familiarity the figure inspires by its disturbing mixture of humanity and animalism evokes the vocabulary of racism.

More telling than this initial association that Prendick establishes between the Beast People and racialized humans, however, are the reversals of understanding Prendick goes through in the course of the novel. Using a narrative strategy that he already had employed in *The Time Machine*, Wells first draws the reader into Prendick's initial interpretation of Moreau's project—that the scientist is turning humans into animals—then overturns this theory with Moreau's explanation that he actually is trying to turn animals into humans. According to Prendick's initial suspicion, then, Moreau resembles a colonial tyrant brutalizing his subjects, while according to Moreau's explanation, he is more like a missionary, a scientific prophet of progress, selflessly pursuing the task set him by his high calling. But rather than settling the allegory into a final shape, this strategy sets up another pair of reversible perspectives. The Beast People, who initially appear as grotesquely racialized others, become, in the Swiftian device of the novel's conclusion, a way of seeing Wells's readers, the inhabitants of London. In the terms Wells uses in "Human Evolution, an Artificial Process," the monstrous artificial man of the scientific colony now stands for the round Paleolithic savage in the square hole of contemporary European civilization. At the same time, the Beast People's quasi-racial ugliness also looks more and more like a disavowed self-recognition. The racialized other becomes the estranged self.

Both of these reversals of perspective are presented by Prendick as if they are progressive revelations in which falsehood gives way to truth, but the strength of Wells's narrative does not lie in unmasking falsehood. It lies in exposing the patterns and motives of misrecognition. No doubt Wells meant for us to draw from *Moreau* the lesson that humans are really animals, as his remark about the "culminating ape" says they are, but it is more to the point that Wells grasps and exposes an ideological attitude, in the relation between Moreau and the Beast People, that makes what appears to be irresponsible cruelty from one perspective look like the pursuit of a noble enterprise from another. The mise-en-scène of racist ideology in *The Island of Dr. Moreau* has more to do with the social relationship of Moreau to the Beast People, with the understanding, or lack of it, Moreau's position allows him to have of them, than with any sort of biological truth about human beings.

Wells's remark about the round savage in the square hole of civilization, in fact, employs an opposition between civilization and savagery that his fiction exposes as something just as unstable and collapsible as the one between animals and humans. The savagery of civilized humans in the novel is obvious enough, not just in Moreau's scientific sadism or in the affinity that Moreau's assistant, Montgomery, professes for the companionship of the Beast People, but also in the drunken cruelty of the captain of the *Ipecacuanha* who maroons Prendick, or in the cannibalism sequence "In the Dingey of the *Lady Vain*" in the opening chapter. If Prendick finds himself threatened with death on several occasions by his supposedly civilized companions acting like animals, the balancing threat from the Beast People is that of finding himself unwillingly dragged into their community, a threat most forcefully dramatized in the scene where he is forced to join them in chanting their Law and its refrain. In the aftermath of Moreau's death, Prendick manages with difficulty to keep himself apart from the Beast People by inheriting Moreau's whip and perpetuating a set of quasi-religious lies about Moreau's power and immortality, but he finds himself at last equalized with them by "the imperious voices of hunger and thirst" (77). This final collapse of the hierarchical difference between civilization and savagery into the monotony of the struggle for existence is no surprise at all, but rather culminates the coherent development of a pervasive theme.

Wells himself holds onto the opposition between savagery and civilization only by reliance on what he calls the "acquired factor," the accumulated effect of tradition and education upon the members of a civilized society. In his essay on "Morals and Civilisation," published in February 1897, he writes, "If, in a night, this artificial, this impalpable mental factor of every human being in the world could be destroyed, the day thereafter would dawn, indeed, upon our cities, our railways, our mighty weapons of warfare, and on our factories and machinery, but it would dawn no more upon a civilised world" (*Early Writings* 221). The way that savagery constantly threatens to intrude itself back into civilization in *The Island of Dr. Moreau*, like the scenario of a degenerate post-human society in *The Time Machine*, expresses Wells's antipathy toward a certain Social Darwinian version of the ideology of progress. Here is how Mike Hawkins describes the logical contradiction within the ideology of progress that Wells is attacking: "moral progress and the triumph of civilisation . . . could be shown to be the work of natural laws such as the struggle for existence," but "the complete realisation of these ideals implied a future state in which the laws of nature were no longer applicable to humans" (108). But Wells is only following the lead of a powerful bunch of Social Darwinian thinkers, including Alfred Russel Wallace, Charles Darwin, and Thomas Huxley, when he holds that natural selection is indeed effectively suspended for the members of a civilized society (Wallace 20; Darwin 168; Huxley 81). Wells's emphasis invariably lies on the fragility of this achievement, and his own ideology of progress in his later writings stresses both the difficulty and the necessity of supplanting the workings of mere natural process with rational social planning.

But the crux of racist ideology is not the opposition between civilization and savagery. It is rather the way scientific racism confuses cultural and natural phenomena. As Joseph Graves demonstrates repeatedly and persuasively, the fundamental error of scientific racism is that of mistaking a relationship for a substance, a cultural construction for a biological necessity, the posture of a slave for an expression of anatomy. Thus the crux of the racist ideological fantasy worked out in Moreau's project is Moreau's identification of his pitilessness as the way of nature itself. Although Moreau himself shows no signs of guilt, this identification is essentially an apologetic strategy that absolves him from responsibility for the atrocities he has produced. This is perhaps where Moreau's project dovetails most tellingly with racial ideology. Even the monogenist Darwin sees the extermination of "savage races" as an inevitable result of natural selection at a social level: "At some future period, not very distant as measured by centuries, the civilised races will almost certainly exterminate and replace throughout the world the savage races" (Darwin 201 * * *). The racial other of polygenist theory remains, as in monogenist versions of evolutionary anthropology, an anachronistic remnant of the civilized observer's past, but one rendered static, trapped in a body that determines its inferiority, not a case of arrested development but rather an evolutionary dead end. The consequent ease of disavowing responsibility for the sometimes-catastrophic consequences of contact between civilized and savage cultures is, in retrospect, one of the most alarming features of colonialism's ideologies. Wells's portrait of Moreau's arrogant, irresponsible, and messianic employment of science is not just about science. Moreau's position as a white colonial master also embodies in horrific form the logic of racial ideology.[3]

---

3. Pushing the logical implications of Moreau's racism to their extreme, Gomel argues for the similarity between Moreau's project and the Nazi holocaust in "From Dr. Moreau to Dr. Mengele: The Biological Sublime." For a reading of Moreau that argues for Wells's own allegiance to a eugenicist program of "vivisection morality," see Leon Stover's introduction to his edition of Moreau. Stover's scholarship is impressive, but his reading of Moreau is seriously weakened by its relative disregard for the novel's satirical strategies.

WORKS CITED

Brody, Jennifer DeVere. *Impossible Purities: Blackness, Femininity, and Victorian Culture* (Durham, NC: Duke UP, 1998).

Christensen, Timothy. "The 'Bestial Mark' of Race in *The Island of Dr. Moreau.*" *Criticism* 46 (2004): 575–95.

Fichman, Martin. *Evolutionary Theory and Victorian Culture* (New York: Humanity Books, 2002).

Gomel, Elana. "From Dr. Moreau to Dr. Mengele: The Biological Sublime." *Poetics Today* 21 (2000): 393–421.

Graves, Joseph L., Jr. *The Emperor's New Clothes: Biological Theories of Race at the Millennium* (New Brunswick, NJ: Rutgers UP, 2001).

Hawkins, Mike. *Social Darwinism in European and American Thought, 1860–1945: Nature as Model and Nature as Threat* (Cambridge: Cambridge UP, 1997).

Stover, Leon. "Introduction." *The Island of Doctor Moreau: A Critical Text of the London 1896 First Edition, with an Introduction and Appendices*. Ed. Leon Stover (Jefferson, NC: McFarland & Co., 1996): 1–54.

Wells, H. G. "Human Evolution as an Artificial Process." In *H. G. Wells: Early Writings in Science and Science Fiction*. Ed. Robert M. Philmus and David Y. Hughes (Berkeley: U of California P, 1975), 211–19.

———. *The Island of Doctor Moreau: A Variorum Text*. Ed. Robert M. Philmus (Athens and London: U of Georgia P, 1993).

———. "Morals and Civilization." *Early Writings*, 220–28.

Žižek, Slavoj. *The Sublime Object of Ideology* (London: Verso, 1989).

MICHAEL PARRISH LEE

Reading Meat in H. G. Wells[†]

The nineteenth-century novel is stuffed with meat—recall Catherine's refusal to eat her goose after Heathcliff's flogging in *Wuthering Heights* (1847), Pip's theft of pork pie for Magwitch in *Great Expectations* (1860–61), or Fred and Rosamond Vincy's quarrel over a grilled bone in *Middlemarch* (1871–72)—and if the subject has been largely passed over by critics in the field, we might attribute

† From *Studies in the Novel* 42.3 (Fall 2010): 249–53, 256–68. Copyright © 2010 by the University of North Texas. Reprinted with permission of Johns Hopkins University Press. The author notes: "I would like to thank Tabitha Sparks, Monique Morgan, Ned Schantz, Gregory Brophy, Joel Deshaye, and Caroline Herbert for their comments on this essay."

this neglect or resistance at least in part to the novel's own apparent tendency to separate bodily appetite from the more "refined" pursuits of knowledge and human understanding that would seem to inhere in the act of reading. For example, in the last of these texts, Fred begins reading a novel without ringing the bell to have his plate cleared away, and Rosamond rebukes him as "vulgar" (100), a judgment which insists on a division between food and book that acquiesces to an Enlightenment tradition that follows Plato in cordoning off gustatory taste from the more "intellectual" senses of vision and hearing (Korsmeyer 1–6, 12–18) and confining appetite like "a wild animal" "as far as might be from the council chamber" of reason (Plato 70e–l, qtd. in Korsmeyer 14; see also Bourdieu 5–6). But while it might be comforting to imagine that eating is indeed truly separate from the "higher" functions of perception and cognition, the spread of evolutionary theory during the second half of the nineteenth century would render this separation at best unstable. As a closer look reveals, soon after *Middlemarch* evokes the division between reading and meat-eating, the novel gives us Tertius Lydgate, "a vigorous animal," going to the library to "hunt" for "a book which might have some freshness for him" (141). The text thus implies a collapse of book into prey, and approaches a working through of its own apparently taken-for-granted division of meat from information. Yet the collapse of this division remains safely metaphorical, and the meat remains dispersed throughout the text. It is not until the early fiction of H. G. Wells, more prepared at the century's close to test the full implications of the human as a "vigorous animal," that the former metaphor takes on extensive narrative force and the division between meat and knowledge is self-consciously and mercilessly taken to task.

In the work of H. G. Wells, meat becomes both something capable of shaping narrative structure and the visceral evidence of an imperial culture in which social interest is inseparable from appetite and illumination is bound to carnage. In both *The Time Machine* (1895) and *The Island of Doctor Moreau* (1896), the seeker of information—the explorer, the scientist, the attentive conversationalist, even the reader of these books—is figured as a sublimated hunter of human meat. So while it is a commonplace in interdisciplinary work on cannibalism that in Western culture the cannibal has long been "a figure associated with absolute alterity and used to enforce boundaries between a civilized 'us' and savage 'them'" (Guest 2), to read early Wells is to find that late nineteenth-century British culture was already beginning to question the viability of a tidy separation between normative civilization and cannibalistic savagery. Indeed, *The Time Machine* and *The Island of Doctor Moreau* ruthlessly dismantle the possibility of holding cannibalism as an "outside" against which we can define our culture, suggesting that the "civilized" desire for knowledge is not essentially different than the cannibalistic hunger for flesh.

The more general blurring, in the Victorian imagination, of the line between "civilization" and "savagery" owes much to the work of Charles Darwin[1] and Darwinian-influenced theories of degeneration (see Lankester, Lombroso, and Nordau). Degeneration theory regarded evolution as a reversible phenomenon, meaning that the so-called "civilized" races of humanity could never be entirely free from potential regressions to savagery and animalism. In the midst of proliferating concerns about the stability of the civilized Western subject, attempts to keep such anxieties at bay sprang up in force. One such form of "anxiety management" was an insatiable hunger for knowledge, and particularly knowledge of an "abnormal" against which to define the "normal." Kelly Hurley, echoing Foucault, notes that the later nineteenth century is a time of "accelerated taxonomical activity, characterized by attempts on all sides to classify and rank the races of men, the natural world, the types and variations of human sexuality, the gradations of insanity and other pathologies" (26). However, this increasing thirst for knowledge of the abnormal was not only at work in those discourses (medical, psychological, criminological, anthropological, penal) that we typically regard, after Foucault, as invasive mechanisms of power. The desire to know and discipline our insides took on a very literal, corporeal manifestation in mid-to-late-nineteenth-century diet reform when enhanced dietary discipline emerged as a method for combating anxieties about the destabilization of the civilized human subject. Most notably, vegetarianism underwent a change during this period. In the Romantic era the meatless diet was a kind of "conceptual bonding with the poor," many of whom could not afford meat (Morton 7). However, in the later nineteenth century, vegetarianism "settled more comfortably within the rhetoric of bourgeois humanitarianism" (7), with increased emphasis by the 1870s on the welfare of animals (Spencer 285).

This shift in emphasis for vegetarianism marks a growing concern about the cannibalistic implications of meat eating after the popularization of evolutionary theory. Geoffrey Sanborn notes that Enlightenment and post-Enlightenment travelers "compulsively sought out"

---

1. The upheavals in Victorian cultural identity caused by the "Darwinian revolution" have been recognized through studies such as those by Beer and Levine. H. G. Wells took a course with Thomas Henry Huxley (known as "Darwin's Bulldog") at the Normal School of Science that influenced him immensely (Mackenzie & Mackenzie 57). In Wells's *Experiment in Autobiography* (1934), he discusses the importance of Darwin and Huxley (199–206) and declares, "That year I spent in Huxley's class was, beyond all question, the most educational year of my life" (201). For criticism that notes the influence of evolutionary theory on Wells's early work, see for example Glendening, Gomel and McConnell.

evidence of cannibalism among foreign peoples (194). He argues that "the figure of the cannibal has been *especially* necessary to the constitution of the humane western subject," because, "[m]ore than any other figure of 'savagery,' cannibalism has functioned" as "the 'constitutive outside' of the western ideology of humanity" (193). For Sanborn, cannibalism "is constitutive of humanity" because "it is the limit that humanity requires in order to know itself *as* itself" (194). However, with the rise of Darwinism, cannibalism could no longer be strictly consigned to the "outside" realm of the savage other. Now Victorian culture faced the idea that the line between humans and animals might not be one of division but of lineage. For many, this idea triggered the possibility that those animals consumed as meat were not essentially different from the "we" who ate them.

Discourses of vegetarianism increasingly described meat eating as a degenerate practice, pushing civilized culture down the slippery slope to cannibalistic savagery. In *The Ethics of Diet* (1883, 1896), Howard Williams describes the "widespread Degeneration" of contemporary culture as "the direct consequence of wholesale butchery" (337); and in his *Essays on Vegetarianism* (1895), Arnold Frank Hills, the president of the Vegetarian Federal Union, argues that "[c]annibalism is the natural consequence of a carnivorous dietary—to eat a man is the logical conclusion of devouring a sheep" (148). Even more dramatic is the assertion that the so-called "civilized" meat-eater is already only a "cultivated cannibal" (Hills 149), and that "the now prevailing habits of living by the slaughter and suffering of the inferior species—habits different in degree rather than in kind from the old-world barbarism," will come to be regarded "with the same astonishment and horror" as "the once orthodox practices of cannibalism and human sacrifice" (Williams xxv).

This concern that "civilized" culture is slipping or has already slipped into a kind of cannibalistic savagery is taken even further in the early fiction of H. G. Wells, which turns its attention toward late-Victorian culture's most purportedly civilized and civilizing attribute: its unceasing hunt for knowledge. Taken together, *The Time Machine* and *The Island of Dr. Moreau* plot a trajectory of increasing suspicion that the very act of detached observation meant to distinguish the civilized subject is essentially no different than the violent, hungry gaze of the savage cannibal against whom the former seeks to define itself. My analysis thus serves as a gustatory reworking of the Foucaultian readings of late-nineteenth-century culture that see Darwinism as throwing into question the possibility of disinterested observation (see Levine 212–13 and Hurley 26). If, for Foucault, the desire for knowledge is always interested, always invasive (see especially *Discipline and Punish*), I would argue that, for Wells, this desire is also hungry—showing not merely a drive to pry open its objects in order to control them, but betraying too a carnal, corporeal urge to ingest and assimilate them.

*   *   *

In analyzing these texts we necessarily confront a complex overlap between the empirical and the imperial. On one level these texts suggest that seeing, knowing, and examining are essentially linked to appetite, that both our scientific observations and our interactions with other people are fundamentally predicated on the desire to consume the subjects we confront. Yet the appetites evinced in these seemingly basic modes of observation and communication cannot finally be separated from the imperial culture in which Wells's texts arise and of which they are highly critical.[2] *The Time Machine* evokes an imperial encounter between a Western explorer and simple-minded and cannibalistic savages. The Time Traveller is an explorer-anthropologist figure who possesses more sophisticated technologies than the peoples he encounters, and whom his Eloi hosts at one point mistake for a god figure, believing him to have "come from the sun in a thunderstorm" (65). Similarly, Dr. Moreau's island looks like nothing so much as the parody of an island colony, complete with Kanaka missionaries (147). Moreau transplants and "reeducates" his subjects, setting himself up as their master and subjecting them to his "Law" (163). These novels suggest that colonialism itself is a kind of eating, a mode of consumption that participates in the "savage" appetites that it purports to be terrified by and seeks to police.

*   *   *

The Island of Doctor Moreau

Wells further develops the link between knowledge and eating in *The Island of Dr. Moreau*, which begins with the narrator, Edward Prendick, and two other men shipwrecked on a dinghy, eventually drawing lots to decide who will be eaten. * * * *The Island*'s beginning on the dinghy foregrounds the kind of survival cannibalism among "the civilized" that would have been very familiar to a contemporary audience after the famous 1884 trial *Regina v. Dudley and Stephens* surrounding the killing and eating of Richard Parker by his shipmates in the dinghy of the sinking *Mignonette* (see Simpson). The Time Traveller's horror at the appetites of his descendents gives way to Prendick's hunger for the flesh of his contemporaries, as cannibalism, which only reveals itself at the crux of the earlier

2. Hendershot and Gold have also noted imperial themes in Wells's early fiction.

novel, now looms at *The Island*'s starting point. And where *The Time Machine*'s emphasis on the relationship between eating and information-gathering culminates when the content of revelation turns out to be cannibalism, *The Island* begins with a formal pairing of cannibalism and revelation. In a narrative that depends so much on mysteries, secrets, and misunderstanding, *The Island* starts out in a space of free-flowing information. Prendick relates how, after the food and water ran out, he and the two other castaways were "thinking strange things and saying them with our eyes" until "Helmar gave voice to the thing we all had in mind" (63). The knowledge of cannibalistic desire circulates among the crew members without the aid of words, as if one's own desire and the recognition of the desire of the other were more than perfectly coordinated, were indeed the same thing, the same desire, lodged in both the self and the other. By the time the desire is verbalized it has already been shared communally. From the outset, the text makes cannibalism synonymous with revelation and depicts open channels of understanding as being highly invasive—violating the boundaries between self and other, much as the cannibalistic desire that they circulate threatens to violate these boundaries. And so the violent union demanded by same-species hunger is formally replicated in the violently harmonious understanding between individuals who want to eat each other.

The novel thus begins at the point where both hunger and information-exchange are excessive, where both cannibalism and communication threaten to negate the distance between individual selves.[3] But the dinghy's space of too-perfect understanding soon collapses into a fight that ends in the drowning of two of the three would-be cannibals and purportedly exculpates our narrator from the guilt of man-eating. However, this guilt does not vanish, but rather gets redirected outward, onto the meat-eating Beast Folk, a redirection that culminates in the Leopard Man's trial scene.

As John R. Reed suggests, the dinghy scene at the beginning of the story "acquire[s] a greater resonance" because of the "relatively recent" *Regina v. Dudley and Stephens* trial (134). The *Mignonette* trial saw the law penetrating into the then legally uncharted realm of survival cannibalism, the decision establishing that, even in a survival situation, it is illegal to kill someone in order to eat him (134–35). It is within this context that the starving Prendick, after his rescue from the dinghy, himself becomes an object of suspicion. His rescuer, Montgomery, responds to his request for mutton by saying

---

3. In this space, communication becomes akin to Christian communion, the cannibalistic implications of which Kilgour notes (84). The text plays with these implications when, after his failed cannibalism on the dinghy, Prendick is revived by the blood drink that Hammond notes is a nod to the blood of Christ (36).

with a slight hesitation, "you know I'm dying to hear how you came
to be alone in the boat," and Prendick notes that he thinks he detects
"a certain suspicion" (66) in Montgomery's eyes. Away from the
openly cannibalistic space of the dinghy where information passes
clearly and wordlessly between men's eyes, cannibalism now comes
to occupy the realm of subtext and insinuation. Eyes and words now
become suspicious and indirect in their meanings. The distance
between people widens from the intolerable communion threatened
by cannibalism and too-perfect understanding, becoming instead an
intraversable gap that provokes suspicion to an almost paranoid
degree. Prendick suspects that Montgomery suspects him of cannibalism, although neither man learns the veracity of his own (potential) suspicion. Montgomery never hears how Prendick came to be
alone in the boat, although his hinted-at suspicion is reiterated by
the ship's captain, who, upon announcing that Prendick must vacate
the ship along with its livestock and strange crew at Moreau's island,
declares, "This ship ain't for beasts and cannibals, and worse than
beasts, any more" (78).

Once Prendick goes overboard onto the island he becomes free
from such indirect accusations of cannibalism, and the text redirects
its focus onto Prendick's suspicions of others rather than his own
status as a suspect. In refracting and redirecting Prendick's cannibalistic guilt, the text spirits him out of the realm of excessive understanding and plunges him into an uncanny world of secrets,
intrigue, and misunderstanding. Appropriately, this intrigue usually
directly centers on eating or arises in close proximity to food. For
example, Moreau's servant M'ling accidentally reveals his pointed
ears while bringing Prendick his breakfast (88). Prendick unsuccessfully questions Montgomery about these ears during another meal
(92), and it is during this same meal that Prendick hears the mysterious sound of a crying animal that will drive him into the forest
(94). In the forest Prendick finds a strangely mangled rabbit corpse
(97–98) before coming upon a group of "bestial-looking creatures"
speaking indecipherable "gibberish" (98). After the narrative leaves
behind the overwhelmingly open space of the dinghy, meals either
serve as gateways that open onto greater and more impenetrable
mysteries and scenes that baffle communication and understanding,
or else lead, Russian doll–style, to the traces of other, horrific meals.

This model of meals as gateways to secrets only shifts with Prendick's attempted suicide. Misinterpreting the Beast Folk as humans
who have been transformed into animals, Prendick fears his own
animalization and sets about trying to drown himself (126), but
Dr. Moreau finally prevails upon him to come out of the water by
offering a full explanation of the island and its mysteries. In a strange
transition wherein eating comes to signal not the accumulation

of secrets, suspicions and misunderstandings, but the solving of puzzles, Moreau finally, after food and drink, provides Prendick with an explanation of the Beast Folk.

But once this, the text's ostensibly central mystery, is solved, the issue of cannibalistic guilt reemerges, though displaced onto the Leopard Man. The problem that now takes hold of the narrative is that one or some of the Beast Folk have been devouring the island's rabbits contrary to the prohibition against meat eating. As I will explain in more detail in the next section, this dietary transgression has cannibalistic implications because of the radically hybrid and ambiguous status of the Beast Folk. Thus the breaking of a cannibalistic eating taboo now becomes the central problem of the narrative, with Moreau and company seeking proof of cannibalism among the "savages." The trial scene violently pries cannibalism out of the realm of secrecy and subtext, tearing open the intrigue-laden world of the island until it resembles the strangely open world of the dinghy. When Moreau, taking the role of prosecutor, looks into the eyes of the Leopard Man, once again information seems to pass through eyes, but instead of flowing freely as in the dinghy, Moreau's gaze now pulls it forcibly into the open, "dragging the very soul" out of the Leopard Man, the latter's eyes going "aflame and his huge feline tusks flashing out from under his curling lips" (164). This wordless confession—the Leopard Man's pouncing attack—opens the floodgates through which comes an explosion of cannibalism as the Beast Folk begin to turn hungrily on one another.

Appropriately, it is Prendick who manages to catch and execute the Leopard Man, finally cornering his scapegoat and killing it off, destroying the external manifestation of his own guilt (see Glendening 586). For Prendick the execution is also a moment of uncanny recognition: "It may seem a strange contradiction in me . . . but now, seeing the creature there in a perfectly animal attitude . . . and its imperfectly human face distorted with terror, I realised again the fact of its humanity" (166). As Carrie Rohman observes, in the moment when the creature seems the least human, Prendick recognizes its humanity (131). This recognition strengthens the affinity between these two characters who share a willingness to transgress the supreme dietary taboos of their respective cultures. In keeping with the motif that joins understanding with cannibalism, the text only allows this shared humanity to come through a cannibalistic link between the characters. It is also fitting that Prendick's own "humane" gesture towards the Leopard Man that rises out of his recognition of the latter's humanity is an act of murder. Prendick reportedly performs a mercy killing so that the Leopard Man will not have to undergo a punishment of torture in Moreau's laboratory (166). Prendick kills the Leopard Man the moment he begins to identify with him, once again demonstrating the violence that the text sees as implicit in acts of understanding.

We should also read this killing as a form of displaced suicide. After Prendick's own thwarted cannibalism on the dinghy, he hopes to "die quickly" (64). And his later suicide attempt mimics the drowning deaths of the dinghy's other would-be cannibals and comes when Prendick jumps to the conclusion that he will be transformed into a Beast Man—that is, when he assumes that he will literally lose his humanity. In other words, Prendick's virtual loss of humanity at the moment of his acquiescence to cannibalism threatens to return in the highly literalized loss of humanity that would come from the transformation into a man-beast. It is as if Prendick desires on some level to die the same death as his fellow-attempted-cannibals on the dinghy. When Prendick at last confronts the monstrous externalization of his own virtual transgression and loss of humanity in the figure of the Leopard Man, the mercy killing that he performs is also, in a sense, meant for himself.

The Cannibalistic Ambiguity of Meat

* * *

* * * The Beast folk do not so much occupy a liminal space between human and animal as embody the ambiguity and slippage that precludes a clear distinction between "human" and "animal" categories in the first place.

This ambiguity and slippage, then, extends to the status of meat and meat-eating. The law against flesh food, as it applies to the Beast Folk, raises the question of whether non-cannibalistic meat-eating is possible for these hybrids. The Beast Folk derive from such a wide variety of animals, and usually from combinations of various animals grafted together, that the total effect is not so much heterogeneity as "a kind of generalised animalism" (198), so that there is a dissolution of the strict lines between different species that would clearly demarcate what counts as cannibalism (or same-species consumption) and what does not.[4] As opposed to the schema wherein meat-eating signifies the difference between the eater and the eaten and the higher place of the eater on the food chain, in the world of The Island, "meat" stands as a marker of the sameness—the troubling interconnectedness—of all species, dissolving the distinction between interspecies meat-eating and homospecies cannibalism. As in The Time Machine, meat loses its specificity and comes to stand ambiguously for all flesh. Both texts imply what

---

4. We thus have evidence for Dryden's link between the "carnivorous appetites" of the Beast Folk and "the Morlocks' cannibalism" [in The Time Machine] (1963).

late-century vegetarian rhetoric explicitly argues: that meat eating is essentially no different than cannibalism. But while the earlier novel subtly hints at this idea, *The Island* radically tests the lines between cannibal and meat-eater, human and animal through the trope of rapid surgical metamorphosis, as Dr. Moreau attempts, through vivisection, to evolve animals into people.

As an aid to these surgeries, Dr. Moreau elevates the law against flesh-eating above all other laws. In his attempt to curtail "the deep-seated, ever rebellious cravings" of the Beast Folk's "animal natures," he displays "particular solicitude" to keep the Beast Folk "ignorant of the taste of blood," fearing "the inevitable suggestions of that flavour" (150). Moreau's concern manifests an evolutionary anxiety that is also present in late-century vegetarian discourse: the fear that meat-eating might stifle evolutionary "progress." In *Vegetarianism and Evolution* (1887) Abel Andrew describes meat-eating as a remainder from an earlier, cannibalistic stage of evolution "when mankind were all savages" (3). He goes on to collapse together the evolutionary stages of "savage" and "animal" (16), arguing that vegetarianism will help mankind to progress beyond this unpleasant ancestry—that "[t]here is much of the wild animal in all of us, but the confirmed Vegetarian leaves the original savage behind" (8). Andrew views mankind in an evolutionary "transition state" similar to *The Island*'s Beast Folk, suspended in its development between savagery and civilization, animal and human, and argues that "[e]volution and education have done much to subdue the animal and develop the human. Vegetarianism shall complete the process" (9).[5]

It is this very struggle to turn the *"human wild beast"* into the "perfect human being" (Andrew 3) that drives Moreau to perform his experiments compulsively, again and again trying to eliminate the "[c]ravings, instincts," and "desires that harm humanity" (*Island* 146) that stubbornly remain in the Beast Folk, each time reciting his mantra: "This time I will burn out all the animal, this time I will make a rational creature of my own" (146–147). And while it is vivisection rather than vegetarianism that constitutes Moreau's primary tool of evolution, Moreau himself ostensibly refrains from meat-eating and berates Montgomery for not being able to keep his "taste for meat in hand" (161), and he strictly upholds the law against flesh-eating among the Beast Folk for fear that meat would cause them to regress into a more animalistic, violent state (see Kemp 21). This fear turns out to be well-founded when the consumption of rabbit meat appears to unleash the bloodlust and rebellious urges of the

---

5. See also Gregory, who, while not engaging with vegetarian anxieties regarding cannibalism or animalistic degeneration, notes that some Victorians believed that vegetarianism "would enable humanity to ascend a special evolutionary ladder" (96).

Beast Folk. The Beasts now start giving in to savage, indiscriminate appetites for flesh, turning on each other as well as the humans around them. The result is "generalised" massacre and cannibalism (164–84), after which the Beast Folk begin to devolve "very rapidly" (196) into monstrous mixtures of the animals from which they were wrought.

Perhaps the greatest irony surrounding meat-eating in *The Island* is that Moreau's "civilizing" vivisections make his subjects them-selves resemble meat. The narrative proximity and descriptive simi-larity of the partially eaten rabbit corpse to the body of the vivisected puma present these figures as parallel mutilations. It is the cries of the vivisected puma that drive Prendick into the forest (94) where he discovers the rabbit that has been chewed and mangled into meat—into a "thing" surrounded by "scattered blood" (97). * * *

* * *

If *The Time Machine* sets up a model in which the desire to under-stand a subject is bound up with the desire to take this subject inside oneself, Dr. Moreau embodies the narcissistic endpoint of this model where the desire to know a subject is not simply the desire to take the subject in but to assimilate it completely. Thus the doctor cuts open the bodies of others with the hope of discovering himself. He not only captures and rends these bodies; he mixes and masti-cates them with his instruments, attempting to reconstitute them into his own image. He investigates the animal form by seeking to "conquer" it and "burn out all the animal" (146–47) from it. He claims to be interested in discovering "the extreme limit of plastic-ity in a living shape" (141), but he will not be satisfied until that shape becomes "rational" and "[his] own" (146–47). Moreau turns his sub-jects into something resembling meat—liminal, violated objects, like the rabbit corpse in the forest—before assimilating them into the human form. However, the animal subjects are never assim-ilated (or "digested") to Moreau's liking, and "when [he] feel[s] the beast in them" he "turn[s] them out" (147) like so much waste, exil-ing them to the island's forest ghetto.

And while Dr. Moreau expresses frustration at his failure to make the Beast Folk fully "human"—and indeed reprimands and punishes them for their inability to behave sufficiently "civilized"—this fail-ure can be read as the necessary remainder of difference upon which colonialism relies. Barri J. Gold notes the relevance of Homi Bhab-ha's theory of colonial "mimicry" to Moreau's unrealized attempts to civilize the Beast Folk (180–83). For Bhabha, the colonial demand that the colonized subject assimilate carries a hidden condition that the demand never be met successfully. This hidden condition arises out of the imperial "desire for a reformed, recognizable Other" that is *"almost the same, but not quite"* (126). In other words, even as

Moreau strives for total transformation of the Beast Folk into humans, the colonial discourse that Moreau is a part of demands that there remain the "unaccountable blank ends," the "unexpected gaps," the "something that [Moreau] cannot touch" (146) that remain in the Beast Folk of the text. If Moreau then might be said to stand for the colonial demand that that which is different be assimilated, the "failures" that in many ways drive the narrative embody the demand within the demand, the desire that the assimilated subject retain a degree of difference.

However, *The Island* also provides a breakdown of difference, a failure of failure. The "slippage," "excess" and "difference" (Bhabha 126) of the Beast Folk finally comes in the form of an unsettling sameness—an all-too-similar appetite that explodes into cannibalistic revolt. The Leopard Man, tried for his inability or refusal to comply with Moreau's Law, is also on trial for an act that too faithfully replicates Moreau's behavior. The mangled rabbit of the Leopard Man's "savage" appetite not only mirrors Prendick's attempted cannibalism, but uneasily reflects the mangled bodies of Moreau's own imperial-scientific appetite. The trial scene itself is highly ambivalent: Moreau tries to drag from the Leopard Man a confession that would ostensibly be a confession of difference, but what he gets is a "confession" of sameness—an admission of guilt through the rebellious act of a will to do harm equal to Moreau's. His "confession" of cannibalism momentarily breaks down the gap between the two characters, and, appropriately, Prendick sees "the two figures collid[e]" (164). This "collision," this sameness of appetite, repeats the sameness of appetite at work on the dinghy at the beginning of the novel. The ensuing cannibalism among the Beast Folk forms a space in which through seeming difference comes excessive sameness, comes the knowledge that we all want (to eat) the same thing. This unleashing of cannibalistic desire is predicated on the model developed through both *The Time Machine* and *The Island* wherein the desire for knowledge is a kind of hunger. And this scene and the dinghy scene that it mirrors both express the anxiety inherent in this model—that the thing looked at will look back in the same way: hungrily.

*　*　*

WORKS CITED

Andrew, Abel. *Vegetarianism and Evolution; or, What is a Vegetarian?* London: Millington Brothers, 1887.

Beer, Gillian. *Darwin's Plots: Evolutionary Narrative in Darwin, George Eliot and Nineteenth-Century Fiction*. London: Routledge, 1983.

Bhabha, Homi. "Of Mimicry and Man: The Ambivalence of Colonial Discourse." *October* 28 (1984): 125–33.

Bourdieu, Pierre. *Distinction: A Social Critique of the Judgment of Taste*. Trans. Richard Nice. Cambridge: Harvard UP, 1984.

Brönte, Emily. *Wuthering Heights*. 1847. Oxford: Oxford UP, 1981.

Dickens, Charles. *Great Expectations*. 1860–61. London: Penguin Books, 1996.

Dryden, Linda. *The Modern Gothic and Literary Doubles: Stevenson, Wilde, and Wells*. Basingstroke: Palgrave Macmillan, 2003.

Eliot, George. *Middlemarch*. 1871–72. Oxford: Oxford UP, 1997.

Foucault, Michel. *Discipline and Punish: The Birth of the Prison*. Trans. Alan Sheridan. New York: Vintage Books, 1979.

Glendening, John. "'Green Confusion': Evolution and Entanglement in H. G. Wells's *The Island of Doctor Moreau*." *Victorian Literature and Culture* 30.2 (2002): 571–97.

Gold, Barri J. "Reproducing Empire: *Moreau* and Others." *Nineteenth Century Studies* 14 (2000): 173–98.

Gomel, Elana. "Shapes of the Past and the Future: Darwin and the Narratology of Time Travel." *Narrative* 17.3 (2009): 334–52.

Gregory, James. *Of Victorians and Vegetarians: The Vegetarian Movement in Nineteenth-century Britain*. New York: Tauris Academic Studies, 2007.

Guest, Kristen. "Introduction: Cannibalism and the Boundaries of Identity." *Eating Their Words: Cannibalism and the Boundaries of Cultural Identity*. Ed. Kristen Guest. Albany: State U of New York P, 2001. 1–9.

Hammond, J. R. "*The Island of Doctor Moreau*: A Swiftian Parable." *The Wellsian: The Journal of the H. G. Wells Society* 16 (1993): 30–41.

Hendershot, Cyndy. "The Animal Without: Masculinity and Imperialism in *The Island of Doctor Moreau* and 'The Adventures of the Speckled Band.'" *Nineteenth Century Studies* 10 (1996): 1–32.

Hills, Arnold Frank. *Essays on Vegetarianism*. London: The Ideal Publishing Union, 1895.

Hurley, Kelly. *The Gothic Body: Sexuality, Materialism, and Degeneration at Fin de Siècle*. Cambridge: Cambridge UP, 1996.

Kemp, Peter. *H. G. Wells and the Culminating Ape: Biological Imperatives and Imaginative Obsessions*. Basingstoke: Macmillan, 1996.

Kilgour, Maggie. *From Communion to Cannibalism: An Anatomy of Metaphors of Incorporation*. Princeton: Princeton UP, 1990.

Korsmeyer, Carolyn. *Making Sense of Taste: Food and Philosophy*. Ithaca: Cornell UP, 1999.

Lankester, E. Ray, Sir. *Degeneration, a Chapter in Darwinism*. London, 1880.

Levine, George. *Darwin and the Novelists: Patterns of Science in Victorian Fiction*. Cambridge: Harvard UP, 1988.

Lombroso, Cesare. *L'homme criminal, étude anthropologique et médico-légale*. Paris: Alcan, 1887.

Mackenzie, Norman and Jeanne Mackenzie. *The Life of H. G. Wells: The Time Traveller*. London: The Hogarth P, 1987.

McConnell, Frank. *The Science Fiction of H. G. Wells*. Oxford: Oxford UP, 1981.

Morton, Timothy. *Shelley and the Revolution in Taste: The Body and the Natural World*. Cambridge: Cambridge UP, 1994.

Nordau, Max Simon. *Degeneration*. New York: Appleton, 1895.

Plato. *Timaeus*. Trans. Benjamin Jowett. *Plato: Collected Dialogues*. Ed. Edith Hamilton and Huntington Cairns. Princeton: Princeton UP, 1963.

Reed, John R. "The Vanity of Law in *The Island of Doctor Moreau*." *H. G. Wells Under Revision*. Ed. Patrick Parrinder and Christopher Rolfe. Toronto: Associated UPs, 1990. 134–44.

Rohman, Carrie. "Burning Out the Animal: The Failure of Enlightenment Purification in H. G. Wells's *The Island of Dr. Moreau*." *Figuring Animals: Essays on Animal Images in Art, Literature, Philosophy, and Popular Culture*. Ed. Mary Sanders Pollock and Catherine Rainwater. New York: Palgrave Macmillan, 2005. 121–34.

Sanborn, Geoffrey. "The Missed Encounter: Cannibalism and the Literary Critic." *Eating Their Words: Cannibalism and the Boundaries of Cultural Identity*. Ed. Kristen Guest. Albany: State U of New York P, 2001. 187–204.

Simpson, A. W. Brian. *Cannibalism and the Common Law*. Chicago: The U of Chicago P, 1984.

Spencer, Colin. *The Heretic's Feast: A History of Vegetarianism*. Hanover: UP of New England, 1995.

Wells, H. G. *Experiment in Autobiography: Discoveries and Conclusions of a very ordinary Brain (Since 1866)*. Volume I. 1934. London: Victor Gollancz Ltd. and Cresset P Ltd., 1966.

———. *The Island of Doctor Moreau*. 1896. Ed. Leon Stover. Jefferson, NC: McFarland, 1996.

———. *The Time Machine: An Invention*. 1895. Ed. Leon Stover. Jefferson, NC: McFarland, 1996.

Williams, Howard. *The Ethics of Diet: A Catena of Authorities Deprecatory of the Practice of Flesh-Eating*. 1883, 1896. Ed. Howard Williams and Carol J. Adams. Urbana: U of Illinois P, 2003.

RONALD EDWARDS

Big Thinks[†]

Suffering and Philosophy

People have asked me, what's your book about? Technically, human exceptionalism. Historically, evolutionary biology and literature. But emotionally, I have found, it is about pain. Certainly and not trivially, the plot events of [*The Island of Doctor Moreau*] are driven by the pain of bodily harm. This is most dramatically the pain inflicted on nonhuman animals during most of the history of live animal experimentation, and—as Moreau misses completely—it isn't solely about specific receptors in the skin, but rather the pain of helplessness, of fear, and of despair. Pain under torture is the issue. The immediate moral question is how much of this we intend to inflict on others. The bigger look is whether all life is helpless enough to be considered pain under torture. That may sound a little adolescent and melodramatic, but hold that thought for a moment.

Yet the novel also touches on the pain of being alone. When Prendick and the Hyena-Swine face one another on the beach, which I now see as the climax of the story, each is as alone as a person can be: sympathetically speaking, each is alienated from his culture, unable to regard its norms as a cosmic good; and also at his most repellent, each is potentially willing to be a cannibal. Their respective internal solitudes are the same, denied even the most basic metaphysical narrative, the one that says to you, "You are special."

What's worse, each of them hits every one of these buttons for the other. To each, the other is truly the Other—a presence whose perception and judgment cannot be controlled. Here, the terms from psychology, philosophy, and biology link up flawlessly: to our kind of ultrasocial animal, it is nearly intolerable that someone is looking at me in a way different from how I look at myself, and yet he or she has the temerity actually to be in the real world just the way I am. This moment is when we connect or we reject. In a world-experience lacking metaphysics, that becomes the only real question: when confronted by the Other, whether one feels exposed, isolated, foolish, targeted, and more alone than ever; or illuminated, given context, provided with listening, and no longer alone.

† From *The Edge of Evolution: Animality, Inhumanity, and Doctor Moreau* (Oxford: Oxford University Press, 2016), pp. 250–60. Reprinted with permission.

Reversion and Violence

If being a beast rather than a human meant no management over inflicting pain, no power to act against being inflicted with pain, uncontrolled aggression, randomly directed violence, predation arising from fury, eating of whatever presented itself (including one's fellows' bodies)—and if this were a beast's "place," its identity, such that elevating it to the rational state of Man could not help but fail— the "don't meddle" story would be so easy. It would look like this:

- Conversion into human anatomy and cognition (Man)
  - Management and responsibility of inflicting pain
- Reversion into the original animal forms (Beast)
  - Unmanaged aggression and violence
  - Predation
- Cannibalism

But in this story, these components don't lie down neatly into that dichotomized package. Instead, they are all present but curiously isolated from one another, overlapping in different ways and at different points. Their associations are cast into less comfortable forms: Moreau, in his idea of the rational Man, denying his responsibility to consider others' pain and therefore inflicting it to an unutterable degree; Montgomery, with his predilection for bad-tempered deadly force; Prendick, constantly fearful the Beast Folk will rend his flesh, while being the only character who really knows what it means to choose to eat another person.

Instead of the compartmentalized breakdown, you get an overlapping mess, which destroys the Beast + Violent + Cannibal/Man + Civil + Virtuous compartments. This isn't an interpretation or an impression or a symbol; confronting you with the mess is what the story does. Instead of "don't meddle," it's the "reality slap" story. Forget it, "Man." You aren't *what* you thought, you aren't *who* you thought, and in fact, it's not even *about* you. The real manager of violence in the story is M'Ling. The real moral voice regarding pain is the Puma Woman's.

A "don't meddle" story may have thrills and chills, but ultimately it's comforting. This one isn't. It shocks, it confronts, it prompts deflective interpretations that immediately deny the text, and it prompts revisions that alter its content into palatable forms and culturally silence it.

Why has this novel received such a strong recoil? Because if you experience the "reality slap," then you're no longer the hero of the Story of Man, whatever that might be for you. You're a Beast Man or Woman, standing in the Valley. There is no arc cresting in you or a shining goal you may point toward. Nothing in the universe or its processes protects you from crushing agony or death. All you have, and really nothing more, is that like any creature anywhere, you're at least undeniably here for a while—and after the shock, maybe that's enough. It's not *nothing*, literally. We're *something*, we're *someone*, grubby and brief as it might be, and we might think about working something out together, even if there's nothing so very grand about the task.

Questions

The story includes blank spots, apparent only because Prendick sees some hint of things going on outside his perception * * *. I'm not talking about the narrator of the story telling us an out-and-out lie. This isn't a puzzle or a guessing game. Instead, the narration accords strictly with Prendick's outlook and assumptions, but the events show how limited those are, therefore forcing the reader's participation in the story's content.

- Did the Puma Woman secretly weaken her chain in planning her escape?
- Did Prendick have sex with a Beast Woman?
- Did the Sayer of the Law act upon his oath to uphold the new Law when he killed Montgomery, whom he had just seen threaten Prendick?
- Was the Hyena-Swine sneaking up on Prendick on the beach, or trying to talk to him?

The "found document" technique isn't merely a quirk, but literally makes you, the reader, decide "yes" or "no" to these things. It's perhaps the most confrontational feature of the novel and, technically speaking, closes the Man/Beast divide with some force.

* * *

Nothing leads more definitely to a recognition of the identity of the essential nature in animal and human phenomena than a study of zoology and anatomy. (Arthur Schopenhauer, "A Critique of Kant," *On the Basis of Morality*, p. 233)[1]

I don't think Schopenhauer's writings are a recognized school of thought with a codified set of precepts, and even if they were, I'm not interested in the traditional philosophical model of a worldview or a construct to adhere to. Instead, Schopenhauer interests me because he breaks with—and in fact completely leaves behind—the idea of cosmology as a moral directive. The cosmos provides no spiritual or logical guidance, and instead is imbued with the Will—the unexplained

---

1. Arthur Schopenhauer, *On the Basis of Morality*, 1818, included in *Philosophical Writing*, edited by Wolfgang Schirmacher, published by The Continuum Publishing Company, 1994.

and quite unstoppable, defining drive of doing things. Today, I'd talk about this as a feature of thermodynamics, but that doesn't really matter—the idea is that natural forces are amoral and overwhelming, and our own behaviors, drives, and perspectives are local examples.

That's an important point, that Schopenhauer's Will is not merely a fun little celebration of human desire. It's not about saying, "I want a pony," and making that happen. It means that any drive, any sense of achievement or purpose—family love, community or national identity, a political end—is as amoral and potentially full of destruction and suffering as anything else. It's ultimately saying that our sincere sensation of purpose is not the same as having purpose. It's not discoverable through logic, through investigation of the physical world, or through an ideal. Really, you're just "here."

In practice, to the extent that ethical suggestions are even present, these notions fall back on simple daily compassion and trying to muddle through the day without letting your drives sucker you into cruelty or misery, with no concern for a grand design to bask in or to seek.

* * *

*** I might prefer to be an "earthy" animal, in Nietzsche's terms, subject to physicality and history, in the absence of natural law, who can at least try to arrive at less suffering among us, than a higher Man. That higher Man hasn't done very well for us; he seems defined by his empowerment to inflict suffering or, upon being demoted, forced to receive it at another's whim. Maybe after all the pretty talk is past, that's what the higher Man really is: the Master of the House of Pain.

Science and Humanity

What happened to philosophy might be known to other historians and scholars, but it's a mystery to me. All I know is that after about 1900, the discipline's prior connection with natural history evaporated. It has a terrible relationship with nature, which stubbornly refuses to be either a deontological principle or a utilitarian end, and, as far as I can tell, seems to focus strictly on either metaphysics or a disembodied and over-rationalized form of ethics. The twentieth-century extension of Kierkegaard and others, existentialism, went off on its own road with a spiritual notion of personal free will that maintained nothing of Schopenhauer's concept.

I could be missing the boat regarding the most famous philosophers of science, Karl Popper and C. P. Snow, but with all respect to them, their works are over-concerned with epistemology and not enough with content. I don't see that they had much direct contact with science in action or, in Snow's case, at least not much nuts and bolts biology.

As I've encountered it, the philosophical (and eventually others') rejection of science is based on a series of apparently deliberate mistakes, in a specific order.

- First, that reductive causes, or small things making big ones happen, are considered more important than—here a word is lacking—the reverse, with big things making small ones happen. Biologists study both and always have.
- Second, reductive cause is confounded with, or smeared as, reduction-*ism*, the idea that larger-scale phenomena are deprived of their identity or scale-specific properties if their reductive causes are identified.
- Third, reductionism is confounded with atomism, the idea that a phenomenon's features can be identified in full in each of its tiny subunits (genes are particularly vulnerable to this misunderstanding).
- Finally, and most toxic of all, plain and simple material thinking is identified with this weird construct of reductionism + atomism. Therefore to call for a scientific understanding of humans is instantly derided as essentialist, the claim that one is reducing the identity of humans into mindless little particles. * * *

Scientific inquiry is guilty of none of these things, but it did itself no favor internally either. The new social environment of science is riddled with awful, senseless dichotomies, of which the mindless/brainless distinction is a mere echo. These dichotomies—instinct/learning, genetic[s]/environment, nature/culture—are present in force throughout science and non-science, tripping up every effort to link across * * * disciplines. They're perpetuated and reinforced by obfuscating terminology, maintaining the Man/Beast dichotomy at every turn, such that complex and/or social behavior in nonhumans is "instinct" even when it includes learning, memory, and emotions, whereas even simple behavior in humans is "conscious."

* * *

I could kick some shins regarding professionalism in the sciences, too, in how what began as an unconstructed set of grassroots journals become a starchy, risk-aversive, and cloistered activity subordinate to publications, reputations, promotion, and tenure, and effective servitude to university administrations through the financial mechanisms of grants. A certain tension has always existed in scientific education between the implications of (i) professional skill and employment and (ii) specialization and segregation from other branches of knowledge, and it's long overdue for some historical scrutiny.

Academe as a whole went ahead and firewalled the whole damn thing from ourselves, as well, mainly through disciplinary boundaries:

psychologists get the mind, physical anthropologists get the body form and evolution, cultural and social anthropologists get the habits and actions, biologists (or rather, medical physiologists) get the diseases and pathologies, historians get the documentation. These boundaries are not minor—they define job success and the unspoken standards of content for scientific publishing, and quickly became perceived as intrinsic; to be a scientist at all, one had to internalize the standards within each one, separately.

* * *

By the mid-twentieth century, real scientific inquiry wouldn't touch humanity with a ten-foot pole. Dialogue is belittled by appeals to consciousness, to metaphysics, to recent details like industrialization, to the dubious honor of overpopulation, to flat-out untruths, and to disciplinary constructs and constraints. * * * [T]here's a sprayed fog of claims that we are "unlike the animals," or deceptively, "unlike the other animals," and "from the animals but" followed by a false claim. I see hardly a shred of thought toward economics as a subset of ecology, sociology as a subset of behavioral ecology, and psychology as a subset of developmental psychobiology. Instead, those are supposed to be something else, the latest word for that separate high status for humans: culture.

Ah, Culture

* * * Let's see what happens when I look at human culture with Prendick's gaze, but unlike him, without fear. What happens, how terrible is it, to look at the human species just as one looks at a species of gopher?

- It has a phylogenetic and species identity, expressed as a distinct set of developmental events.
- It has an ecological context composed of abilities and constraints.
- It has an identifiable range of behavior and socializing.
- It has regional variants regarding fairly trivial details and a considerable amount of gene flow.

For any and every species, the biologist expects these topics to be integrated and coherent, with acceptable results being in part defined by consistency across different analyses. He or she knows that any of these topics might boom into a rich and nuanced array of history and surprising properties. We're supposed to debate how they work in order to enrich, expand, and revise all possible connections and understanding.

Here, I see a relict species of bipedal ape with its own profile of reproductive, cognitive, and social features; specifically, it records what it communicates—and look, look at what this ape is

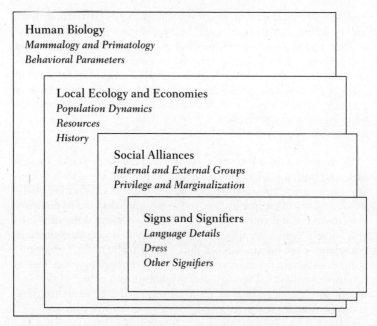

Figure [1] Human cultural biology or biological culture, as you prefer.

doing! Briefly, these creatures communicate with abstractions, and they record their communications—then, the recordings become a learning environment for a new generation. The information, values, standards, and vocabulary for a given location therefore become a distinctive spin, reflecting the history there. So, I see culture, always proliferating and changing, always arriving as a distortion of the past and always affected unexpectedly by what happens next. All right, that's not controversial, it's an observation. No one is going to take that away.

Here's how it works (Figure [1]). The biological animal in a given place has all the usual features: a life-history strategy, a set of behavioral parameters, a population size, a resource base with specific geographic properties, and any number of details like local parasites. Given its abilities with social organizing and symbolic communication, various subcultures of effort, exchange, and recompense are operating there, however contentiously and with however much pain and exploitation; these operations and their history are absolutely the historical products of the creature's biology, including cognition, in this place. These social arrangements become themselves an operating environment, learned and experienced as rock-solid identities and tensions, reinforced through education, but also subject to revision and upheaval as conditions in the underlying power and resources change. These identities and tensions are made explicit through local terms and symbols, in every means of expression.

It's clear, sensible, and easy. I haven't dented or devalued anything concrete stated by any of these other disciplines, I haven't said they're "nothing but" biology, and I haven't said that we as humans don't do those things. The only thing that's added is to expect that these different levels make sense relative to one another, such that no set of physical rules gets to be magically isolated from any others. The only things now missing are presumed elevated functionality, special history composed of heroic narrative elements, intrinsically admirable achievements, and a presumed destiny.

The past couple of centuries have brought some new details: industrial technology and notable population abundance, currently undergoing exponential growth. All right, that can be a new topic, and maybe this construct can help us change dilemmas into questions.

Morals

I have no intention of trying to argue anyone out of the Man/Beast divide—it is a very deeply felt, unexamined thing, and there's literally no way anyone will be dislodged from his or her side of it through confrontation. I'm here to talk about what it's like to see no categorical difference between humans and nonhumans at all, using the term "animal" to mean both, and significantly, seeing absolutely no implications concerning ethical or social capabilities by using that word. My criticism is that *this* viewpoint, although present and identifiable in individuals like myself, has no general cultural voice. It died on the vine right around 1900, even in the sciences, and therefore has failed to develop any philosophical, ethical, political, or artistic identity for over a century. We need to recognize that failure, to identify its origins, and effectively, to call it *out*.

Specifically: if you find yourself, like me, unable to identify any fundamental distinction between humans and all other animals, and if you are similarly baffled by the implications so deeply felt by others, then the question for us must be, "What ethics do you stand by, and where do they come from?" And again less formally, "Well, then, who *do* you think you are?" Furthermore, these questions are not merely individual curiosities, but must be extended outward, socially, intellectually, and politically, to their applications in society, whatever those may be.

Huxley thought he knew, or at least he phrased it optimistically in the last few minutes of his talk.[2] Scientific context and new

2. Edwards refers here to T. H. Huxley's essay "Evolution and Ethics," originally presented as a Romanes Lecture in 1893. For an excerpt from Huxley's essay, see pp. 180–84 above [*Editor's note*].

ethical thinking would bring us around, to solve it somehow or to save us, in the 1890s or by a century later, to blossom into a way actually to live among one another. He was praising the gains in understanding in astronomy, physics, and chemistry, using them as a model for what * * * other disciplines may become. "Physiology, Psychology, Ethics, Political Science must submit to the same ordeal" (*Evolution and Ethics*, p. 84 in original; p. 142 in Princeton University Press edn.). This was his key to arriving at a more just society, his "great work of helping one another" in the constant negative context of a grim history and array of easily tapped grim behaviors.

Boy, was he ever wrong on that one. Astronomy, physics, and chemistry arrived all right, transforming the world into a war ecology and war economy, with a global impact on ecology best described as disastrous. The disciplines he hoped to see develop have become methods of political control beyond anyone's imaginings.

Was Huxley even theoretically right? One would have to admit to a century of dedicated "not quite there yet," an unstopping reiteration of the 1890s and 19-oughts—the same peripheral imperial assault on the central empire of Eurasia, the same extraction from all economies to support it, the framework of the Boer War, the opium trade, the destruction of the Ottoman Empire, all still in place, repeated in new places, and elaborated upon with more propaganda, more atrocity, and more cumulative misery, like a horrific Mandelbrot's snowflake. I may be a pessimist, but I'm inclined to say that Huxley's future ethical developments, the ones he said would be "irrational to doubt," aren't coming.

Is there a morality to discover? Can some perspective on the biological human, however battered and dismembered, be recovered enough even to see whether it helps us, as he put it, help one another? Maybe, if by "morality" we mean common ground for discussion, a context rather than a directive. Maybe, if we can keep biology from becoming a cosmology, a story in which we hold the starring role. Maybe, if we can grasp that basic ethics does not translate easily into sustained policy. * * * Maybe, if we don't succumb to the Naturalistic Fallacy of saying "what's biological is right" or—in the lack of a name for it—the corresponding Humanistic Fallacy of claiming culture and policy exist free-floating from our biology. And finally, maybe if we can decide that nothing about morality or an ethos is about making anyone happy, but about reducing misery, that it works not because everyone is satisfied but because we have some agreed-upon idea of what shows we're better off than we were.

And after that, I want a pony.

Science and Fiction

All that is too heady for me, even in Ape Man mode. This was a book about a book, and staying down in that scope, it turns out that over the years, science fiction—or speculative fiction—has plenty to offer in its confrontational mode. When I was in college in the 1980s, professors reacted to the suggestion that "genre fiction" had something to offer with contempt, even nausea. Times have changed, though, and some room has been made after all. Two references that could form the basis for a whole new subdiscipline along these lines include Jonathan Gottschall's *The Storytelling Animal* (2012) and Sherryl Vint's *Animal Alterity* (2012), as well as her paper "Animals and Animality from the Island of Moreau to the Uplift Universe," in the *Yearbook of English Studies* (2007).[3]

* * *

I'm talking about reading science fiction not as prediction but rather as contemporary insight, dated exactly at the moment of its writing. Its trappings and excess aren't escapism, or not entirely, but rather act as genuine confrontation. I think the whole array of science fiction, fantasy, and horror can express and develop sensitive real-life topics in ways that naturalistic stories and essays cannot.

* * *

Well, that's it for the "Big Thinks": "read some science fiction." It seems a feeble thing, but where formal philosophy and science have fallen short, maybe *The Island of Doctor Moreau* still shows the way.

SARAH COLE

Bio = Life[†]

We will begin our summary [of *The Science of Life*][1] by asking what is meant by life? What are its distinctive characteristics? . . . Firstly, a living thing moves about. . . . Life may move as swiftly as a flying bird, or as slowly as an expanding turnip, but it moves. It moves in response to an inner impulse. . . . And not only does it move of itself, but it feeds. . . . In addition, life seems always to be

---

3. Vint's paper is excerpted on pp. 335–47 above [*Editor's note*].
† From *Inventing Tomorrow: H. G. Wells and the Twentieth Century* (New York: Columbia University Press, 2019), pp. 239, 241–46, 253–63, 342–43. Copyright © 2019 Columbia University Press. Reprinted with permission of Columbia University Press. Unless otherwise indicated, notes are by Cole.
1. *The Science of Life*, 3 vols. (New York: Doubleday, 1931). Cited hereafter as *SL*. *The Science of Life*, which Wells coauthored with his son zoologist George Philip Wells (1901–1985) and English evolutionary biologist Julian Huxley (1887–1975), is a three-volume compendium of biological knowledge written for a popular audience [*Editor's note*].

produced by pre-existing life. It presents itself as a multitude of
individuals which have been produced by division or the detachment of parts from other individuals, and most of which will in
their time give rise to another generation. The existence in the
form of distinct individuals which directly or indirectly reproduce their kind by a sort of inherent necessity is a third distinction between living and non-living things.

(SL 1:4–5)

* * *

* * * For Wells, what it means to seek life is not to plumb "the dark
places of psychology" (Woolf) or to assert that "it is art that *makes*
life" (James, his italics) but rather to dramatize the foundational qualities of living beings—that they move, interact with the biological
world around them, and belong in a generational trajectory.[2] From
these will follow innumerable scenarios, some of them frightening,
others sobering, still others exhilarating; the human animal finds
its quintessential qualities when it is closest to its past, its future,
or its near kin. And vice versa: "It may seem a strange contradiction
in me," says Prendick in *The Island of Doctor Moreau* (1896) at a
late moment in the narrative of the beast people. "I cannot explain
the fact—but now, seeing the creature in a perfectly animal attitude, with the light gleaming in its eyes, and its imperfectly human
face distorted with terror, I realized again the fact of its humanity."[3]

Wells begins his definition of life with movement, and all of his
engagements with life muster around one particular form of slow
movement and transformation, evolution. If there ever was a master
narrative, one that gives shape and significance to the place of the
human in the scheme of the world, it is evolution. And if ever there
was a theory that stood ready to provide a thick account of origins
right where religion falls short, this is it too. "Evolution is," Wells puts
it simply in *The Science of Life*, "*the* life-process" (*SL*, 1:317, italics in
the original). Numerous critics have described Wells as an apostle
to evolution, its literary avatar as Huxley was its scientific prosely-
tizer. Huxley's place in Wells's imagination, and Darwin's before him,
was indeed profound, including in his writerly techniques. Huxley's
science writings in particular provided the model for Wells's own
efforts, straddling as they do the line between addressing specialists
and lay readers. These writings covered many topics; one important
category includes works like *Man's Place in Nature* (1863), in which
Huxley patiently, carefully, slowly makes his case for seeing humans

2. Virginia Woolf, *The Common Reader* (New York: Harcourt, 1984), 152; [Leon] Edel and
   [Gordon N.] Ray, *Henry James and H. G. Wells*[: *A Record of Their Friendship, Their
   Debate on the Art of Fiction, and Their Quarrel* (Urbana: U of Illinois P, 1958)], 267.
3. H. G. Wells, *The Island of Doctor Moreau* (London: Penguin, 2005), 94. Cited hereafter as *IDM*.

in proper relation to other apes and primates. Man is an ape, that's the sensational point for which he argues, but Huxley gets there by working calmly and evenly through the details of comparative anatomy—of, say, the enormous importance of the structure of a hip joint, or the bones in the hand, and of course the all-important jaw bone. Such temperate persistence is the hallmark of biology in general, and Huxley's gift in writing for a wider audience was to build edifices, slowly and without melodrama, that nevertheless ultimately undo expectations and confront conventional thinking about the biological world and the scientific structure of the universe.

And Huxley knows how to use an extended conceit, to create the kind of analogy essential to all scientific writing for nonspecialists, a legacy that reaches far into the twentieth century, and that, of course characterizes Wells's science writings. In a wonderful essay, "On the Method of Zadig" (1880), first published in *The Nineteenth Century*, as an example, Huxley begins his analysis of what we might today call "scientific method" with the case of the (fictional) Babylonian philosopher Zadig, whose seemingly miraculous predictive talents were, according to him, merely the consequence of exemplary attention to detail. In essence, Huxley wants to say that there is nothing in scientific research that differs in kind from our ordinary habits of perception and documentation. Or, in "Evolution and Ethics" (1893),[4] an essay Wells took to heart, among other things, for its rendering of life as perpetual movement, Huxley argues that evolution, far from being a new discovery, presents the essential principle of chaotic violence against which all religions, Eastern and Western, have launched their ethical visions. This essay, with its pitting of evolution against human ethical community, stands at the heart of Wells's endeavor in so many writings, where the imperative to work toward human betterment seems taunted by the longer time schemes and other evolutionary realities that render such efforts laughable. Most generally, in seeing science, especially biology, entirely intertwined with intellectual change, Huxley stands as the predecessor that Wells sought, a father figure par excellence (in real life Huxley remained the great man and Wells the distant student and admirer).[5] Too, Huxley is credited with coining the term "agnostic," cementing the ties between secularism and evolution, a pairing Wells went far to encourage. Wells was known by some as an enemy of religion—even if he often characterized his world state as a new

---

4. Excerpts from Huxley's essay are reprinted on pp. 180–84 above [*Editor's note*].
5. Jeanne and Norman MacKenzie note that the closest Wells came to a personal interaction with Huxley at the Normal School was to hold a door open for him. Meanwhile, however, the paternal and professional relationship Wells later developed with Julian Huxley might make for a juicy addition to the psychological story of these men. [Jeanne and Norman Mackenzie, *The Life of H. G. Wells: The Time Traveller* (London: Hogarth, 1987).]

"religion" and regularly enlists God on his side—and this avowed antagonism to the inherited religions certainly finds affinity with Darwinian discoveries and Huxley's elaborations.

It is hard to overstate the centrality of evolution, and of Huxley, in Wells's vision.[6] Roslynn Haynes notes that "the chief formative influence on Wells's thought was that of Huxley," and more fully, "evolutionary theory . . . seemed to Wells . . . the nearest approach to a unifying factor in contemporary thought. . . . No other concept ever made an equivalent impact on Wells—rather the criteria of biology became his yardstick to measure the claims of all other disciplines—astronomy, physics, sociology, politics, even theology and art."[7] Michael Page agrees, writing that "in the anonymity of Huxley's lecture hall and through Huxley's writings, Wells found the evolutionary vision that was to dominate his career as writer and public figure."[8] These and other critics have stressed a neat line from Darwin, to Huxley, to Wells, each later writer a disseminator and creative reimaginer of the earlier. Such a line might, of course, be too straight; thus Leon Stover asks, "But does it follow that just because he worshiped Huxley as man and teacher, Wells stuck to the man's teachings?" Stover's answer is no: "far from adhering to [Huxley's 'Evolution and Ethics'], Wells contradicts it."[9] Stover is right to challenge the assumption that Wells slavishly followed Huxley. Huxley's ideas fueled Wells's intellectual projects, but Wells runs along his own lines, and his lifelong interest in evolution, which produced ongoing imaginative ferment, intersects with Huxley's even as it veers off in new, often unsettling, directions.[1]

But what is impossible to miss is the presence, urgency, and longevity of evolution in Wells's writing. Evolution is an underlying principle from his first novel *The Time Machine* (1895), an evolutionary parable at the level of class and species, to his last work *The Mind at the End of Its Tether* (1945), an evolutionary riff on how the

6. But the point about Wells's attachment to evolution can easily be misconstrued. To take a particularly extreme case, the famous historian A. J. P. Taylor wrote in a 1966 commentary on Wells's career that Wells failed to understand the basics of evolution, asserting that Wells believed man could evolve within a few hundred years to suit Wells's own plans for the future. It is a spectacularly wrongheaded discussion. A. J. P. Taylor, "The Man Who Tried to Work Miracles," in *Critical Essays on H. G. Wells*, ed. John Huntington (Boston: G. K. Hall, 1991), 127–35.

7. Roslynn D. Haynes, *H. G. Wells: Discoverer of the Future: The Influence of Science on His Thought* (New York: NYU Press, 1980), 16.

8. Michael R. Page, *The Literary Imagination from Erasmus Darwin to H. G. Wells: Science, Evolution, Ecology* (Farnham: Ashgate, 2012), 151.

9. Leon Stover, "Applied Natural History: Wells v. Huxley," in *H. G. Wells Under Revision*, ed. Patrick Parrinder and Christopher Rolfe (Selinsgrove, PA: Susquehanna University Press, 1990), 125.

1. Huxley and Darwin represent the most prominent, though far from the only, scientific influences on Wells's thought. For a discussion of Wells and a variety of scientific debates of the 1890s, see John McNabb, "The Beast Within: H. G. Wells, *The Island of Doctor Moreau*, and Human Evolution in the mid-1890s," *Geological Journal* 50 (2015): 383–97.

running down of the world registers in one whirling consciousness. Sometimes evolution is the active subject, at others a principle of growth and change, at still others a way to give narrative to some of the anxieties about biological life that haunted his generation and Wells himself. Evolution takes many forms in Wells's writing; it can be a solid truth, what he calls in *The Science of Life* "The Incontrovertible Fact of Evolution," or a check to human hubris on the model of his early science journalism (recall those giant reptiles who think themselves the pinnacle and endpoint of life on earth). It is an endlessly fertile source of imagination and forecast, and a reminder, finally, that these vast processes governing the history and future of the planet are not so much irrespective of individual life as arrows shooting through it. Wells described his scientific education, and especially biology, in terms of imaginative reorganization and stimulation, "an extraordinary mental enlargement as my mind passed from the printed sciences within book covers to these intimate real things and then radiated outward to a realization that the synthesis of the sciences composed a vital interpretation of the world" (*EA*, 160).[2] Vitality, growth, and synthesis are the tenets of both evolution and life, and thus in framing his own learning in their terms, he enfolds his developing mind within their broad capacities.

However dominant it was as an idea in Wells's corpus, evolution is no subject for veneration. He was particularly contemptuous of Social Darwinism, which he felt was based on a skewed understanding of evolution, an excessive adherence to the non-Darwinian idea of "survival of the fittest," a conservative and self-serving ideology that gave the entire enterprise of evolutionary theory a bad name. Among the other problems with such models is that they mistake the time scale of evolution. * * * Wells stressed in his works the disproportionate temporal scale of human, and especially historical, existence versus the vastness of time in more evolutionary, geological, or cosmological schemes. He reminds his readers regularly, even obsessively, of the cave-man's red eyes staring through ours—all of ours, not specified by any narrow inheritance. In an early essay, very much influenced by Huxley, he tries to be as plain as he can, in declaring "that man (allowing for racial blendings) is still mentally, morally, and physically what he was during the later Palaeolithic period, that we are, and that the race is likely to remain, for (humanly speaking) a vast period of time, at the level of the Stone Age. The only considerable evolution that has occurred since then, so far as

2. *EA*: Wells's 1934 *Experiment in Autobiography: Discoveries and Conclusions of a Very Ordinary Brain (Since 1866)* (New York: Macmillan, 1934) [*Editor's note*].

man is concerned, has been, it is here asserted, a different sort of
evolution altogether, an evolution of suggestions and ideas."[3]

* * *

We might think of evolution in Wells's works as akin, say, to social
and racial difference in Forster's writing or sexuality in Lawrence's,
one of the large, organizing facts of human experience. Even if we
cannot see evolution (or, rather, because we cannot), its power and
presence course through Wells's universe. It is the source of plots
and action but also, more revealingly, a pervasive force in the world,
that which is always acting on and through us, a reality that can
never be superseded. But then, need it be one's destiny? * * * Wells
* * * will never quite reach a conclusion about how, if at all, we go
about overcoming the aspects of biology that seem tied to destiny
versus controlling our collective future. It is an especially thorny
knot because the idea of destiny is so central to Wells's optimism in
general. Evolution, made up of untold millions of random changes
over millions of years, despite the misleading rhetoric that has
always surrounded it, is neither predictable nor friendly. As early as
1895, Wells cautioned against "Bio-Optimism," declaring, "The
names of the sculptor who carves out the new forms of life are, and
so far as human science goes at present they must ever be, Pain and
Death. And the phenomena of degeneration rob one of any confidence that the new forms will be in any case or in a majority of cases
'higher' (by any standard except present adaptation to circumstance)
than the old" (EWS, 209).[4] * * *

It is in The Island of Doctor Moreau, above all, that Wells offers a
stinging and unforgettable dramatization of what it might mean to
forge humanity. Preceding Mankind in the Making by nearly a
decade, it registers what no amount of activist biopower is ready to
recognize, that taken to its logical extreme, such making is no better than unmaking, to use the word in Elaine Scarry's sense from
The Body in Pain: The Making and Unmaking of the World (1985),
where unmaking stands against and undoes creation, language,
and the alleviation of bodily pain. If we believe Foucault and his
followers, such is the inevitable insight about biopolitics, that it
delivers state power (governmentality) enacted through bodies,

3. H. G. Wells, Early Writings in Science and Science Fiction, ed. Robert M. Philmus and
   David Y. Hughes (Berkeley: University of California Press, 1975), 211. Cited hereafter
   as EWS.
4. Here Wells shows his debt, in particular, to Ray Lankester, the evolutionary biologist
   whose book Degeneration: A Chapter in Darwinism (1880) is particularly germane. For
   a discussion of Wells and Lankester, see Richard Barnett, "Education or Degeneration:
   E. Ray Lankester, H. G. Wells, and The Outline of History," Studies in History and
   Philosophy of Science Part C: Studies in History and Philosophy of Biological and Biomedical Sciences 37, no. 2 (June 2006): 203–29. [Lankester's book is excerpted on
   pp. 155–59 above —Editor.]

hence representing the most chilling outcomes of modernity and its controls, always in the interest of power itself. But *The Island of Doctor Moreau* registers the terrors of man making, rather, in the quintessentially Wellsian form of literalization. Doctor Moreau's experiments, of creating human beings out of animals imported for the purpose, sears through the metaphor, and that is just the beginning of the trespasses in this short, explosive tale of revelation, culminating in the death of Moreau and the return of the beast people to their previous states.

It is a book that defies categories and expectations. Published in 1896, one year after the success of *The Time Machine*, *The Island of Doctor Moreau* dismayed readers right from the start. Compared to its predecessor, *The Island of Doctor Moreau* drained away the charm of protagonist and setting, the wonder of scientific imagining, and the safety of a story set nearly a million years in the future to force an even harsher and more violent view of the status of humanity. The island, with its sealed nature and its overt unreality, may be a classic literary setting for testing out the limits and possibilities of the social, but Wells took his anti-Eden a few steps further than readers cared to go. Some samples of early reviews include:

> The distinction between legitimate and illegitimate use of horror seems to lie not in the form of the horror, but in the purpose for which it is used . . . the disgusting descriptions arouse loathing without any equivalent personal interest. The sufferings inflicted in the course of the story have absolutely no adequate artistic reason.
>
> (*Athenaeum*)

> We should have thought it impossible for any work of fiction to surpass in gruesome horror some of the problem-novels relating to the great sexual question which have been recently published, if we had not read the *Island of Doctor Moreau*, by H. G. Wells. Having read it, we are bound to admit that there are still lower depths of nastiness, and still cruder manifestations of fantastic imbecility.
>
> (*Speaker*)

> Those who have delighted in the singular talent of Mr. Wells will read *The Island of Doctor Moreau* with dismay. . . . For Mr. Wells has put his talent to the most flagitious usury.[5]
>
> (*Saturday Review*)

The overwhelming sense is of horror, a word that comes up repeatedly in these responses to the novel, as reviewers lashed out at Wells

5. All quoted in Patrick Parrinder, ed., *H. G. Wells: The Critical Heritage* (London: Routledge, 1972), 51, 50, 43–44.

for pushing too far in the direction of blood and disgust, "nastiness," as well as for the story's scientific extravagance (reviewers questioned the verisimilitude of the outcome of Moreau's experiments). Perhaps a deeper uneasiness about what such transgressions are expressing stands at the base of these critiques. But there is, in truth, a great deal of blood in *Moreau*, much of it dripping, splashing, forming pools and puddles, and of course awash through the enclosed yard Moreau has converted to a vivisection chamber. An alarming amount of it is also consumed—even by Prendick, or so it might be, his first drink after being rescued by the *Ipecacuanha* being "some scarlet stuff, iced. It tasted like blood, and made me feel stronger" (*IDM*, 10). As Peter Kemp has noted in delectable detail, the drinking of blood is a replete Wellsian trope; in Kemp's phrase, the Wellsian human is "The Edible Predator."[6]

But the difficulty of *Moreau* is not only its ferocious attack on the niceties of Victorian fictional decorum ("decency") or the relentlessness of its focus on physically revolting details, including the regular feature of blood-drenched faces. There is a larger question in all of this, of what this short novel is trying to *do*. If we are asked to experience these grotesqueries, there must be a reason, a larger message, as the anonymous *Athenaeum* reviewer stressed. And the story does seem to demand an allegorical reading; everything seems to point toward allegory, from the setting in a magical yet sinister island to its creation myth and religious ritual, its robust literary associations, and its tapping into basic questions of what constitutes human nature. Yet it is not entirely clear whether allegorical technique is even appropriate, let alone what the referent might be. Given the literalization at the story's center, that is, allegorical reading seems pitted against a different kind of hermeneutical force, as if the concretizing of one central metaphor—making men—wreaks havoc on the more general metaphor-using habits to which readers of fiction are accustomed. The violence of vivisection, made not so much visible as audible, wafts through the story, continually calling us back to the primal scene of the female puma being torn apart and reconstructed, similar to the way the beast people are kept in line by being constantly drawn back in memory to the House of Pain. Wells makes the initial experience of the puma's torture nearly unbearable, for Prendick, who is driven out into the island by her howls, and also for the reader, who may not share Prendick's opinion that "surely, and especially to another scientific man, there was nothing so horrible in vivisection" (*IDM*, 35). Wells, in the introduction to the Atlantic Edition (1924), wrote this about the question of allegory:

6. Peter Kemp, *H. G. Wells and the Culminating Ape: Biological Imperatives and Imaginative Obsessions* (London: Macmillan, 1996).

There was a scandalous trial about that time [of Oscar Wilde], the graceless and pitiful downfall of a man of genius, and this story was the response of an imaginative mind to the reminder that humanity is but animal rough-hewn to a reasonable shape and in perpetual internal conflict between instinct and injunction. This story embodies this ideal, but apart from this embodiment it has no allegorical quality. It is written just to give the utmost possible vividness to that conception of men as hewn and confused and tormented beasts.[7]

Of course, we need not follow Wells's exhortation to avoid allegory (much less his takeaway from the Wilde trials), and, as Jorge Luis Borges and many other readers have noticed, *Moreau* distills a sense of human truth that seems to promise widening circles of meaning: "Not only do [Wells's scientific fantasies like *Moreau*] tell an ingenious story; but they tell a story symbolic of processes that are somehow inherent in all human destinies."[8] Wells and Borges are in agreement, perhaps, that the way meaning works in *Moreau* is less by allegory than by holding before us, in a contained space and a time seemingly out of time, a series of provocations about what it means to be human, and also animal, what evolution shows us about ourselves.

Such questions are at the heart of the story and of Wells's more general investigation into the principle of life, but we might, before shifting to the knot at the tale's center, linger further on the question of allegory and other symbolic reading habits, to ask: what—if we want to pursue these for a moment—would it be allegorizing? Most directly, it reads as a conservative fable about the folly of colonial attempts to "civilize the savage." Neatly put by Paul A. Cantor and Peter Hufnagel, "The Beast People Moreau creates correspond to natives in the British colonial imagination; imperialist romances often pictured non-Europeans as animals (think of Kipling's *Jungle Books*). Indeed Moreau's fear that his creations will be unable to abide by the laws he has laid down for them reflects the central concern of British colonial rule."[9] In such a scenario, that project is hopeless, since the beast people can never be more than parodies of men and will revert, in any case, back to their animal ways. These are mimic men par excellence. Such an allegory of colonization has a number of supporting themes,

7. H. G. Wells, "Preface," in *The Works of H. G. Wells* (New York: Scribner, 1927), 2:ix.
8. Parrinder, *Critical Heritage*, 331.
9. Paul A. Cantor and Peter Hufnagel, "The Empire of the Future: Imperialism and Modernism in H. G. Wells," *Studies in the Novel* 38, no. 1 (Spring 2006): 52. See also Jennifer DeVere Brody, *Impossible Purities: Blackness, Femininity, and Victorian Culture* (Durham, NC: Duke University Press, 1998); Timothy Christensen, "The Bestial Mark of Race in *The Island of Dr. Moreau*," *Criticism* 46, no. 4 (Fall 2004): 575–95; John Rieder, *Colonialism and the Emergence of Science Fiction* (Middletown, CT: Wesleyan University Press, 2012); Payal Taneja, "The Tropical Empire: Exotic Animals and Beastly Men in *The Island of Dr. Moreau*," *English Studies in Canada* 39, no. 2/3 (June–September 2013): 139–59. [For Rieder's analysis of Wells, see pp. 347–54 above —*Editor.*]

the white-haired Moreau playing the part of the White Man, even Europe (as with Kurtz after him, it could be said that all of Europe went into the making of Moreau), the savages who can never be real men, the parodic European community set up on the island, even the expected catastrophe for whites who go native: Montgomery's fate, he who "half likes some of these beasts" is fittingly to be killed in a drunken confab with his bestial pals (*IDM*, 78). Wells also pushes against this reading, in the sense that Moreau's version of empire is bereft of all that Wells, for one, felt the empire was supposed to be doing: there is no project here other than experiment and egotism.

More urgent, perhaps, than the complex substitution demanded by allegory, *Moreau* offers the simpler reading formula of fable: about the dangers of science, playing God, the human aspiration to tinker with the universe. As we have noted, Wells's dialectical thinking is never greater than when science is the topic—science, our savior, that which will allow us to tackle our own biological infelicities, conquer matter, perfect our lives and our institutions, and build our utopia, but also science, our downfall, that which acutely shows how much humans are capable of achieving and how inescapably inadequate they are to such discoveries. It is a decidedly sinister moment when Moreau notes, learning that Prendick has some scientific training, "'That alters the case a little . . . As it happens, we are biologists here. This is a biological station—of a sort'" (*IDM*, 29). A biological station: perhaps the yoking of the laboratory to the outpost, of an undertaking that thrives only through publication and collaboration to the rule-free universe of the colonial enclave, necessitates the corruption. Here on the outer edge beyond the populated world, science can carry on without the social restraints epitomized in the novel by Moreau's earlier exposures back in the Western metropolis, the press reports that drove him out of London. The result of unfettered scientific investigation is this, the island of Doctor Moreau. Science left alone, without its culture, becomes a matter of egomania triumphing over the common good. Restraint, as we see in other stories too (*The Food of the Gods*, *The Invisible Man*), becomes an essential accessory to ethical science.

In plumbing the question of scientific ethics in a sensational and unforgettable riff on creation, Wells's Dr. Moreau keeps company with various literary antecedents and especially with Shelley's Dr. Frankenstein. The parallels between the tales are clear, from the excitement of scientific discovery, to the blurring of the line between art and science under the rich sign of "creation," to the violence that eventually overtakes the narrative, to the ultimate showdown between creator and creation. And it is not only *Frankenstein* that Wells's tale calls up; of all his scientific fantasies, *The Island of Doctor Moreau* is the most saturated in literary history. *Frankenstein*,

Robinson Crusoe, *Faust*, the Bible, *The Origin of Species*, *The Tempest*, *Comus*, "The Rime of the Ancient Mariner," Aesop's *Fables*, *The Odyssey*, *Treasure Island* . . . and the list continues.[1] Yet there is a strange way in which none of these literary references adds perceptibly to the experience of reading or helps in decoding the tale's meaning. Almost the reverse—these affinities show how ruthless and intransigent Wells's story is and underscore the essentiality of its central idea. *Moreau* is after something primal, raw, almost impervious to literary technique. Even under the rubric of the fable or parable, the moral import remains murky, a fact that very palpably worried all of the early reviewers quoted earlier. Returning to the question of the island's activity being offered as an allegory for the "civilizing" mission of the British Empire, what the story does, rather, is to degrade the foundations of that ideology by diluting the meaning of its stabilizing principles: civilization, higher and lower forms of mankind, progress, the value of Christian law and practice. Wells's own later assessment, that the tale was an attempt to get right down to the hewn human animal, rightly steers the reader toward something other than the substitutive logic of allegory. Yet in other ways, Wells's judgment does not entirely help matters, since the novella never heeds the call of clarity.

Rather, *The Island of Doctor Moreau* confounds categories as its primary mechanism, beginning with the central axis of human and animal. Take the excessive blood drinking that touches nearly every aspect of the story. The Law stipulates several key proscriptions against regression for the beast people: chasing other creatures, scratching on trees, lapping water from on all fours, and, above all, meat eating. Reciting the law (or rather chanting it, in a combination of self-hypnosis and crowd intoxication) as a prophylactic to prevent backsliding, the beast people go about their human ways—though, right from start, as early as Prendick's first exploration of the island, signs abound of their transgressions. As Moreau rues it, "First one animal trait, then another, creeps to the surface and stares at me . . . As soon as my hand is taken from them, the beast begins to creep back, begins to assert itself again" (*IDM*, 78). One transgression naturally stands above the rest as a threat to the system and a sign of resurgent instinct, the eating of prey, figured in the text largely as a matter of drinking blood (and as we know, once tasted . . .). But what is odd and symptomatic in all of this is that many of the animals figured as reverting to their blood-drinking ways are not natural predators. Certainly a leopard, puma, or hyena would be a frightening

1. Margaret Atwood's excellent introduction to Penguin *The Island of Doctor Moreau* includes a discussion of the import of some of these literary forebears and adds others, such as "Goblin Market." Margaret Atwood, introduction to H. G. Wells, *The Island of Doctor Moreau* (London: Penguin, 2005), xiii–xxvi.

killer once returned to that identity, but why an ape? Or the swine men and women, not an appealing lot, are seen "bloodstained . . . about the mouth," and this follows immediately from the most domesticated of all the beast people, M'ling, displaying "ominous brown stains" around his jaws, though with some bear and dog in his pedigree, we can forgive him (*IDM*, 101, 100). Meanwhile, to state the obvious, humans on their side belong to the omnivore designation, and in Wells's fiction they are a heartily meat-eating species, beginning with the Time Traveller's craving for mutton, which so disconcertingly marks his return from the future, where he only just escaped the flesh-loving Morlocks (who of course favor their meat uncooked). Prendick too seems undaunted by an "ill-cooked rabbit" for breakfast on the morning after his conversation with Moreau, despite his encounter with a mutilated rabbit as the first sign of violence on the island (*IDM*, 80). Indeed, as Kemp points out, the Wellsian world divides with suspicious regularity into a game of predator and prey; on Moreau's island the question of who's who is part of the suspense, but what's missing in the menagerie is the possibility of any creature who does not harbor the predatory tendency. Even the rabbit-like creatures on the island, purpose-built by Moreau for food, end up eating their young. Wells the biologist is after something other than species fidelity, clearly. At the level of plot, such miscegenation makes sense, since what the island dramatizes is the mixture, confusion, and criss-crossing of different kinds of being.

Once the animal/human divide has been so entirely breached, it seems that all categories break down; "a kind of generalized animalism" emerges, in lieu of the distinct categorizations beloved of biologists, and also of the nineteenth century's cataloguing and displaying zeitgeist (*IDM*, 124). * * * Wells recognized the natural history museum as one of the quintessential institutions of his century. It is a place where his fiction often tends and lingers, but could there be an aisle for the beast people, who stand against the ordering compulsion that defines Victorian ethnography, natural history, biology? Some of the island's creatures, after all, are composed of several different animals—the hyena-swine and so on—and Prendick regularly uses the term "monster" and its cognates to describe all of the beast people (or beast monsters, as he also dubs them). In his first conversation with Moreau, he uses the term "abomination," picking up a religious intonation, another stride away from biology. From the natural history museum to the freak show might indeed be less of a distance than these distinctive attractions would proclaim.[2] The

---

2. For a brilliant discussion of the freak in American culture, see Rachel Adams, *Sideshow USA: Freaks and the American Cultural Imagination* (Chicago: University of Chicago Press, 2001).

monstrous is a loaded term, one with powerful cultural implications in the late nineteenth century (as today), but on the island, it stands above all for the erasure of distinctiveness, a quality of indeterminacy that hovers over the beast people, with their species impurity, and seems to turn one and all into blood-drinking threats.

There is, of course, no monstrosity (or abomination) in biology. To the extent that the novel's speakers take recourse to its figuration, they enter a different terrain, where issues of essence and being come to the fore, raw forces in the world that cannot be fitted into proper scientific categories. Moreau, who presents himself as the pure investigator unbothered by ethics or consequences, waves away Prendick's concerns about the beast people being "abominations," yet he too recognizes that there is something in the animal that he cannot control, fix, or eliminate. "'But I will conquer yet,'" he insists, "'Each time I dip a living creature into the bath of burning pain, I say: this time I will burn out all the animal'" (*IDM*, 78). Moreau knows that the "animal" cannot be burned out, since the human is no less animal than any other, and so, in a sense, he has created a nonscientific goal for himself, an end in the realm of fantasy rather than material reality. And Prendick, for his part, is no scientist at all. Moreau may welcome him (warily and unenthusiastically, it is true) into the biological circle, but Prendick has few qualifications for the task. By his own account his "eye has no training in details— and unhappily I cannot sketch" (in his biology textbook of 1893, Wells reminds his would-be science students that anatomical drawing is a crucial skill for them), and of course observation of detail is a given for biology, as Huxley had so deftly argued in "On the Method of Zadig" (*IDM*, 82). More generally, as readers inevitably notice, Prendick is an unimpressive figure for the task at hand, given to fatigue and terror, utterly unresourceful. Rescued from the *Lady Vain*, our Prendick does not progress far from the laxity such a name promises, more the plaything of fate than its maker; this is no bildungsroman. Prendick is unreliable as a scientific guide, then, and his attachment to the idea of monstrosity is also shared around the text, as it takes us from the realm of biological classification to that of fantasy, folklore, and, more generally, literature.

Once again we feel the force of *Frankenstein*'s presence; after all, Mary Shelley made little effort to convince readers of the biological likelihood of her protagonist's creation. Wells takes pivotal biological questions and, releasing them into the hothouse atmosphere of the possible, infuses the narrative with a combination of biological and fantasmatic urgency. *The Island of Doctor Moreau* seems to grip the Victorian imagination by the throat, insisting that it watch its own most potent fears reach culmination. Like so many monstrous figures in literary history, the beast people play out the drama of admixture, kinds and differences that won't keep to their places, in a form that upends key principles in the culture of late-century, high-imperial Britain. Gillian Beer places the novella in the context of the Victorian obsession with "the missing link," that half-century-long reckoning with evolution's troubling provocation: what actually separates us from the apes? Wells, as we have seen, generally follows Huxley in reframing the question, considering the hermeneutical puzzles of man's genealogy, looking for common ancestry, asking where and when the split happened, deducing hypotheses from the careful study of animal and human anatomy.

Yet here in the novel, no such comparative biological conversation is underway. It is a place, rather, where the uses of science, and its overarching aura, create a surround for the novel's richer ore, the challenges to human self-understanding that abound in the face of what Moreau has constructed. In an article published the same year, Wells considered the "limits of plasticity," suggesting in his journalistic voice that such work as his novella imagines could one day be actualized in reality.[3] And so we ask again, what makes a human? * * * Prendick's response to the confusions is clear. Once he has experienced the beast people, neither category can ever return to its simpler status. The animal staring defensively on all fours from the bushes suddenly displays its residual humanity (in a passage quoted early in this chapter, "seeing the creature in a perfectly animal attitude, with the light gleaming in its eyes, and its imperfectly human face distorted with terror, I realized again the fact of its humanity"). And back at home, the tarnishing to human dignity evinced by the island's experiments with hybridity becomes permanent. The beast people of the island hover over the ordinary people of London, a kind of photographic transparency pressed over the picture to alter the view. "Then I look about me at my fellow men," says Prendick, "And I go in fear. I see faces keen and bright, others dull or dangerous, others unsteady, insincere; none that have the calm authority of a reasonable soul. I feel as though the animal was surging up through them; that presently the degradation of the Islanders will be played over again on a larger scale" (IDM, 130). Prendick may filter the experience as his own anxiety ("I go in fear . . . will be played out on a larger scale"), but Wells wants us to feel it too, to worry that we cannot specify the line that demarcates our humanity, that the hairy ears or coarse snout or ravening jaws of the beast people are, after all, not so very unlike our own features. We are mammalian at the core—and with the exception of the early failed snake-man, Moreau sticks to mammals for his creations.

---

3. H. G. Wells, "The Limits of Individual Plasticity," *Saturday Evening Review*, January 19, 1895; reprinted in *EWS*, 39 [excerpted on pp. 242–44 above —*Editor*].

But what makes *The Island of Doctor Moreau* such an unforgettable reading experience is not solely the hybridity it literalizes or
its narrative arc of sensational discovery, but the way we watch species return to their norms. "They were reverting," is how Prendick
describes the situation on the island after Moreau's death and the
disintegration of the Law—"and reverting very rapidly" (*IDM*, 123).
As Moreau had rued, the time of species admixture has a half-life,
and some of the most wonderful, haunting sequences in the novel
transpire in the last few chapters, when the beast people slowly,
almost imperceptibly, revert to their animal natures. They move back
to the trees and the forest, lose their ability to walk upright, and their
use of language gradually slides into grunts and howls—"Can you
imagine language," Prendick asks the reader, "once clear-cut and
exact, softening and guttering, losing shape and import, becoming
mere lumps of sound again?" (*IDM*, 122). One thinks of Elaine Scarry's magisterial account of the creation of language out of pain,
here inverted; as often with Wells, it reads like a film effect, now in
reverse, the acquisition of language from "mere lumps of sound"
reeling backward. Thus Prendick's loyal companion becomes, once
again, an actual dog. In some ways, these returns have the feel of
cosmic order, each back to its place. Yet not quite. For all that
Moreau's experiments are unjustified and loathsome on ethical
grounds, once here in the world, the beast people exert a certain calling. The challenge they have offered to the natural order, with all the
ideological weight that carries, has been almost exhilarating, and the
creatures made by human hubris, whether by Frankenstein or
Moreau, have about them a true pathos, not least when they begin to
fall out of the human pantheon. "The change was slow and inevitable," Prendick says of these forces, somewhat contradicting his com-
ment of rapid reversion made on the same page, as he tries to hash out
what these forms of change mean, in time among other dimensions
(*IDM*, 123). The reversion can seem simultaneously fast and slow in
part because we only notice change when confronted by some jolting
symptom. Wells was often thinking about the many ways time refuses
to be measured or experienced singly, and his reflections on regression can be especially Bergsonian in this novel. Thus Prendick
"scarcely noticed the transition from the companion on my right hand
to the lurching dog at my side," but then, "the dwindling shreds of
their humanity still startled me every now and then, a momentary
recrudescence of speech perhaps, an unexpected dexterity of the fore
feet, a pitiful attempt to walk erect" (*IDM*, 123, 124).

These mixed qualities of recognition come, too, because Wells is
playing throughout the novel with the temporality of evolution and
indeed more generally with the principles underlying evolution as
an idea and a force in the natural arena. As noted, Wells consistently

probed the question of what kind of force, exactly, evolution is, what the nature of its presence might be in the lived, contemporary world, and whether its powers should be understood as a matter solely for biological learning or, like alchemy in the past, as a potency that might be captured by the skilled practitioner (Victor Frankenstein, we recall, began his own career with alchemy). We know what eugenics says: yes, through selective breeding and even extermination, the gene pool can be manipulated, improved, ultimately perfected. Moreau's island is the site for a different kind of genetic experimentation, a laboratory where the premise that humans have evolved from earlier forms of animal life can be tested in the present as a matter of will. Moreau may not so much be playing god, then, as channeling Darwin, and the setting of this unnamed island in the vague Pacific vicinity of the Galapagos points to the analogy between these sites of species scrutiny. Of course, nothing in Moreau's work actually corresponds to the principles of evolution: his species cannot reproduce (their offspring almost always die), their adaptability to habitat is decreased rather than increased by virtue of his interventions, and, above all, the longue durée needed to account for evolution is missing here in this eleven-month stay, itself the last portion of a mere ten-year experiment. Moreau is not replicating evolution, then, but is conjuring its inner dynamics, the way species ultimately generate surprising variation, adding new traits to old, each animal a composite of what has come before in its line. There is, in evolution, always that fact of ghostly remainder, inherited traits and qualities from the long past, and these are grist for Wells's mill. What stares through us with its red eyes is not so much some foreign, earlier being but the substance that constitutes ourselves. "We have the same family secrets in our embryonic cupboards as the rest of our mammalian relatives," Wells writes in *The Science of Life*, and every one of us "began his existence as a single cell, passed from the stage of protozoan resemblance through the stage of the cell-colony . . . recalled the furry, four-footed stage of his genealogy by his tail, all ready to be wagged, and his coat of flaxen down; and even, after birth, was unable to help recalling what he later regarded as a blot on his escutcheon—his simian past. . . . We are thus no exception to life's rule" (*SL*, 1:416–18). And at the same time, the experiment fails; there is no engineering of new beings, no common animality either to be made or to be burned out of us, no acceleration of evolution, which must always function according to its own slow logic. One can manipulate, plan, extend, transform, mutate in a certain circumscribed sphere, but life, in the end, cannot really be made. It has its own mysterious power.

H. G. Wells: A Chronology

1866   Born September 21 in Bromley, Kent, the fourth and youngest child of Joseph Wells, a gardener, shopkeeper, and professional cricketer of modest means, and his wife Sarah, who before her marriage served as a lady's maid at Uppark, country home of the Fetherstonhaugh family in Sussex.

1874   Breaks leg, leaving him bedridden, and becomes a voracious reader during convalescence. Begins attending Bromley Academy, a school for tradesmen's sons run by Thomas Morley.

1877   Joseph falls from a ladder and fractures his thigh. The family finances, always precarious, collapse into disarray.

1880   Apprenticed to a draper in Windsor, who soon lets him go. Works equally briefly as a pupil-teacher at a village school in Somerset. Sarah takes a position as resident housekeeper at Uppark, where Wells immerses himself in the household's extensive library (introducing him to the works of Plato, More, Defoe, Swift, and Voltaire, among many others).

1881   Apprenticed to a pharmacist in Midhurst. Begins taking lessons at Midhurst Grammar School. Leaves the pharmacy to take an apprenticeship at Hyde's Drapery Emporium in Southsea.

1883   Convinces parents to release him from draper's apprenticeship; taken on as a pupil-teacher at Midhurst Grammar School. Broadens program of self-education, reading widely in natural science and political economy. Prepares for national exams in science education.

1884   Wins government scholarship to the Normal School (later the Royal College) of Science, in Kensington, London. Attends lectures on biology and zoology by T. H. Huxley, dean of the Normal School.

1885   Receives first-class honors in summer exams; has his scholarship renewed.

1886   Interests widen to include literature and politics while commitment to his formal studies declines rapidly. Attends Socialist meetings at the home of William Morris. Delivers paper on socialism to college debating society. Founds and (until April 1887) edits the *Science Schools Journal*. Meets his first cousin, Isabel Mary Wells.

1887   Fails final examination in geology, loses scholarship, and leaves the Normal School without a degree. Takes teaching post at Holt Academy in northern Wales. Suffers crushed kidney and lung hemorrhages as a result of a collision in a school rugby match and is forced to resign from Holt. Convalesces at Uppark, devotes himself to intense reading (especially in Romantic and later-nineteenth-century authors).

1888   Takes teaching position at Henley House School, London, where the headmaster's son, A. A. Milne, was among his pupils. *The Chronic Argonauts* serialized in *Science Schools Journal*.

1890   Passes exams at London University's External Programme for degree of B.Sc., with first-class honors in biology and second-class in geology. Elected fellow of the Zoological Society. Hired by University Correspondence College to tutor students in biology.

1891   "The Rediscovery of the Unique," the first of his scientific essays to be accepted by a major periodical, appears in the *Fortnightly Review*. Continuing to write what will become by the middle of the 1890s a spate of essays concerned with evolution, publishes "Zoological Retrogression" later in the year. Marries Isabel in October.

1892   Meets Amy Catherine Robbins ("Jane"), his pupil.

1893   Lung hemorrhage recurs. Decides to give up teaching and focus exclusively on writing. Begins placing short stories, fiction, and drama reviews, and essays on topics both serious and flighty, in a variety of London publications. Publishes *Text-Book of Biology* and "On Extinction."

1894   Separates from Isabel, elopes with Jane. Seven episodes of what would become *The Time Machine* appear in the *National Observer* (March–June). Publishes "The Province of Pain." Moves to Sevenoaks.

1895   Divorces Isabel and marries Jane. Moves to Woking. *The Time Machine* serialized in the *New Review* (January–May); first edition published by Heinemann in May. Also publishes two collections of short stories (*Select Conversations with an Uncle* and *The Stolen Bacillus and Other Incidents*), a novel (*The Wonderful Visit*), and several scientific essays, including "The Limits of Individual Plasticity" and "Bio-Optimism."

1896   Moves to Worcester Park, Surrey. Meets George Gissing. Hires J. B. Pinker as literary agent. Publishes "Under the Knife," "Human Evolution, an Artificial Process," and *The Island of Doctor Moreau*, the second of his "scientific romances," first in London (by Heinemann), then in the United States (by Stone & Kimball); also publishes a domestic novel, *The Wheels of Chance*.

1897   Begins a lifelong correspondence with Arnold Bennett. Publications include *The Invisible Man*, *The Plattner Story and Others*, and *Certain Personal Matters*.

1898   Lung hemorrhage recurs. Convalesces on the south coast. Meets Henry James, Joseph Conrad, Ford Madox Hueffer (later Ford), and Stephen Crane. Travels to Italy with Gissing. Publishes *The War of the Worlds*.

1899   Publishes *When the Sleeper Wakes* and *Tales of Space and Time*.

1900   Publishes *Love and Mr. Lewisham*. Builds Spade House in Sandgate, Kent.

1901   First child, George Philip ("Gip"), born. Publishes *The First Men in the Moon* and "A Dream of Armageddon," as well as the sociological study *Anticipations*. First essay on T. H. Huxley appears in *Royal College of Science Magazine*.

1902   Invited to address the Royal Institution. Publishes a work of fiction, *The Sea Lady*, and of nonfiction, *The Discovery of the Future*. The latter impresses members of the Socialist Fabian Society, including George Bernard Shaw.

1903   Second child, Frank Richard, born. Joins the Fabian Society. Participates in the discussion group known as the Co-Efficients and becomes a member of the Society's Executive Committee. Becomes friends with Shaw, Sidney and Beatrice Webb, and Vernon Lee. Publishes *Twelve Stories and a Dream* and the nonfictional *Mankind in the Making*.

1904   Publishes *The Food of the Gods*, a scientific romance.

1905   Sarah Wells dies. Publishes two novels, *A Modern Utopia* and *Kipps*.

1906   A busy year includes a lecture tour in the United States; meetings with Theodore Roosevelt, Maxim Gorky, and Booker T. Washington; affairs with Dorothy Richardson, Rosamund Bland, and Amber Reeves; and the publication of a scientific romance, *In the Days of the Comet*, and two works of nonfiction, *The Future in America* and *Socialism and the Family*.

1908   Differences with Shaw and the Webbs lead to forced resignation from the Fabian Society, though Wells remains an active Socialist. Helps found the Royal College of Science Association (RCSA), soon becoming its first president. Publishes a scientific romance, *The War in the Air*, and two works of nonfiction, *New Worlds for Old* and *First and Last Things*.

1909   Wells's daughter, Anna Jane Blanco-White, born to Amber Reeves. Moves with Jane to Hampstead, London. Publishes two novels, *Tono-Bungay* and *Ann Veronica*.

1910   Joseph Wells dies. Publishes *The History of Mr. Polly*. Begins affair with Elizabeth von Arnim.

1911   Publishes two collections of stories, *The Country of the Blind and Other Stories* and *The Door in the Wall and Other Stories*; a novel, *The New Machiavelli*; and a work of nonfiction, *Floor Games*.

1912   Publishes *Marriage*, a novel. Moves to Dunmow, Essex.

1913   Publishes *The Passionate Friends*, a novel, and *Little Wars*, a work of nonfiction. Begins affair with Rebecca West.

1914   Visits Russia in January. His son, Anthony West, born to Rebecca West. Publishes two novels, *The World Set Free* and *The Wife of Sir Isaac Harman*, and two works of nonfiction, *An Englishman Looks at the World* and *The War That Will End War*. Horrified by outbreak of war, but in contrast to many fellow Socialists supports British involvement.

1915   Gradual falling out with Henry James made irreparable by Wells's satiric portrait of him in *Boon*. Publishes *Bealby*, *The Research Magnificent*, and *The Peace of the World*, the first two novels, the last a work of nonfiction.

1916   Tours battlefronts in France and Italy. The war is the main subject of the novel *Mr. Britling Sees It Through* and two nonfictional works, *What Is Coming?* and *The Elements of Reconstruction*.

1917   Brief religious phase results in *The Soul of a Bishop*, a novel, and *God the Invisible King*, a work of nonfiction.

1918   Recruited to produce war propaganda for the Ministry of Information. Joins committee charged with setting up the League of Nations. Publishes *In the Fourth Year: Anticipations of World Peace* and *British Nationalism and the League of Nations*.

1919   Publishes *The Undying Fire*, a novel.

1920   Visits Russia, meets Lenin, Trotsky, Gorky, Moura Budberg. Publishes *Russia in the Shadows* and the immensely popular *Outline of History*.

1921   Visits the United States to cover the World Disarmament Conference in Washington, D.C. Affair with Margaret Sanger. Publishes *The New Teaching of History*.

1922   Publishes *A Short History of the World* and a revised *Outline of History*, as well as *Washington and the Hope of Peace* and the novel *The Secret Places of the Heart*. Joins the Labour Party and stands unsuccessfully for Parliament.

1923   A second unsuccessful run for Parliament. Begins habit of wintering in Grasse in Provence. Meets and begins affair with Odette Keun. Publications include the novels *Men Like Gods* and *The Dream*, the nonfictional *Socialism and the Scientific Motive* and *The Labour Ideal of Education*, and a biographical study, *The Story of a Great Schoolmaster*.

1924   The Atlantic Edition of *The Works of H. G. Wells* published.

1925   Publishes the fictional *Christina Alberta's Father* and the nonfictional *Forecast of the World's Affairs*.

1926   Controversy with the Catholic writer Hilaire Belloc over the *Outline of History*. Publishes the novel *The World of William Clissold*.

1927   Builds house with Odette Keun in Grasse. Publishes *The Short Stories of H. G. Wells* in addition to a new novel, *Meanwhile*, and a new work of nonfiction, *Democracy under Revision*. Jane Wells dies in October.

1928   Publishes his tribute to Jane, *The Book of Catherine Wells*. Other publications include *The Way the World Is Going* and *The Open Conspiracy* (both nonfiction) and the novel *Mr. Blettworthy on Rampole Island*.

1929   First BBC radio talk. Delivers speech in German Reichstag, published as *The Common-Sense of World Peace*. Publishes a screenplay, *The King Who Was a King*, and a children's book, *The Adventures of Tommy*.

1930   With his son G. P. Wells and Julian Huxley, publishes the textbook *The Science of Life*. Moves to Chiltern Court, London. Publishes *The Autocracy of Mr. Parham*, a novel, and *The Way to World Peace*, a work of nonfiction.

1931   Diagnosed with diabetes. Breakup with Odette Keun. Death of Isabel Wells.

1932   Publications include a novel, *The Bulpington of Blup*; a textbook, *The Work, Wealth, and Happiness of Mankind*; and a work of nonfiction, *After Democracy*.

1933   Collects seven of his most popular works in the one-volume *Scientific Romances*. Also publishes the novel *The Shape of Things to Come*. Assumes presidency of PEN, the international writers' association. Begins affair with Moura Budberg.

1934   Visits Soviet Union and United States, meets with Joseph Stalin and Franklin Roosevelt. Cofounds the Diabetic Association (today Diabetes UK). Publishes *Experiment in Autobiography*.

1935   Collaborates with director Alexander Korda on film version of *The Shape of Things to Come* (released in 1936 as *Things to Come*). Moves to Regent's Park, London. Second essay on T. H. Huxley appears in the *Listener*.

1936   PEN dinner in honor of his seventieth birthday. Nonfiction publications include *The Anatomy of Frustration* and *The Idea of a World Encyclopedia*. Fictional works include a novel, *The Croquet Player*, and a screenplay, *The Man Who Could Work Miracles*.

1937   Assumes chair of Section I of the British Association for the Advancement of Science. Publishes three works of fiction: *Star Begotten*, *Brynhild*, and *The Camford Visitation*.

1938   Publishes two works of fiction, *The Brothers* and *Apropos of Dolores*, and the nonfictional *World Brain*. Embarks on lecture tour of Australia.

1939   Publishes a novel, *The Holy Terror*, and three works of nonfiction: *Travels of a Republican Radical in Search of Hot Water*, *The Fate of Homo Sapiens*, and *The New World Order*.

1940   Remains in London during the Blitz. Autumn lecture tour in the United States. Publications include *The Rights of Man*, *The Common Sense of War and Peace*, and *Two Hemispheres or One World?* (all nonfiction) and the fictions *Babes in the Darkling Wood* and *All Aboard for Ararat*.

1941   Publishes what proves to be his final novel, *You Can't Be Too Careful*, as well as *Guide to the New World*.

1942   Publishes *Science and the World Mind*, *The Conquest of Time*, and *Phoenix* in addition to his University of London D.Sc. thesis in zoology, *On the Quality of Illusion in the Continuity of Individual Life in the Higher Metazoa, with Particular Reference to the Species Homo Sapiens*.

1943   Awarded the D.Sc. degree by the University of London. Publishes *Crux Ansata*.

1944   Publishes a collection of essays, *'42 to '44*.

1945   Publishes *Mind at the End of Its Tether*. Health slowly failing.

1946   Dies at home on August 13. Nominated for the Nobel Prize in Literature for the fourth time (the others being 1921, 1932, and 1935).

Selected Bibliography

Annotated Editions of The Island of Doctor Moreau

Wells, H. G., *The Island of Doctor Moreau*. Ed. Mason Harris. Toronto: Broadview Press, 2009.
————. *The Island of Doctor Moreau*. Ed. Darryl Jones. Oxford: Oxford UP, 2017.
————. *The Island of Doctor Moreau*. Ed. Patrick Parrinder. New York: Penguin Classics, 2005.
————. *The Island of Doctor Moreau: A Variorum Text*. Ed. Robert M. Philmus. Athens: U of Georgia P, 1993.
————. *The Island of Doctor Moreau* Ed. Leon Stover. Jefferson, NC: McFarland & Company, 1996.

Collections of Wells's Works

The Annotated H. G. Wells. Ed. Leon Stover, Jefferson, NC: McFarland & Company, 1996–2007.
The Atlantic Edition of the Works of H. G. Wells. 28 vols. London: T. Fisher, Unwin, 1924; New York: Charles Scribner's Sons, 1924.
The Complete Short Stories of H. G. Wells. London: J. M. Dent, 1998.
H. G. Wells: Early Writings in Science and Science Fiction. Ed. Robert M. Philmus and David Y. Hughes. Berkeley and London: U of California P, 1975.
H. G. Wells's Literary Criticism. Ed. Patrick Parrinder and Robert M. Philmus. Brighton: Harvester Press, 1980.
The H. G. Wells Reader: A Complete Anthology from Science Fiction to Social Satire. Ed. John Huntington. Lanham, MD: Taylor Trade Publishing, 2003.
Project Gutenberg: Works by H. G. Wells.
The Scientific Romances of H. G. Wells. London: Gollancz, 1933.

Correspondence

Edel, Leon, and Gordon N. Ray, eds. *Henry James and H. G. Wells: A Record of Their Friendship, Their Debate on the Art of Fiction, and Their Quarrel*. London: Hart-Davis, 1958; Urbana: U of Illinois P, 1958.
Gettmann, Royal A., ed. *George Gissing and H. G. Wells: Their Friendship and Correspondence*. Urbana: U of Illinois P, 1961.
Smith, David C., ed. *The Correspondence of H. G. Wells*. 4 vols. London and Brookfield, VT: Pickering & Chatto, 1995.
Smith, J. Percy, ed. *Bernard Shaw and H. G. Wells*. Toronto and Buffalo: U of Toronto P, 1995.
Wilson, Harris, ed. *Arnold Bennett and H. G. Wells: A Record of a Personal and a Literary Friendship*. London: Hart-Davis, 1960; Urbana: U of Illinois P, 1960.

Biography and Autobiography

Dickson, Lovar. *H. G. Wells: His Turbulent Life and Times.* New York: Atheneum, 1969.

Hammond, H. R., ed. *H. G. Wells: Interviews and Recollections.* London: Macmillan, 1980.

Mackenzie, Norman, and Jeanne Mackenzie. *H. G. Wells: A Biography.* New York: Simon and Schuster, 1973.

Ray, Gordon H. *H. G. Wells and Rebecca West.* New Haven: Yale UP, 1974.

Roberts, Adam. *H. G. Wells: A Literary Life.* London: Palgrave Macmillan, 2019.

Smith, David C. *H. G. Wells: Desperately Mortal: A Biography.* New Haven and London: Yale UP, 1986.

Sherborne, Michael. *H. G. Wells: Another Kind of Life.* London: Peter Owen, 2010.

Tomalin, Claire. *The Young H. G. Wells: Changing the World.* New York: Penguin Press, 2021.

Wells, G. P., ed. *H. G. Wells in Love: Postscript to "An Experiment in Autobiography."* London: Faber and Faber, 1984; Boston: Little, Brown, 1984.

Wells, H. G. *Experiment in Autobiography: Discoveries and Conclusions of a Very Ordinary Brain (since 1866).* London: Victor Gollancz, and New York: Macmillan, 1934.

West, Anthony. "H. G. Wells." In Bernard Bergonzi, ed. *H. G. Wells: A Collection of Critical Essays.* Englewood Cliffs, NJ: Prentice-Hall, 1976 [1957]. 8–24.

West, Geoffrey. *H. G. Wells: A Sketch for a Portrait.* London: Gerald Howe and New York: Norton, 1930.

Bibliographies

Hammond, J. R. *Herbert George Wells: An Annotated Bibliography of His Works.* New York and London: Garland, 1977.

H. G. Wells: A Comprehensive Bibliography. Rev. ed. London: H. G. Wells Society, 1985.

Hughes, David Y. "Criticism in English of H. G. Wells's Science Fiction: A Select Annotated Bibliography." *Science Fiction Studies* 6.3 (1979): 303–19.

Mullen, Richard D. "The Books and Principal Pamphlets of H. G. Wells: A Chronological Survey." *Science Fiction Studies* 1.2 (1973): 114–35.

Scheick, William J., and J. Randolph Cox. *H. G. Wells: A Reference Guide.* Boston: G. K. Hall, 1988.

Smith, David C. *The Definitive Bibliography of Herbert George Wells.* Oss, Netherlands: Equilibris, 2007.

———. *The Journalism of H. G. Wells: An Annotated Bibliography.* Ed. Patrick Parrinder. Oss, Netherlands: Equilibris, 2012.

Criticism

• Indicates a work included or excerpted in this Norton Critical Edition.

Antor, Heinz. *Monsters and Monstrosity.* Berlin, Munich, and Boston: Walter de Gruyter, 2019.

Asker, D. B. S. "H. G. Wells and Regressive Evolution." *Dutch Quarterly Review of Anglo-American Letters* 12.1 (1982): 15–20.

Atwood, Margaret. Introduction to H. G. Wells, *The Island of Doctor Moreau.* Ed. Patrick Parrinder. New York: Penguin Classics, 2005. xiii–xxvii.

Batchelor, John. *H. G. Wells.* Cambridge: Cambridge UP, 1985.

Bergonzi, Bernard. *The Early H. G. Wells: A Study of the Scientific Romances.* Manchester: Manchester UP, 1961.

———, ed. *H. G. Wells: A Collection of Critical Essays.* Englewood Cliffs, NJ: Prentice-Hall, 1976.

Beuchamp, Gorman. "*The Island of Dr. Moreau* as Theological Grotesque." *Papers on Language & Literature* 15.4 (Fall 1979): 408–17.

Bishop, Andrew. "Making Sympathy 'Vicious' on *The Island of Dr. Moreau.*" *Nineteenth-Century Contexts* 43.2 (2021): 205–20.

Bowen, Roger. "Science, Myth, and Fiction in H. G. Wells's *Island of Dr. Moreau.*" *Studies in the Novel* 8.3 (1976): 318–35.

Bowler, Peter J. *A History of the Future: Prophets of Progress from H. G. Wells to Isaac Asimov.* Cambridge: Cambridge UP, 2017.

Bozzetto, R. M. P., and Russell Taylor. "Moreau's Tragi-Farcical Island." *Science Fiction Studies* 20.1 (1993): 33–44.

Brody, Jennifer DeVere. "Deforming Island Races." In *Impossible Purities: Blackness, Femininity, and Victorian Culture.* Durham and London: Duke UP, 1998. 130–69.

Brooks, Van Wyck. *The World of H. G. Wells.* New York: Mitchell Kennerley, 1915.

Caleb, Amanda Mordavsky. "Amoral Animality: H. G. Wells' *The Island of Dr. Moreau.*" In *Restoring the Mystery of the Rainbow,* ed. Valerie Tinkler-Villani and C. C. Barfoot. Amsterdam: Brill, 2011. 313–31.

Cantor, Paul A., and Peter Hufnagel. "The Empire of the Future: Imperialism and Modernism in H. G. Wells." *Studies in the Novel* 38.1 (2006): 36–56.

Caudwell, Christopher. "H. G. Wells: A Study in Utopianism." In *Studies in a Dying Culture.* London: Allen Lane, 1971. 73–95.

Christensen, Timothy. "The 'Bestial Mark' of Race in *The Island of Dr. Moreau.*" *Criticism* 46.4 (2004): 575–95.

• Cole, Sarah. *Inventing Tomorrow: H. G. Wells and the Twentieth Century.* New York: Columbia UP, 2020.

Danahay, Martin. "Wells, Galton, and Biopower: Breeding Human Animals." *Journal of Victorian Culture* 17.4 (2012): 468–79.

Danta, Chris. "The Future Will Have Been Animal: Dr. Moreau and the Aesthetics of Monstrosity." *Textual Practice* 26.4 (2012): 687–705.

Devine, Christine. *Class in Turn-of-the Century Novels of Gissing, James, Hardy and Wells.* Aldershot: Ashgate, 2005.

Draper, Michael. *H. G. Wells.* London: Macmillan, 1987.

• Edwards, Ronald. *The Edge of Evolution: Animality, Inhumanity, and Doctor Moreau.* Oxford: Oxford UP, 2016.

Ferguson, Christine. *Language, Science and Popular Fiction in the Victorian Fin-de-Siècle: The Brutal Tongue.* Burlington, VT: Ashgate, 1988; Aldershot: Ashgate, 2006.

Firchow, Peter Edgerly. *Modern Utopian Fictions: From H. G. Wells to Iris Murdoch.* Washington, D.C.: Catholic UP of America, 2007.

Fried, Michael. "Impressionist Monsters: H. G. Wells's *The Island of Dr. Moreau.*" In *Frankenstein Creation and Monstrosity.* Ed. Stephen Bann. London: Reaktion Books, 1994. 95–112.

Generani, Gustavo. "*The Island of Doctor Moreau* by H. G. Wells: A Pre-Freudian Reply to Darwinian Imperialism." *English* 67.258 (2018): 235–61.

Gill, Stephen. *Scientific Romances of H. G. Wells: A Critical Study.* Cornwall, ON: Vesta Publications, 1977.

• Glendening, John. "'Green Confusion': Evolution and Entanglement in H. G. Wells's *The Island of Doctor Moreau.*" *Victorian Literature and Culture* 30.2 (September 2002): 571–97.

Gold, Barri J. "Reproducing Empire: 'Moreau' and Others." *Nineteenth Century Studies* 14 (2000): 173–98.

Gomel, Elana. "From Dr. Moreau to Dr. Mengele: The Biological Sublime." *Poetics Today* 21.2 (2000): 393–421.

Graff, Ann-Barbara. "'Administrative Nihilism': Evolution, Ethics and Victorian Utopian Satire." *Utopian Studies* 12.2 (2001): 33–52.

Greenslade, William. *Degeneration, Culture and the Novel: 1880–1940*. Cambridge: Cambridge UP, 1994.

Greiner, Rae. *Sympathetic Realism in Nineteenth-Century British Fiction*. Baltimore: Johns Hopkins UP, 2012.

Hamilton, Craig A. "'The World Was a Confusion': Imagining the Hybrids of H. G. Wells's *The Island of Dr. Moreau*." *Undying Fire* 2 (2003): 28–36.

Hammond, J. R. "*The Island of Doctor Moreau*: A Swiftian Parable." *The Wellsian: Journal of the H. G. Wells Society* 16 (1976): 30–41.

Hardy, Sylvia. "A Story of the Days to Come: H. G. Wells and the Language of Science Fiction." *Language and Literature* 12.3 (2003): 199–212.

Harris, Mason. "Vivisection, the Culture of Science, and Intellectual Uncertainty in *The Island of Doctor Moreau*." *Gothic Studies* 4 (2002): 99–115.

Haynes, Roslynn D. *H. G. Wells: Discoverer of the Future: The Influence of Science on His Thought*. New York: New York UP, 1980.

———. "Wells's Debt to Huxley and the Myth of Dr. Moreau." *Cahiers Victoriens et Edouardiens* 13 (1981): 31–41.

———. "The Unholy Alliance of Science in *The Island of Doctor Moreau*." In *The Wellsian: Selected Essays on H. G. Wells*. Ed. John S. Partington. Oss, Netherlands: Equilibris, 2003. 55–67.

• Hendershot, Cyndy. *The Animal Within: Masculinity and the Gothic*. Ann Arbor: U of Michigan P, 1998.

Hillegas, Mark R. *The Future as Nightmare: H. G. Wells and the Anti-Utopians*. New York: Oxford UP, 1967.

Hoad, Neville. "Cosmetic Surgeons of the Social: Darwin, Freud, and Wells and the Limits of Sympathy on *The Island of Dr. Moreau*." In *Compassion: The Culture and Politics of an Emotion*, ed. Lauren Berlant. London and New York: Routledge, 2004. 187–217.

Hurley, Kelly. *The Gothic Body: Sexuality, Materialism, and Degeneration at the "Fin de Siècle"*. Cambridge: Cambridge UP, 1996.

Jackson, Kimberly. "Vivisected Language in H. G. Wells's *The Island of Doctor Moreau*." *The Wellsian* 29 (2006): 20–35.

James, Simon J. *Maps of Utopia: H. G. Wells, Modernity and the End of Culture*. New York: Oxford UP, 2012.

Kemp, Peter. *H. G. Wells and the Culminating Ape: Biological Imperatives and Imaginative Obsessions*. London: Macmillan, 1996, [1982].

Kiang, Shun Yin. "Human Intervention and More-Than-Human Humanity in H. G. Wells's *The Island of Dr. Moreau*." In *Victorian Environmental Nightmares*, ed. Laurence W. Mazzeno and Ronald D. Morrison. London: Palgrave Macmillan, 2019. 207–25.

Krumm, Pascale. "*The Island of Doctor Moreau*, or the Case of Devolution." *Foundation* 75 (1999): 51–62.

• Lee, Michael Parrish. "Reading Meat in H. G. Wells." *Studies in the Novel* 42.3 (2010): 249–68.

Lehman, Steven. "The Motherless Child in Science Fiction: *Frankenstein* and *Moreau*." *Science Fiction Studies* 18 (1992): 49–57.

Levine, Suzanne Jill. "Science versus the Library in *The Island of Dr. Moreau*, *La Invención de Morel*, and *Plan de Evasión*." *Latin American Literary Review* 9.18 (1981): 17–26.

Luckhurst, Roger. *Science Fiction*. Cambridge: Polity Press, 2005. 30–49, 250–55.

MacDonald, Alex. "'Passionate Intensity' in Wells's *The Island of Doctor Moreau* and Yeats's 'The Second Coming': Constructing an Echo." *ANQ* 9.4 (1996): 40–43.

McConnell, Frank. *The Science Fiction of H. G. Wells*. New York: Oxford UP, 1981.

McLean, Steven. *The Early Fiction of H. G. Wells: Fantasies of Science*. Basingstoke: Palgrave Macmillan, 2009.

McNabb, John. "The Beast Within: *The Island of Doctor Moreau*, and Human Evolution in the mid-1890s." *Geological Journal* 50 (2015): 383–97.

Parrinder, Patrick. *Shadows of the Future: H. G. Wells, Science Fiction and Prophecy*. Liverpool: Liverpool UP, 1995.

Parrinder, Patrick, ed. *H. G. Wells: The Critical Heritage*. London and Boston: Routledge, 1972.

Partridge, Eric, ed. *H. G. Wells's Fin-de-Siècle: Twenty-First-Century Reflections on the Early H. G. Wells*. Frankfurt: Peter Lang, 2007.

Philmus, Robert M. *Into the Unknown: The Evolution of Science Fiction from Francis Godwin to H. G. Wells*. Berkeley and Los Angeles: U of California P, 1970.

———. "Revisions of His Past: Wells's Anatomy of Frustration." *Texas Studies in Literature and Language* 20.2 (1978): 249–66.

———. "The Satiric Ambivalence of 'The Island of Doctor Moreau.'" *Science Fiction Studies* 8.1 (1981): 2–11.

———. "Textual Authority: The Strange Case of *The Island of Doctor Moreau*." *Science Fiction Studies* 17.1 (1990): 64–70.

Planinc, Emma. "Catching Up with Wells: The Political Theory of H. G. Wells's Science Fiction." *Political Theory* 45.5 (2017): 637–58.

Platzner, Robert L. "H. G. Wells's 'Jungle Book': The Influence of Kipling on *The Island of Dr. Moreau*." *Victorian Newsletter* 36 (1969): 16–22.

Quinn, Emelia. *Reading Veganism: The Monstrous Vegan, 1818 to Present*. Oxford: Oxford UP, 2021.

Redfern, Nick. "Abjection and Evolution in *The Island of Doctor Moreau*." *The Wellsian* 27 (2004): 37–47.

Reed, John R. *The Natural History of H. G. Wells*. Athens: Ohio UP, 1981.

———. "The Vanity of Law in *The Island of Doctor Moreau*." In *H. G. Wells Under Revision: Proceedings of the International H. G. Wells Symposium*, ed. Patrick Parrinder and Christopher Rolfe. Selinsgrove: Susquehanna UP, 1990. 134–44.

• Rieder, John. *Colonialism and the Emergence of Science Fiction*. Middletown, CT: Wesleyan UP, 2012.

• Rohman, Carrie. "Burning Out the Animal: The Failure of Enlightenment Purification in H. G. Wells's *The Island of Dr. Moreau*." In *Figuring Animals: Essays on Animal Images in Art, Literature, Philosophy, and Popular Culture*, ed. Mary Sanders Pollock and Catherine Rainwater. London: Palgrave Macmillan, 2005. 121–34.

Showalter, Elaine. "The Apocalyptic Fictions of H. G. Wells." In *Fin de Siècle/Fin du Globe: Fears and Fantasies of the Late Nineteenth Century*, ed. John Stokes. New York: St. Martin's, 1992. 69–83.

Starr, Michael. *Wells Meets Deleuze: The Scientific Romances Reconsidered*. Jefferson, NC: McFarland & Company, 2017.

Stiles, Anne. "Literature in 'Mind': H. G. Wells and the Evolution of the Mad Scientist." *Journal of the History of Ideas* 7.2 (2009): 317–39.

Stover, Leon. "Applied Natural History: Wells vs. Huxley." In *H. G. Wells Under Revision: Proceedings of the International H. G. Wells Symposium*, ed. Patrick Parrinder and Christopher Rolfe. Selinsgrove: Susquehanna UP, 1990. 125–33.

Snyder, E. E. "Moreau and the Monstrous: Evolution, Religion, and the Beast on the Island." *Preternature: Critical and Historical Studies on the Preternatural* 2.2 (2013): 213–39.

Taneja, Payal. "The Tropical Empire: Exotic Animals and Beastly Men in *The Island of Doctor Moreau*." *ESC* 39.2–3 (2013): 139–59.

Vallorani, Nicoletta. "Hybridizing Science: The 'Patchwork Biology' of Dr. Moreau." *Cahiers Victoriens et Edouardiens* 46 (1997): 245–61.

Vernier, J. P. "Evolution as a Literary Theme in H. G. Wells's Science Fiction." In *H. G. Wells and Modern Science Fiction*, ed. Darko Suvin and Robert M. Philmus. Cranbury, NJ: Associated U Presses, 1977. 70–89.

• Vint, Sherryl. "Animals and Animality on the Island of Moreau." *Yearbook of English Studies* 37.2 (2007): 85–102.

Weaver-Hightower, Rebecca. *Empire Islands* (Minneapolis, MN: U of Minnesota P), 2007.

Weaver-Hightower, Rebecca, and Rachel Piwarski. "The Gothic Uncanny as Colonial Allegory in *The Island of Doctor Moreau*." *Gothic Studies* 20.1–2 (2018): 358–72.

Woodcock, George. "The Darkness Violated by Light: A Revisionist View of H. G. Wells." *Malahat Review* 26 (1973): 144–60.